Also by Stuart Gibbs

The FunJungle series
Belly Up
Poached
Big Game
Panda-monium
Lion Down
Tyrannosaurus Wrecks
Bear Bottom

The Spy School series
Spy School
Spy Camp
Evil Spy School
Spy Ski School
Spy School Secret Service
Spy School Goes South
Spy School British Invasion
Spy School Revolution
Spy School at Sea

The Moon Base Alpha series
Space Case
Spaced Out
Waste of Space

The Charlie Thorne series
Charlie Thorne and the Last Equation
Charlie Thorne and the Lost City

The Last Musketeer

STUART GIBBS

ILLUSTRATED BY **ANJAN SARKAR**

spy school

THE GRAPHIC NOVEL

Simon & Schuster Books for Young Readers
New York London Toronto Sydney New Delhi

SIMON & SCHUSTER BOOKS FOR YOUNG READERS
An imprint of Simon & Schuster Children's Publishing Division
1230 Avenue of the Americas, New York, New York 10020

SIMON & SCHUSTER BOOKS FOR YOUNG READERS
and related marks are trademarks of Simon & Schuster, Inc.
For information about special discounts for bulk purchases, please contact
Simon & Schuster Special Sales at 1-866-506-1949 or business@simonandschuster.com.
The Simon & Schuster Speakers Bureau can bring authors to your live event.
For more information or to book an event, contact the Simon & Schuster
Speakers Bureau at 1-866-248-3049 or visit our website at www.simonspeakers.com.
Also available in a Simon & Schuster Books for Young Readers paperback edition
The text for this book was set in Memphis LT Std.
The illustrations for this book were rendered digitally
Special thanks to Rob Richardson, for his invaluable help with background design,
and to Yuko Noda and Lauren Auty, who assisted with coloring and shading.
Manufactured in China
1121 SCP
First Simon & Schuster Books for Young Readers hardcover edition February 2022
10 9 8 7 6 5 4 3 2 1
Library of Congress Cataloging-in-Publication Data
Names: Gibbs, Stuart, 1969– author. | Sarkar, Anjan, illustrator.
Title: Spy School : the graphic novel / Stu Gibbs ; illustrated by Anjan Sarkar.
Description: First Simon & Schuster hardcover edition. | New York : Simon & Schuster
Books for Young Readers, 2022. | Audience: Ages 8–12. | Audience: Grades 4–6. |
Summary: "Ben Ripley is recruited for a magnet school with a focus on science—
but he's entirely shocked to discover that the school is actually a front for a junior
C.I.A. academy. Ben becomes an undercover agent and goes on his first assignment
in this graphic novel adaptation of SPY SCHOOL"— Provided by publisher.
Identifiers: LCCN 2020050956 | ISBN 9781534455436 (hardcover) |
ISBN 9781534455429 (paperback) | ISBN 9781534455443 (ebook)
Subjects: LCSH: Graphic novels. | CYAC: Graphic novels. | Spies—Fiction. |
Schools—Fiction.
Classification: LCC PZ7.7.G5324 Spy 2022 | DDC 741.5/973—dc23
LC record available at https://lccn.loc.gov/2020050956

For Dashiell and Violet—S. G.

For Yuko—ごめんね!—A. S.

From:
Office of CIA Internal Investigations
CIA Headquarters
Langley, Virginia

To:
[redacted]
Director of Covert Affairs
The White House
Washington, DC

Classified Documents Enclosed
Security Level AA2
For Your Eyes Only

As part of the continuing investigation into Operation Creeping Badger, the following pages have been transcribed from 53 hours of debriefings of Mr. Benjamin Ripley, aka Smokescreen, age 12, a first year student at the Academy of Espionage.

Mr. Ripley's acceptance to the academy, while unprecedented, was sanctioned by [redacted] and [redacted], Director of the CIA, as part of the operation.

As Operation Creeping Badger did not proceed as planned, given the events of [redacted], this investigation has been launched to determine exactly what went wrong, why it went wrong, and who should be terminated for it.

After reading these documents, they are to be destroyed immediately, in accordance with CIA Security Directive 163-12A. No discussion of these pages will be tolerated, except during the review, which will be conducted in [redacted]. Please note that no weapons will be allowed at said meeting.

I look forward to hearing your thoughts.

[redacted]
Director of Internal Investigations

Cc:
[redacted]

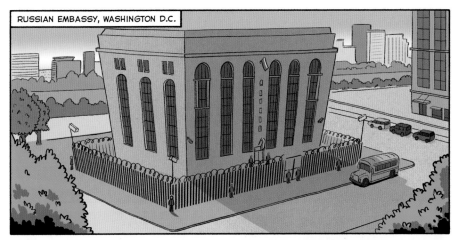

RUSSIAN EMBASSY, WASHINGTON D.C.

AMERICAN CHILDREN, PLEASE FOLLOW ME TO HALL OF HEROES WHERE YOU WILL SEE WHAT REAL LEADERS ARE LIKE...

1

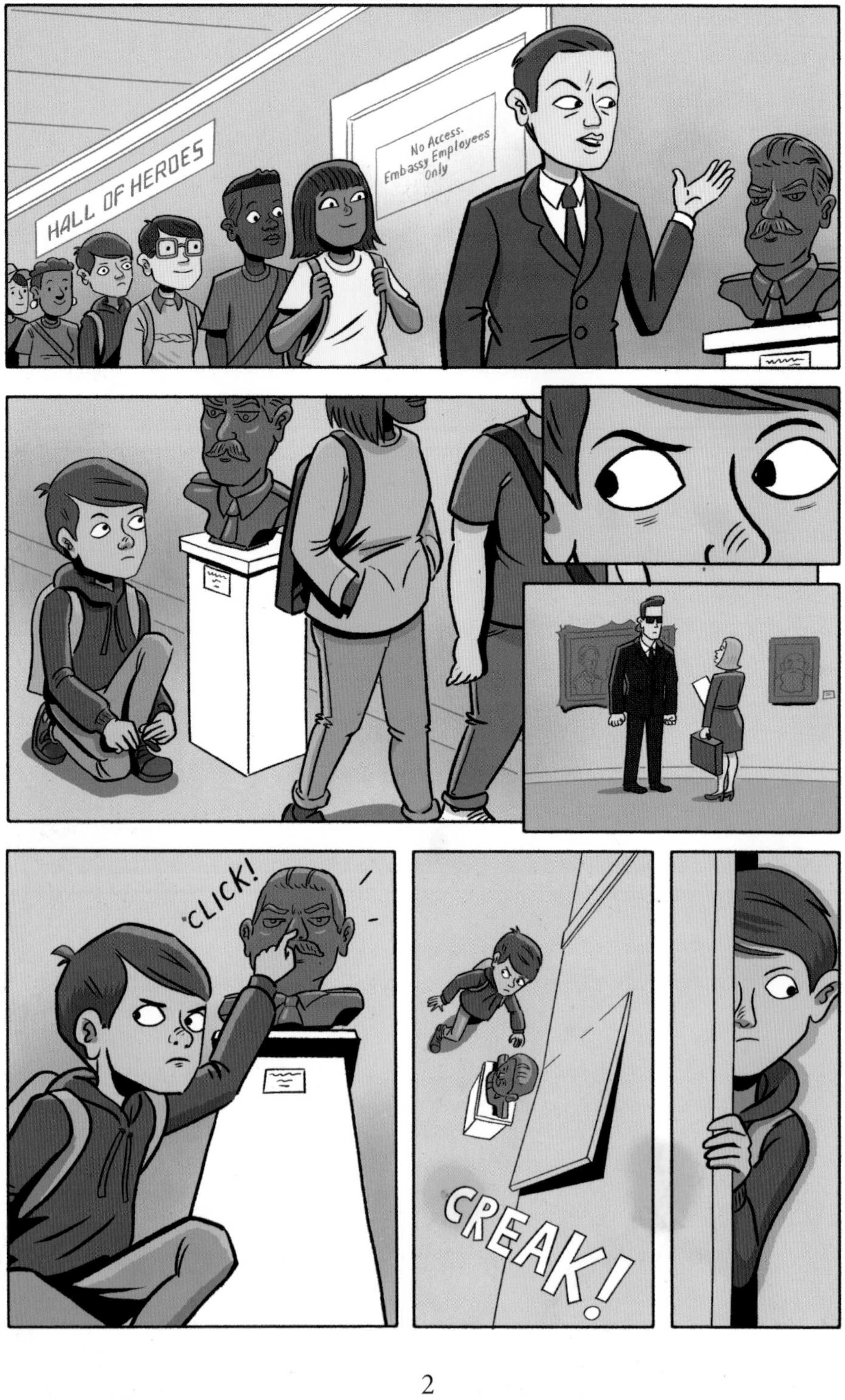
HALL OF HEROES
No Access.
Embassy Employees
Only
CLICK!
CREAK!

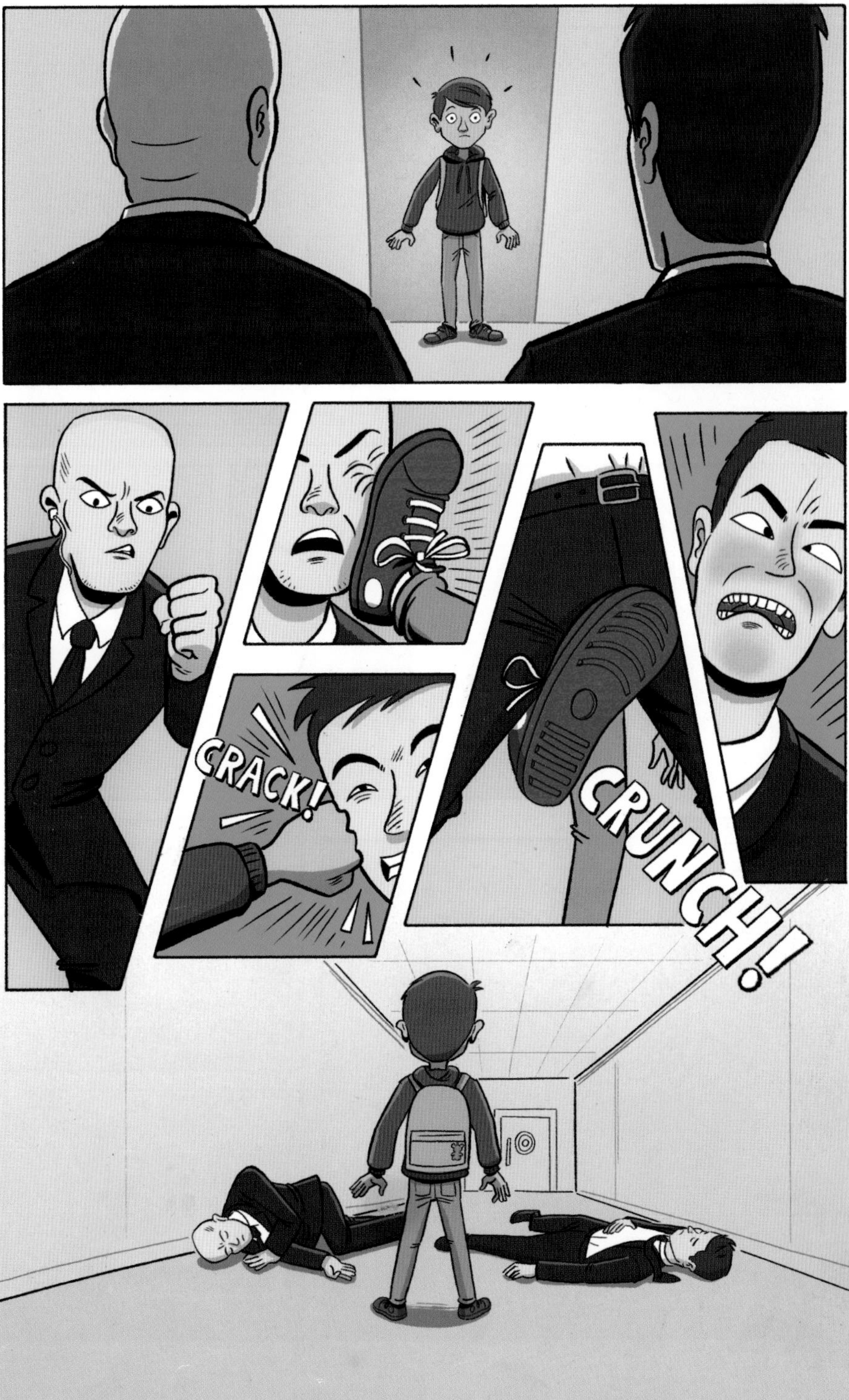
CRACK!
CRUNCH!

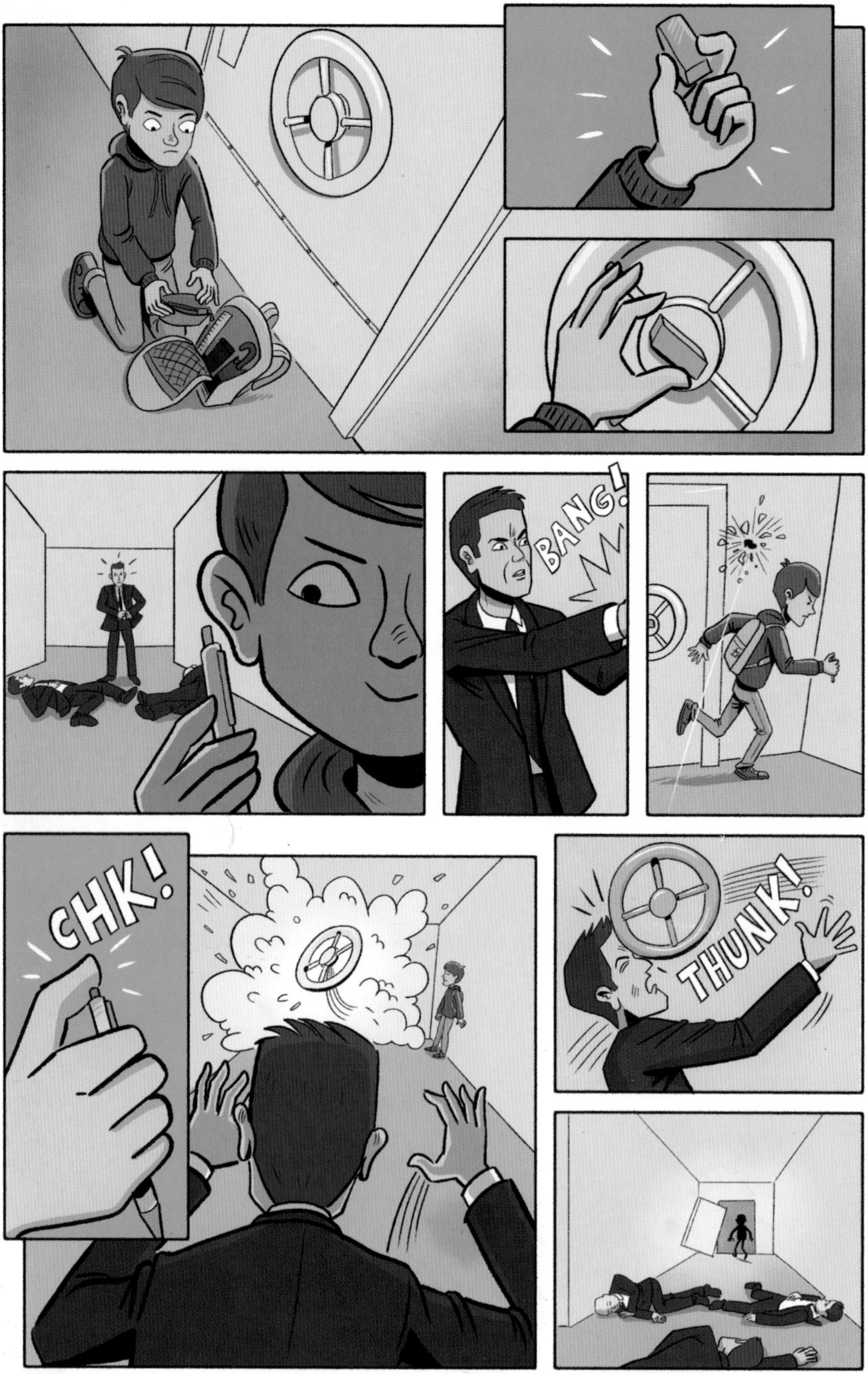
BANG!
CHK!
THUNK!

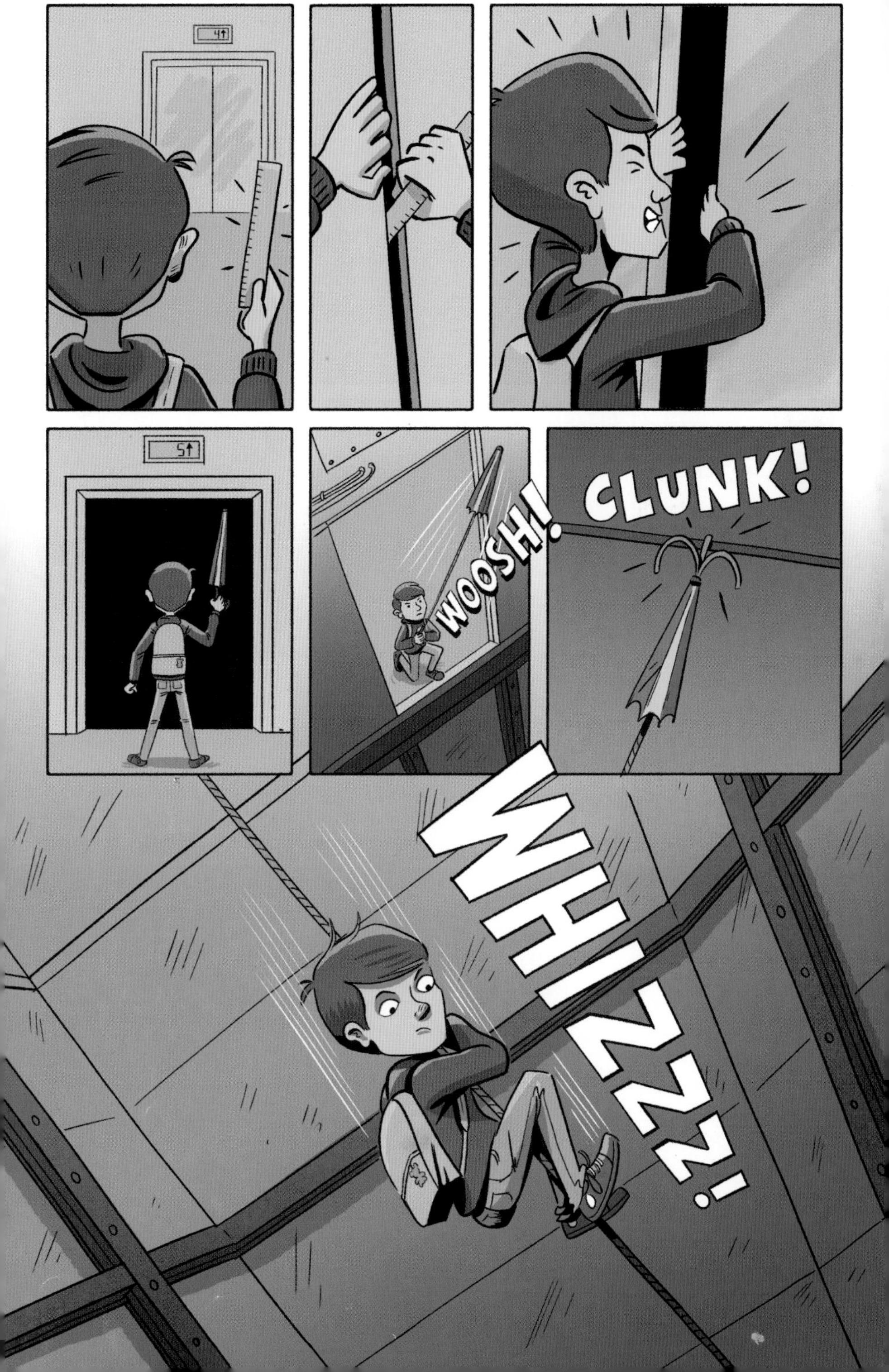
4↑
5↑
WOOSH!
CLUNK!
WHIZZZ!

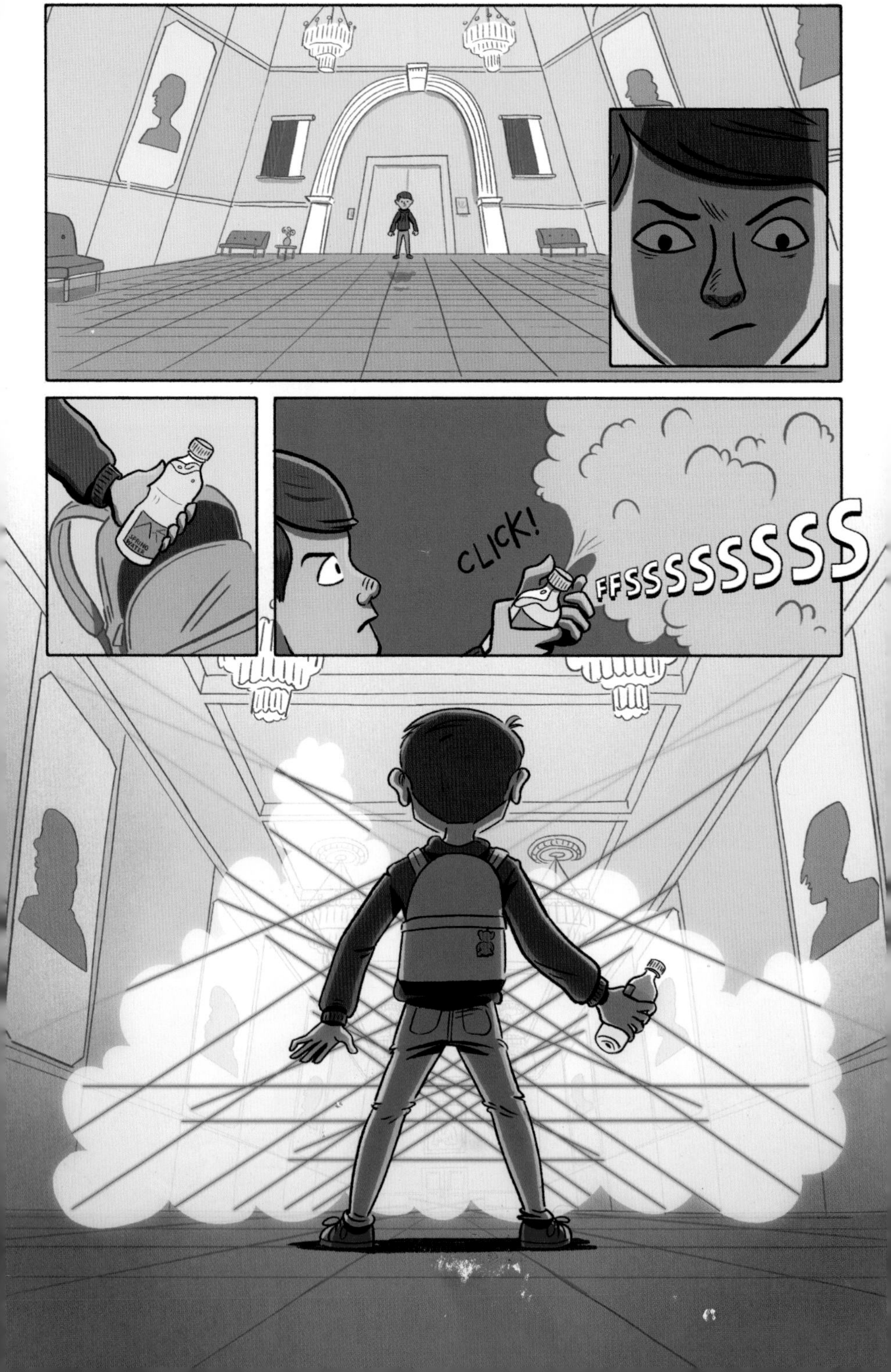
SPRING WATER
CLICK!
FFSSSSSSSSS

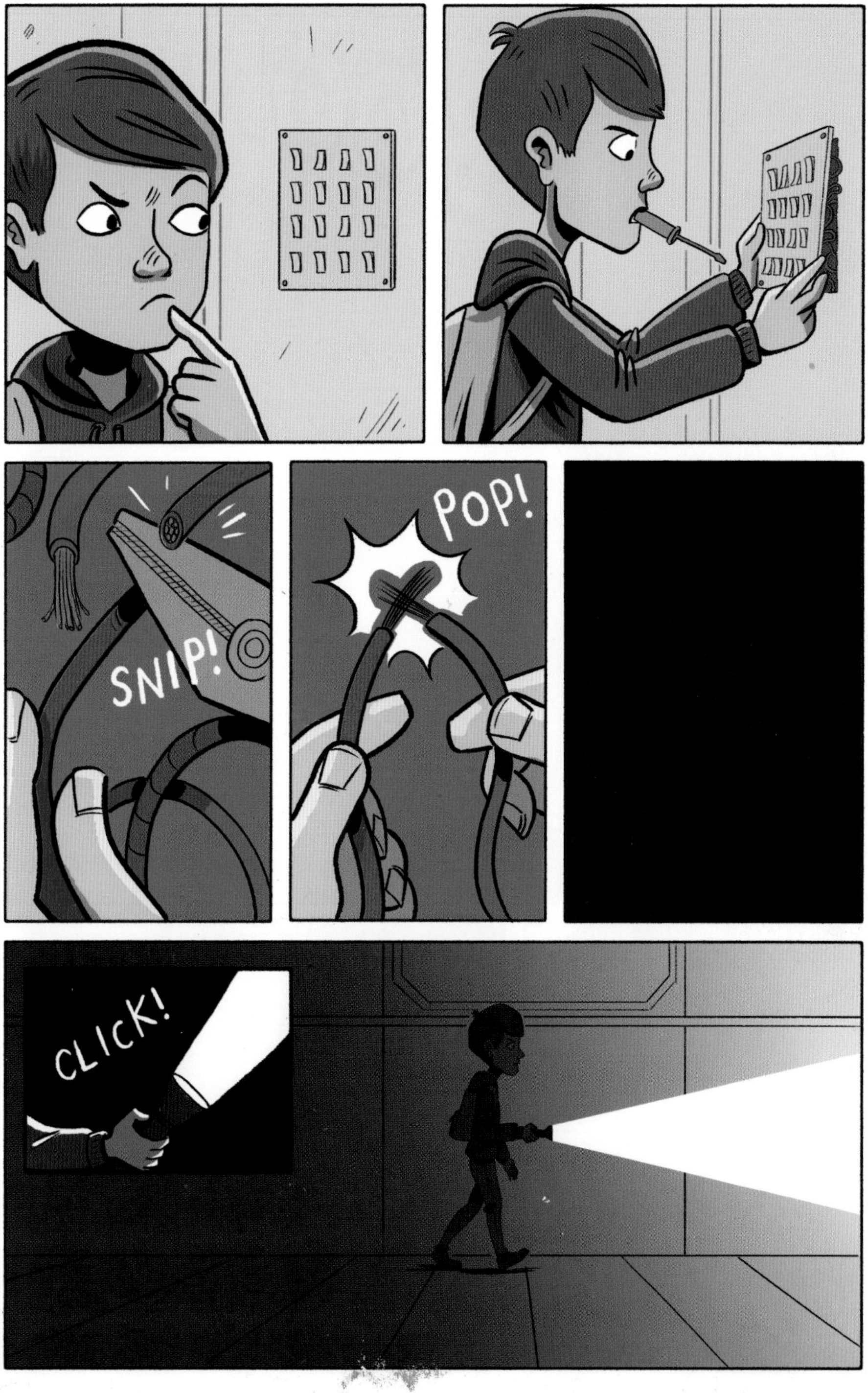
SNIP!
POP!
CLICK!

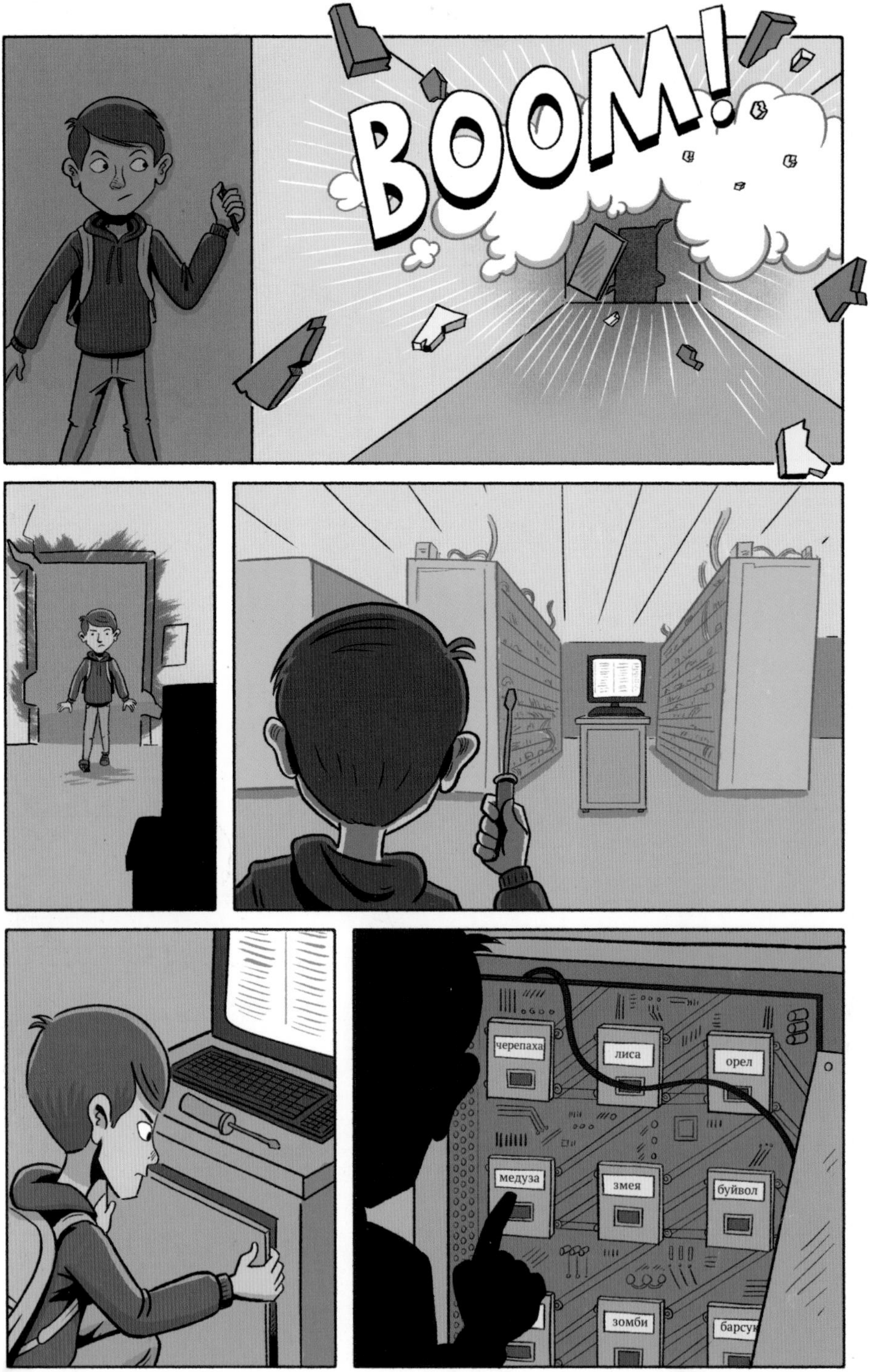
BOOM!
черепаха
лиса
орел
медуза
змея
буйвол
зомби
барсук

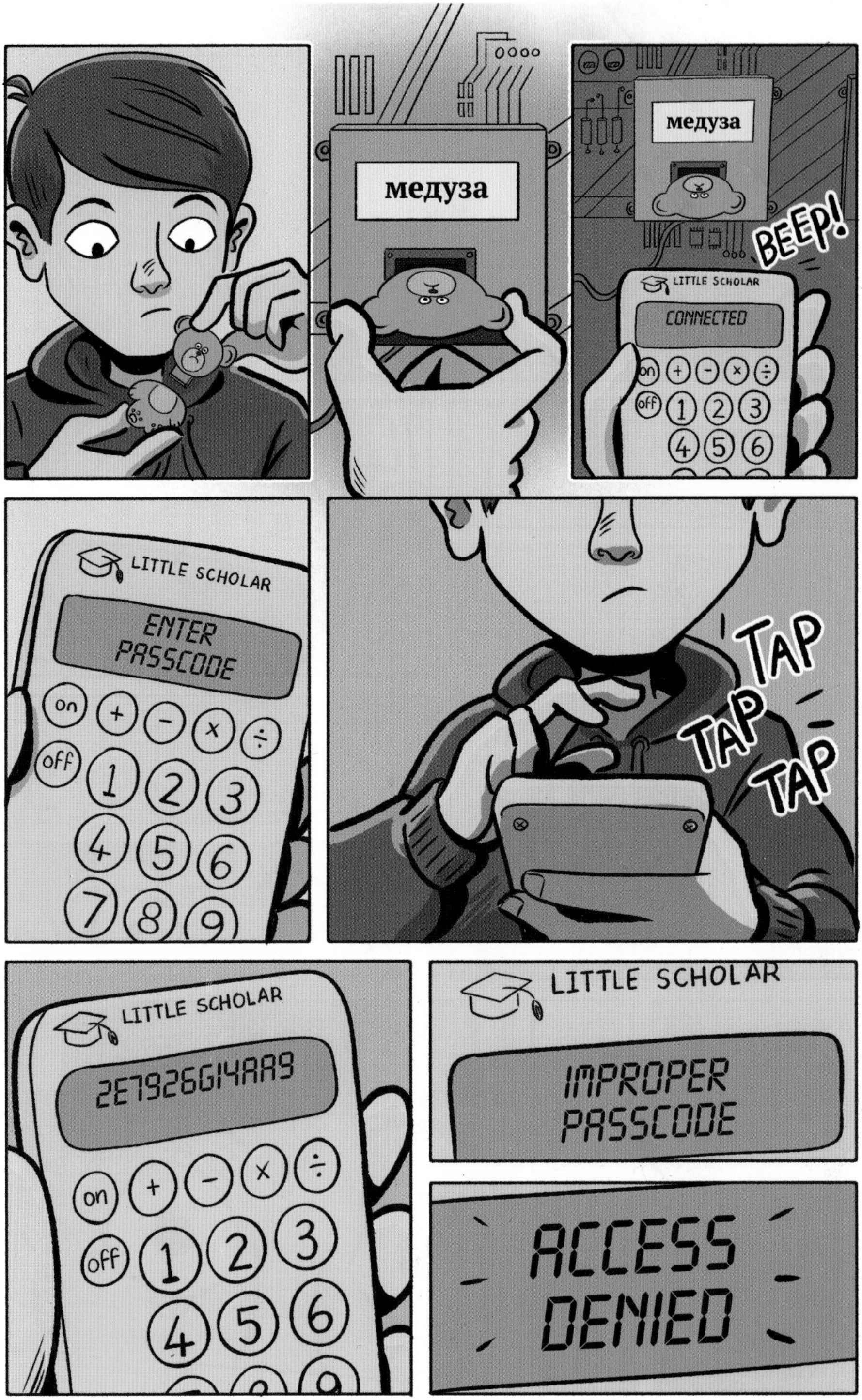
медуза
медуза
BEEP!
LITTLE SCHOLAR
CONNECTED
LITTLE SCHOLAR
ENTER PASSCODE
TAP TAP TAP TAP
LITTLE SCHOLAR
2E7926G14AA9
LITTLE SCHOLAR
IMPROPER PASSCODE
ACCESS DENIED

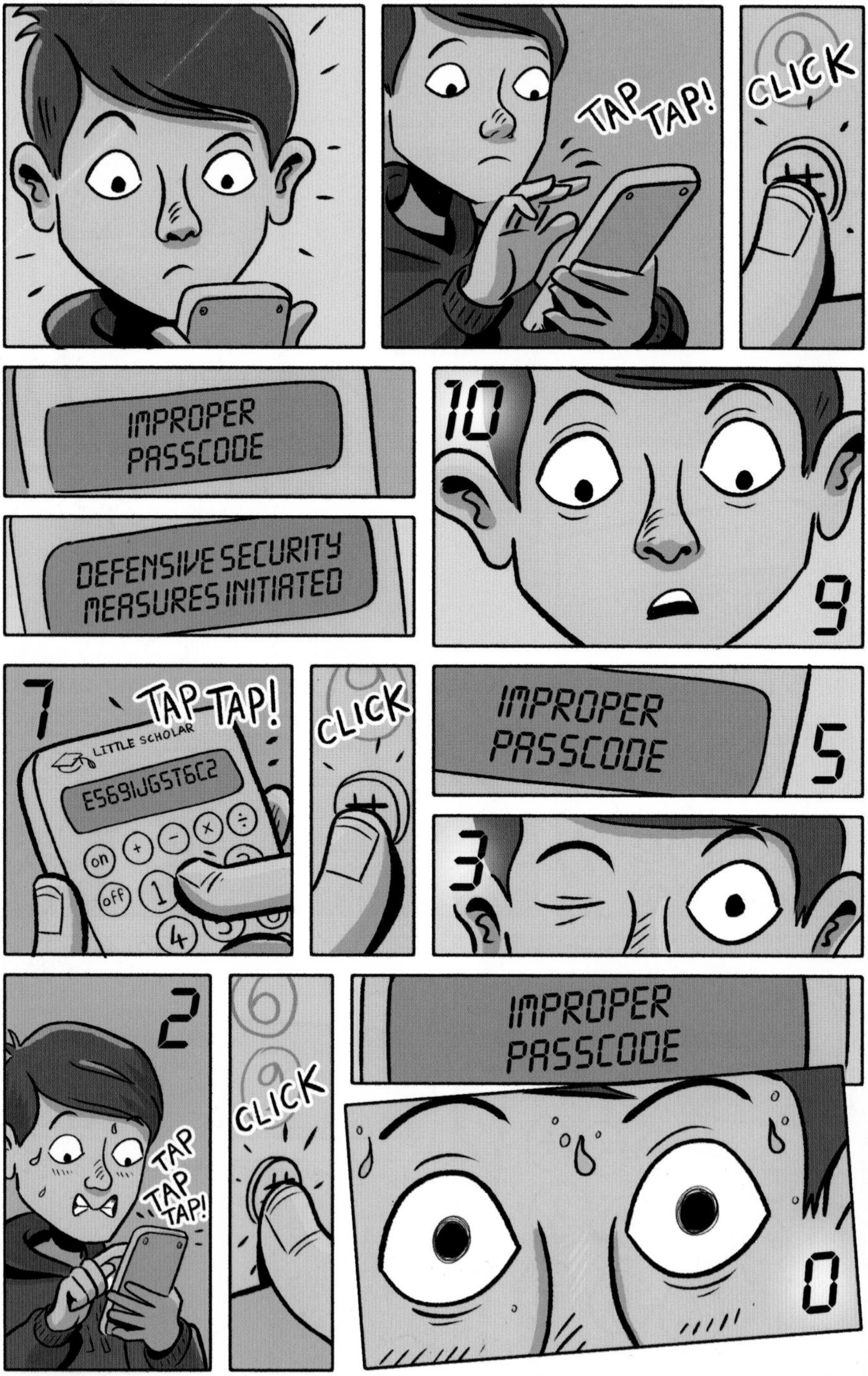

TAP TAP!
CLICK
IMPROPER PASSCODE
DEFENSIVE SECURITY MEASURES INITIATED
10
9
7
TAP TAP!
LITTLE SCHOLAR
E5691JG5T6C2
on
off
+
−
×
÷
1
4
CLICK
IMPROPER PASSCODE
5
3
2
TAP TAP TAP!
CLICK
IMPROPER PASSCODE
0

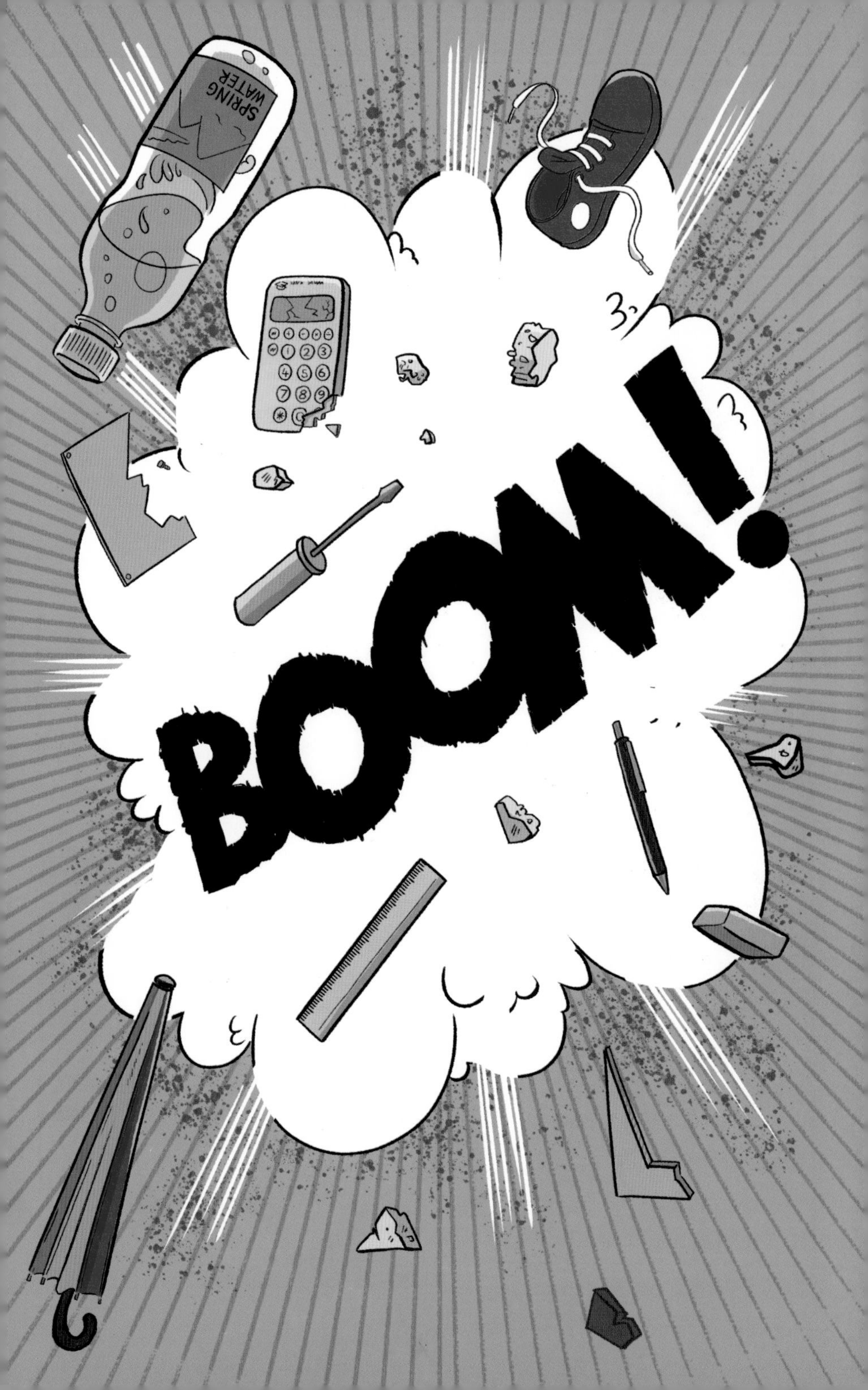
BOOM!
SPRING WATER

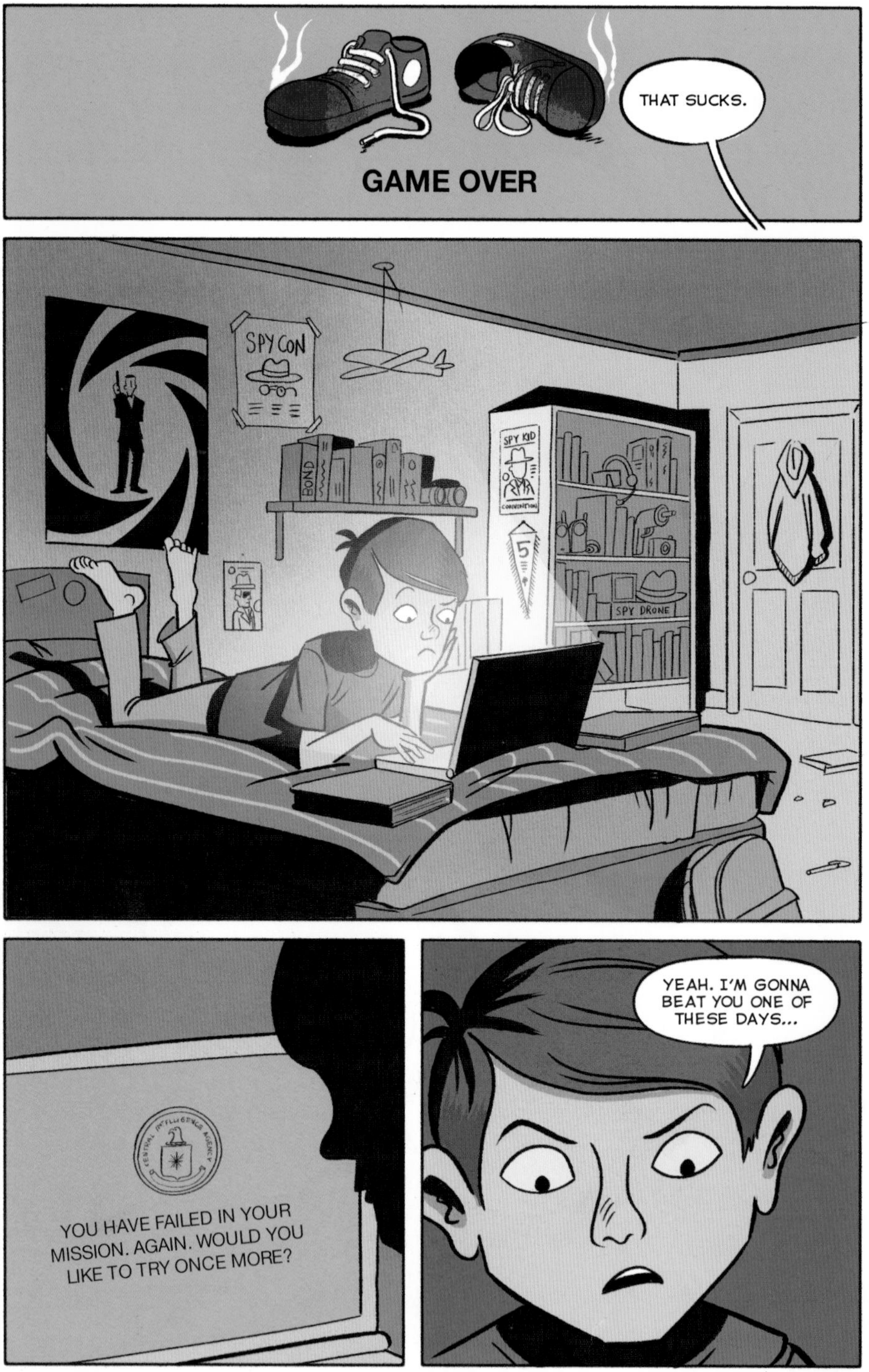
GAME OVER
THAT SUCKS.
SPY CON
BOND
SPY KID
CONVENTION
5
SPY DRONE
YOU HAVE FAILED IN YOUR MISSION. AGAIN. WOULD YOU LIKE TO TRY ONCE MORE?
YEAH. I'M GONNA BEAT YOU ONE OF THESE DAYS...

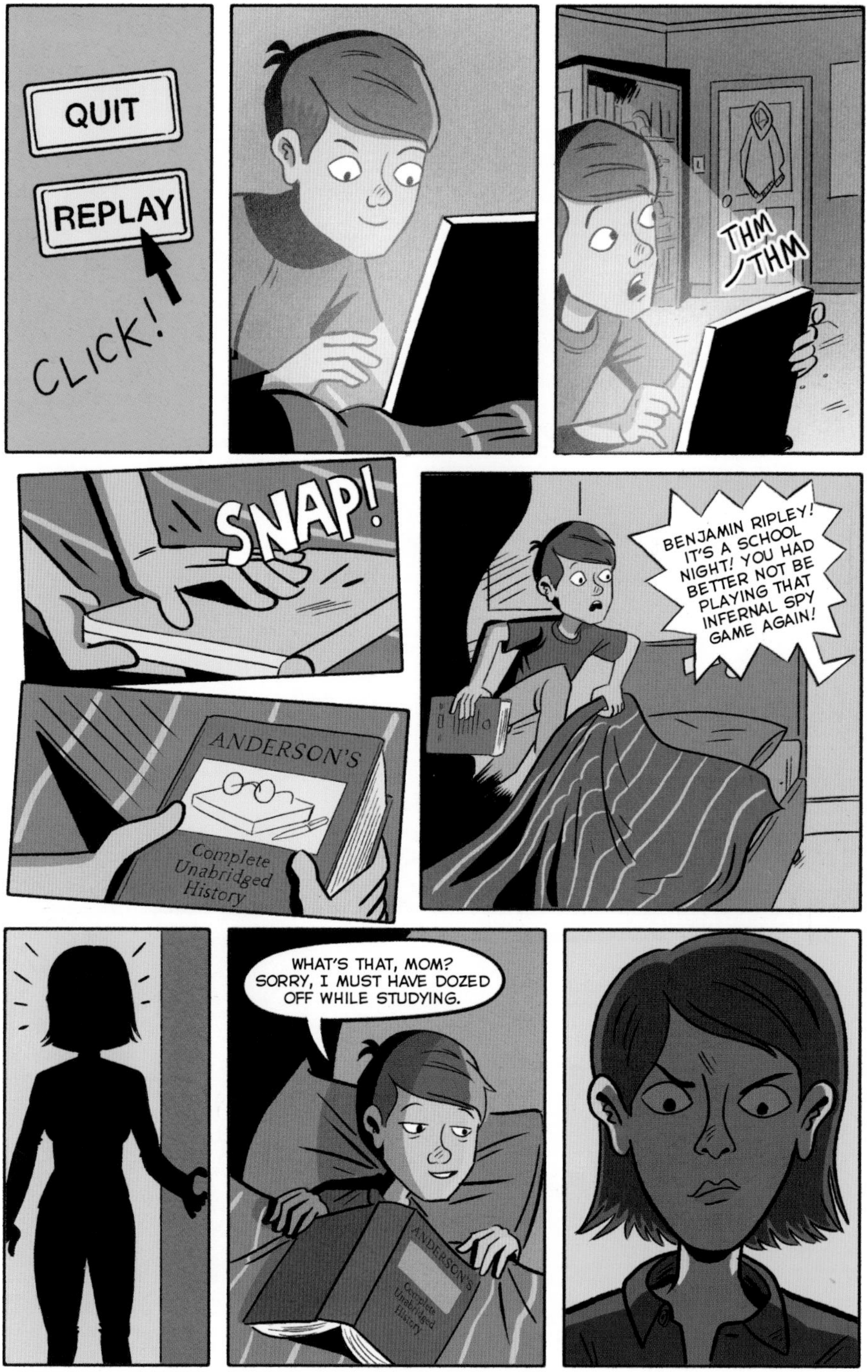
QUIT
REPLAY
CLICK!
THM THM
SNAP!
ANDERSON'S
Complete Unabridged History
BENJAMIN RIPLEY! IT'S A SCHOOL NIGHT! YOU HAD BETTER NOT BE PLAYING THAT INFERNAL SPY GAME AGAIN!
WHAT'S THAT, MOM? SORRY, I MUST HAVE DOZED OFF WHILE STUDYING.
ANDERSON'S Complete Unabridged History

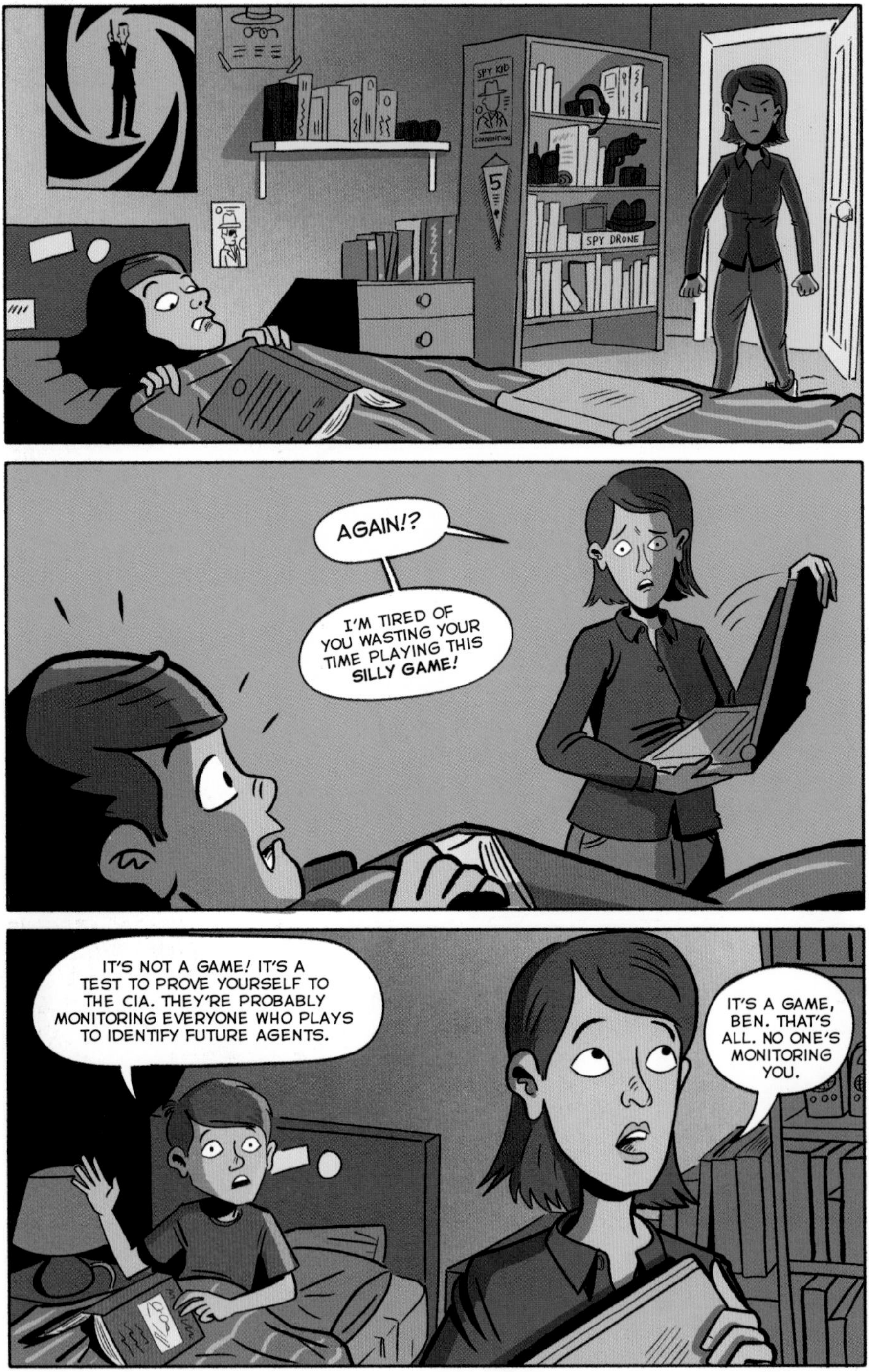
SPY KID
CONVENTION
SPY DRONE
AGAIN!?
I'M TIRED OF YOU WASTING YOUR TIME PLAYING THIS SILLY GAME!
IT'S NOT A GAME! IT'S A TEST TO PROVE YOURSELF TO THE CIA. THEY'RE PROBABLY MONITORING EVERYONE WHO PLAYS TO IDENTIFY FUTURE AGENTS.
IT'S A GAME, BEN. THAT'S ALL. NO ONE'S MONITORING YOU.

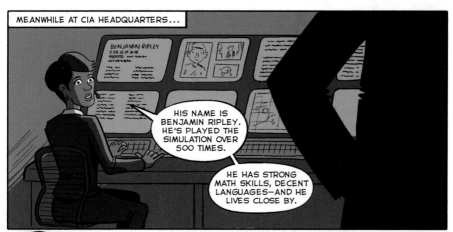

MEANWHILE AT CIA HEADQUARTERS...

BENJAMIN RIPLEY

HIS NAME IS BENJAMIN RIPLEY. HE'S PLAYED THE SIMULATION OVER 500 TIMES.

HE HAS STRONG MATH SKILLS, DECENT LANGUAGES—AND HE LIVES CLOSE BY.

SOUNDS LIKE THE PERFECT PATSY. BRING HIM IN.

YES SIR.

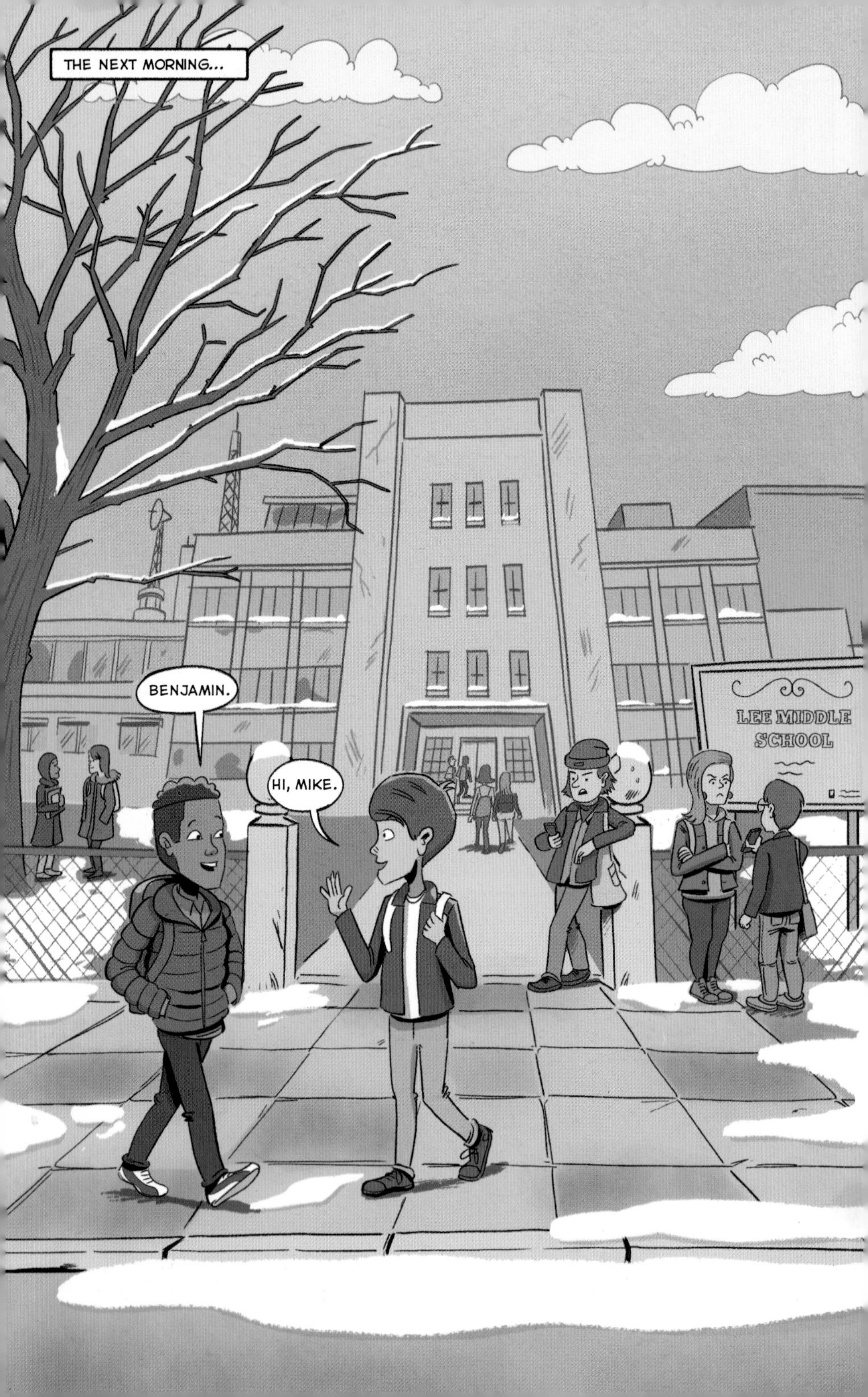
THE NEXT MORNING...
BENJAMIN.
HI, MIKE.
LEE MIDDLE SCHOOL

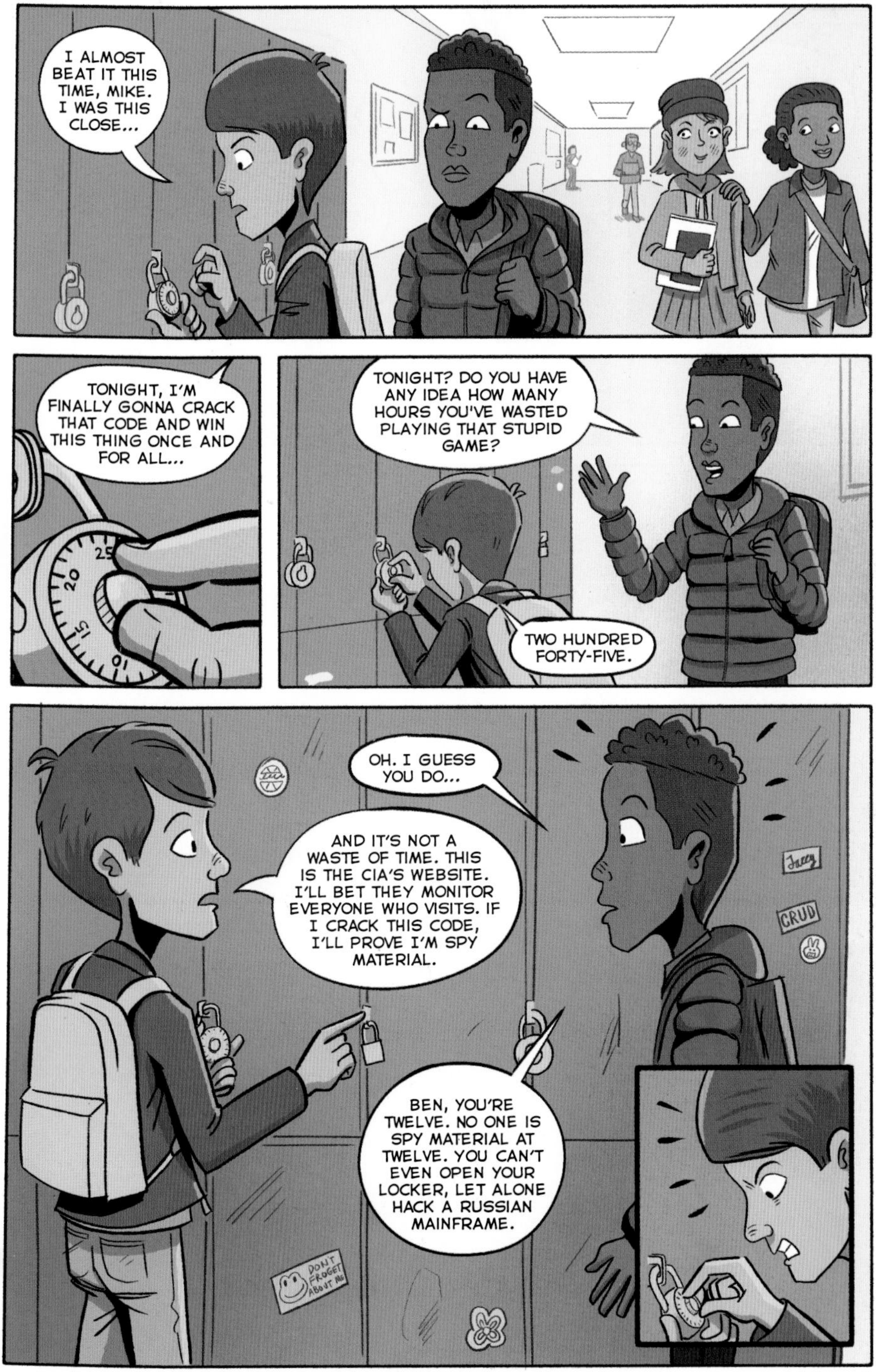
I ALMOST BEAT IT THIS TIME, MIKE. I WAS THIS CLOSE...
TONIGHT, I'M FINALLY GONNA CRACK THAT CODE AND WIN THIS THING ONCE AND FOR ALL...
TONIGHT? DO YOU HAVE ANY IDEA HOW MANY HOURS YOU'VE WASTED PLAYING THAT STUPID GAME?
TWO HUNDRED FORTY-FIVE.
OH. I GUESS YOU DO...
AND IT'S NOT A WASTE OF TIME. THIS IS THE CIA'S WEBSITE. I'LL BET THEY MONITOR EVERYONE WHO VISITS. IF I CRACK THIS CODE, I'LL PROVE I'M SPY MATERIAL.
CRUD
BEN, YOU'RE TWELVE. NO ONE IS SPY MATERIAL AT TWELVE. YOU CAN'T EVEN OPEN YOUR LOCKER, LET ALONE HACK A RUSSIAN MAINFRAME.

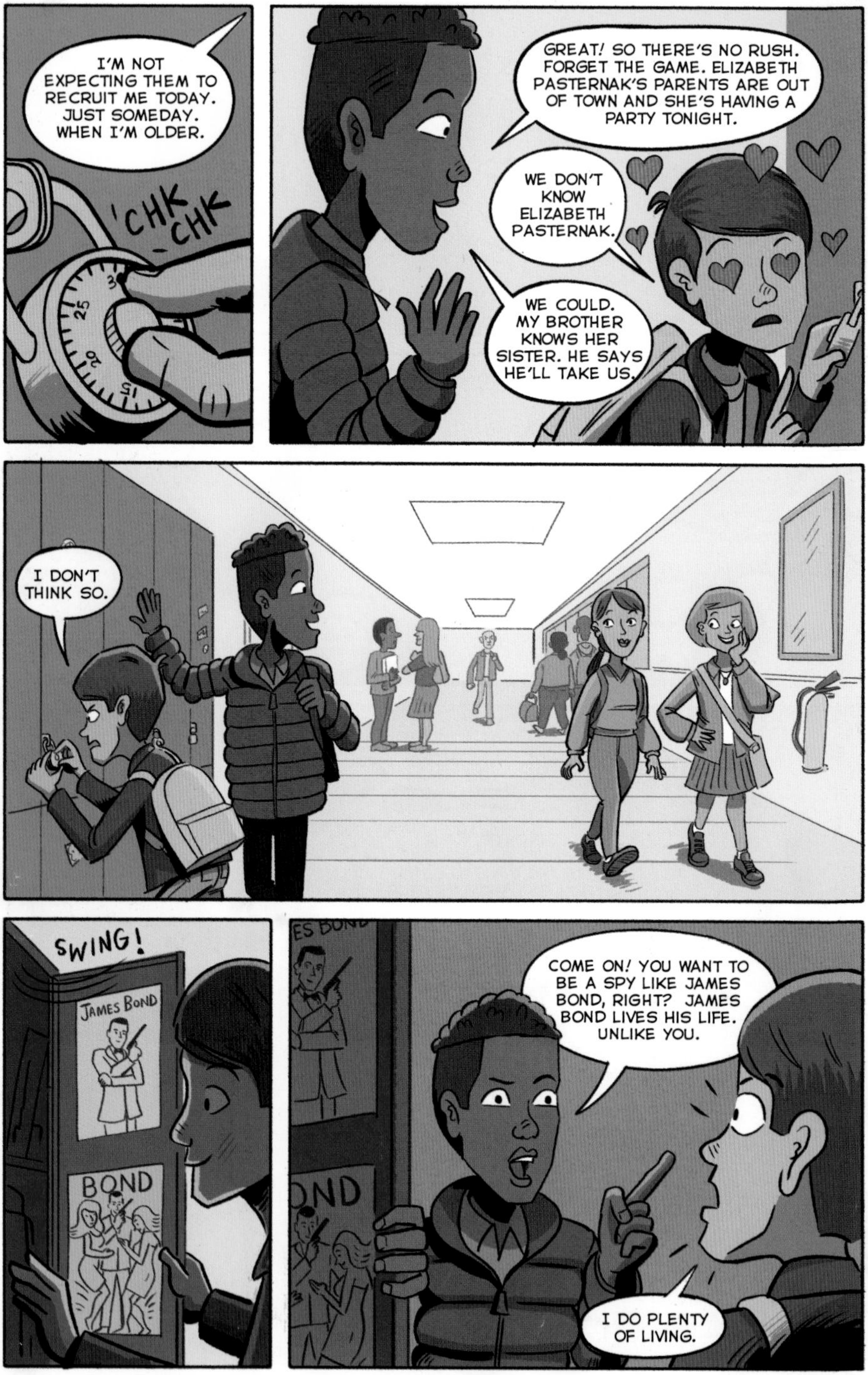
I'M NOT EXPECTING THEM TO RECRUIT ME TODAY. JUST SOMEDAY. WHEN I'M OLDER.
CHK CHK
GREAT! SO THERE'S NO RUSH. FORGET THE GAME. ELIZABETH PASTERNAK'S PARENTS ARE OUT OF TOWN AND SHE'S HAVING A PARTY TONIGHT.
WE DON'T KNOW ELIZABETH PASTERNAK.
WE COULD. MY BROTHER KNOWS HER SISTER. HE SAYS HE'LL TAKE US.
I DON'T THINK SO.
SWING!
JAMES BOND
BOND
COME ON! YOU WANT TO BE A SPY LIKE JAMES BOND, RIGHT? JAMES BOND LIVES HIS LIFE. UNLIKE YOU.
I DO PLENTY OF LIVING.

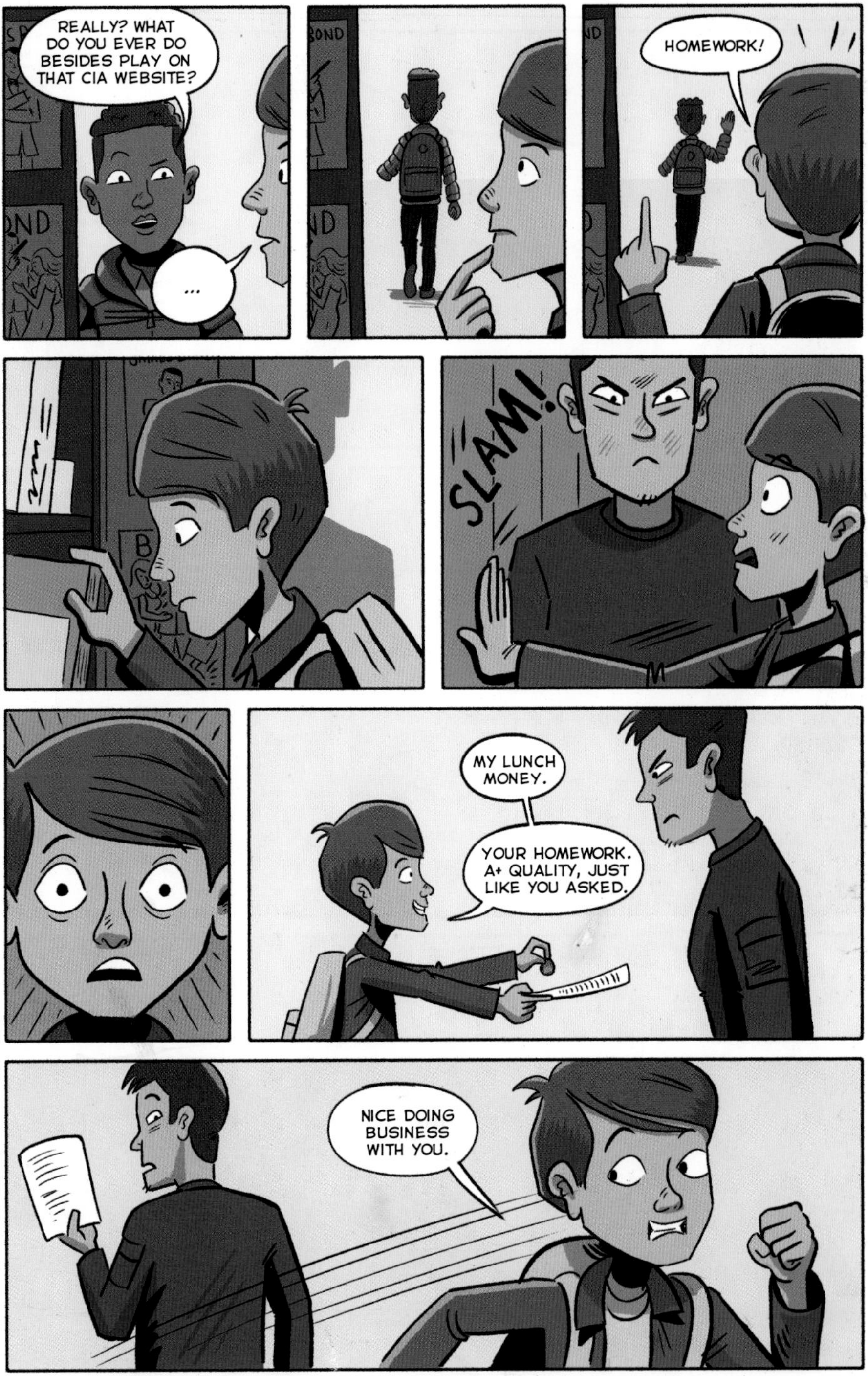
REALLY? WHAT DO YOU EVER DO BESIDES PLAY ON THAT CIA WEBSITE?
...
HOMEWORK!
SLAM!
MY LUNCH MONEY.
YOUR HOMEWORK. A+ QUALITY, JUST LIKE YOU ASKED.
NICE DOING BUSINESS WITH YOU.

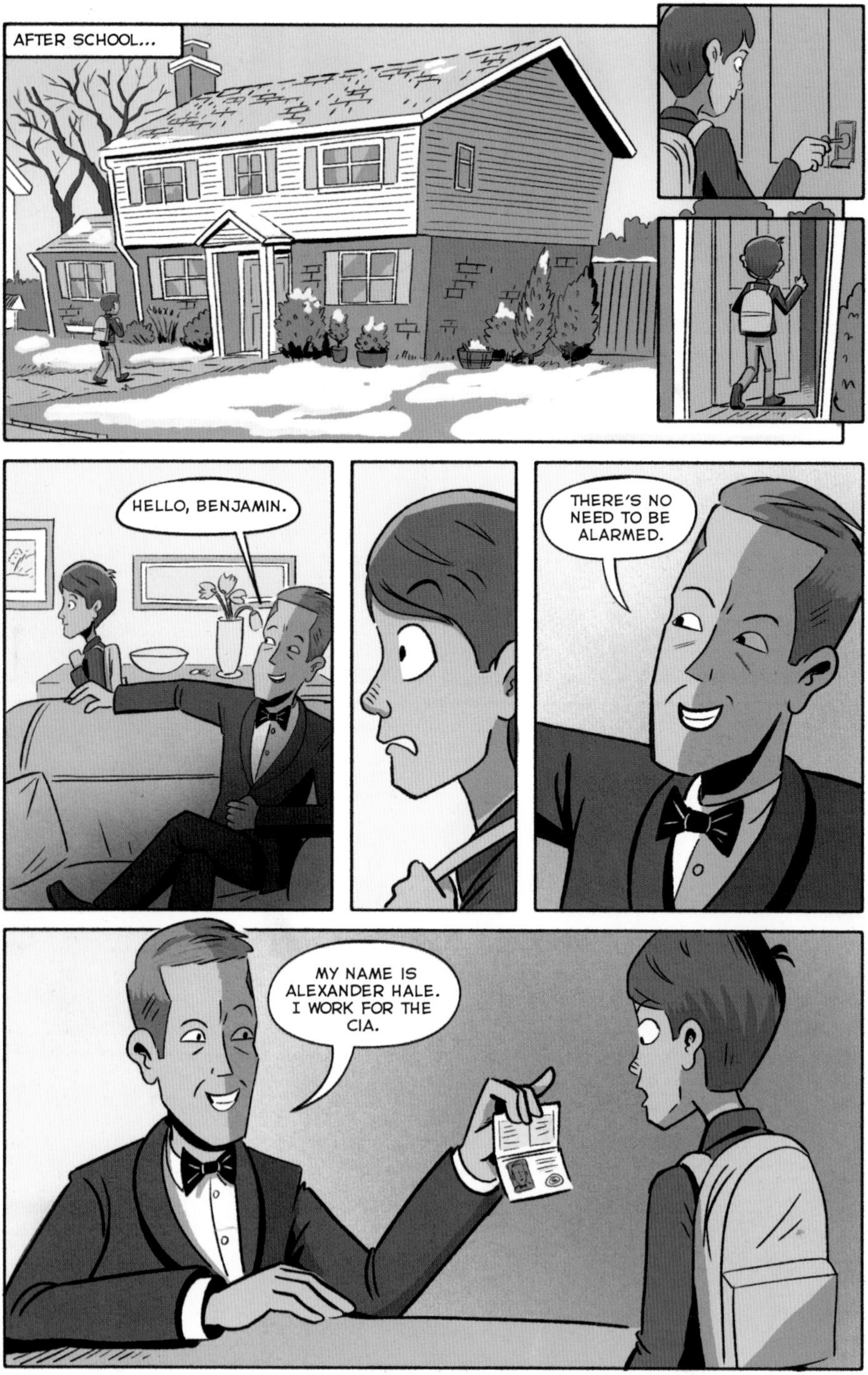
AFTER SCHOOL...
HELLO, BENJAMIN.
THERE'S NO NEED TO BE ALARMED.
MY NAME IS ALEXANDER HALE. I WORK FOR THE CIA.

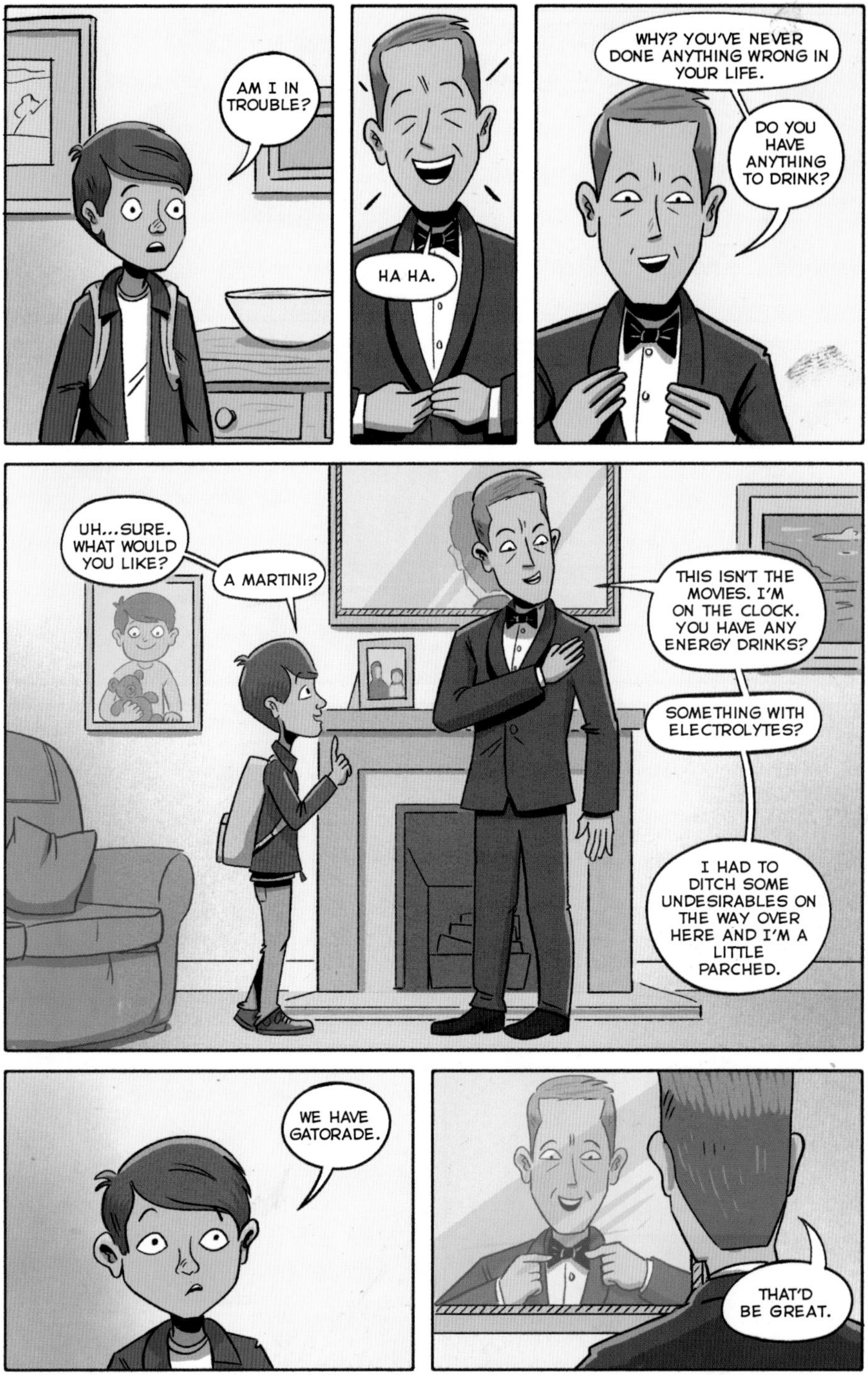
AM I IN TROUBLE?
HA HA.
WHY? YOU'VE NEVER DONE ANYTHING WRONG IN YOUR LIFE.
DO YOU HAVE ANYTHING TO DRINK?
UH...SURE. WHAT WOULD YOU LIKE?
A MARTINI?
THIS ISN'T THE MOVIES. I'M ON THE CLOCK. YOU HAVE ANY ENERGY DRINKS?
SOMETHING WITH ELECTROLYTES?
I HAD TO DITCH SOME UNDESIRABLES ON THE WAY OVER HERE AND I'M A LITTLE PARCHED.
WE HAVE GATORADE.
THAT'D BE GREAT.

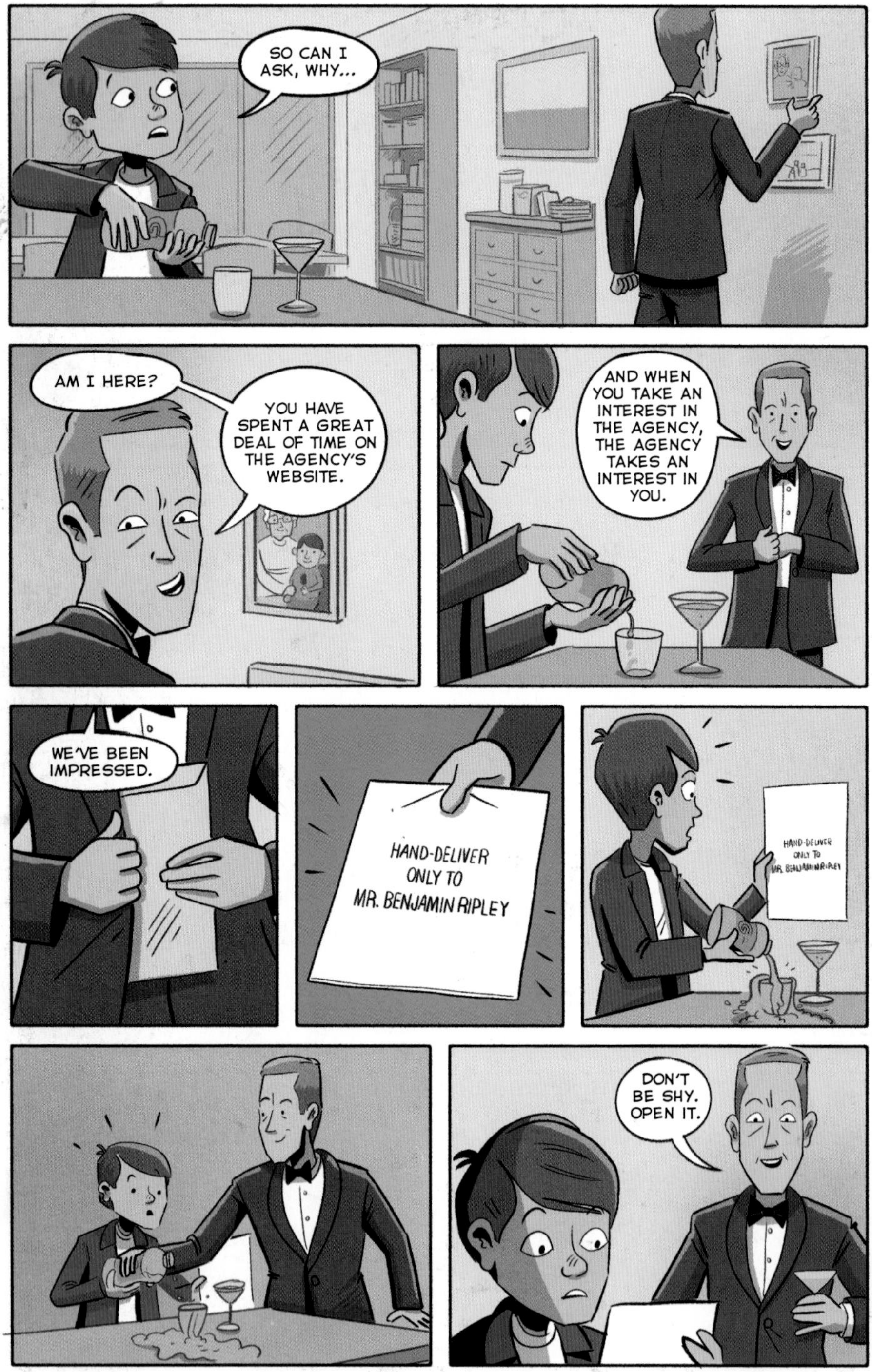
SO CAN I ASK, WHY...
AM I HERE?
YOU HAVE SPENT A GREAT DEAL OF TIME ON THE AGENCY'S WEBSITE.
AND WHEN YOU TAKE AN INTEREST IN THE AGENCY, THE AGENCY TAKES AN INTEREST IN YOU.
WE'VE BEEN IMPRESSED.
HAND-DELIVER ONLY TO MR. BENJAMIN RIPLEY
HAND-DELIVER ONLY TO MR. BENJAMIN RIPLEY
DON'T BE SHY. OPEN IT.

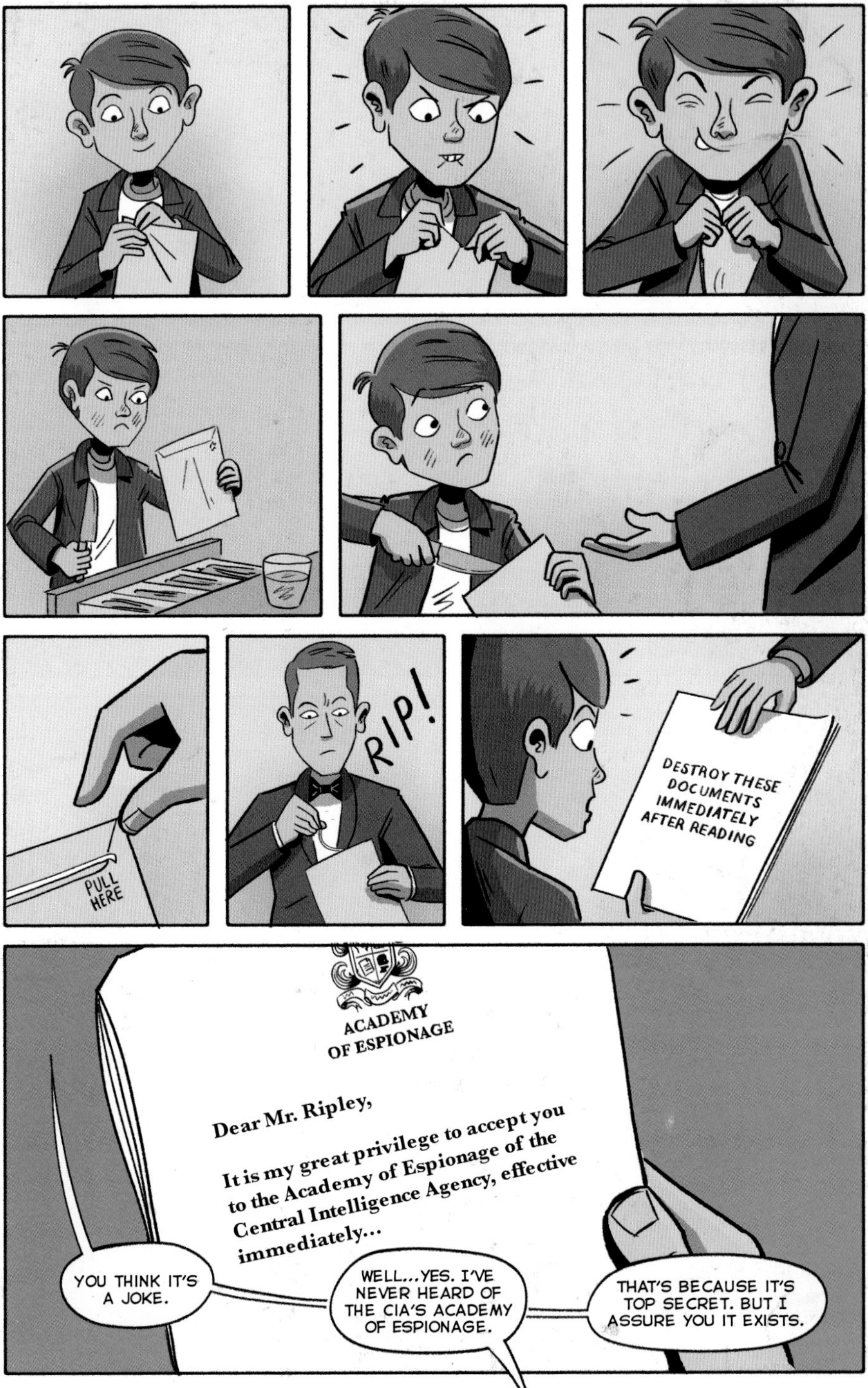
PULL HERE
RIP!
DESTROY THESE DOCUMENTS IMMEDIATELY AFTER READING
ACADEMY OF ESPIONAGE
Dear Mr. Ripley,
It is my great privilege to accept you to the Academy of Espionage of the Central Intelligence Agency, effective immediately...
YOU THINK IT'S A JOKE.
WELL...YES. I'VE NEVER HEARD OF THE CIA'S ACADEMY OF ESPIONAGE.
THAT'S BECAUSE IT'S TOP SECRET. BUT I ASSURE YOU IT EXISTS.

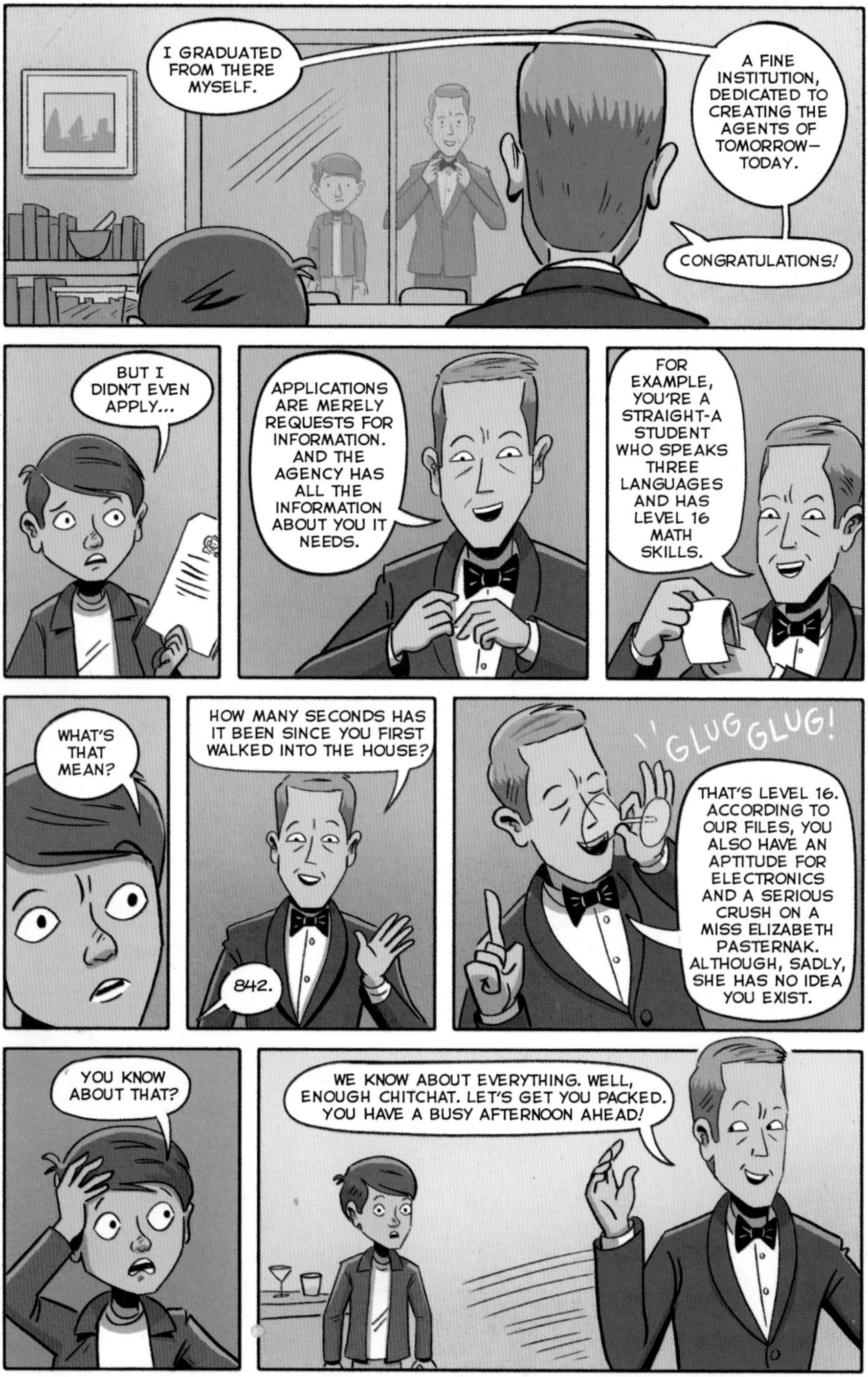
I GRADUATED FROM THERE MYSELF.
A FINE INSTITUTION, DEDICATED TO CREATING THE AGENTS OF TOMORROW— TODAY.
CONGRATULATIONS!
BUT I DIDN'T EVEN APPLY...
APPLICATIONS ARE MERELY REQUESTS FOR INFORMATION. AND THE AGENCY HAS ALL THE INFORMATION ABOUT YOU IT NEEDS.
FOR EXAMPLE, YOU'RE A STRAIGHT-A STUDENT WHO SPEAKS THREE LANGUAGES AND HAS LEVEL 16 MATH SKILLS.
WHAT'S THAT MEAN?
HOW MANY SECONDS HAS IT BEEN SINCE YOU FIRST WALKED INTO THE HOUSE?
842.
GLUG GLUG!
THAT'S LEVEL 16. ACCORDING TO OUR FILES, YOU ALSO HAVE AN APTITUDE FOR ELECTRONICS AND A SERIOUS CRUSH ON A MISS ELIZABETH PASTERNAK. ALTHOUGH, SADLY, SHE HAS NO IDEA YOU EXIST.
YOU KNOW ABOUT THAT?
WE KNOW ABOUT EVERYTHING. WELL, ENOUGH CHITCHAT. LET'S GET YOU PACKED. YOU HAVE A BUSY AFTERNOON AHEAD!

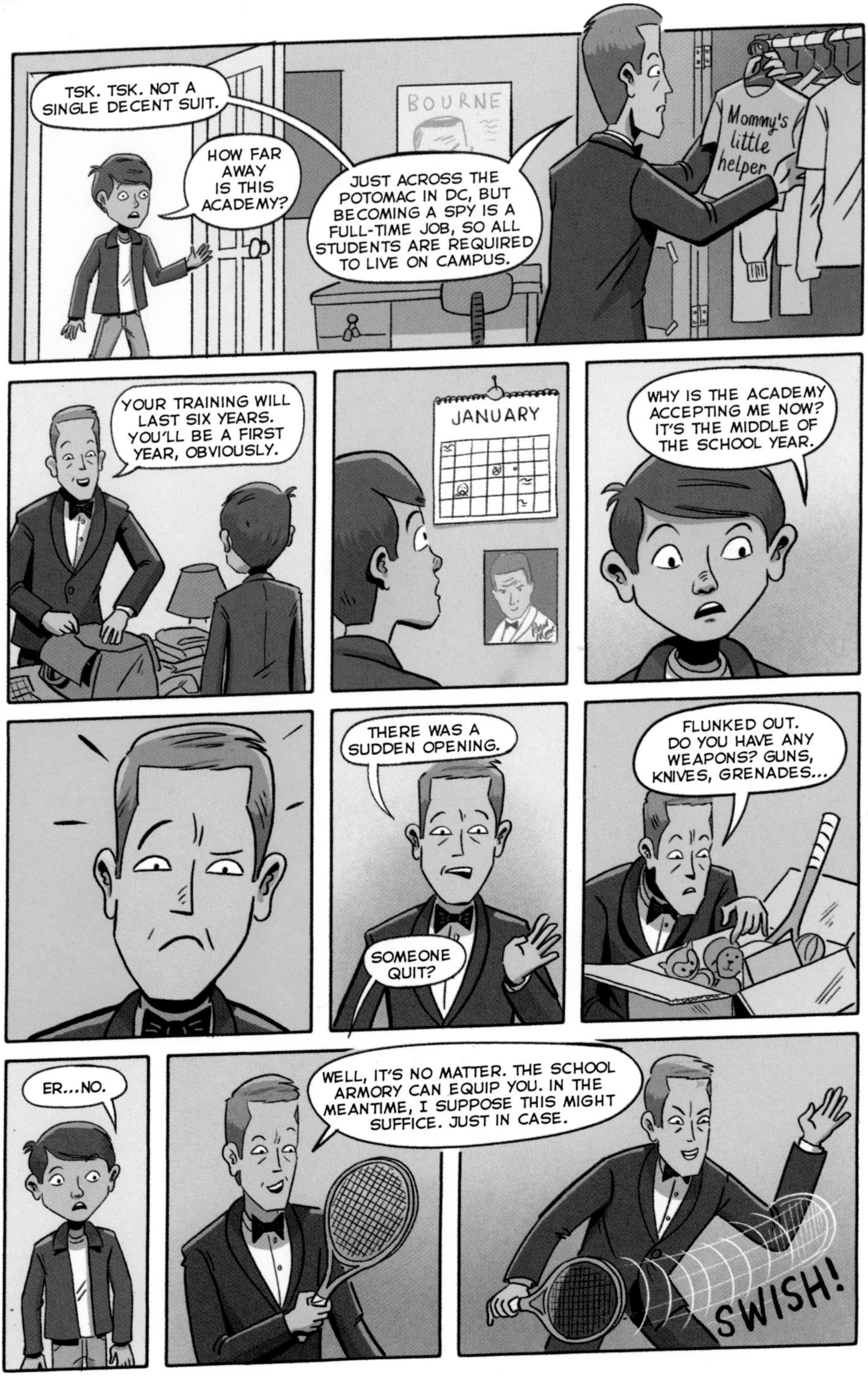
TSK. TSK. NOT A SINGLE DECENT SUIT.
HOW FAR AWAY IS THIS ACADEMY?
JUST ACROSS THE POTOMAC IN DC, BUT BECOMING A SPY IS A FULL-TIME JOB, SO ALL STUDENTS ARE REQUIRED TO LIVE ON CAMPUS.
BOURNE
Mommy's little helper
YOUR TRAINING WILL LAST SIX YEARS. YOU'LL BE A FIRST YEAR, OBVIOUSLY.
JANUARY
WHY IS THE ACADEMY ACCEPTING ME NOW? IT'S THE MIDDLE OF THE SCHOOL YEAR.
THERE WAS A SUDDEN OPENING.
SOMEONE QUIT?
FLUNKED OUT. DO YOU HAVE ANY WEAPONS? GUNS, KNIVES, GRENADES...
ER...NO.
WELL, IT'S NO MATTER. THE SCHOOL ARMORY CAN EQUIP YOU. IN THE MEANTIME, I SUPPOSE THIS MIGHT SUFFICE. JUST IN CASE.
SWISH!

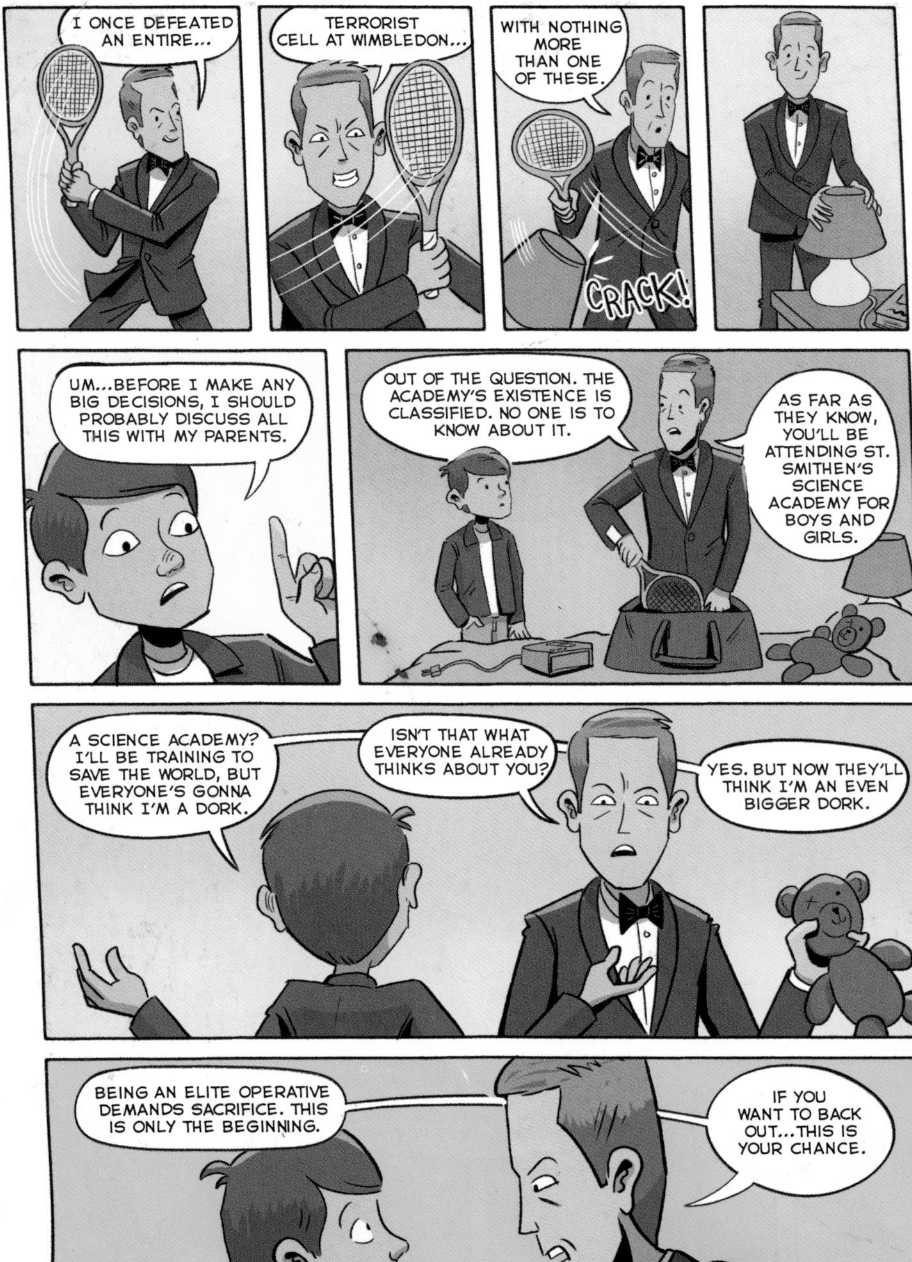

I ONCE DEFEATED AN ENTIRE...
TERRORIST CELL AT WIMBLEDON...
WITH NOTHING MORE THAN ONE OF THESE.
CRACK!
UM...BEFORE I MAKE ANY BIG DECISIONS, I SHOULD PROBABLY DISCUSS ALL THIS WITH MY PARENTS.
OUT OF THE QUESTION. THE ACADEMY'S EXISTENCE IS CLASSIFIED. NO ONE IS TO KNOW ABOUT IT.
AS FAR AS THEY KNOW, YOU'LL BE ATTENDING ST. SMITHEN'S SCIENCE ACADEMY FOR BOYS AND GIRLS.
A SCIENCE ACADEMY? I'LL BE TRAINING TO SAVE THE WORLD, BUT EVERYONE'S GONNA THINK I'M A DORK.
ISN'T THAT WHAT EVERYONE ALREADY THINKS ABOUT YOU?
YES. BUT NOW THEY'LL THINK I'M AN EVEN BIGGER DORK.
BEING AN ELITE OPERATIVE DEMANDS SACRIFICE. THIS IS ONLY THE BEGINNING.
IF YOU WANT TO BACK OUT...THIS IS YOUR CHANCE.

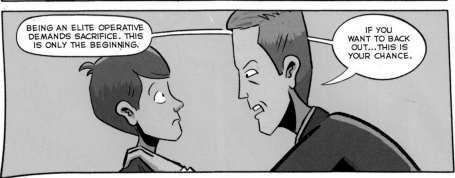

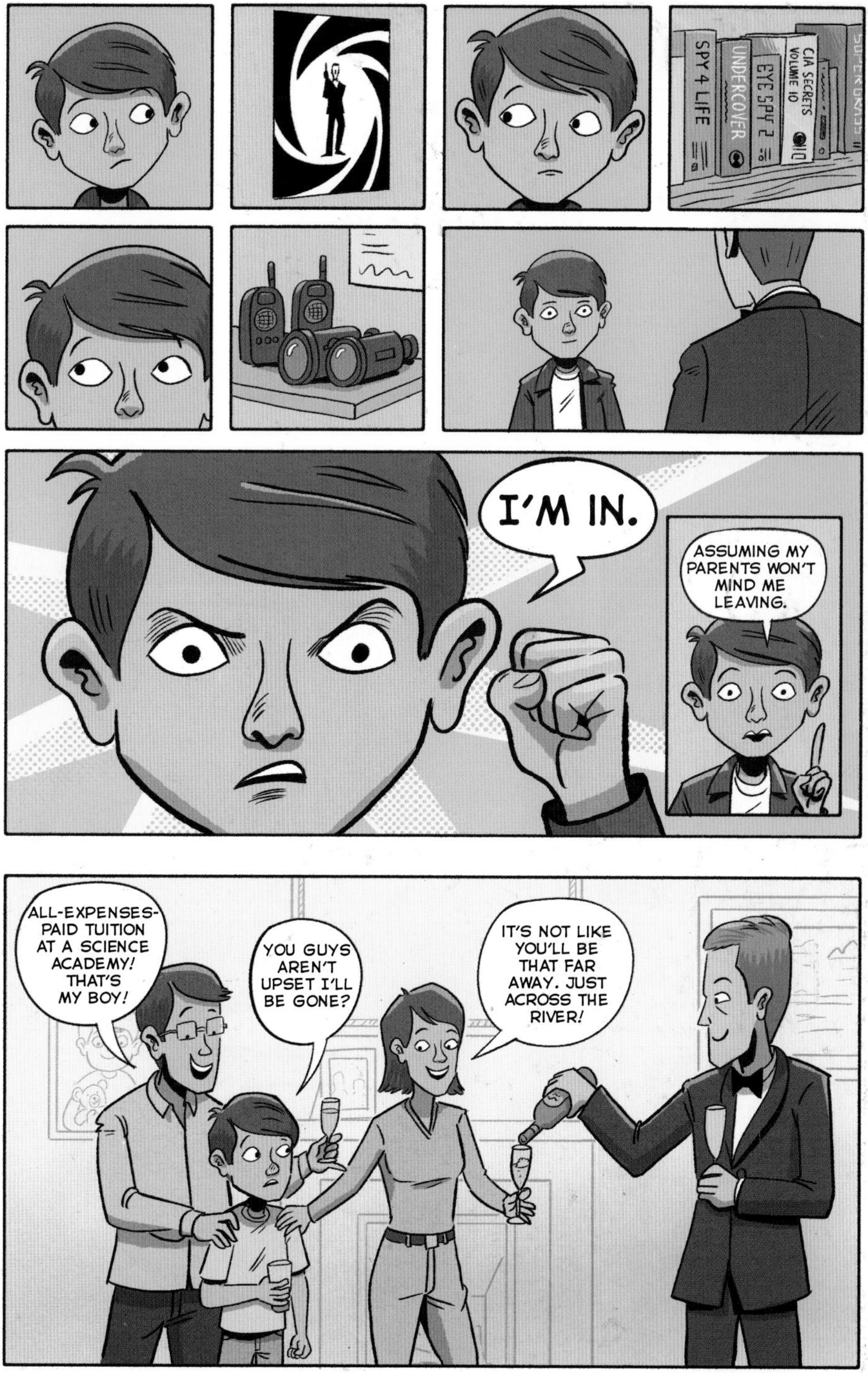
SPY 4 LIFE
UNDERCOVER
EYE SPY 2
CIA SECRETS VOLUME 10
I'M IN.
ASSUMING MY PARENTS WON'T MIND ME LEAVING.
ALL-EXPENSES-PAID TUITION AT A SCIENCE ACADEMY! THAT'S MY BOY!
YOU GUYS AREN'T UPSET I'LL BE GONE?
IT'S NOT LIKE YOU'LL BE THAT FAR AWAY. JUST ACROSS THE RIVER!

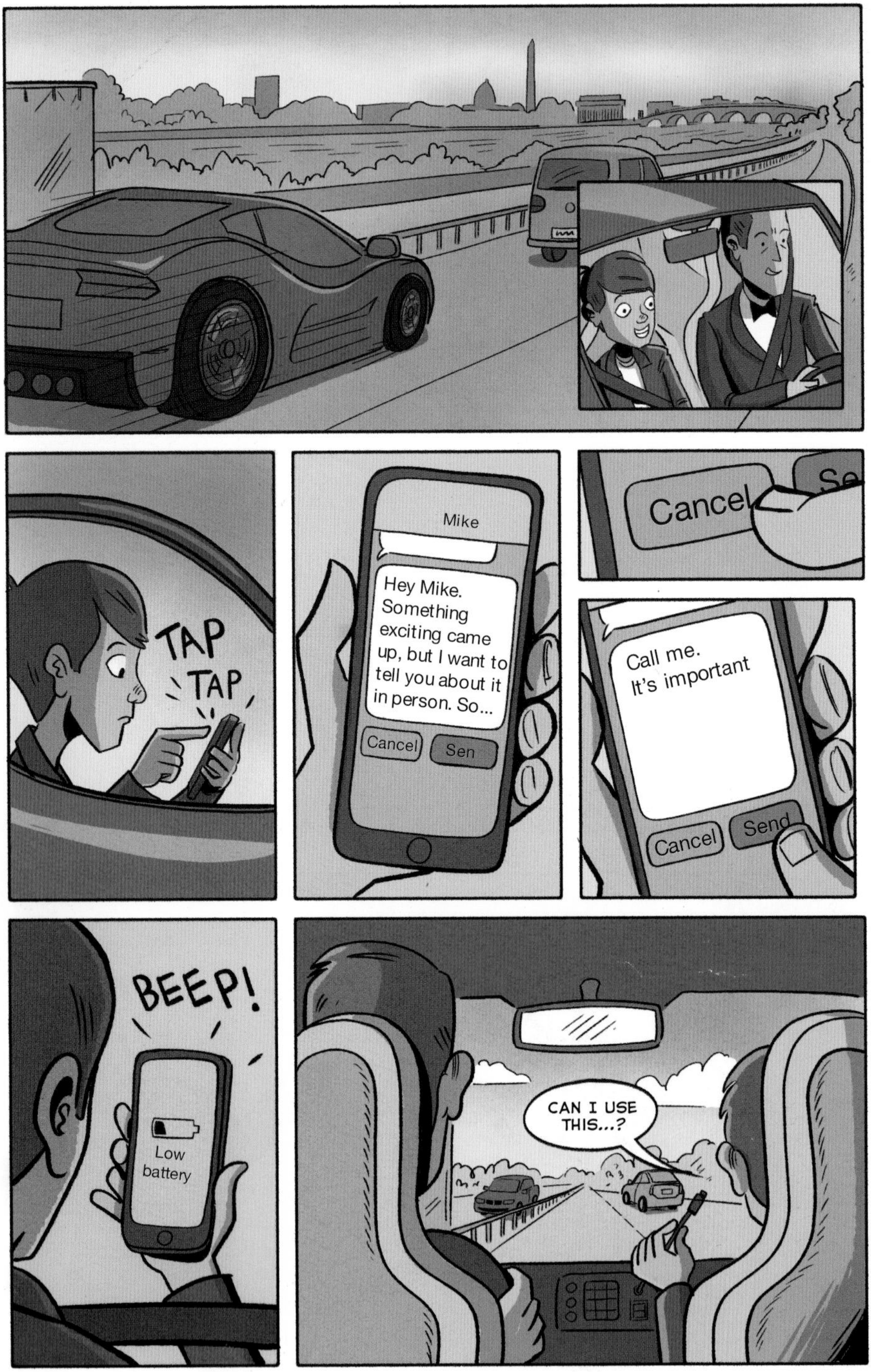
Mike
TAP
TAP
Hey Mike. Something exciting came up, but I want to tell you about it in person. So...
Cancel
Sen
Cancel
Se
Call me. It's important
Cancel
Send
BEEP!
Low battery
CAN I USE THIS...?

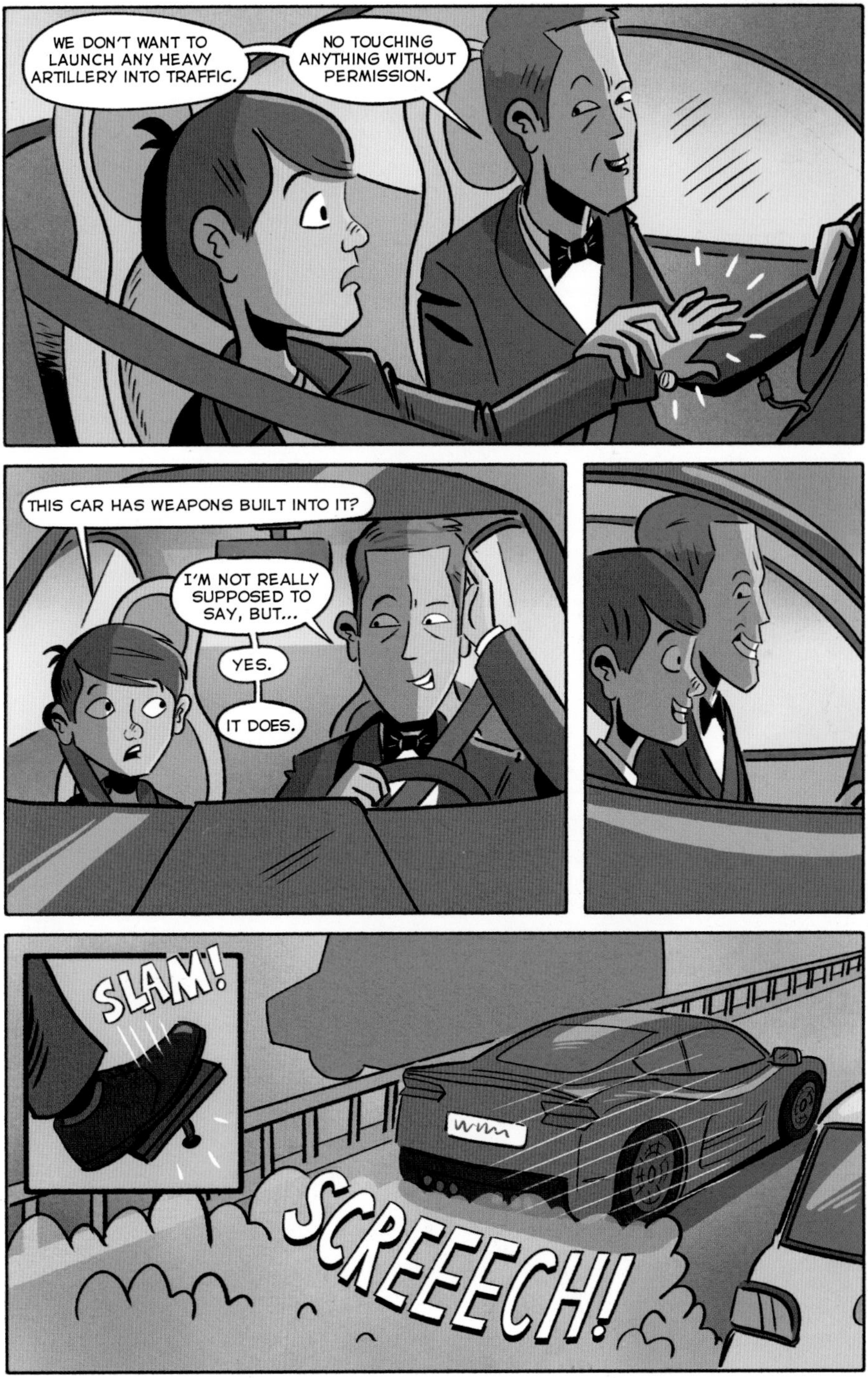
WE DON'T WANT TO LAUNCH ANY HEAVY ARTILLERY INTO TRAFFIC.
NO TOUCHING ANYTHING WITHOUT PERMISSION.
THIS CAR HAS WEAPONS BUILT INTO IT?
I'M NOT REALLY SUPPOSED TO SAY, BUT...
YES.
IT DOES.
SLAM!
SCREEECH!

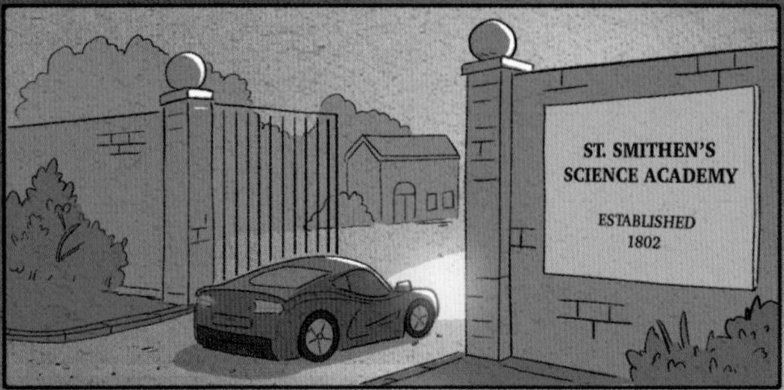
ST. SMITHEN'S
SCIENCE ACADEMY
ESTABLISHED
1802

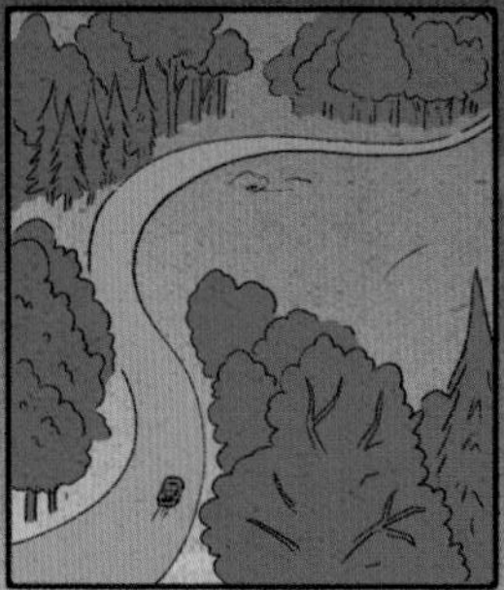

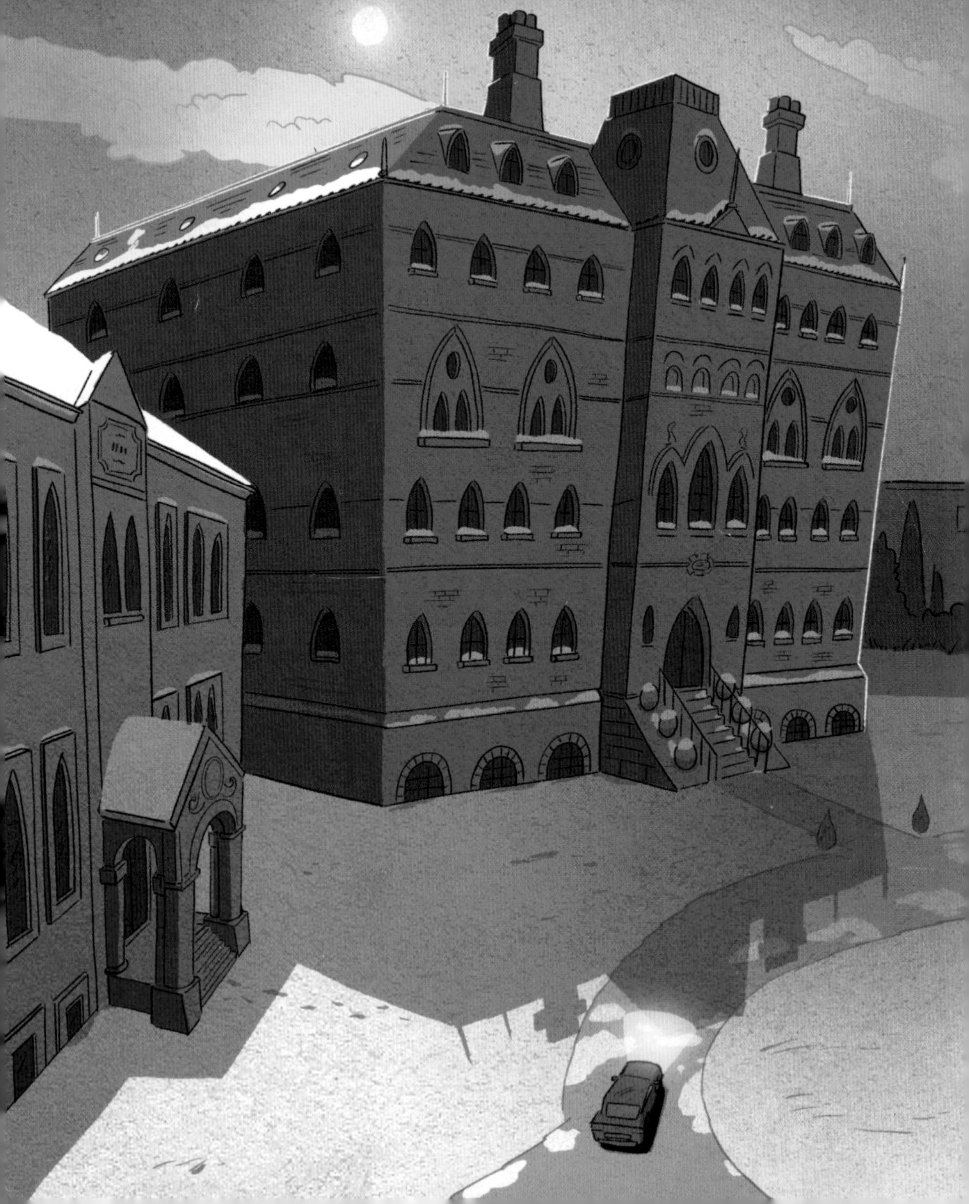

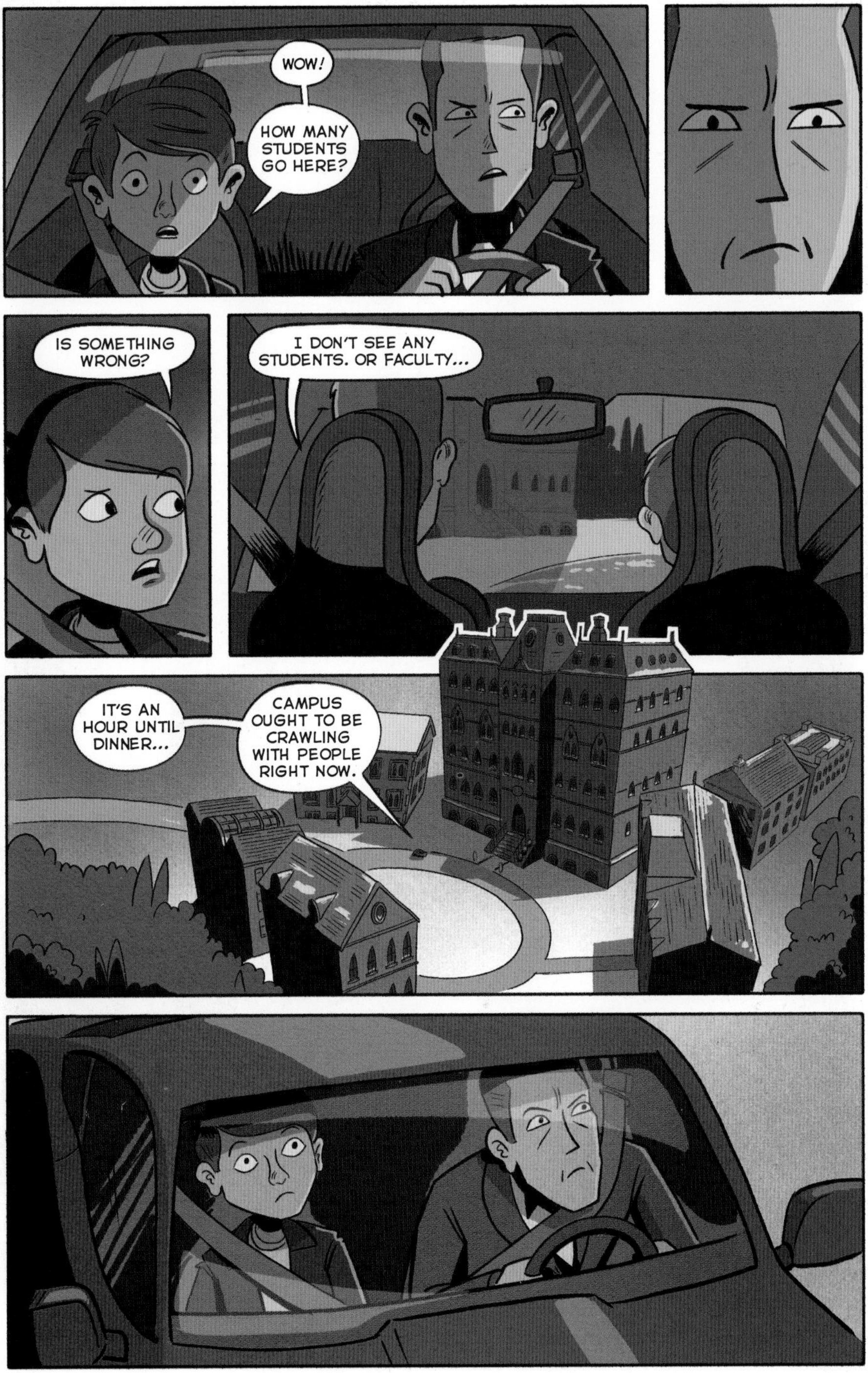
WOW!
HOW MANY STUDENTS GO HERE?
IS SOMETHING WRONG?
I DON'T SEE ANY STUDENTS. OR FACULTY...
IT'S AN HOUR UNTIL DINNER...
CAMPUS OUGHT TO BE CRAWLING WITH PEOPLE RIGHT NOW.

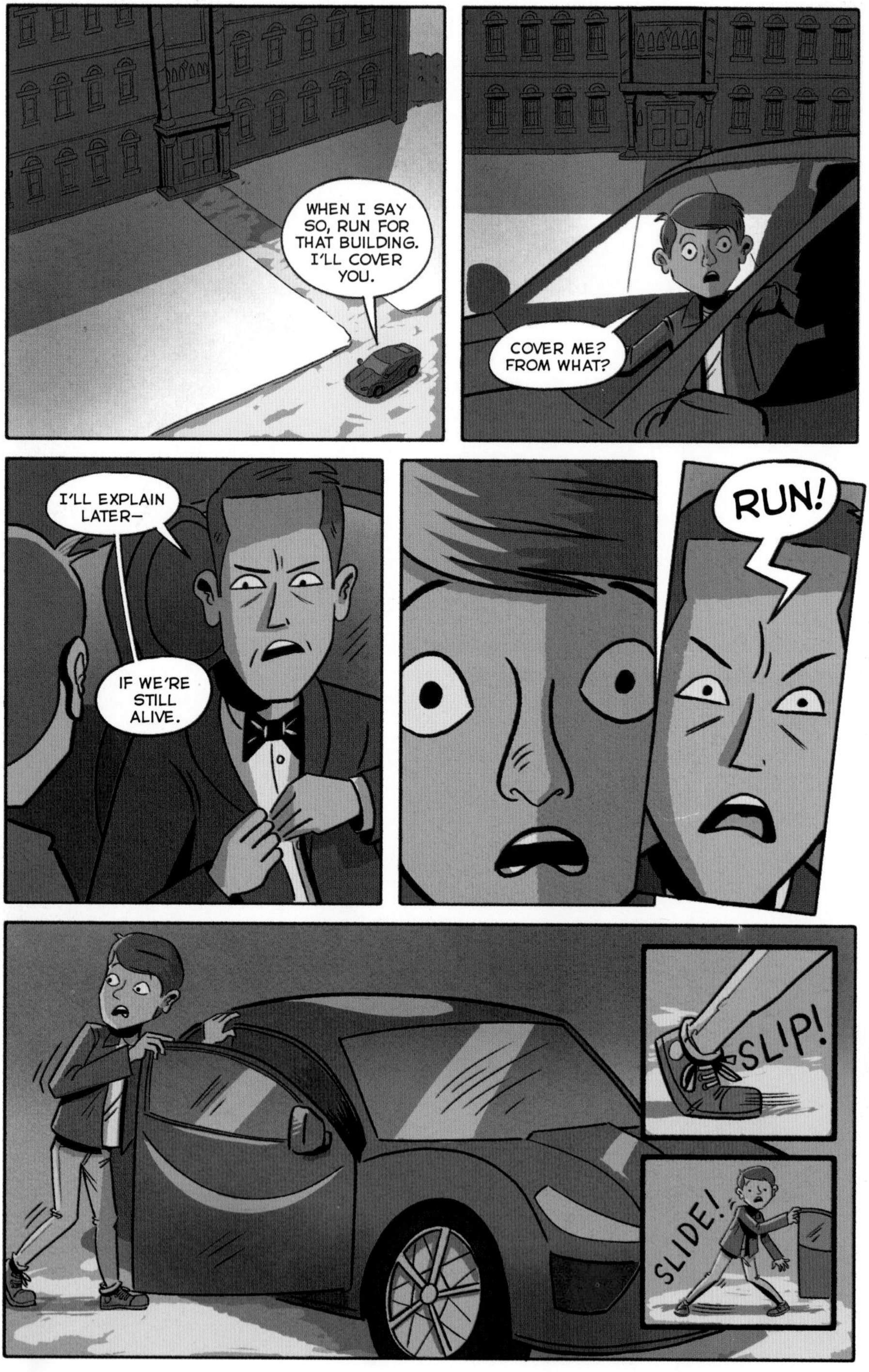
WHEN I SAY SO, RUN FOR THAT BUILDING. I'LL COVER YOU.
COVER ME? FROM WHAT?
I'LL EXPLAIN LATER—
IF WE'RE STILL ALIVE.
RUN!
SLIP!
SLIDE!

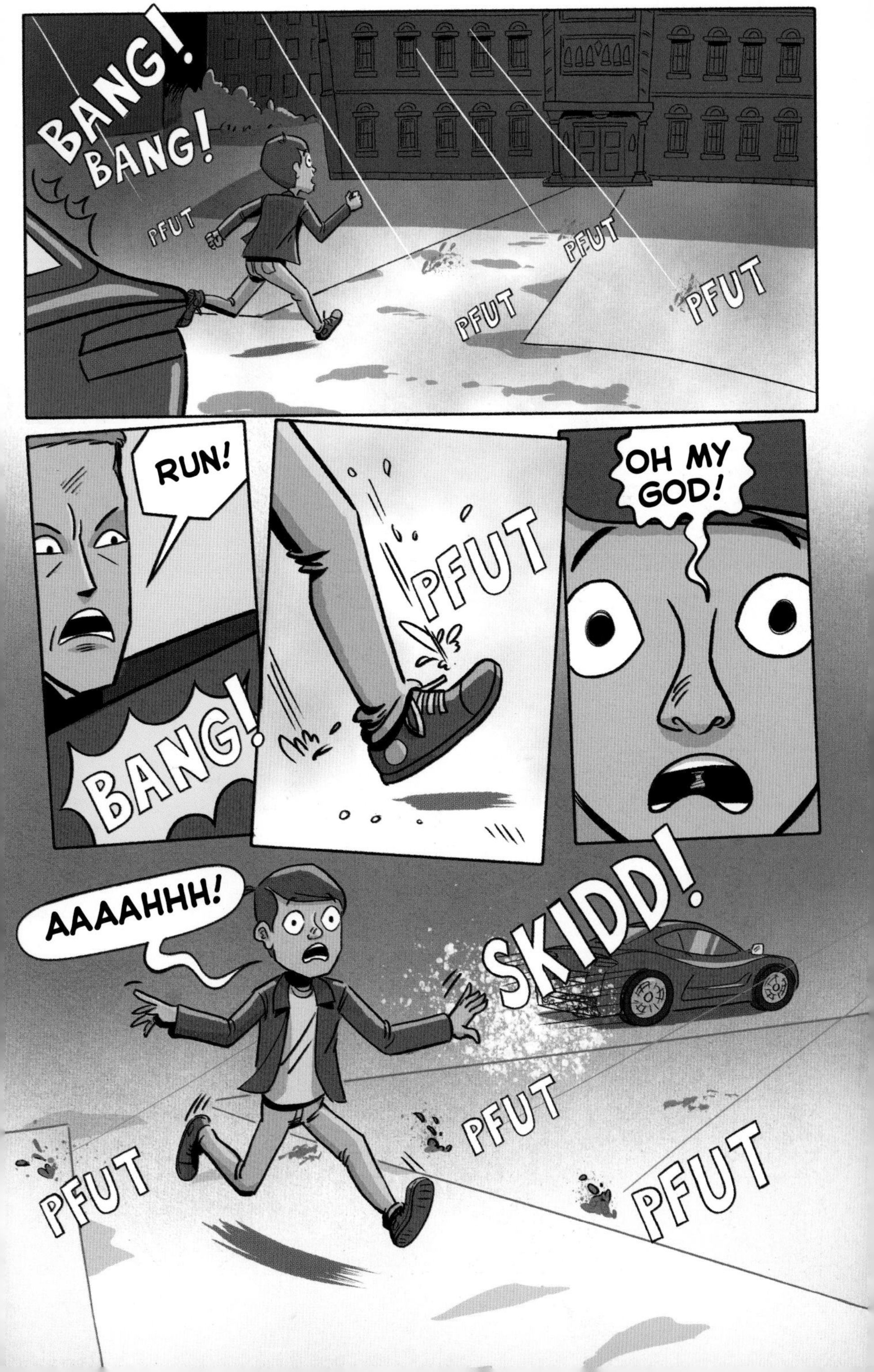
BANG!
BANG!
PFUT
PFUT
PFUT
PFUT
RUN!
BANG!
PFUT
OH MY GOD!
AAAAHHH!
SKIDD!
PFUT
PFUT
PFUT

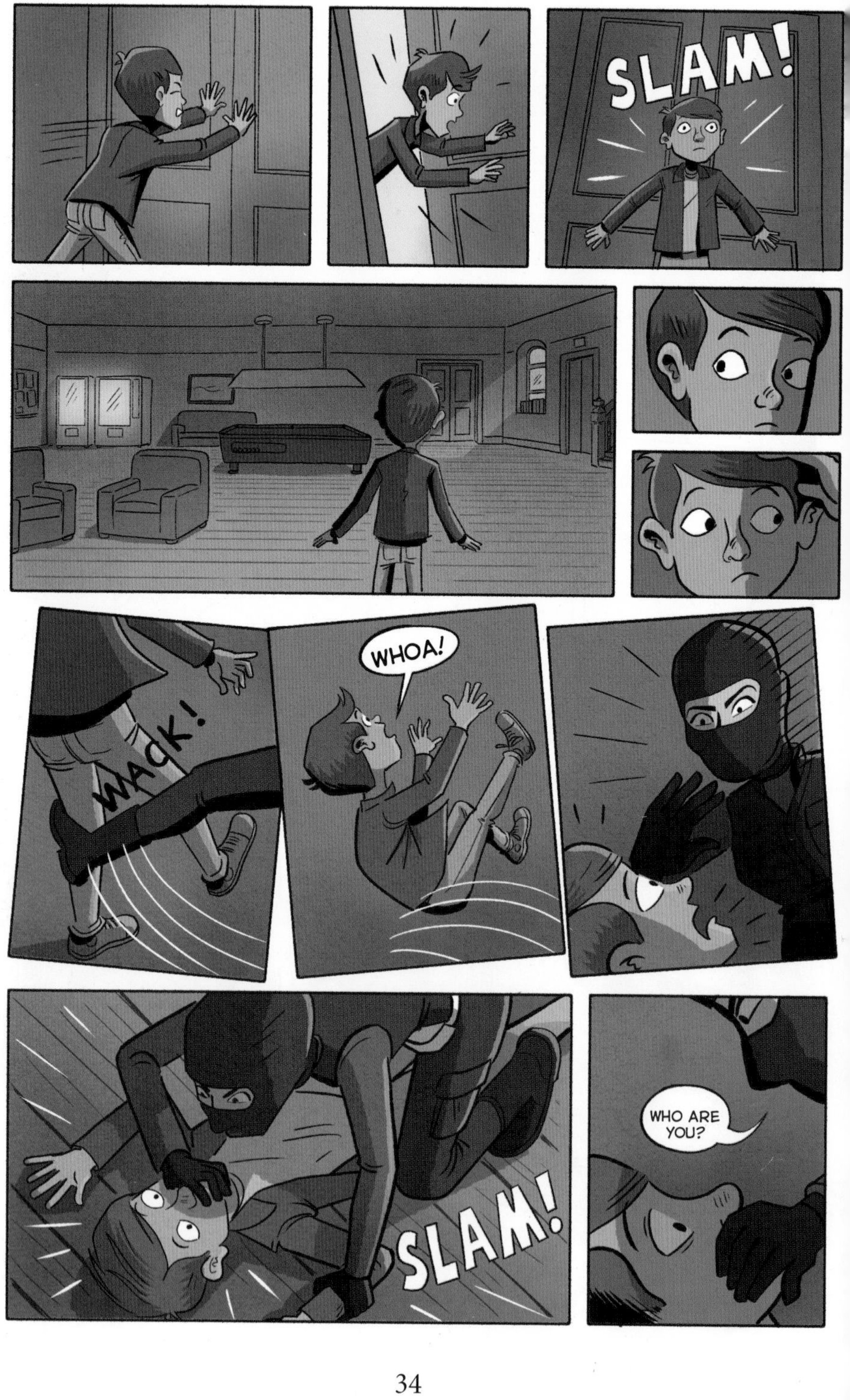
SLAM!
WACK!
WHOA!
SLAM!
WHO ARE YOU?

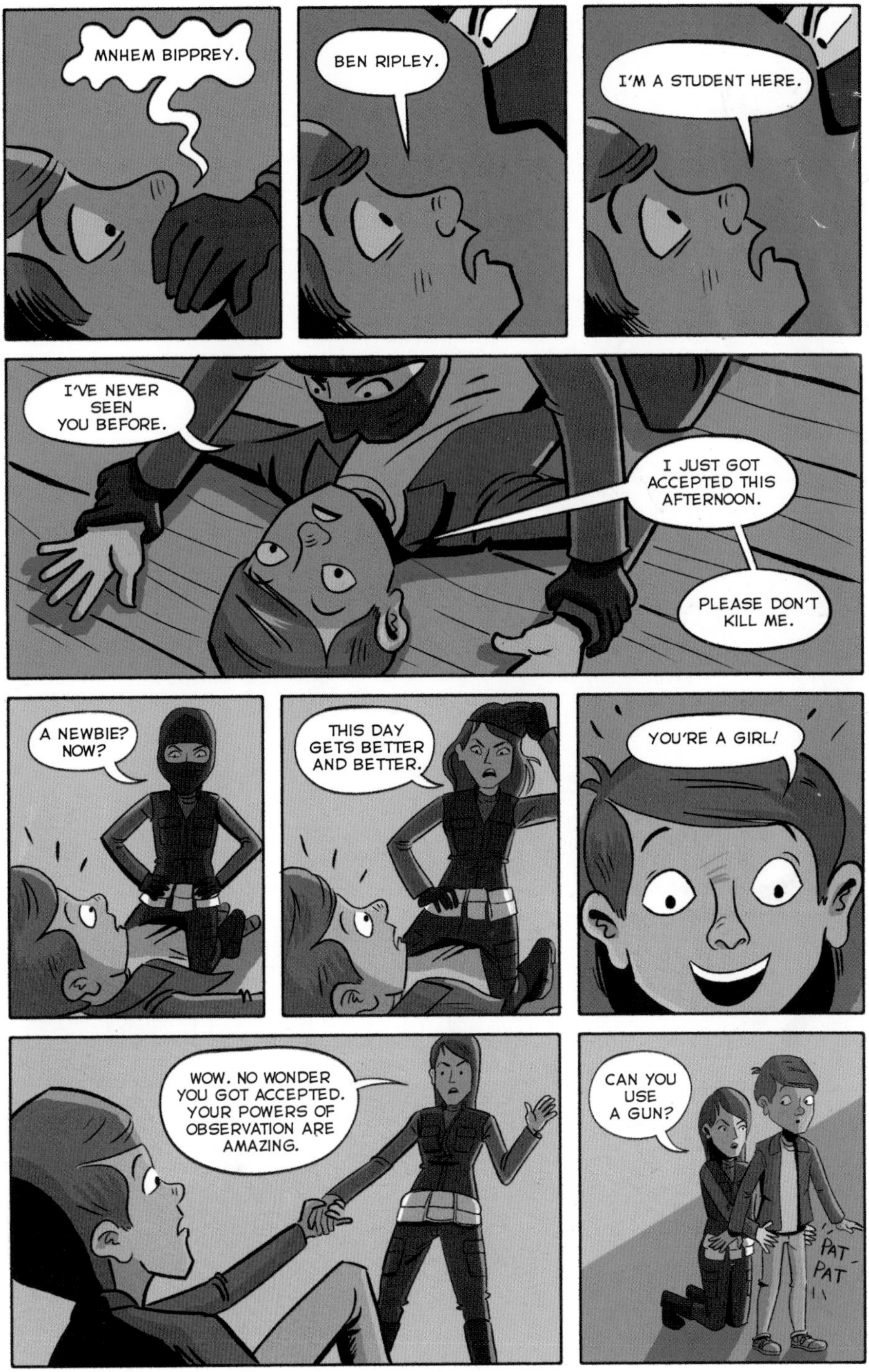
MNHEM BIPPREY.
BEN RIPLEY.
I'M A STUDENT HERE.
I'VE NEVER SEEN YOU BEFORE.
I JUST GOT ACCEPTED THIS AFTERNOON.
PLEASE DON'T KILL ME.
A NEWBIE? NOW?
THIS DAY GETS BETTER AND BETTER.
YOU'RE A GIRL!
WOW. NO WONDER YOU GOT ACCEPTED. YOUR POWERS OF OBSERVATION ARE AMAZING.
CAN YOU USE A GUN?
PAT PAT

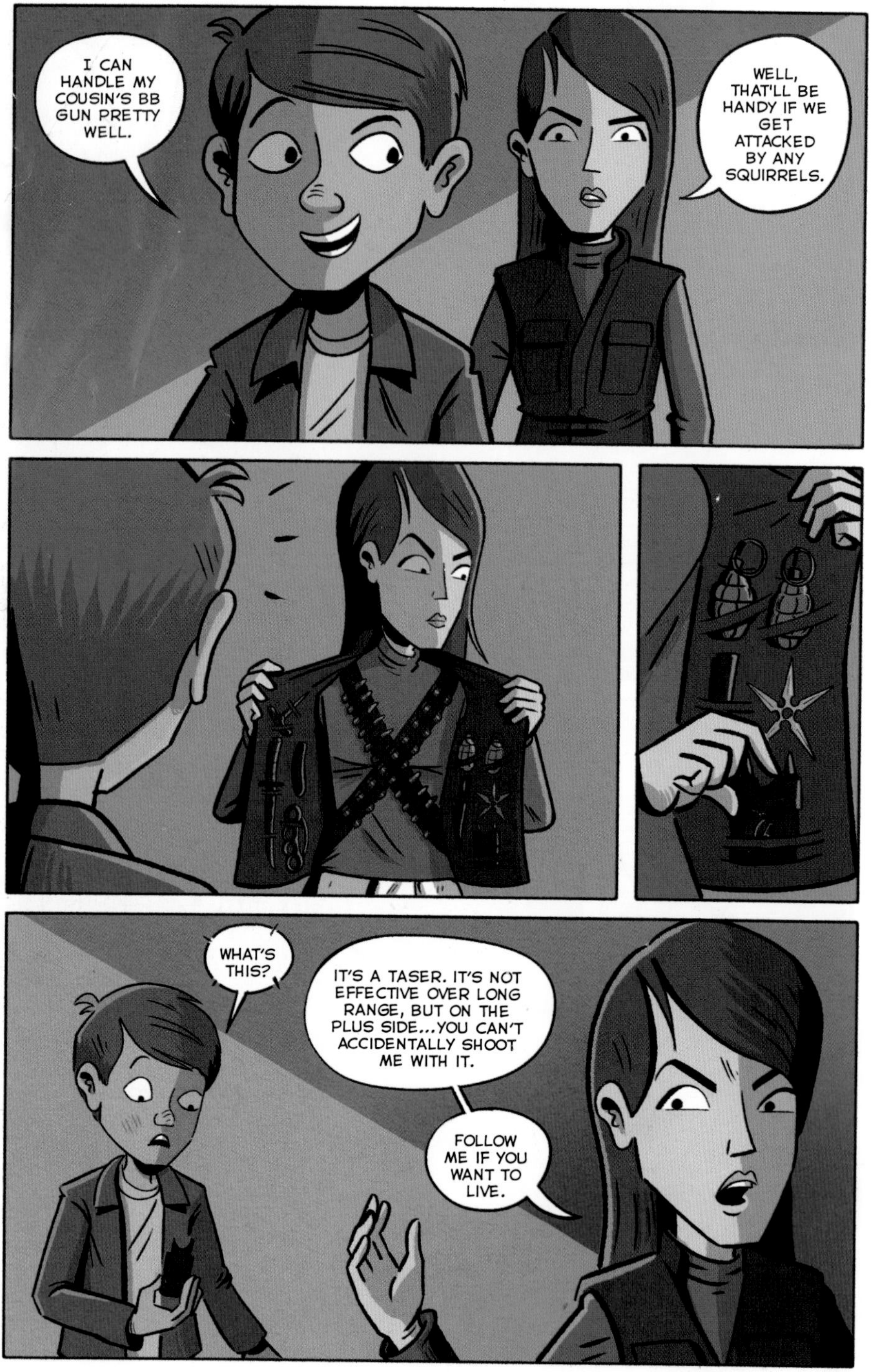
I CAN HANDLE MY COUSIN'S BB GUN PRETTY WELL.
WELL, THAT'LL BE HANDY IF WE GET ATTACKED BY ANY SQUIRRELS.
WHAT'S THIS?
IT'S A TASER. IT'S NOT EFFECTIVE OVER LONG RANGE, BUT ON THE PLUS SIDE...YOU CAN'T ACCIDENTALLY SHOOT ME WITH IT.
FOLLOW ME IF YOU WANT TO LIVE.

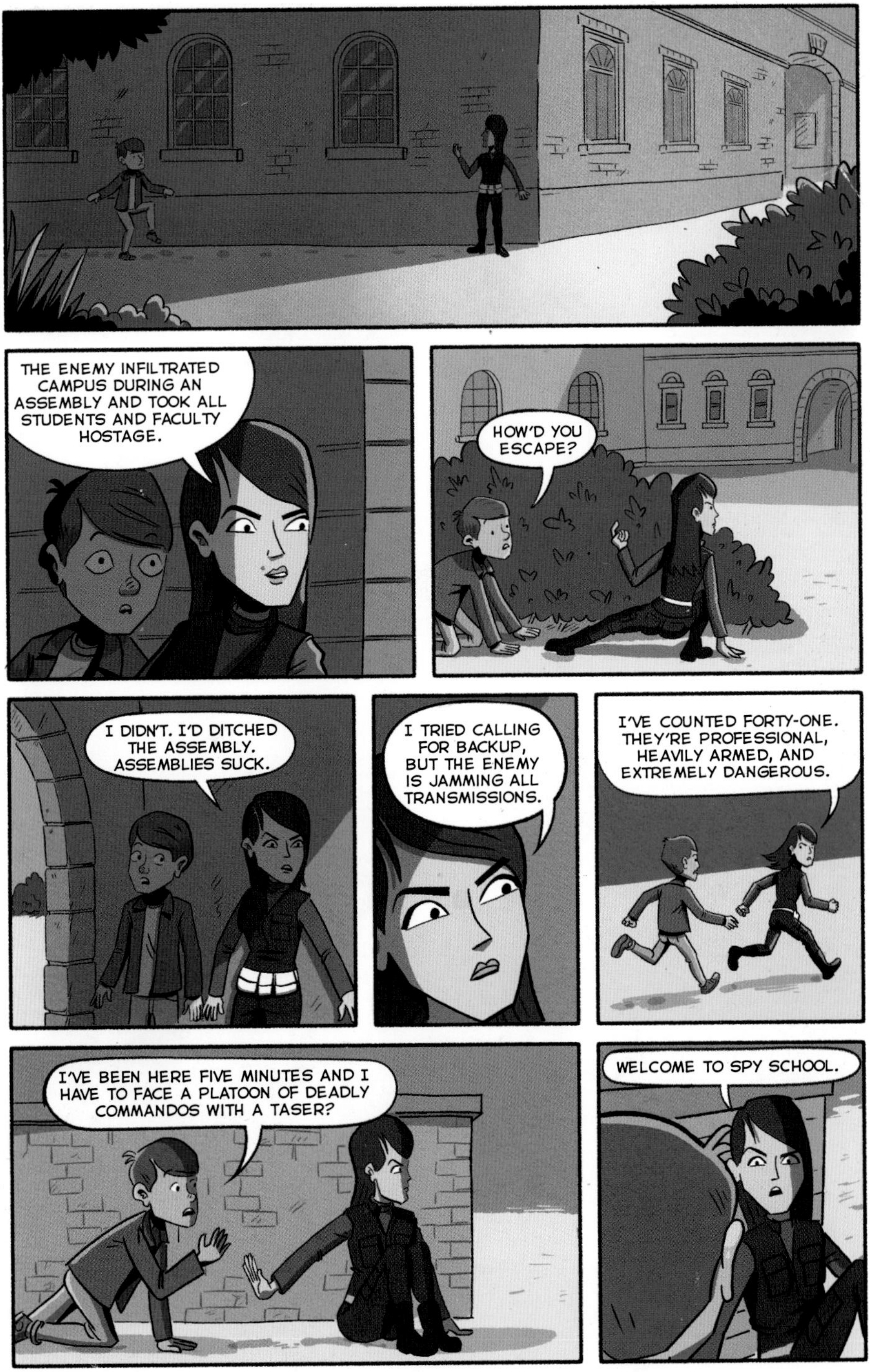
THE ENEMY INFILTRATED CAMPUS DURING AN ASSEMBLY AND TOOK ALL STUDENTS AND FACULTY HOSTAGE.
HOW'D YOU ESCAPE?
I DIDN'T. I'D DITCHED THE ASSEMBLY. ASSEMBLIES SUCK.
I TRIED CALLING FOR BACKUP, BUT THE ENEMY IS JAMMING ALL TRANSMISSIONS.
I'VE COUNTED FORTY-ONE. THEY'RE PROFESSIONAL, HEAVILY ARMED, AND EXTREMELY DANGEROUS.
I'VE BEEN HERE FIVE MINUTES AND I HAVE TO FACE A PLATOON OF DEADLY COMMANDOS WITH A TASER?
WELCOME TO SPY SCHOOL.

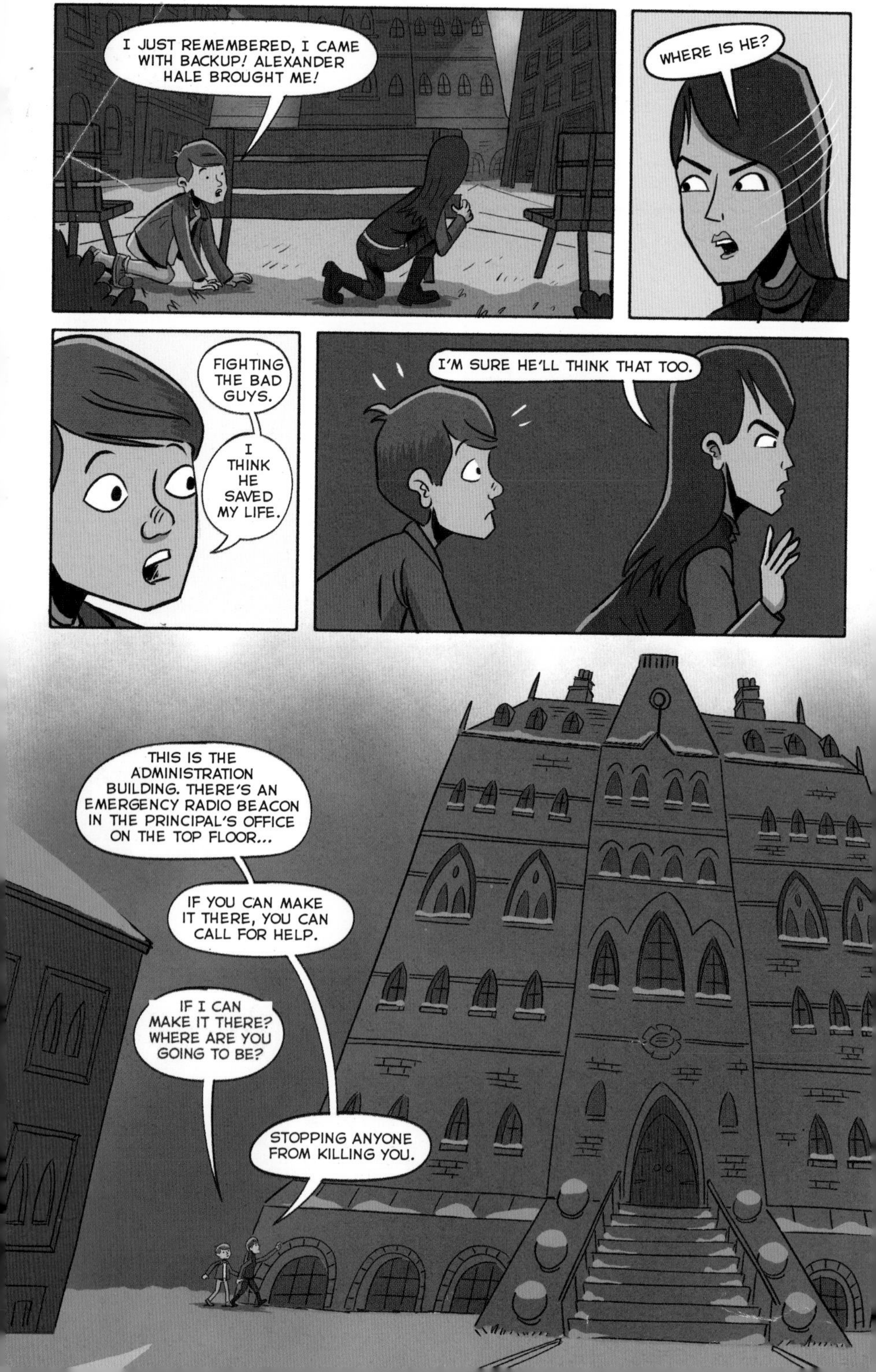
I JUST REMEMBERED, I CAME WITH BACKUP! ALEXANDER HALE BROUGHT ME!
WHERE IS HE?
FIGHTING THE BAD GUYS.
I THINK HE SAVED MY LIFE.
I'M SURE HE'LL THINK THAT TOO.
THIS IS THE ADMINISTRATION BUILDING. THERE'S AN EMERGENCY RADIO BEACON IN THE PRINCIPAL'S OFFICE ON THE TOP FLOOR...
IF YOU CAN MAKE IT THERE, YOU CAN CALL FOR HELP.
IF I CAN MAKE IT THERE? WHERE ARE YOU GOING TO BE?
STOPPING ANYONE FROM KILLING YOU.

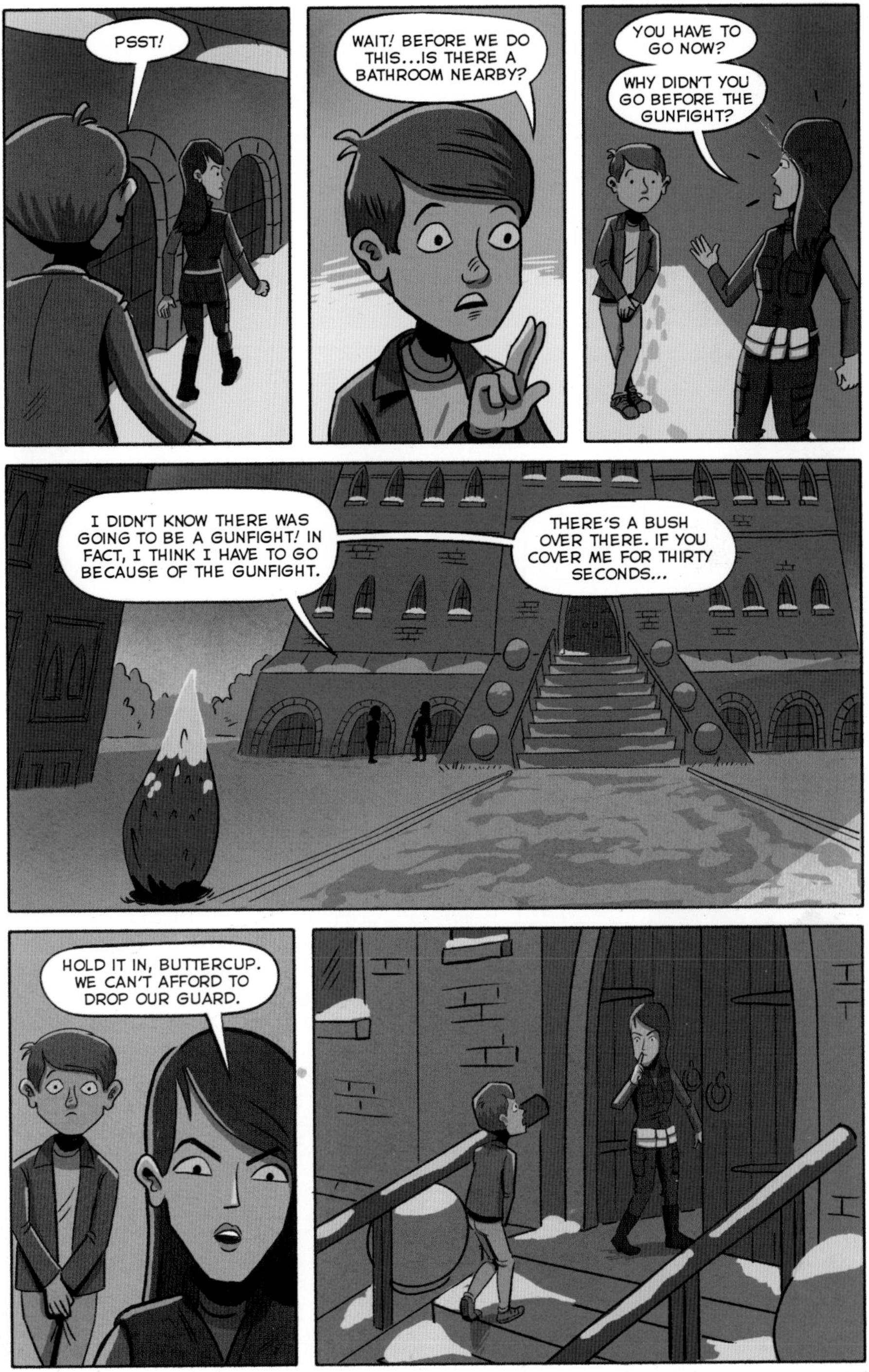
PSST!
WAIT! BEFORE WE DO THIS...IS THERE A BATHROOM NEARBY?
YOU HAVE TO GO NOW?
WHY DIDN'T YOU GO BEFORE THE GUNFIGHT?
I DIDN'T KNOW THERE WAS GOING TO BE A GUNFIGHT! IN FACT, I THINK I HAVE TO GO BECAUSE OF THE GUNFIGHT.
THERE'S A BUSH OVER THERE. IF YOU COVER ME FOR THIRTY SECONDS...
HOLD IT IN, BUTTERCUP. WE CAN'T AFFORD TO DROP OUR GUARD.

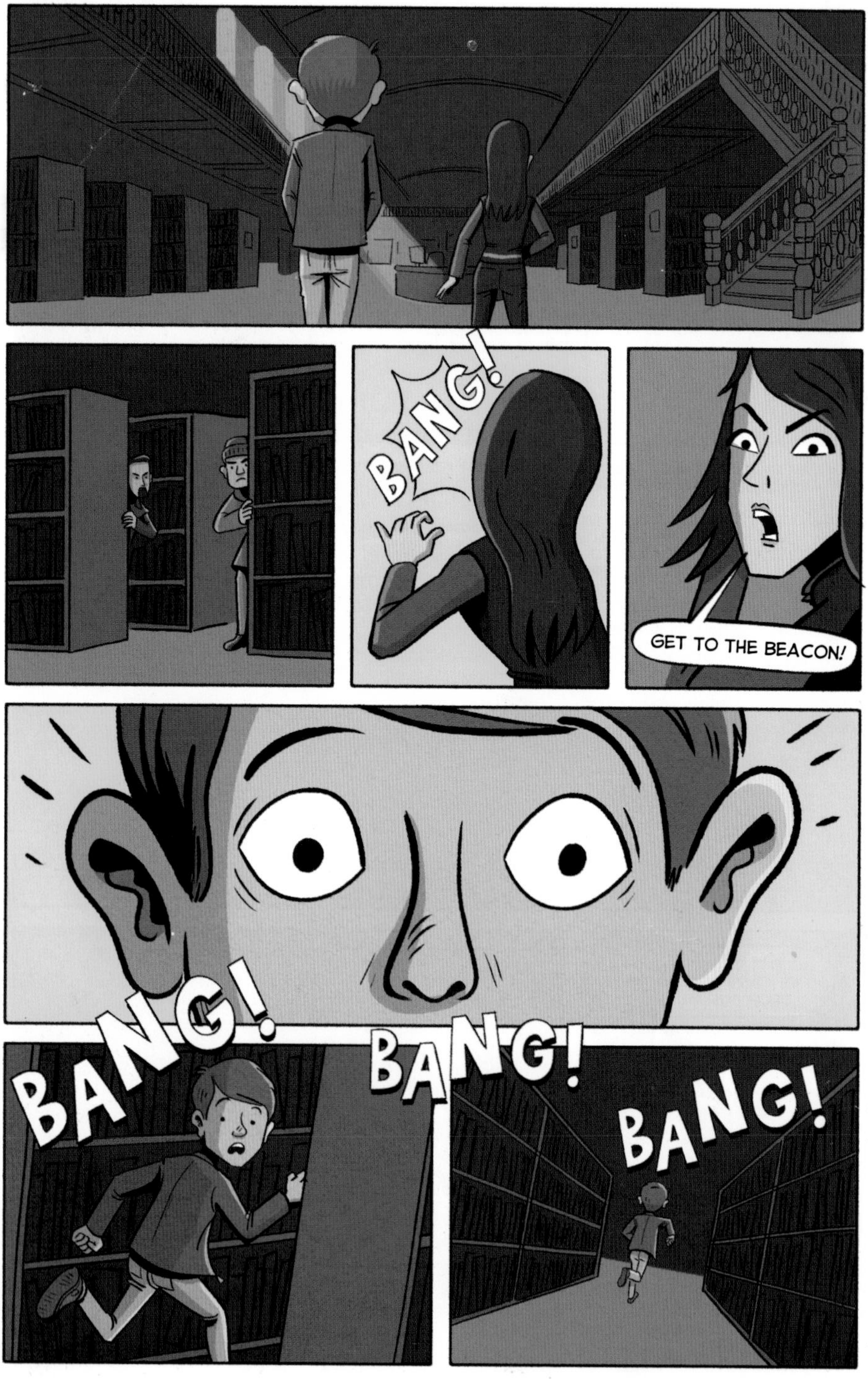
BANG!
GET TO THE BEACON!
BANG!
BANG!
BANG!

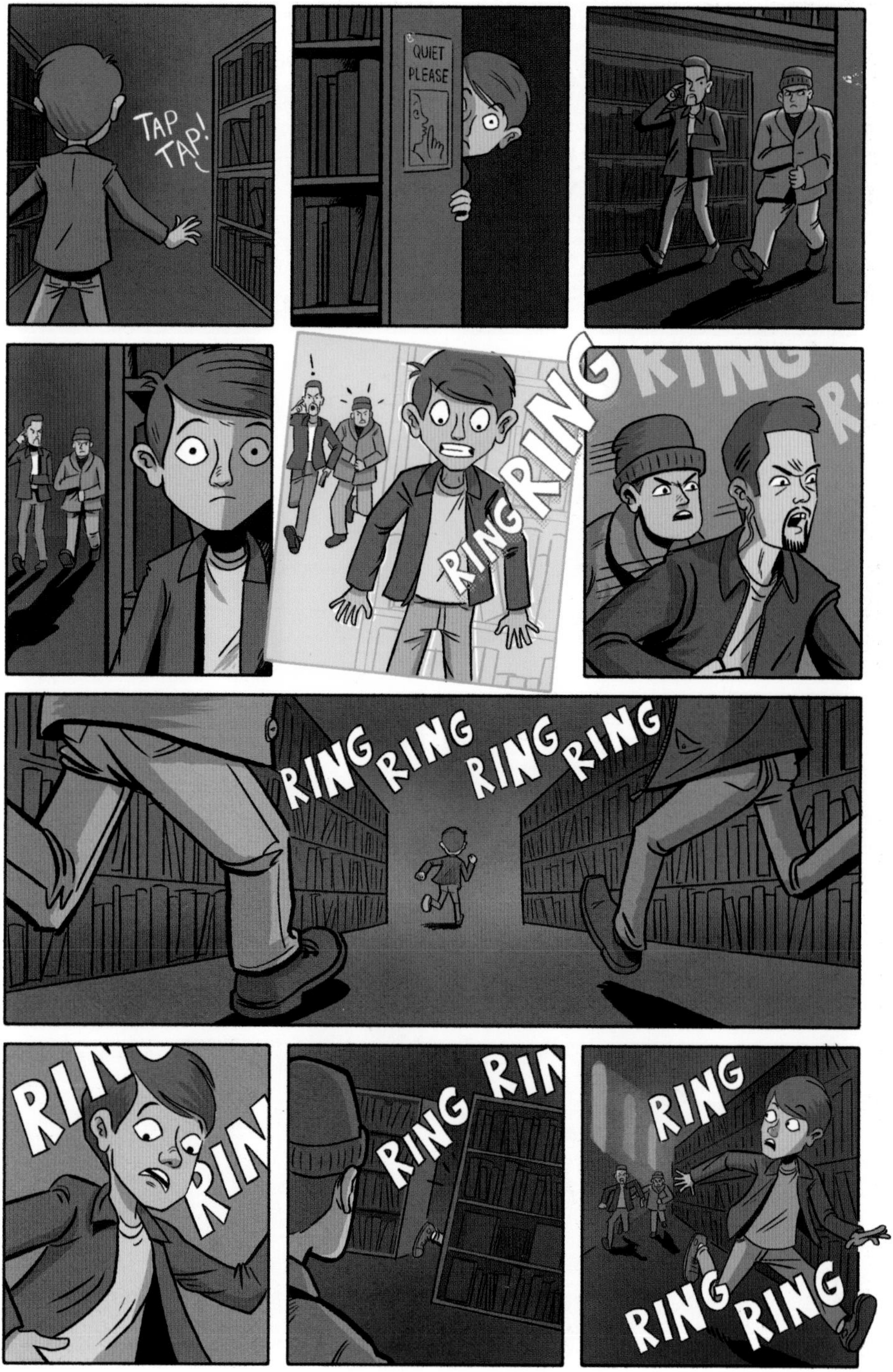
TAP TAP!
QUIET PLEASE
!
RING RING
RING
RING
RING RING RING RING
RIN
RIN
RING RIN
RING
RING RING

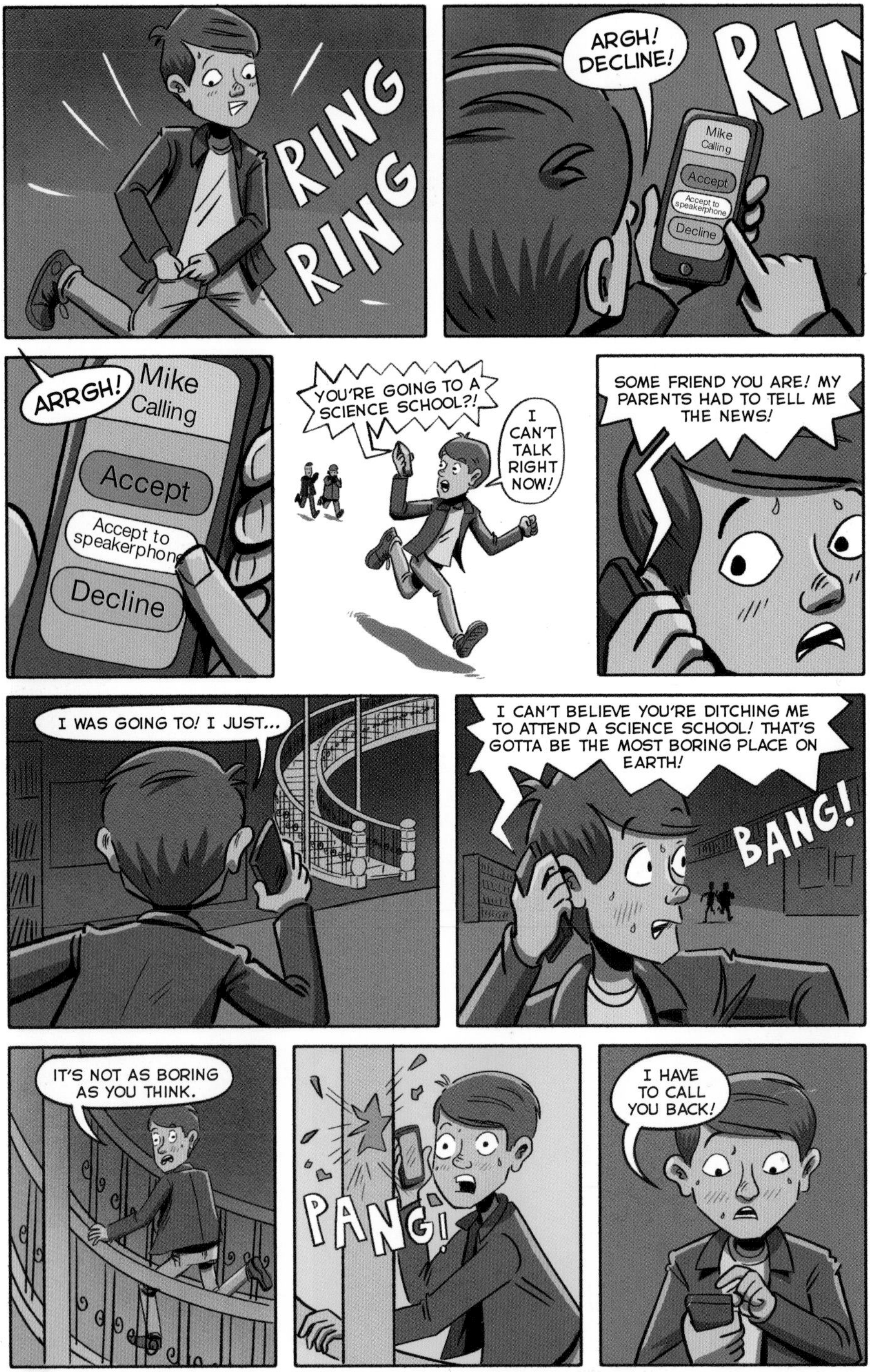
RING
RING
ARGH! DECLINE!
RIN
Mike
Calling
Accept
Accept to speakerphone
Decline
ARRGH!
Mike
Calling
Accept
Accept to speakerphone
Decline
YOU'RE GOING TO A SCIENCE SCHOOL?!
I CAN'T TALK RIGHT NOW!
SOME FRIEND YOU ARE! MY PARENTS HAD TO TELL ME THE NEWS!
I WAS GOING TO! I JUST...
I CAN'T BELIEVE YOU'RE DITCHING ME TO ATTEND A SCIENCE SCHOOL! THAT'S GOTTA BE THE MOST BORING PLACE ON EARTH!
BANG!
IT'S NOT AS BORING AS YOU THINK.
PANG!
I HAVE TO CALL YOU BACK!

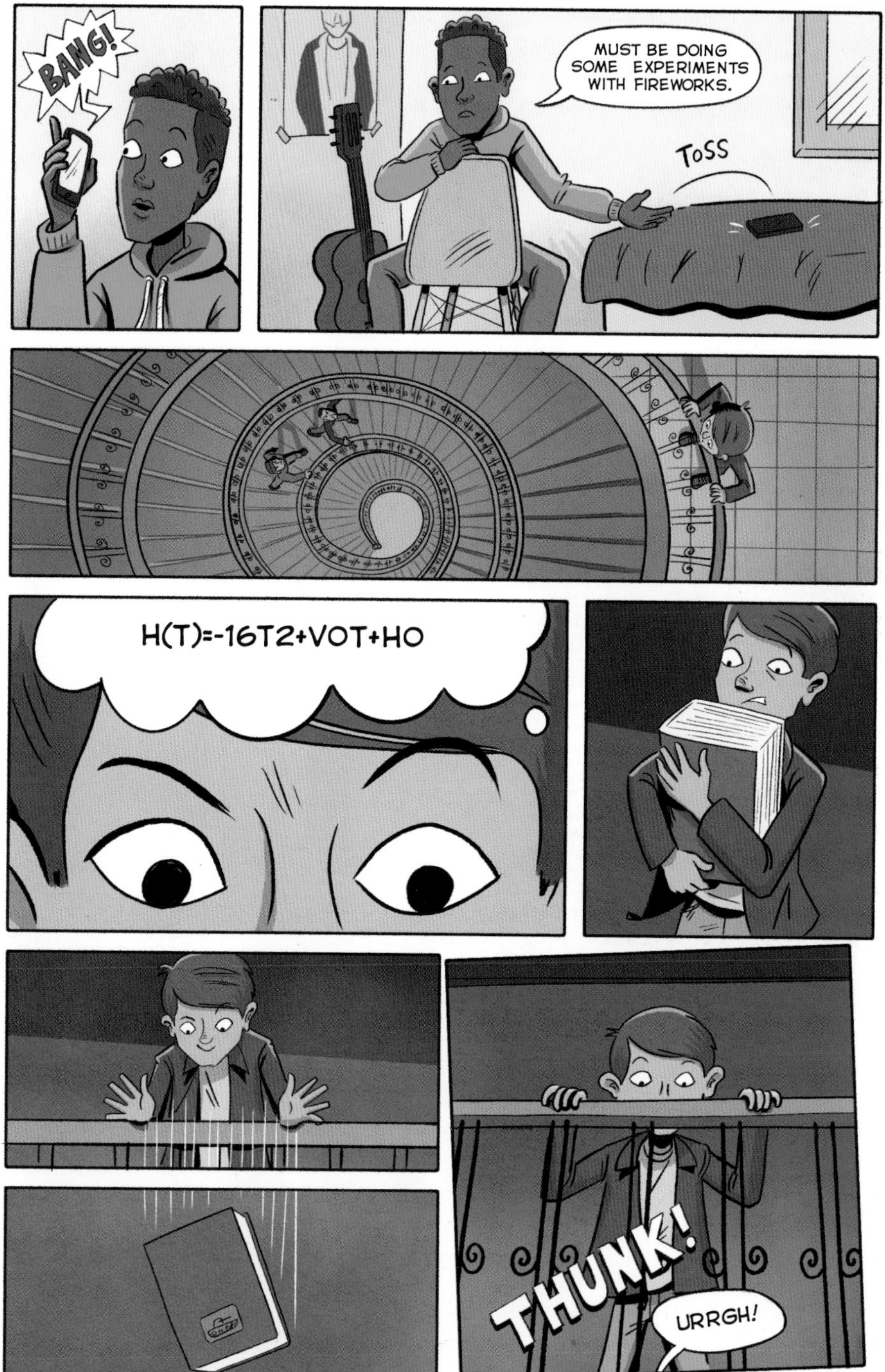
BANG!
MUST BE DOING SOME EXPERIMENTS WITH FIREWORKS.
TOSS
H(T)=-16T2+VOT+HO
THUNK!
URRGH!

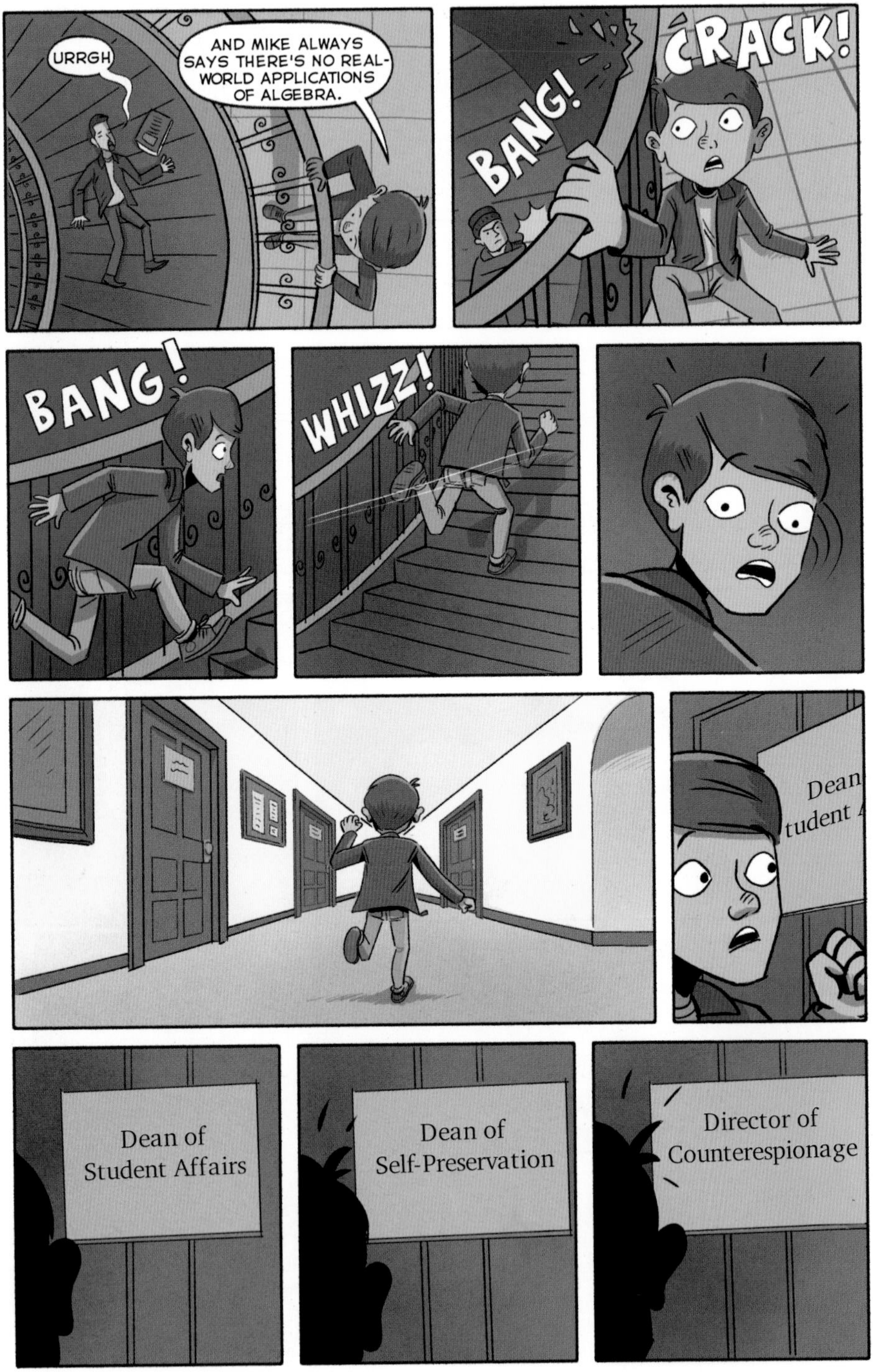
URRGH
AND MIKE ALWAYS SAYS THERE'S NO REAL-WORLD APPLICATIONS OF ALGEBRA.
BANG!
CRACK!
BANG!
WHIZZ!
Dean of Student Affairs
Dean of Self-Preservation
Director of Counterespionage

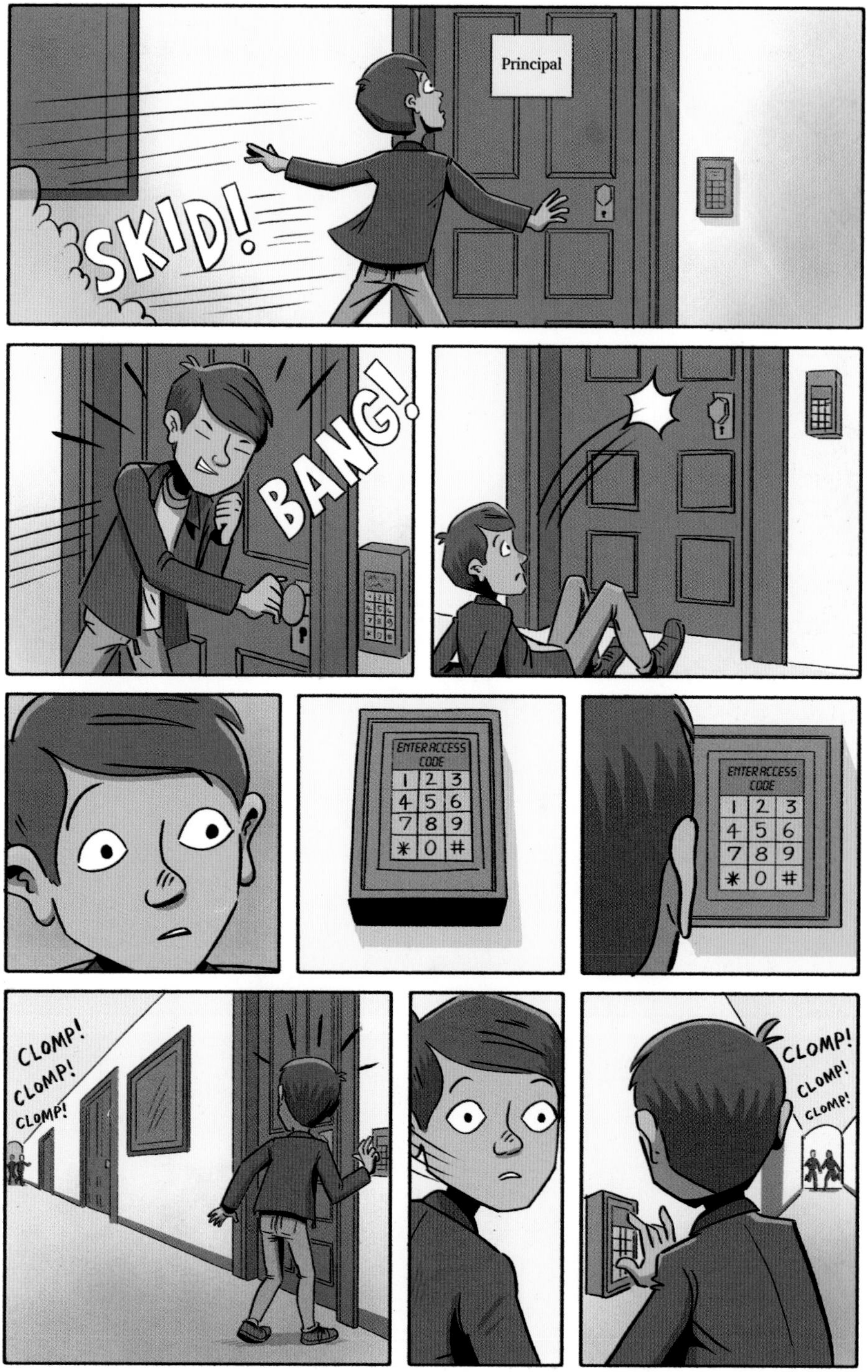
Principal
SKID!
BANG!
ENTER ACCESS CODE
1 2 3
4 5 6
7 8 9
* 0 #
ENTER ACCESS CODE
1 2 3
4 5 6
7 8 9
* 0 #
CLOMP!
CLOMP!
CLOMP!
CLOMP!
CLOMP!
CLOMP!

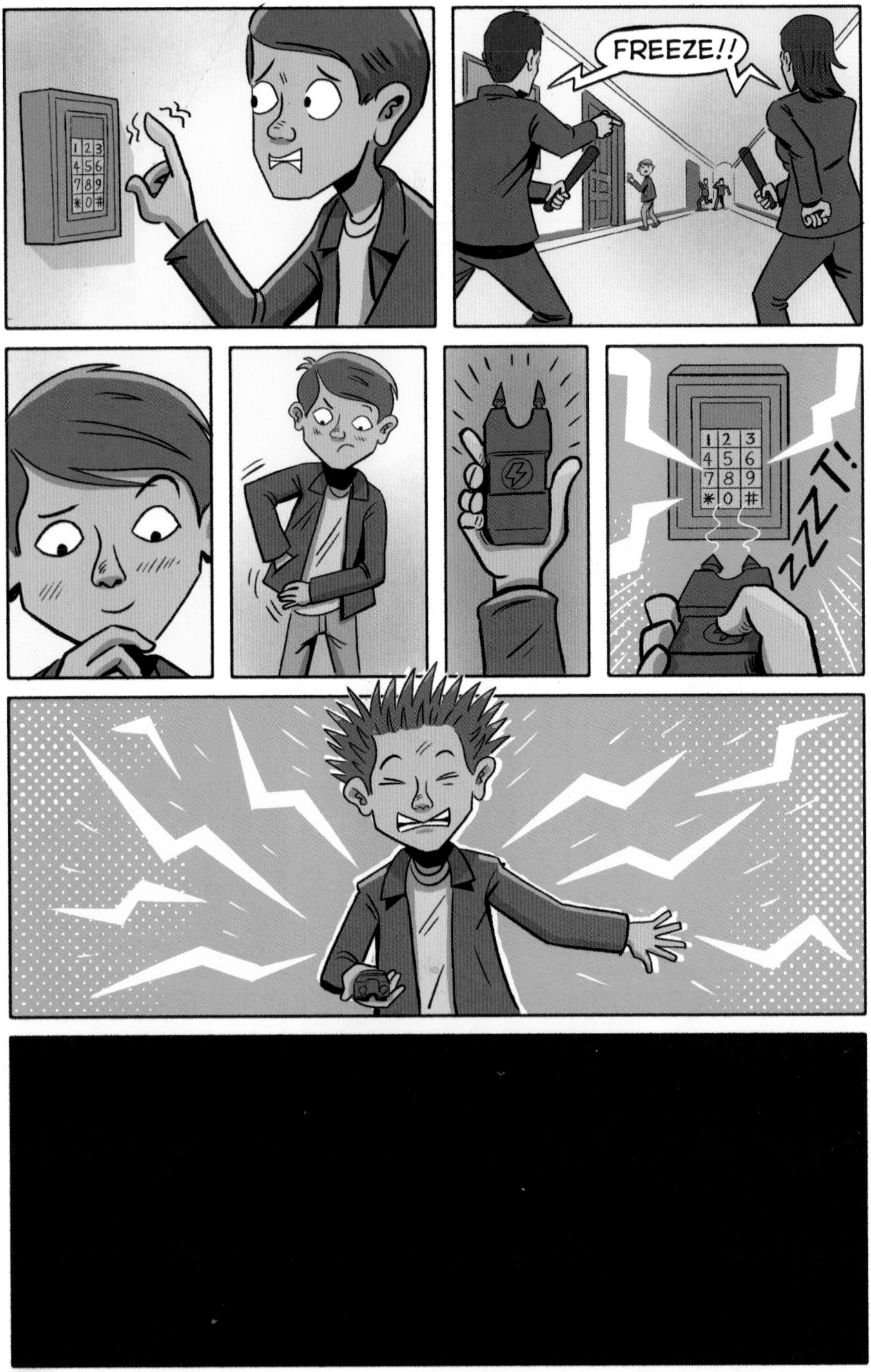
FREEZE!!
ZZZT!

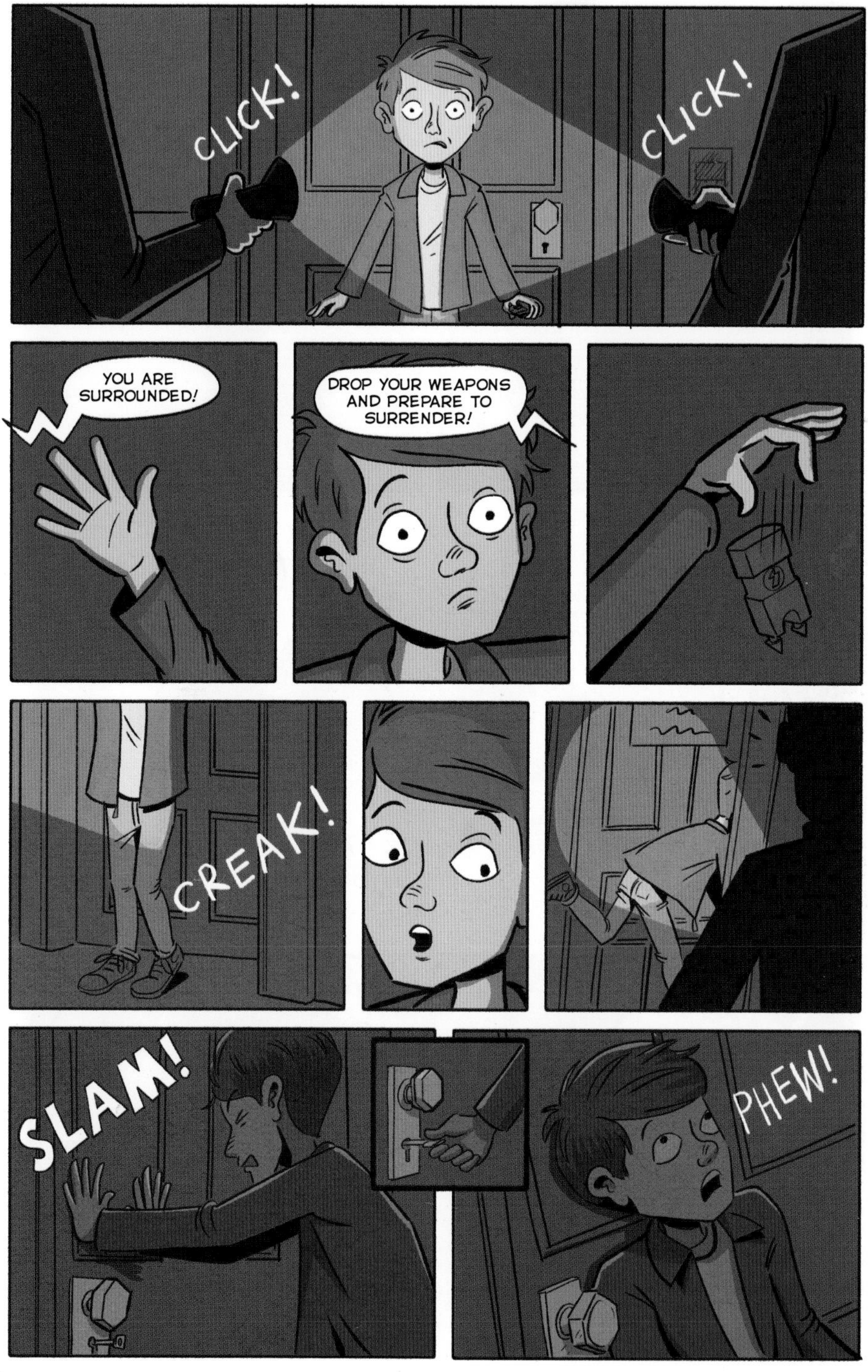
CLICK!
CLICK!
YOU ARE SURROUNDED!
DROP YOUR WEAPONS AND PREPARE TO SURRENDER!
CREAK!
SLAM!
PHEW!

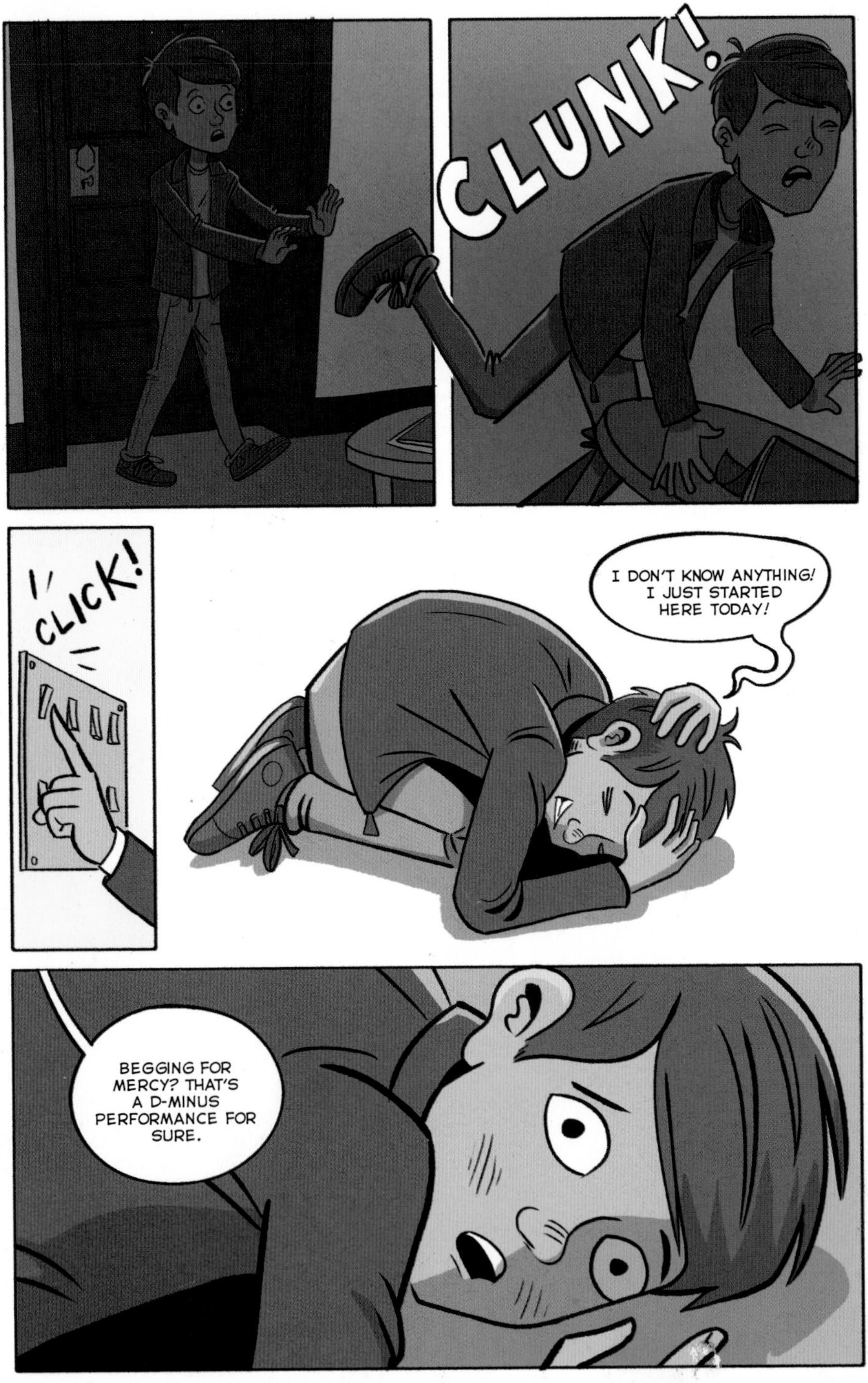
CLUNK!
CLICK!
I DON'T KNOW ANYTHING! I JUST STARTED HERE TODAY!
BEGGING FOR MERCY? THAT'S A D-MINUS PERFORMANCE FOR SURE.

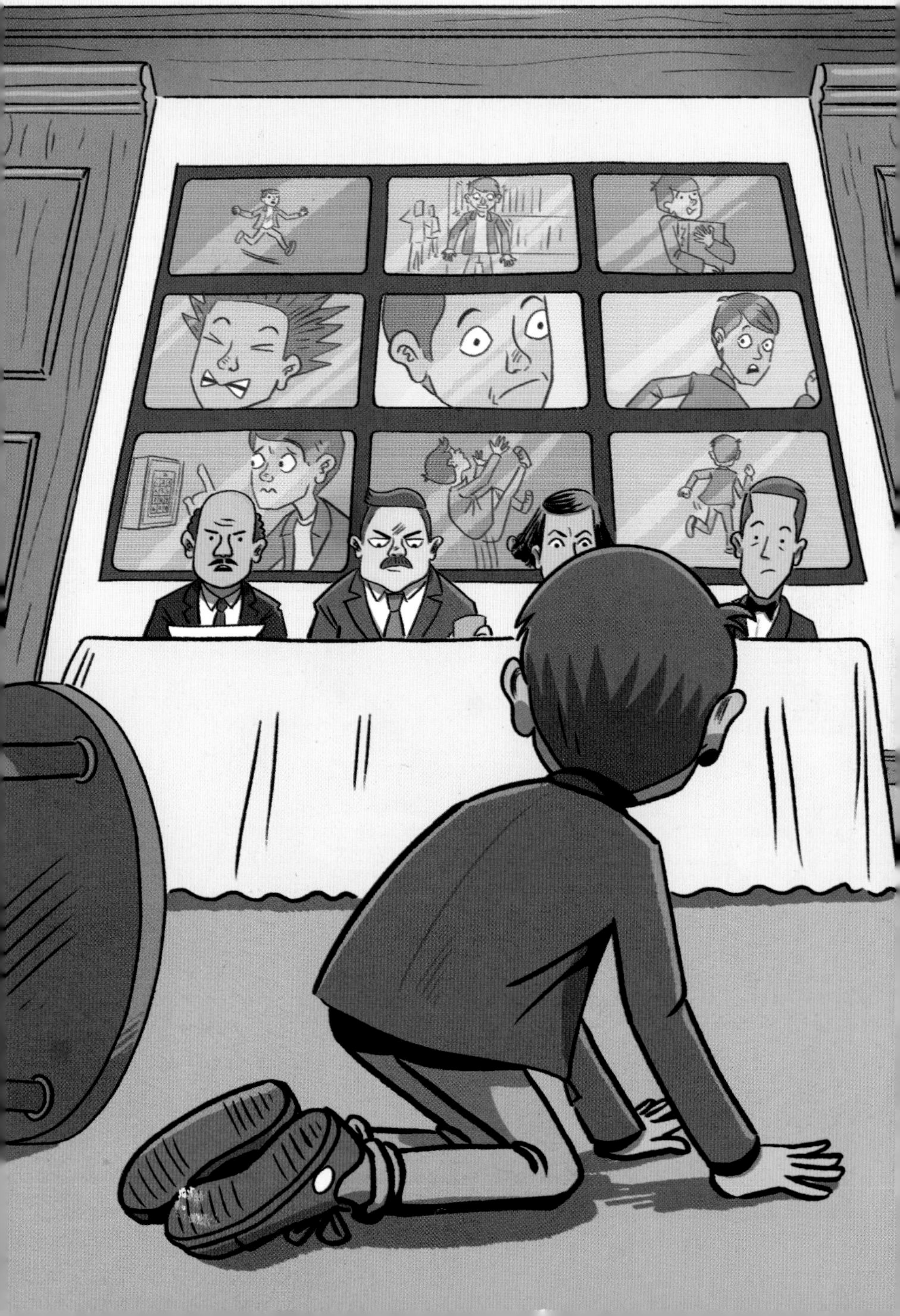

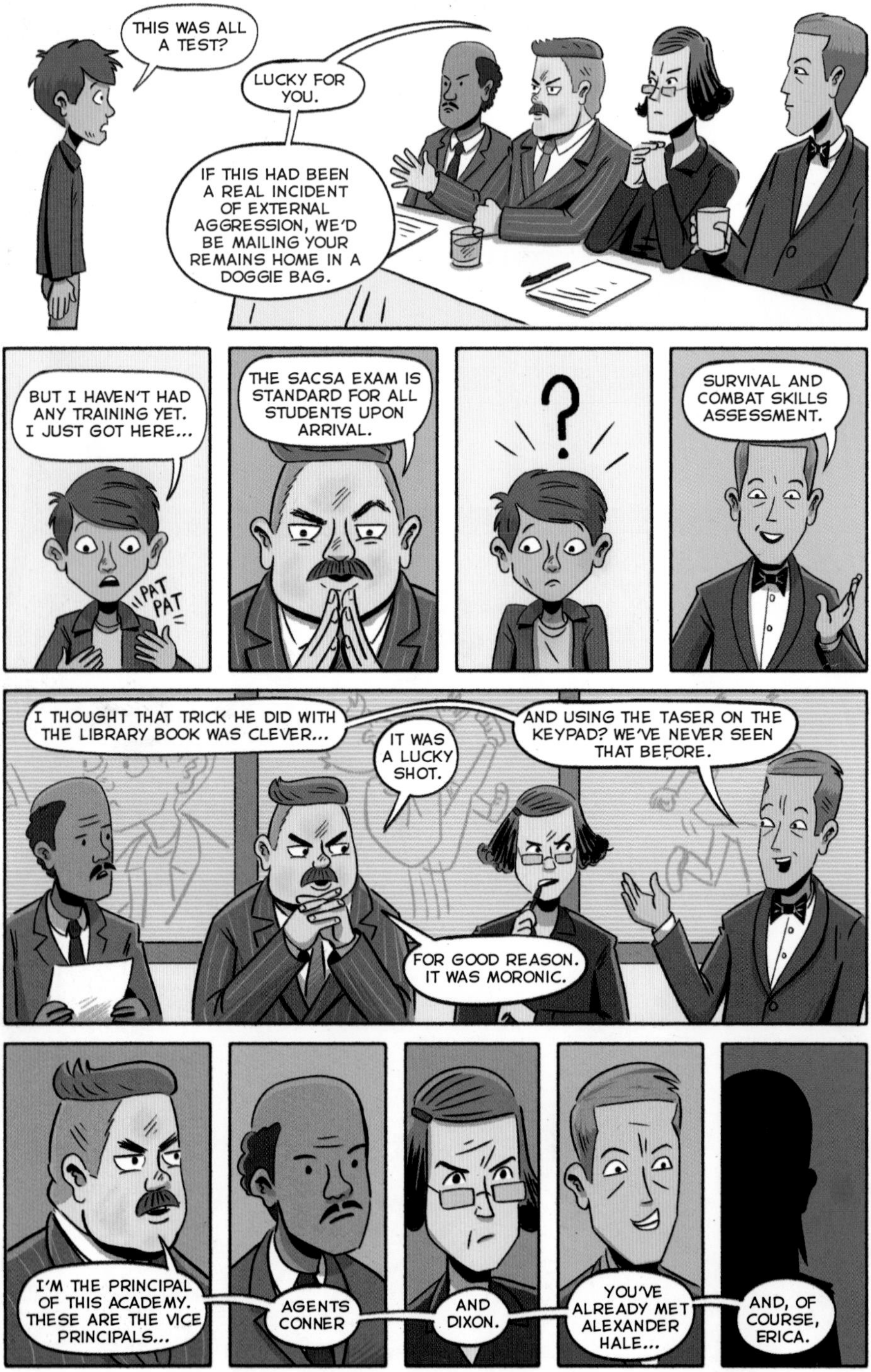
THIS WAS ALL A TEST?
LUCKY FOR YOU.
IF THIS HAD BEEN A REAL INCIDENT OF EXTERNAL AGGRESSION, WE'D BE MAILING YOUR REMAINS HOME IN A DOGGIE BAG.
BUT I HAVEN'T HAD ANY TRAINING YET. I JUST GOT HERE...
PAT PAT
THE SACSA EXAM IS STANDARD FOR ALL STUDENTS UPON ARRIVAL.
?
SURVIVAL AND COMBAT SKILLS ASSESSMENT.
I THOUGHT THAT TRICK HE DID WITH THE LIBRARY BOOK WAS CLEVER...
IT WAS A LUCKY SHOT.
AND USING THE TASER ON THE KEYPAD? WE'VE NEVER SEEN THAT BEFORE.
FOR GOOD REASON. IT WAS MORONIC.
I'M THE PRINCIPAL OF THIS ACADEMY. THESE ARE THE VICE PRINCIPALS...
AGENTS CONNER
AND DIXON.
YOU'VE ALREADY MET ALEXANDER HALE...
AND, OF COURSE, ERICA.

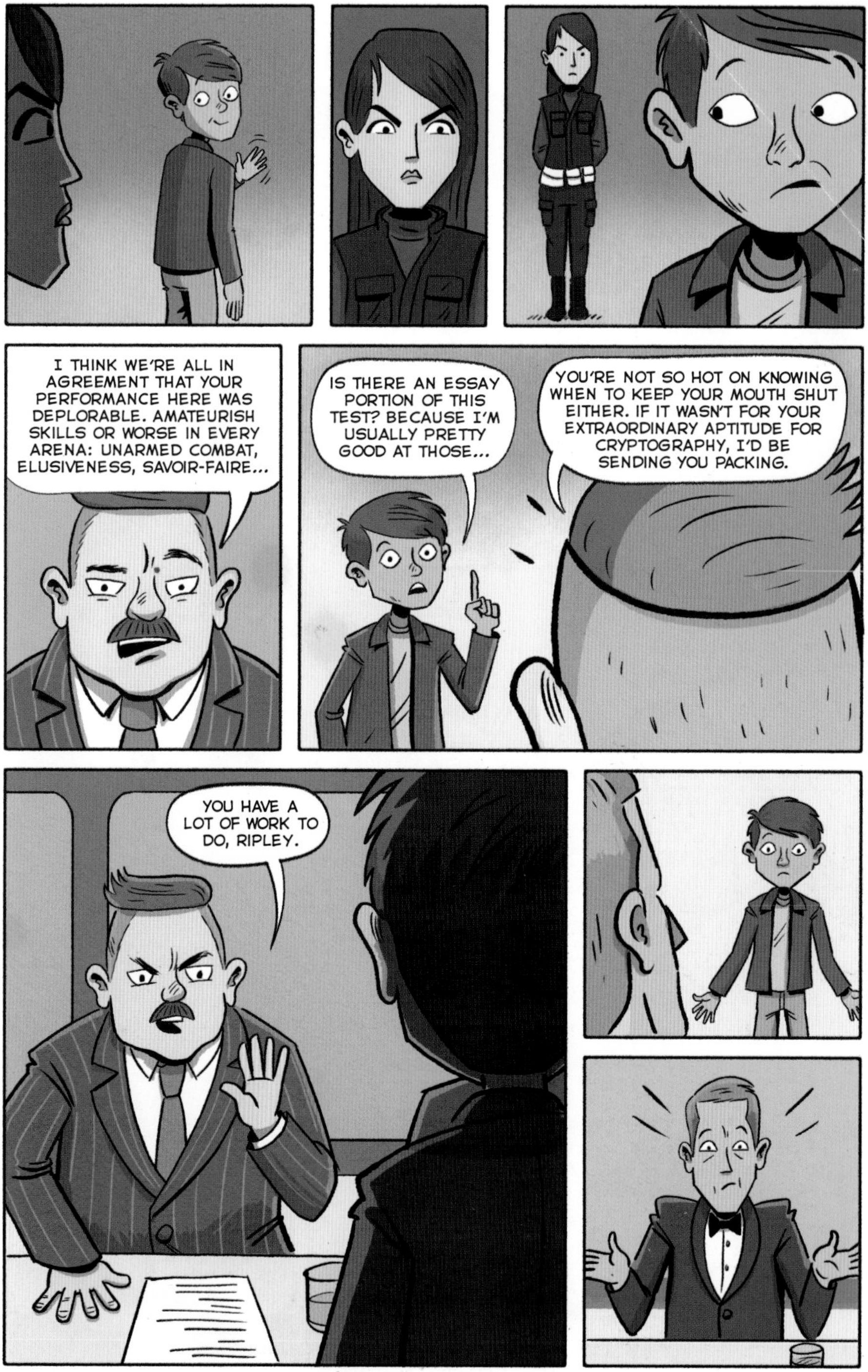
I THINK WE'RE ALL IN AGREEMENT THAT YOUR PERFORMANCE HERE WAS DEPLORABLE. AMATEURISH SKILLS OR WORSE IN EVERY ARENA: UNARMED COMBAT, ELUSIVENESS, SAVOIR-FAIRE...
IS THERE AN ESSAY PORTION OF THIS TEST? BECAUSE I'M USUALLY PRETTY GOOD AT THOSE...
YOU'RE NOT SO HOT ON KNOWING WHEN TO KEEP YOUR MOUTH SHUT EITHER. IF IT WASN'T FOR YOUR EXTRAORDINARY APTITUDE FOR CRYPTOGRAPHY, I'D BE SENDING YOU PACKING.
YOU HAVE A LOT OF WORK TO DO, RIPLEY.

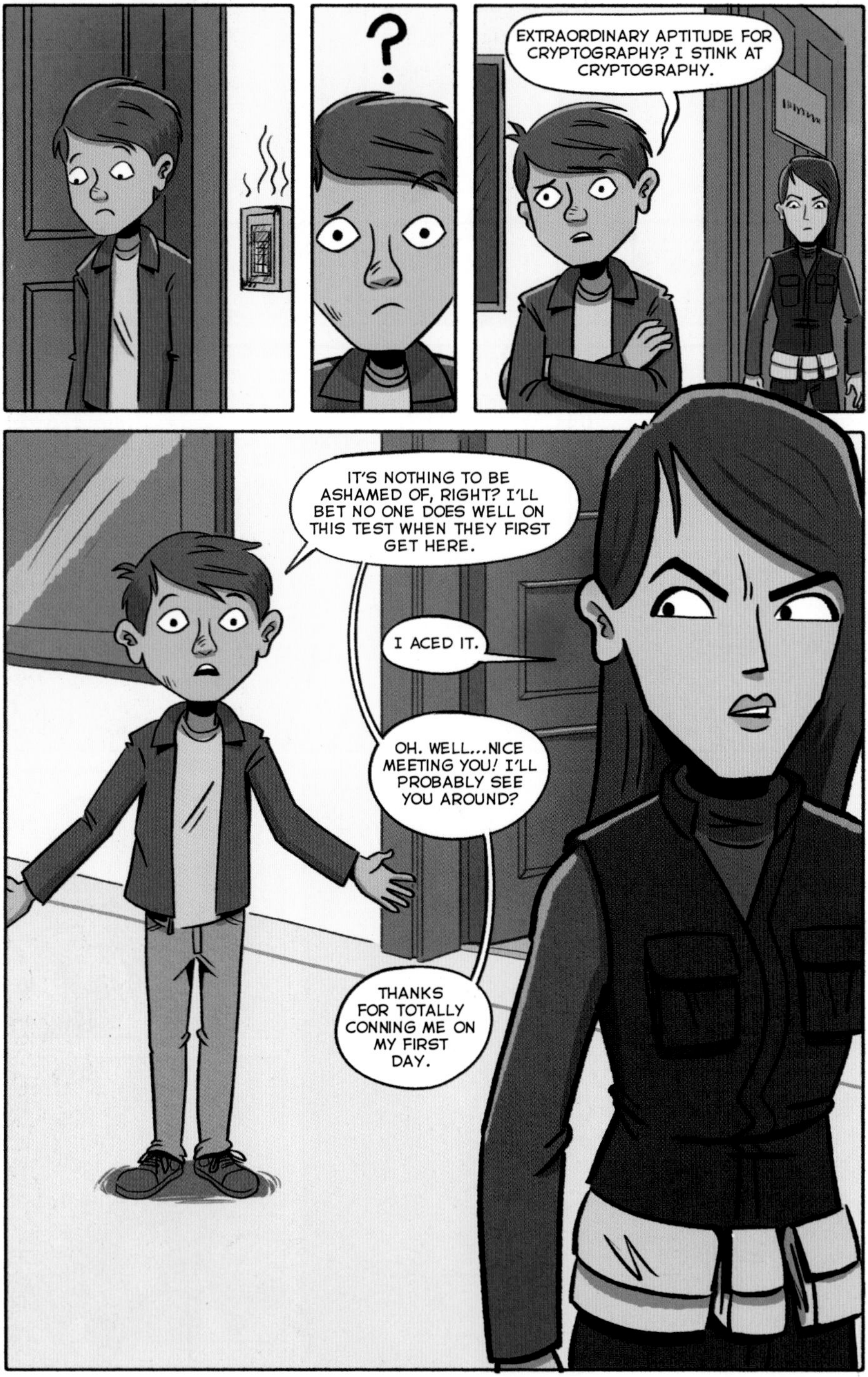
?
EXTRAORDINARY APTITUDE FOR CRYPTOGRAPHY? I STINK AT CRYPTOGRAPHY.
IT'S NOTHING TO BE ASHAMED OF, RIGHT? I'LL BET NO ONE DOES WELL ON THIS TEST WHEN THEY FIRST GET HERE.
I ACED IT.
OH. WELL...NICE MEETING YOU! I'LL PROBABLY SEE YOU AROUND?
THANKS FOR TOTALLY CONNING ME ON MY FIRST DAY.

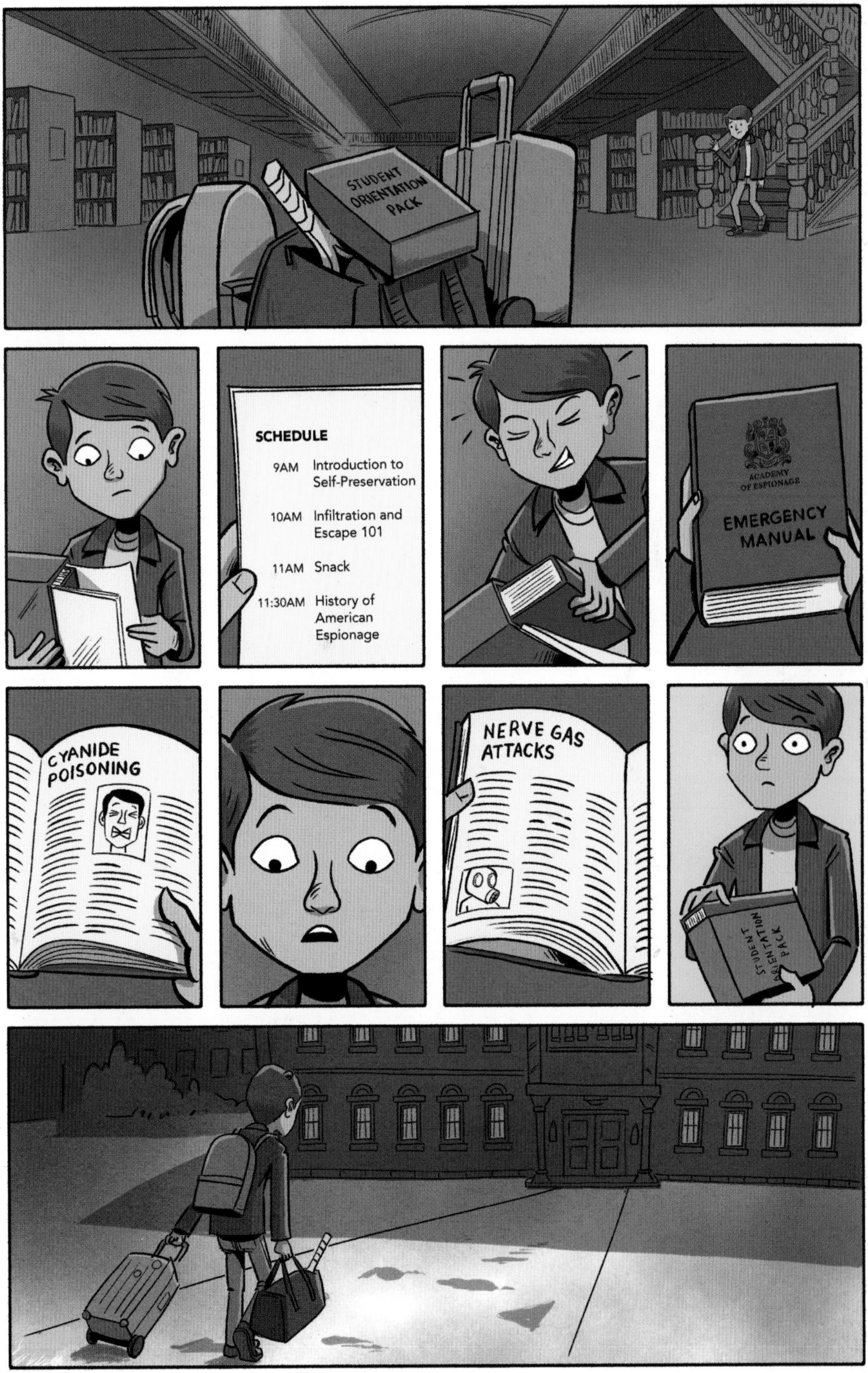
STUDENT ORIENTATION PACK
SCHEDULE
9AM Introduction to Self-Preservation
10AM Infiltration and Escape 101
11AM Snack
11:30AM History of American Espionage
ACADEMY OF ESPIONAGE
EMERGENCY MANUAL
CYANIDE POISONING
NERVE GAS ATTACKS
STUDENT ORIENTATION PACK

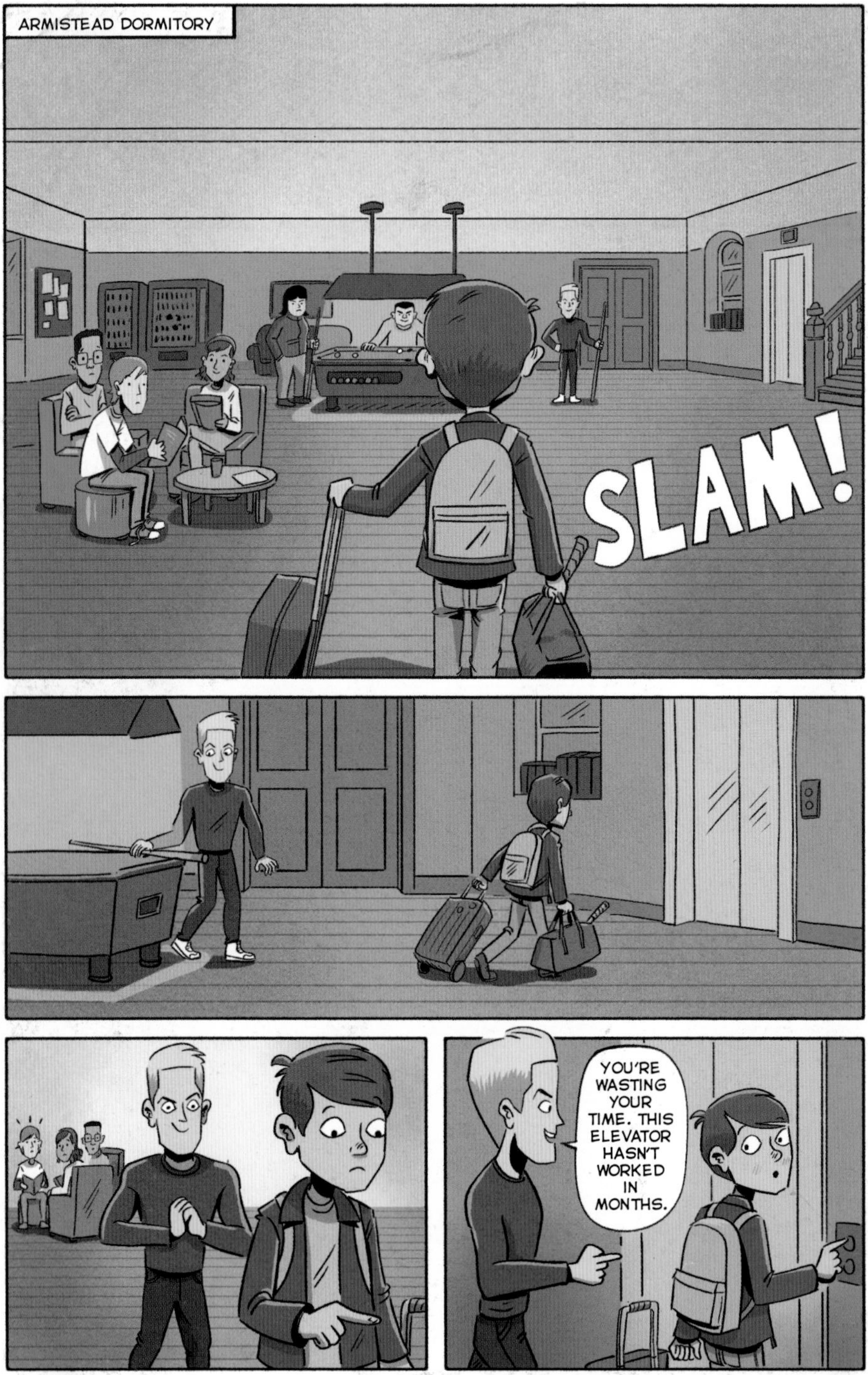
ARMISTEAD DORMITORY
SLAM!
YOU'RE WASTING YOUR TIME. THIS ELEVATOR HASN'T WORKED IN MONTHS.

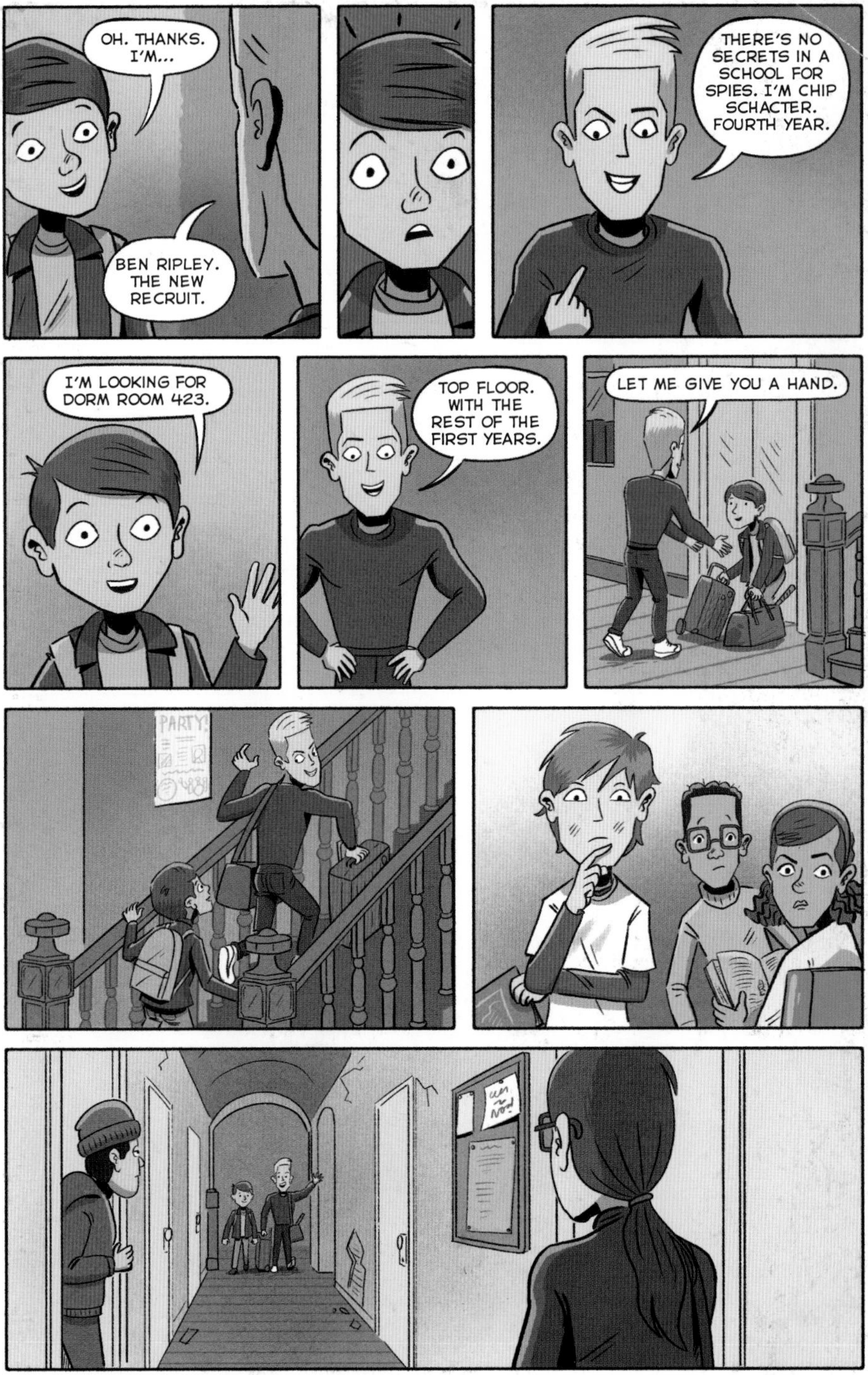
OH. THANKS. I'M...
BEN RIPLEY. THE NEW RECRUIT.
THERE'S NO SECRETS IN A SCHOOL FOR SPIES. I'M CHIP SCHACTER. FOURTH YEAR.
I'M LOOKING FOR DORM ROOM 423.
TOP FLOOR. WITH THE REST OF THE FIRST YEARS.
LET ME GIVE YOU A HAND.
PARTY!

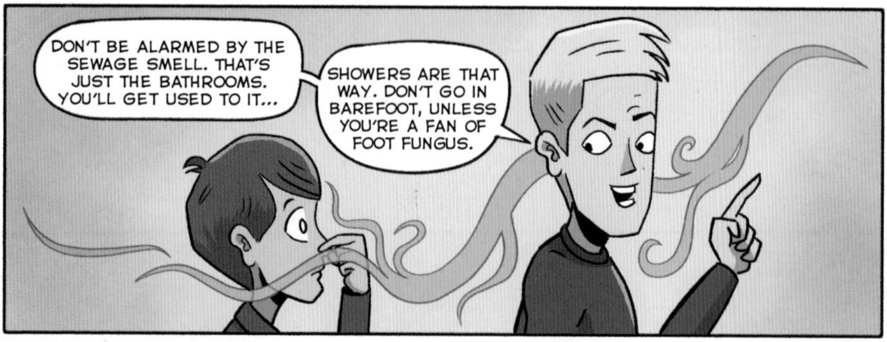
DON'T BE ALARMED BY THE SEWAGE SMELL. THAT'S JUST THE BATHROOMS. YOU'LL GET USED TO IT...
SHOWERS ARE THAT WAY. DON'T GO IN BAREFOOT, UNLESS YOU'RE A FAN OF FOOT FUNGUS.

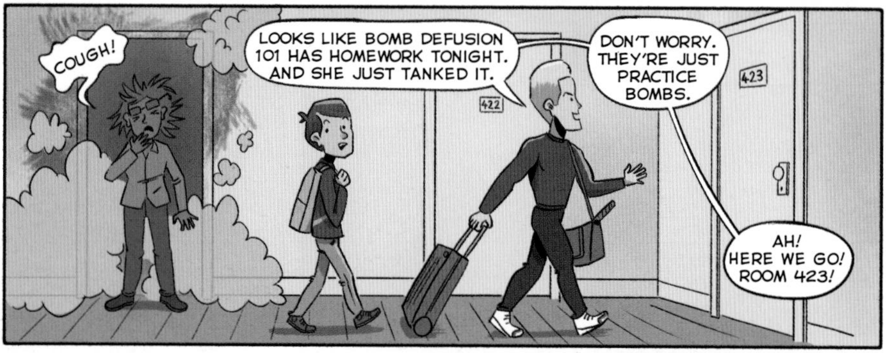
COUGH!
LOOKS LIKE BOMB DEFUSION 101 HAS HOMEWORK TONIGHT. AND SHE JUST TANKED IT.
DON'T WORRY. THEY'RE JUST PRACTICE BOMBS.
422
423
AH! HERE WE GO! ROOM 423!

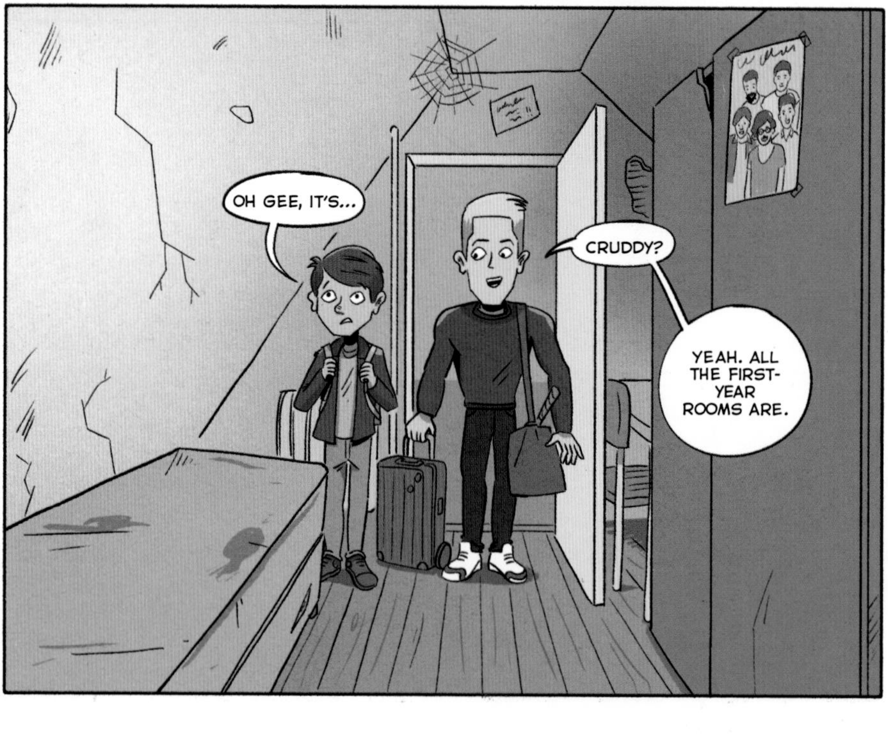
OH GEE, IT'S...
CRUDDY?
YEAH. ALL THE FIRST-YEAR ROOMS ARE.

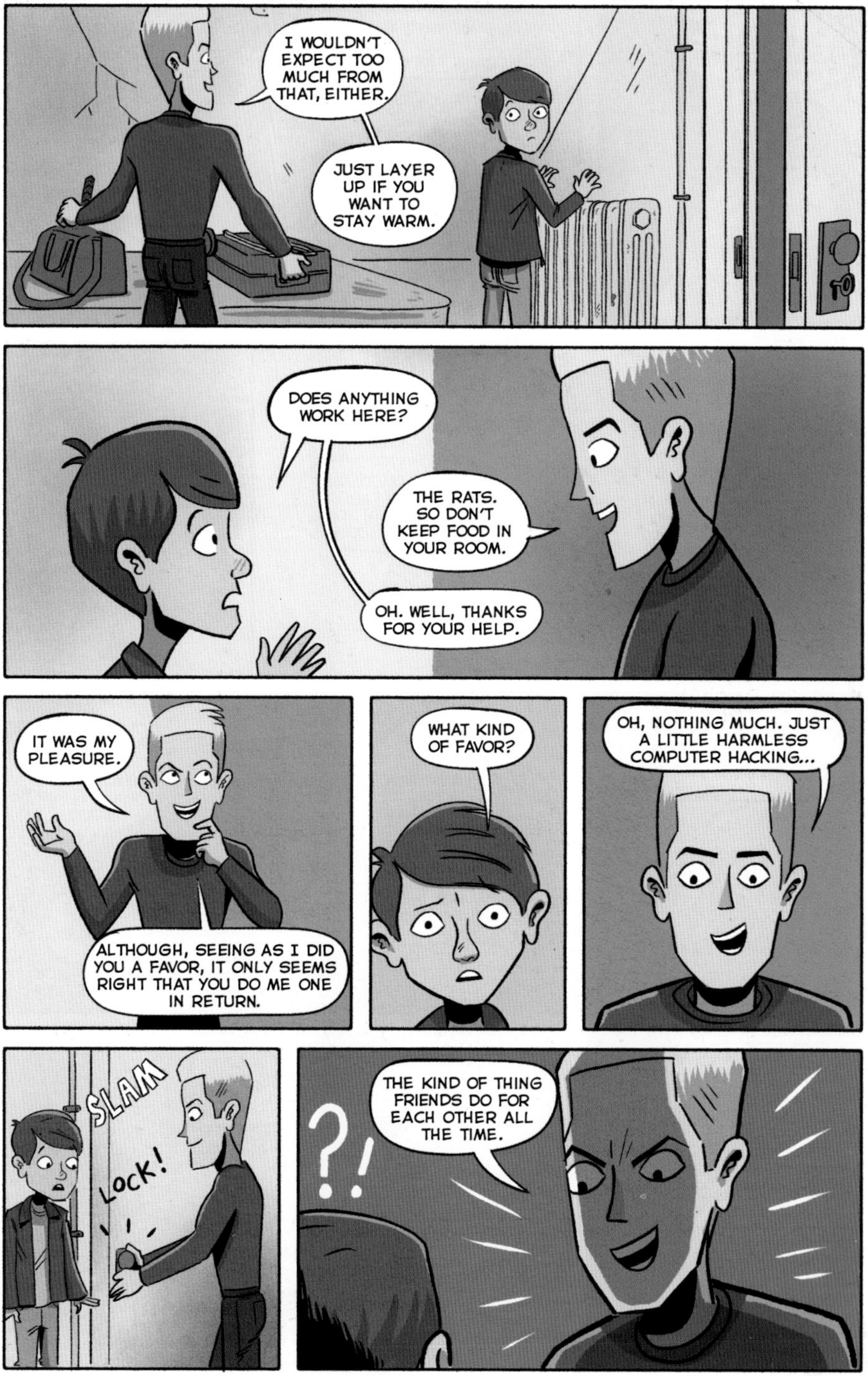
I WOULDN'T EXPECT TOO MUCH FROM THAT, EITHER.
JUST LAYER UP IF YOU WANT TO STAY WARM.
DOES ANYTHING WORK HERE?
THE RATS. SO DON'T KEEP FOOD IN YOUR ROOM.
OH. WELL, THANKS FOR YOUR HELP.
IT WAS MY PLEASURE.
ALTHOUGH, SEEING AS I DID YOU A FAVOR, IT ONLY SEEMS RIGHT THAT YOU DO ME ONE IN RETURN.
WHAT KIND OF FAVOR?
OH, NOTHING MUCH. JUST A LITTLE HARMLESS COMPUTER HACKING...
SLAM
LOCK!
?!
THE KIND OF THING FRIENDS DO FOR EACH OTHER ALL THE TIME.

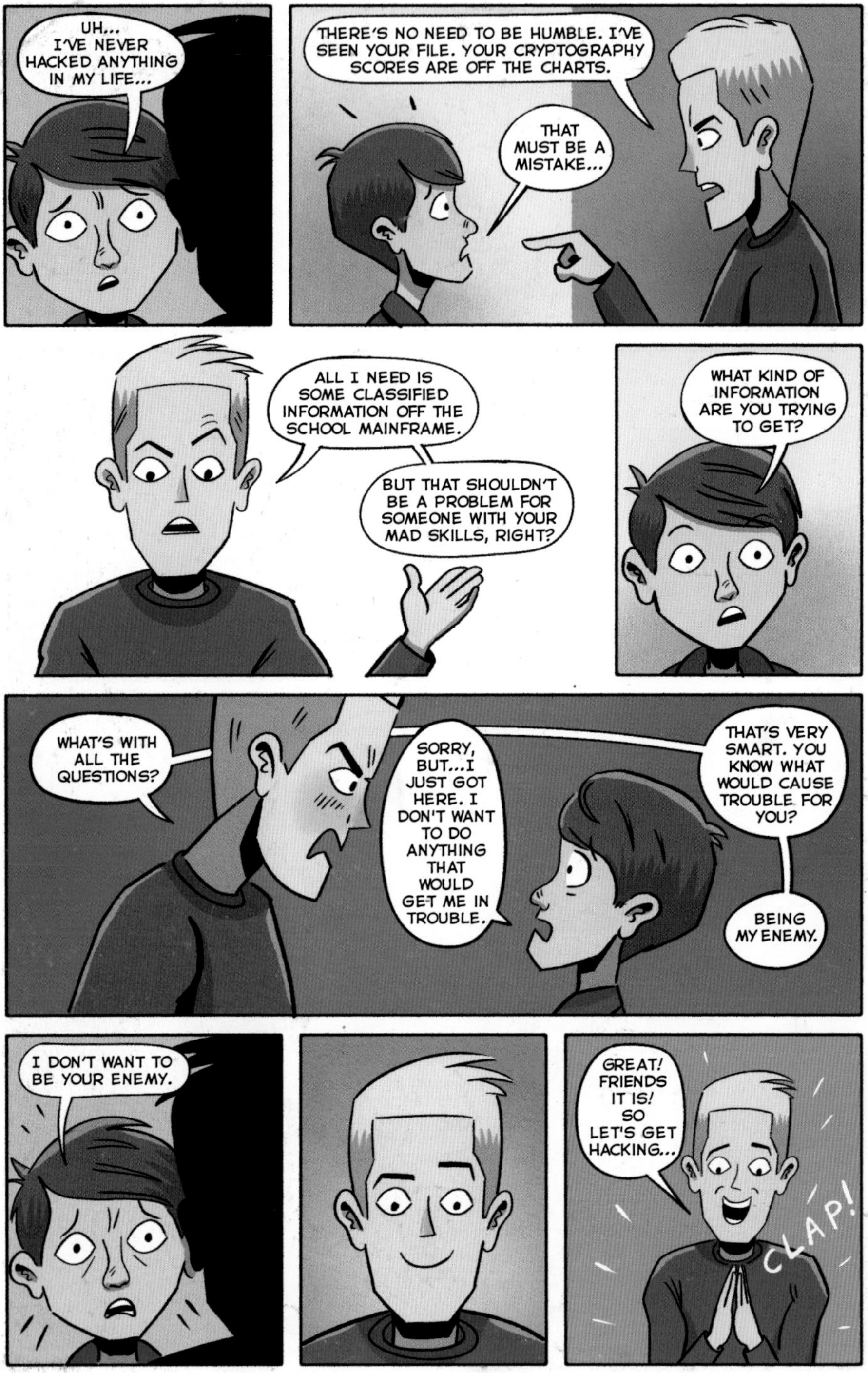
UH... I'VE NEVER HACKED ANYTHING IN MY LIFE...
THERE'S NO NEED TO BE HUMBLE. I'VE SEEN YOUR FILE. YOUR CRYPTOGRAPHY SCORES ARE OFF THE CHARTS.
THAT MUST BE A MISTAKE...
ALL I NEED IS SOME CLASSIFIED INFORMATION OFF THE SCHOOL MAINFRAME.
BUT THAT SHOULDN'T BE A PROBLEM FOR SOMEONE WITH YOUR MAD SKILLS, RIGHT?
WHAT KIND OF INFORMATION ARE YOU TRYING TO GET?
WHAT'S WITH ALL THE QUESTIONS?
SORRY, BUT...I JUST GOT HERE. I DON'T WANT TO DO ANYTHING THAT WOULD GET ME IN TROUBLE.
THAT'S VERY SMART. YOU KNOW WHAT WOULD CAUSE TROUBLE FOR YOU?
BEING MY ENEMY.
I DON'T WANT TO BE YOUR ENEMY.
GREAT! FRIENDS IT IS! SO LET'S GET HACKING...
CLAP!

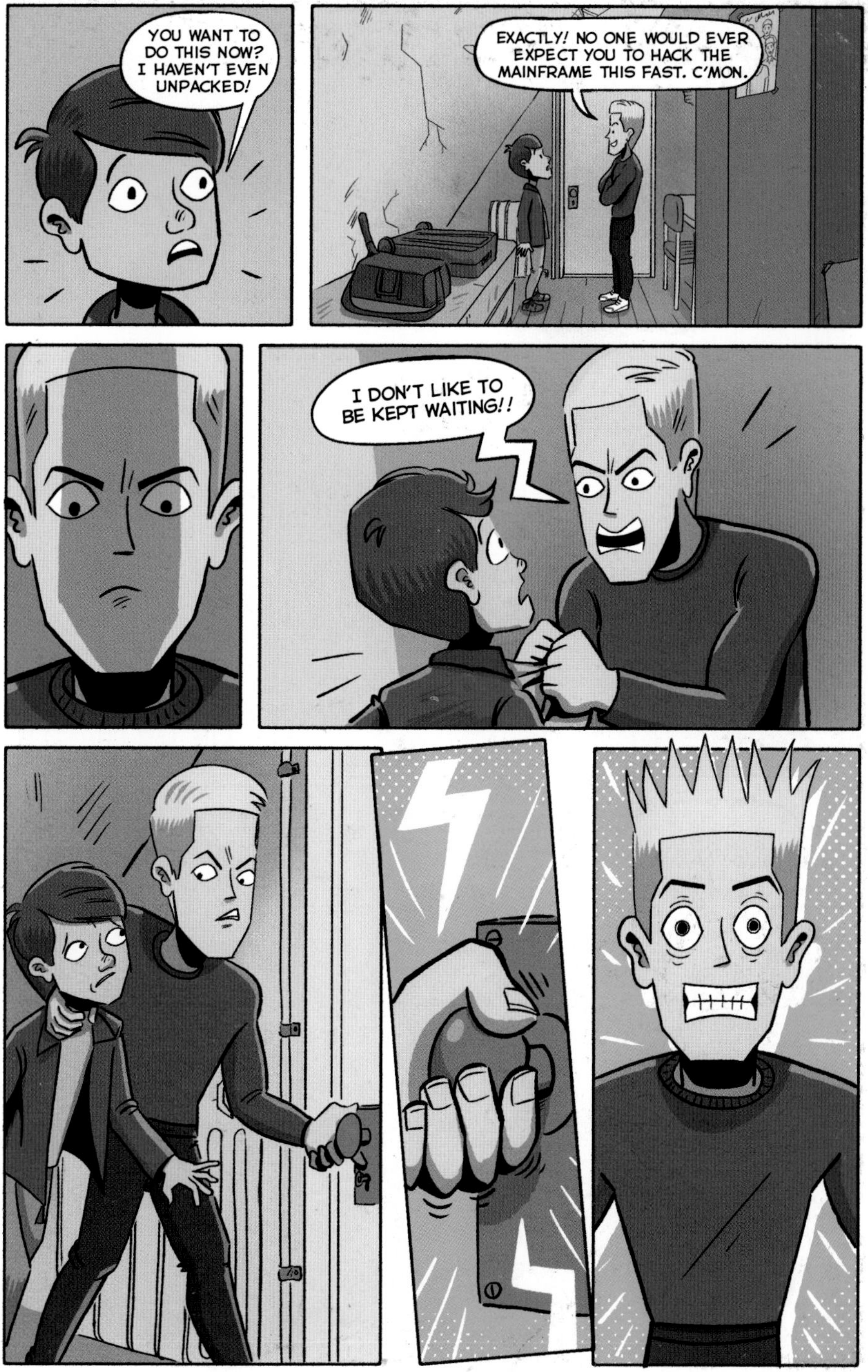
YOU WANT TO DO THIS NOW? I HAVEN'T EVEN UNPACKED!
EXACTLY! NO ONE WOULD EVER EXPECT YOU TO HACK THE MAINFRAME THIS FAST. C'MON.
I DON'T LIKE TO BE KEPT WAITING!!

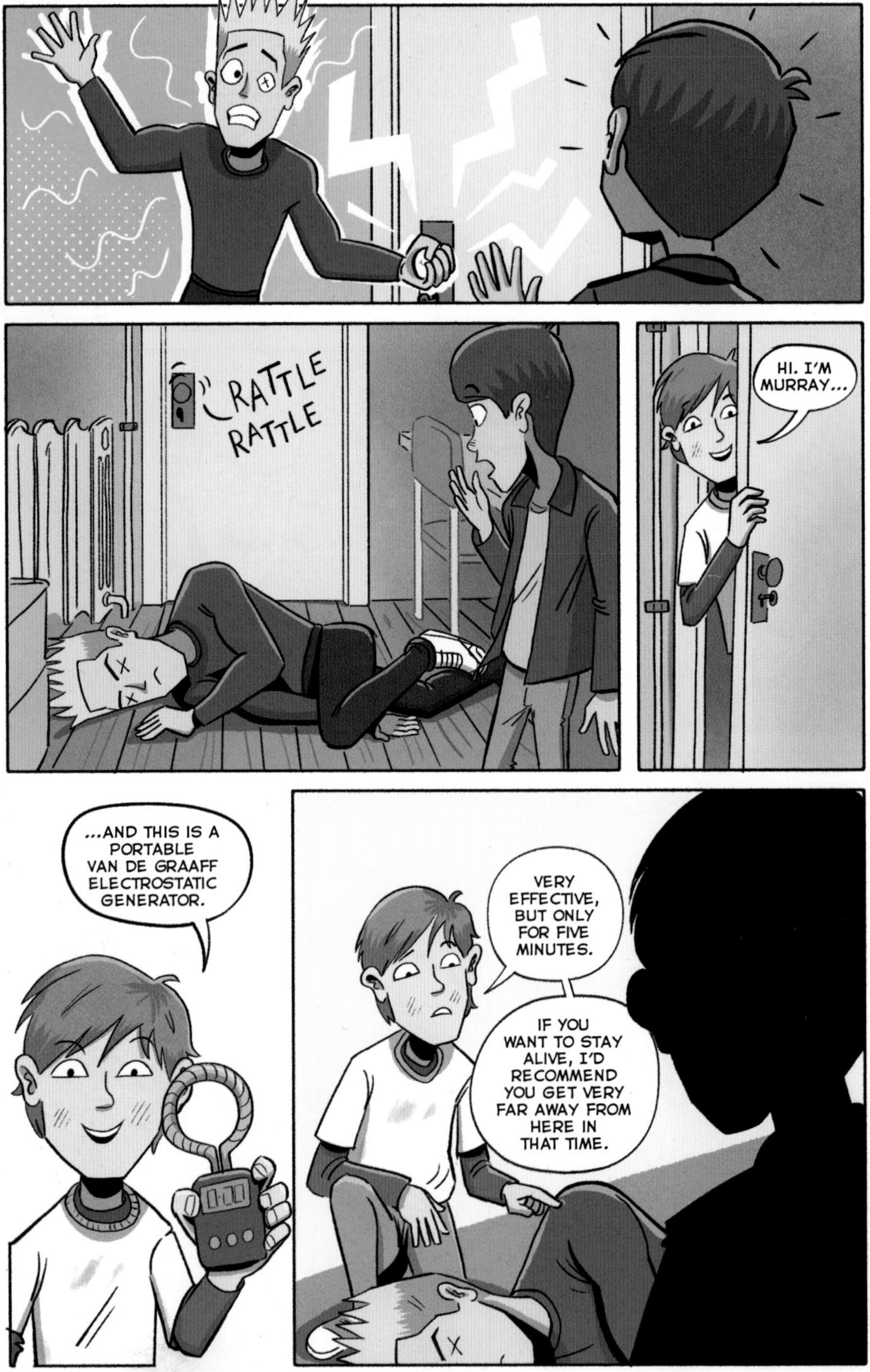
RATTLE
RATTLE
HI. I'M MURRAY...
...AND THIS IS A PORTABLE VAN DE GRAAFF ELECTROSTATIC GENERATOR.
VERY EFFECTIVE, BUT ONLY FOR FIVE MINUTES.
IF YOU WANT TO STAY ALIVE, I'D RECOMMEND YOU GET VERY FAR AWAY FROM HERE IN THAT TIME.

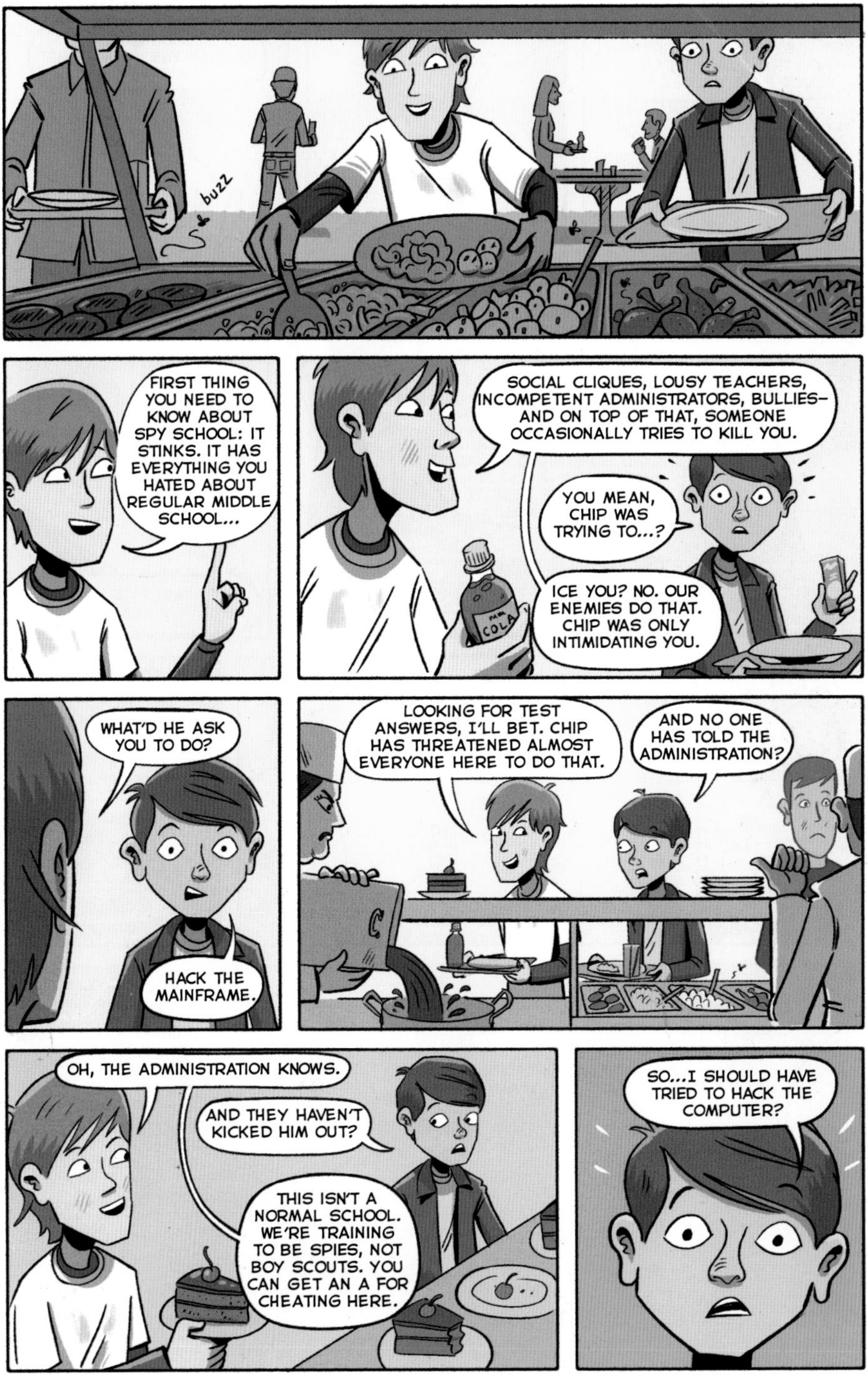
buzz
FIRST THING YOU NEED TO KNOW ABOUT SPY SCHOOL: IT STINKS. IT HAS EVERYTHING YOU HATED ABOUT REGULAR MIDDLE SCHOOL...
SOCIAL CLIQUES, LOUSY TEACHERS, INCOMPETENT ADMINISTRATORS, BULLIES— AND ON TOP OF THAT, SOMEONE OCCASIONALLY TRIES TO KILL YOU.
YOU MEAN, CHIP WAS TRYING TO...?
ICE YOU? NO. OUR ENEMIES DO THAT. CHIP WAS ONLY INTIMIDATING YOU.
COLA
WHAT'D HE ASK YOU TO DO?
HACK THE MAINFRAME.
LOOKING FOR TEST ANSWERS, I'LL BET. CHIP HAS THREATENED ALMOST EVERYONE HERE TO DO THAT.
AND NO ONE HAS TOLD THE ADMINISTRATION?
OH, THE ADMINISTRATION KNOWS.
AND THEY HAVEN'T KICKED HIM OUT?
THIS ISN'T A NORMAL SCHOOL. WE'RE TRAINING TO BE SPIES, NOT BOY SCOUTS. YOU CAN GET AN A FOR CHEATING HERE.
SO...I SHOULD HAVE TRIED TO HACK THE COMPUTER?

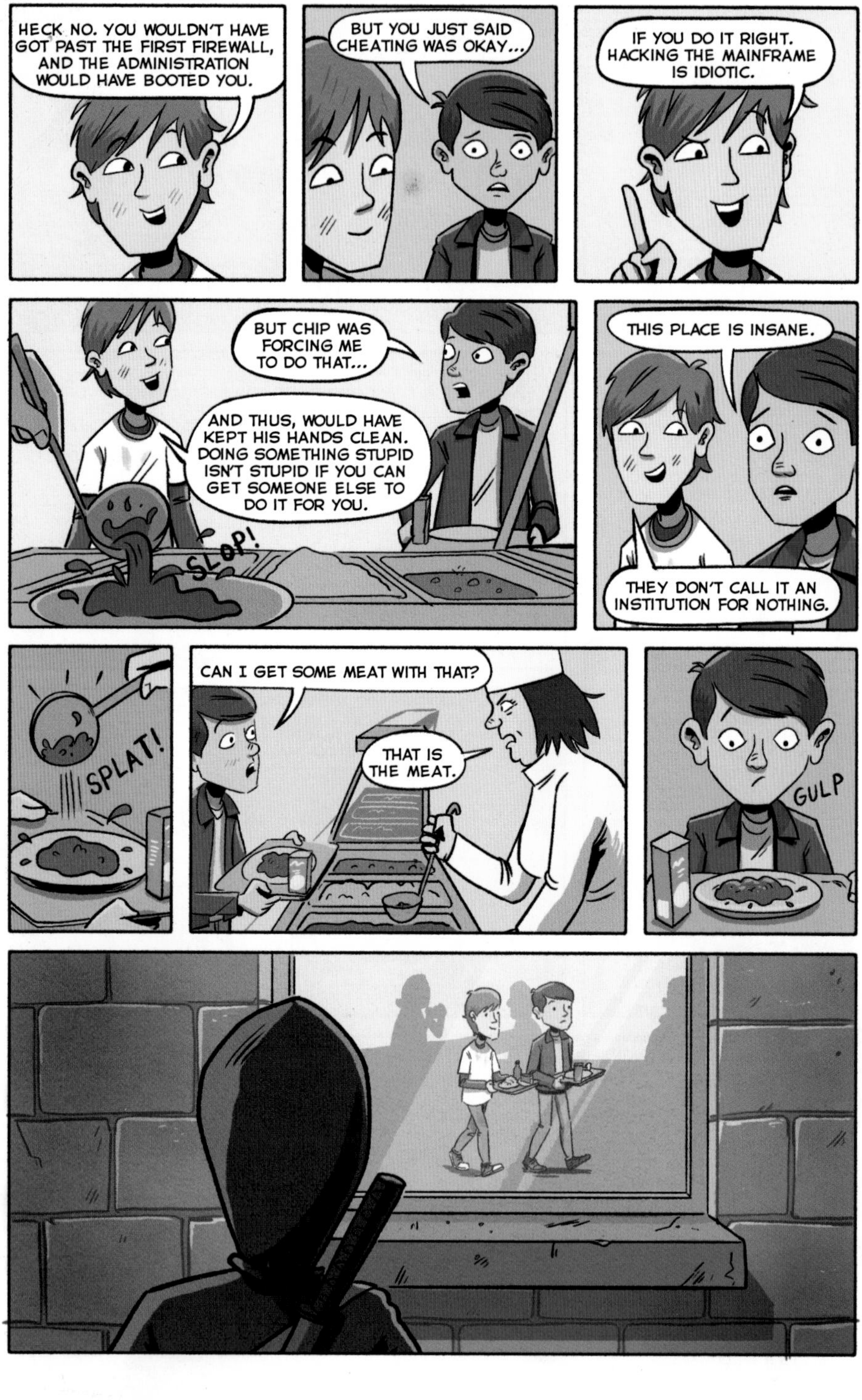
HECK NO. YOU WOULDN'T HAVE GOT PAST THE FIRST FIREWALL, AND THE ADMINISTRATION WOULD HAVE BOOTED YOU.
BUT YOU JUST SAID CHEATING WAS OKAY...
IF YOU DO IT RIGHT. HACKING THE MAINFRAME IS IDIOTIC.
BUT CHIP WAS FORCING ME TO DO THAT...
AND THUS, WOULD HAVE KEPT HIS HANDS CLEAN. DOING SOMETHING STUPID ISN'T STUPID IF YOU CAN GET SOMEONE ELSE TO DO IT FOR YOU.
SLOP!
THIS PLACE IS INSANE.
THEY DON'T CALL IT AN INSTITUTION FOR NOTHING.
SPLAT!
CAN I GET SOME MEAT WITH THAT?
THAT IS THE MEAT.
GULP

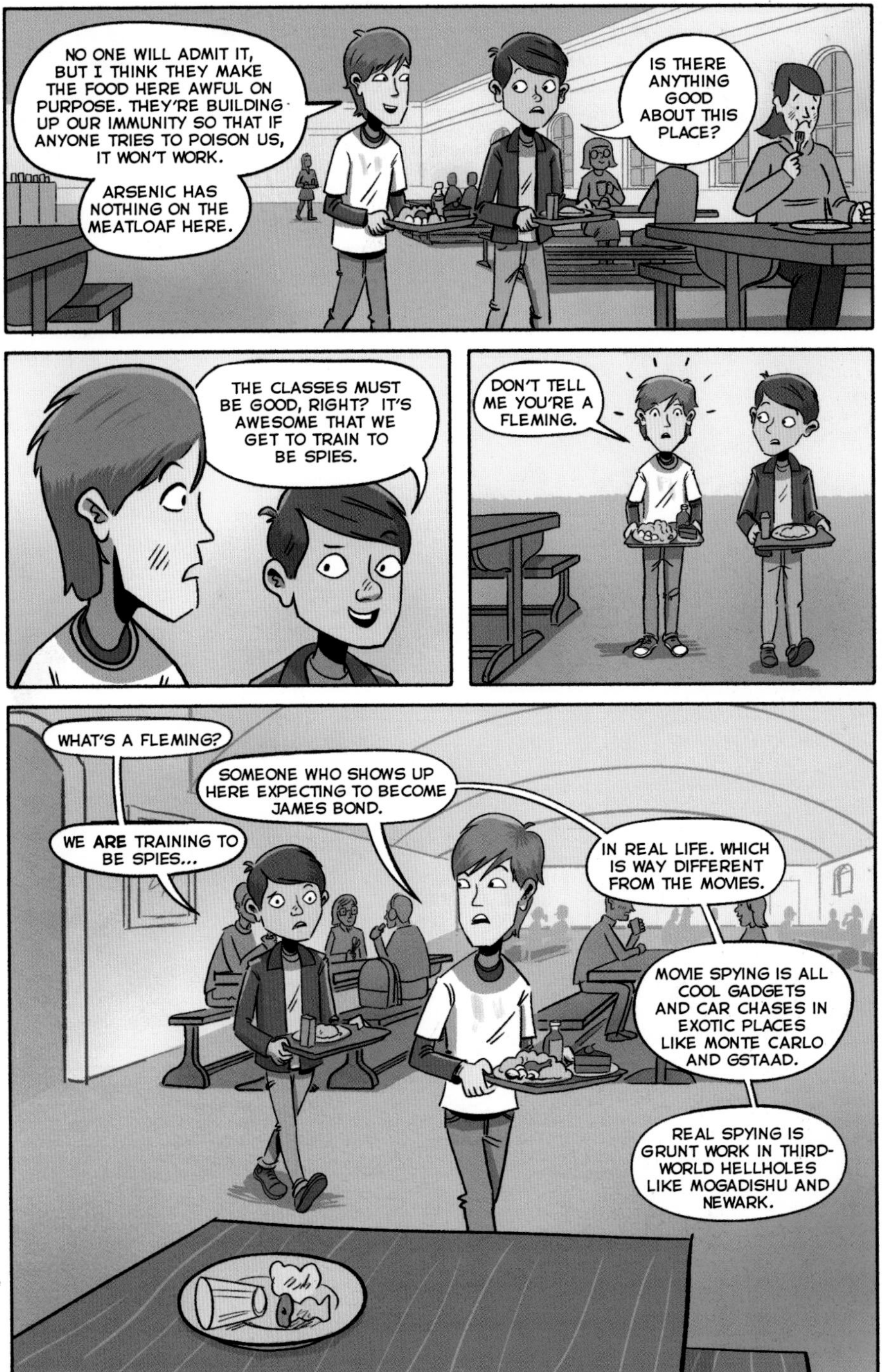
NO ONE WILL ADMIT IT, BUT I THINK THEY MAKE THE FOOD HERE AWFUL ON PURPOSE. THEY'RE BUILDING UP OUR IMMUNITY SO THAT IF ANYONE TRIES TO POISON US, IT WON'T WORK.
ARSENIC HAS NOTHING ON THE MEATLOAF HERE.
IS THERE ANYTHING GOOD ABOUT THIS PLACE?
THE CLASSES MUST BE GOOD, RIGHT? IT'S AWESOME THAT WE GET TO TRAIN TO BE SPIES.
DON'T TELL ME YOU'RE A FLEMING.
WHAT'S A FLEMING?
SOMEONE WHO SHOWS UP HERE EXPECTING TO BECOME JAMES BOND.
WE **ARE** TRAINING TO BE SPIES...
IN REAL LIFE. WHICH IS WAY DIFFERENT FROM THE MOVIES.
MOVIE SPYING IS ALL COOL GADGETS AND CAR CHASES IN EXOTIC PLACES LIKE MONTE CARLO AND GSTAAD.
REAL SPYING IS GRUNT WORK IN THIRD-WORLD HELLHOLES LIKE MOGADISHU AND NEWARK.

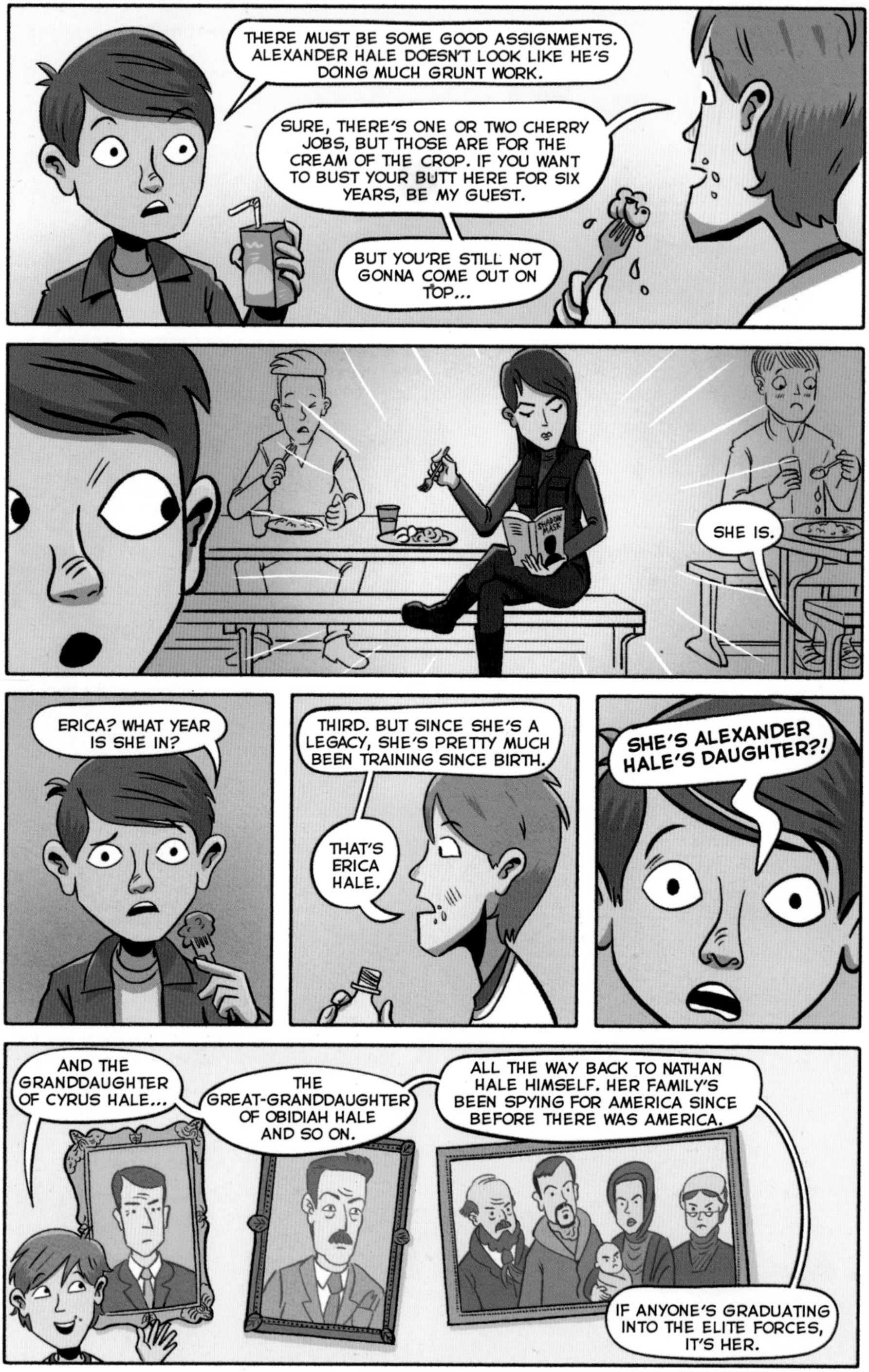
THERE MUST BE SOME GOOD ASSIGNMENTS. ALEXANDER HALE DOESN'T LOOK LIKE HE'S DOING MUCH GRUNT WORK.
SURE, THERE'S ONE OR TWO CHERRY JOBS, BUT THOSE ARE FOR THE CREAM OF THE CROP. IF YOU WANT TO BUST YOUR BUTT HERE FOR SIX YEARS, BE MY GUEST.
BUT YOU'RE STILL NOT GONNA COME OUT ON TOP...
SHADOW MASK
SHE IS.
ERICA? WHAT YEAR IS SHE IN?
THIRD. BUT SINCE SHE'S A LEGACY, SHE'S PRETTY MUCH BEEN TRAINING SINCE BIRTH.
THAT'S ERICA HALE.
SHE'S ALEXANDER HALE'S DAUGHTER?!
AND THE GRANDDAUGHTER OF CYRUS HALE...
THE GREAT-GRANDDAUGHTER OF OBIDIAH HALE AND SO ON.
ALL THE WAY BACK TO NATHAN HALE HIMSELF. HER FAMILY'S BEEN SPYING FOR AMERICA SINCE BEFORE THERE WAS AMERICA.
IF ANYONE'S GRADUATING INTO THE ELITE FORCES, IT'S HER.

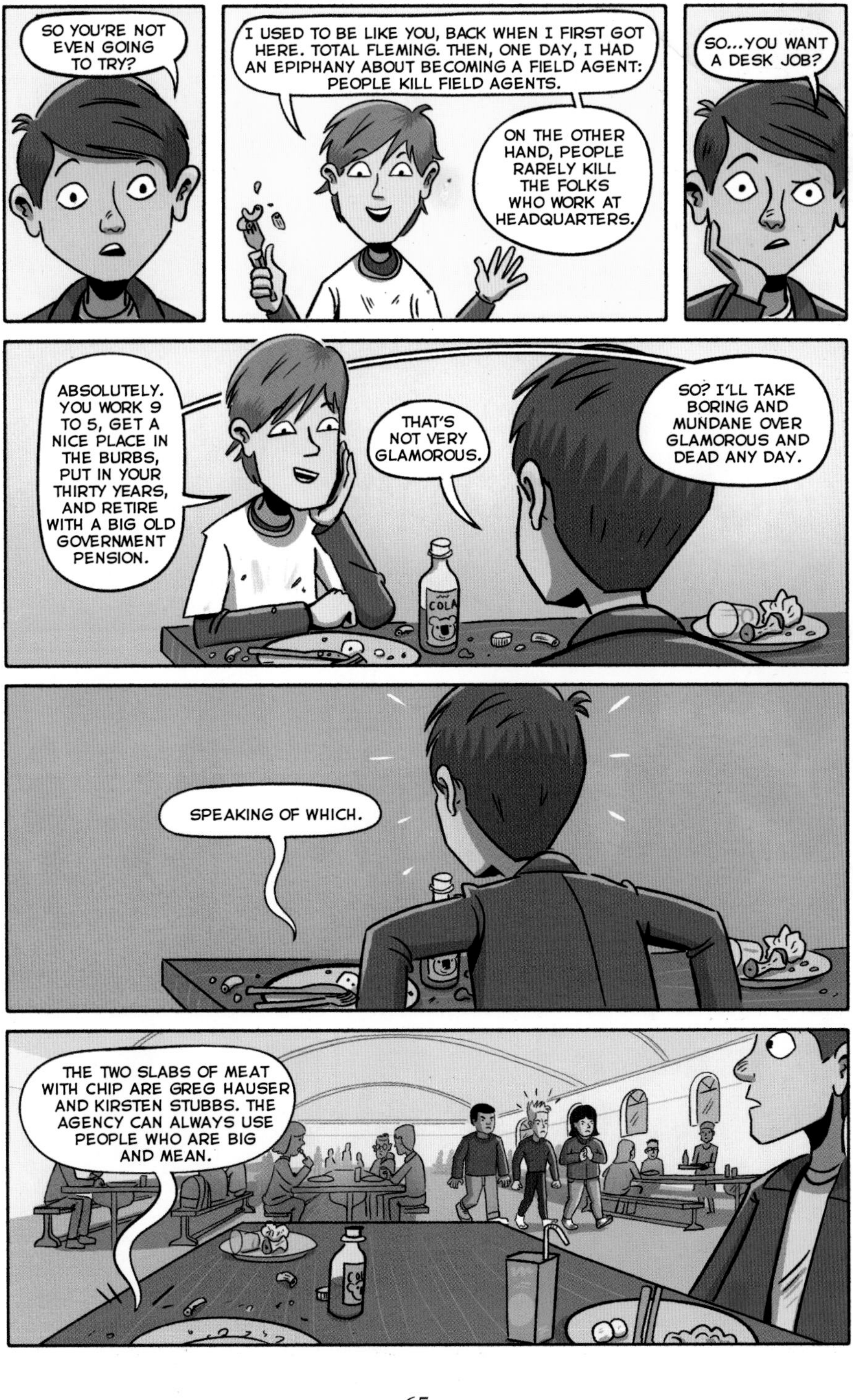
SO YOU'RE NOT EVEN GOING TO TRY?
I USED TO BE LIKE YOU, BACK WHEN I FIRST GOT HERE. TOTAL FLEMING. THEN, ONE DAY, I HAD AN EPIPHANY ABOUT BECOMING A FIELD AGENT: PEOPLE KILL FIELD AGENTS.
ON THE OTHER HAND, PEOPLE RARELY KILL THE FOLKS WHO WORK AT HEADQUARTERS.
SO...YOU WANT A DESK JOB?
ABSOLUTELY. YOU WORK 9 TO 5, GET A NICE PLACE IN THE BURBS, PUT IN YOUR THIRTY YEARS, AND RETIRE WITH A BIG OLD GOVERNMENT PENSION.
THAT'S NOT VERY GLAMOROUS.
SO? I'LL TAKE BORING AND MUNDANE OVER GLAMOROUS AND DEAD ANY DAY.
COLA
SPEAKING OF WHICH.
THE TWO SLABS OF MEAT WITH CHIP ARE GREG HAUSER AND KIRSTEN STUBBS. THE AGENCY CAN ALWAYS USE PEOPLE WHO ARE BIG AND MEAN.

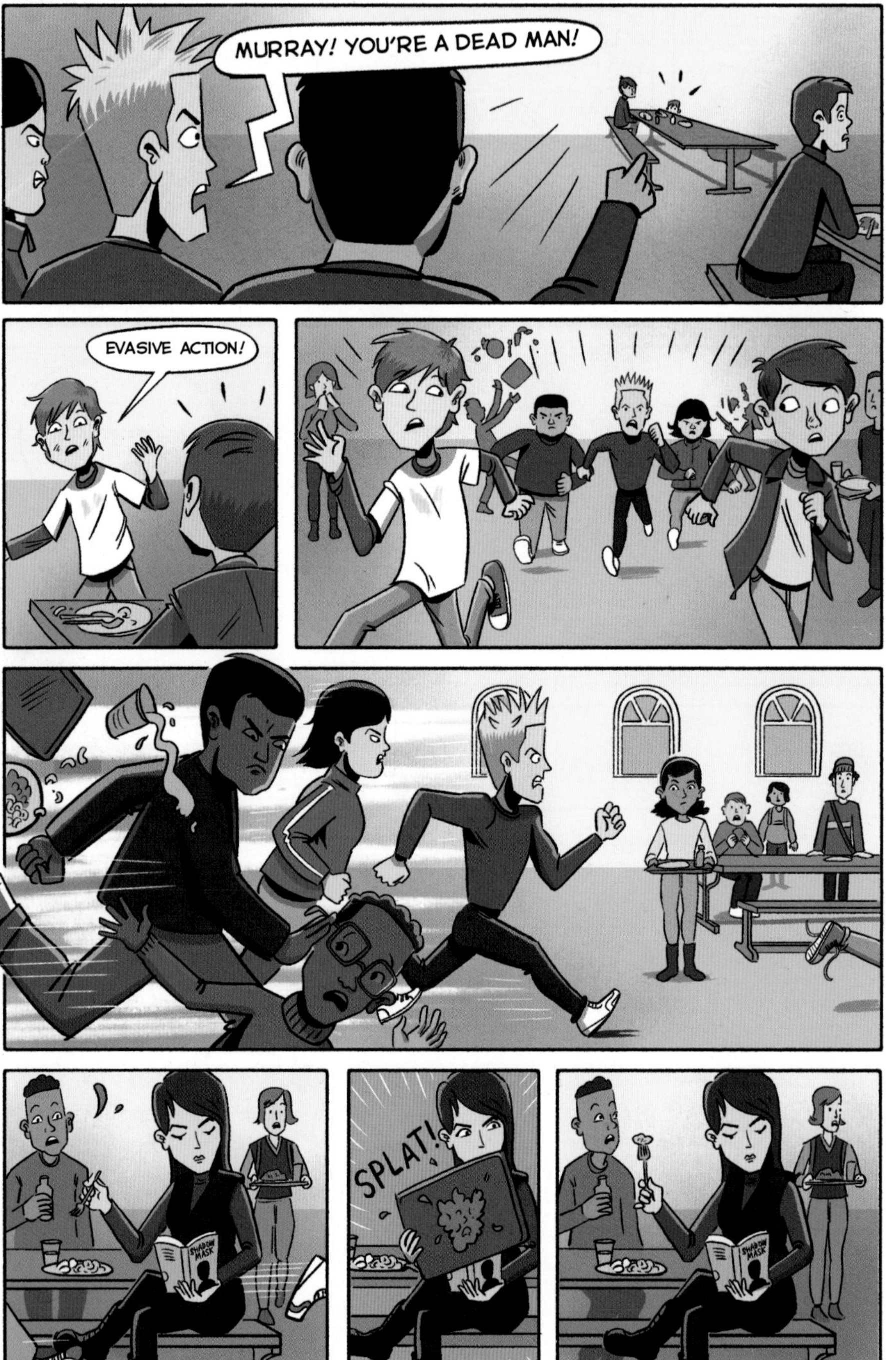
MURRAY! YOU'RE A DEAD MAN!
EVASIVE ACTION!
SHADOW MASK
SPLAT!
SHADOW MASK

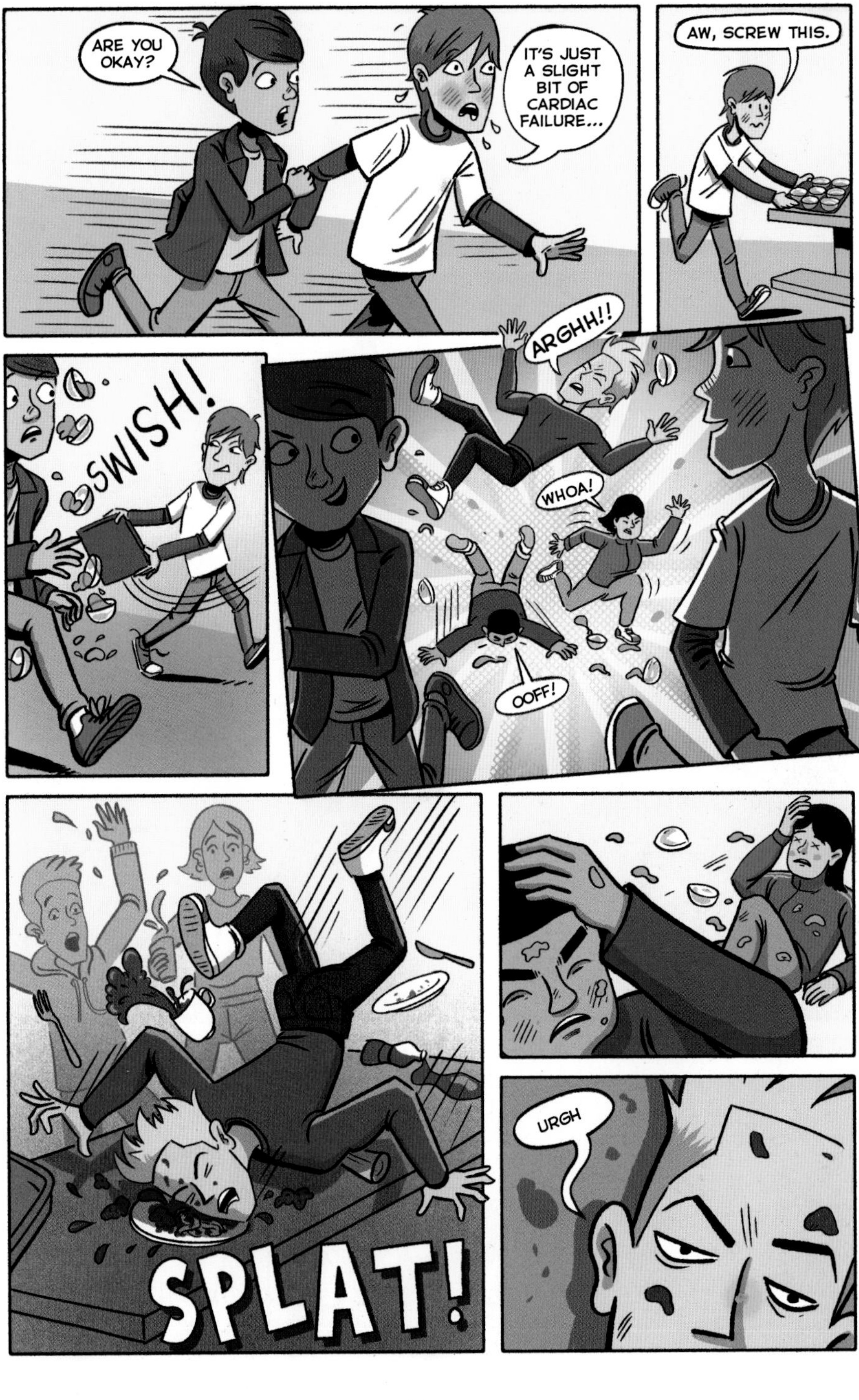
ARE YOU OKAY?
IT'S JUST A SLIGHT BIT OF CARDIAC FAILURE...
AW, SCREW THIS.
SWISH!
ARGHH!!
WHOA!
OOFF!
SPLAT!
URGH

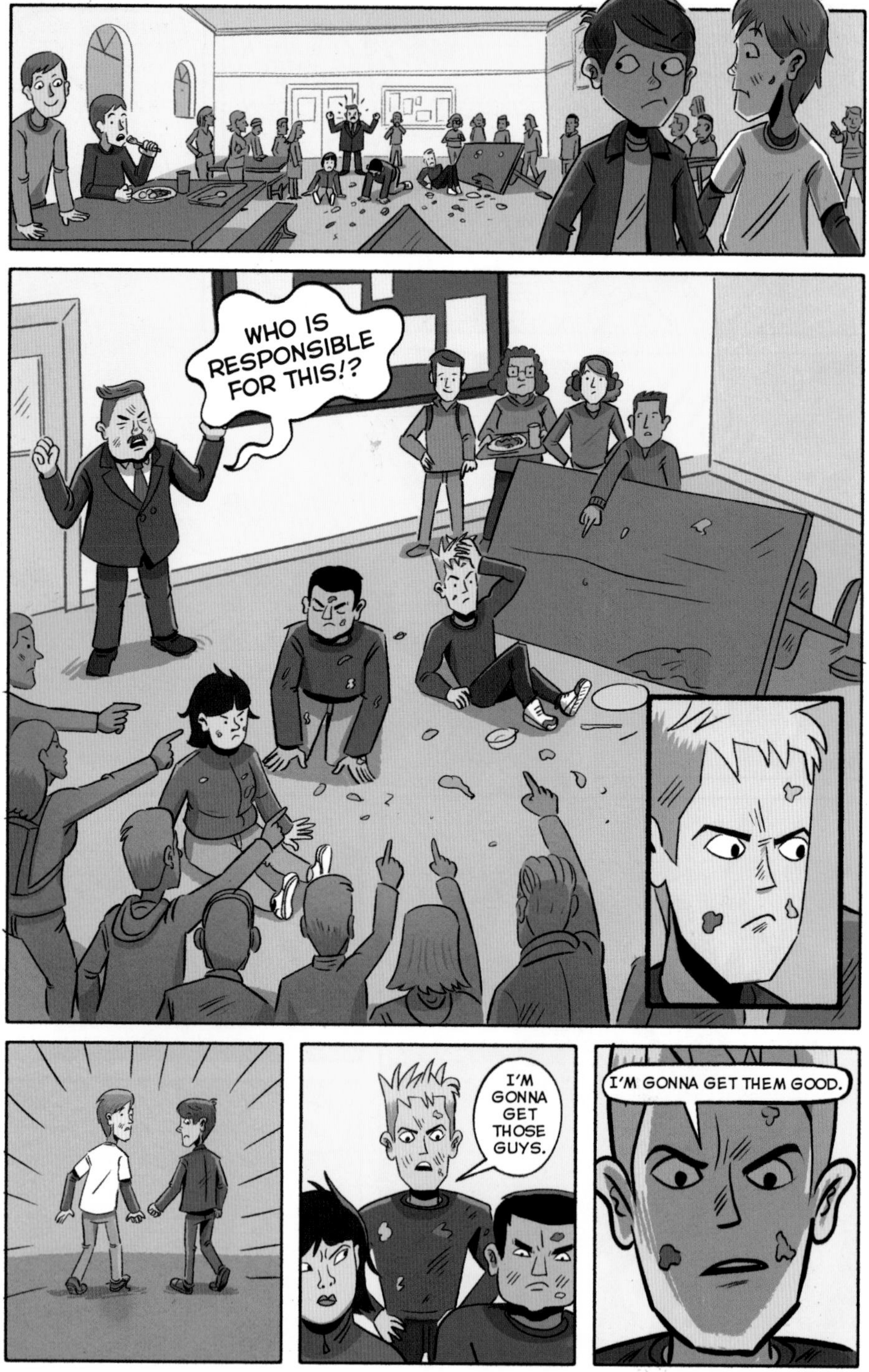
WHO IS RESPONSIBLE FOR THIS!?
I'M GONNA GET THOSE GUYS.
I'M GONNA GET THEM GOOD.

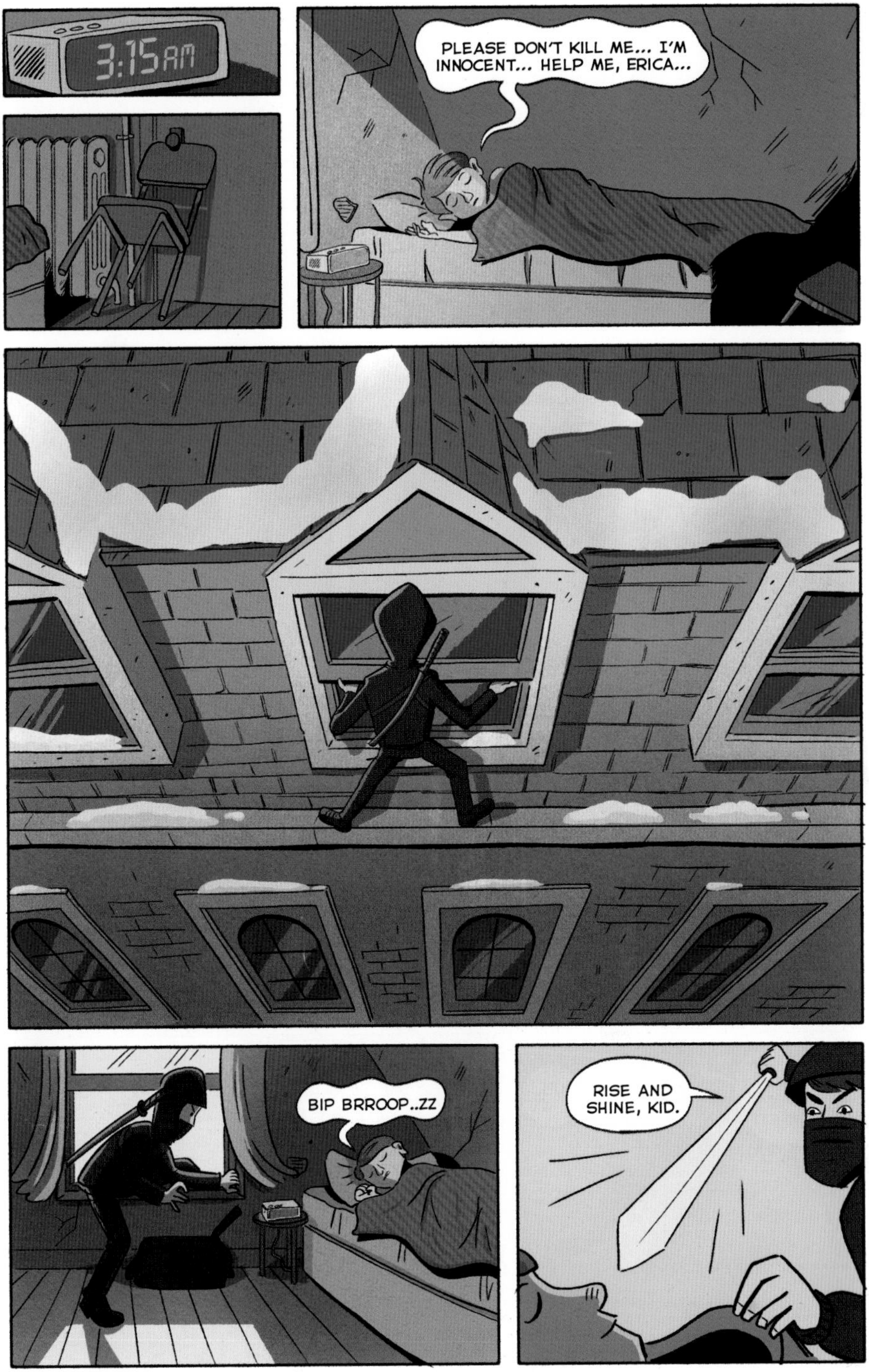
3:15AM
PLEASE DON'T KILL ME... I'M INNOCENT... HELP ME, ERICA...
BIP BRROOP..ZZ
RISE AND SHINE, KID.

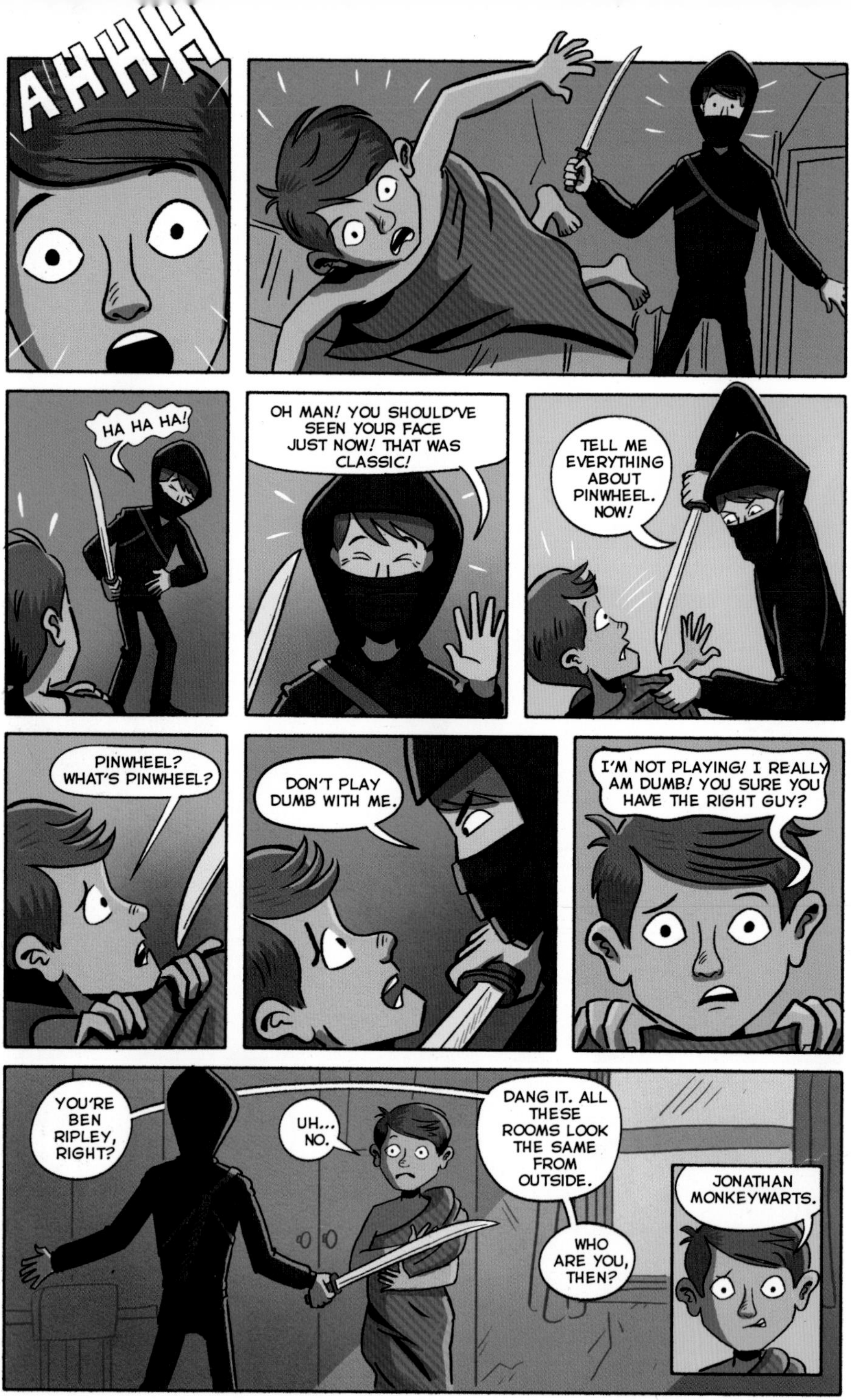
AHHHH
HA HA HA!
OH MAN! YOU SHOULD'VE SEEN YOUR FACE JUST NOW! THAT WAS CLASSIC!
TELL ME EVERYTHING ABOUT PINWHEEL. NOW!
PINWHEEL? WHAT'S PINWHEEL?
DON'T PLAY DUMB WITH ME.
I'M NOT PLAYING! I REALLY AM DUMB! YOU SURE YOU HAVE THE RIGHT GUY?
YOU'RE BEN RIPLEY, RIGHT?
UH... NO.
DANG IT. ALL THESE ROOMS LOOK THE SAME FROM OUTSIDE.
WHO ARE YOU, THEN?
JONATHAN MONKEYWARTS.

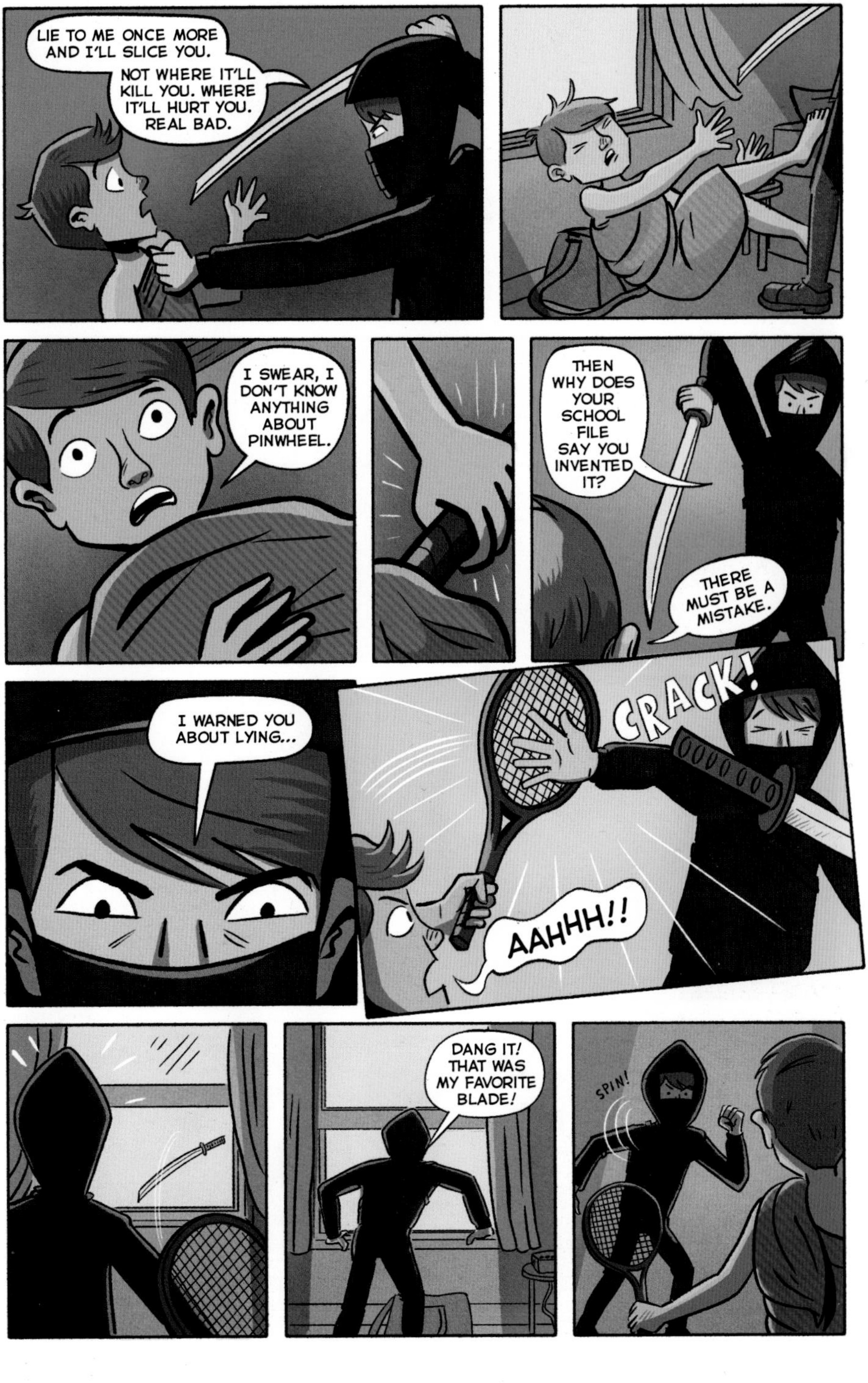
LIE TO ME ONCE MORE AND I'LL SLICE YOU.
NOT WHERE IT'LL KILL YOU. WHERE IT'LL HURT YOU. REAL BAD.
I SWEAR, I DON'T KNOW ANYTHING ABOUT PINWHEEL.
THEN WHY DOES YOUR SCHOOL FILE SAY YOU INVENTED IT?
THERE MUST BE A MISTAKE.
I WARNED YOU ABOUT LYING...
CRACK!
AAHHH!!
DANG IT! THAT WAS MY FAVORITE BLADE!
SPIN!

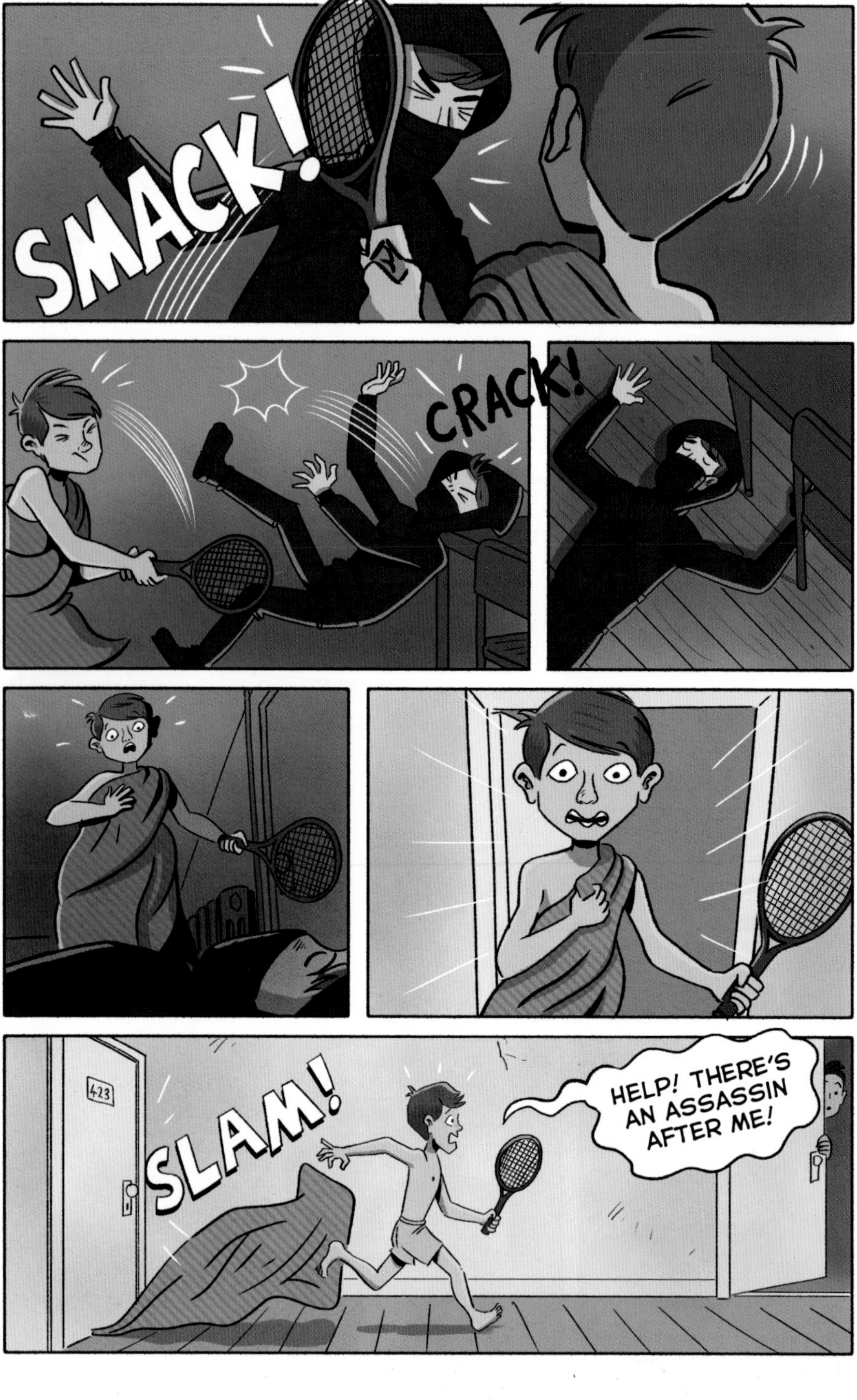
SMACK!
CRACK!
423
SLAM!
HELP! THERE'S AN ASSASSIN AFTER ME!

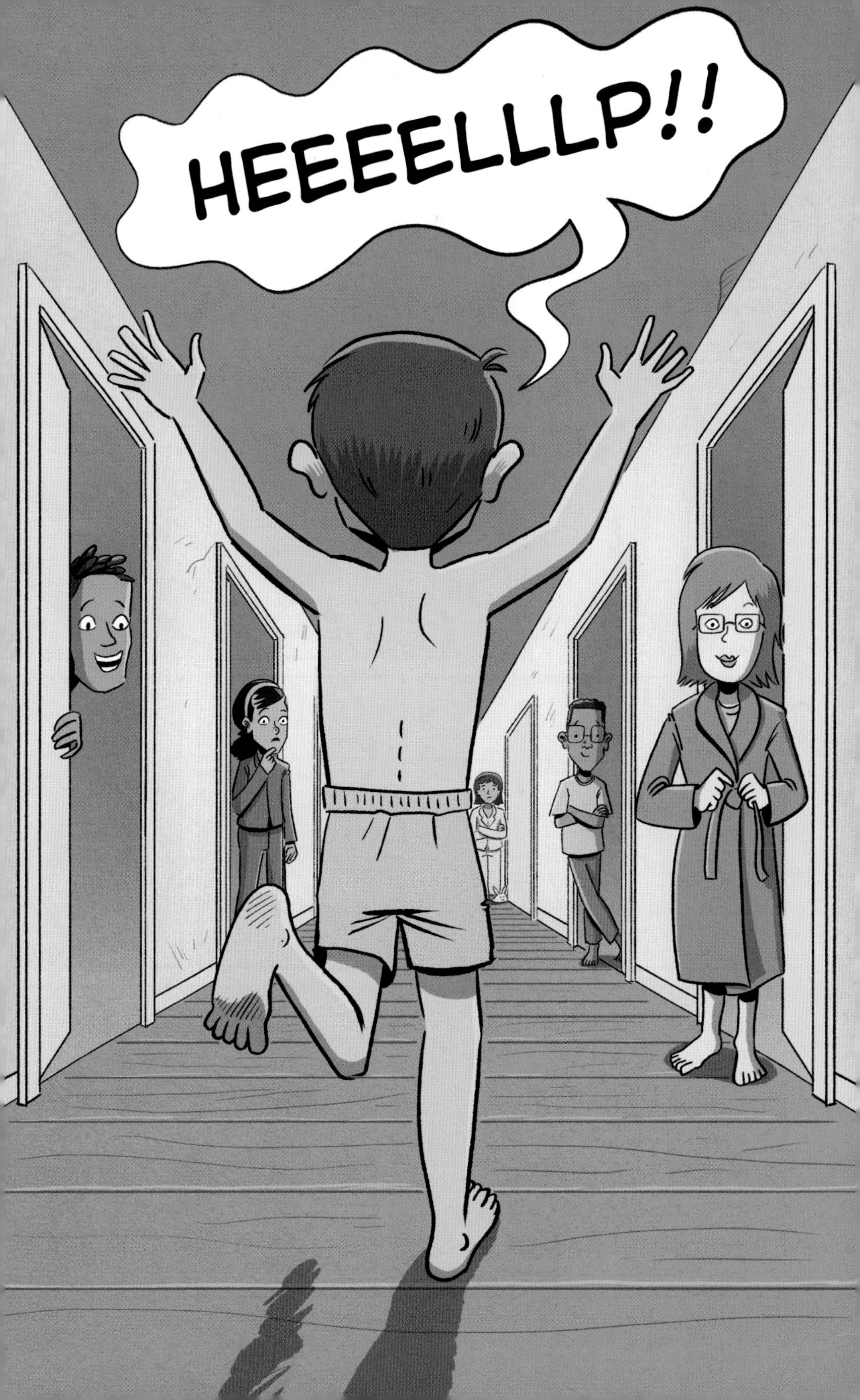
HEEEEELLLLP!!

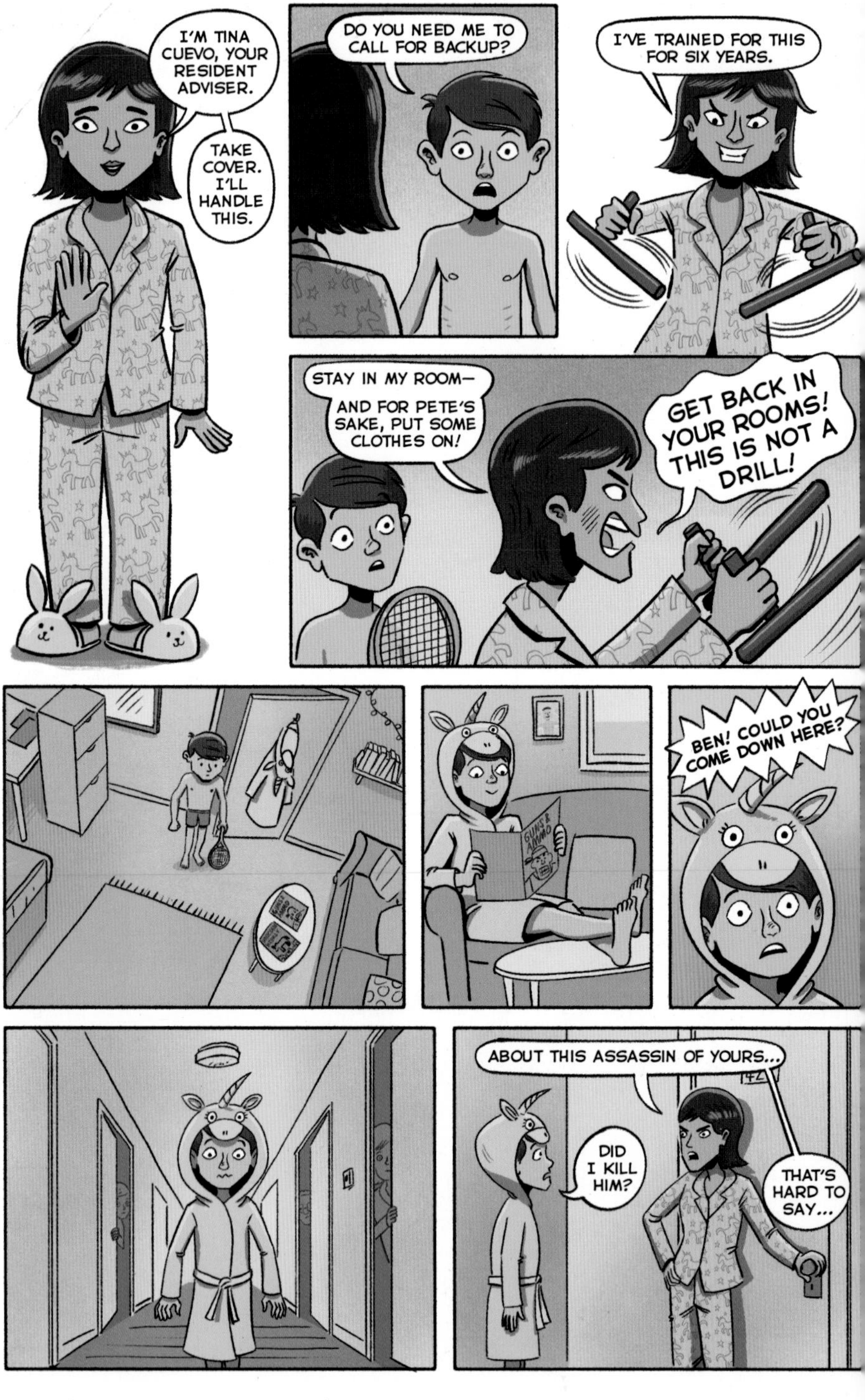
I'M TINA CUEVO, YOUR RESIDENT ADVISER.
TAKE COVER. I'LL HANDLE THIS.
DO YOU NEED ME TO CALL FOR BACKUP?
I'VE TRAINED FOR THIS FOR SIX YEARS.
STAY IN MY ROOM—
AND FOR PETE'S SAKE, PUT SOME CLOTHES ON!
GET BACK IN YOUR ROOMS! THIS IS NOT A DRILL!
GUNS & AMMO
BEN! COULD YOU COME DOWN HERE?
ABOUT THIS ASSASSIN OF YOURS...
DID I KILL HIM?
THAT'S HARD TO SAY...

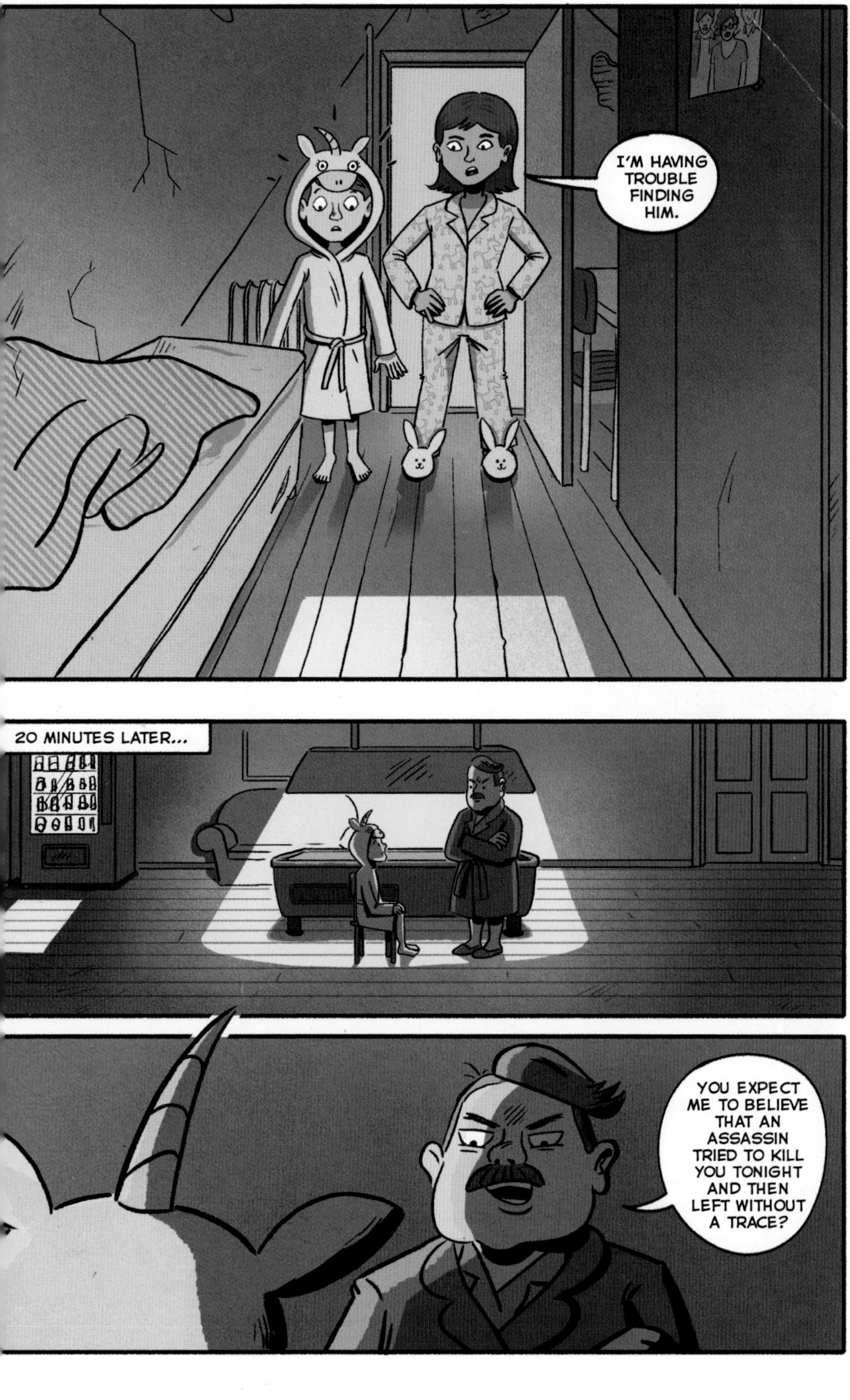
I'M HAVING TROUBLE FINDING HIM.
20 MINUTES LATER...
YOU EXPECT ME TO BELIEVE THAT AN ASSASSIN TRIED TO KILL YOU TONIGHT AND THEN LEFT WITHOUT A TRACE?

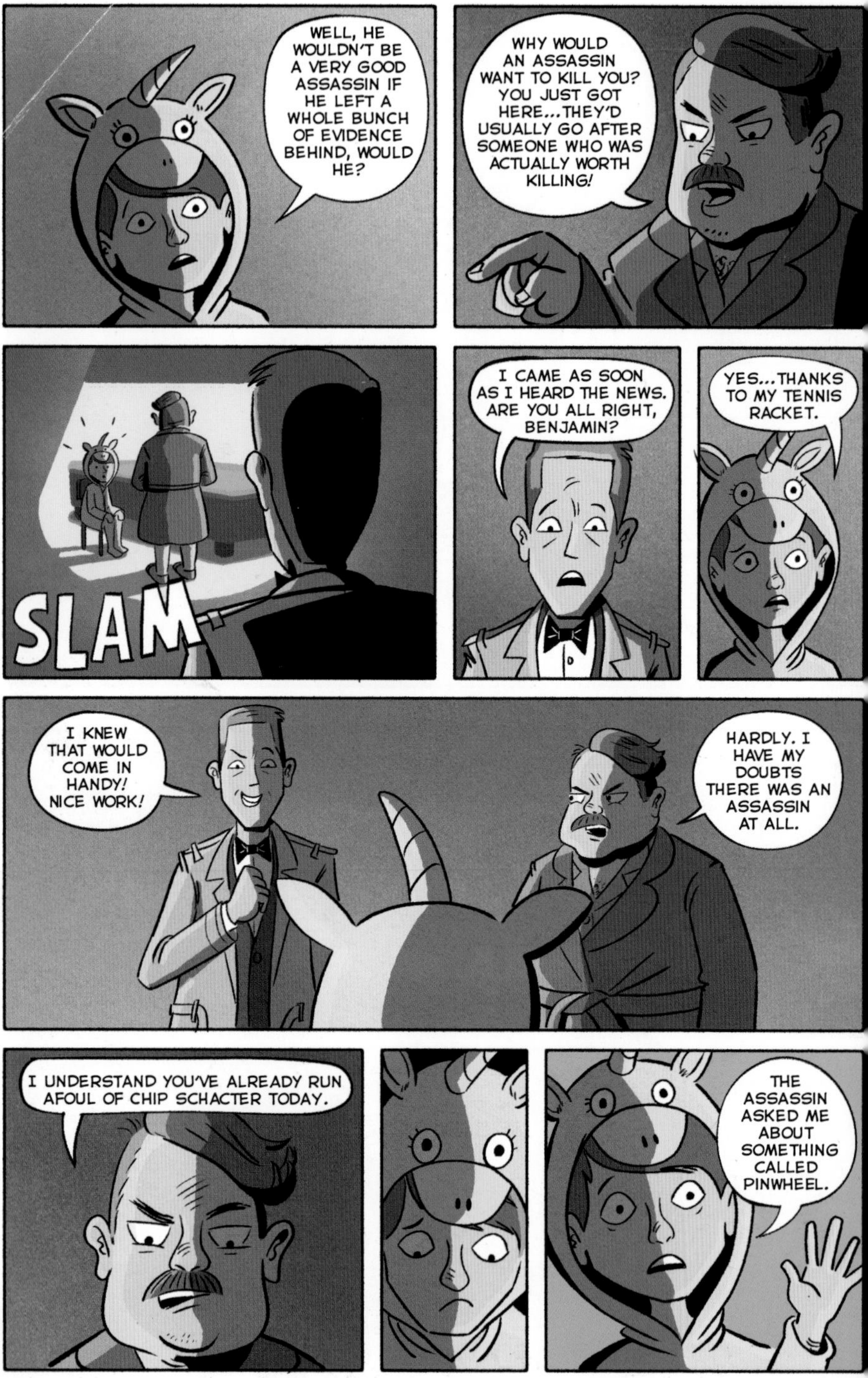
WELL, HE WOULDN'T BE A VERY GOOD ASSASSIN IF HE LEFT A WHOLE BUNCH OF EVIDENCE BEHIND, WOULD HE?
WHY WOULD AN ASSASSIN WANT TO KILL YOU? YOU JUST GOT HERE...THEY'D USUALLY GO AFTER SOMEONE WHO WAS ACTUALLY WORTH KILLING!
SLAM
I CAME AS SOON AS I HEARD THE NEWS. ARE YOU ALL RIGHT, BENJAMIN?
YES...THANKS TO MY TENNIS RACKET.
I KNEW THAT WOULD COME IN HANDY! NICE WORK!
HARDLY. I HAVE MY DOUBTS THERE WAS AN ASSASSIN AT ALL.
I UNDERSTAND YOU'VE ALREADY RUN AFOUL OF CHIP SCHACTER TODAY.
THE ASSASSIN ASKED ME ABOUT SOMETHING CALLED PINWHEEL.

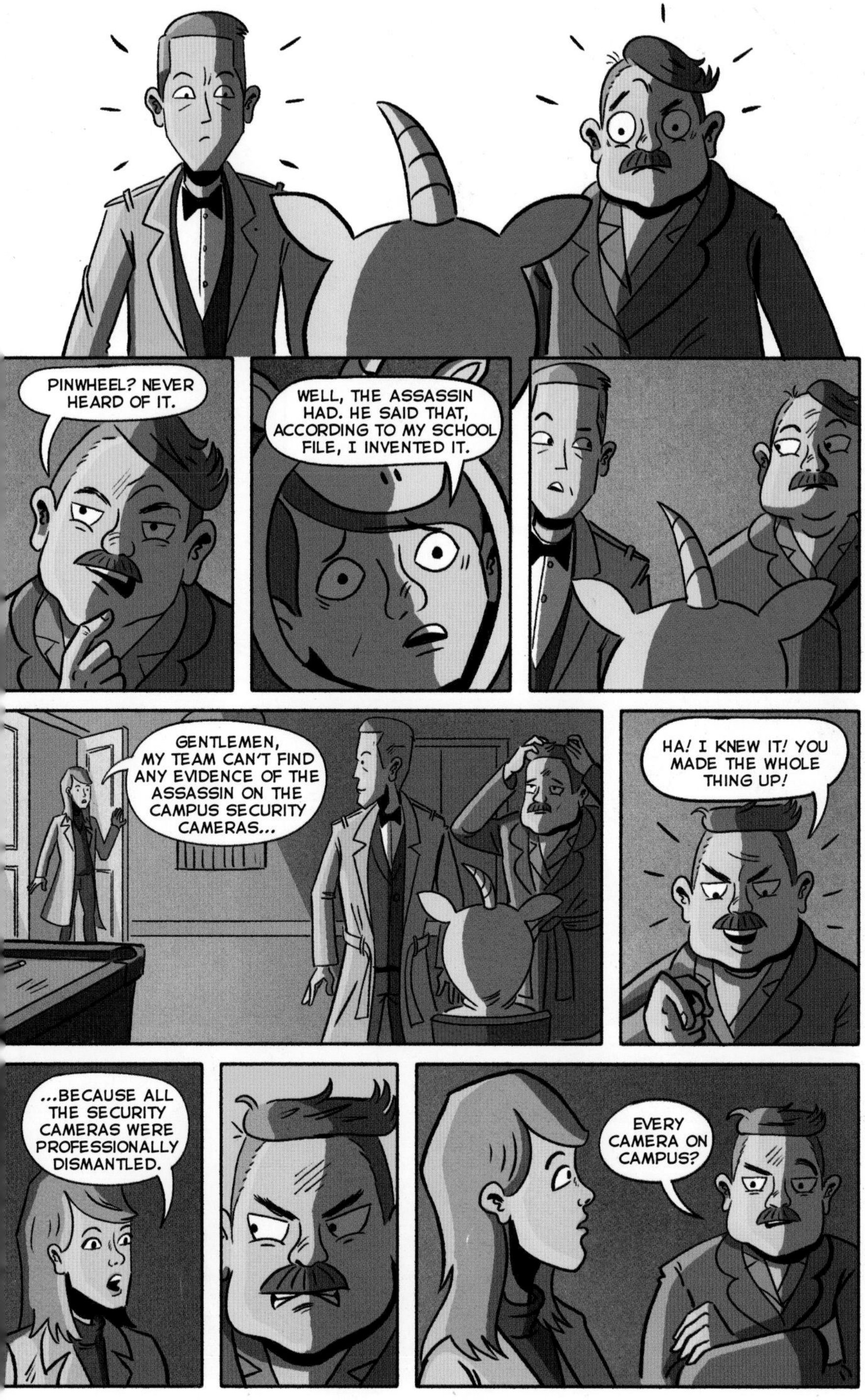
PINWHEEL? NEVER HEARD OF IT.
WELL, THE ASSASSIN HAD. HE SAID THAT, ACCORDING TO MY SCHOOL FILE, I INVENTED IT.
GENTLEMEN, MY TEAM CAN'T FIND ANY EVIDENCE OF THE ASSASSIN ON THE CAMPUS SECURITY CAMERAS...
HA! I KNEW IT! YOU MADE THE WHOLE THING UP!
...BECAUSE ALL THE SECURITY CAMERAS WERE PROFESSIONALLY DISMANTLED.
EVERY CAMERA ON CAMPUS?

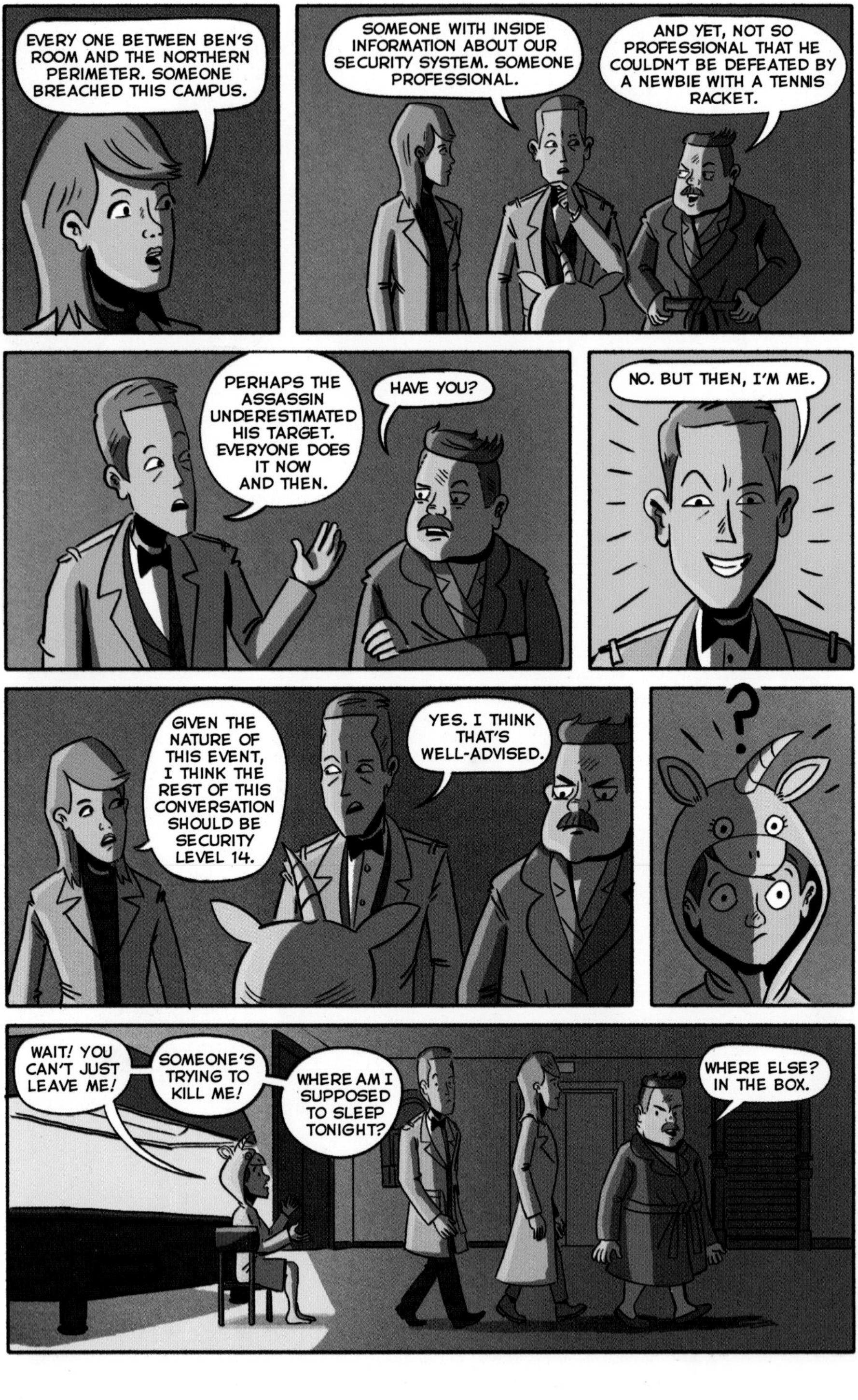
EVERY ONE BETWEEN BEN'S ROOM AND THE NORTHERN PERIMETER. SOMEONE BREACHED THIS CAMPUS.
SOMEONE WITH INSIDE INFORMATION ABOUT OUR SECURITY SYSTEM. SOMEONE PROFESSIONAL.
AND YET, NOT SO PROFESSIONAL THAT HE COULDN'T BE DEFEATED BY A NEWBIE WITH A TENNIS RACKET.
PERHAPS THE ASSASSIN UNDERESTIMATED HIS TARGET. EVERYONE DOES IT NOW AND THEN.
HAVE YOU?
NO. BUT THEN, I'M ME.
GIVEN THE NATURE OF THIS EVENT, I THINK THE REST OF THIS CONVERSATION SHOULD BE SECURITY LEVEL 14.
YES. I THINK THAT'S WELL-ADVISED.
?
WAIT! YOU CAN'T JUST LEAVE ME!
SOMEONE'S TRYING TO KILL ME!
WHERE AM I SUPPOSED TO SLEEP TONIGHT?
WHERE ELSE? IN THE BOX.

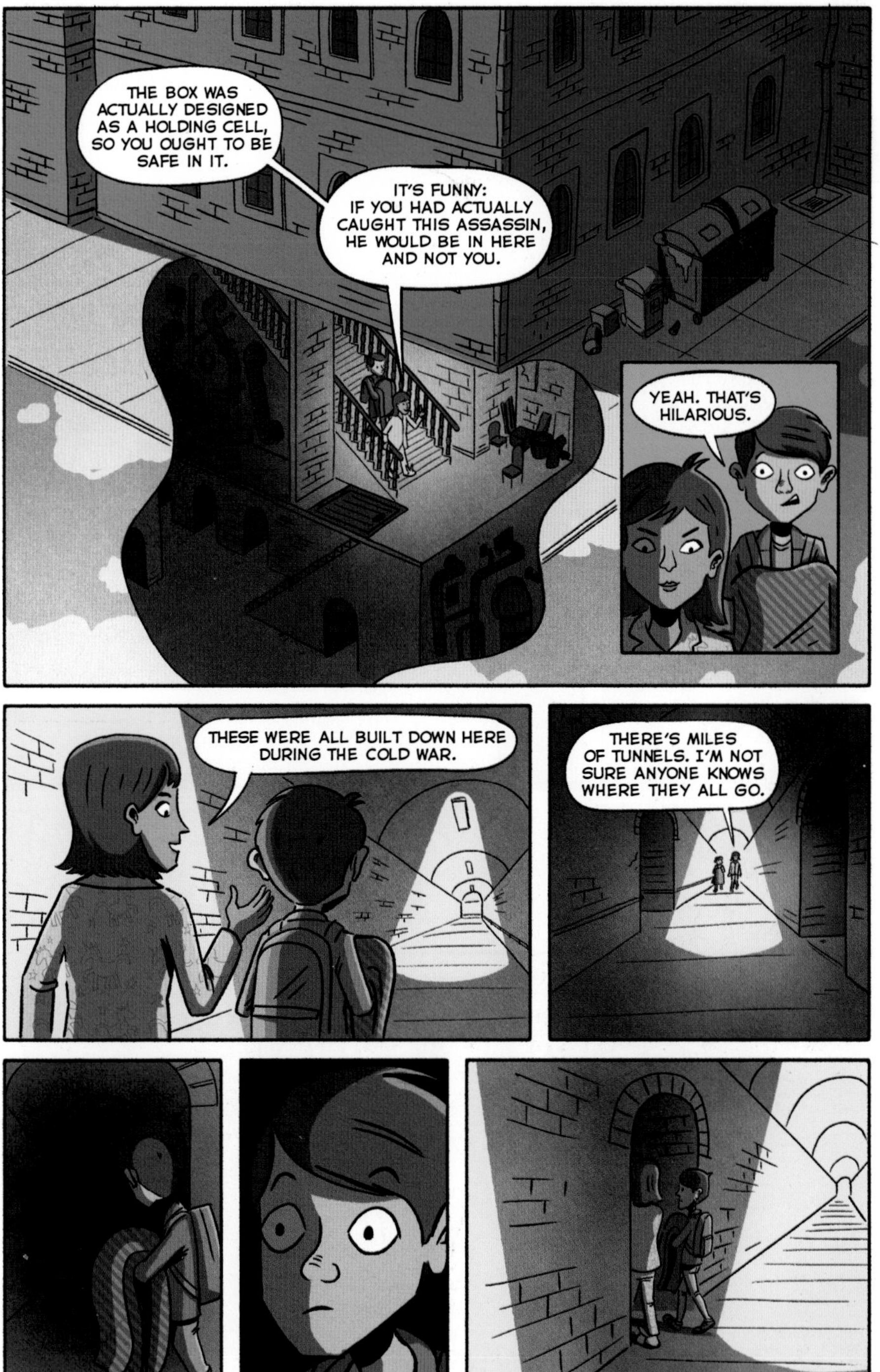
THE BOX WAS ACTUALLY DESIGNED AS A HOLDING CELL, SO YOU OUGHT TO BE SAFE IN IT.
IT'S FUNNY: IF YOU HAD ACTUALLY CAUGHT THIS ASSASSIN, HE WOULD BE IN HERE AND NOT YOU.
YEAH. THAT'S HILARIOUS.
THESE WERE ALL BUILT DOWN HERE DURING THE COLD WAR.
THERE'S MILES OF TUNNELS. I'M NOT SURE ANYONE KNOWS WHERE THEY ALL GO.

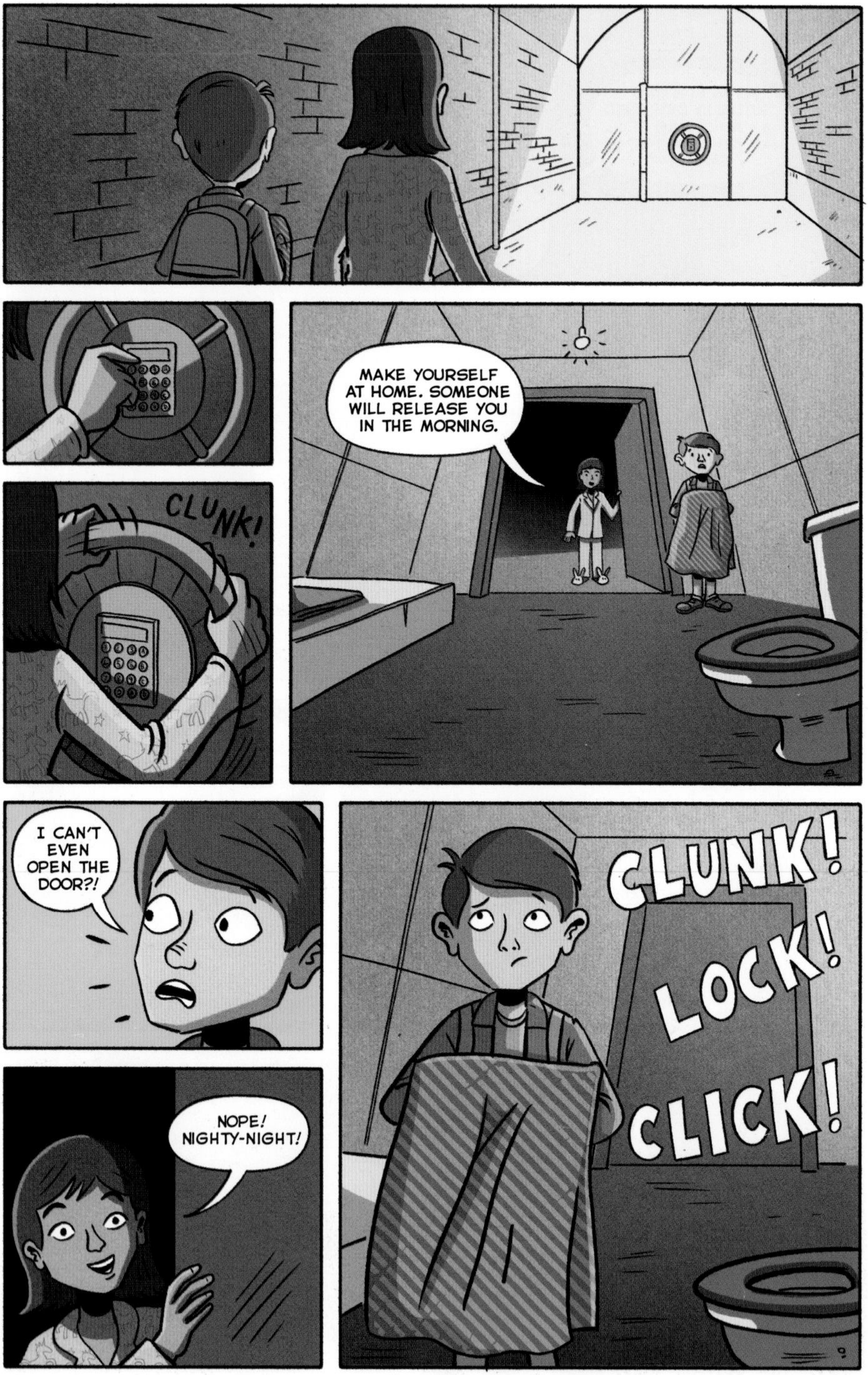
CLUNK!
MAKE YOURSELF AT HOME. SOMEONE WILL RELEASE YOU IN THE MORNING.
I CAN'T EVEN OPEN THE DOOR?!
NOPE! NIGHTY-NIGHT!
CLUNK!
LOCK!
CLICK!

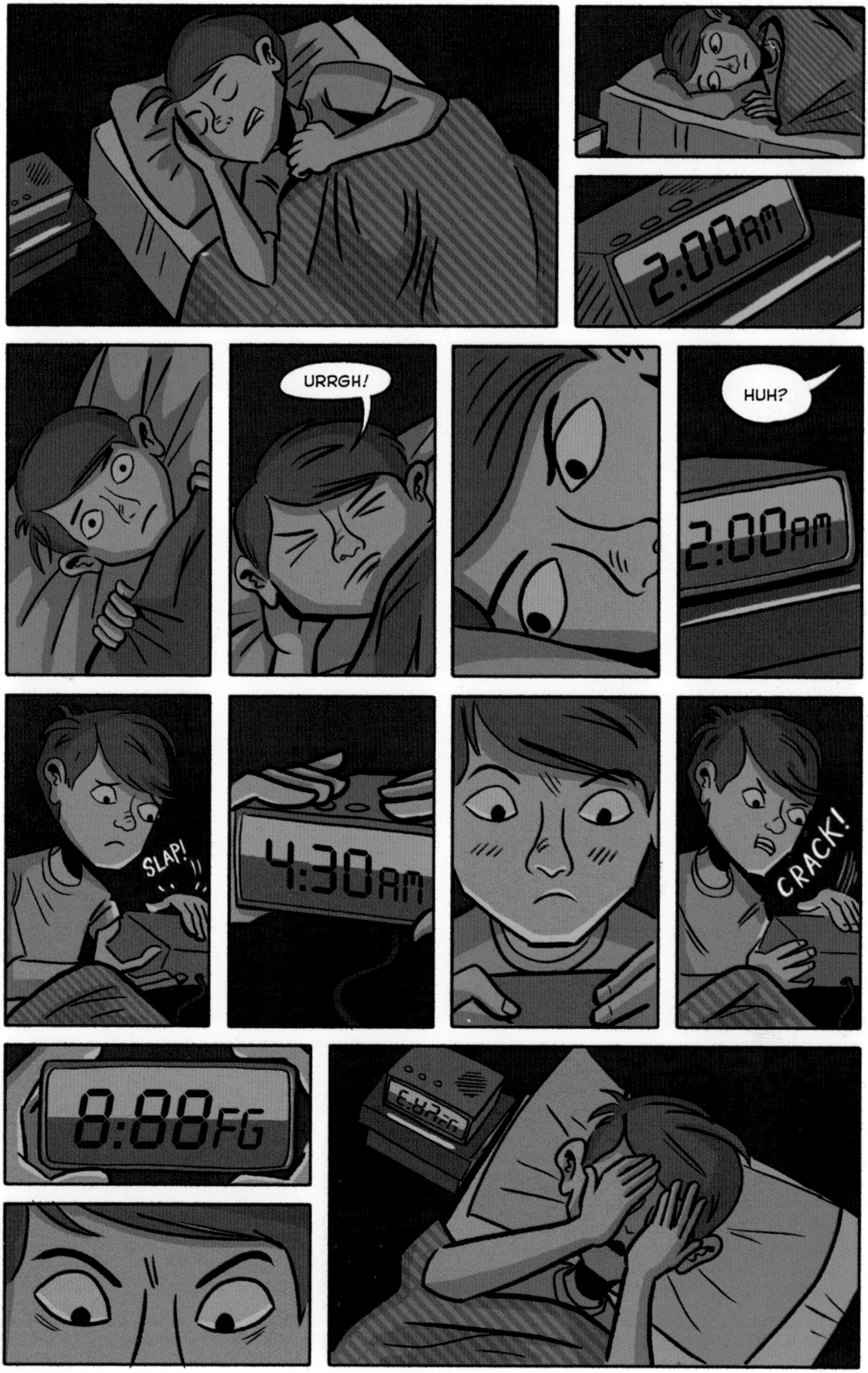
2:00AM
URRGH!
HUH?
2:00AM
SLAP!
4:30AM
CRACK!
8:88FG

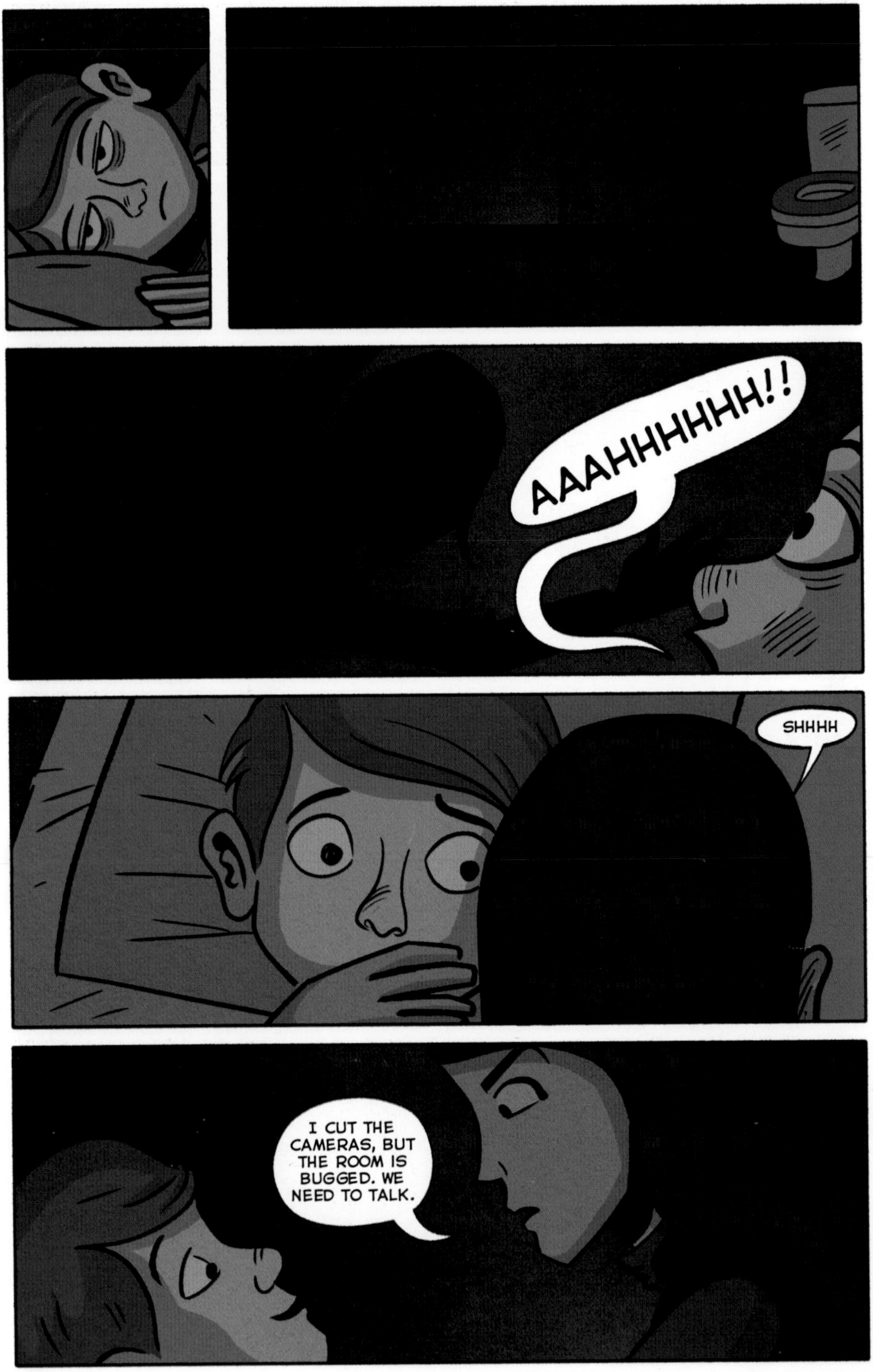
AAAHHHHHH!!
SHHHH
I CUT THE CAMERAS, BUT THE ROOM IS BUGGED. WE NEED TO TALK.

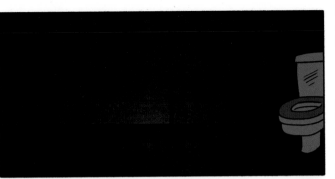

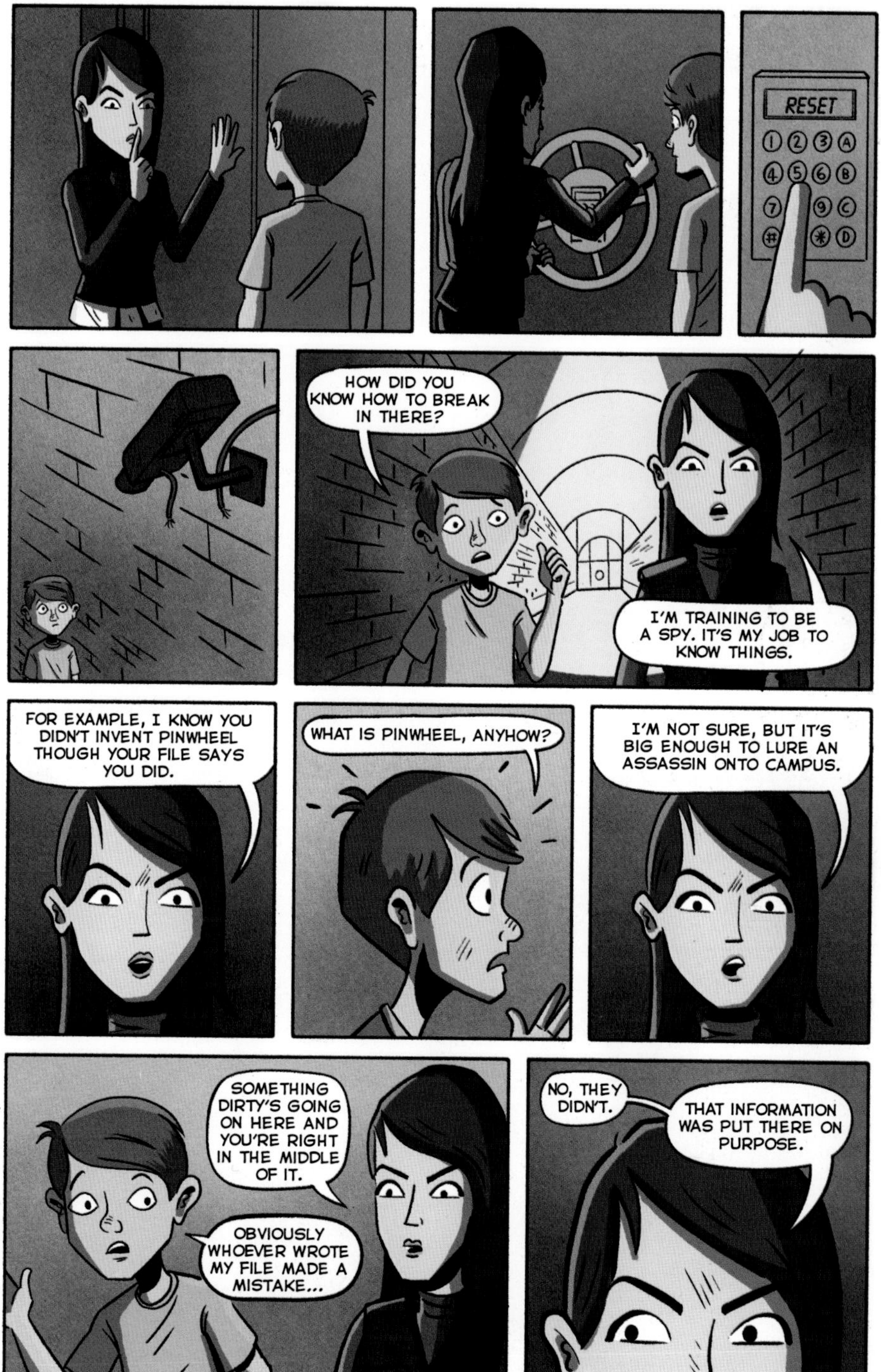
RESET
HOW DID YOU KNOW HOW TO BREAK IN THERE?
I'M TRAINING TO BE A SPY. IT'S MY JOB TO KNOW THINGS.
FOR EXAMPLE, I KNOW YOU DIDN'T INVENT PINWHEEL THOUGH YOUR FILE SAYS YOU DID.
WHAT IS PINWHEEL, ANYHOW?
I'M NOT SURE, BUT IT'S BIG ENOUGH TO LURE AN ASSASSIN ONTO CAMPUS.
SOMETHING DIRTY'S GOING ON HERE AND YOU'RE RIGHT IN THE MIDDLE OF IT.
OBVIOUSLY WHOEVER WROTE MY FILE MADE A MISTAKE...
NO, THEY DIDN'T.
THAT INFORMATION WAS PUT THERE ON PURPOSE.

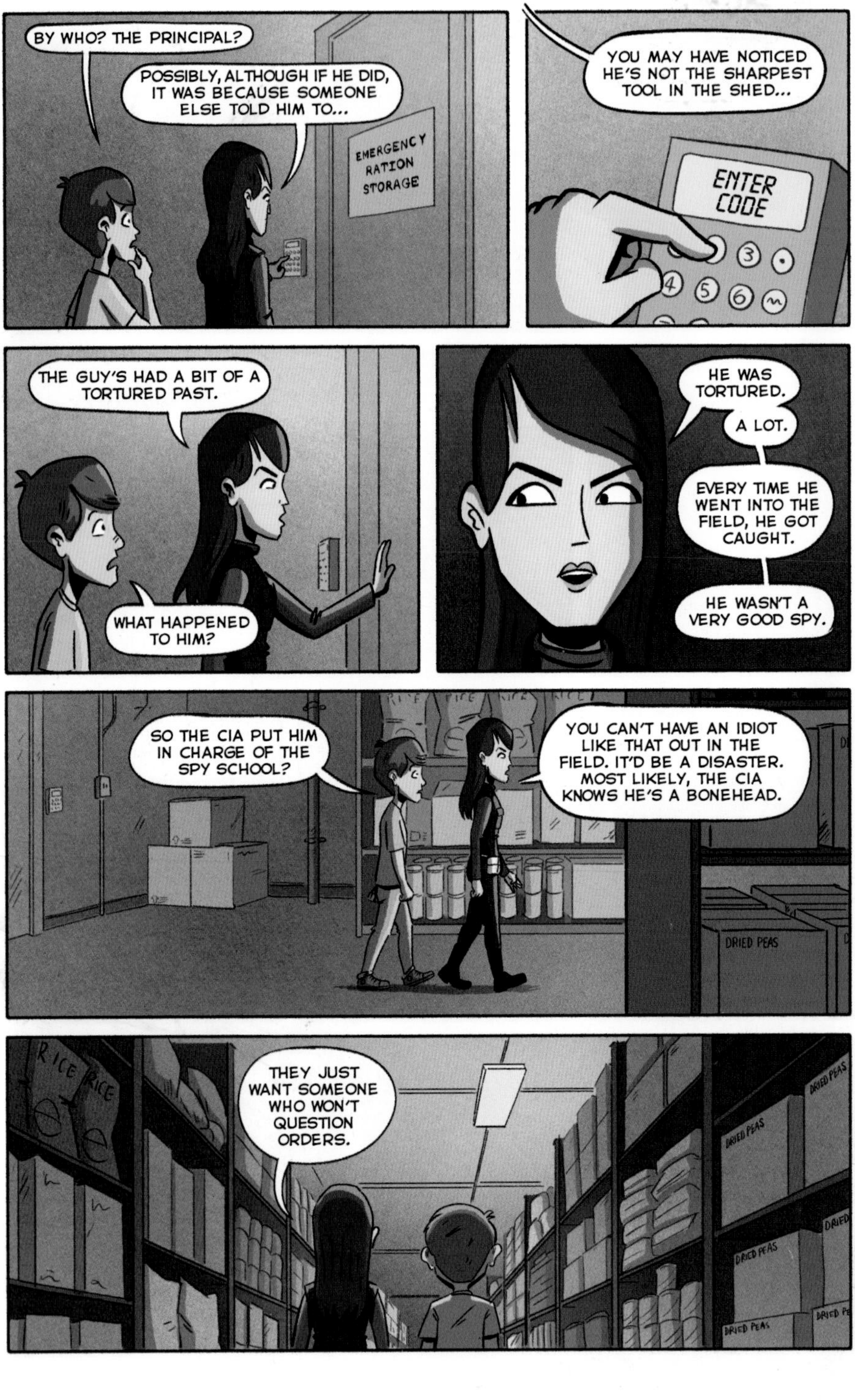
BY WHO? THE PRINCIPAL?
POSSIBLY, ALTHOUGH IF HE DID, IT WAS BECAUSE SOMEONE ELSE TOLD HIM TO...
EMERGENCY RATION STORAGE
YOU MAY HAVE NOTICED HE'S NOT THE SHARPEST TOOL IN THE SHED...
ENTER CODE
THE GUY'S HAD A BIT OF A TORTURED PAST.
WHAT HAPPENED TO HIM?
HE WAS TORTURED.
A LOT.
EVERY TIME HE WENT INTO THE FIELD, HE GOT CAUGHT.
HE WASN'T A VERY GOOD SPY.
SO THE CIA PUT HIM IN CHARGE OF THE SPY SCHOOL?
YOU CAN'T HAVE AN IDIOT LIKE THAT OUT IN THE FIELD. IT'D BE A DISASTER. MOST LIKELY, THE CIA KNOWS HE'S A BONEHEAD.
DRIED PEAS
THEY JUST WANT SOMEONE WHO WON'T QUESTION ORDERS.
RICE
RICE
DRIED PEAS
DRIED PEAS
DRIED PEAS

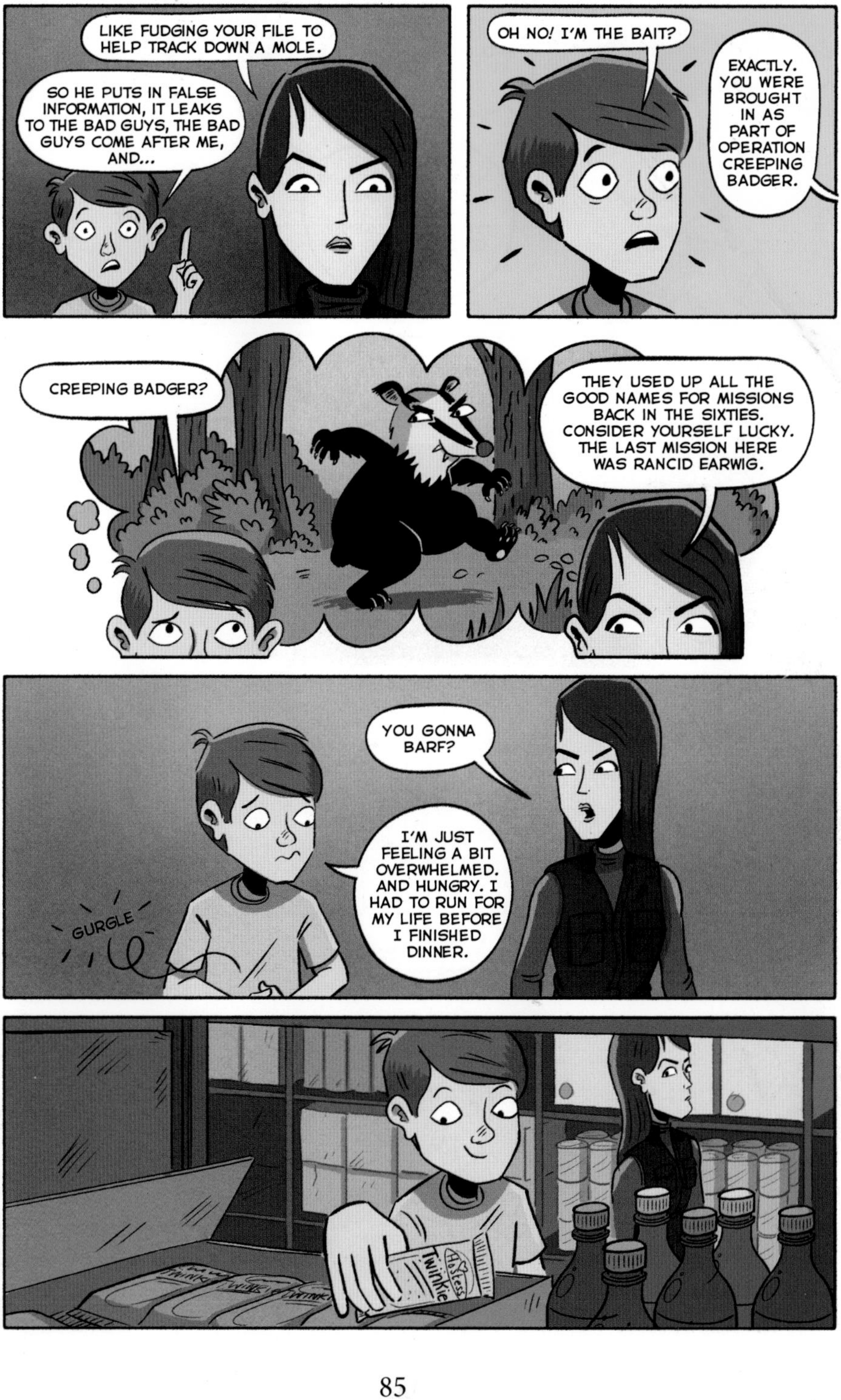
LIKE FUDGING YOUR FILE TO HELP TRACK DOWN A MOLE.
SO HE PUTS IN FALSE INFORMATION, IT LEAKS TO THE BAD GUYS, THE BAD GUYS COME AFTER ME, AND...
OH NO! I'M THE BAIT?
EXACTLY. YOU WERE BROUGHT IN AS PART OF OPERATION CREEPING BADGER.
CREEPING BADGER?
THEY USED UP ALL THE GOOD NAMES FOR MISSIONS BACK IN THE SIXTIES. CONSIDER YOURSELF LUCKY. THE LAST MISSION HERE WAS RANCID EARWIG.
YOU GONNA BARF?
I'M JUST FEELING A BIT OVERWHELMED. AND HUNGRY. I HAD TO RUN FOR MY LIFE BEFORE I FINISHED DINNER.
GURGLE
Hostess
Twinkie

IF I WAS ONLY BROUGHT IN AS BAIT... AM I EVEN QUALIFIED TO GO TO THIS SCHOOL?

NO. I THINK THEY PICKED YOU BECAUSE YOU LOOK GOOD ON PAPER. AND YOU LIVE CLOSE BY, SO THEY DIDN'T HAVE TO SPRING FOR AIRFARE.

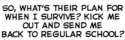

SO, WHAT'S THEIR PLAN FOR WHEN I SURVIVE? KICK ME OUT AND SEND ME BACK TO REGULAR SCHOOL?

OH, THEY CAN'T DO THAT. YOU KNOW THE ACADEMY EXISTS. FRANKLY, I DON'T THINK ANYONE EXPECTED YOU TO SURVIVE THIS LONG.

EVEN YOUR FATHER? HE RECRUITED ME.

HE MUST HAVE BEEN GIVEN SOME INTELLIGENCE ON THIS.

MUNCH! MUNCH!

MY FATHER DOESN'T HAVE AS MUCH INTELLIGENCE AS YOU'D THINK.

DOES THAT TASTE FUNNY TO YOU?

SHOULD IT?

POSSIBLY. IT'S BEEN DOWN HERE FOR SIXTY YEARS.

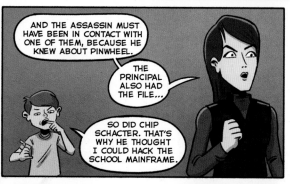

BLEURGH!

MY FATHER **WAS** ONE OF THE FEW PEOPLE WITH ACCESS TO YOUR FILE, THOUGH.

AND THE ASSASSIN MUST HAVE BEEN IN CONTACT WITH ONE OF THEM, BECAUSE HE KNEW ABOUT PINWHEEL.

THE PRINCIPAL ALSO HAD THE FILE...

SO DID CHIP SCHACTER. THAT'S WHY HE THOUGHT I COULD HACK THE SCHOOL MAINFRAME.

THAT IDIOT. IT'S ALMOST IMPOSSIBLE TO HACK THE SCHOOL MAINFRAME.

WE NEED TO GET A LIST OF EVERYONE WHO WAS GIVEN A COPY OF YOUR FILE.

HOW?

WE'LL HAVE TO HACK THE SCHOOL MAINFRAME.

YOU JUST SAID THAT WAS IMPOSSIBLE!

NO, I SAID ALMOST IMPOSSIBLE. THERE'S A DIFFERENCE.

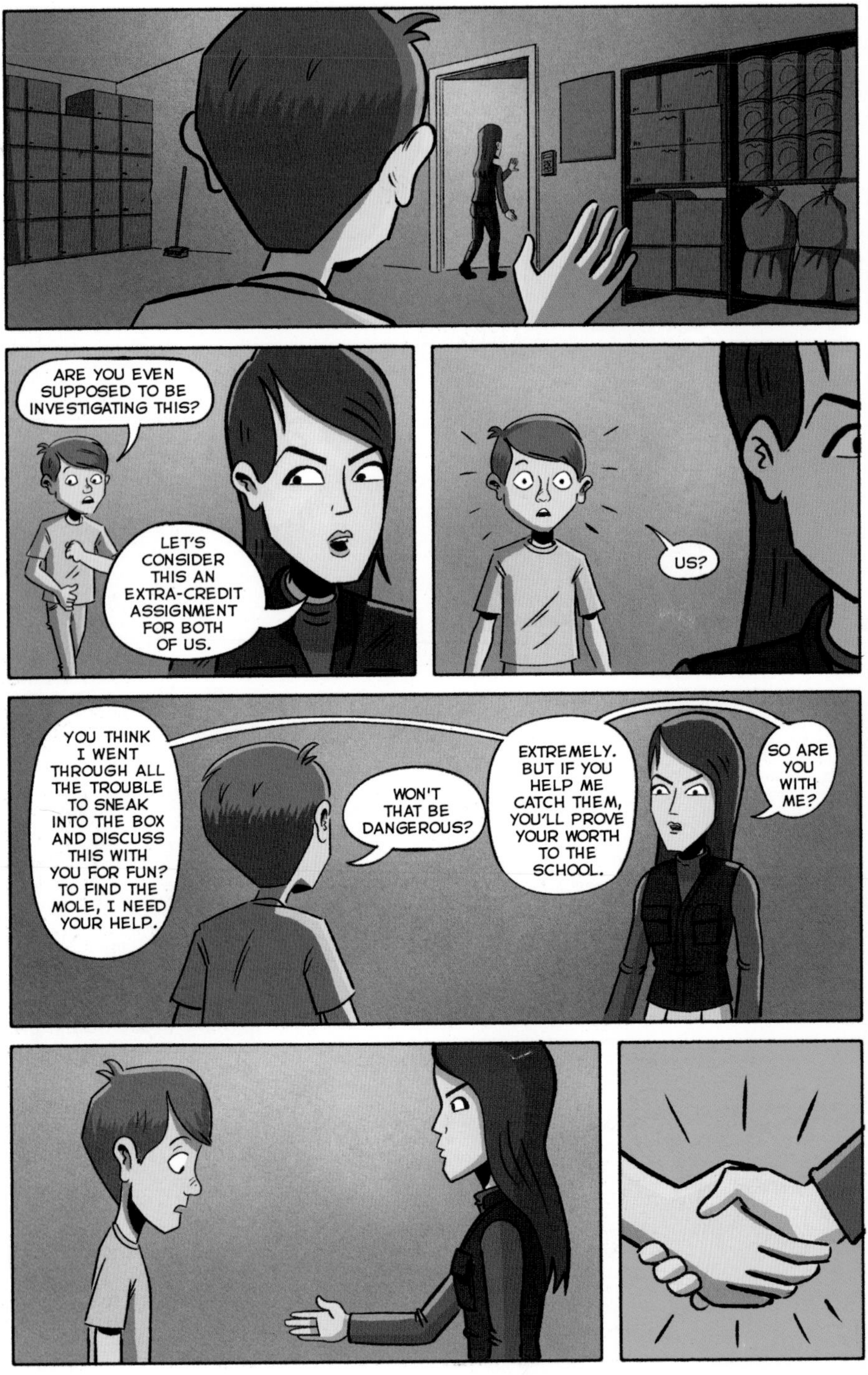
ARE YOU EVEN SUPPOSED TO BE INVESTIGATING THIS?
LET'S CONSIDER THIS AN EXTRA-CREDIT ASSIGNMENT FOR BOTH OF US.
US?
YOU THINK I WENT THROUGH ALL THE TROUBLE TO SNEAK INTO THE BOX AND DISCUSS THIS WITH YOU FOR FUN? TO FIND THE MOLE, I NEED YOUR HELP.
WON'T THAT BE DANGEROUS?
EXTREMELY. BUT IF YOU HELP ME CATCH THEM, YOU'LL PROVE YOUR WORTH TO THE SCHOOL.
SO ARE YOU WITH ME?

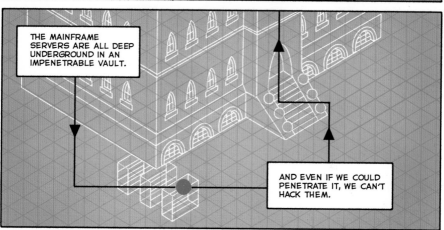

THE MAINFRAME SERVERS ARE ALL DEEP UNDERGROUND IN AN IMPENETRABLE VAULT.

AND EVEN IF WE COULD PENETRATE IT, WE CAN'T HACK THEM.

SO WE TARGET THE WEAKEST LINK IN ANY COMPUTER'S SYSTEM...

THE HUMAN ONE.

THE PRINCIPAL KNOWS HOW TO ACCESS THE SERVER.

SO WE USE HIM.

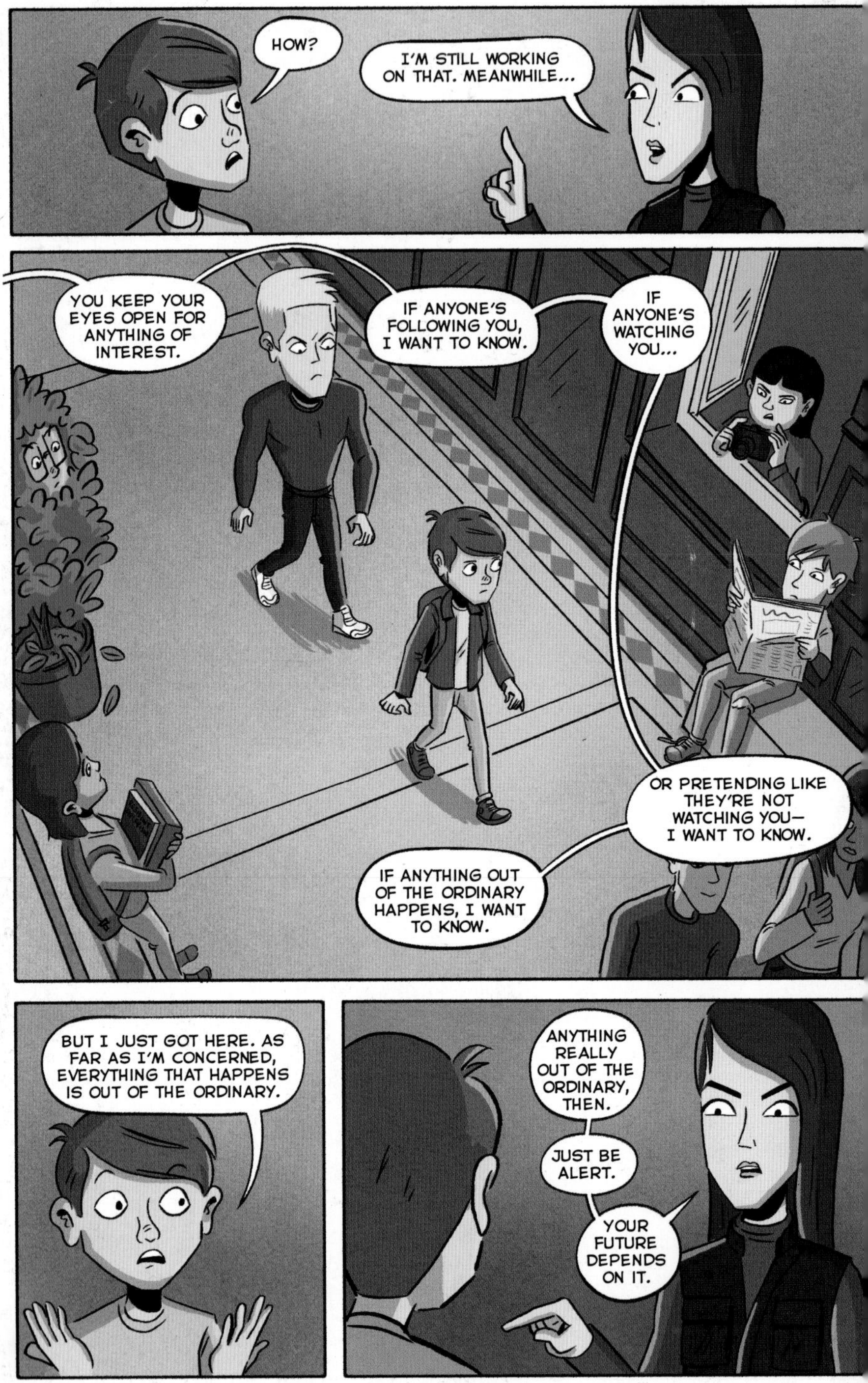
HOW?
I'M STILL WORKING ON THAT. MEANWHILE...
YOU KEEP YOUR EYES OPEN FOR ANYTHING OF INTEREST.
IF ANYONE'S FOLLOWING YOU, I WANT TO KNOW.
IF ANYONE'S WATCHING YOU...
OR PRETENDING LIKE THEY'RE NOT WATCHING YOU— I WANT TO KNOW.
IF ANYTHING OUT OF THE ORDINARY HAPPENS, I WANT TO KNOW.
BUT I JUST GOT HERE. AS FAR AS I'M CONCERNED, EVERYTHING THAT HAPPENS IS OUT OF THE ORDINARY.
ANYTHING REALLY OUT OF THE ORDINARY, THEN.
JUST BE ALERT.
YOUR FUTURE DEPENDS ON IT.

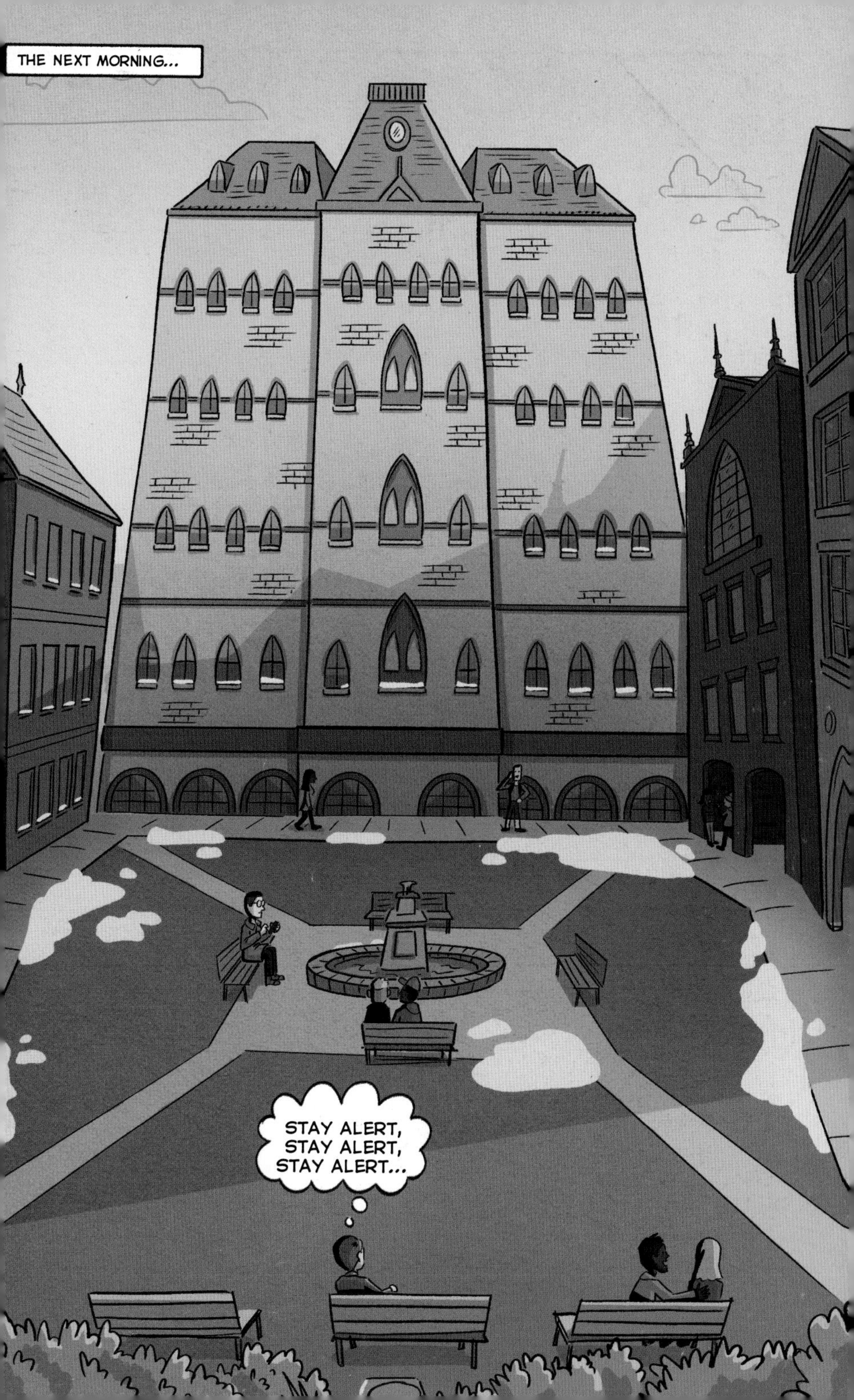
THE NEXT MORNING...
STAY ALERT, STAY ALERT, STAY ALERT...

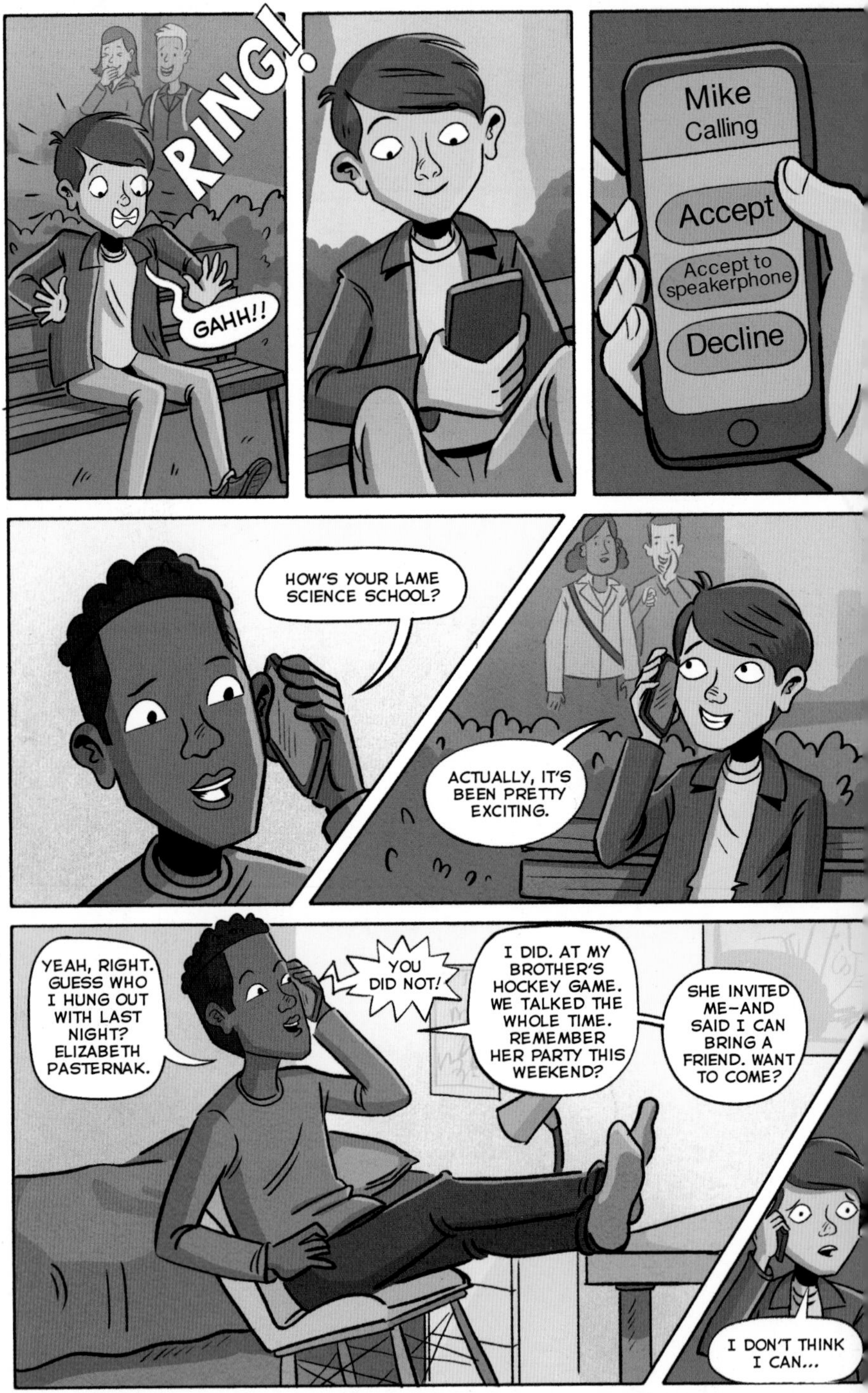
RING!
GAHH!!
Mike
Calling
Accept
Accept to speakerphone
Decline
HOW'S YOUR LAME SCIENCE SCHOOL?
ACTUALLY, IT'S BEEN PRETTY EXCITING.
YEAH, RIGHT. GUESS WHO I HUNG OUT WITH LAST NIGHT? ELIZABETH PASTERNAK.
YOU DID NOT!
I DID. AT MY BROTHER'S HOCKEY GAME. WE TALKED THE WHOLE TIME. REMEMBER HER PARTY THIS WEEKEND?
SHE INVITED ME—AND SAID I CAN BRING A FRIEND. WANT TO COME?
I DON'T THINK I CAN...

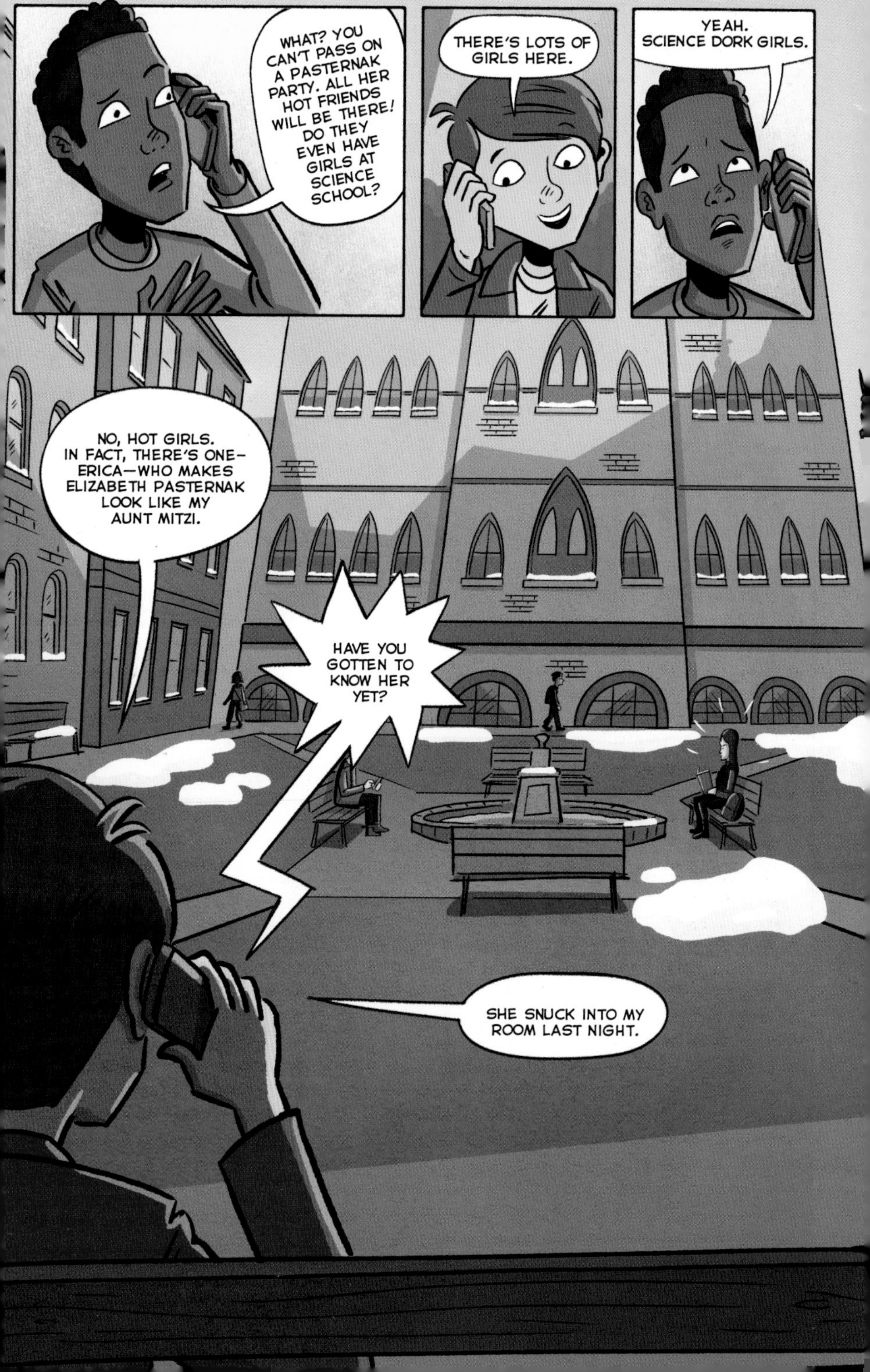
WHAT? YOU CAN'T PASS ON A PASTERNAK PARTY. ALL HER HOT FRIENDS WILL BE THERE! DO THEY EVEN HAVE GIRLS AT SCIENCE SCHOOL?
THERE'S LOTS OF GIRLS HERE.
YEAH. SCIENCE DORK GIRLS.
NO, HOT GIRLS. IN FACT, THERE'S ONE–ERICA—WHO MAKES ELIZABETH PASTERNAK LOOK LIKE MY AUNT MITZI.
HAVE YOU GOTTEN TO KNOW HER YET?
SHE SNUCK INTO MY ROOM LAST NIGHT.

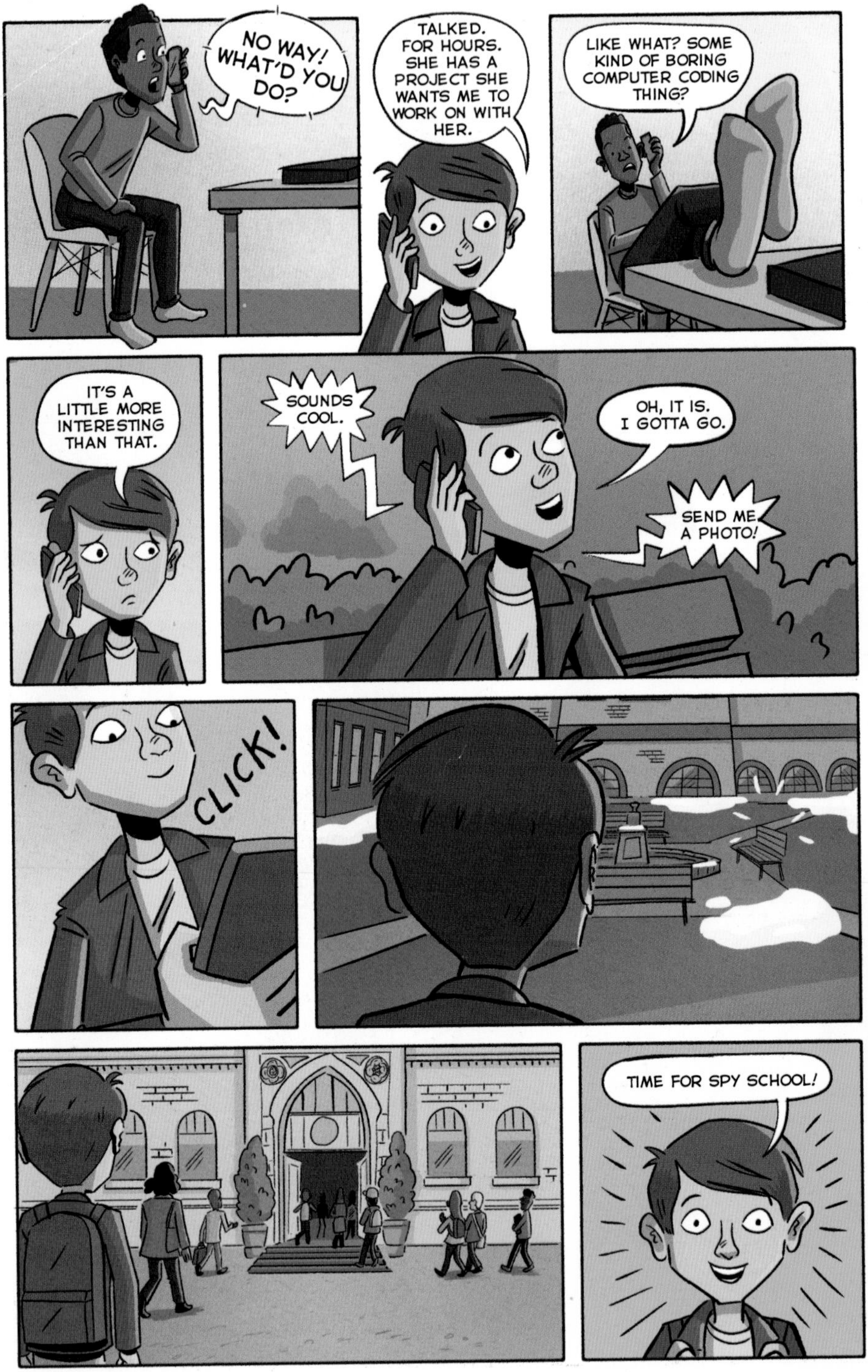
NO WAY! WHAT'D YOU DO?
TALKED. FOR HOURS. SHE HAS A PROJECT SHE WANTS ME TO WORK ON WITH HER.
LIKE WHAT? SOME KIND OF BORING COMPUTER CODING THING?
IT'S A LITTLE MORE INTERESTING THAN THAT.
SOUNDS COOL.
OH, IT IS. I GOTTA GO.
SEND ME A PHOTO!
CLICK!
TIME FOR SPY SCHOOL!

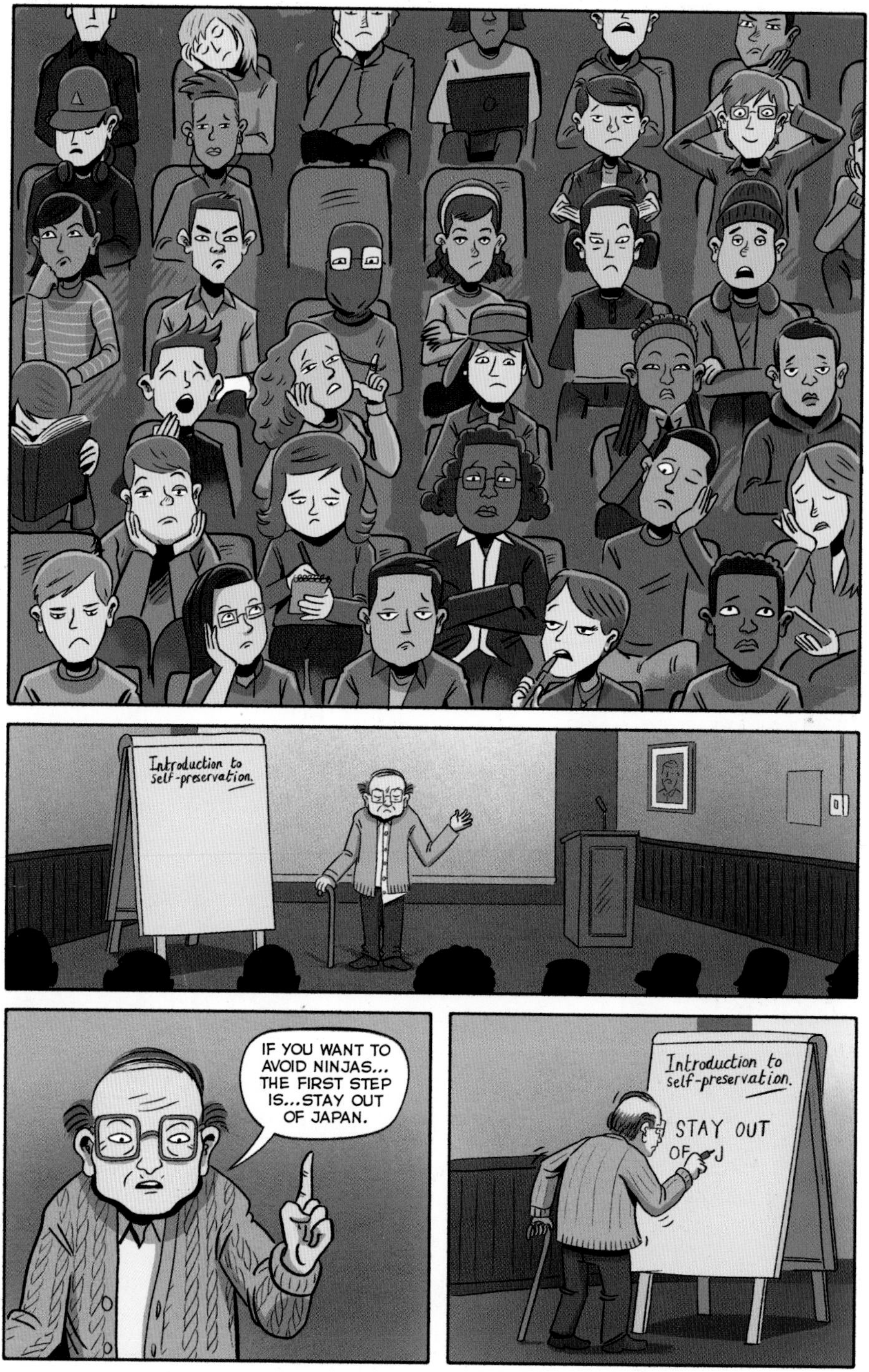
Introduction to self-preservation.
IF YOU WANT TO AVOID NINJAS... THE FIRST STEP IS...STAY OUT OF JAPAN.
Introduction to self-preservation.
STAY OUT OF J

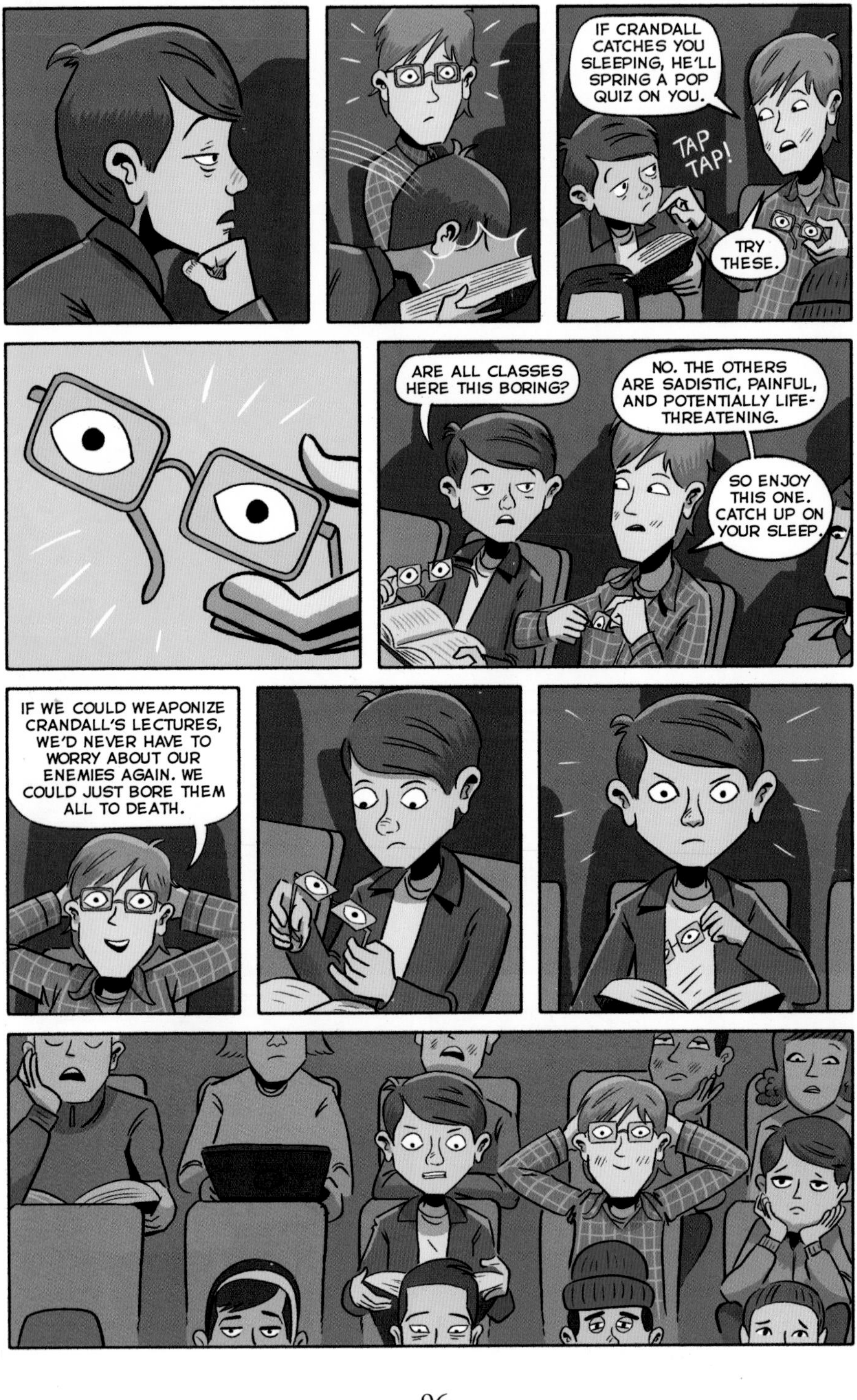
IF CRANDALL CATCHES YOU SLEEPING, HE'LL SPRING A POP QUIZ ON YOU.
TAP TAP!
TRY THESE.
ARE ALL CLASSES HERE THIS BORING?
NO. THE OTHERS ARE SADISTIC, PAINFUL, AND POTENTIALLY LIFE-THREATENING.
SO ENJOY THIS ONE. CATCH UP ON YOUR SLEEP.
IF WE COULD WEAPONIZE CRANDALL'S LECTURES, WE'D NEVER HAVE TO WORRY ABOUT OUR ENEMIES AGAIN. WE COULD JUST BORE THEM ALL TO DEATH.

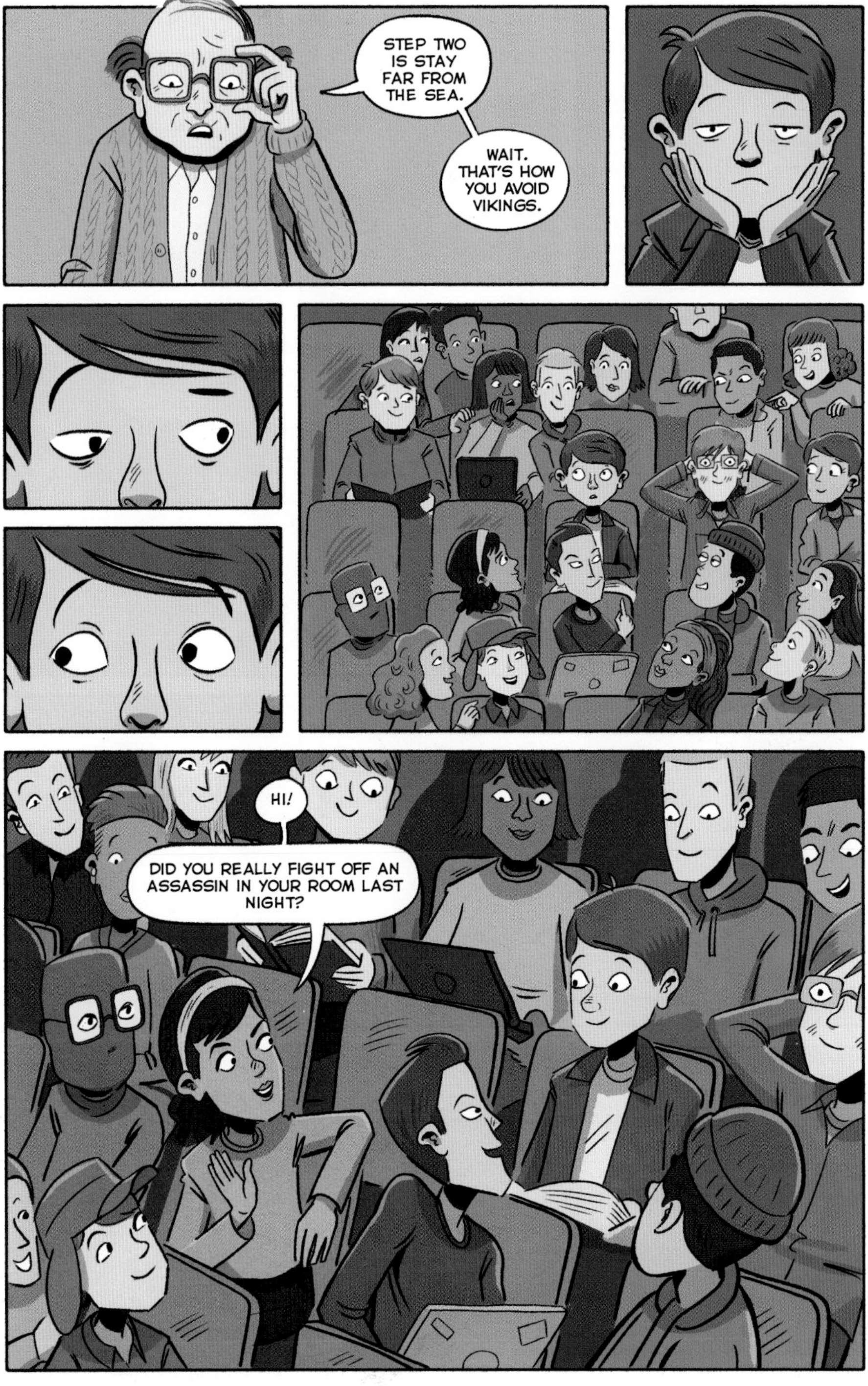
STEP TWO IS STAY FAR FROM THE SEA.
WAIT. THAT'S HOW YOU AVOID VIKINGS.
HI!
DID YOU REALLY FIGHT OFF AN ASSASSIN IN YOUR ROOM LAST NIGHT?

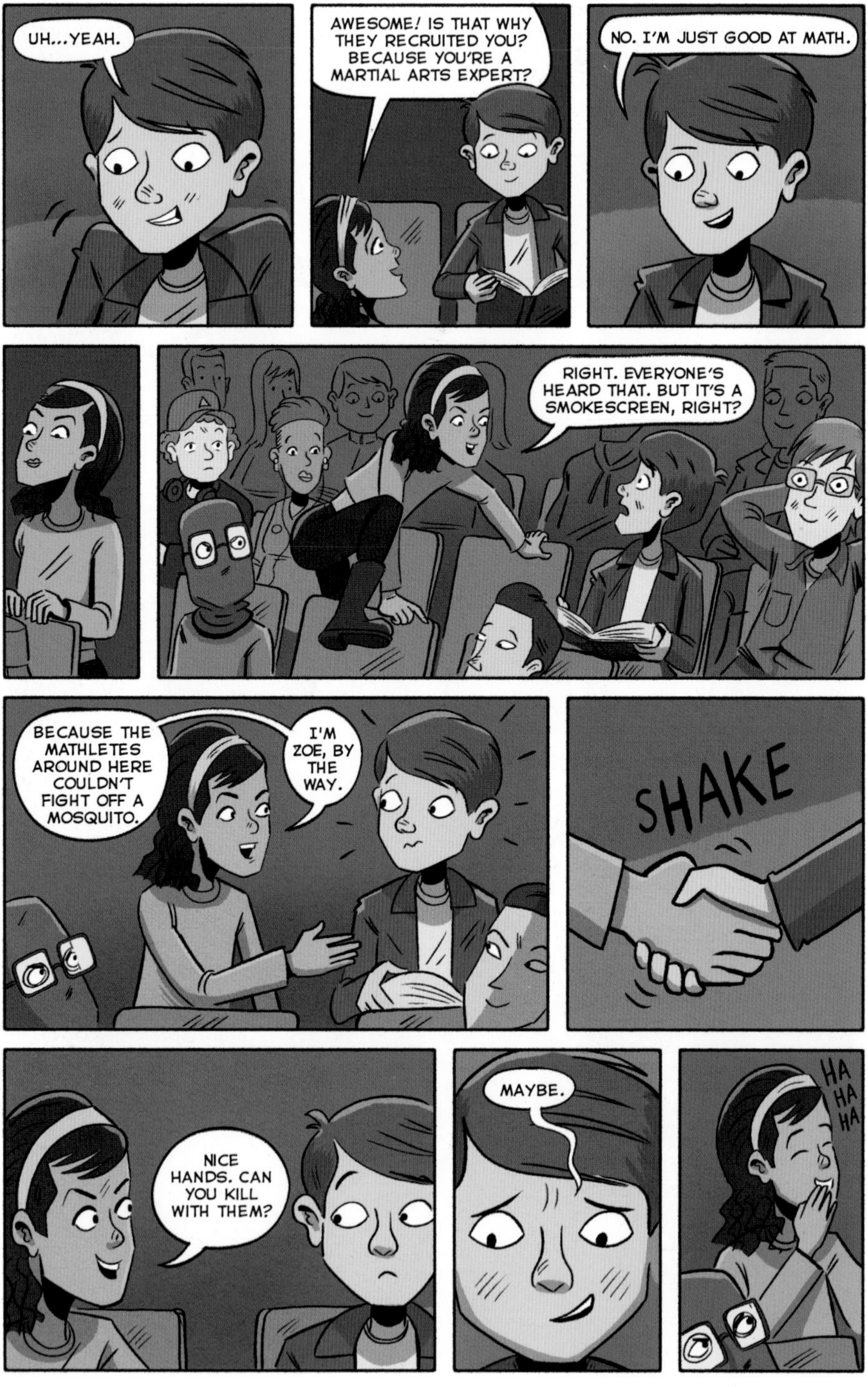
UH...YEAH.
AWESOME! IS THAT WHY THEY RECRUITED YOU? BECAUSE YOU'RE A MARTIAL ARTS EXPERT?
NO. I'M JUST GOOD AT MATH.
RIGHT. EVERYONE'S HEARD THAT. BUT IT'S A SMOKESCREEN, RIGHT?
BECAUSE THE MATHLETES AROUND HERE COULDN'T FIGHT OFF A MOSQUITO.
I'M ZOE, BY THE WAY.
SHAKE
NICE HANDS. CAN YOU KILL WITH THEM?
MAYBE.
HA HA HA

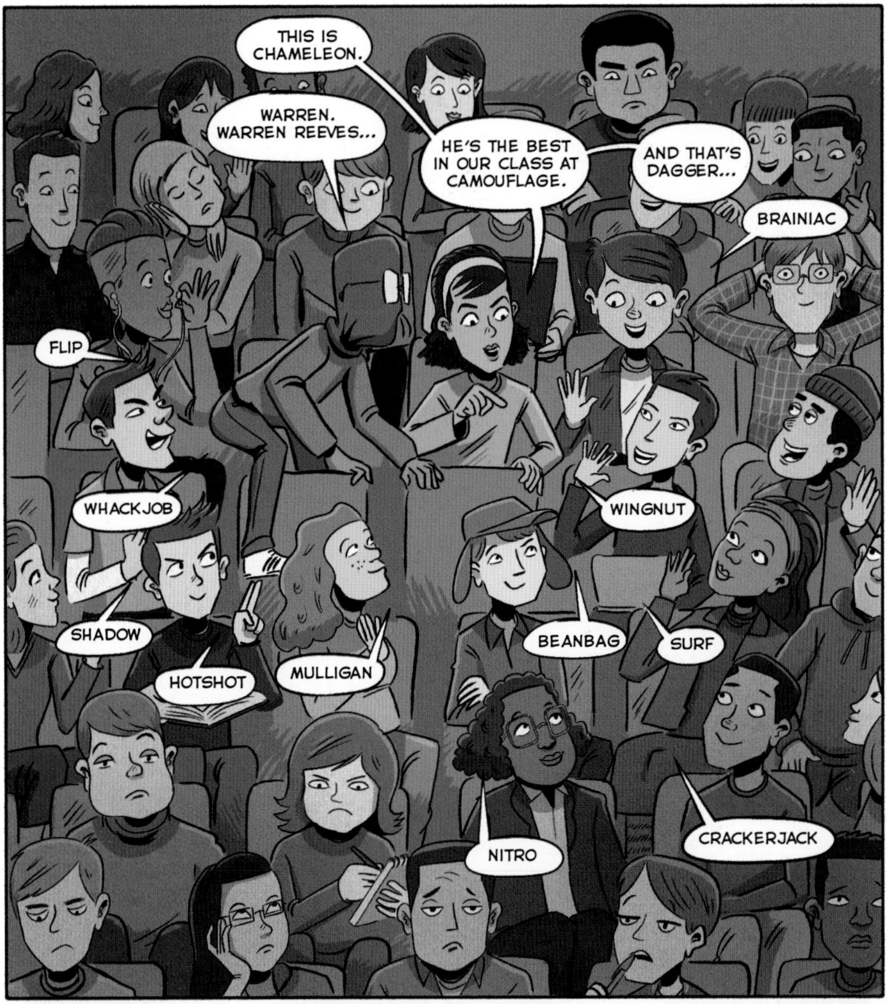
THIS IS CHAMELEON.
WARREN. WARREN REEVES...
HE'S THE BEST IN OUR CLASS AT CAMOUFLAGE.
AND THAT'S DAGGER...
BRAINIAC
FLIP
WHACKJOB
WINGNUT
SHADOW
HOTSHOT
MULLIGAN
BEANBAG
SURF
NITRO
CRACKERJACK

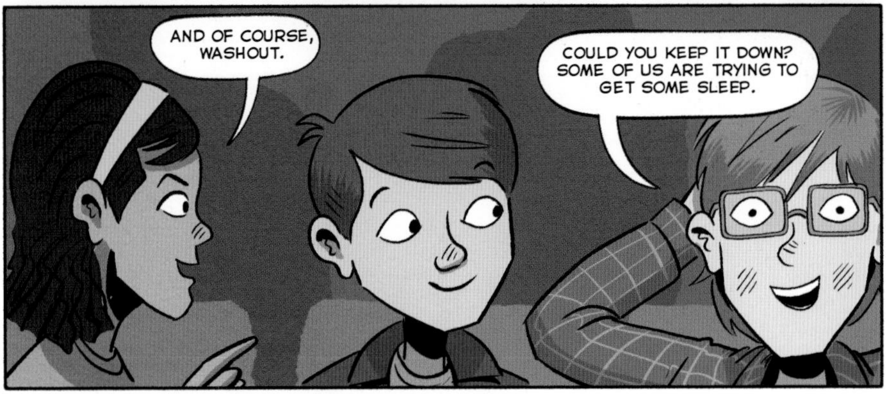
AND OF COURSE, WASHOUT.
COULD YOU KEEP IT DOWN? SOME OF US ARE TRYING TO GET SOME SLEEP.

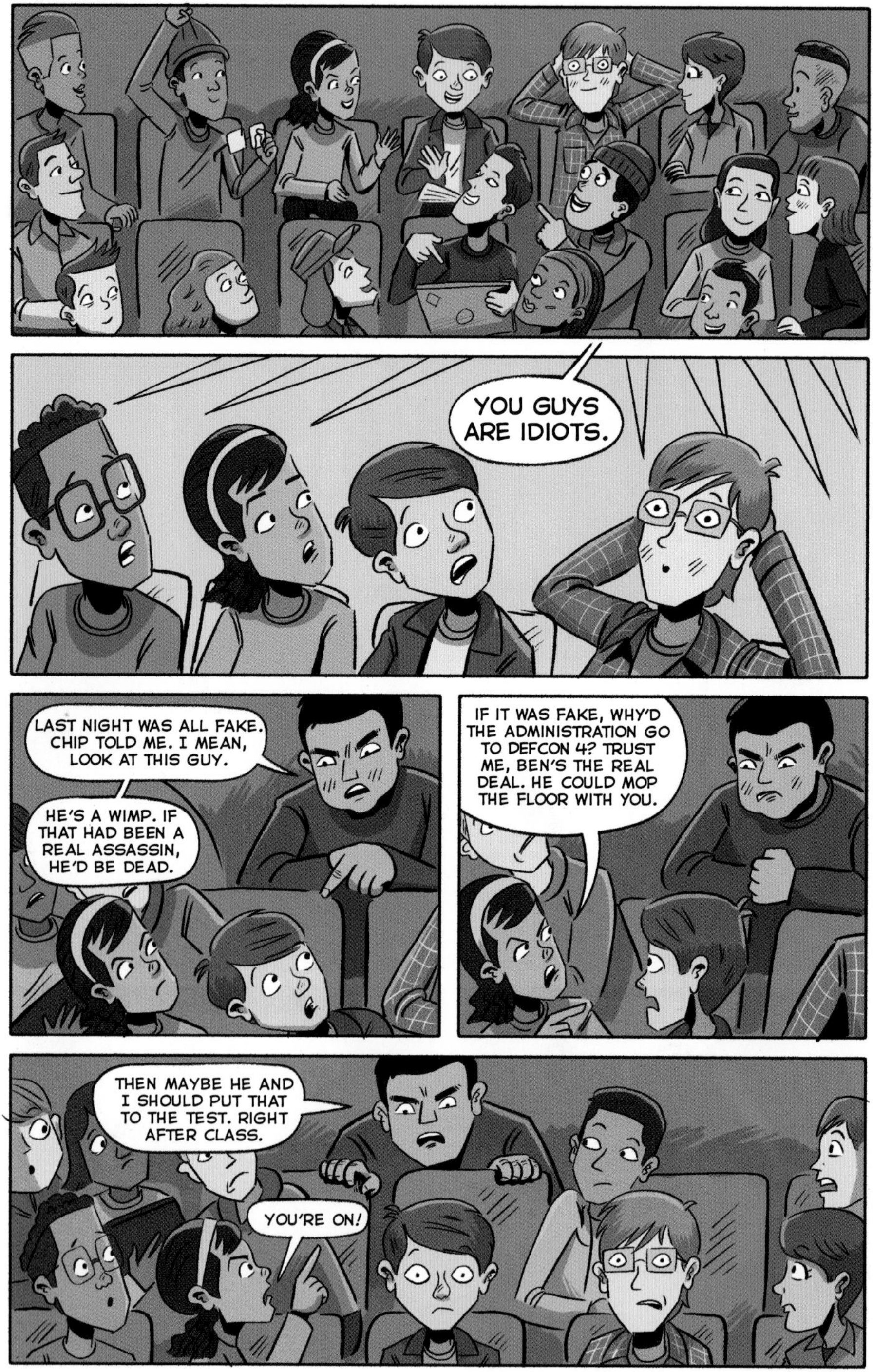
YOU GUYS ARE IDIOTS.
LAST NIGHT WAS ALL FAKE. CHIP TOLD ME. I MEAN, LOOK AT THIS GUY.
HE'S A WIMP. IF THAT HAD BEEN A REAL ASSASSIN, HE'D BE DEAD.
IF IT WAS FAKE, WHY'D THE ADMINISTRATION GO TO DEFCON 4? TRUST ME, BEN'S THE REAL DEAL. HE COULD MOP THE FLOOR WITH YOU.
THEN MAYBE HE AND I SHOULD PUT THAT TO THE TEST. RIGHT AFTER CLASS.
YOU'RE ON!

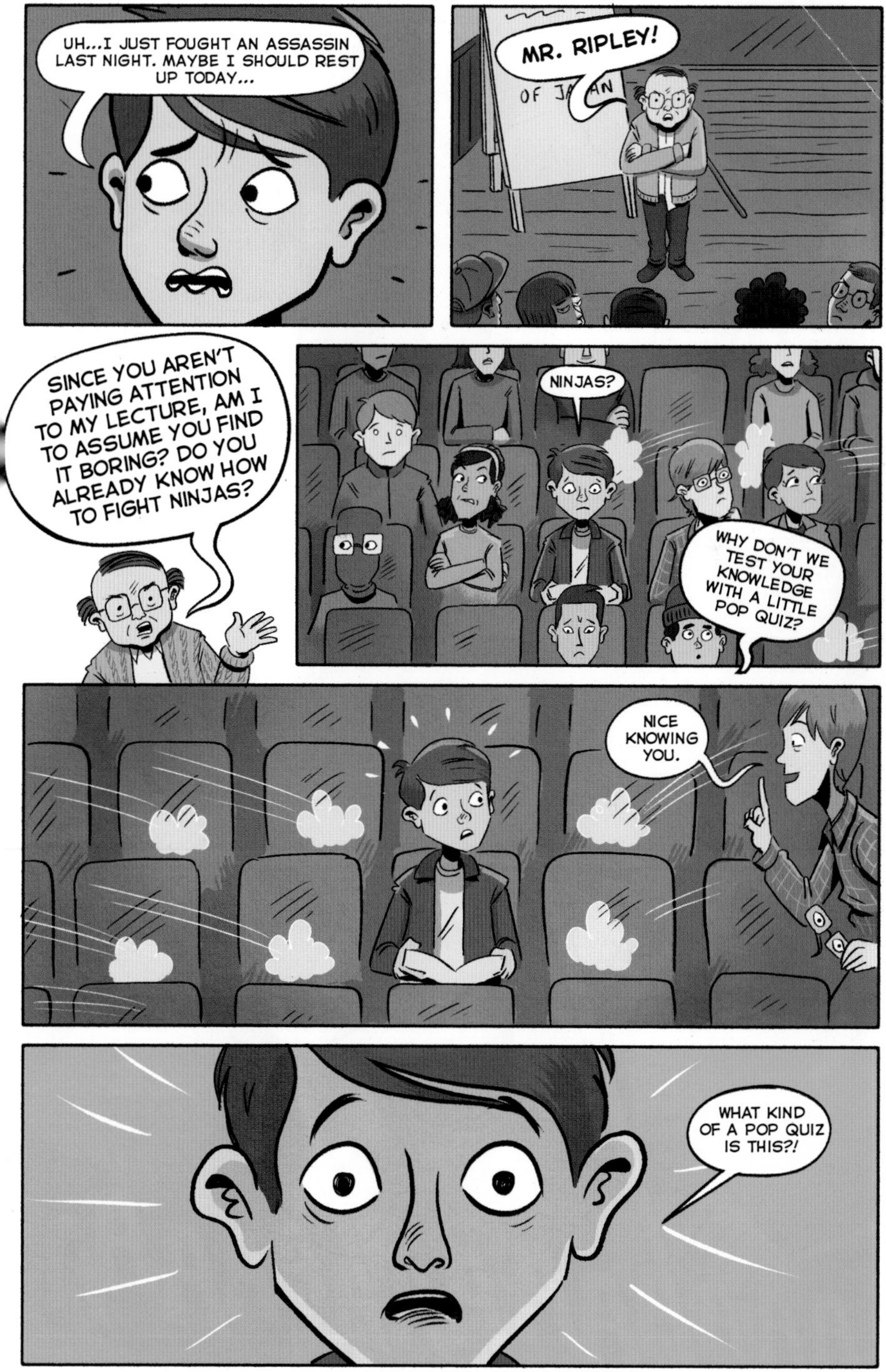
UH...I JUST FOUGHT AN ASSASSIN LAST NIGHT. MAYBE I SHOULD REST UP TODAY...
MR. RIPLEY!
SINCE YOU AREN'T PAYING ATTENTION TO MY LECTURE, AM I TO ASSUME YOU FIND IT BORING? DO YOU ALREADY KNOW HOW TO FIGHT NINJAS?
NINJAS?
WHY DON'T WE TEST YOUR KNOWLEDGE WITH A LITTLE POP QUIZ?
NICE KNOWING YOU.
WHAT KIND OF A POP QUIZ IS THIS?!

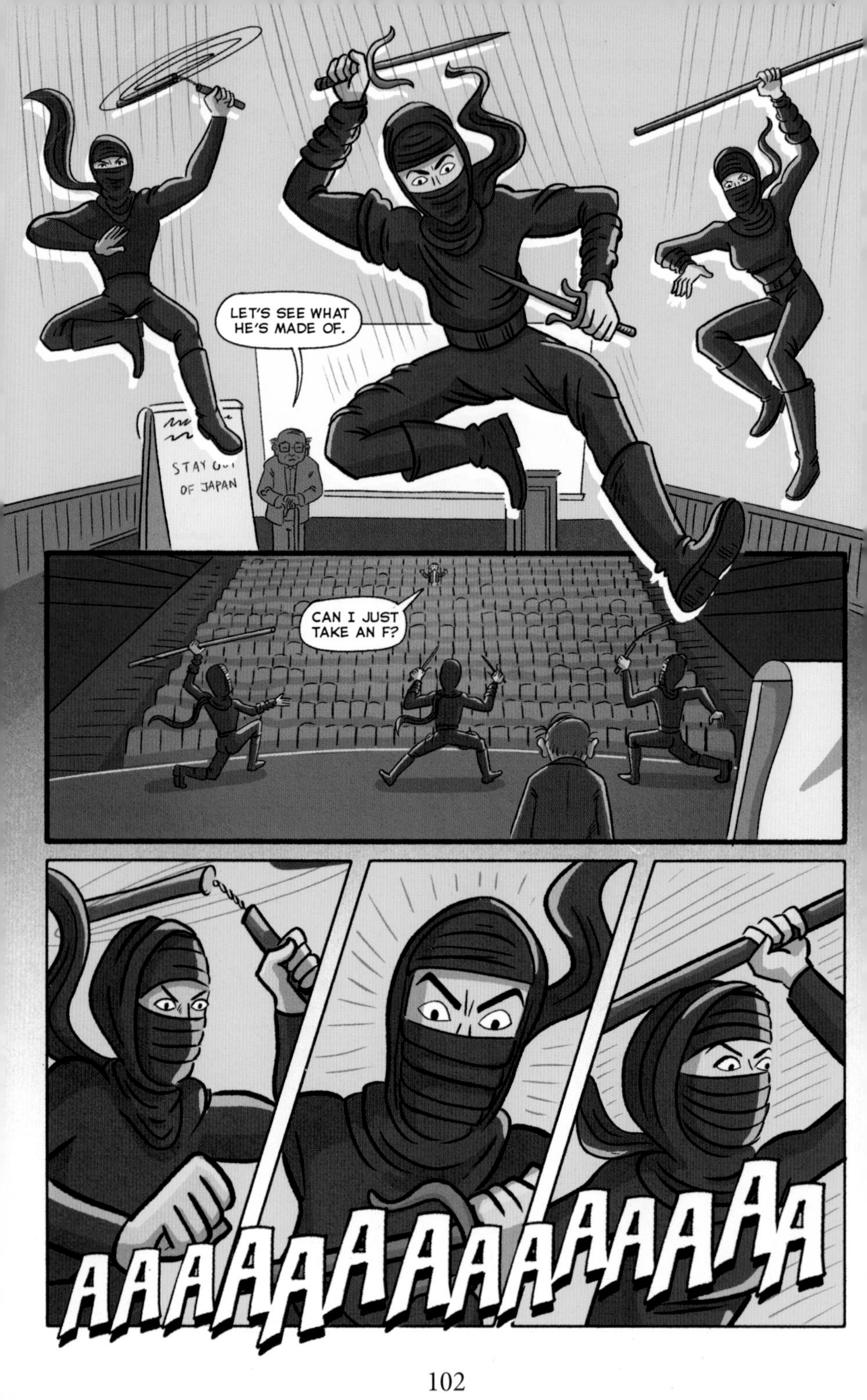
STAY OUT OF JAPAN
LET'S SEE WHAT HE'S MADE OF.
CAN I JUST TAKE AN F?
AAAAAAAAAAAAAAAA

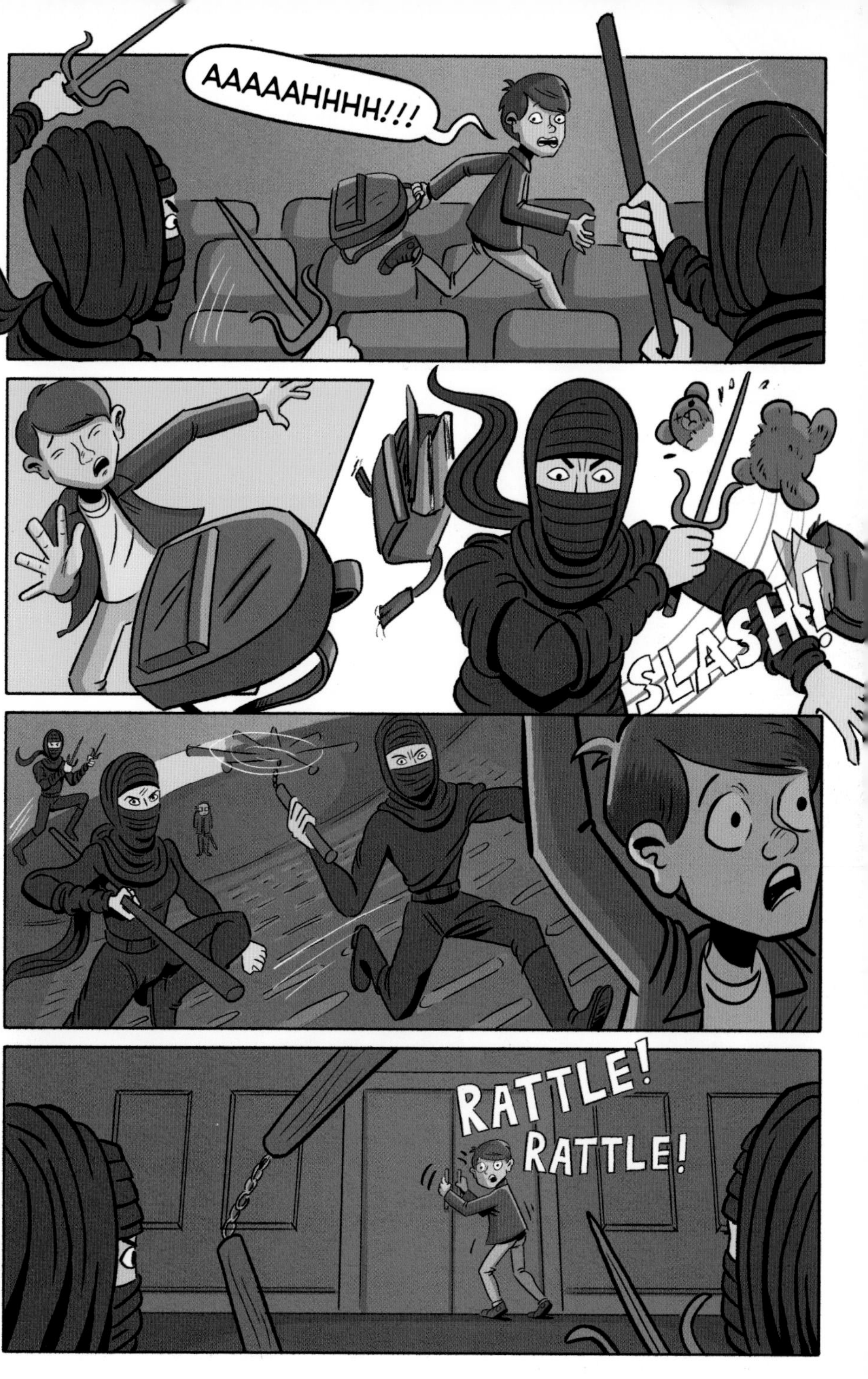
AAAAAHHHH!!!
SLASH!
RATTLE!
RATTLE!

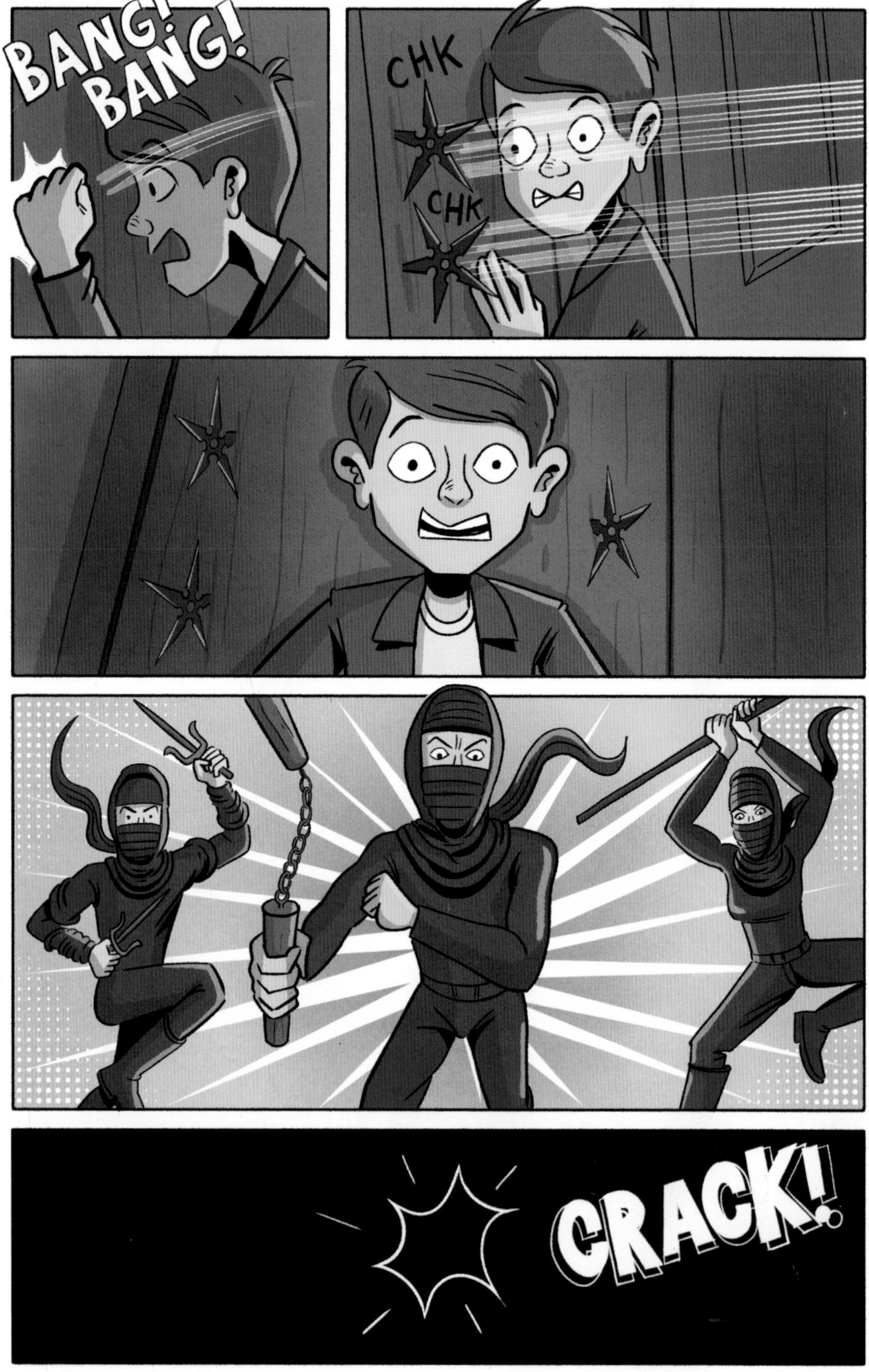
BANG! BANG!
CHK
CHK
CRACK!

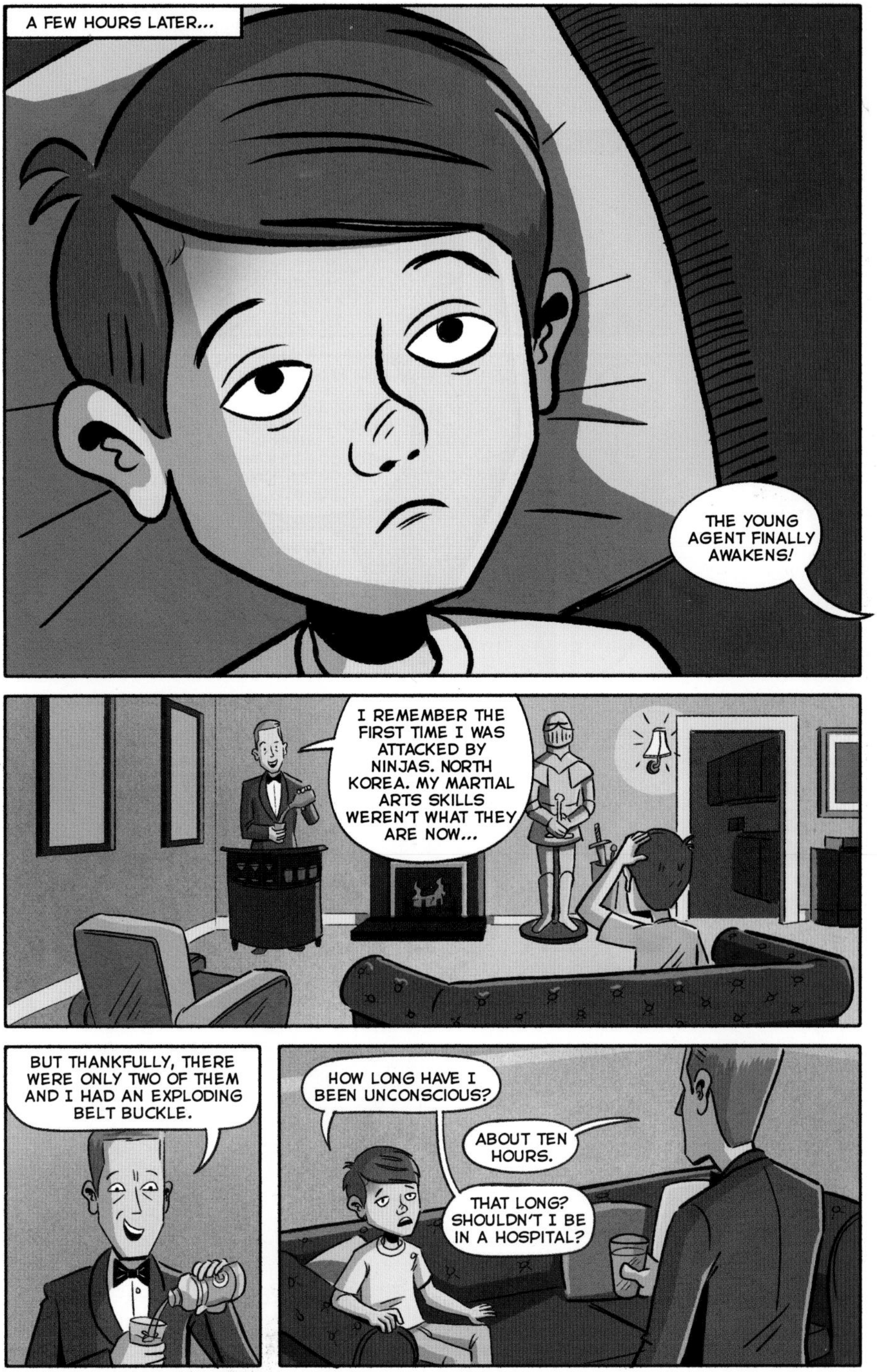
A FEW HOURS LATER...
THE YOUNG AGENT FINALLY AWAKENS!
I REMEMBER THE FIRST TIME I WAS ATTACKED BY NINJAS. NORTH KOREA. MY MARTIAL ARTS SKILLS WEREN'T WHAT THEY ARE NOW...
BUT THANKFULLY, THERE WERE ONLY TWO OF THEM AND I HAD AN EXPLODING BELT BUCKLE.
HOW LONG HAVE I BEEN UNCONSCIOUS?
ABOUT TEN HOURS.
THAT LONG? SHOULDN'T I BE IN A HOSPITAL?

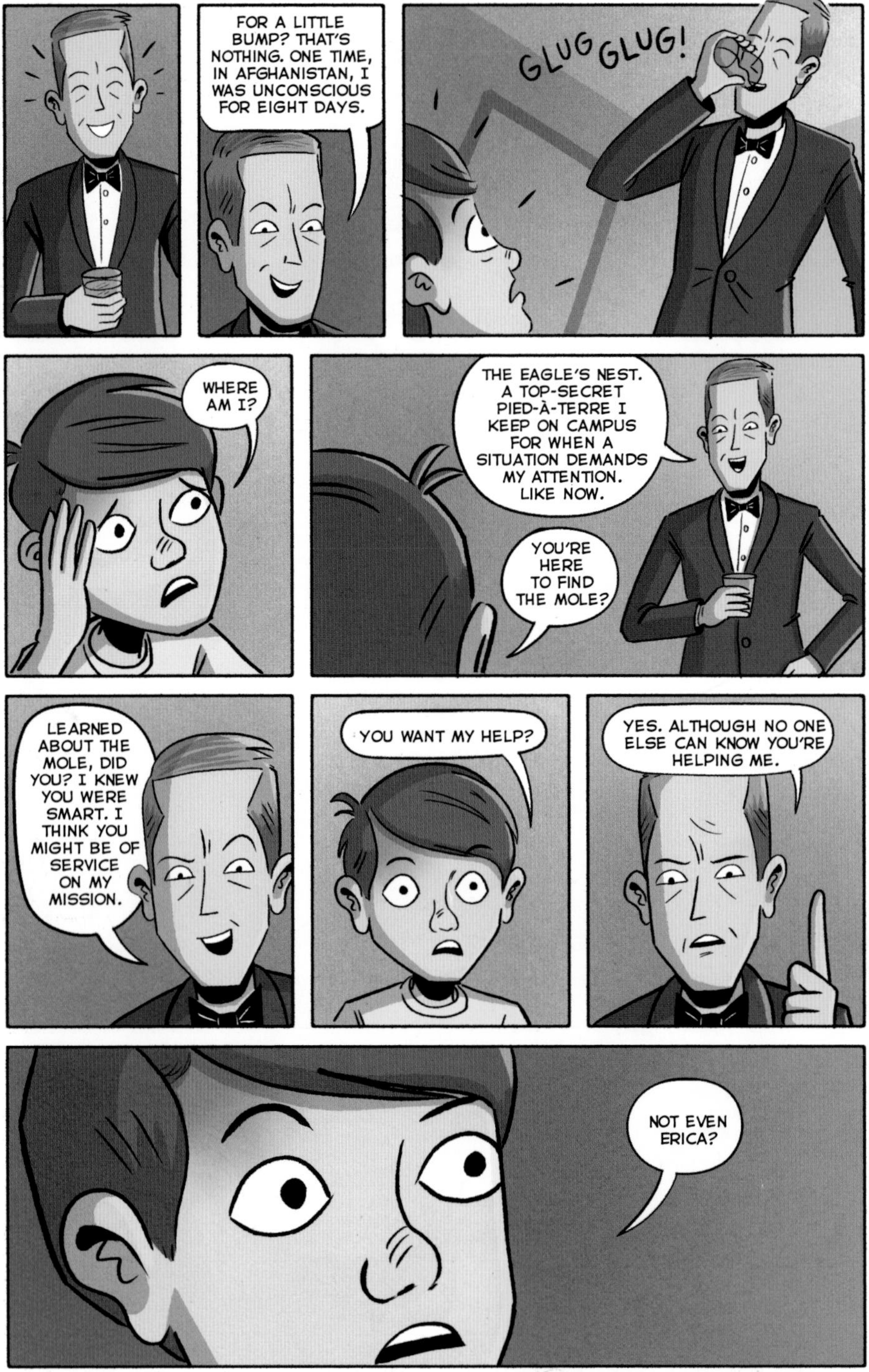
FOR A LITTLE BUMP? THAT'S NOTHING. ONE TIME, IN AFGHANISTAN, I WAS UNCONSCIOUS FOR EIGHT DAYS.
GLUG GLUG!
WHERE AM I?
THE EAGLE'S NEST. A TOP-SECRET PIED-À-TERRE I KEEP ON CAMPUS FOR WHEN A SITUATION DEMANDS MY ATTENTION. LIKE NOW.
YOU'RE HERE TO FIND THE MOLE?
LEARNED ABOUT THE MOLE, DID YOU? I KNEW YOU WERE SMART. I THINK YOU MIGHT BE OF SERVICE ON MY MISSION.
YOU WANT MY HELP?
YES. ALTHOUGH NO ONE ELSE CAN KNOW YOU'RE HELPING ME.
NOT EVEN ERICA?

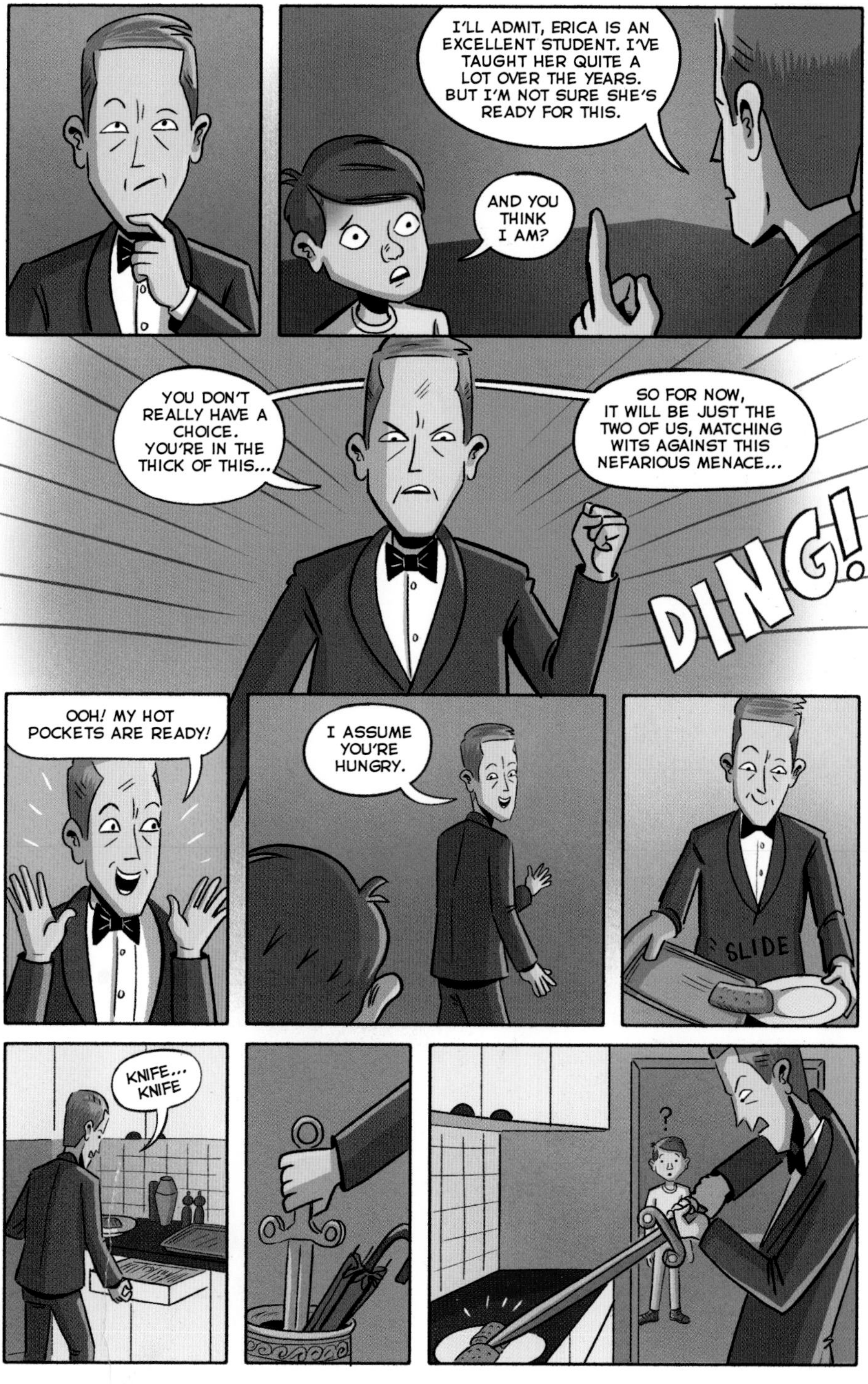
I'LL ADMIT, ERICA IS AN EXCELLENT STUDENT. I'VE TAUGHT HER QUITE A LOT OVER THE YEARS. BUT I'M NOT SURE SHE'S READY FOR THIS.
AND YOU THINK I AM?
YOU DON'T REALLY HAVE A CHOICE. YOU'RE IN THE THICK OF THIS...
SO FOR NOW, IT WILL BE JUST THE TWO OF US, MATCHING WITS AGAINST THIS NEFARIOUS MENACE...
DING!
OOH! MY HOT POCKETS ARE READY!
I ASSUME YOU'RE HUNGRY.
SLIDE
KNIFE... KNIFE
?

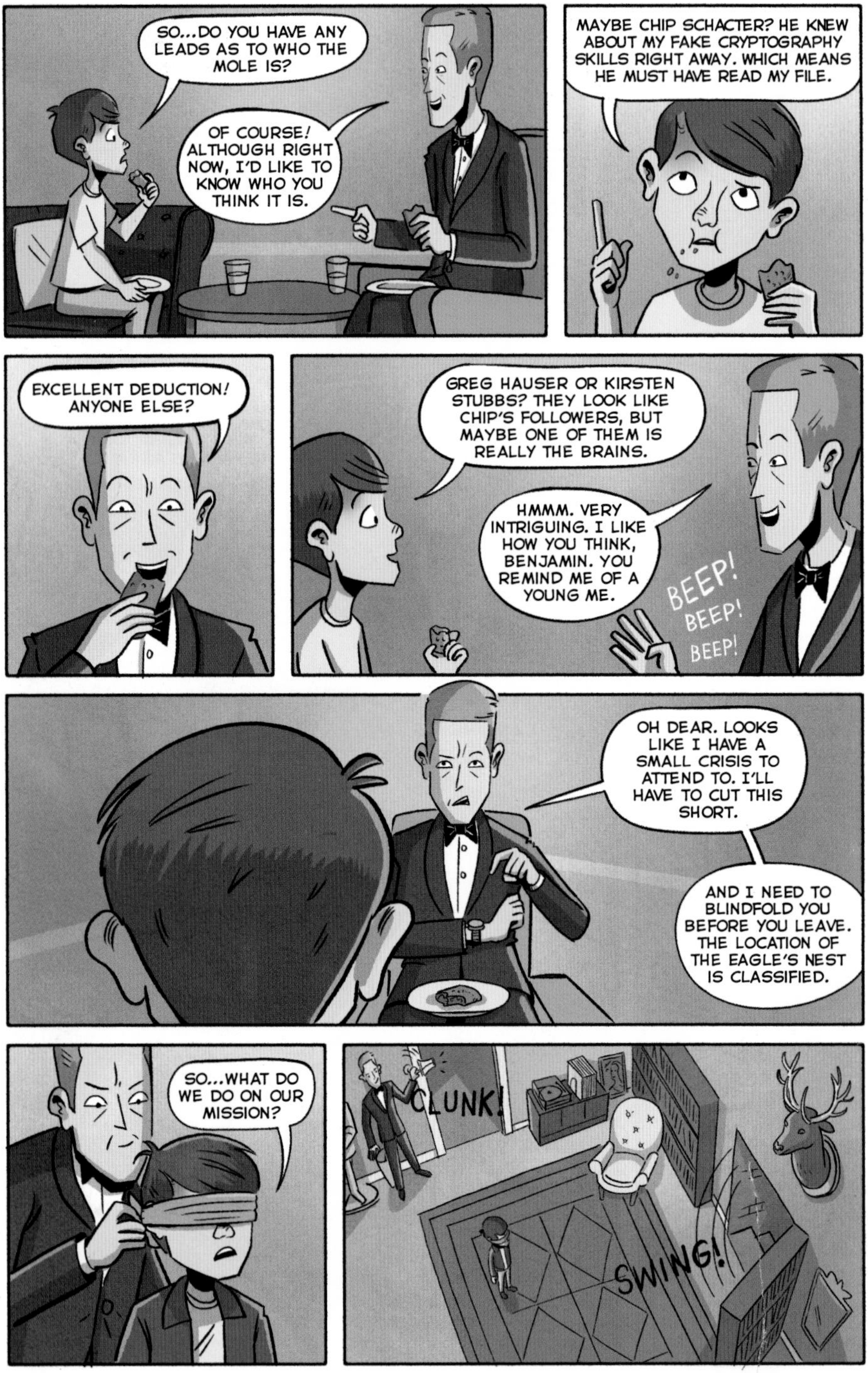
SO...DO YOU HAVE ANY LEADS AS TO WHO THE MOLE IS?
OF COURSE! ALTHOUGH RIGHT NOW, I'D LIKE TO KNOW WHO YOU THINK IT IS.
MAYBE CHIP SCHACTER? HE KNEW ABOUT MY FAKE CRYPTOGRAPHY SKILLS RIGHT AWAY. WHICH MEANS HE MUST HAVE READ MY FILE.
EXCELLENT DEDUCTION! ANYONE ELSE?
GREG HAUSER OR KIRSTEN STUBBS? THEY LOOK LIKE CHIP'S FOLLOWERS, BUT MAYBE ONE OF THEM IS REALLY THE BRAINS.
HMMM. VERY INTRIGUING. I LIKE HOW YOU THINK, BENJAMIN. YOU REMIND ME OF A YOUNG ME.
BEEP!
BEEP!
BEEP!
OH DEAR. LOOKS LIKE I HAVE A SMALL CRISIS TO ATTEND TO. I'LL HAVE TO CUT THIS SHORT.
AND I NEED TO BLINDFOLD YOU BEFORE YOU LEAVE. THE LOCATION OF THE EAGLE'S NEST IS CLASSIFIED.
SO...WHAT DO WE DO ON OUR MISSION?
CLUNK!
SWING!

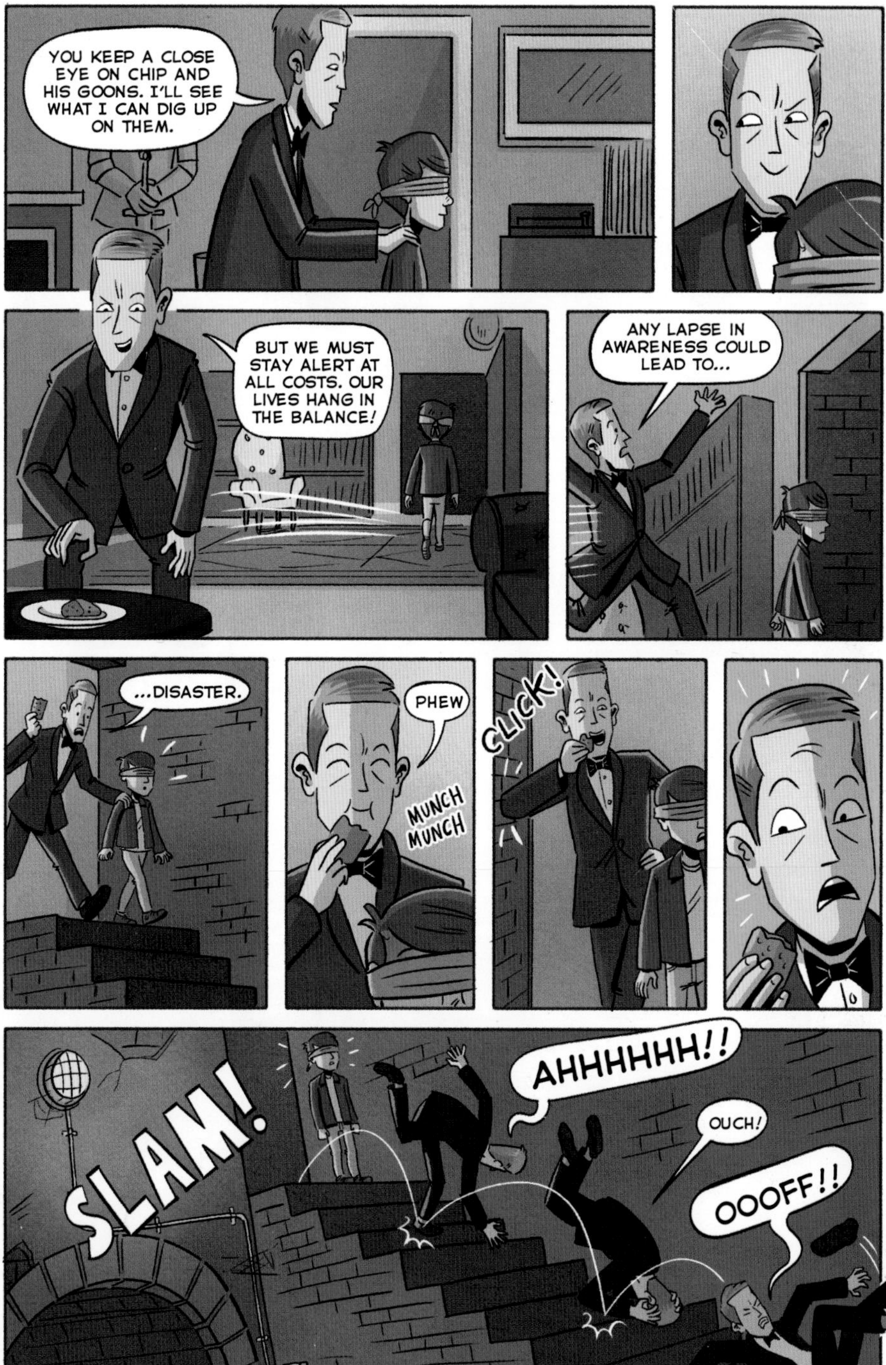
YOU KEEP A CLOSE EYE ON CHIP AND HIS GOONS. I'LL SEE WHAT I CAN DIG UP ON THEM.
BUT WE MUST STAY ALERT AT ALL COSTS. OUR LIVES HANG IN THE BALANCE!
ANY LAPSE IN AWARENESS COULD LEAD TO...
...DISASTER.
PHEW
MUNCH MUNCH
CLICK!
SLAM!
AHHHHHH!!
OUCH!
OOOFF!!

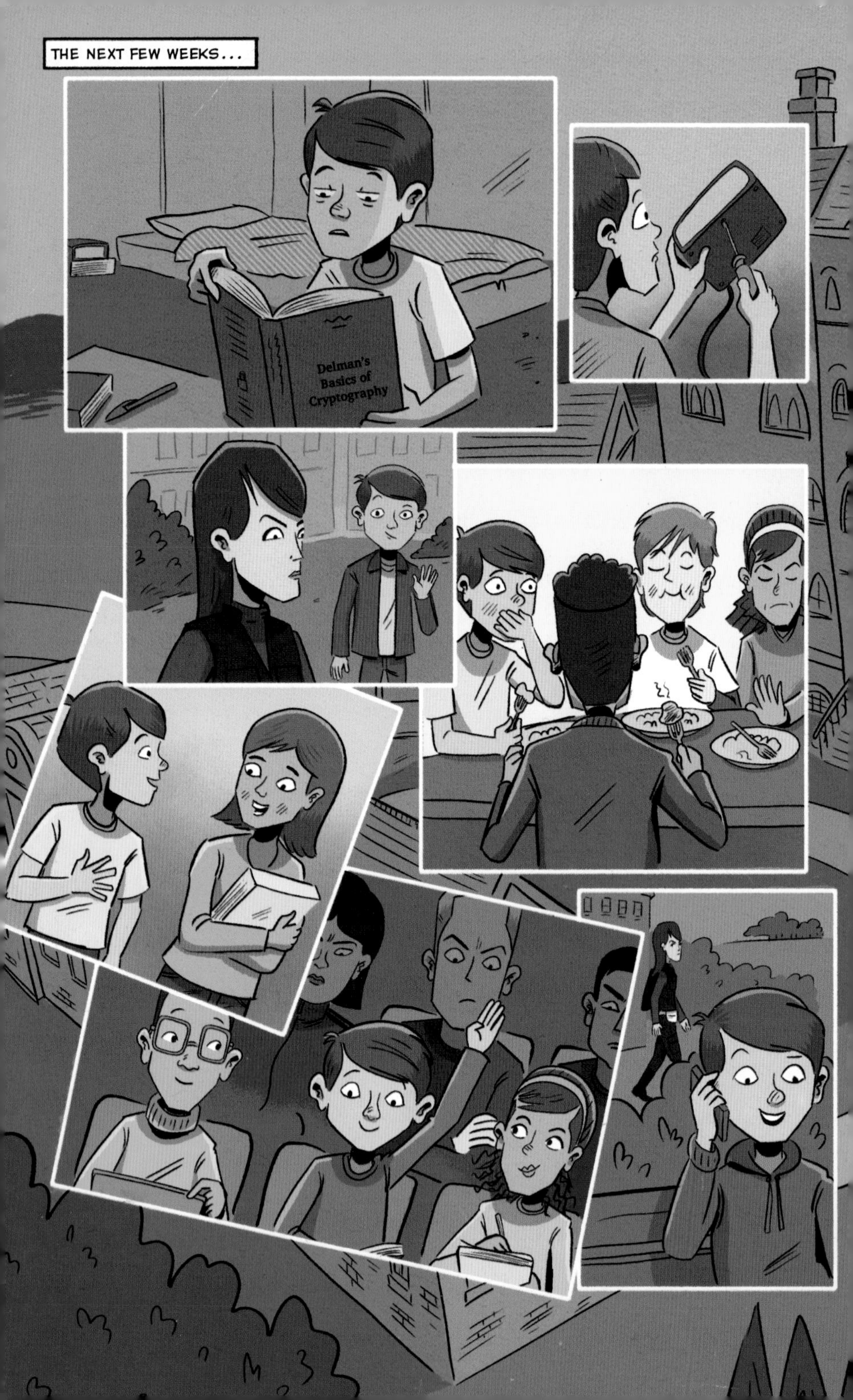
THE NEXT FEW WEEKS...
Delman's Basics of Cryptography

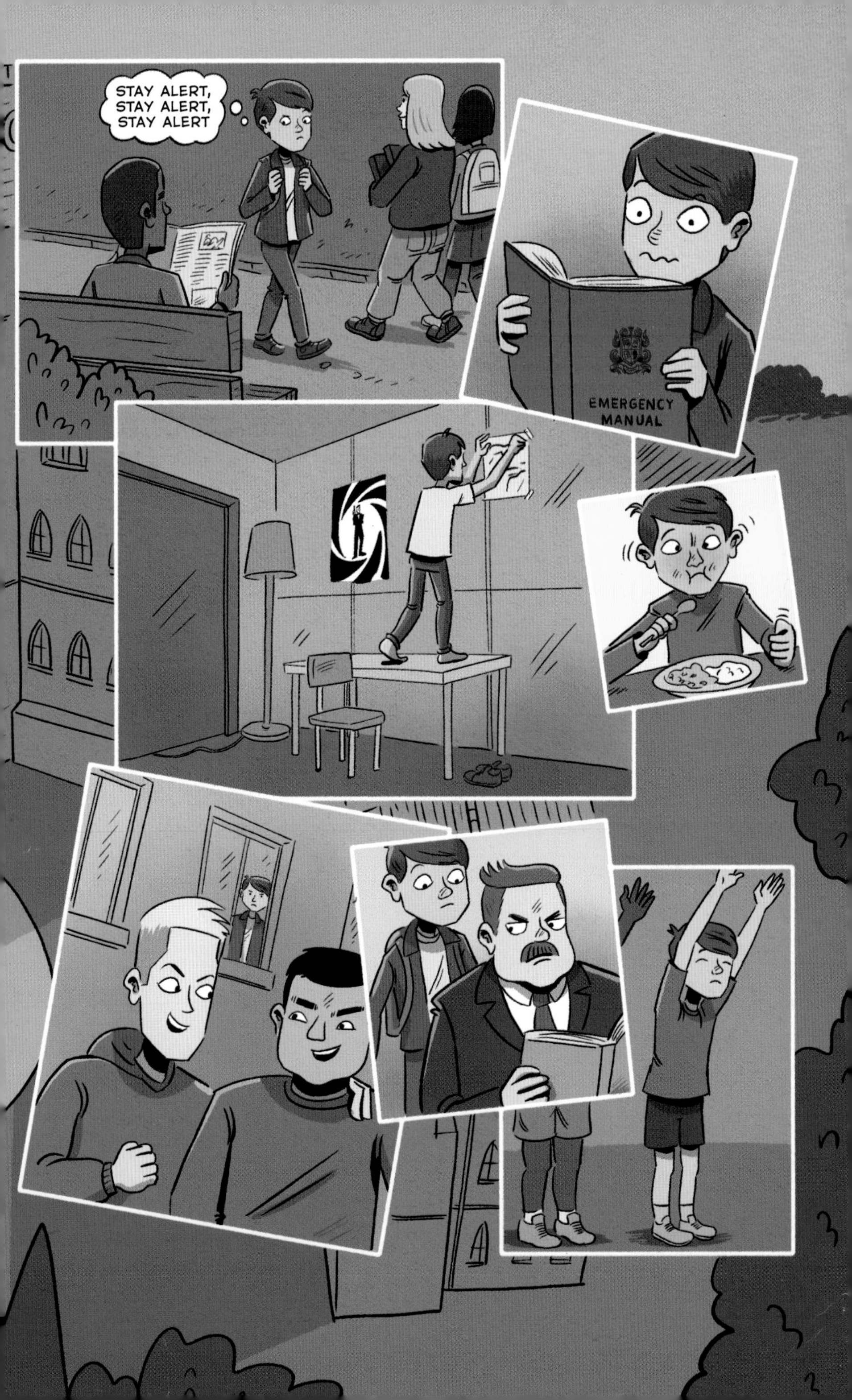
STAY ALERT, STAY ALERT, STAY ALERT
EMERGENCY MANUAL

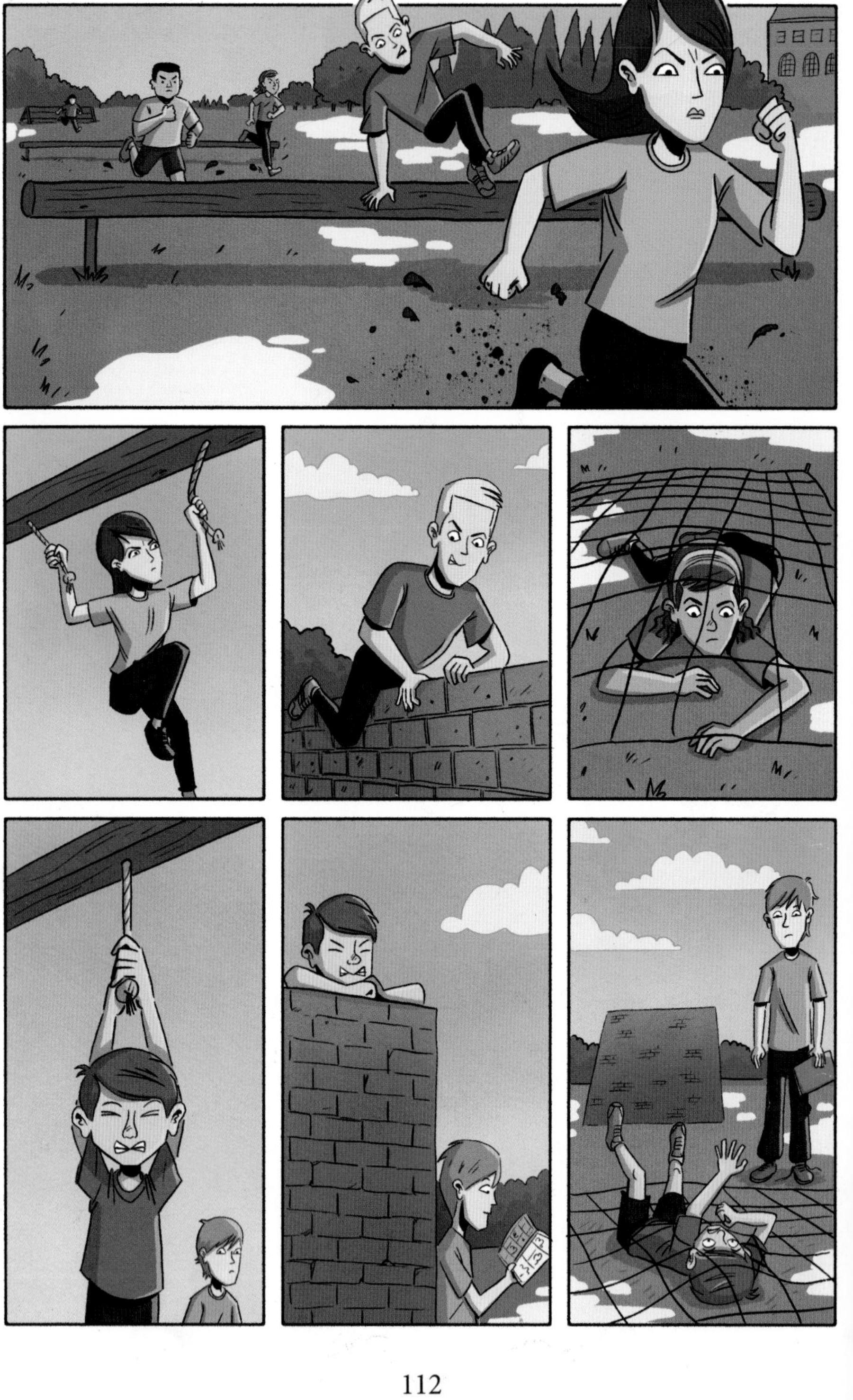

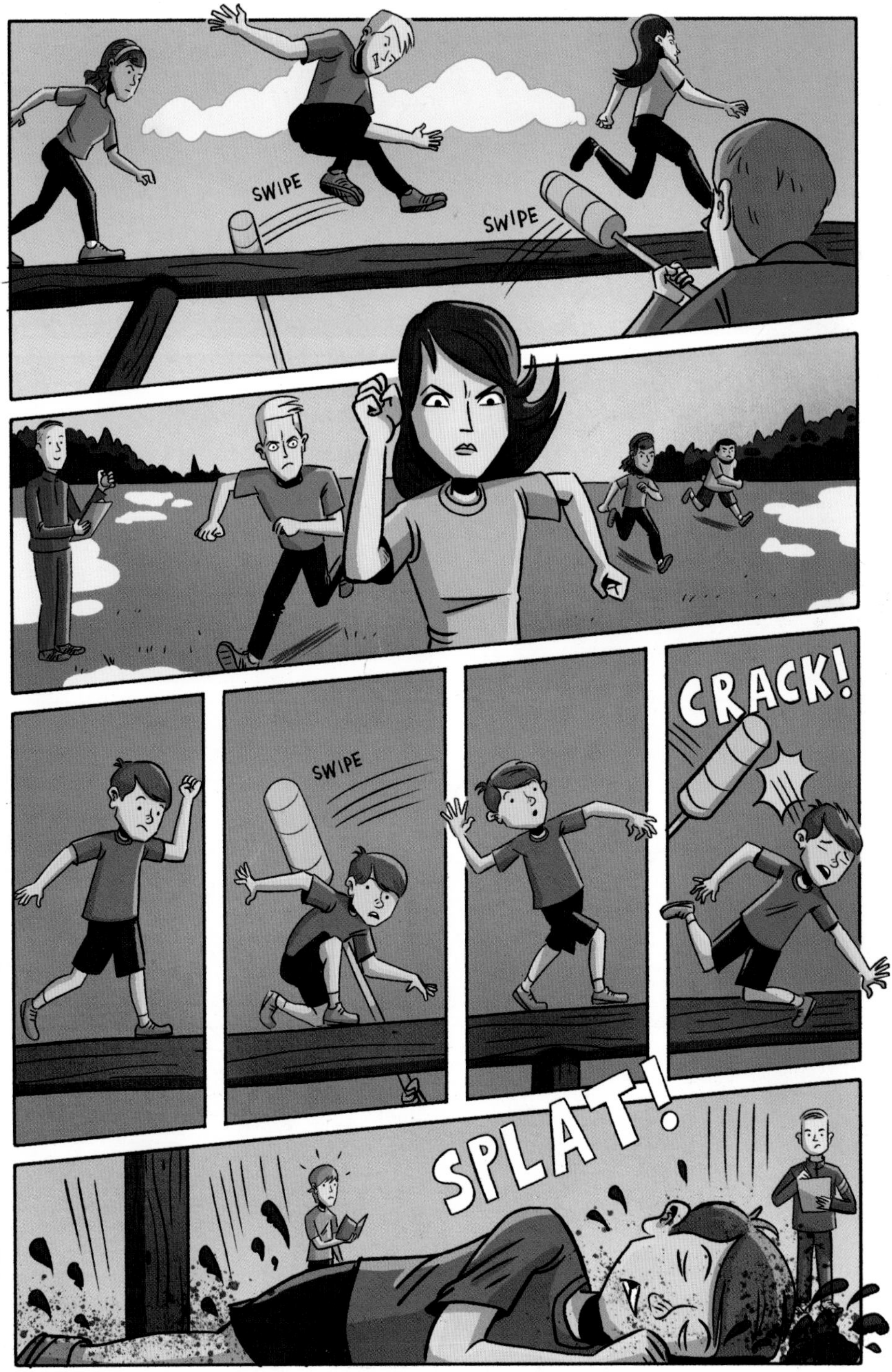
SWIPE
SWIPE
SWIPE
CRACK!
SPLAT!

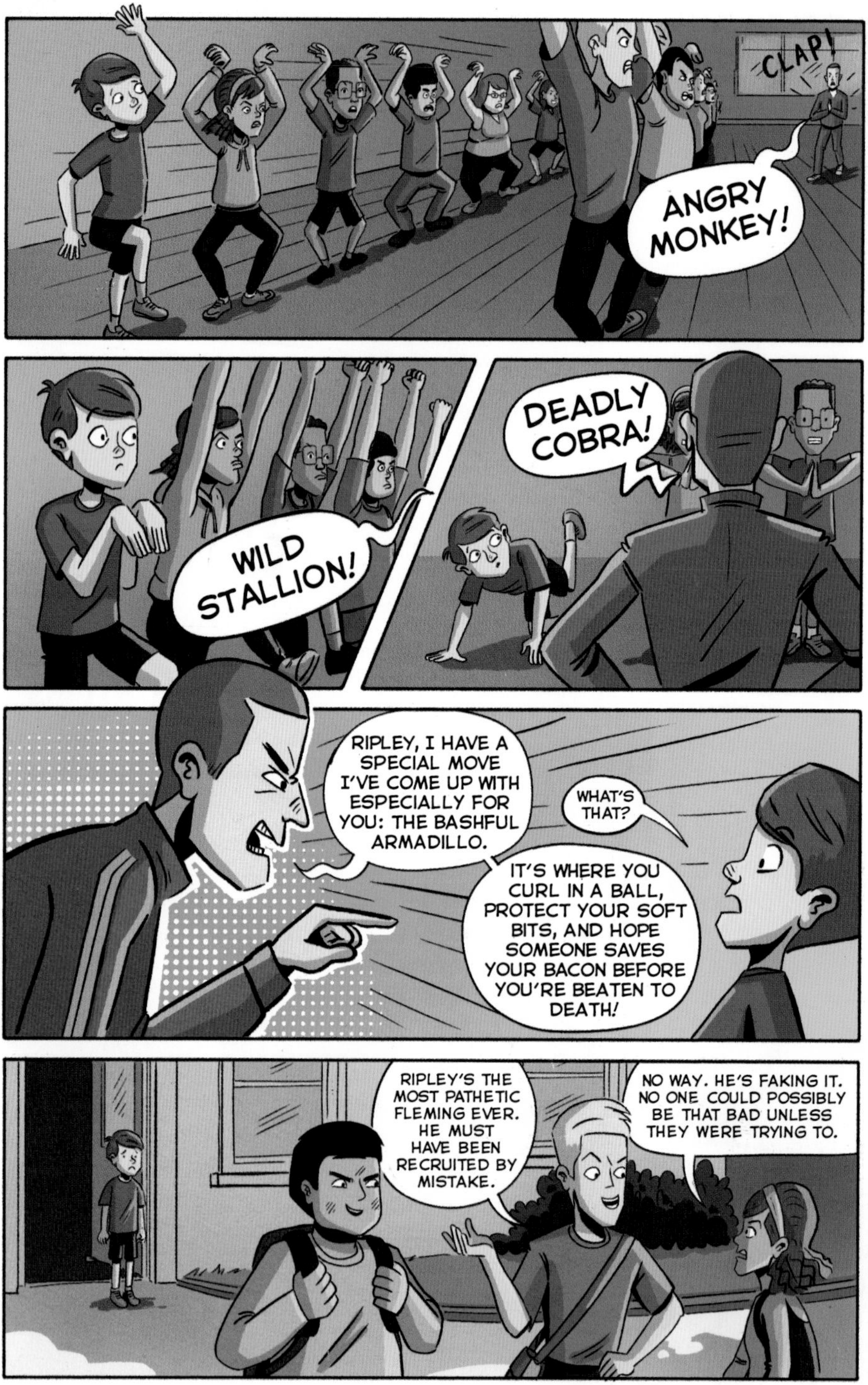
CLAP!
ANGRY MONKEY!
WILD STALLION!
DEADLY COBRA!
RIPLEY, I HAVE A SPECIAL MOVE I'VE COME UP WITH ESPECIALLY FOR YOU: THE BASHFUL ARMADILLO.
WHAT'S THAT?
IT'S WHERE YOU CURL IN A BALL, PROTECT YOUR SOFT BITS, AND HOPE SOMEONE SAVES YOUR BACON BEFORE YOU'RE BEATEN TO DEATH!
RIPLEY'S THE MOST PATHETIC FLEMING EVER. HE MUST HAVE BEEN RECRUITED BY MISTAKE.
NO WAY. HE'S FAKING IT. NO ONE COULD POSSIBLY BE THAT BAD UNLESS THEY WERE TRYING TO.

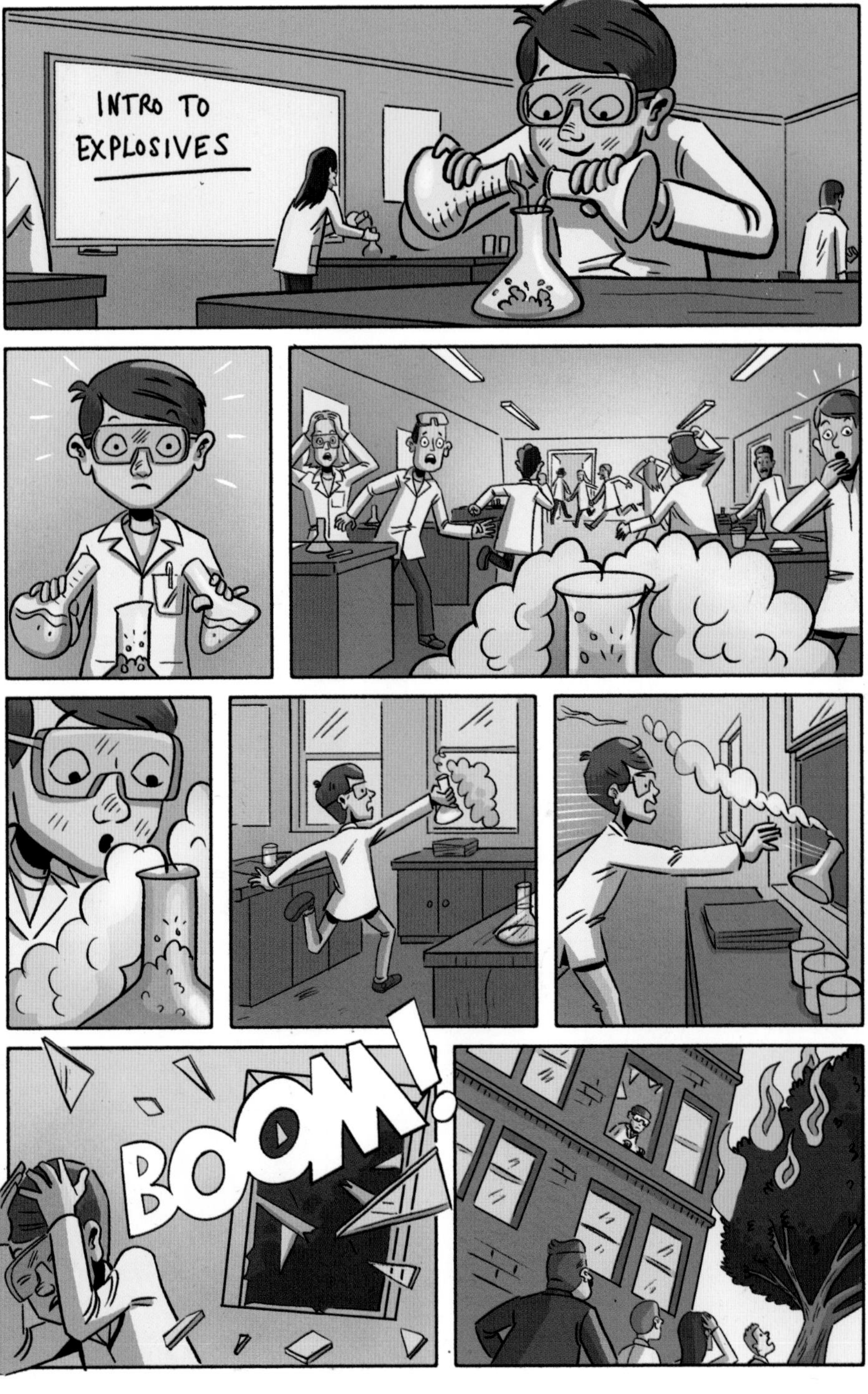
INTRO TO
EXPLOSIVES
BOOM!

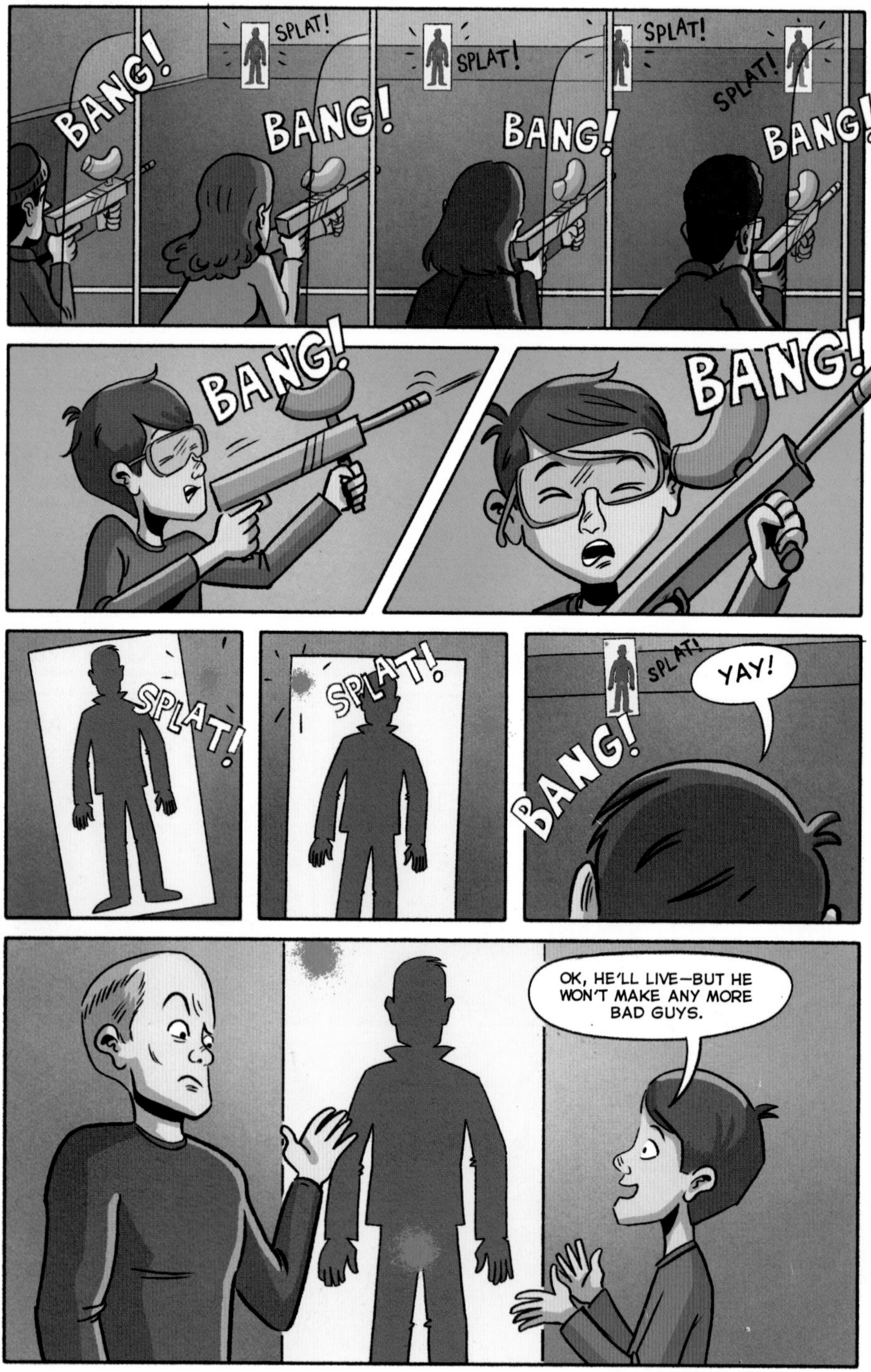
BANG!
SPLAT!
BANG!
SPLAT!
BANG!
SPLAT!
BANG!
SPLAT!
BANG!
BANG!
SPLAT!
SPLAT!
SPLAT!
YAY!
BANG!
OK, HE'LL LIVE—BUT HE WON'T MAKE ANY MORE BAD GUYS.

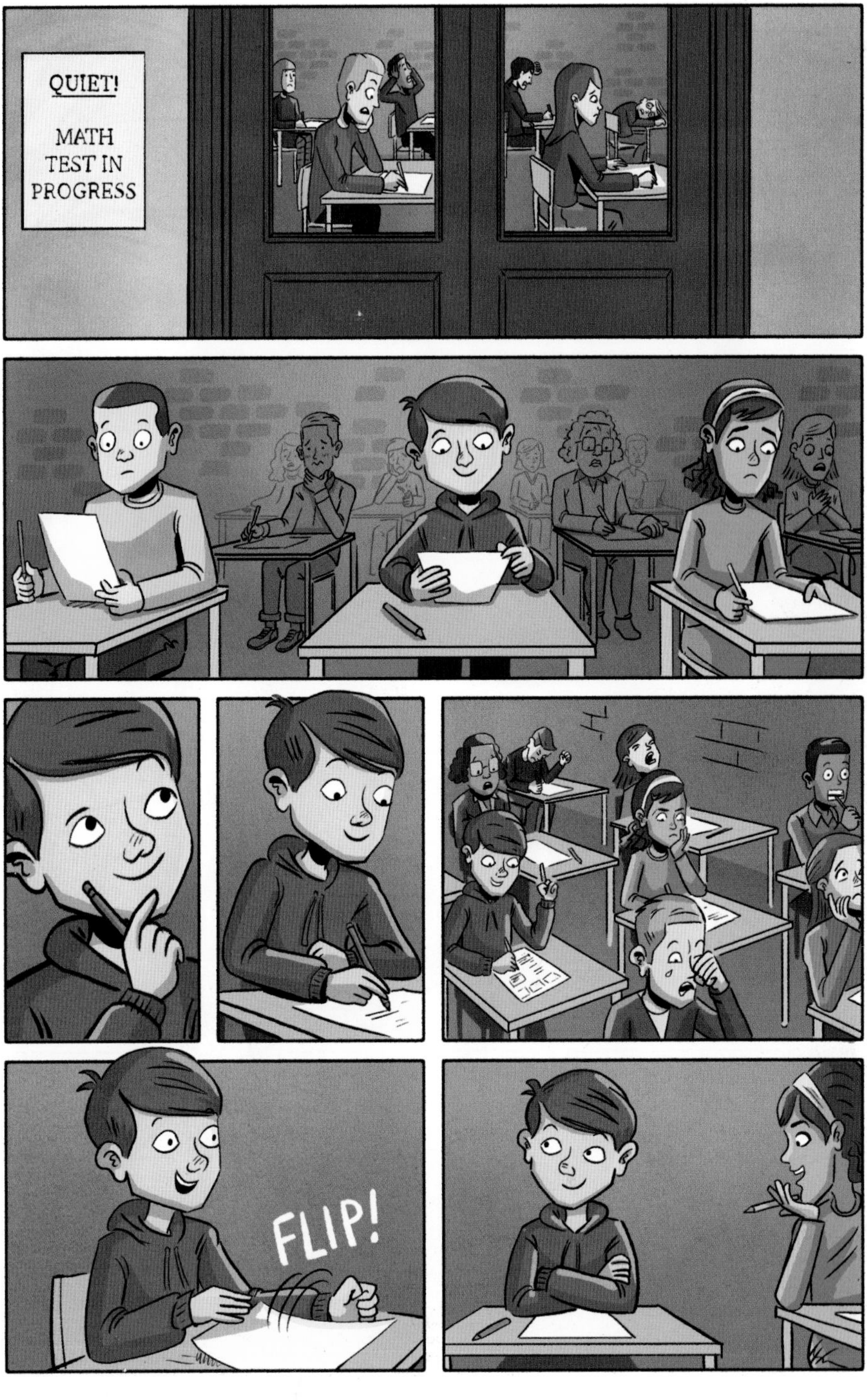
QUIET!
MATH TEST IN PROGRESS
FLIP!

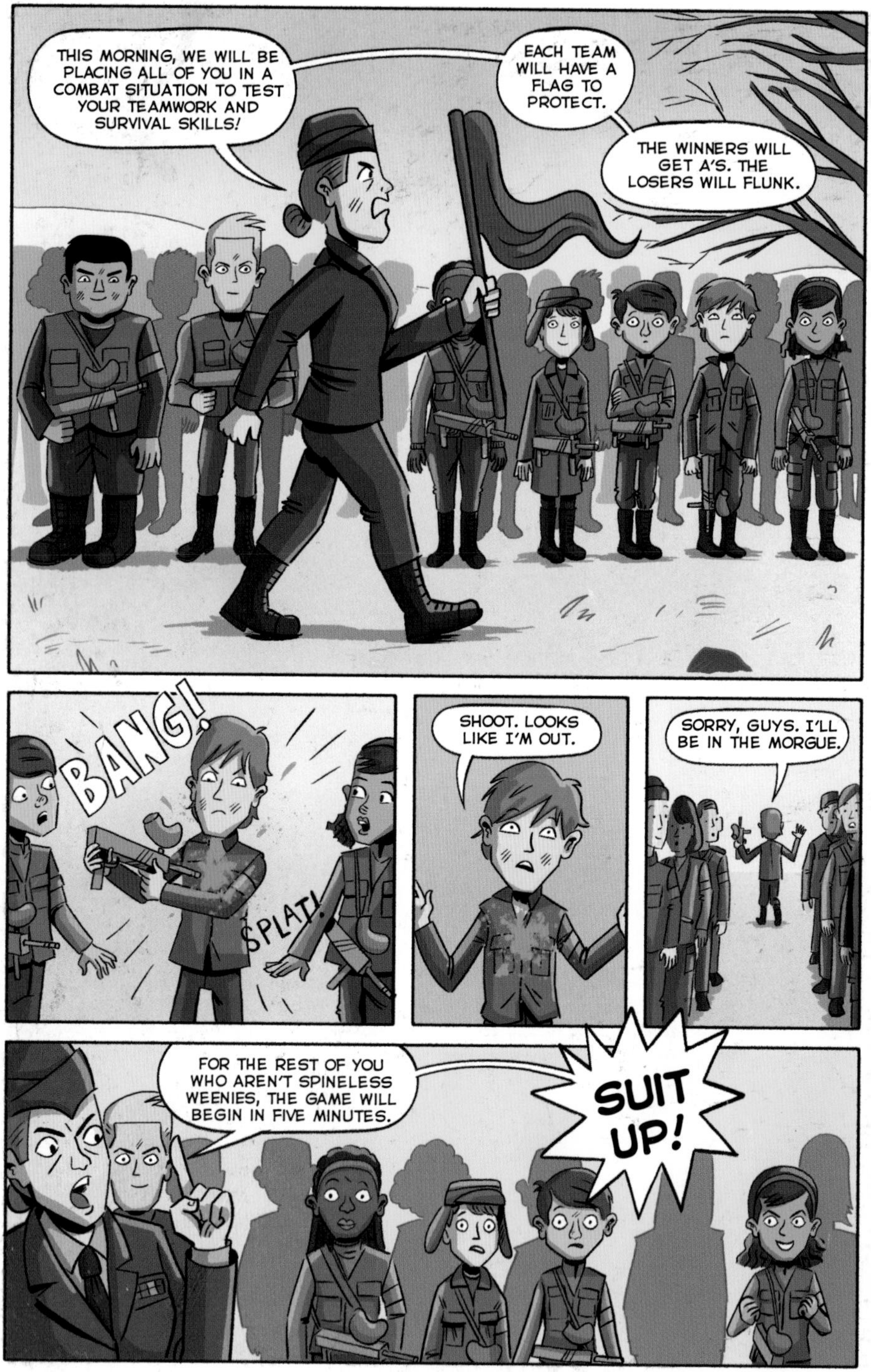
THIS MORNING, WE WILL BE PLACING ALL OF YOU IN A COMBAT SITUATION TO TEST YOUR TEAMWORK AND SURVIVAL SKILLS!
EACH TEAM WILL HAVE A FLAG TO PROTECT.
THE WINNERS WILL GET A'S. THE LOSERS WILL FLUNK.
BANG!
SPLAT!
SHOOT. LOOKS LIKE I'M OUT.
SORRY, GUYS. I'LL BE IN THE MORGUE.
FOR THE REST OF YOU WHO AREN'T SPINELESS WEENIES, THE GAME WILL BEGIN IN FIVE MINUTES.
SUIT UP!

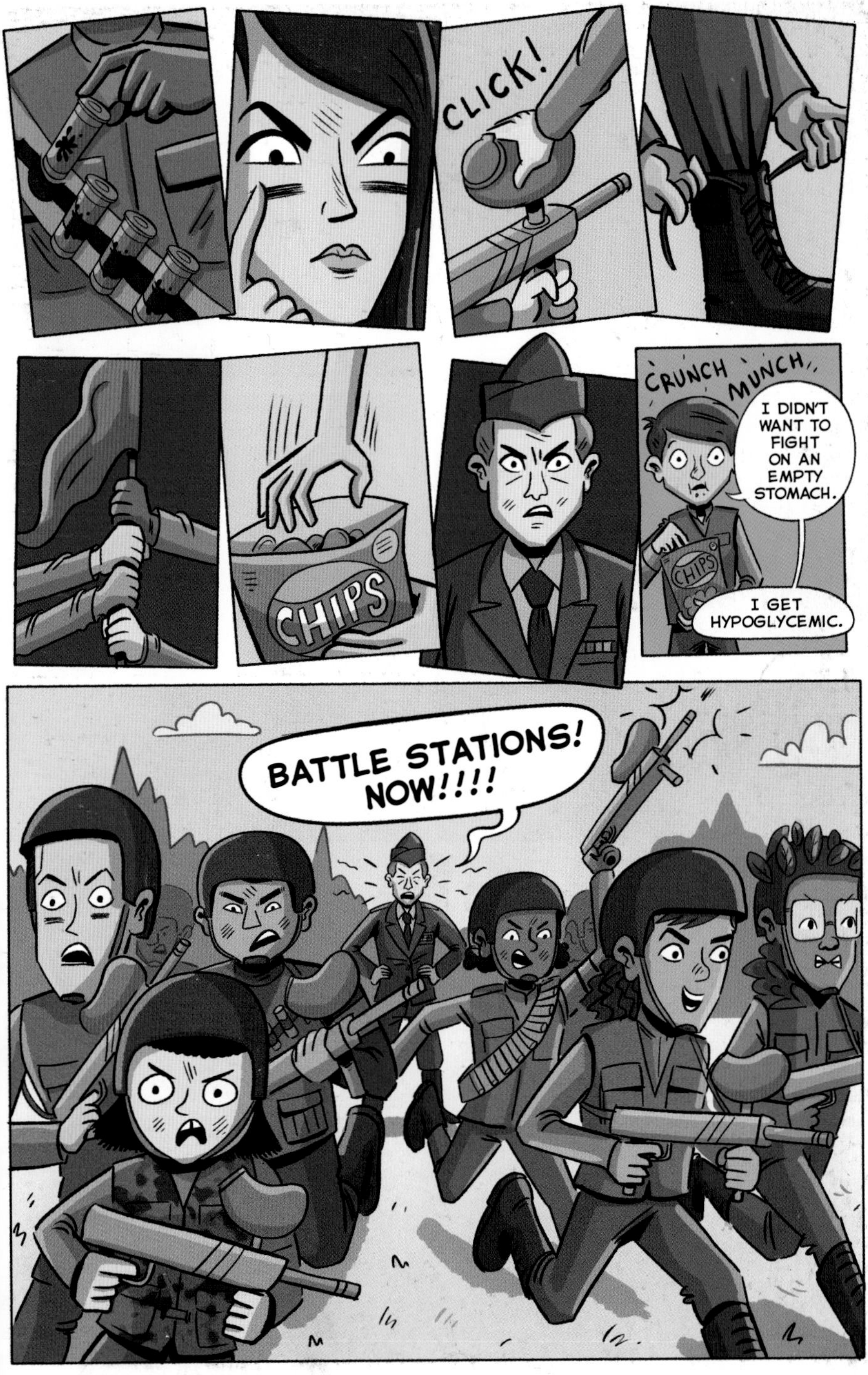
CLICK!
CRUNCH
MUNCH
I DIDN'T WANT TO FIGHT ON AN EMPTY STOMACH.
I GET HYPOGLYCEMIC.
CHIPS
CHIPS
BATTLE STATIONS! NOW!!!!

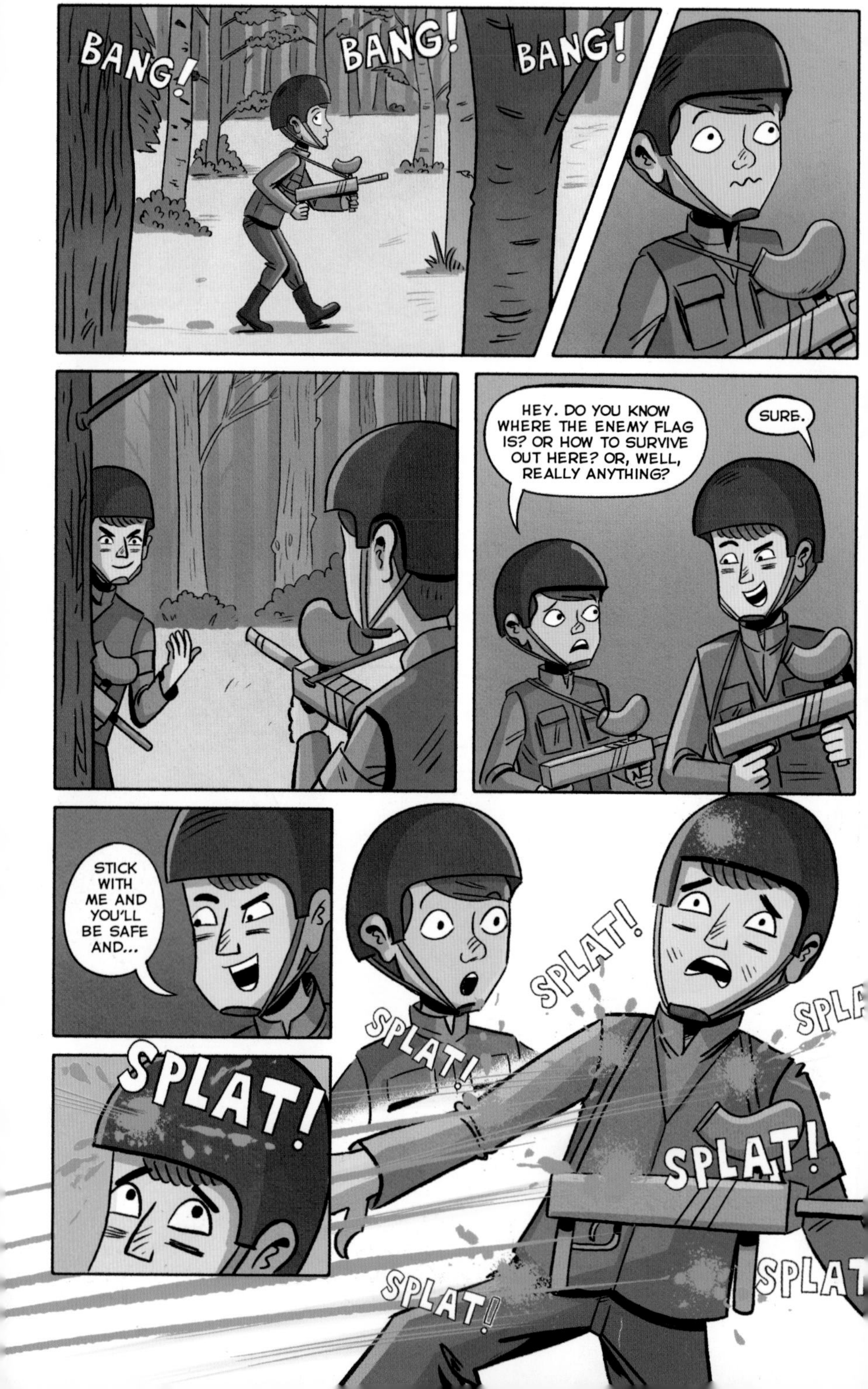
BANG!
BANG!
BANG!
HEY. DO YOU KNOW WHERE THE ENEMY FLAG IS? OR HOW TO SURVIVE OUT HERE? OR, WELL, REALLY ANYTHING?
SURE.
STICK WITH ME AND YOU'LL BE SAFE AND...
SPLAT!
SPLAT!
SPLAT!
SPLAT!
SPLAT!

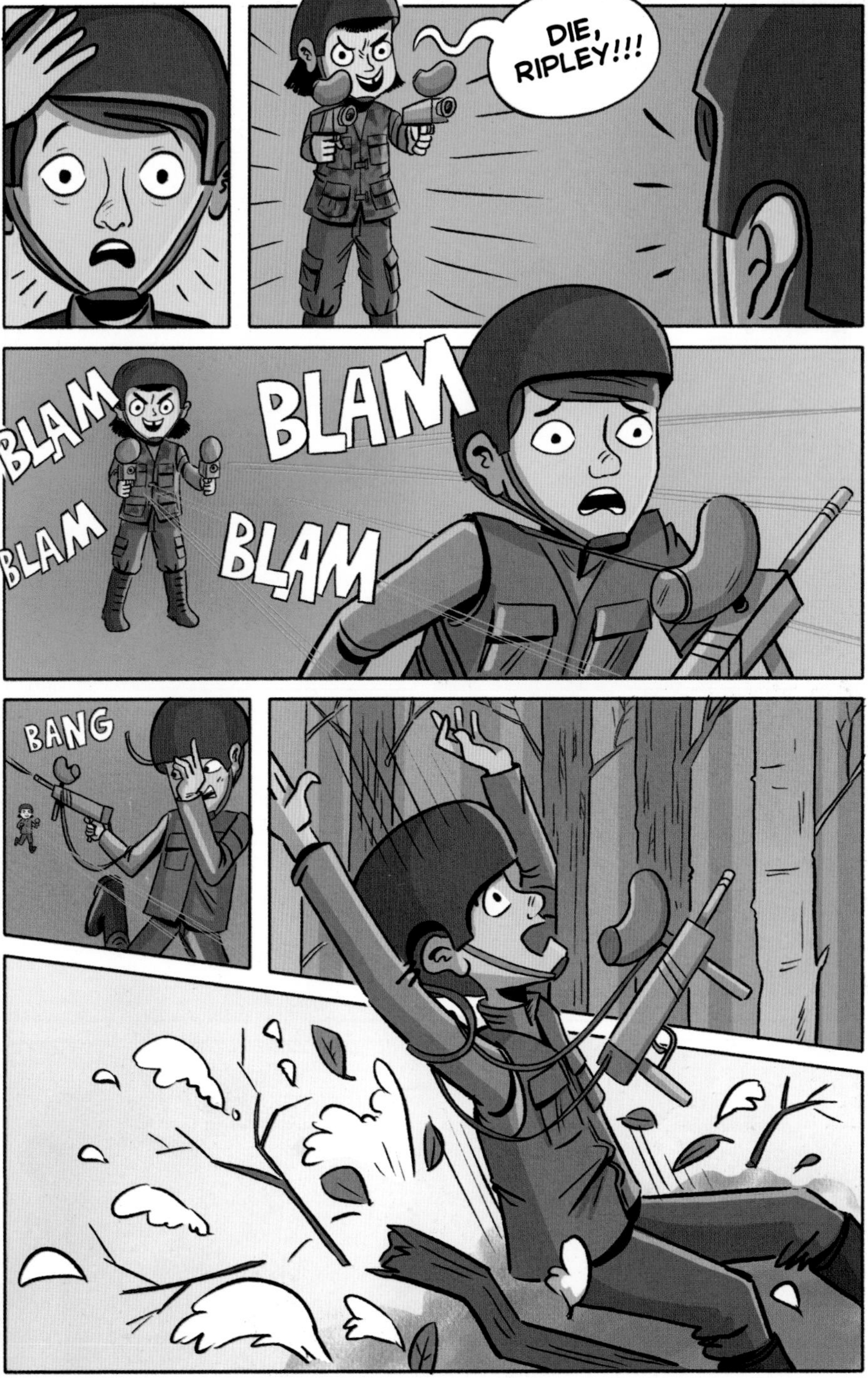
DIE, RIPLEY!!!
BLAM
BLAM
BLAM
BLAM
BANG

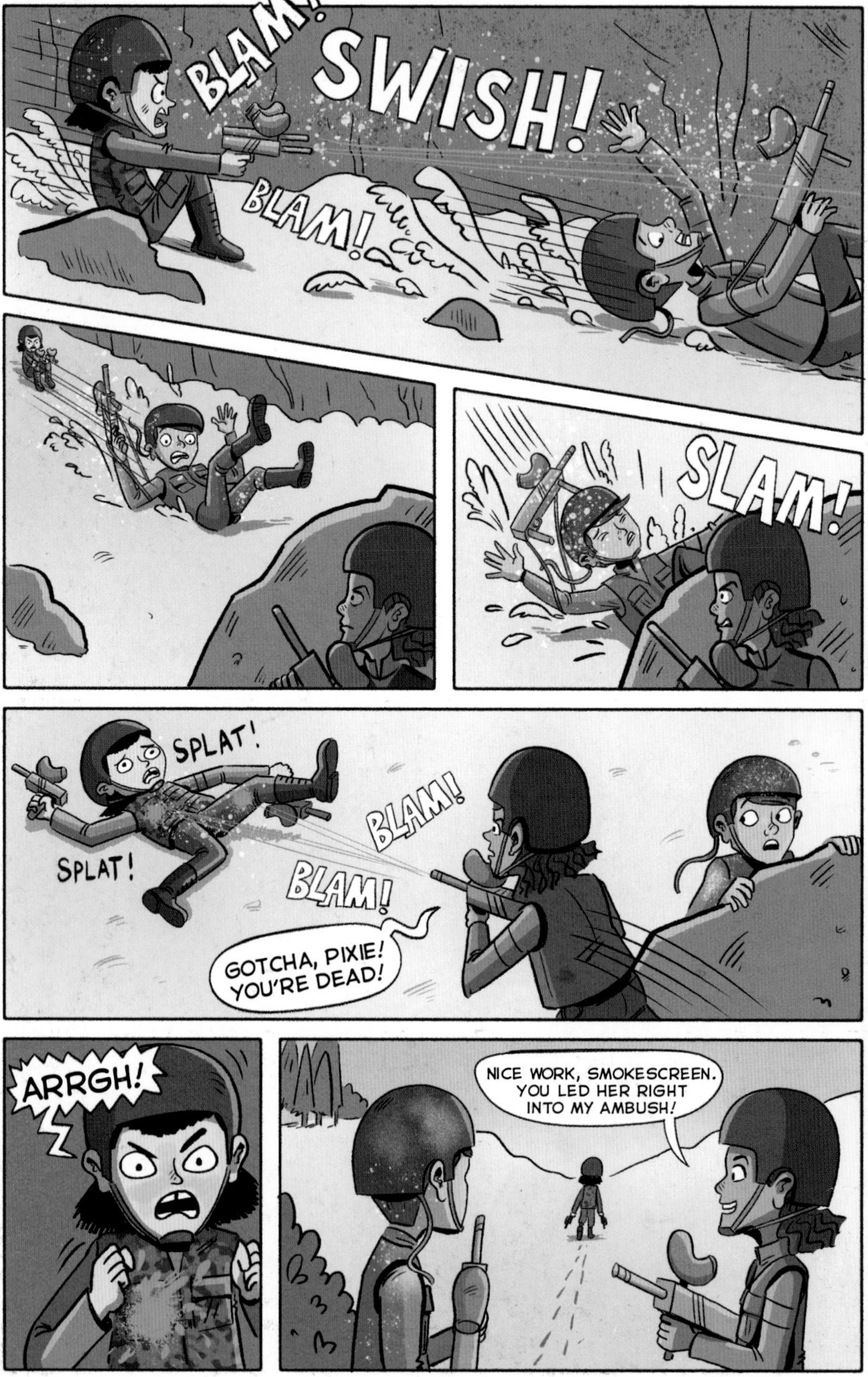
BLAM!
SWISH!
BLAM!
SLAM!
SPLAT!
SPLAT!
BLAM!
BLAM!
GOTCHA, PIXIE! YOU'RE DEAD!
ARRGH!
NICE WORK, SMOKESCREEN. YOU LED HER RIGHT INTO MY AMBUSH!

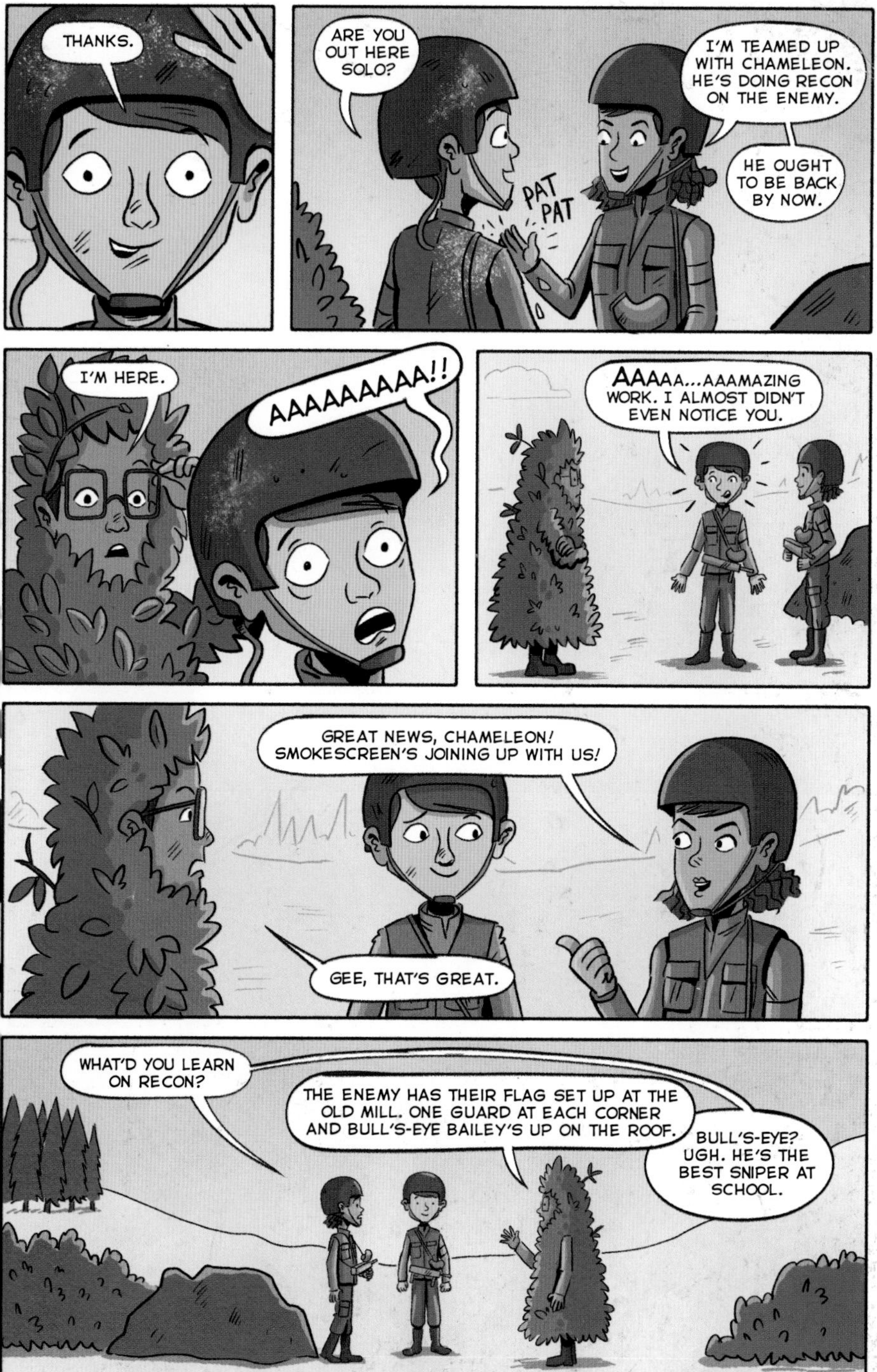
THANKS.
ARE YOU OUT HERE SOLO?
I'M TEAMED UP WITH CHAMELEON. HE'S DOING RECON ON THE ENEMY.
PAT PAT
HE OUGHT TO BE BACK BY NOW.
I'M HERE.
AAAAAAAAA!!
AAAAA...AAAMAZING WORK. I ALMOST DIDN'T EVEN NOTICE YOU.
GREAT NEWS, CHAMELEON! SMOKESCREEN'S JOINING UP WITH US!
GEE, THAT'S GREAT.
WHAT'D YOU LEARN ON RECON?
THE ENEMY HAS THEIR FLAG SET UP AT THE OLD MILL. ONE GUARD AT EACH CORNER AND BULL'S-EYE BAILEY'S UP ON THE ROOF.
BULL'S-EYE? UGH. HE'S THE BEST SNIPER AT SCHOOL.

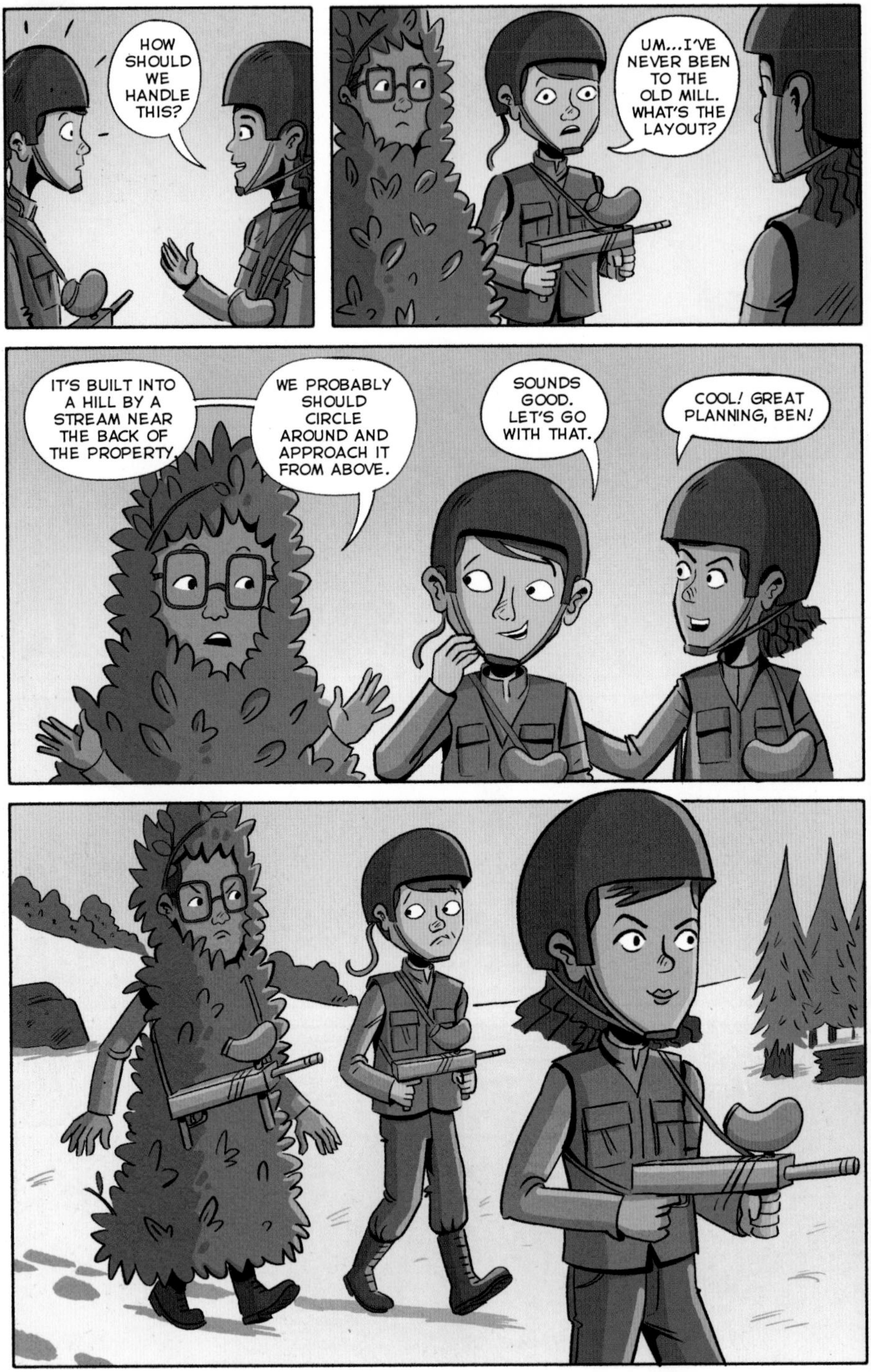
HOW SHOULD WE HANDLE THIS?
UM...I'VE NEVER BEEN TO THE OLD MILL. WHAT'S THE LAYOUT?
IT'S BUILT INTO A HILL BY A STREAM NEAR THE BACK OF THE PROPERTY.
WE PROBABLY SHOULD CIRCLE AROUND AND APPROACH IT FROM ABOVE.
SOUNDS GOOD. LET'S GO WITH THAT.
COOL! GREAT PLANNING, BEN!

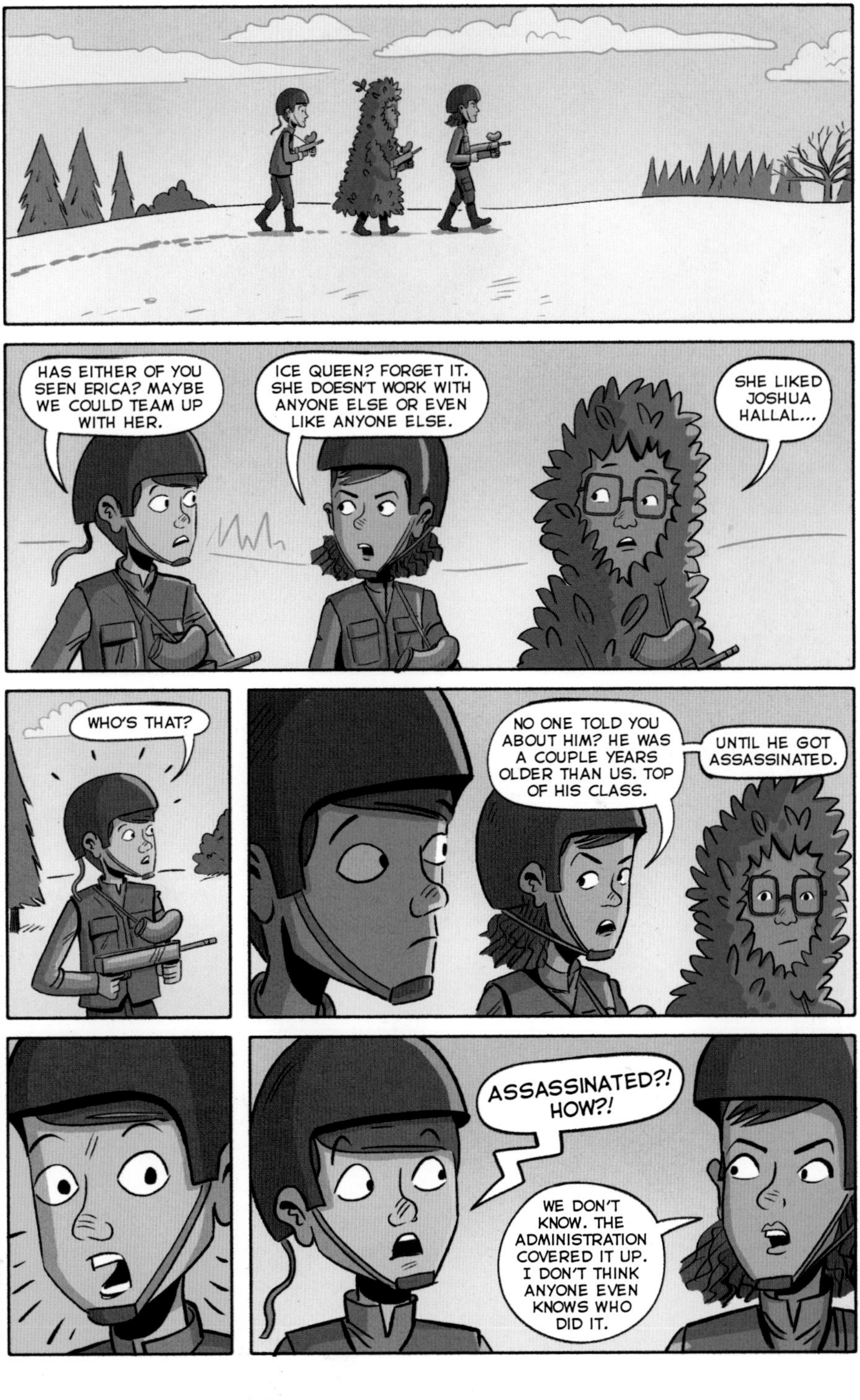
HAS EITHER OF YOU SEEN ERICA? MAYBE WE COULD TEAM UP WITH HER.
ICE QUEEN? FORGET IT. SHE DOESN'T WORK WITH ANYONE ELSE OR EVEN LIKE ANYONE ELSE.
SHE LIKED JOSHUA HALLAL...
WHO'S THAT?
NO ONE TOLD YOU ABOUT HIM? HE WAS A COUPLE YEARS OLDER THAN US. TOP OF HIS CLASS.
UNTIL HE GOT ASSASSINATED.
ASSASSINATED?! HOW?!
WE DON'T KNOW. THE ADMINISTRATION COVERED IT UP. I DON'T THINK ANYONE EVEN KNOWS WHO DID IT.

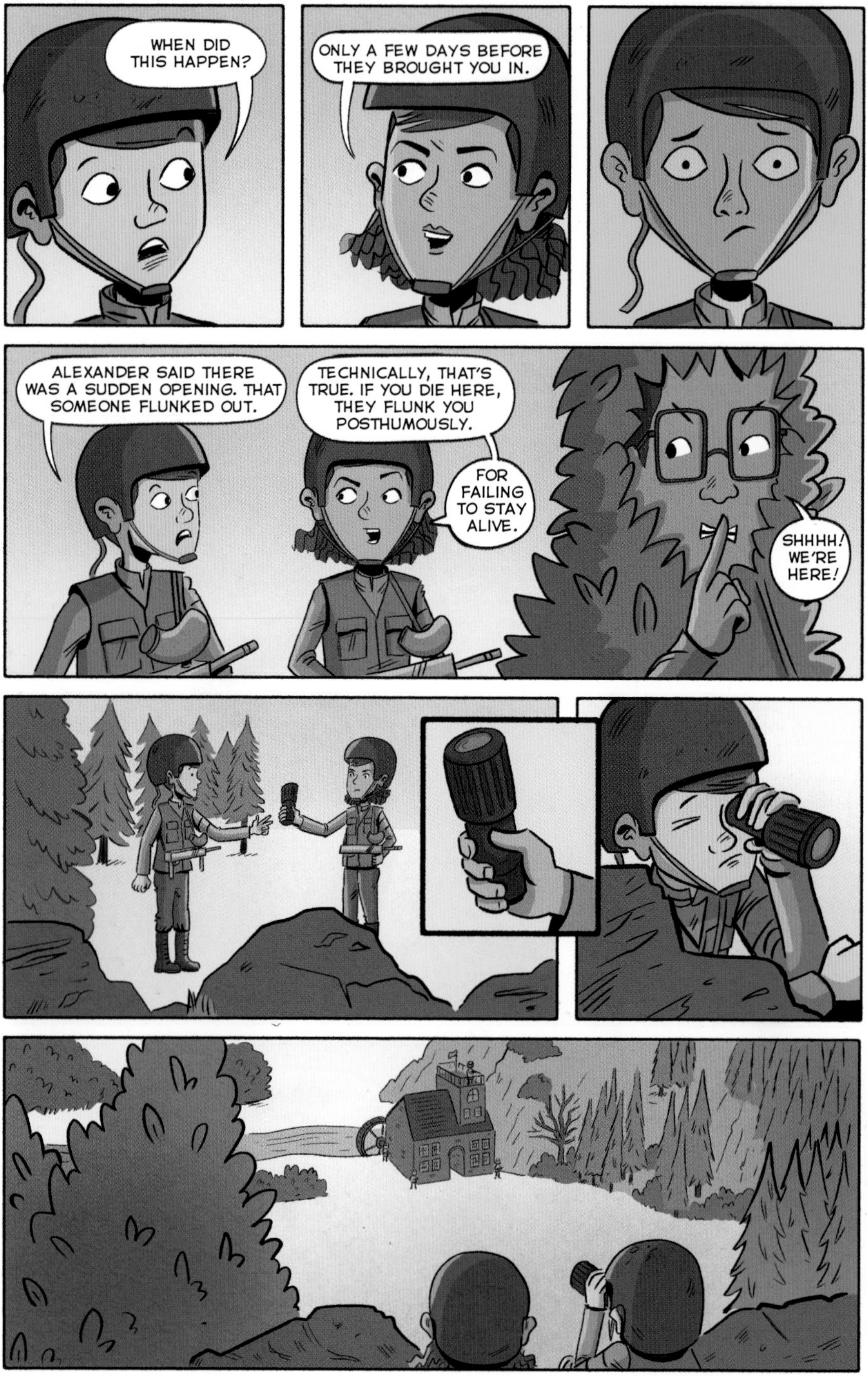
WHEN DID THIS HAPPEN?
ONLY A FEW DAYS BEFORE THEY BROUGHT YOU IN.
ALEXANDER SAID THERE WAS A SUDDEN OPENING. THAT SOMEONE FLUNKED OUT.
TECHNICALLY, THAT'S TRUE. IF YOU DIE HERE, THEY FLUNK YOU POSTHUMOUSLY.
FOR FAILING TO STAY ALIVE.
SHHHH! WE'RE HERE!

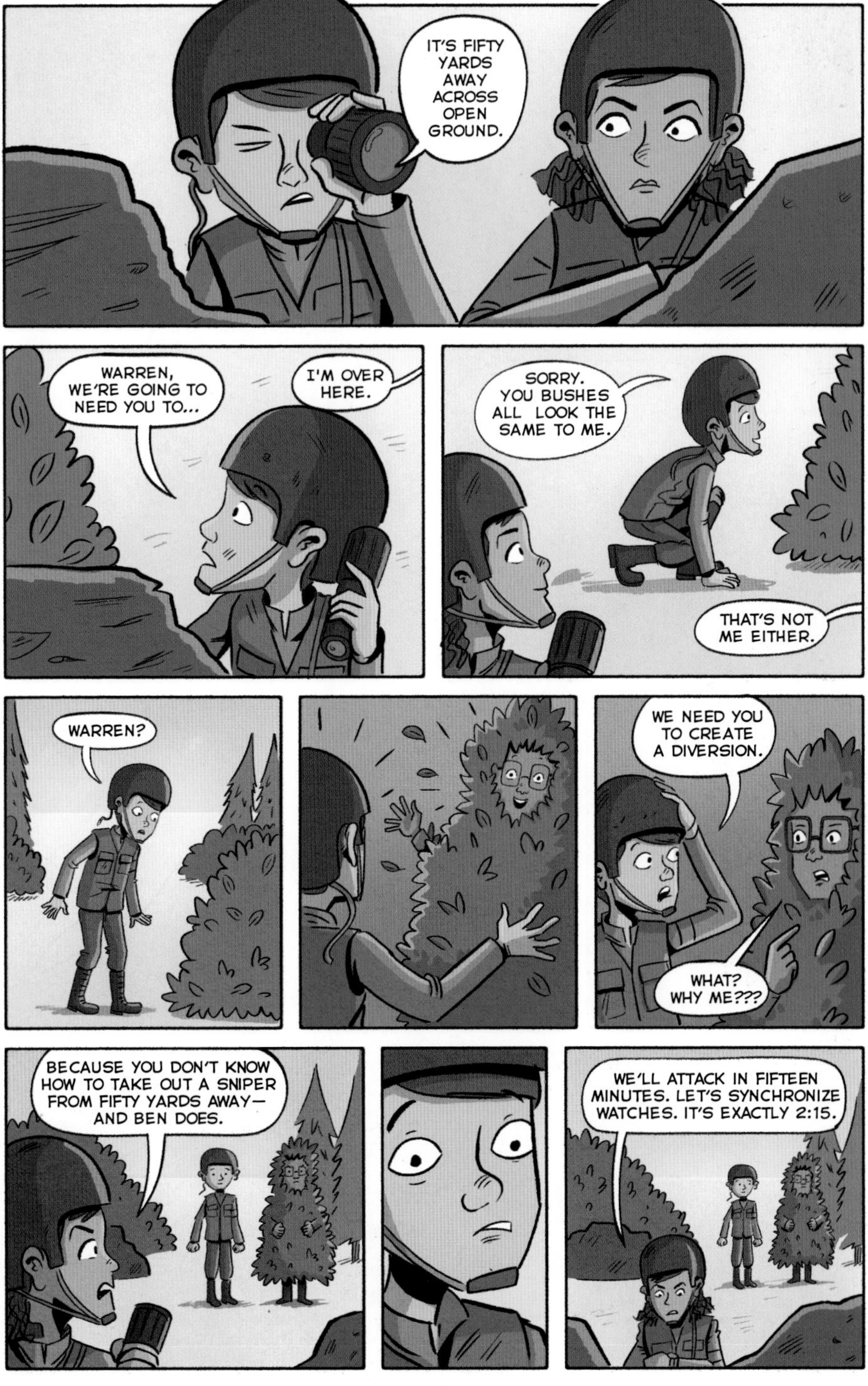
IT'S FIFTY YARDS AWAY ACROSS OPEN GROUND.
WARREN, WE'RE GOING TO NEED YOU TO...
I'M OVER HERE.
SORRY. YOU BUSHES ALL LOOK THE SAME TO ME.
THAT'S NOT ME EITHER.
WARREN?
WE NEED YOU TO CREATE A DIVERSION.
WHAT? WHY ME???
BECAUSE YOU DON'T KNOW HOW TO TAKE OUT A SNIPER FROM FIFTY YARDS AWAY— AND BEN DOES.
WE'LL ATTACK IN FIFTEEN MINUTES. LET'S SYNCHRONIZE WATCHES. IT'S EXACTLY 2:15.

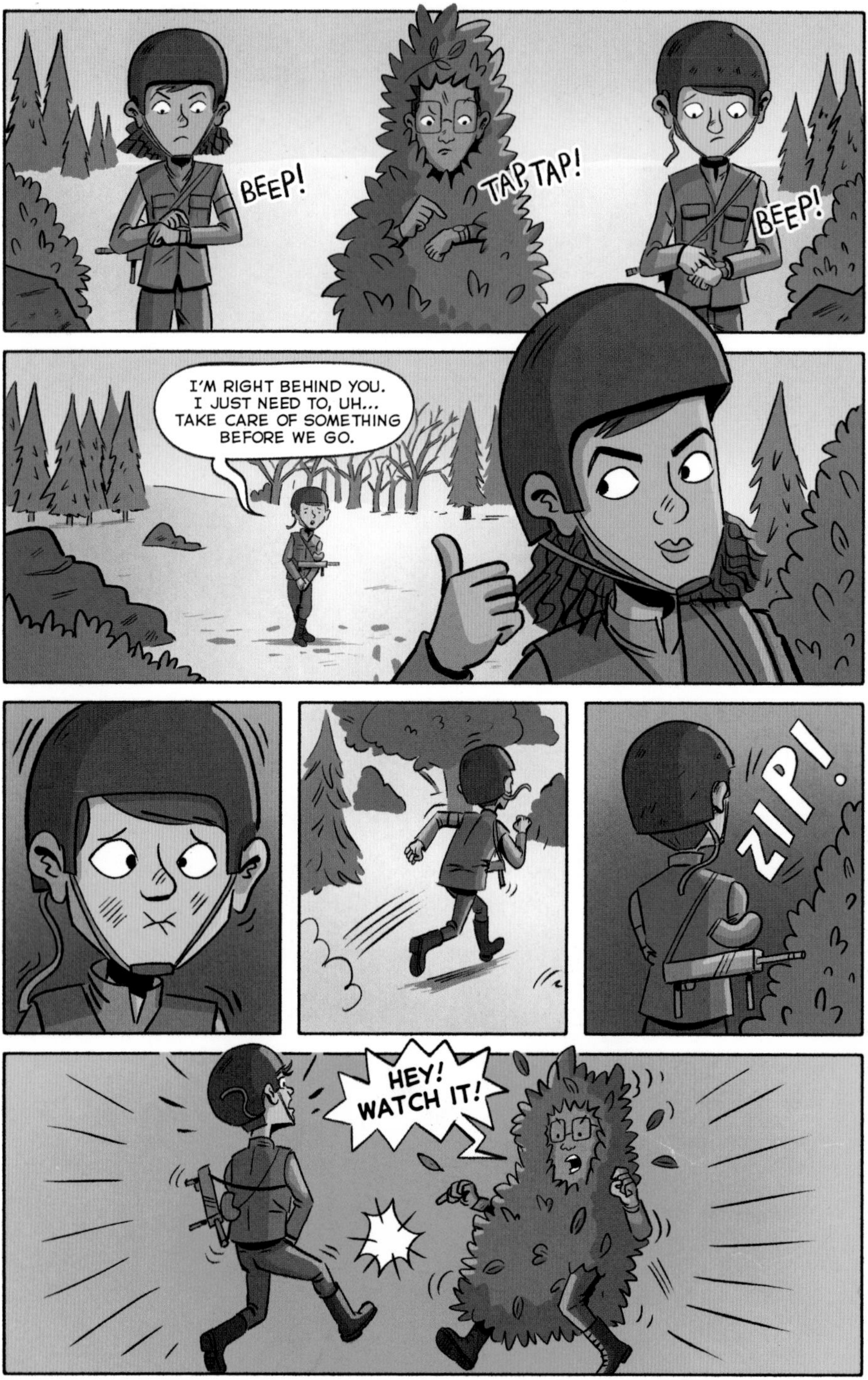
BEEP!
TAP, TAP!
BEEP!
I'M RIGHT BEHIND YOU. I JUST NEED TO, UH... TAKE CARE OF SOMETHING BEFORE WE GO.
ZIP!
HEY! WATCH IT!

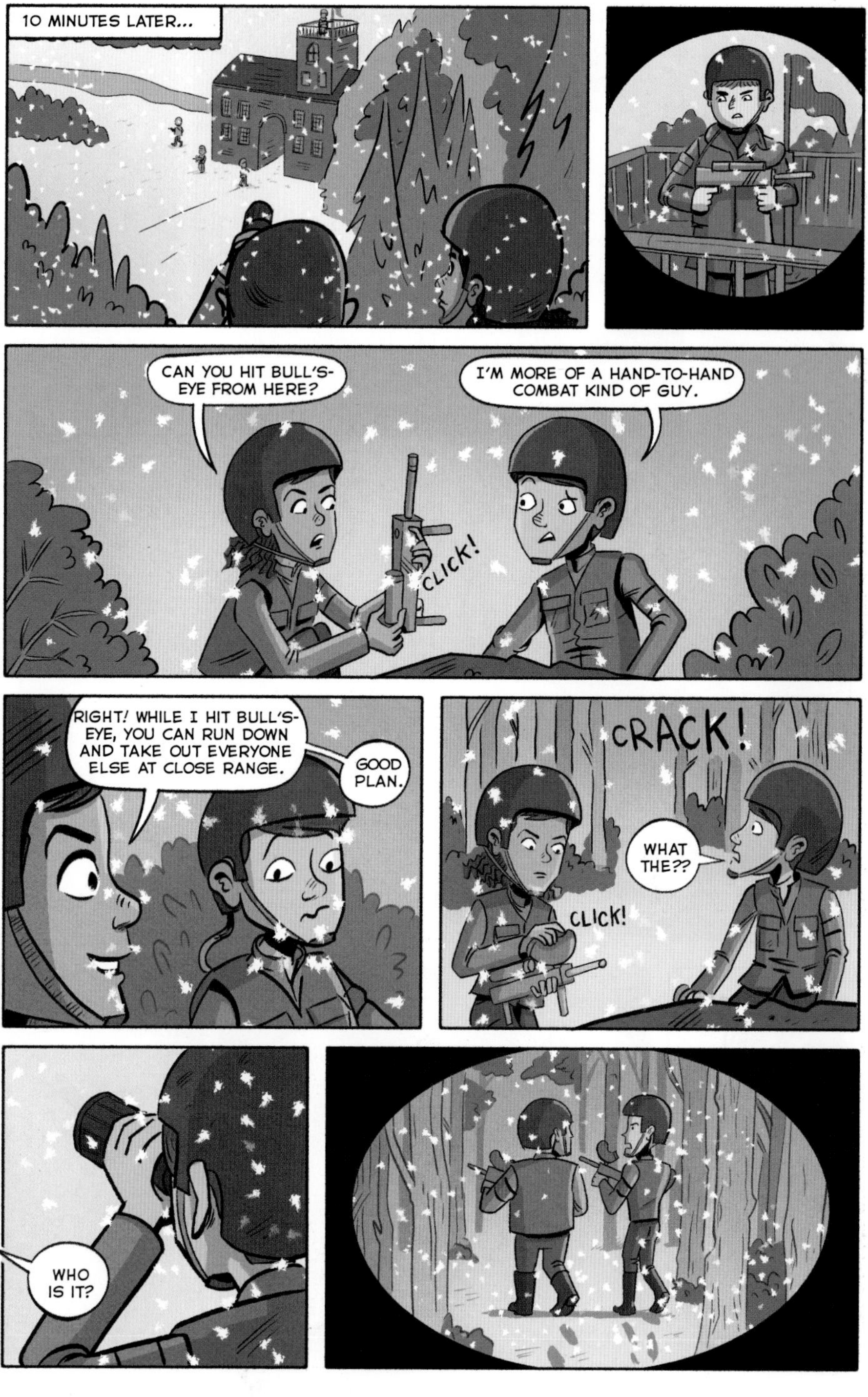
10 MINUTES LATER...
CAN YOU HIT BULL'S-EYE FROM HERE?
CLICK!
I'M MORE OF A HAND-TO-HAND COMBAT KIND OF GUY.
RIGHT! WHILE I HIT BULL'S-EYE, YOU CAN RUN DOWN AND TAKE OUT EVERYONE ELSE AT CLOSE RANGE.
GOOD PLAN.
CRACK!
WHAT THE??
CLICK!
WHO IS IT?

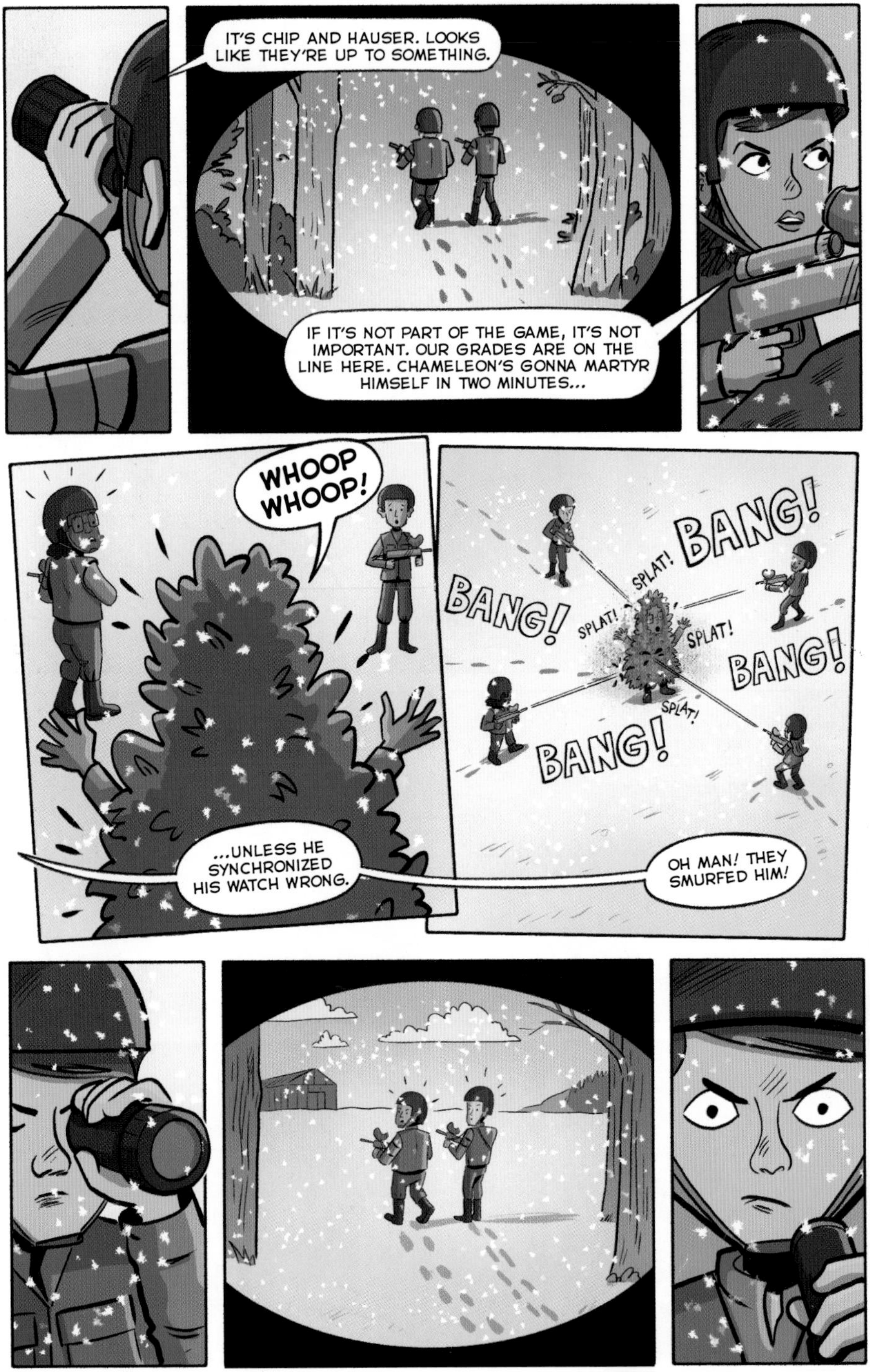
IT'S CHIP AND HAUSER. LOOKS LIKE THEY'RE UP TO SOMETHING.
IF IT'S NOT PART OF THE GAME, IT'S NOT IMPORTANT. OUR GRADES ARE ON THE LINE HERE. CHAMELEON'S GONNA MARTYR HIMSELF IN TWO MINUTES...
WHOOP WHOOP!
BANG!
SPLAT!
BANG!
SPLAT!
SPLAT!
BANG!
SPLAT!
BANG!
...UNLESS HE SYNCHRONIZED HIS WATCH WRONG.
OH MAN! THEY SMURFED HIM!

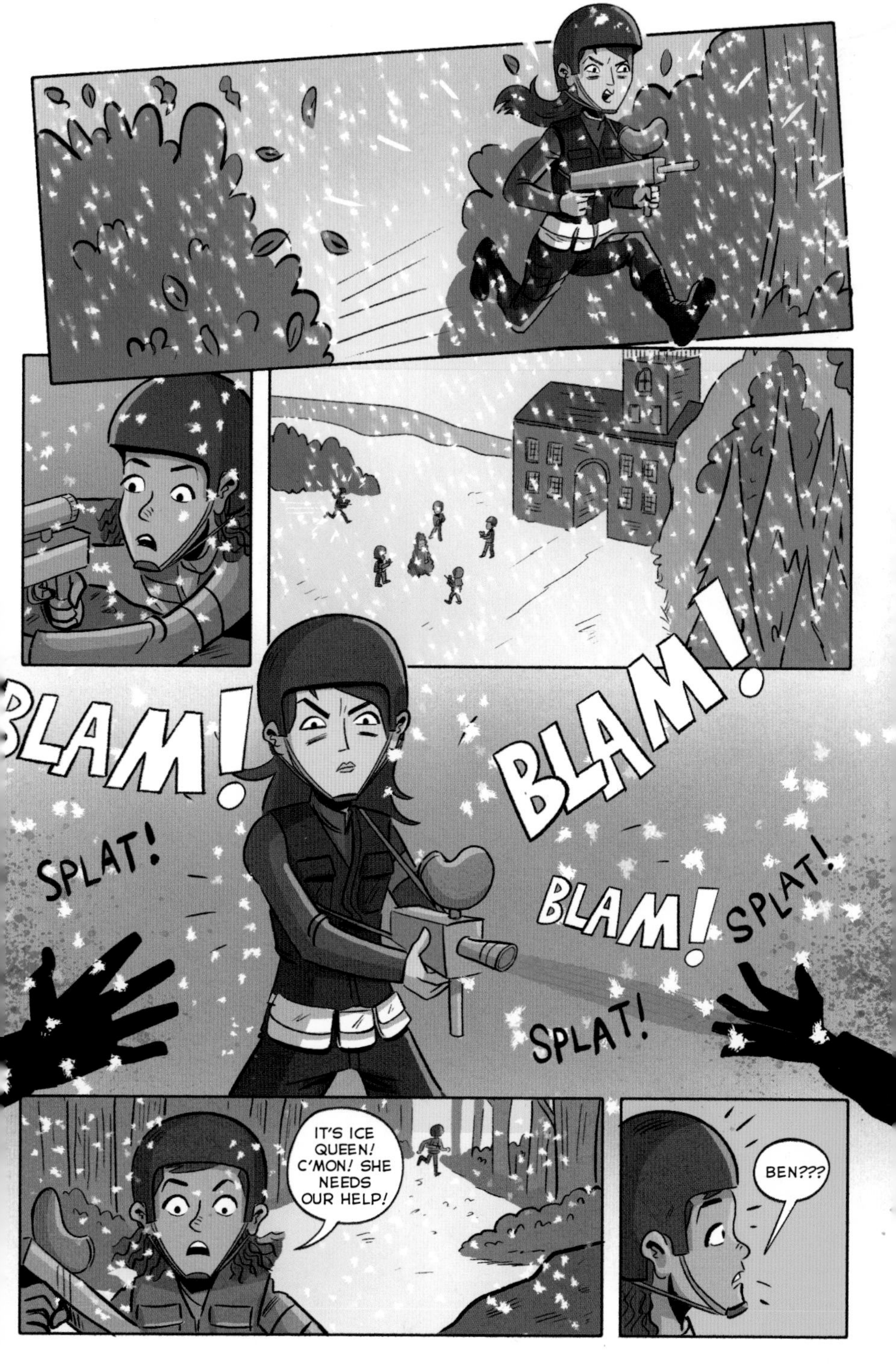
BLAM!
BLAM!
SPLAT!
BLAM!
SPLAT!
SPLAT!
IT'S ICE QUEEN! C'MON! SHE NEEDS OUR HELP!
BEN???

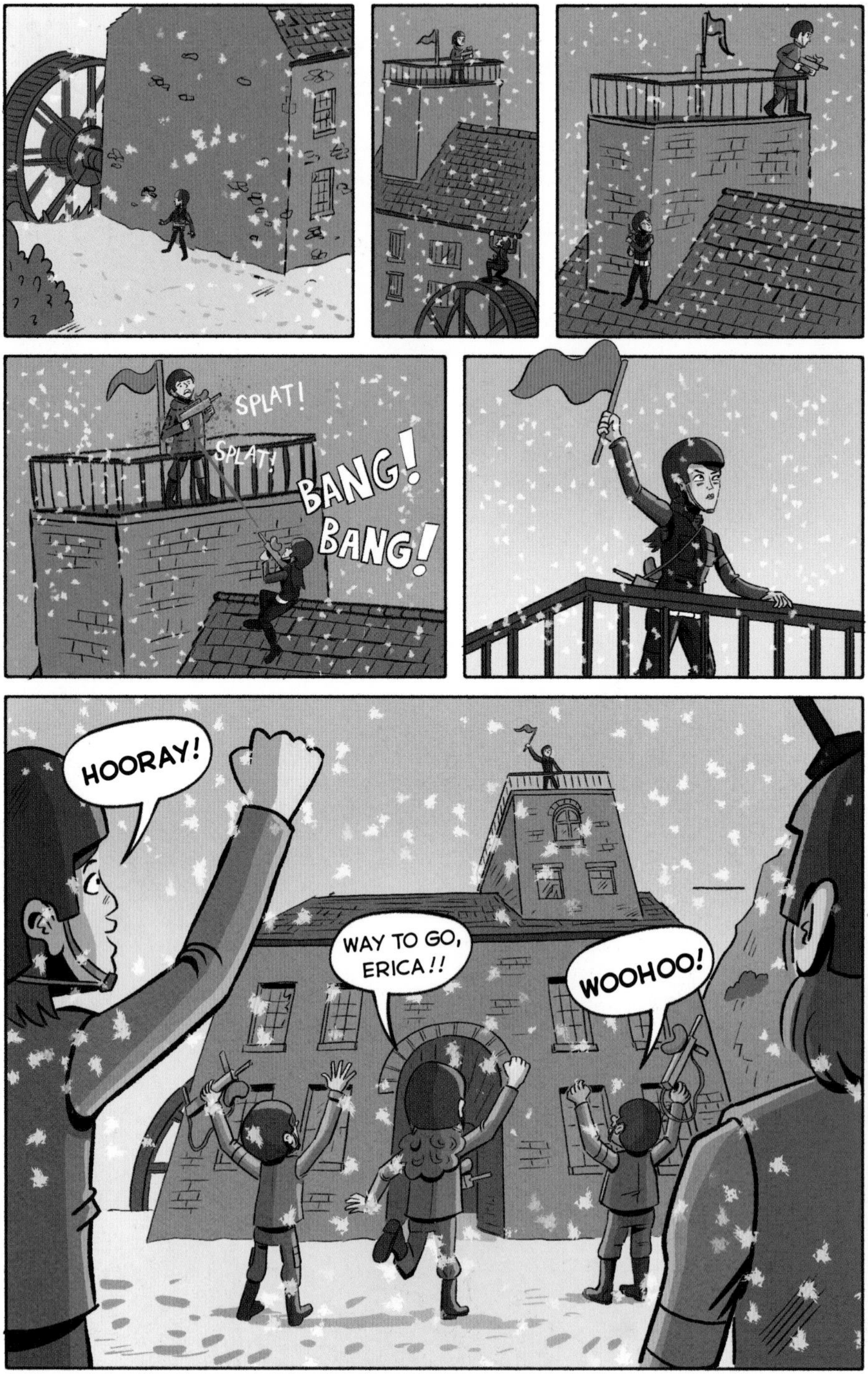
SPLAT!
SPLAT!
BANG!
BANG!
HOORAY!
WAY TO GO, ERICA!!
WOOHOO!

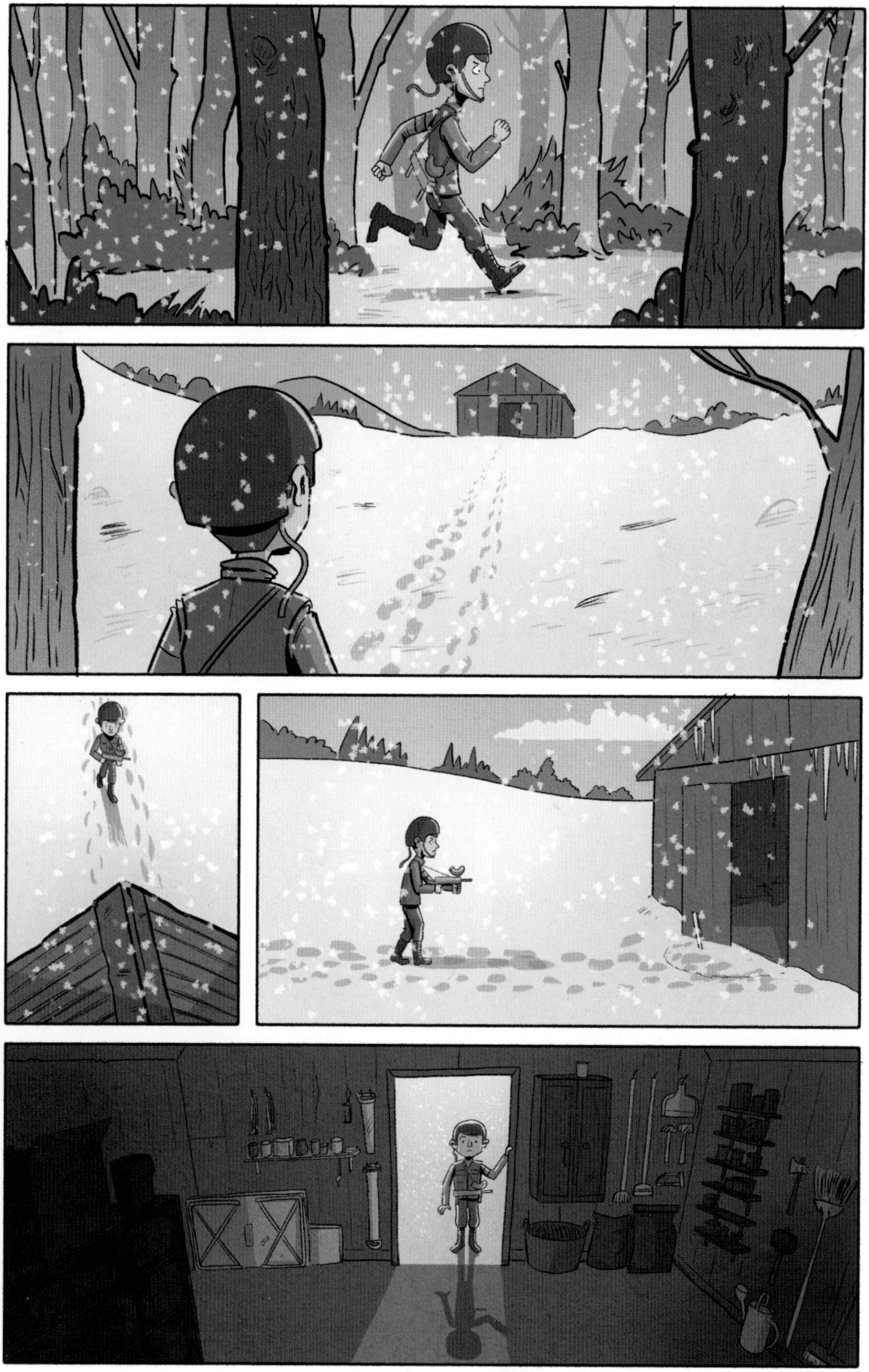

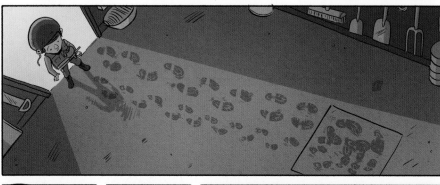

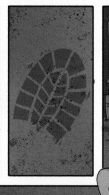

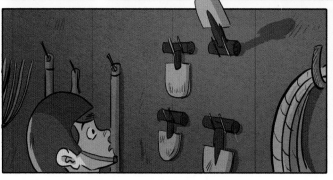

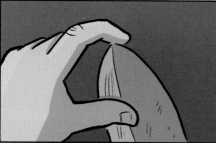

CLUNK!

HISSS

135

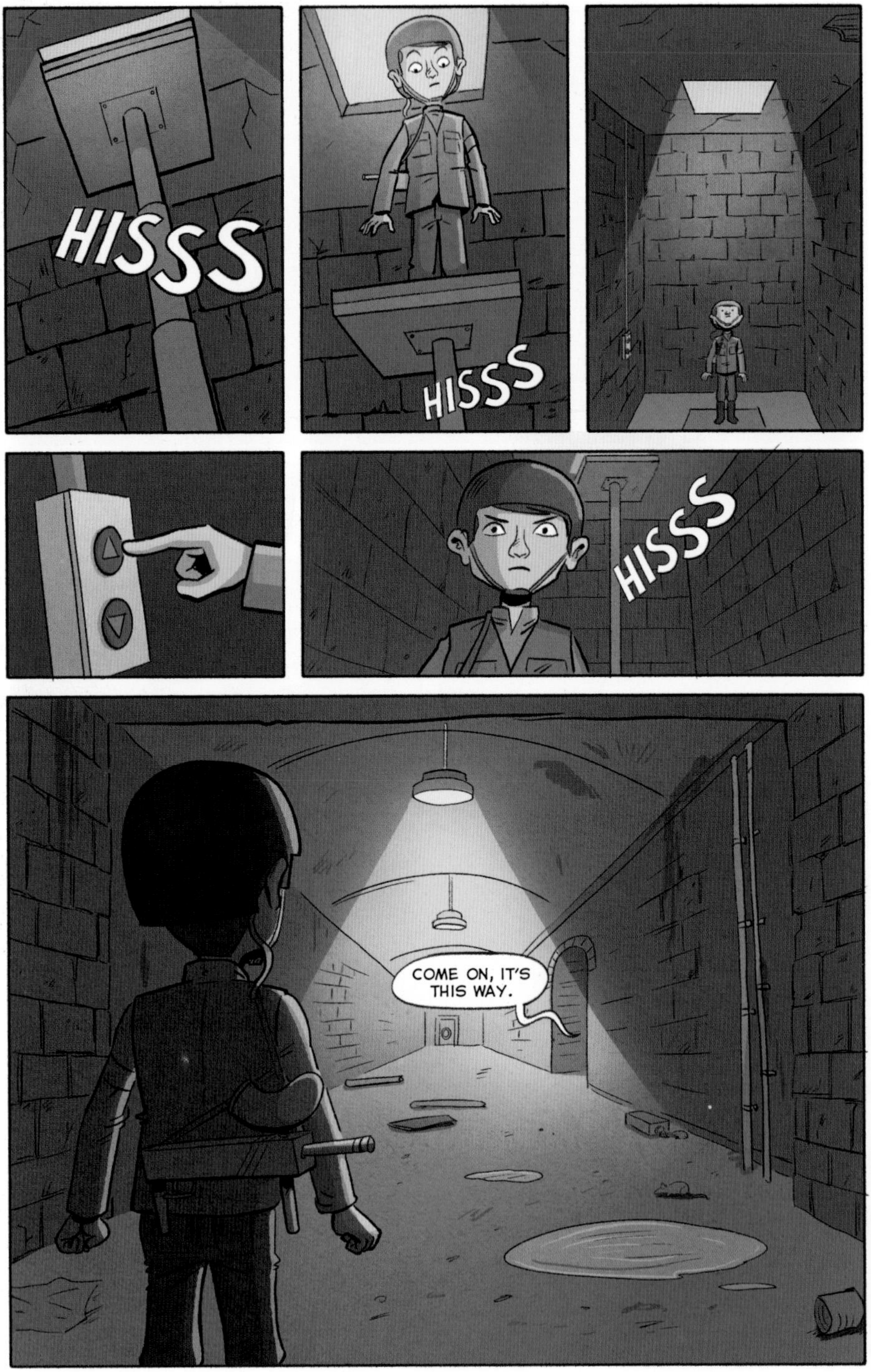
HISSS
HISSS
HISSS
COME ON, IT'S THIS WAY.

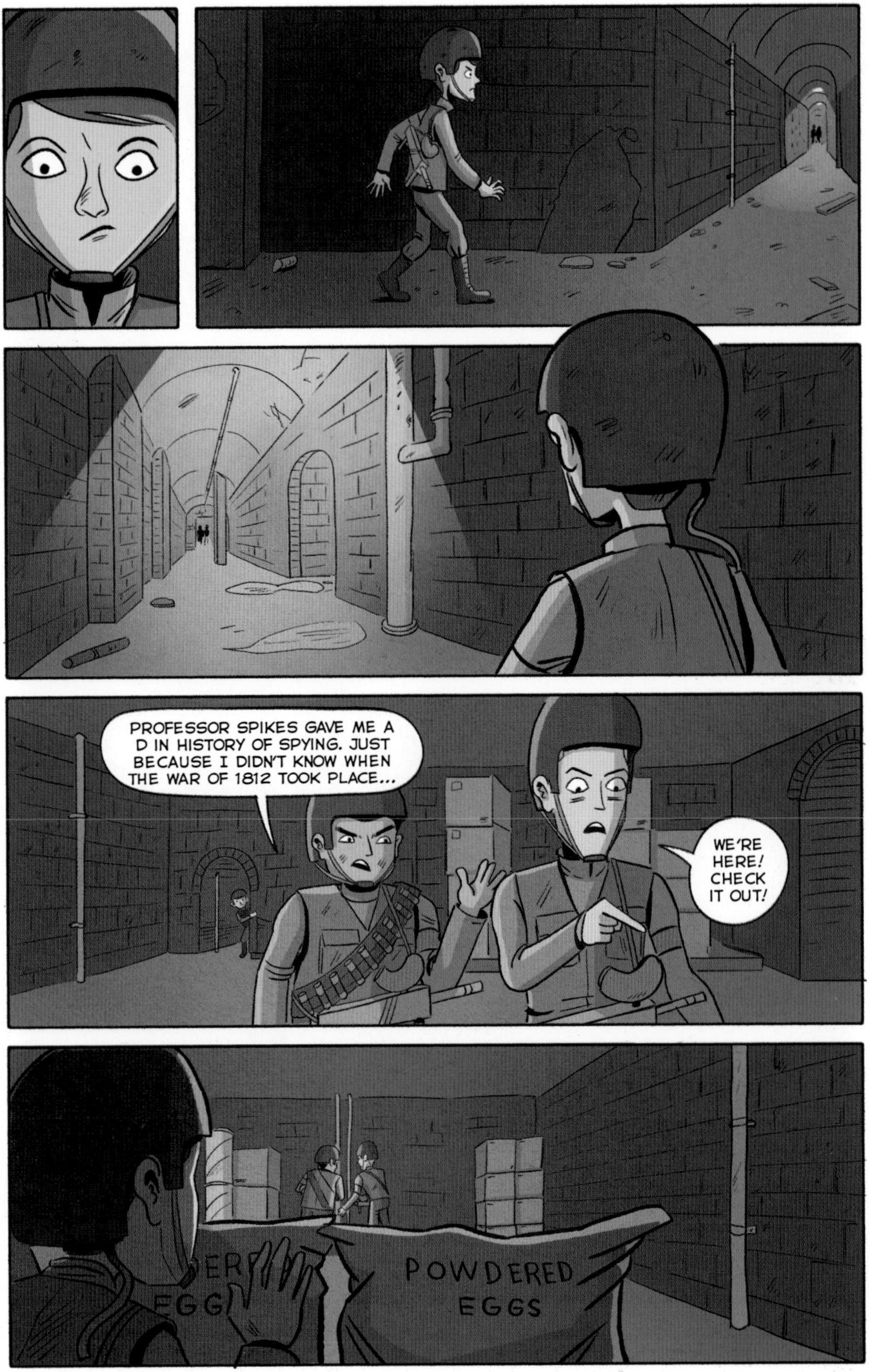
PROFESSOR SPIKES GAVE ME A D IN HISTORY OF SPYING. JUST BECAUSE I DIDN'T KNOW WHEN THE WAR OF 1812 TOOK PLACE...
WE'RE HERE! CHECK IT OUT!
POWDERED EGGS

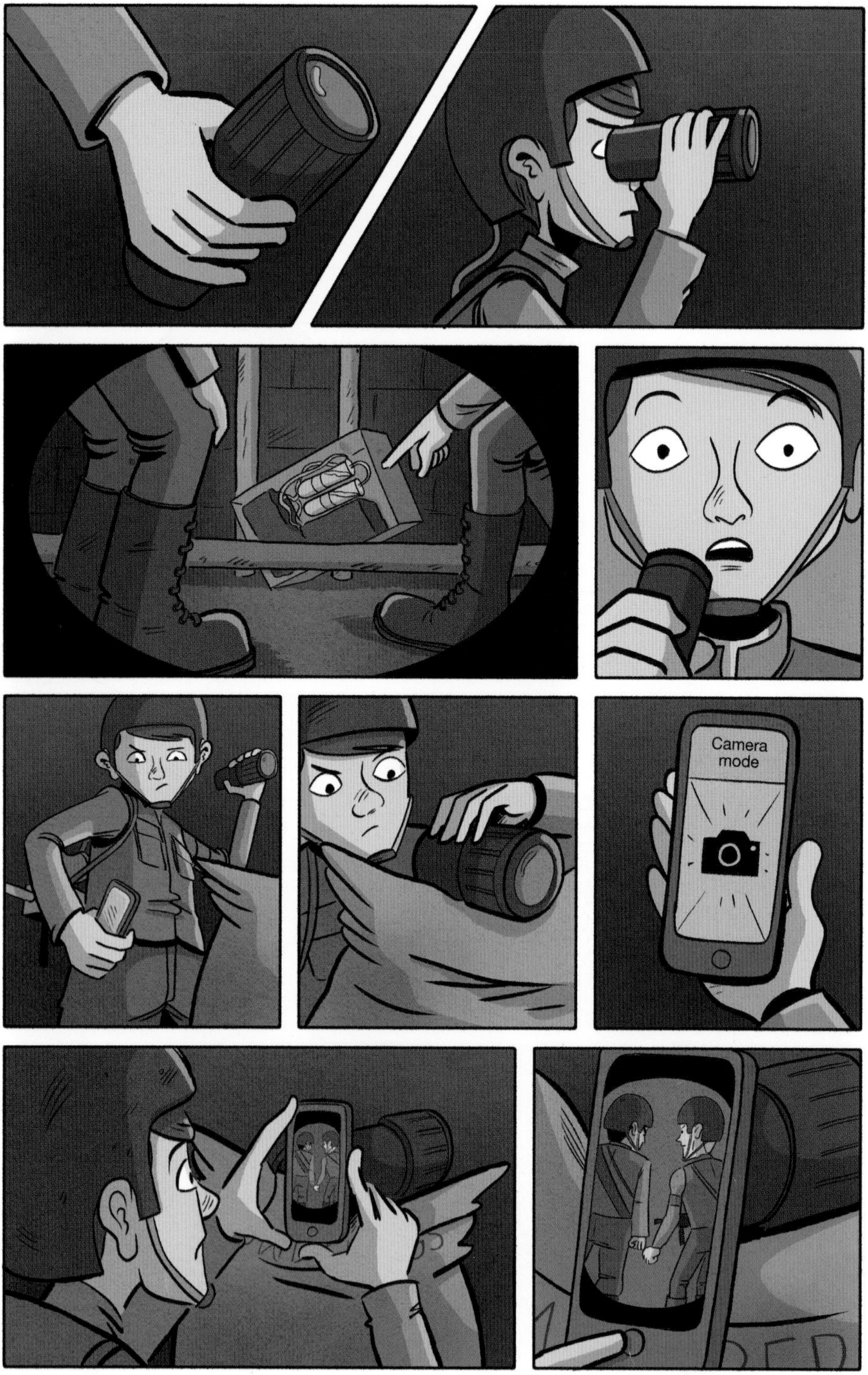
Camera
mode

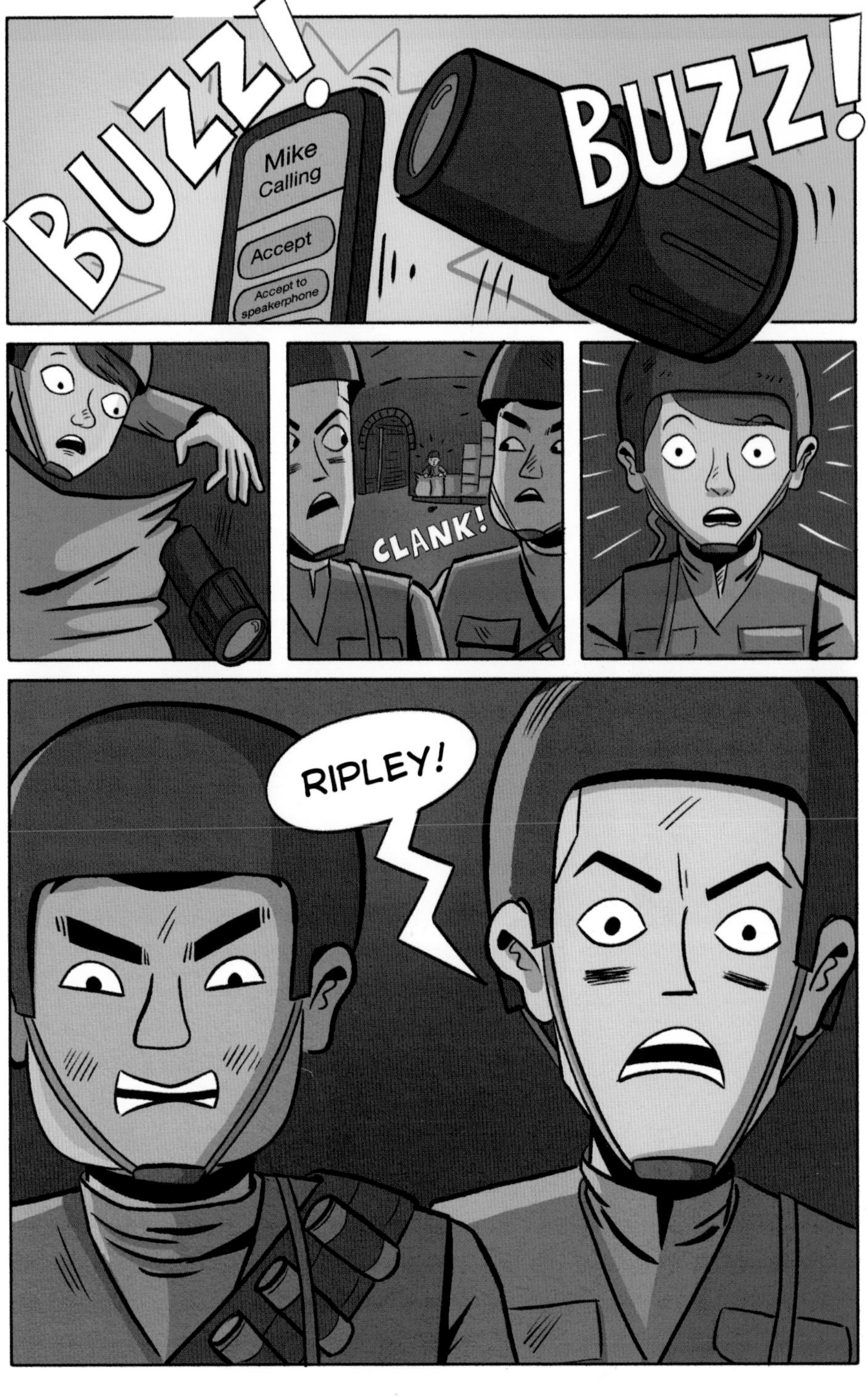
BUZZ!
Mike
Calling
Accept
Accept to
speakerphone
BUZZ!
CLANK!
RIPLEY!

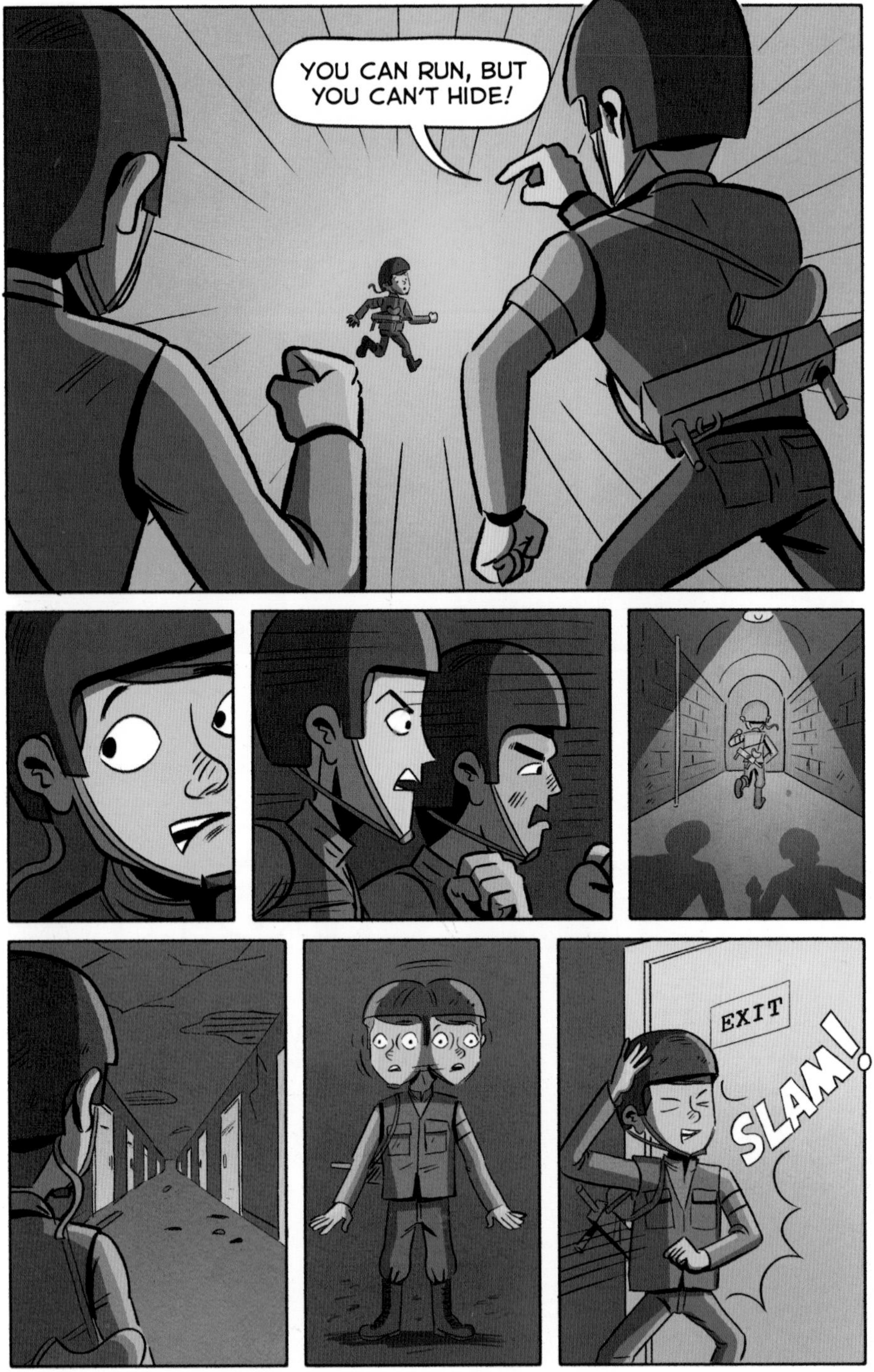
YOU CAN RUN, BUT YOU CAN'T HIDE!
EXIT
SLAM!

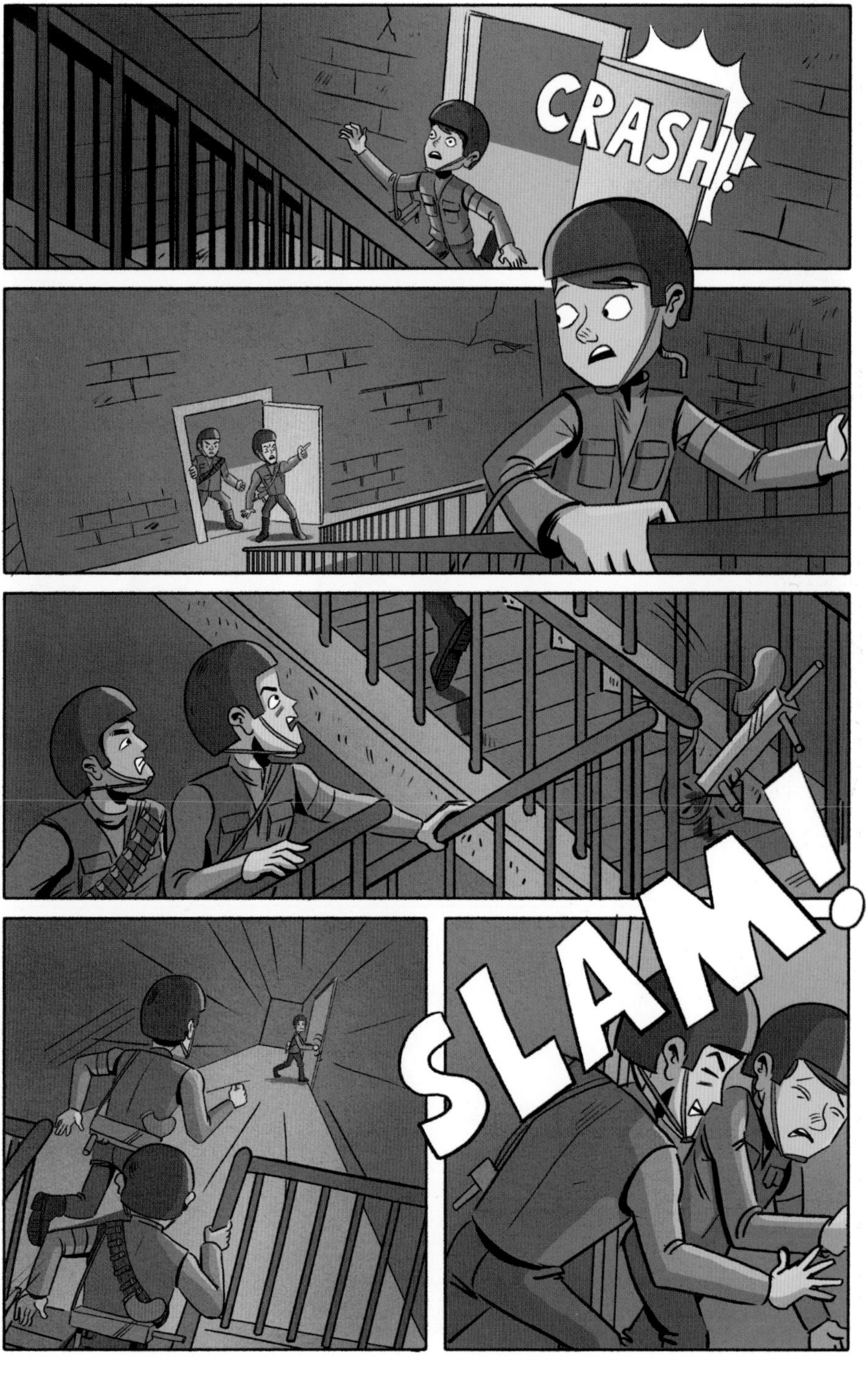
CRASH!
SLAM!

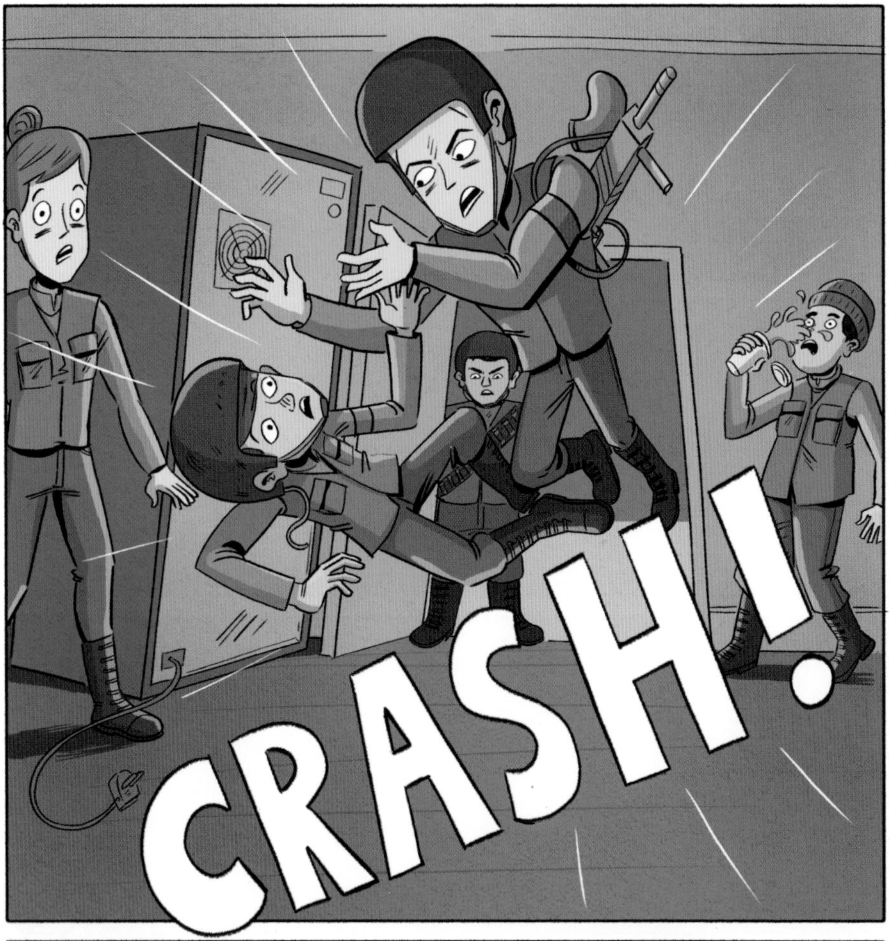
CRASH!

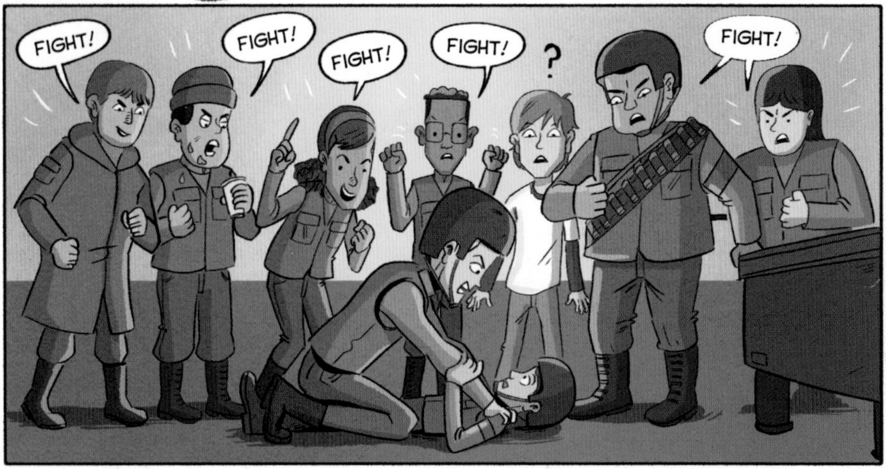
FIGHT!
FIGHT!
FIGHT!
FIGHT!
?
FIGHT!

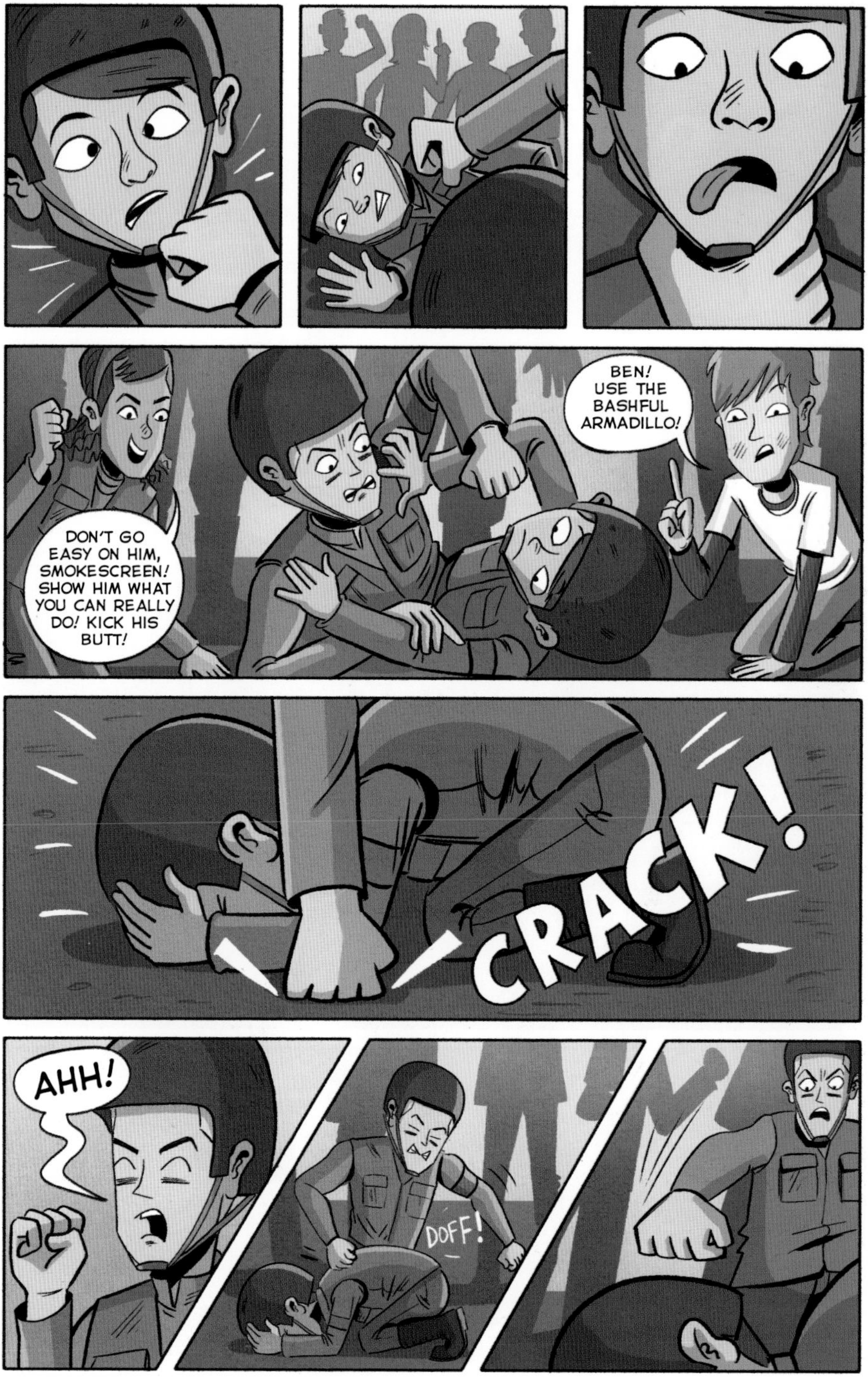
BEN!
USE THE
BASHFUL
ARMADILLO!
DON'T GO
EASY ON HIM,
SMOKESCREEN!
SHOW HIM WHAT
YOU CAN REALLY
DO! KICK HIS
BUTT!
CRACK!
AHH!
DOFF!

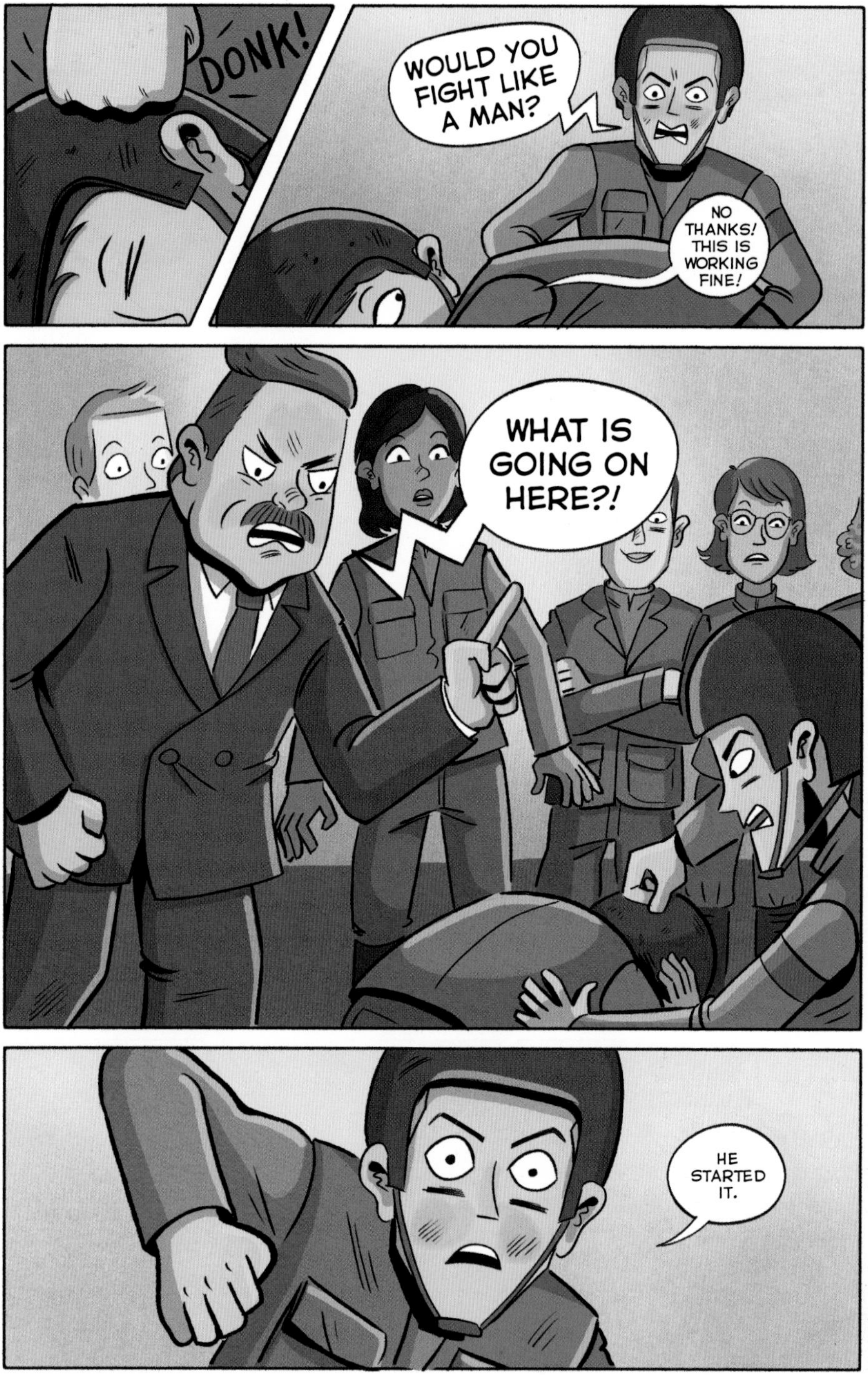
DONK!
WOULD YOU FIGHT LIKE A MAN?
NO THANKS! THIS IS WORKING FINE!
WHAT IS GOING ON HERE?!
HE STARTED IT.

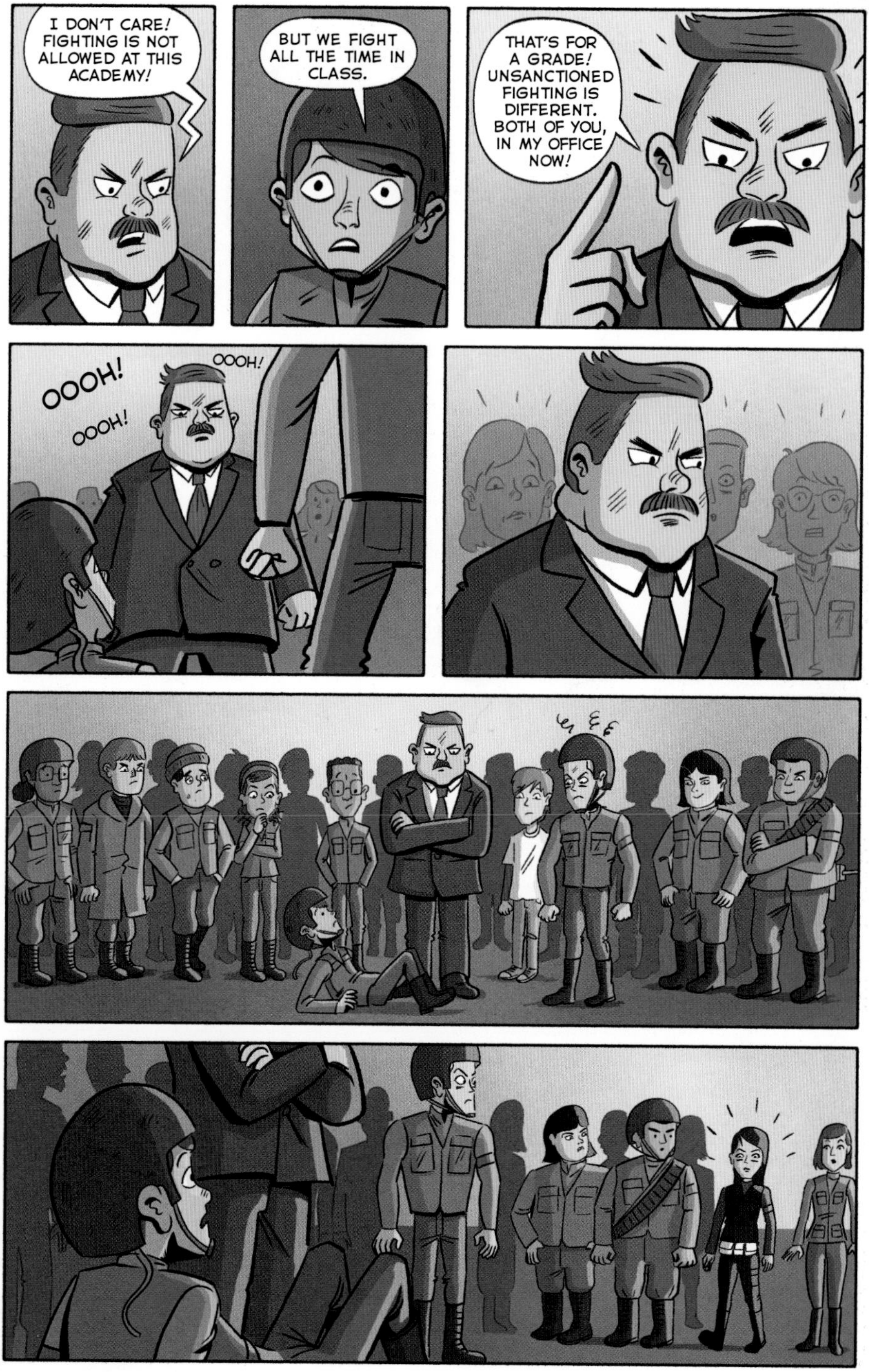
I DON'T CARE! FIGHTING IS NOT ALLOWED AT THIS ACADEMY!
BUT WE FIGHT ALL THE TIME IN CLASS.
THAT'S FOR A GRADE! UNSANCTIONED FIGHTING IS DIFFERENT. BOTH OF YOU, IN MY OFFICE NOW!
OOOH!
OOOH!
OOOH!

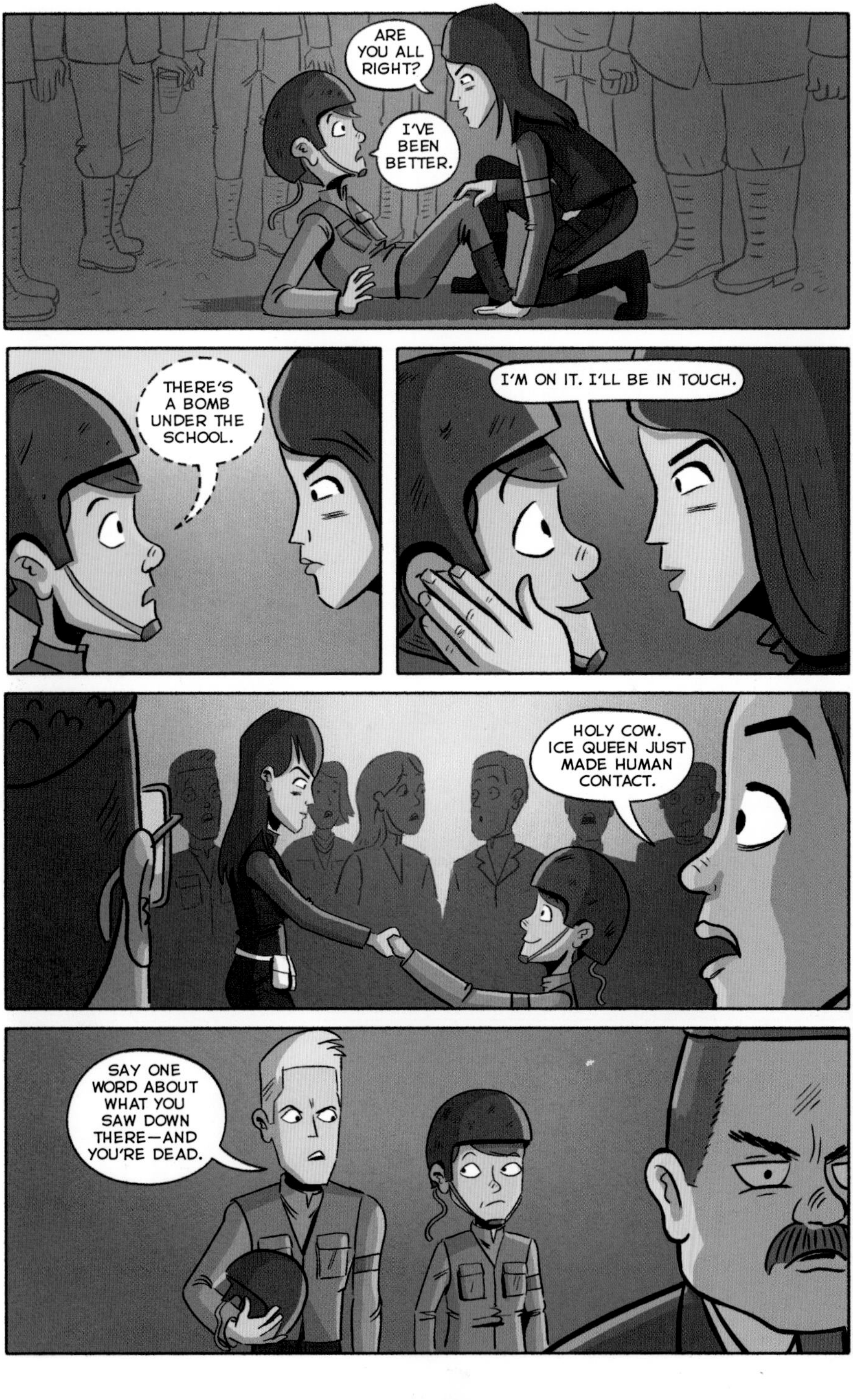
ARE YOU ALL RIGHT?
I'VE BEEN BETTER.
THERE'S A BOMB UNDER THE SCHOOL.
I'M ON IT. I'LL BE IN TOUCH.
HOLY COW. ICE QUEEN JUST MADE HUMAN CONTACT.
SAY ONE WORD ABOUT WHAT YOU SAW DOWN THERE—AND YOU'RE DEAD.

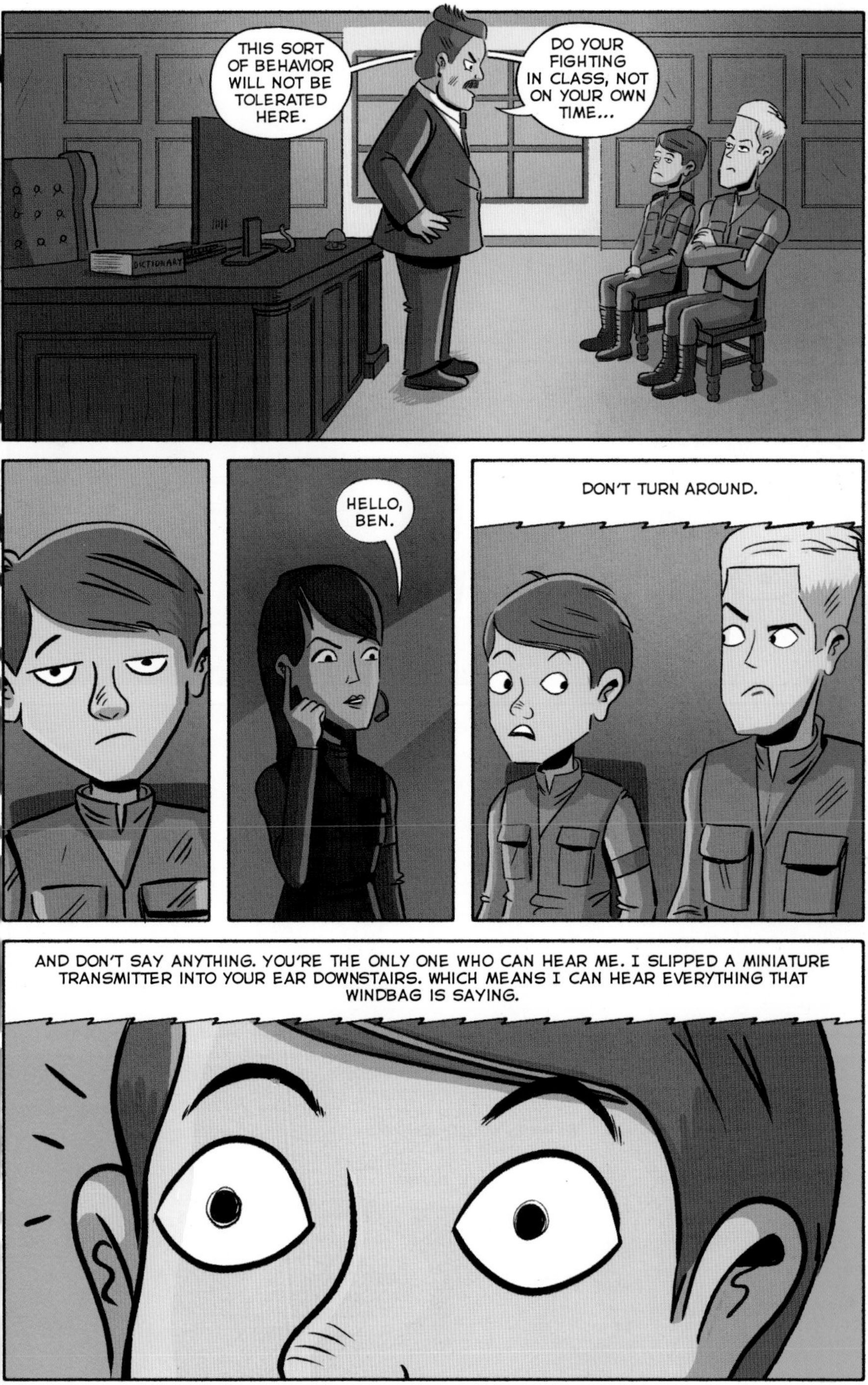
THIS SORT OF BEHAVIOR WILL NOT BE TOLERATED HERE.
DO YOUR FIGHTING IN CLASS, NOT ON YOUR OWN TIME...
DICTIONARY
HELLO, BEN.
DON'T TURN AROUND.
AND DON'T SAY ANYTHING. YOU'RE THE ONLY ONE WHO CAN HEAR ME. I SLIPPED A MINIATURE TRANSMITTER INTO YOUR EAR DOWNSTAIRS. WHICH MEANS I CAN HEAR EVERYTHING THAT WINDBAG IS SAYING.

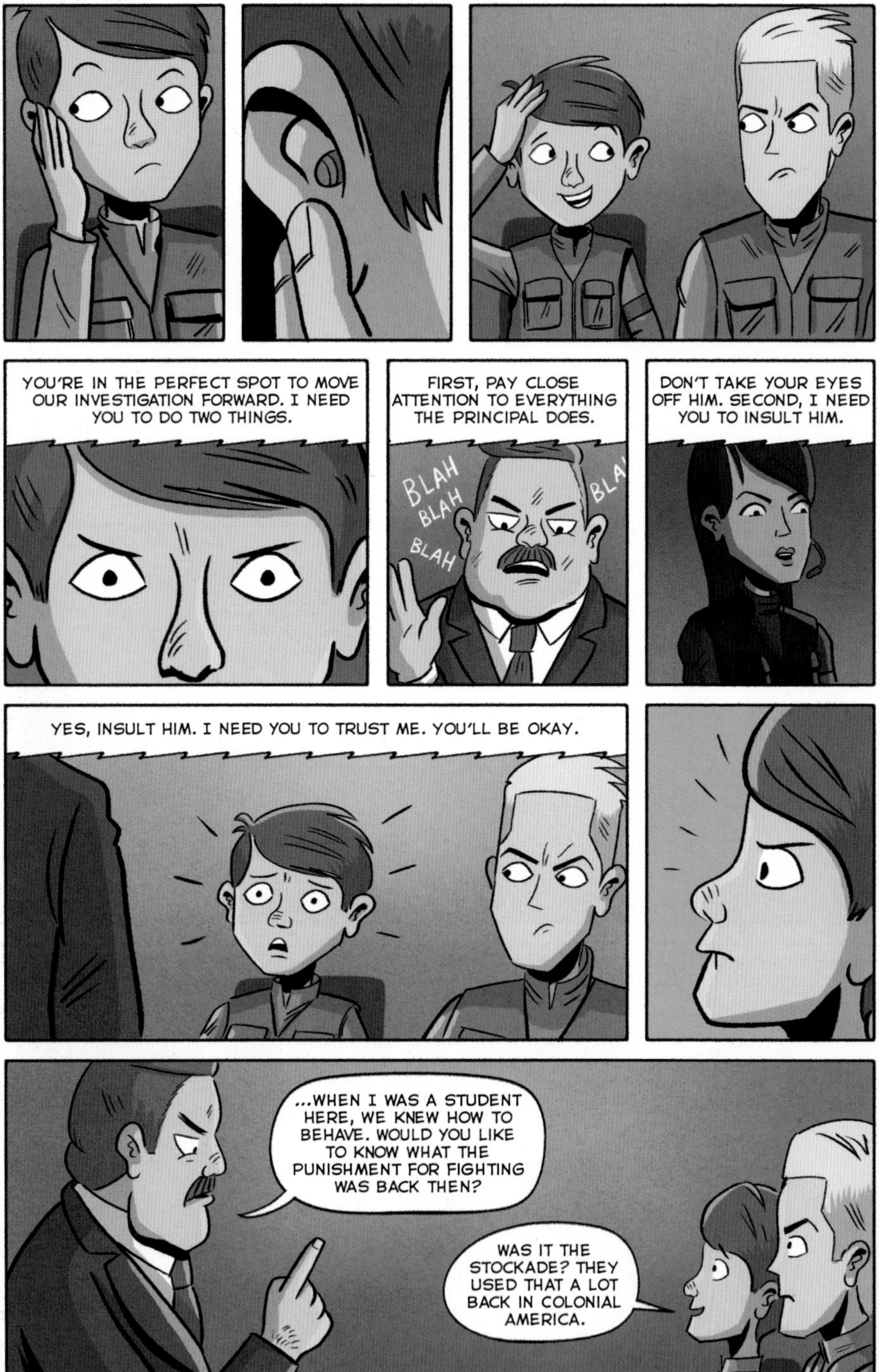
YOU'RE IN THE PERFECT SPOT TO MOVE OUR INVESTIGATION FORWARD. I NEED YOU TO DO TWO THINGS.
FIRST, PAY CLOSE ATTENTION TO EVERYTHING THE PRINCIPAL DOES.
BLAH BLAH BLAH
DON'T TAKE YOUR EYES OFF HIM. SECOND, I NEED YOU TO INSULT HIM.
YES, INSULT HIM. I NEED YOU TO TRUST ME. YOU'LL BE OKAY.
...WHEN I WAS A STUDENT HERE, WE KNEW HOW TO BEHAVE. WOULD YOU LIKE TO KNOW WHAT THE PUNISHMENT FOR FIGHTING WAS BACK THEN?
WAS IT THE STOCKADE? THEY USED THAT A LOT BACK IN COLONIAL AMERICA.

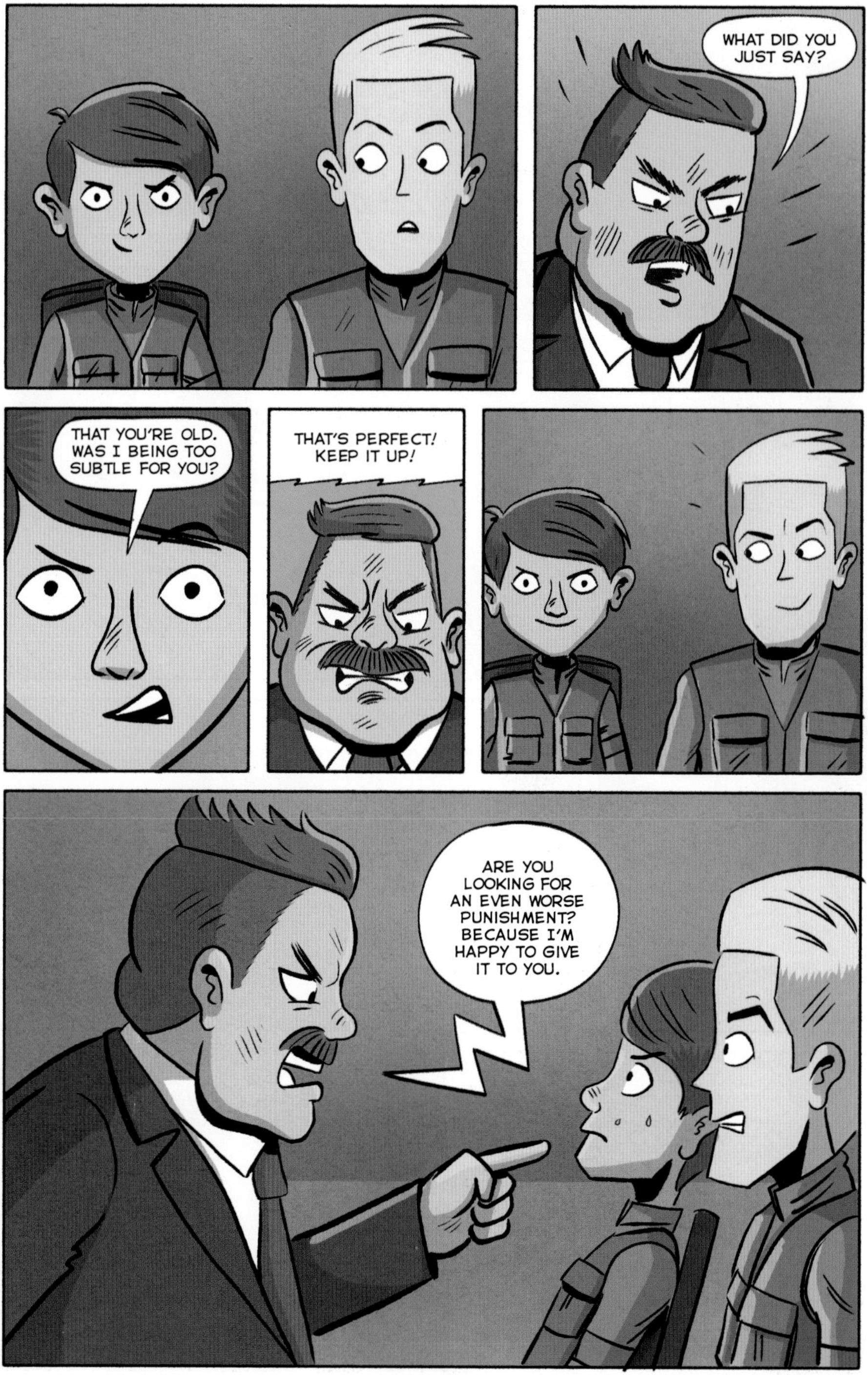
WHAT DID YOU JUST SAY?
THAT YOU'RE OLD. WAS I BEING TOO SUBTLE FOR YOU?
THAT'S PERFECT! KEEP IT UP!
ARE YOU LOOKING FOR AN EVEN WORSE PUNISHMENT? BECAUSE I'M HAPPY TO GIVE IT TO YOU.

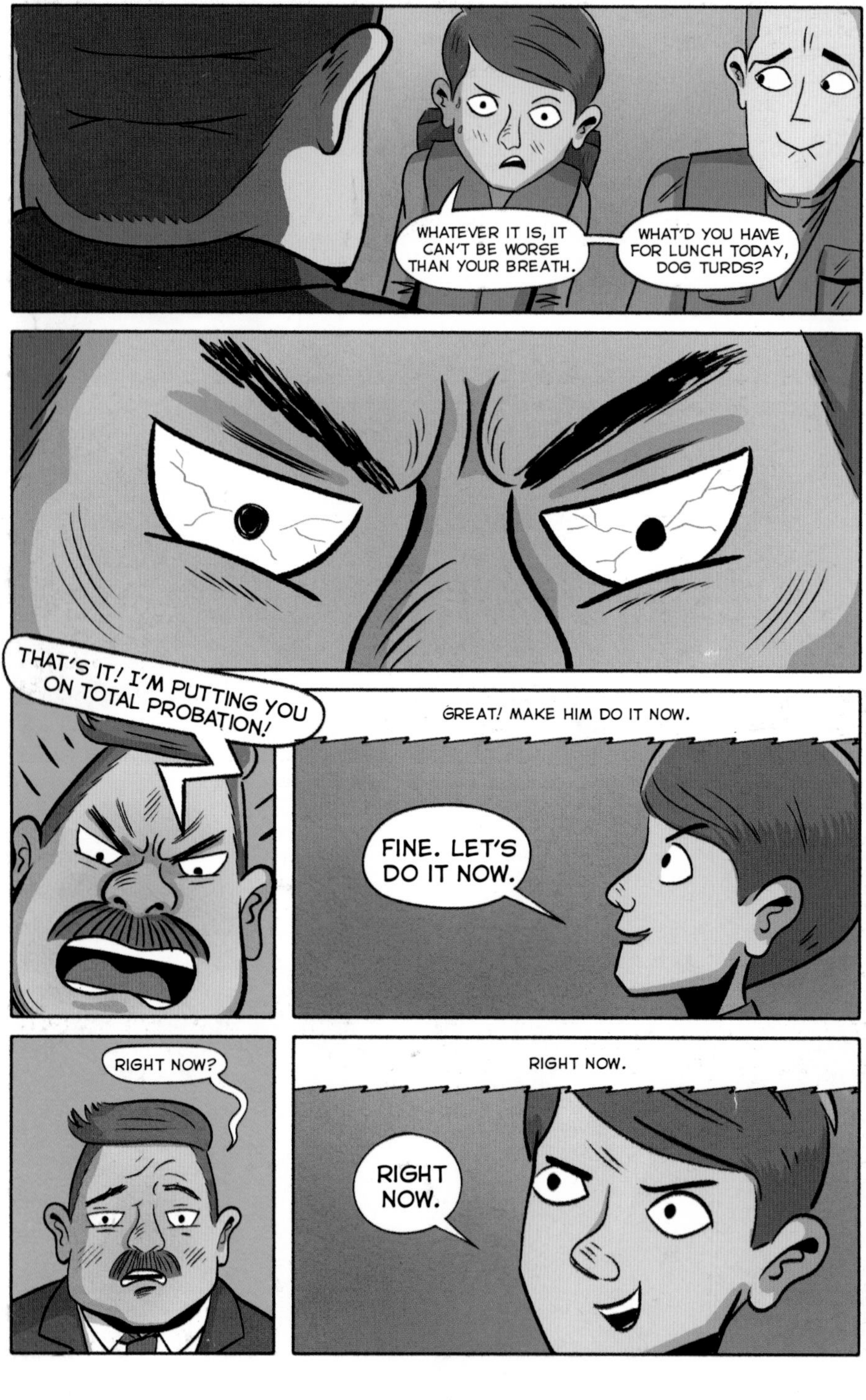
WHATEVER IT IS, IT CAN'T BE WORSE THAN YOUR BREATH.
WHAT'D YOU HAVE FOR LUNCH TODAY, DOG TURDS?
THAT'S IT! I'M PUTTING YOU ON TOTAL PROBATION!
GREAT! MAKE HIM DO IT NOW.
FINE. LET'S DO IT NOW.
RIGHT NOW?
RIGHT NOW.
RIGHT NOW.

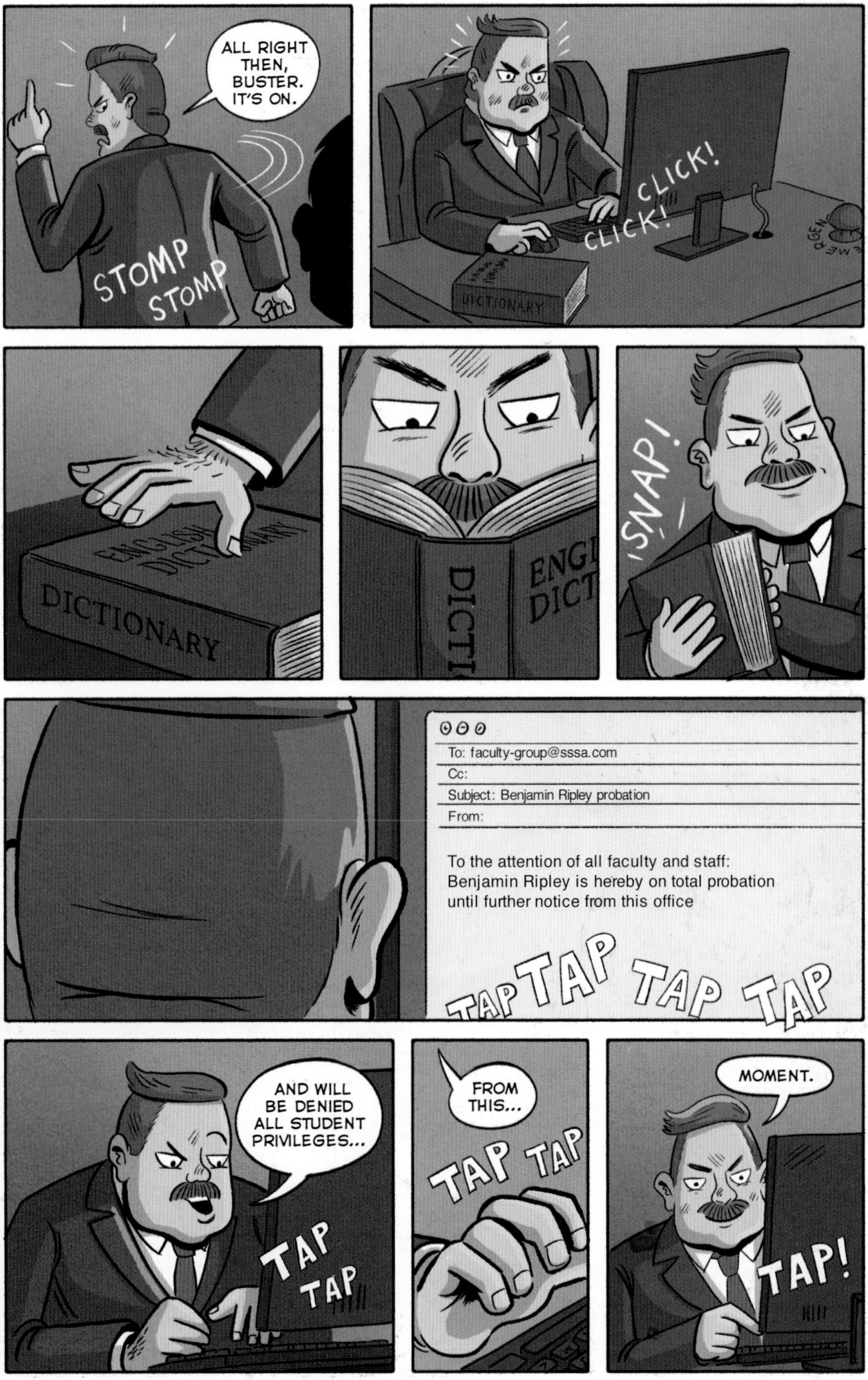
ALL RIGHT THEN, BUSTER. IT'S ON.
STOMP STOMP
CLICK! CLICK!
DICTIONARY
ENGLISH DICTIONARY
DICTIONARY
SNAP!
To: faculty-group@sssa.com
Cc:
Subject: Benjamin Ripley probation
From:
To the attention of all faculty and staff:
Benjamin Ripley is hereby on total probation
until further notice from this office
TAP TAP TAP TAP
AND WILL BE DENIED ALL STUDENT PRIVILEGES...
TAP TAP
FROM THIS...
TAP TAP
MOMENT.
TAP!

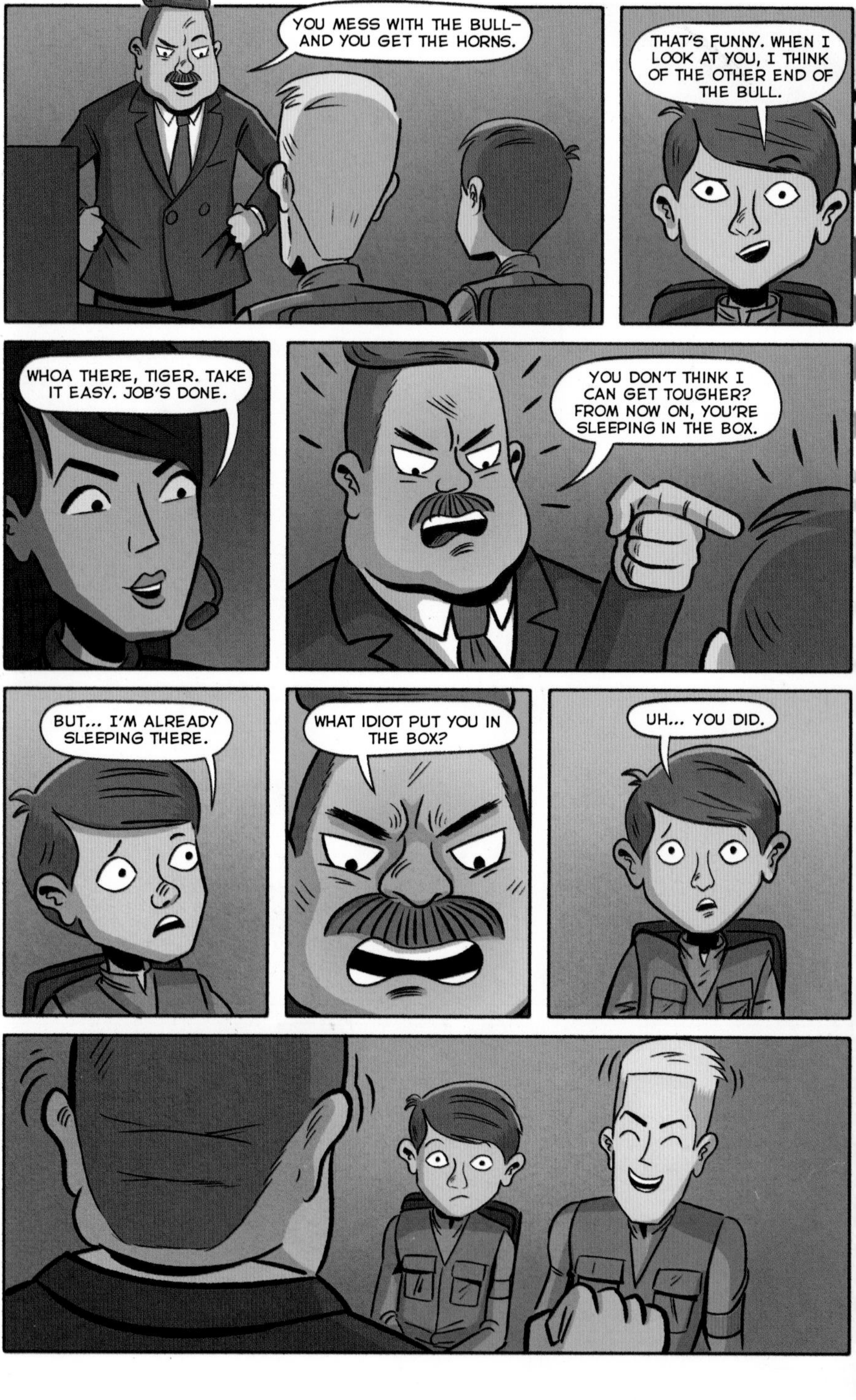
YOU MESS WITH THE BULL– AND YOU GET THE HORNS.
THAT'S FUNNY. WHEN I LOOK AT YOU, I THINK OF THE OTHER END OF THE BULL.
WHOA THERE, TIGER. TAKE IT EASY. JOB'S DONE.
YOU DON'T THINK I CAN GET TOUGHER? FROM NOW ON, YOU'RE SLEEPING IN THE BOX.
BUT... I'M ALREADY SLEEPING THERE.
WHAT IDIOT PUT YOU IN THE BOX?
UH... YOU DID.

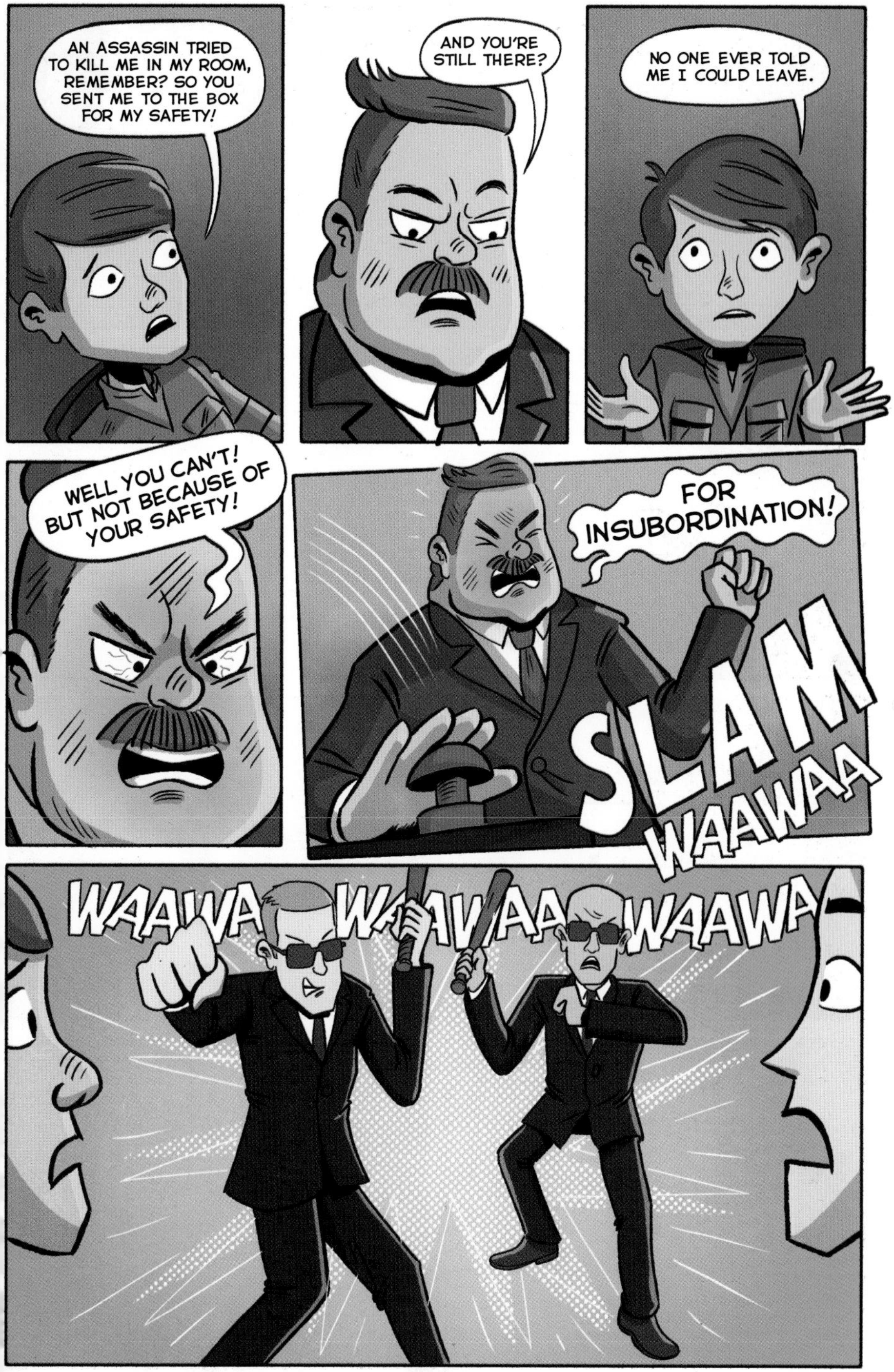
AN ASSASSIN TRIED TO KILL ME IN MY ROOM, REMEMBER? SO YOU SENT ME TO THE BOX FOR MY SAFETY!
AND YOU'RE STILL THERE?
NO ONE EVER TOLD ME I COULD LEAVE.
WELL YOU CAN'T! BUT NOT BECAUSE OF YOUR SAFETY!
FOR INSUBORDINATION!
SLAM
WAAWAA
WAAWA
WAAWAA
WAAWA

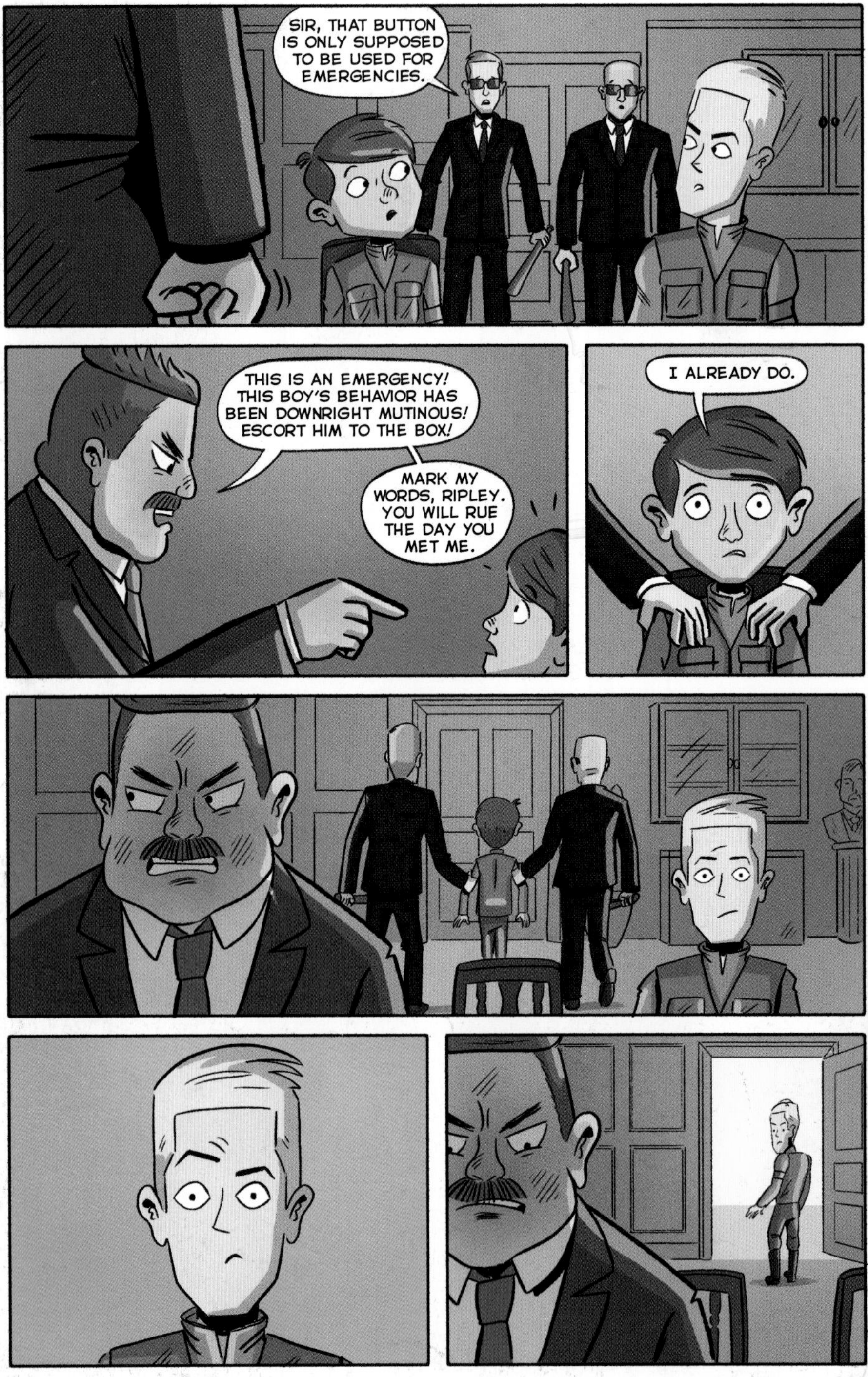
SIR, THAT BUTTON IS ONLY SUPPOSED TO BE USED FOR EMERGENCIES.
THIS IS AN EMERGENCY! THIS BOY'S BEHAVIOR HAS BEEN DOWNRIGHT MUTINOUS! ESCORT HIM TO THE BOX!
MARK MY WORDS, RIPLEY. YOU WILL RUE THE DAY YOU MET ME.
I ALREADY DO.

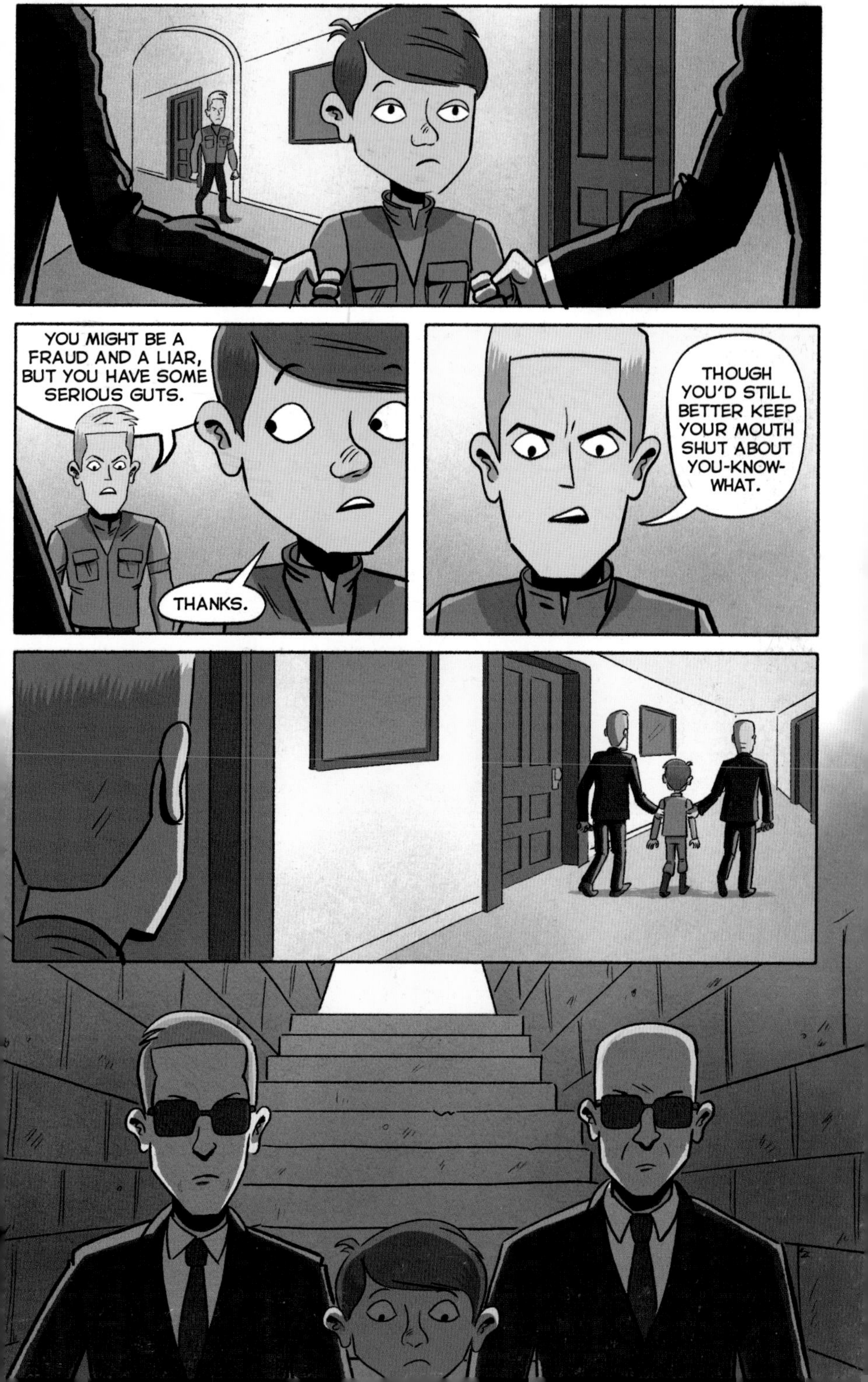
YOU MIGHT BE A FRAUD AND A LIAR, BUT YOU HAVE SOME SERIOUS GUTS.
THANKS.
THOUGH YOU'D STILL BETTER KEEP YOUR MOUTH SHUT ABOUT YOU-KNOW-WHAT.

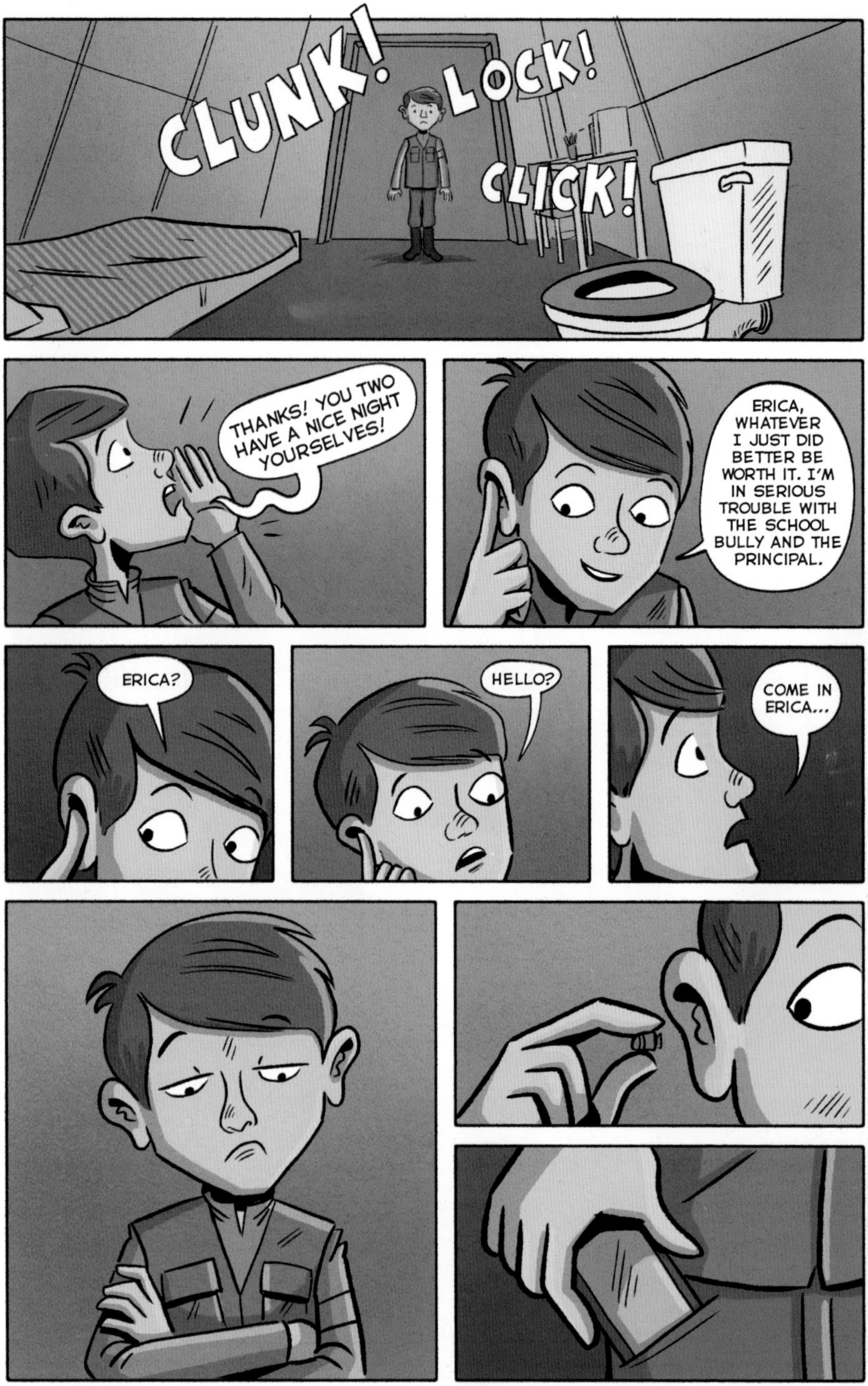
CLUNK!
LOCK!
CLICK!
THANKS! YOU TWO HAVE A NICE NIGHT YOURSELVES!
ERICA, WHATEVER I JUST DID BETTER BE WORTH IT. I'M IN SERIOUS TROUBLE WITH THE SCHOOL BULLY AND THE PRINCIPAL.
ERICA?
HELLO?
COME IN ERICA...

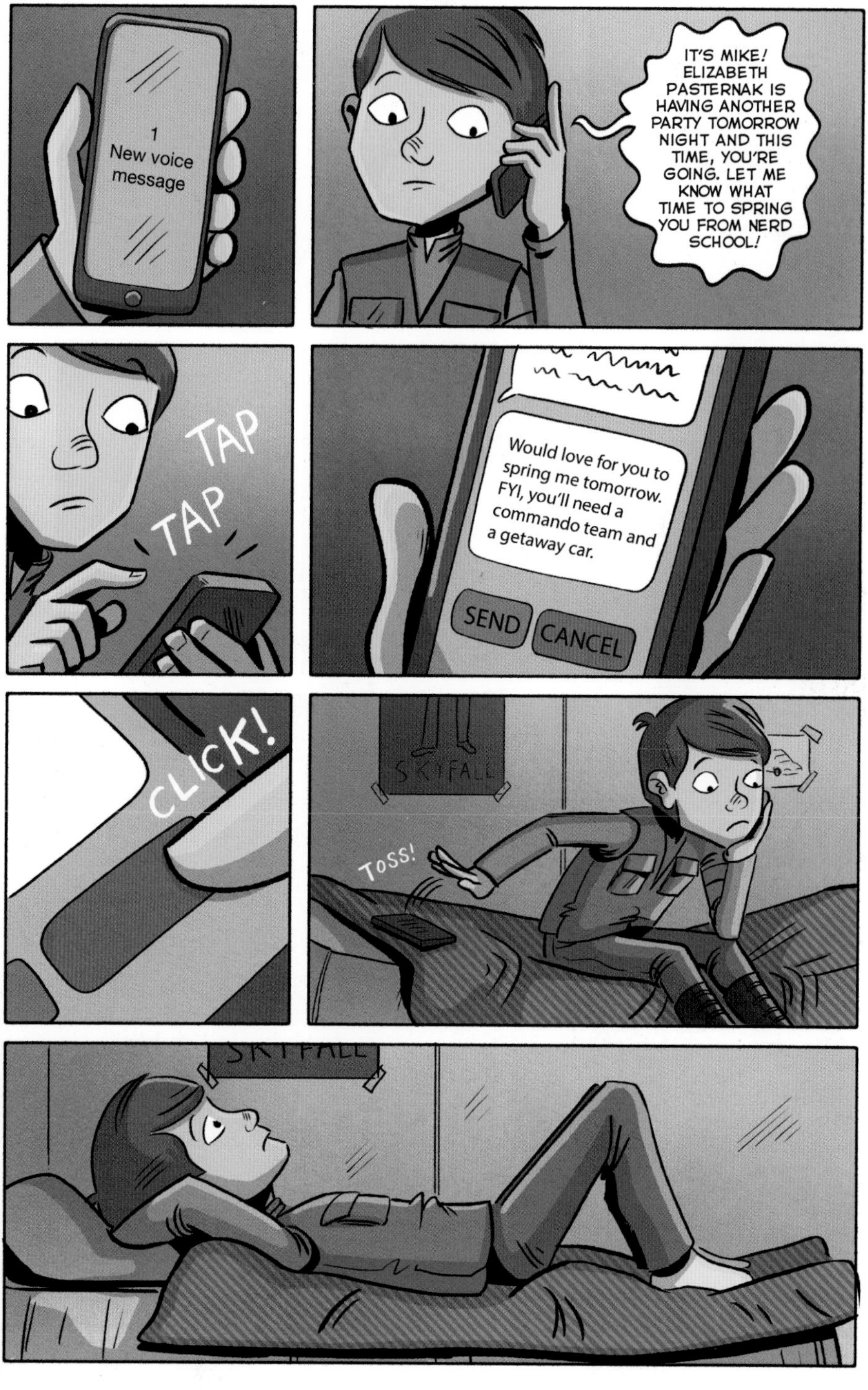
1
New voice
message
IT'S MIKE! ELIZABETH PASTERNAK IS HAVING ANOTHER PARTY TOMORROW NIGHT AND THIS TIME, YOU'RE GOING. LET ME KNOW WHAT TIME TO SPRING YOU FROM NERD SCHOOL!
TAP
TAP
Would love for you to spring me tomorrow. FYI, you'll need a commando team and a getaway car.
SEND
CANCEL
CLICK!
SKYFALL
TOSS!
SKYFALL

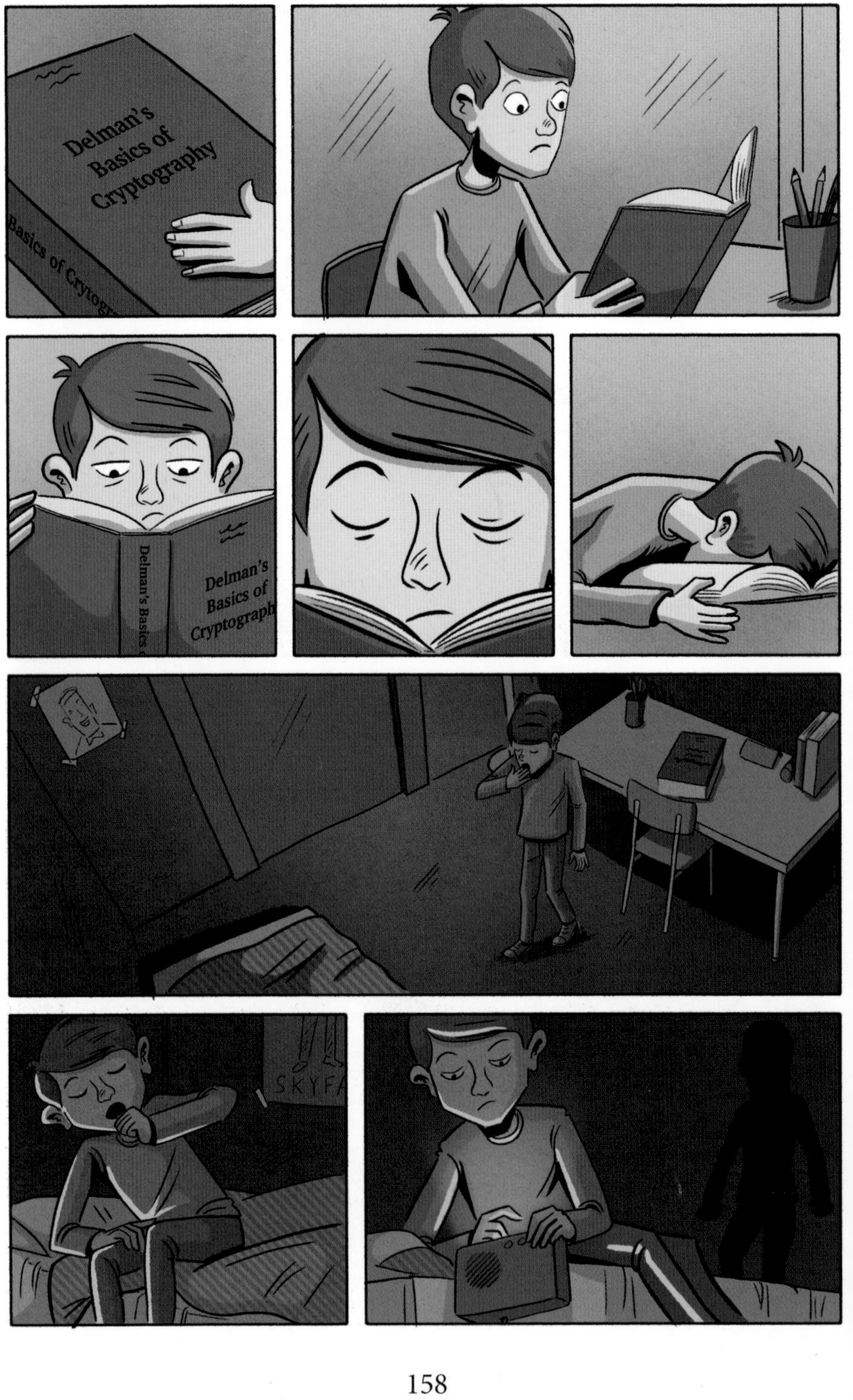
Delman's
Basics of
Cryptography

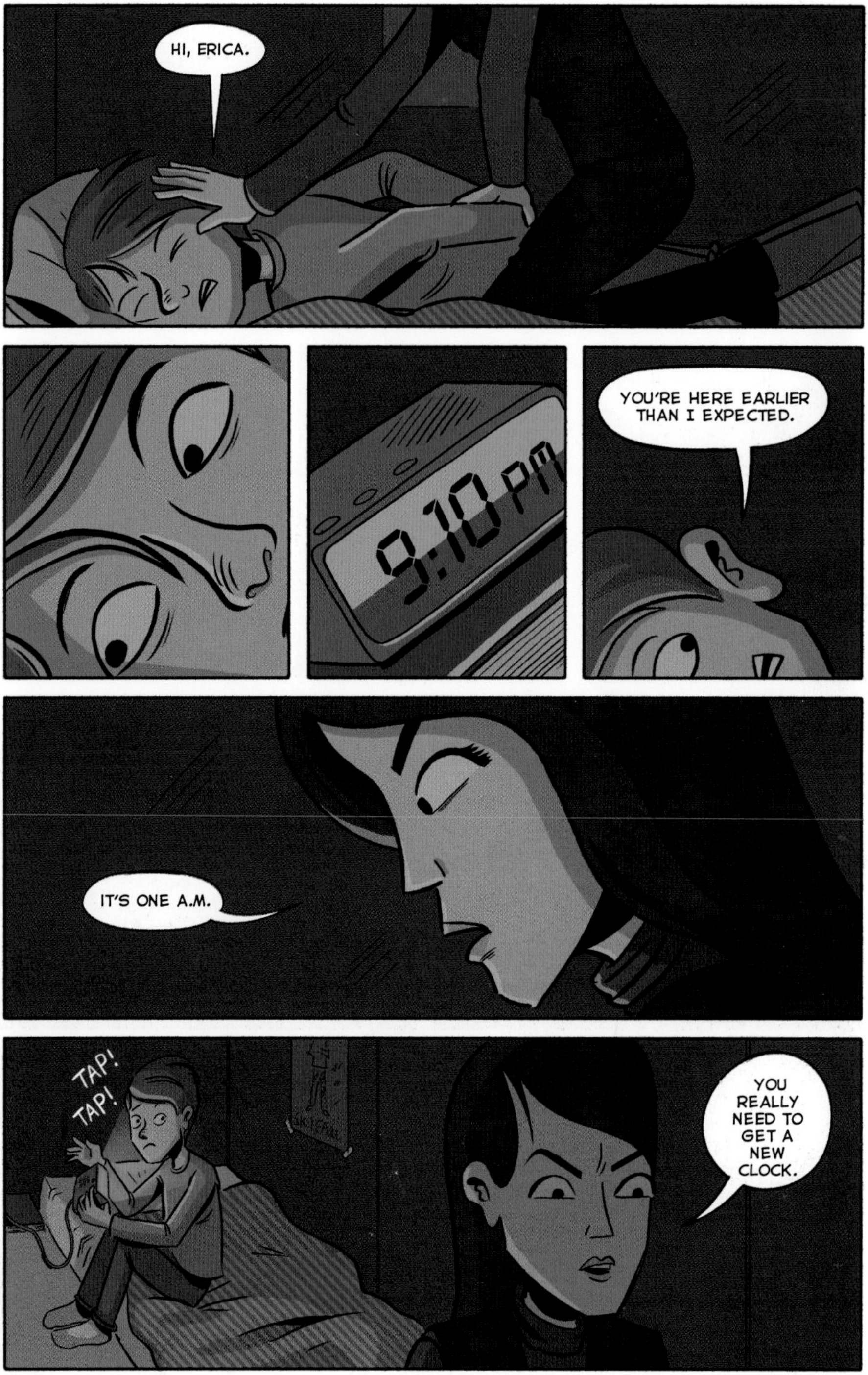
HI, ERICA.
9:10 PM
YOU'RE HERE EARLIER THAN I EXPECTED.
IT'S ONE A.M.
TAP! TAP!
YOU REALLY NEED TO GET A NEW CLOCK.

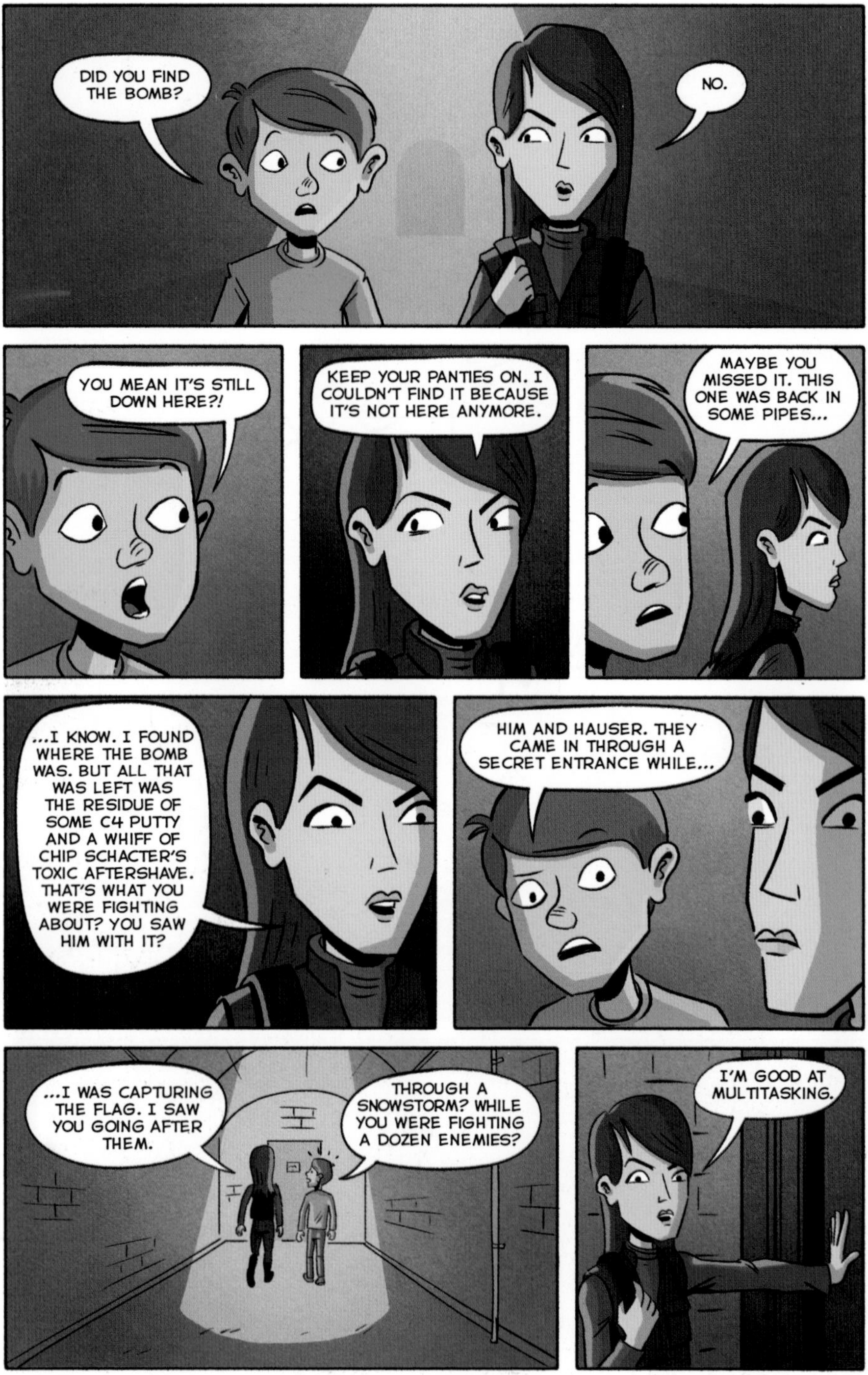
DID YOU FIND THE BOMB?
NO.
YOU MEAN IT'S STILL DOWN HERE?!
KEEP YOUR PANTIES ON. I COULDN'T FIND IT BECAUSE IT'S NOT HERE ANYMORE.
MAYBE YOU MISSED IT. THIS ONE WAS BACK IN SOME PIPES...
...I KNOW. I FOUND WHERE THE BOMB WAS. BUT ALL THAT WAS LEFT WAS THE RESIDUE OF SOME C4 PUTTY AND A WHIFF OF CHIP SCHACTER'S TOXIC AFTERSHAVE. THAT'S WHAT YOU WERE FIGHTING ABOUT? YOU SAW HIM WITH IT?
HIM AND HAUSER. THEY CAME IN THROUGH A SECRET ENTRANCE WHILE...
...I WAS CAPTURING THE FLAG. I SAW YOU GOING AFTER THEM.
THROUGH A SNOWSTORM? WHILE YOU WERE FIGHTING A DOZEN ENEMIES?
I'M GOOD AT MULTITASKING.

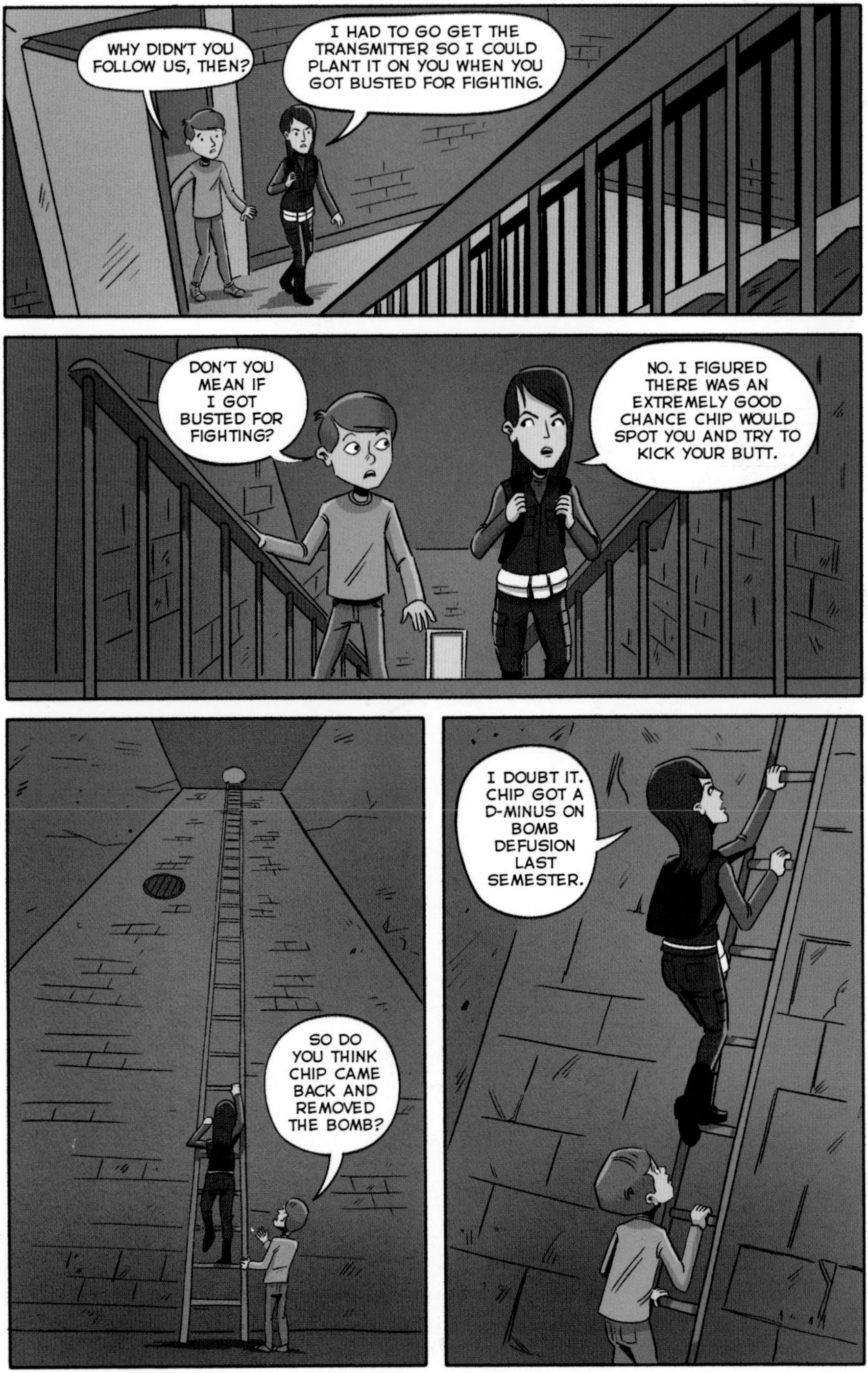

WHY DIDN'T YOU FOLLOW US, THEN?
I HAD TO GO GET THE TRANSMITTER SO I COULD PLANT IT ON YOU WHEN YOU GOT BUSTED FOR FIGHTING.
DON'T YOU MEAN IF I GOT BUSTED FOR FIGHTING?
NO. I FIGURED THERE WAS AN EXTREMELY GOOD CHANCE CHIP WOULD SPOT YOU AND TRY TO KICK YOUR BUTT.
SO DO YOU THINK CHIP CAME BACK AND REMOVED THE BOMB?
I DOUBT IT. CHIP GOT A D-MINUS ON BOMB DEFUSION LAST SEMESTER.

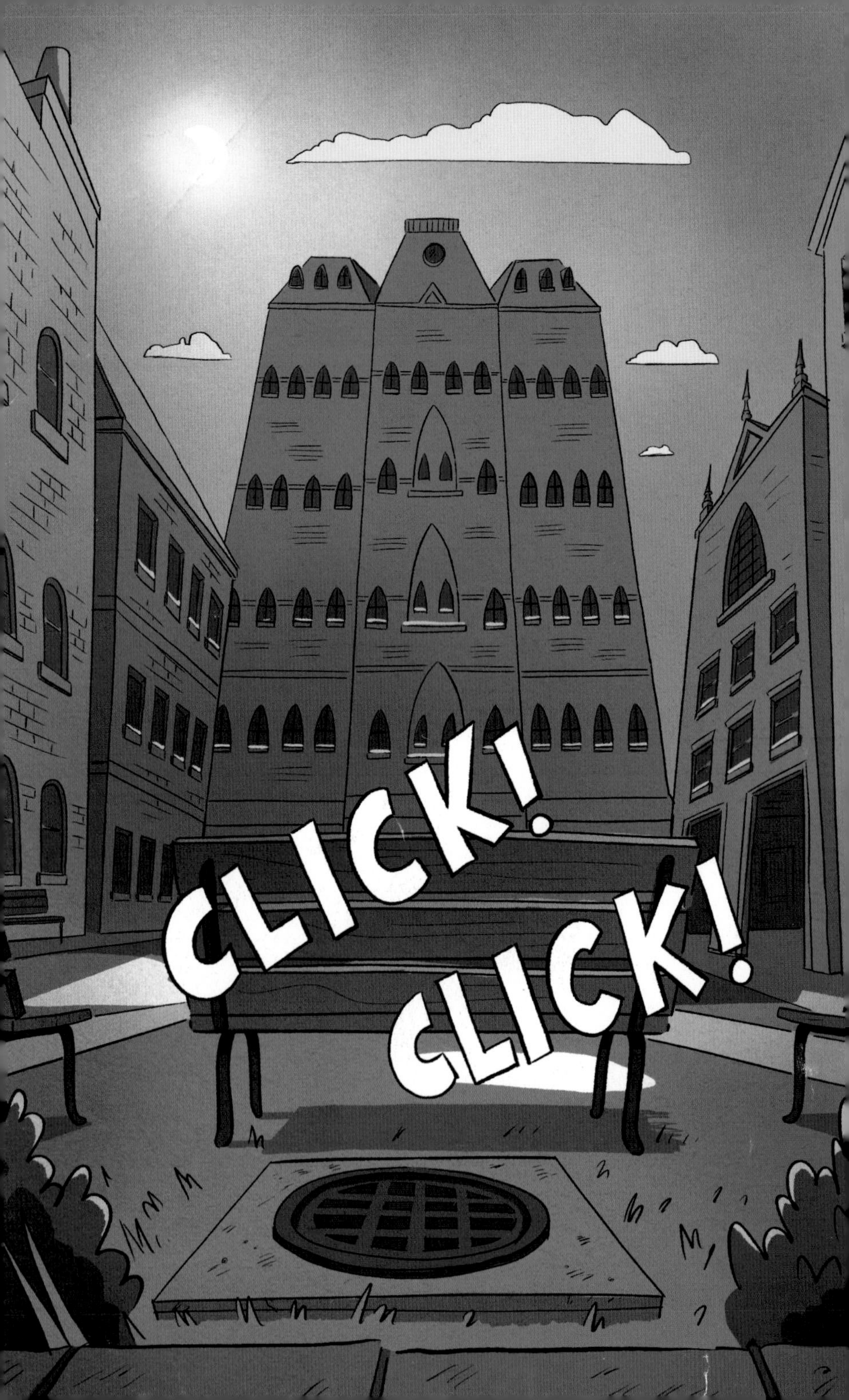
CLICK!
CLICK!

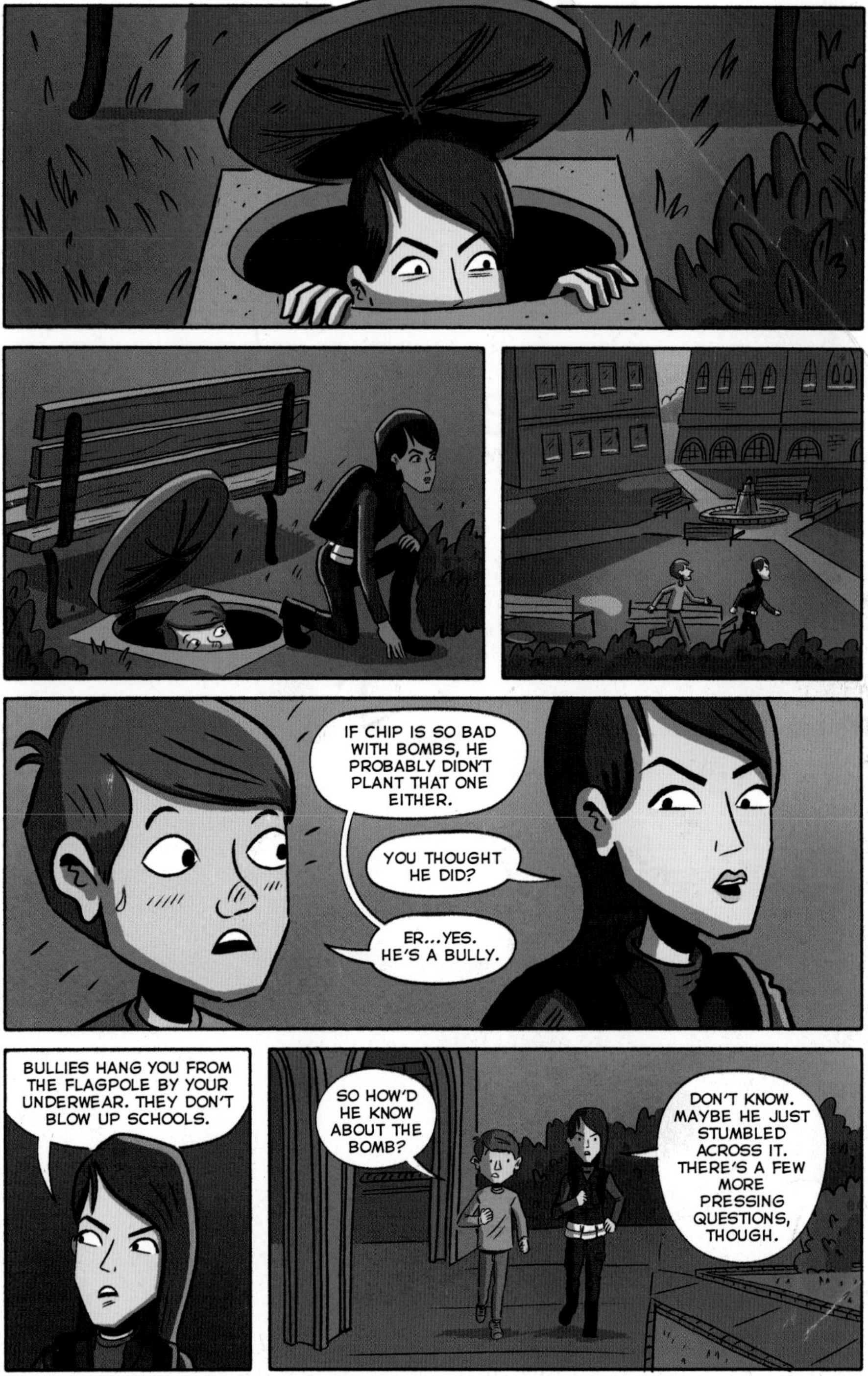
IF CHIP IS SO BAD WITH BOMBS, HE PROBABLY DIDN'T PLANT THAT ONE EITHER.
YOU THOUGHT HE DID?
ER...YES. HE'S A BULLY.
BULLIES HANG YOU FROM THE FLAGPOLE BY YOUR UNDERWEAR. THEY DON'T BLOW UP SCHOOLS.
SO HOW'D HE KNOW ABOUT THE BOMB?
DON'T KNOW. MAYBE HE JUST STUMBLED ACROSS IT. THERE'S A FEW MORE PRESSING QUESTIONS, THOUGH.

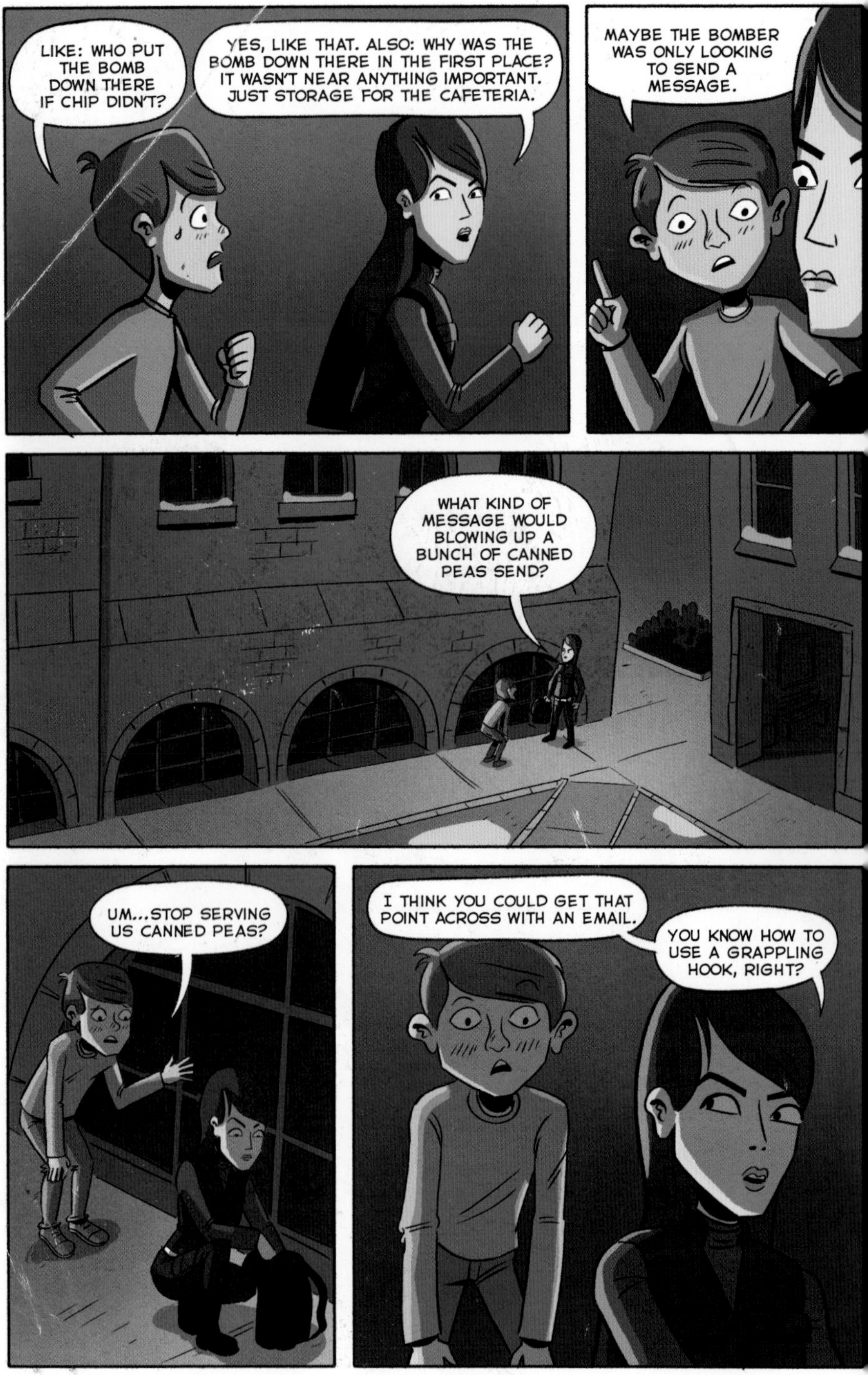
LIKE: WHO PUT THE BOMB DOWN THERE IF CHIP DIDN'T?
YES, LIKE THAT. ALSO: WHY WAS THE BOMB DOWN THERE IN THE FIRST PLACE? IT WASN'T NEAR ANYTHING IMPORTANT. JUST STORAGE FOR THE CAFETERIA.
MAYBE THE BOMBER WAS ONLY LOOKING TO SEND A MESSAGE.
WHAT KIND OF MESSAGE WOULD BLOWING UP A BUNCH OF CANNED PEAS SEND?
UM...STOP SERVING US CANNED PEAS?
I THINK YOU COULD GET THAT POINT ACROSS WITH AN EMAIL.
YOU KNOW HOW TO USE A GRAPPLING HOOK, RIGHT?

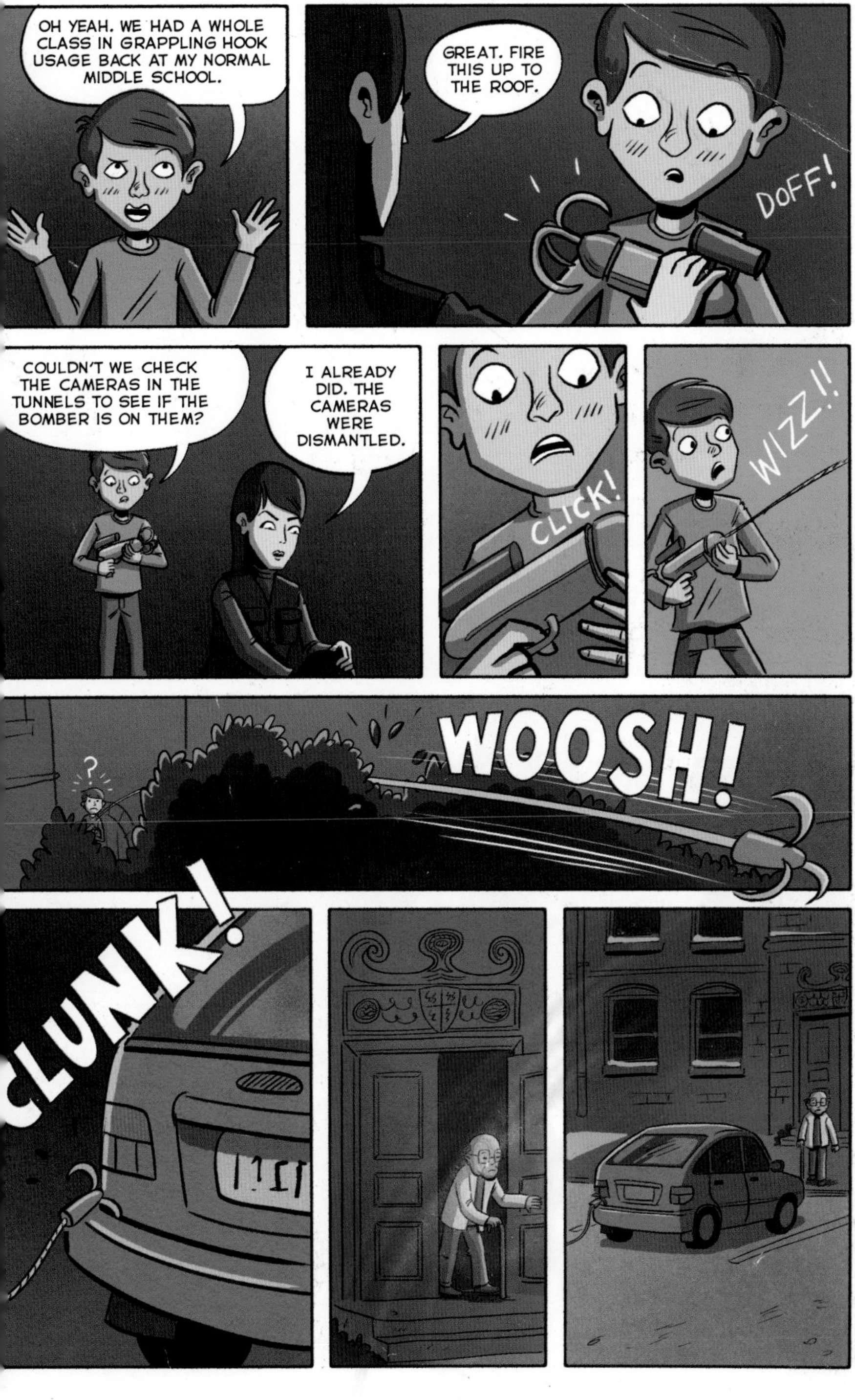

OH YEAH. WE HAD A WHOLE CLASS IN GRAPPLING HOOK USAGE BACK AT MY NORMAL MIDDLE SCHOOL.
GREAT. FIRE THIS UP TO THE ROOF.
DOFF!
COULDN'T WE CHECK THE CAMERAS IN THE TUNNELS TO SEE IF THE BOMBER IS ON THEM?
I ALREADY DID. THE CAMERAS WERE DISMANTLED.
CLICK!
WIZZ!!
?
WOOSH!
CLUNK!

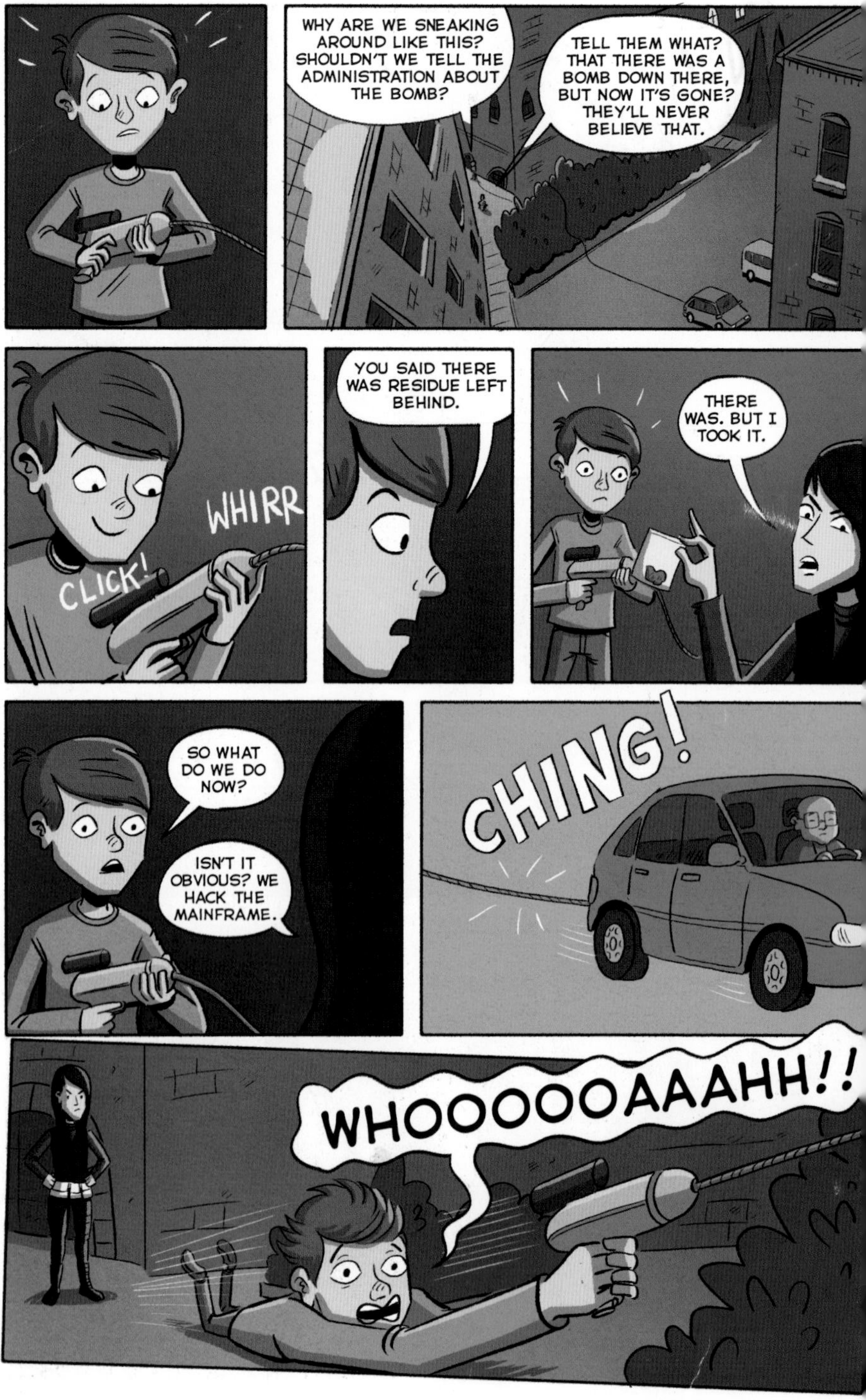
WHY ARE WE SNEAKING AROUND LIKE THIS? SHOULDN'T WE TELL THE ADMINISTRATION ABOUT THE BOMB?
TELL THEM WHAT? THAT THERE WAS A BOMB DOWN THERE, BUT NOW IT'S GONE? THEY'LL NEVER BELIEVE THAT.
WHIRR
CLICK!
YOU SAID THERE WAS RESIDUE LEFT BEHIND.
THERE WAS. BUT I TOOK IT.
SO WHAT DO WE DO NOW?
ISN'T IT OBVIOUS? WE HACK THE MAINFRAME.
CHING!
WHOOOOOAAAHH!!

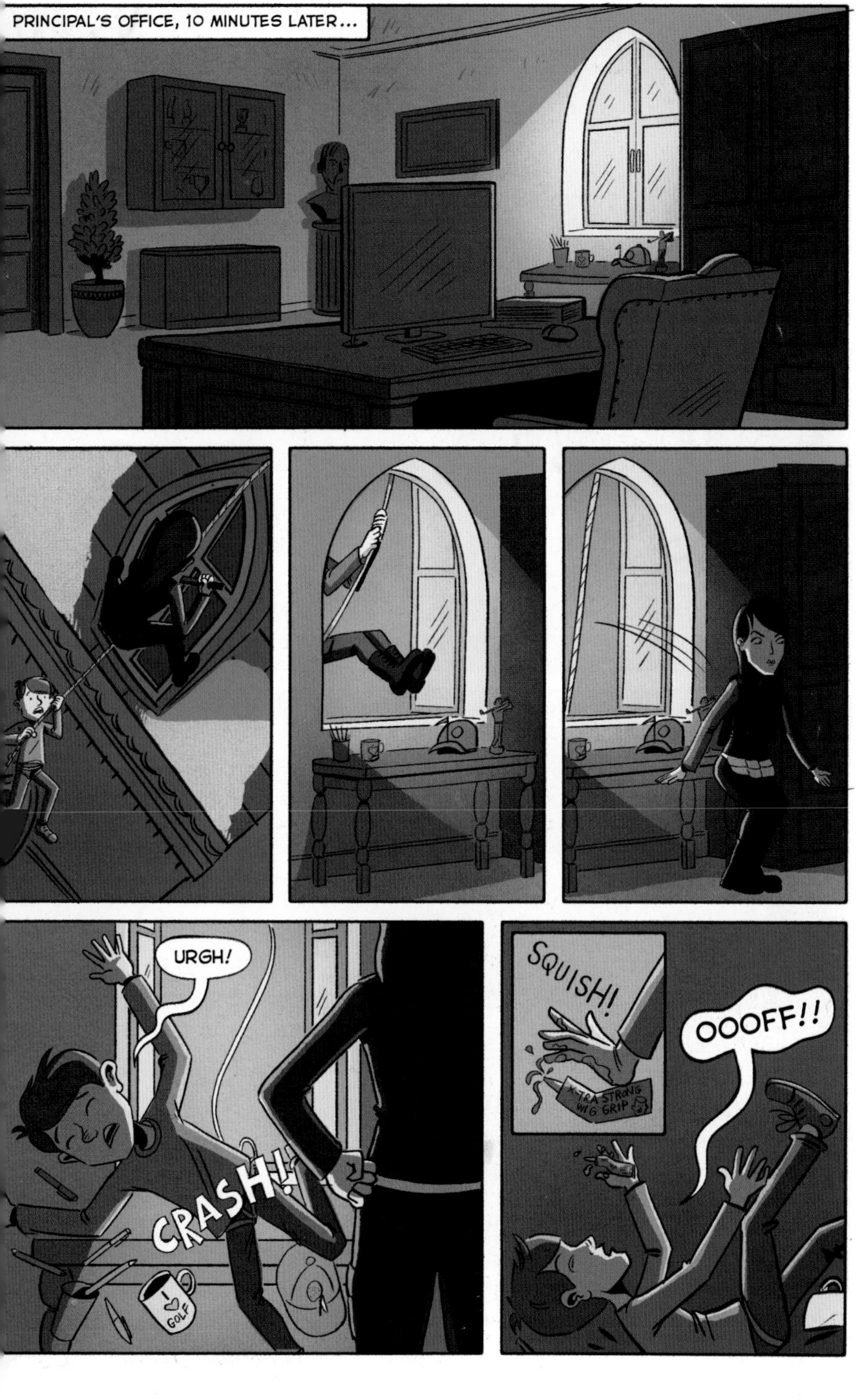
PRINCIPAL'S OFFICE, 10 MINUTES LATER...
URGH!
CRASH!
I ♥ GOLF
SQUISH!
X-TRA STRONG WIG GRIP
OOOFF!!

LIKE I SAID, THIS ISN'T GOING TO BE EASY. THE ACCESS CODE HAS SIXTEEN-BIT DAISY-CHAIN ENCRYPTION ON IT.

WHAT IS THAT, ANYWAY?

CREAK!

HAVEN'T YOU READ DELMAN'S *BASICS OF CRYPTOGRAPHY* YET?

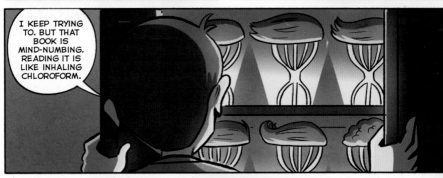
I KEEP TRYING TO. BUT THAT BOOK IS MIND-NUMBING. READING IT IS LIKE INHALING CHLOROFORM.

YOU'VE OBVIOUSLY NEVER INHALED CHLOROFORM.

THE DAISY CHAIN IS A SIXTEEN-CHARACTER CODE RANDOMLY SELECTED BY A CIA COMPUTER...

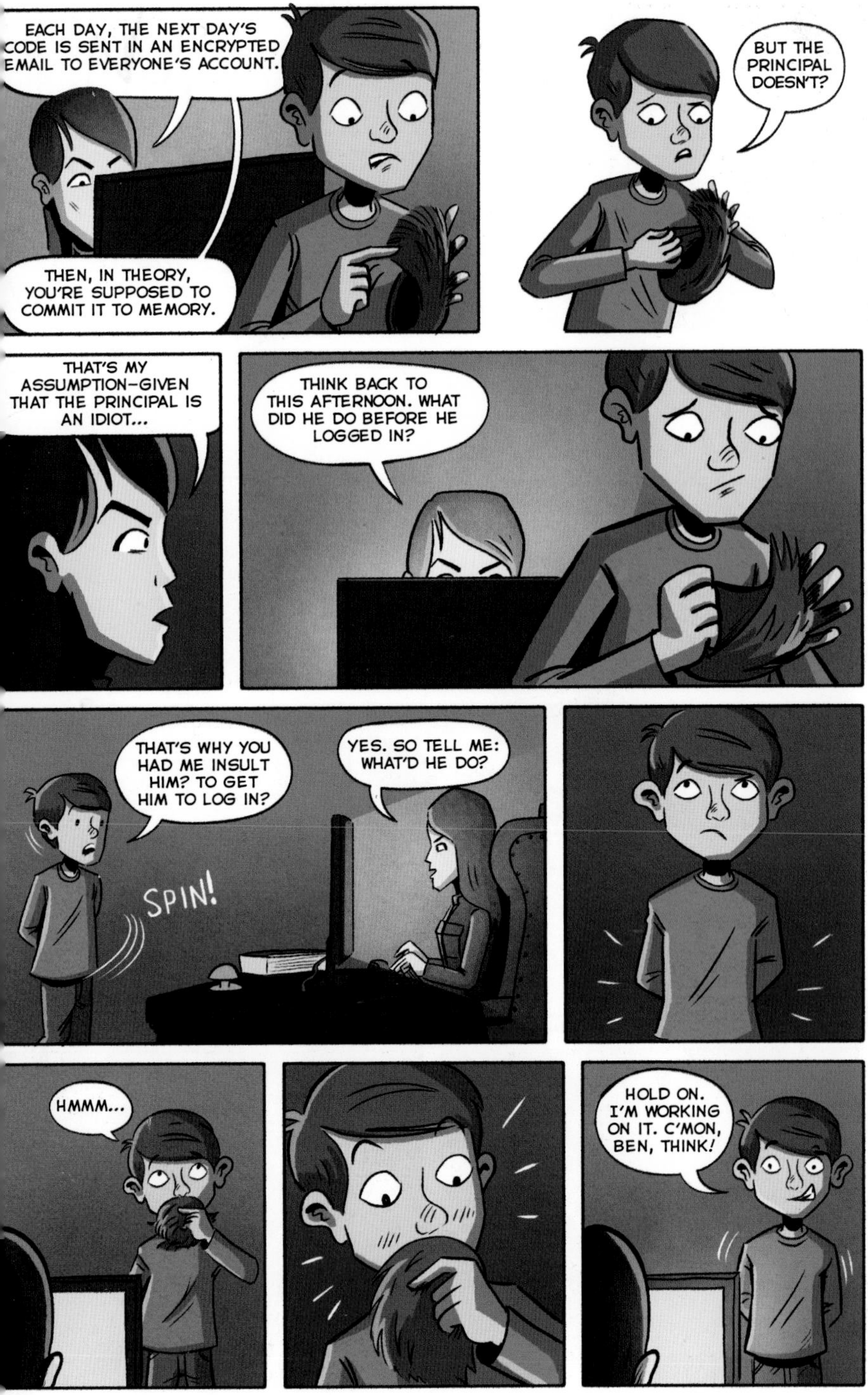
EACH DAY, THE NEXT DAY'S CODE IS SENT IN AN ENCRYPTED EMAIL TO EVERYONE'S ACCOUNT.
THEN, IN THEORY, YOU'RE SUPPOSED TO COMMIT IT TO MEMORY.
BUT THE PRINCIPAL DOESN'T?
THAT'S MY ASSUMPTION–GIVEN THAT THE PRINCIPAL IS AN IDIOT...
THINK BACK TO THIS AFTERNOON. WHAT DID HE DO BEFORE HE LOGGED IN?
THAT'S WHY YOU HAD ME INSULT HIM? TO GET HIM TO LOG IN?
YES. SO TELL ME: WHAT'D HE DO?
SPIN!
HMMM...
HOLD ON. I'M WORKING ON IT. C'MON, BEN, THINK!

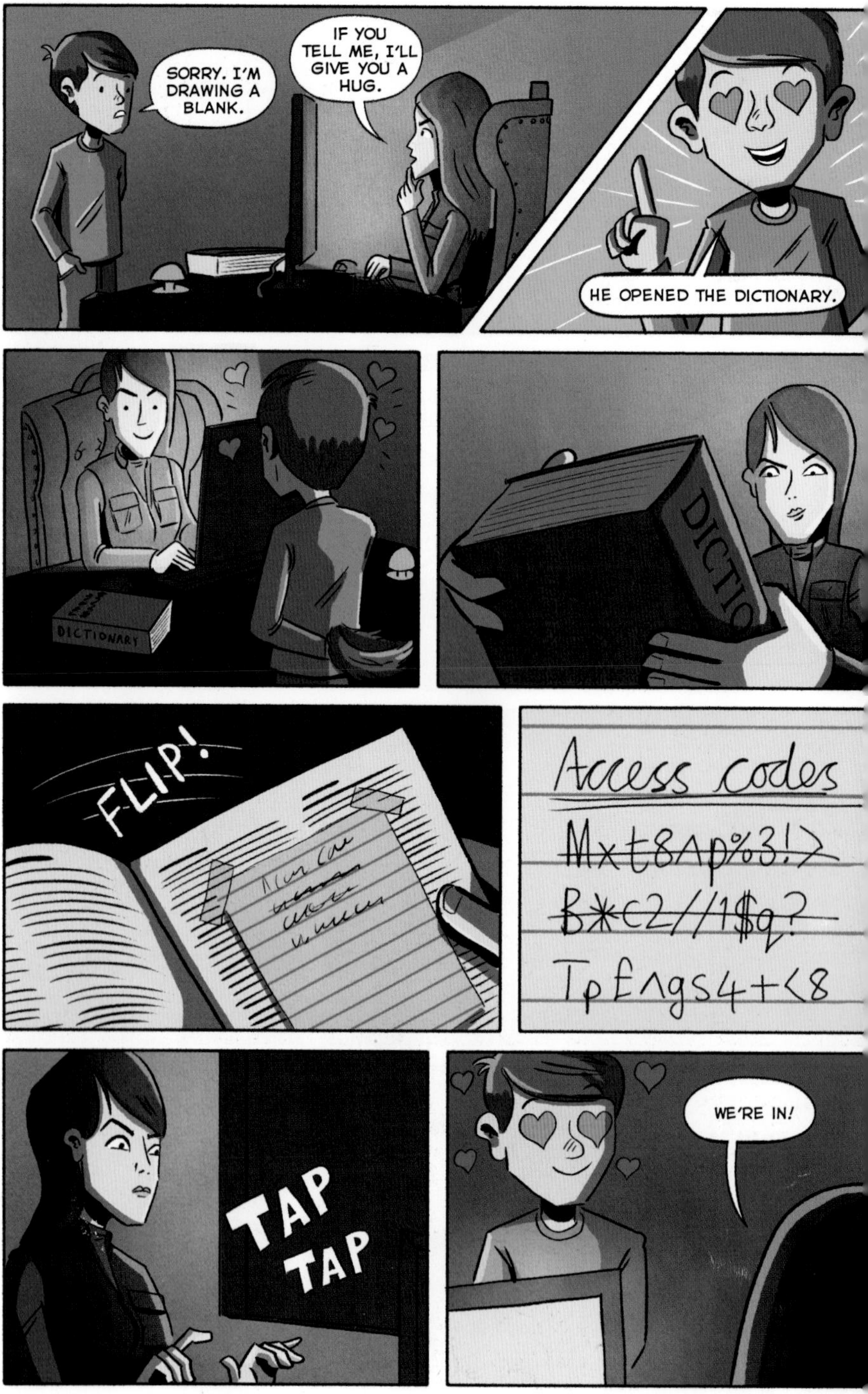
SORRY. I'M DRAWING A BLANK.
IF YOU TELL ME, I'LL GIVE YOU A HUG.
HE OPENED THE DICTIONARY.
DICTIONARY
DICTIO
FLIP!
Access codes
Mxt8^p%3!>
B*c2//1$q?
Tp£^gs4+<8
TAP
TAP
WE'RE IN!

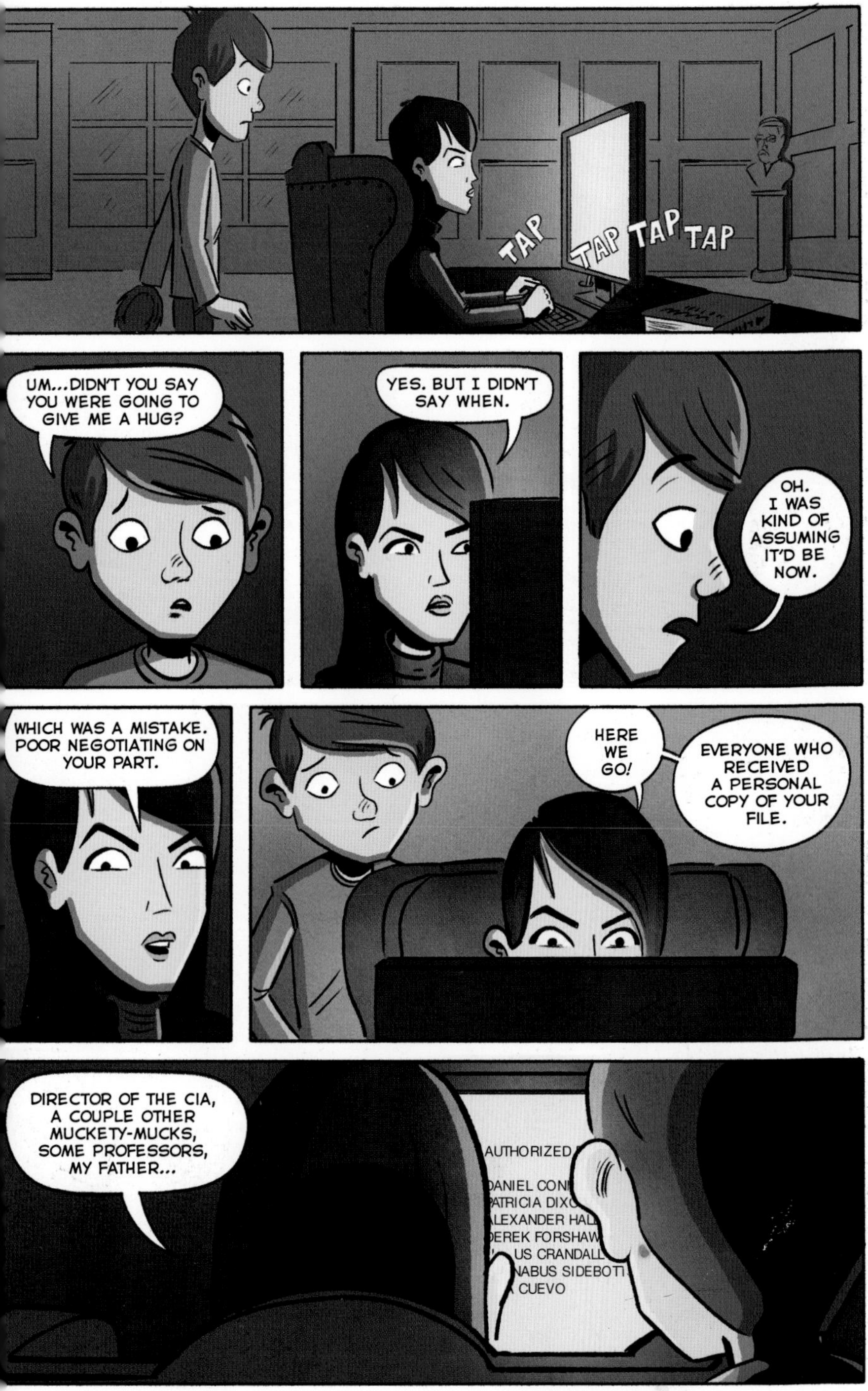
TAP
TAP TAP TAP
UM...DIDN'T YOU SAY YOU WERE GOING TO GIVE ME A HUG?
YES. BUT I DIDN'T SAY WHEN.
OH. I WAS KIND OF ASSUMING IT'D BE NOW.
WHICH WAS A MISTAKE. POOR NEGOTIATING ON YOUR PART.
HERE WE GO!
EVERYONE WHO RECEIVED A PERSONAL COPY OF YOUR FILE.
DIRECTOR OF THE CIA, A COUPLE OTHER MUCKETY-MUCKS, SOME PROFESSORS, MY FATHER...
AUTHORIZED
DANIEL CON
PATRICIA DIXO
ALEXANDER HAL
DEREK FORSHAW
US CRANDALL
NABUS SIDEBOT
CUEVO

PROFESSOR CRANDALL? WHO'D TRUST HIM WITH ANYTHING CLASSIFIED? AND WHO'S BARNABUS SIDEBOTTOM?

YOU'RE IN HIS OFFICE RIGHT NOW.

DANIEL CONNER
PATRICIA DIXON
ALEXANDER HALE
DEREK FORSHAW
LUCAS CRANDALL
BARNABUS SIDEBOTTOM
TINA CUEVO

TINA CUEVO? SHE'S ONLY A STUDENT.

BUT SHE WAS SUPPOSED TO BE YOUR RESIDENT ADVISER...UNTIL YOU ENDED UP IN THE BOX. SO SHE HAD TO KNOW ABOUT YOU.

OKAY. TIME FOR PHASE TWO.

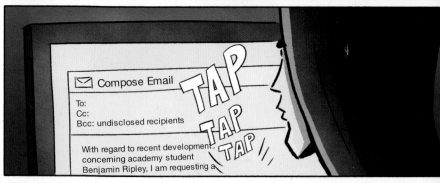

✉ Compose Email

To:
Cc:
Bcc: undisclosed recipients

With regard to recent development concerning academy student Benjamin Ripley, I am requesting a

TAP
TAP
TAP

THINK CHIP GOT MY FILE FROM TINA?

NO WAY. TINA'S RANKED THIRD IN HER CLASS. SHE WOULD NEVER SHARE CLASSIFIED INFORMATION.

MAYBE SHE ACCIDENTALLY LEFT IT WHERE HE COULD ACCESS IT.

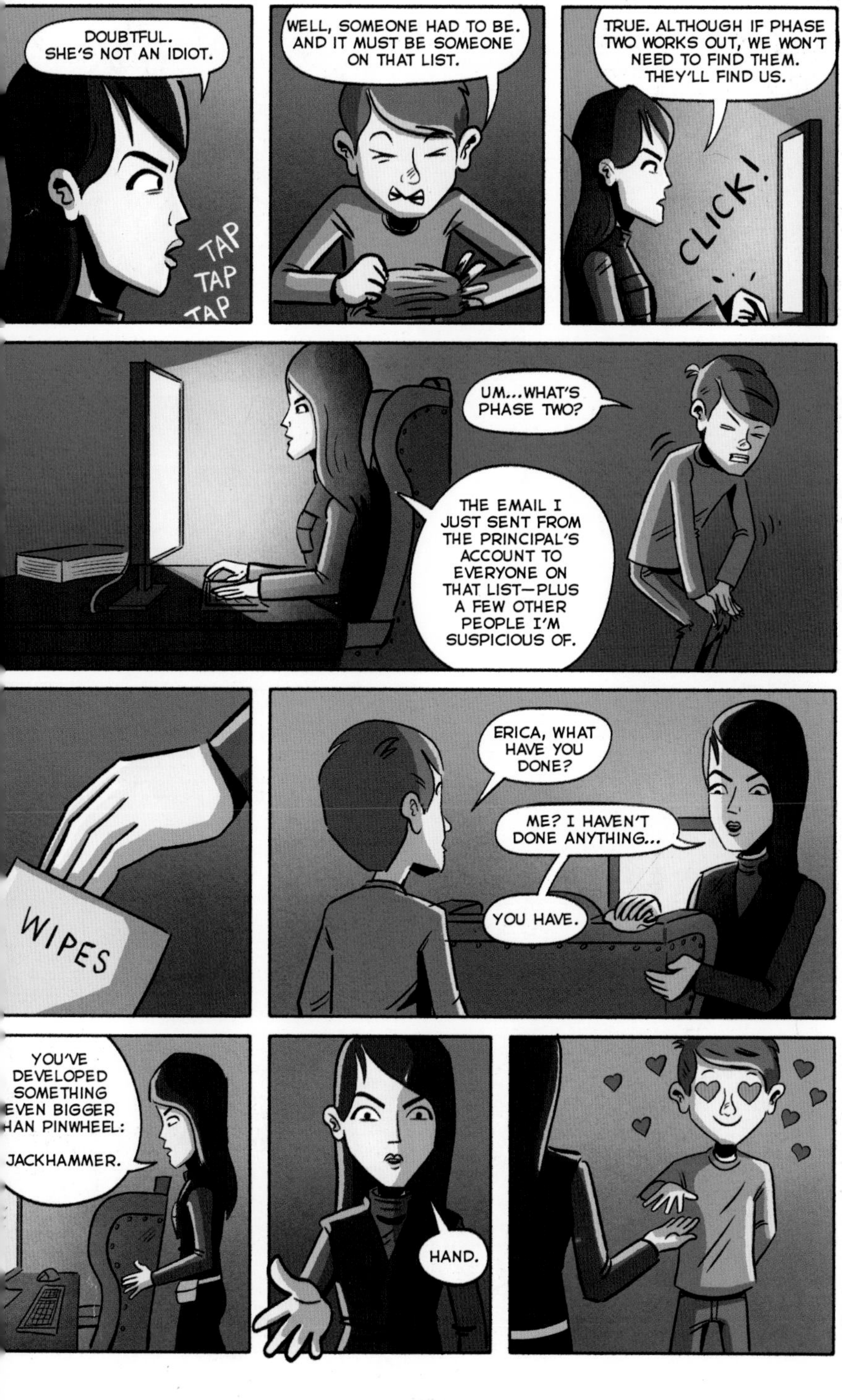
DOUBTFUL. SHE'S NOT AN IDIOT.
TAP TAP TAP
WELL, SOMEONE HAD TO BE. AND IT MUST BE SOMEONE ON THAT LIST.
TRUE. ALTHOUGH IF PHASE TWO WORKS OUT, WE WON'T NEED TO FIND THEM. THEY'LL FIND US.
CLICK!
UM...WHAT'S PHASE TWO?
THE EMAIL I JUST SENT FROM THE PRINCIPAL'S ACCOUNT TO EVERYONE ON THAT LIST—PLUS A FEW OTHER PEOPLE I'M SUSPICIOUS OF.
WIPES
ERICA, WHAT HAVE YOU DONE?
ME? I HAVEN'T DONE ANYTHING...
YOU HAVE.
YOU'VE DEVELOPED SOMETHING EVEN BIGGER HAN PINWHEEL:
JACKHAMMER.
HAND.

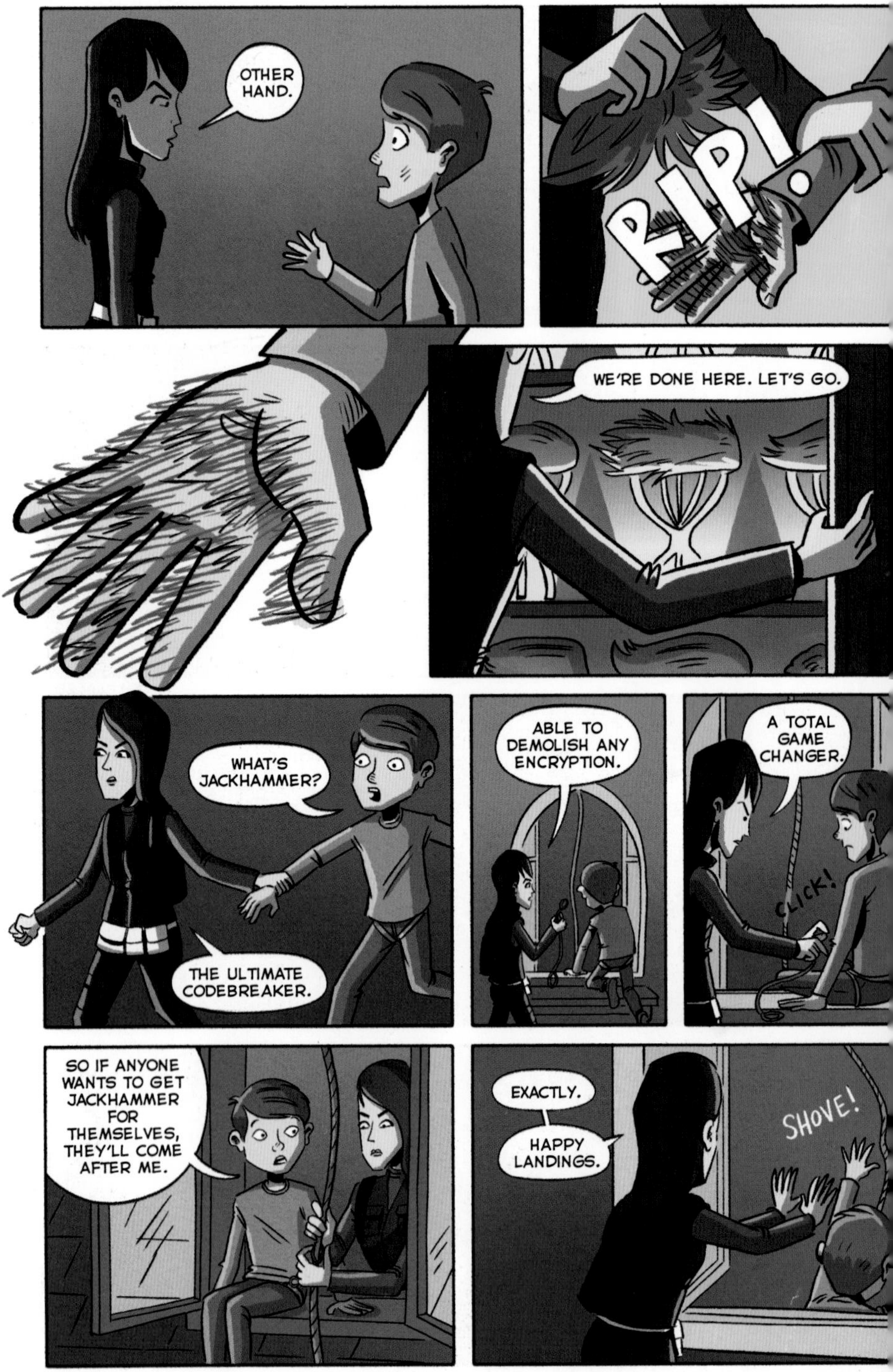
OTHER HAND.
RIP!
WE'RE DONE HERE. LET'S GO.
WHAT'S JACKHAMMER?
THE ULTIMATE CODEBREAKER.
ABLE TO DEMOLISH ANY ENCRYPTION.
A TOTAL GAME CHANGER.
CLICK!
SO IF ANYONE WANTS TO GET JACKHAMMER FOR THEMSELVES, THEY'LL COME AFTER ME.
EXACTLY.
HAPPY LANDINGS.
SHOVE!

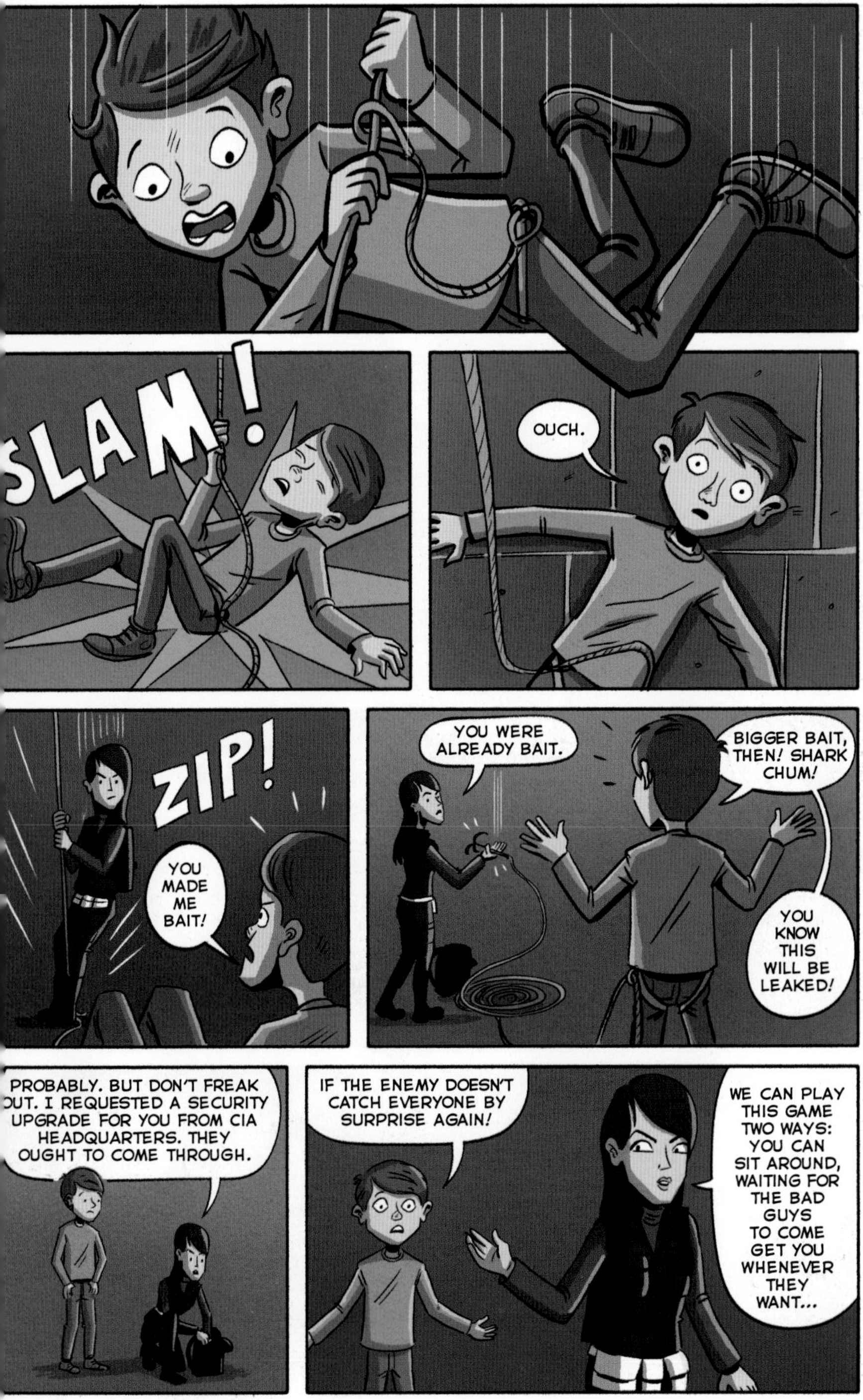
SLAM!
OUCH.
ZIP!
YOU MADE ME BAIT!
YOU WERE ALREADY BAIT.
BIGGER BAIT, THEN! SHARK CHUM!
YOU KNOW THIS WILL BE LEAKED!
PROBABLY. BUT DON'T FREAK OUT. I REQUESTED A SECURITY UPGRADE FOR YOU FROM CIA HEADQUARTERS. THEY OUGHT TO COME THROUGH.
IF THE ENEMY DOESN'T CATCH EVERYONE BY SURPRISE AGAIN!
WE CAN PLAY THIS GAME TWO WAYS: YOU CAN SIT AROUND, WAITING FOR THE BAD GUYS TO COME GET YOU WHENEVER THEY WANT...

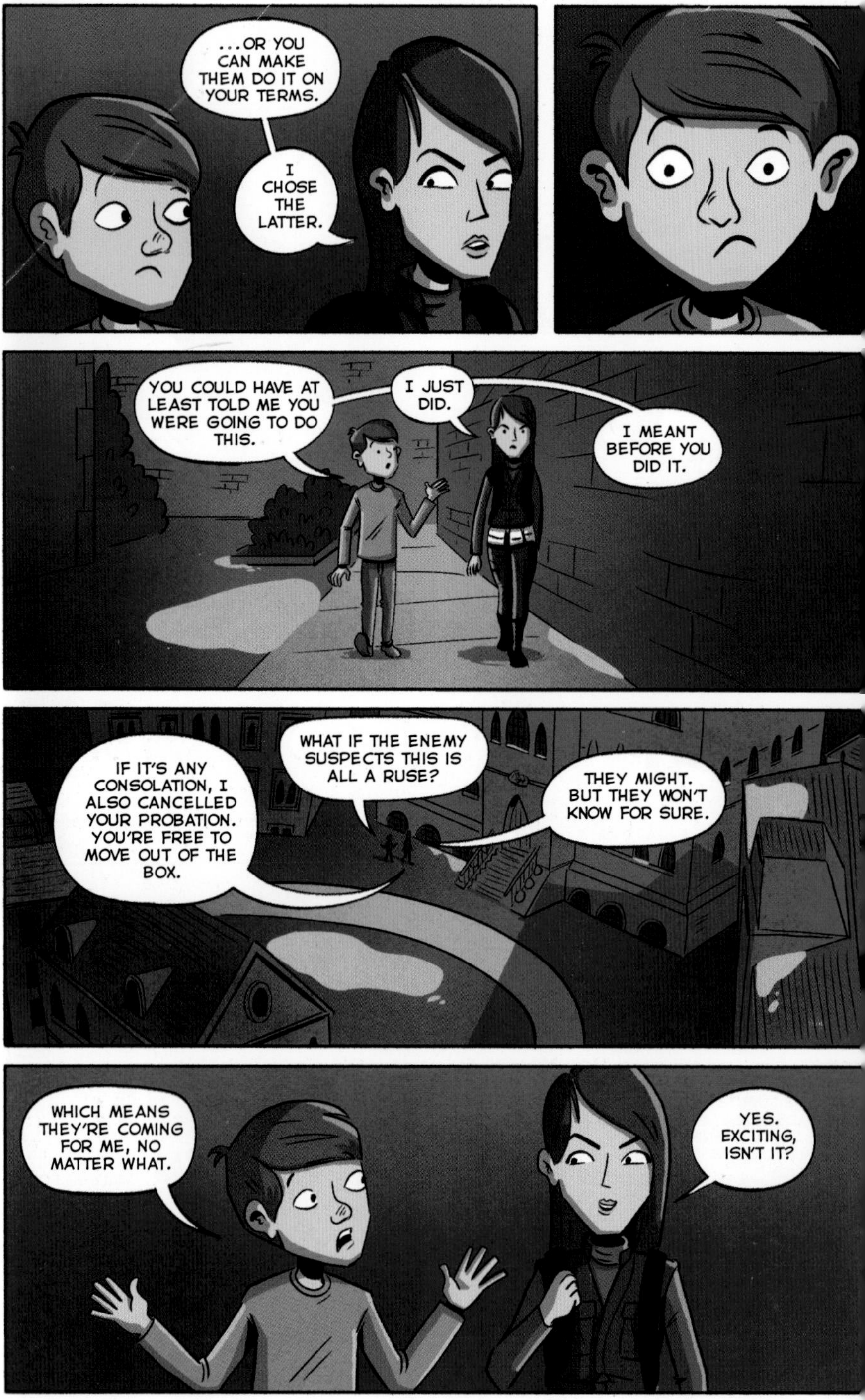
...OR YOU CAN MAKE THEM DO IT ON YOUR TERMS.
I CHOSE THE LATTER.
YOU COULD HAVE AT LEAST TOLD ME YOU WERE GOING TO DO THIS.
I JUST DID.
I MEANT BEFORE YOU DID IT.
IF IT'S ANY CONSOLATION, I ALSO CANCELLED YOUR PROBATION. YOU'RE FREE TO MOVE OUT OF THE BOX.
WHAT IF THE ENEMY SUSPECTS THIS IS ALL A RUSE?
THEY MIGHT. BUT THEY WON'T KNOW FOR SURE.
WHICH MEANS THEY'RE COMING FOR ME, NO MATTER WHAT.
YES. EXCITING, ISN'T IT?

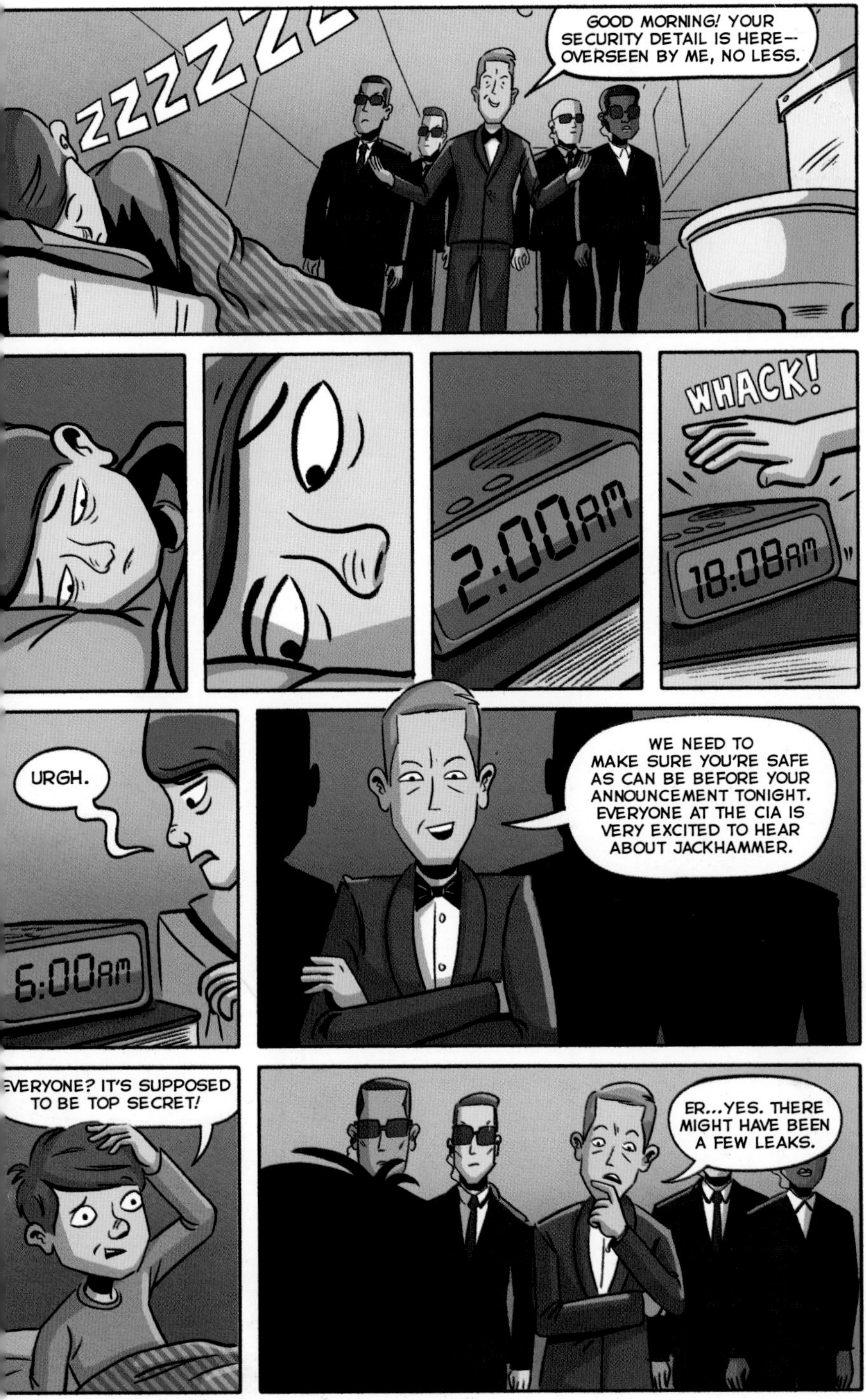
ZZZZZZ
GOOD MORNING! YOUR SECURITY DETAIL IS HERE-- OVERSEEN BY ME, NO LESS.
2:00AM
WHACK!
18:08AM
URGH.
6:00AM
WE NEED TO MAKE SURE YOU'RE SAFE AS CAN BE BEFORE YOUR ANNOUNCEMENT TONIGHT. EVERYONE AT THE CIA IS VERY EXCITED TO HEAR ABOUT JACKHAMMER.
EVERYONE? IT'S SUPPOSED TO BE TOP SECRET!
ER...YES. THERE MIGHT HAVE BEEN A FEW LEAKS.

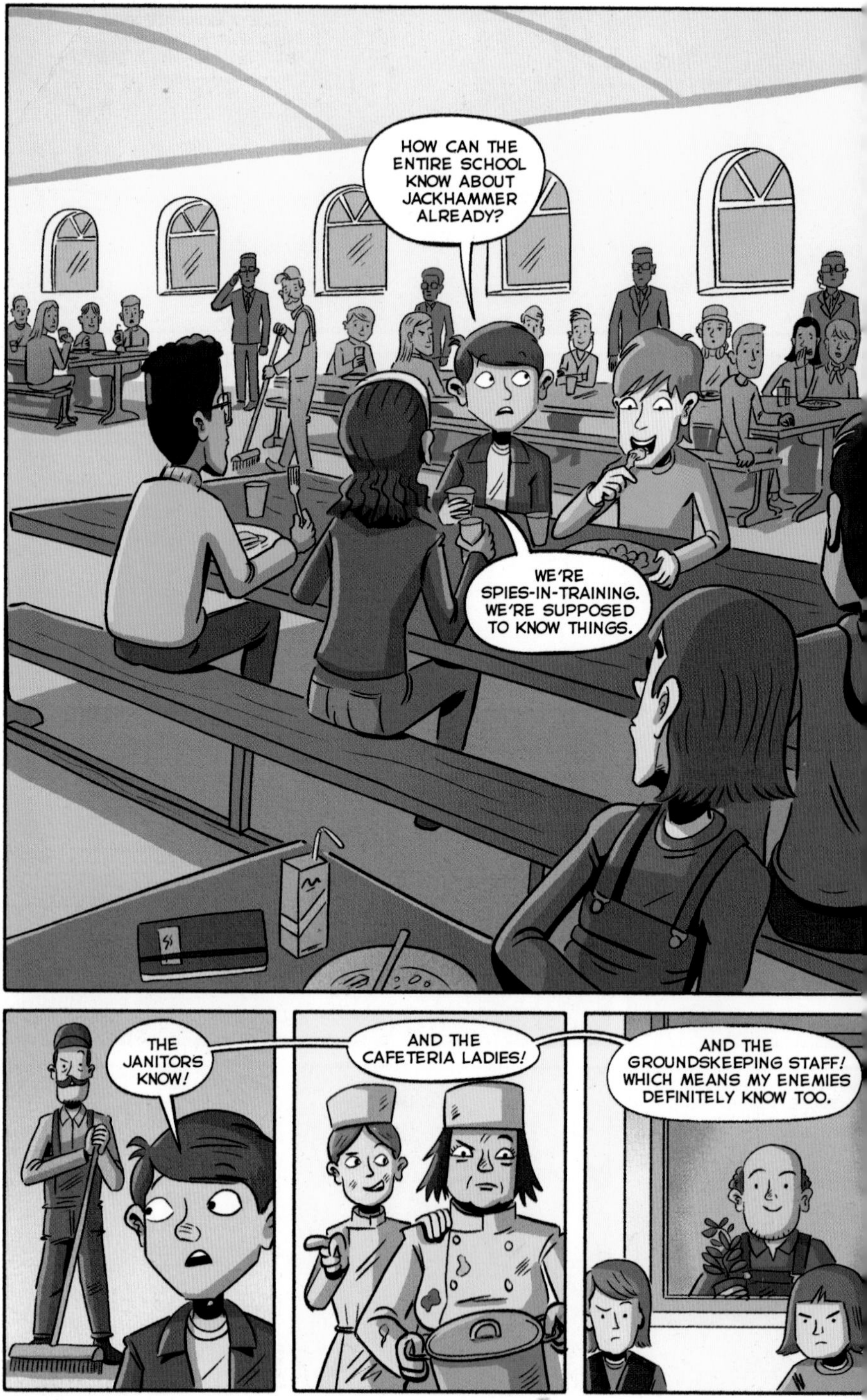
HOW CAN THE ENTIRE SCHOOL KNOW ABOUT JACKHAMMER ALREADY?
WE'RE SPIES-IN-TRAINING. WE'RE SUPPOSED TO KNOW THINGS.
THE JANITORS KNOW!
AND THE CAFETERIA LADIES!
AND THE GROUNDSKEEPING STAFF! WHICH MEANS MY ENEMIES DEFINITELY KNOW TOO.

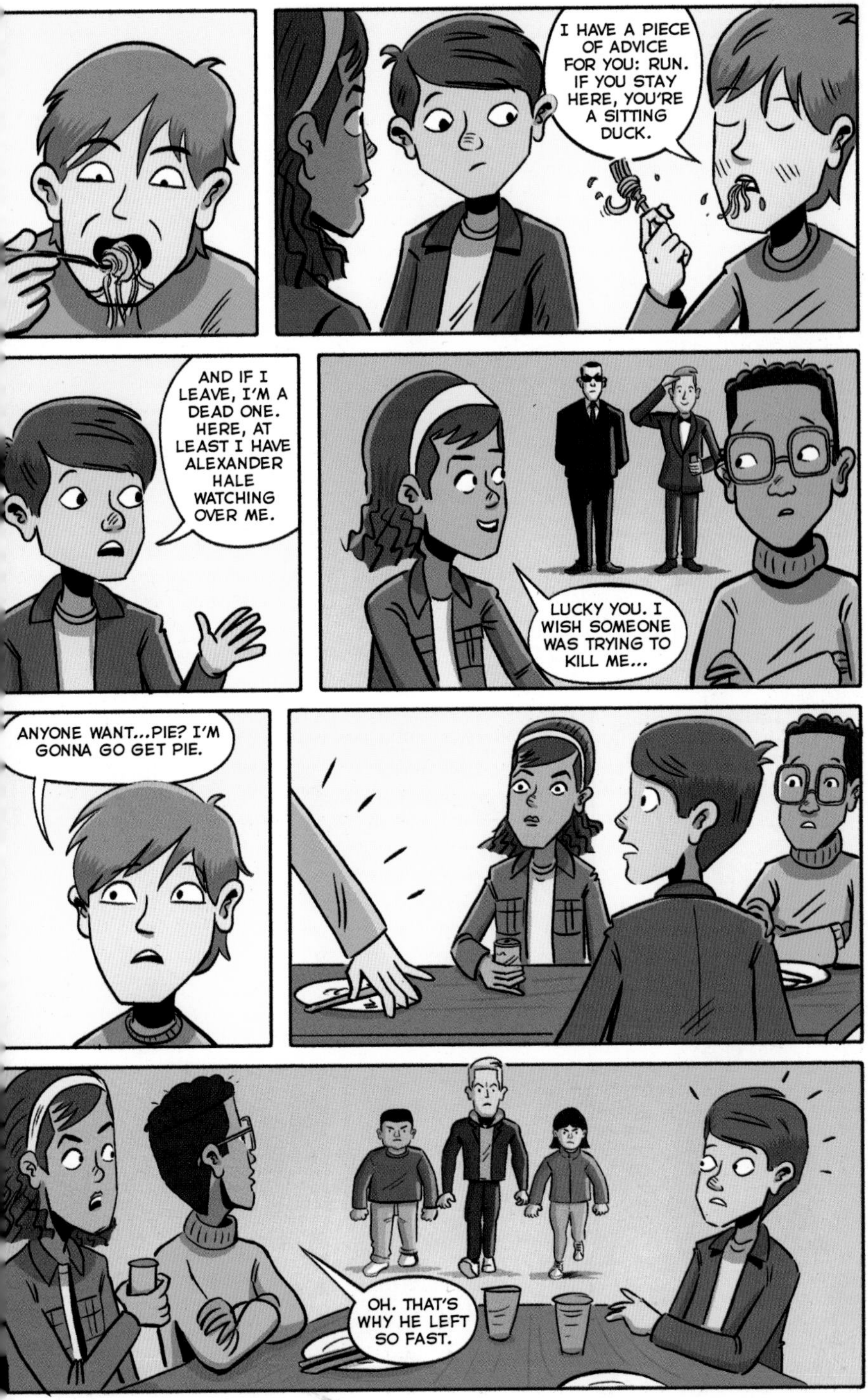
I HAVE A PIECE OF ADVICE FOR YOU: RUN. IF YOU STAY HERE, YOU'RE A SITTING DUCK.
AND IF I LEAVE, I'M A DEAD ONE. HERE, AT LEAST I HAVE ALEXANDER HALE WATCHING OVER ME.
LUCKY YOU. I WISH SOMEONE WAS TRYING TO KILL ME...
ANYONE WANT...PIE? I'M GONNA GO GET PIE.
OH. THAT'S WHY HE LEFT SO FAST.

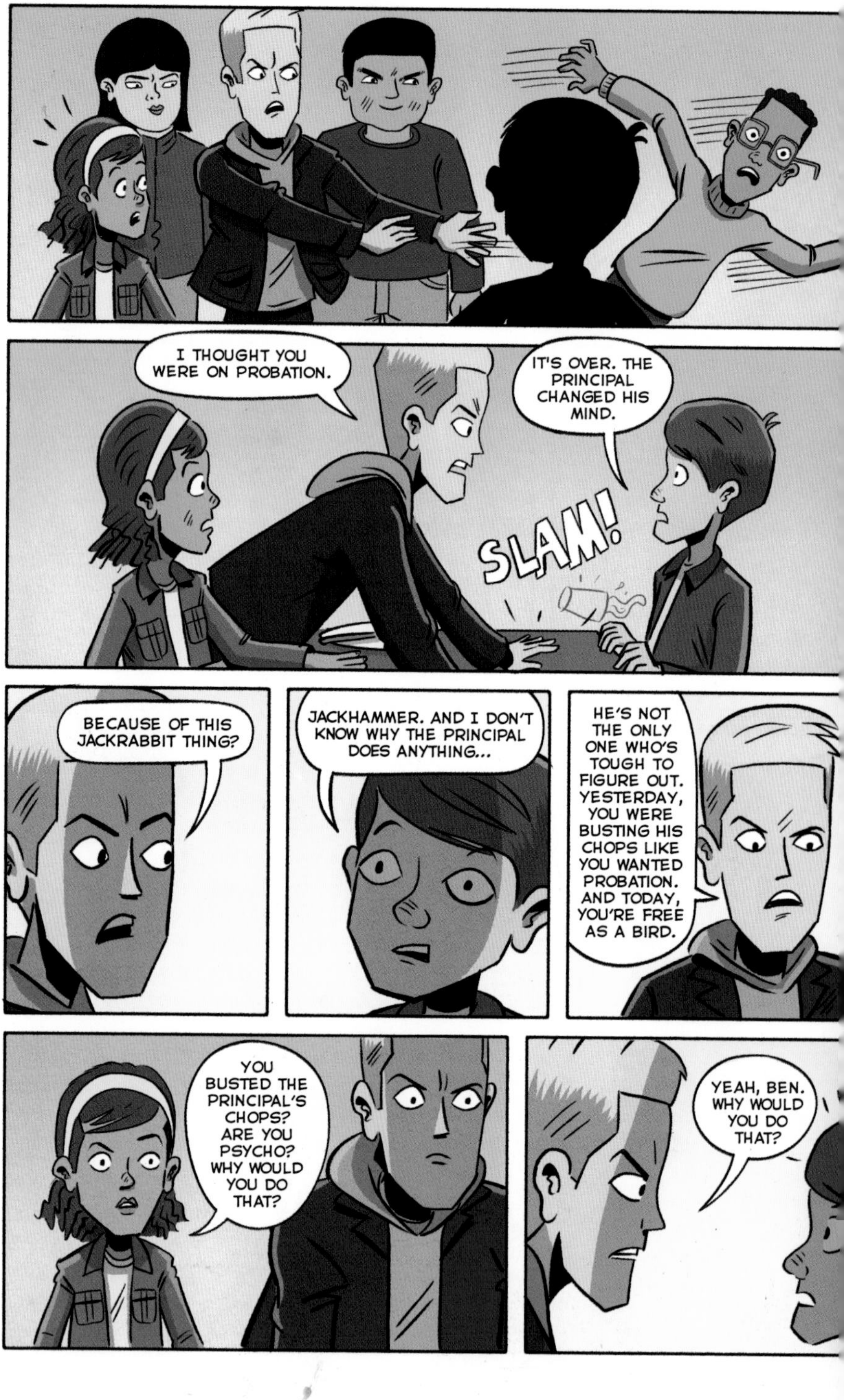
I THOUGHT YOU WERE ON PROBATION.
IT'S OVER. THE PRINCIPAL CHANGED HIS MIND.
SLAM!
BECAUSE OF THIS JACKRABBIT THING?
JACKHAMMER. AND I DON'T KNOW WHY THE PRINCIPAL DOES ANYTHING...
HE'S NOT THE ONLY ONE WHO'S TOUGH TO FIGURE OUT. YESTERDAY, YOU WERE BUSTING HIS CHOPS LIKE YOU WANTED PROBATION. AND TODAY, YOU'RE FREE AS A BIRD.
YOU BUSTED THE PRINCIPAL'S CHOPS? ARE YOU PSYCHO? WHY WOULD YOU DO THAT?
YEAH, BEN. WHY WOULD YOU DO THAT?

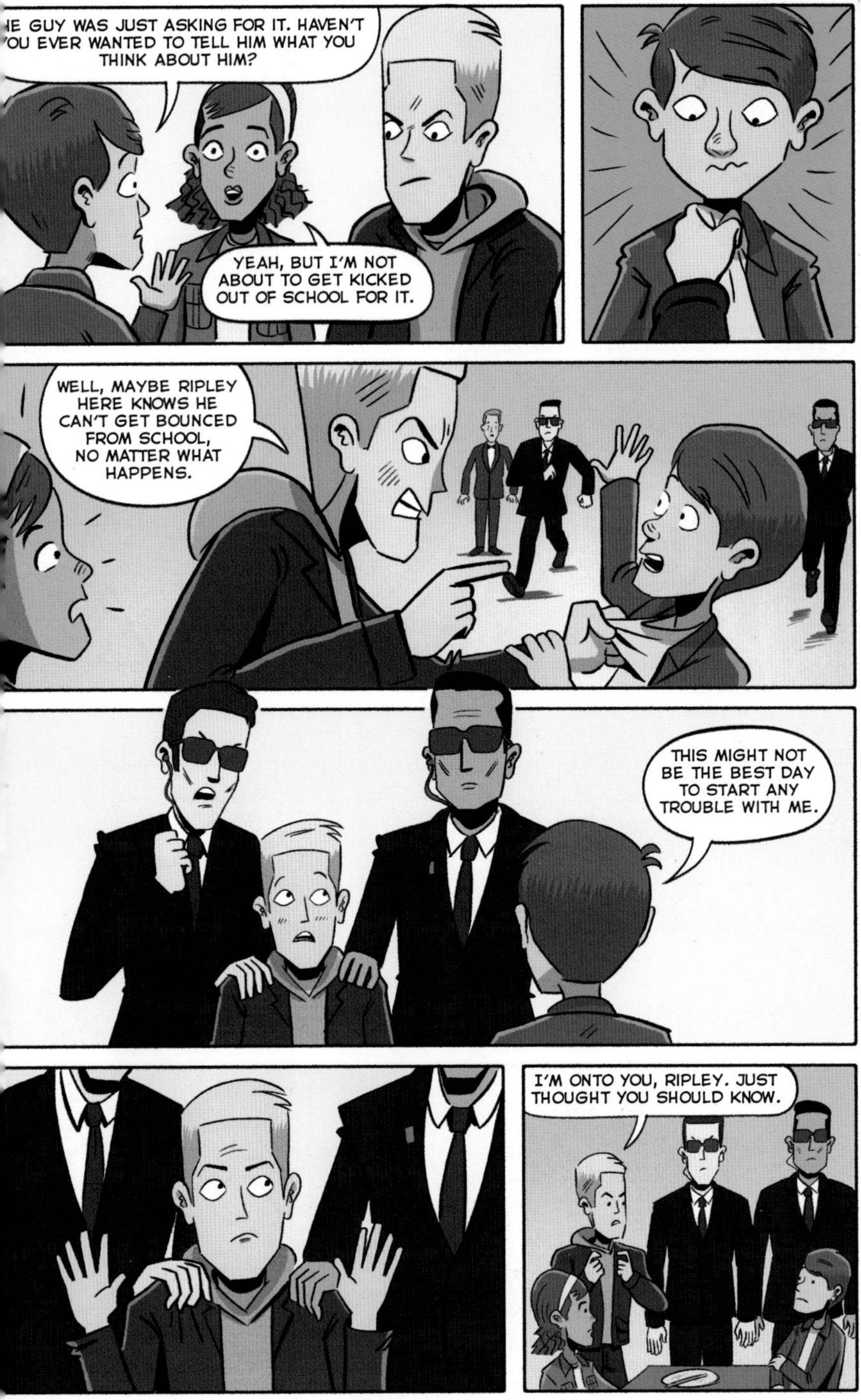
HE GUY WAS JUST ASKING FOR IT. HAVEN'T YOU EVER WANTED TO TELL HIM WHAT YOU THINK ABOUT HIM?
YEAH, BUT I'M NOT ABOUT TO GET KICKED OUT OF SCHOOL FOR IT.
WELL, MAYBE RIPLEY HERE KNOWS HE CAN'T GET BOUNCED FROM SCHOOL, NO MATTER WHAT HAPPENS.
THIS MIGHT NOT BE THE BEST DAY TO START ANY TROUBLE WITH ME.
I'M ONTO YOU, RIPLEY. JUST THOUGHT YOU SHOULD KNOW.

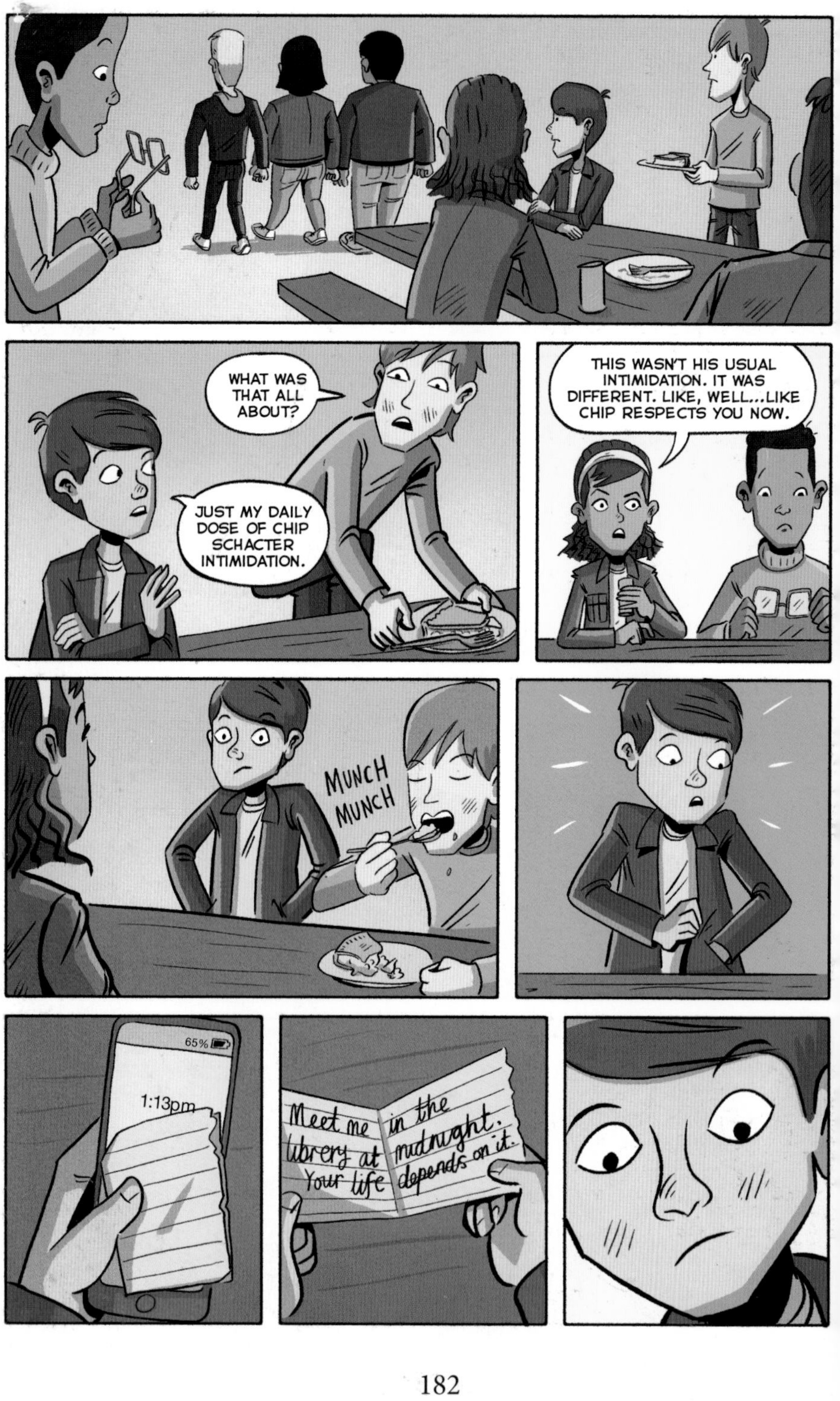
WHAT WAS THAT ALL ABOUT?
JUST MY DAILY DOSE OF CHIP SCHACTER INTIMIDATION.
THIS WASN'T HIS USUAL INTIMIDATION. IT WAS DIFFERENT. LIKE, WELL...LIKE CHIP RESPECTS YOU NOW.
MUNCH MUNCH
65%
1:13pm
Meet me in the library at midnight. Your life depends on it.

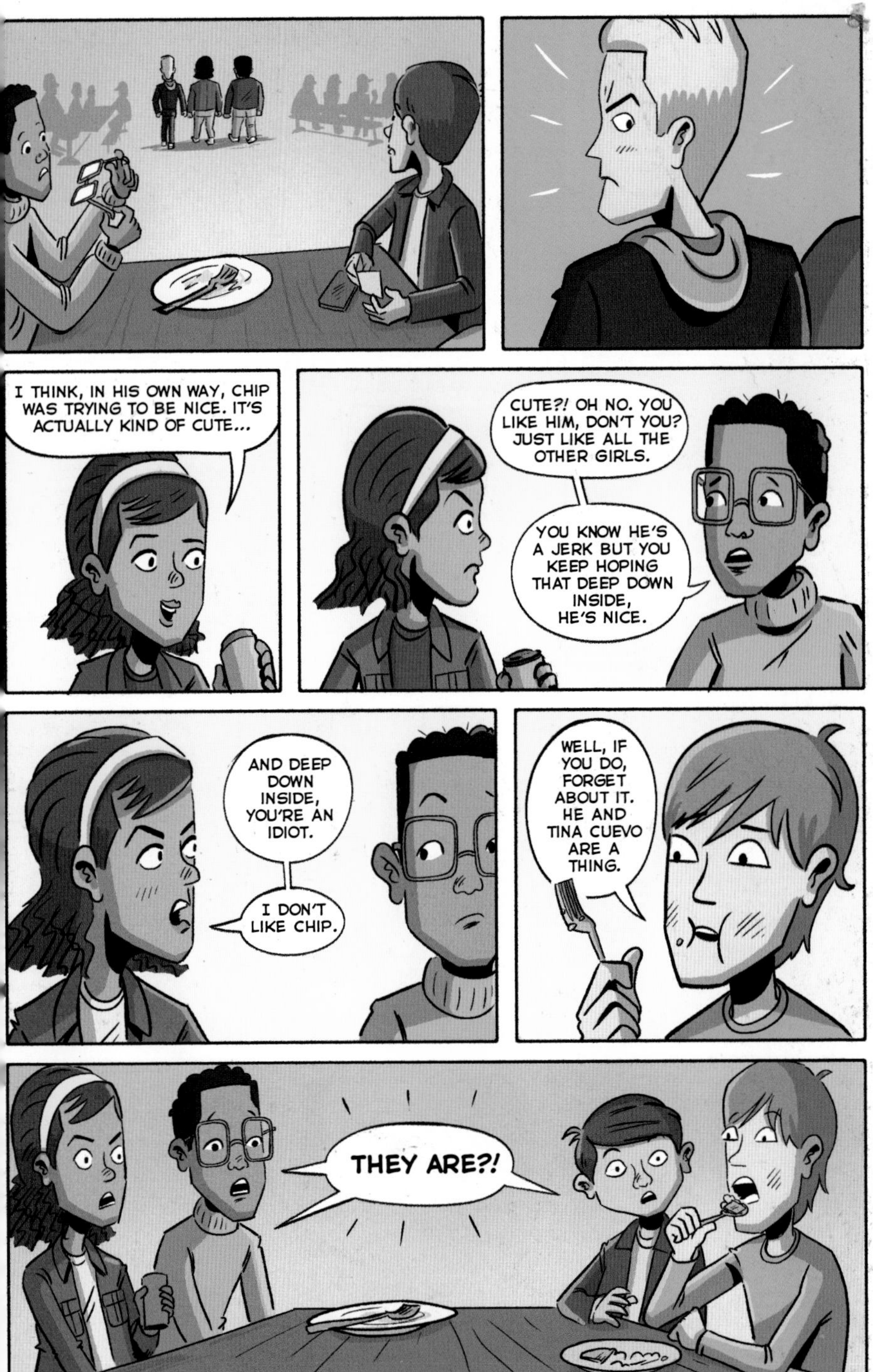
I THINK, IN HIS OWN WAY, CHIP WAS TRYING TO BE NICE. IT'S ACTUALLY KIND OF CUTE...
CUTE?! OH NO. YOU LIKE HIM, DON'T YOU? JUST LIKE ALL THE OTHER GIRLS.
YOU KNOW HE'S A JERK BUT YOU KEEP HOPING THAT DEEP DOWN INSIDE, HE'S NICE.
AND DEEP DOWN INSIDE, YOU'RE AN IDIOT.
I DON'T LIKE CHIP.
WELL, IF YOU DO, FORGET ABOUT IT. HE AND TINA CUEVO ARE A THING.
THEY ARE?!

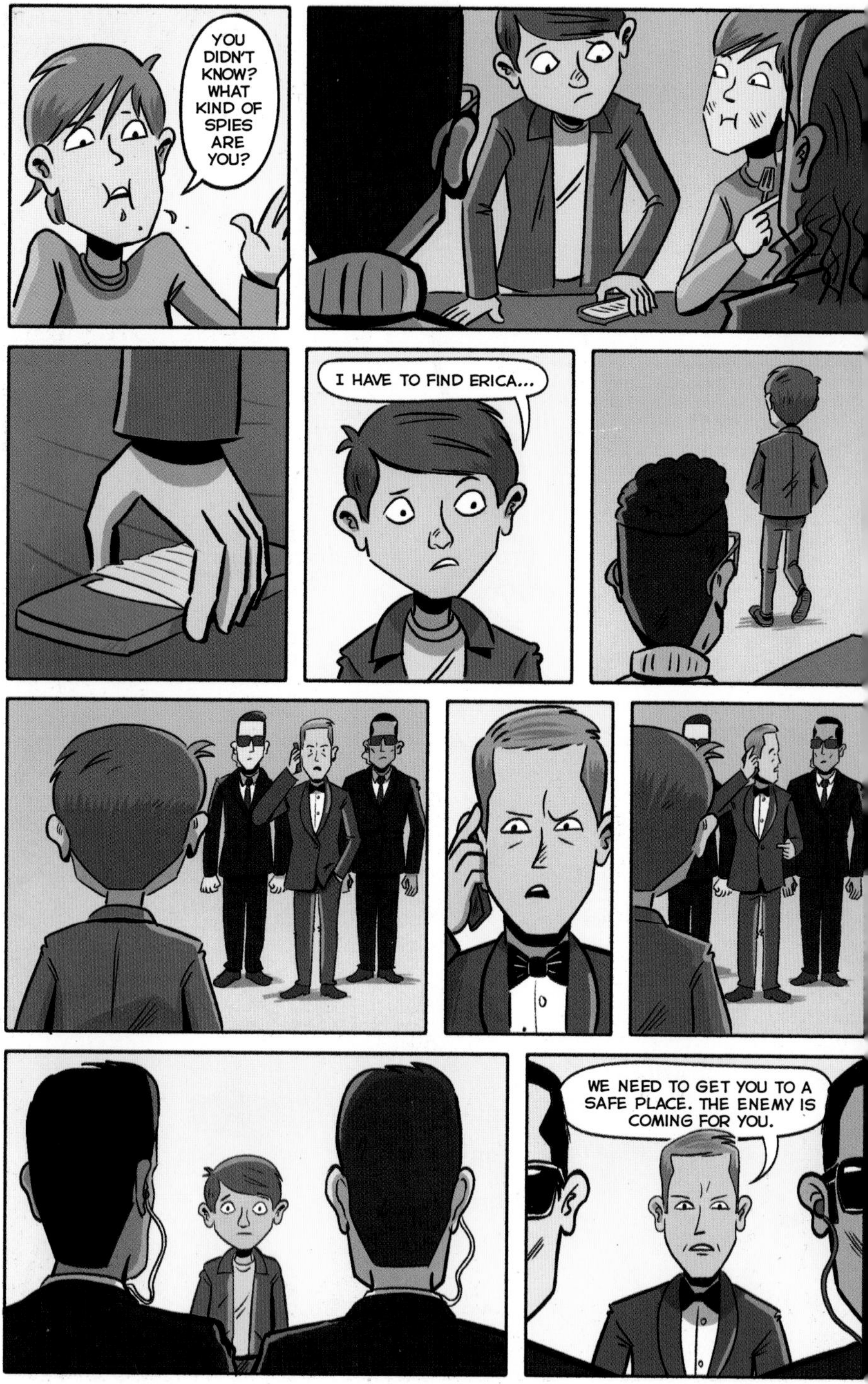
YOU DIDN'T KNOW? WHAT KIND OF SPIES ARE YOU?
I HAVE TO FIND ERICA...
WE NEED TO GET YOU TO A SAFE PLACE. THE ENEMY IS COMING FOR YOU.

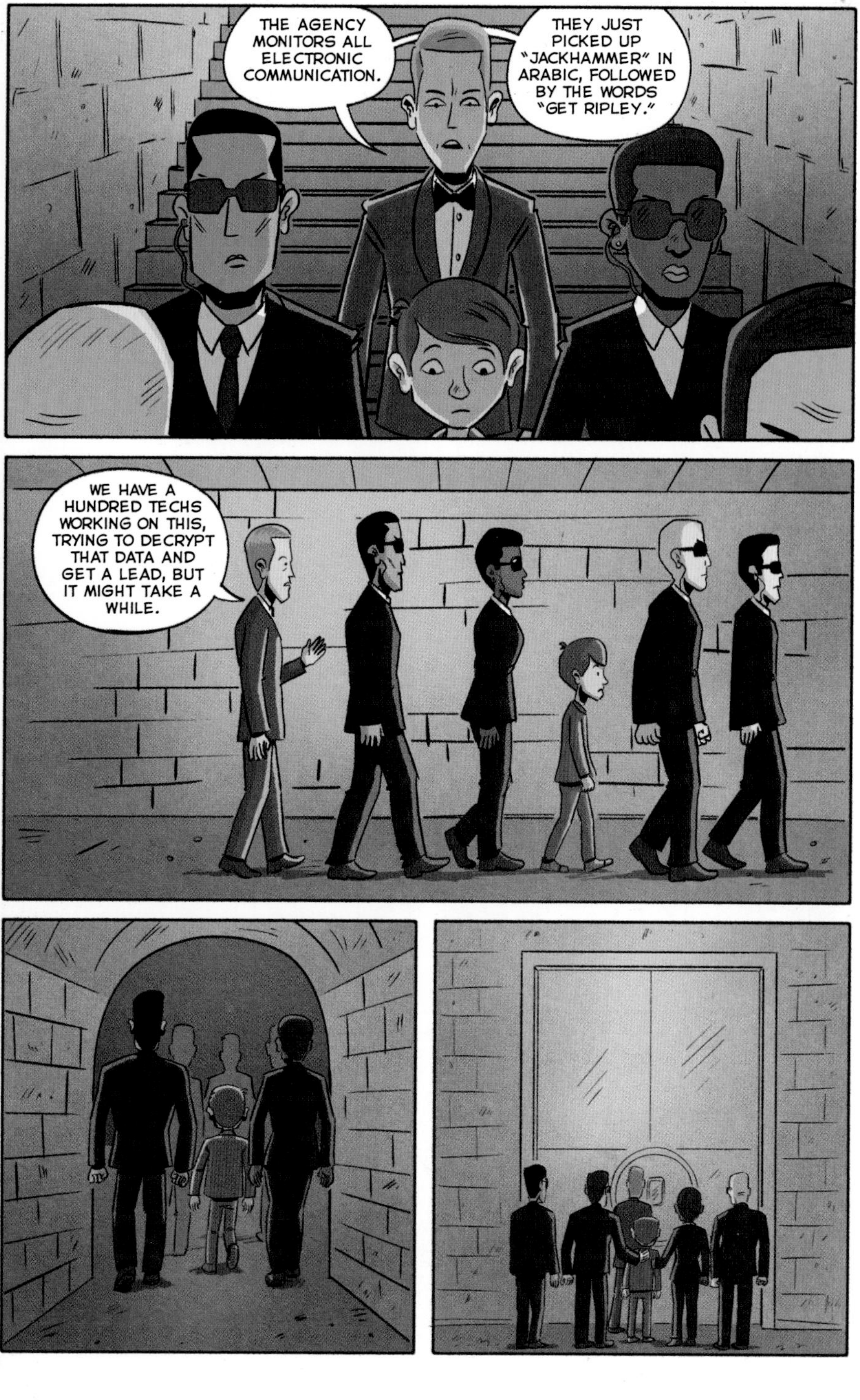
THE AGENCY MONITORS ALL ELECTRONIC COMMUNICATION.
THEY JUST PICKED UP "JACKHAMMER" IN ARABIC, FOLLOWED BY THE WORDS "GET RIPLEY."
WE HAVE A HUNDRED TECHS WORKING ON THIS, TRYING TO DECRYPT THAT DATA AND GET A LEAD, BUT IT MIGHT TAKE A WHILE.

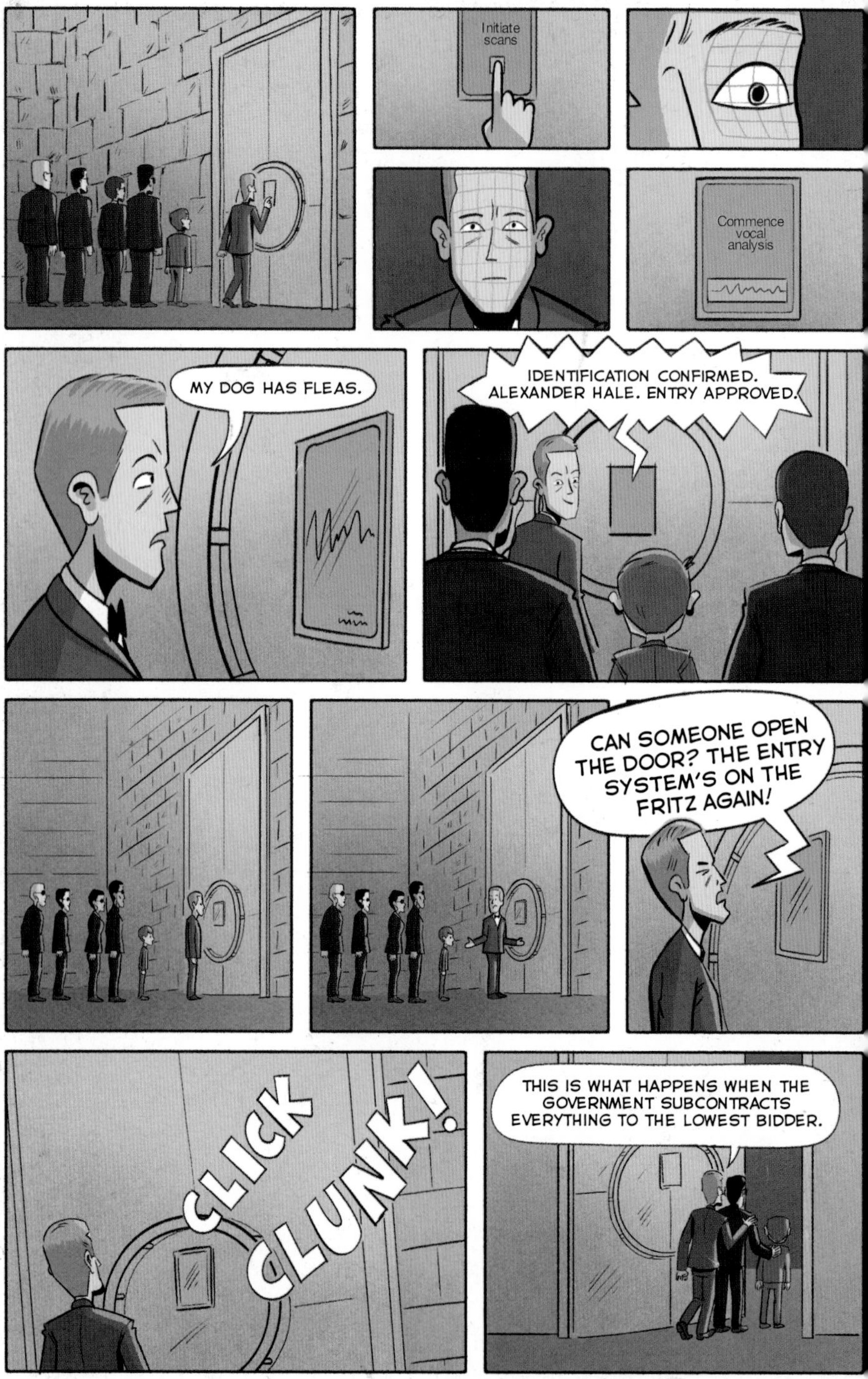
Initiate scans
Commence vocal analysis
MY DOG HAS FLEAS.
IDENTIFICATION CONFIRMED. ALEXANDER HALE. ENTRY APPROVED.
CAN SOMEONE OPEN THE DOOR? THE ENTRY SYSTEM'S ON THE FRITZ AGAIN!
CLICK
CLUNK!
THIS IS WHAT HAPPENS WHEN THE GOVERNMENT SUBCONTRACTS EVERYTHING TO THE LOWEST BIDDER.

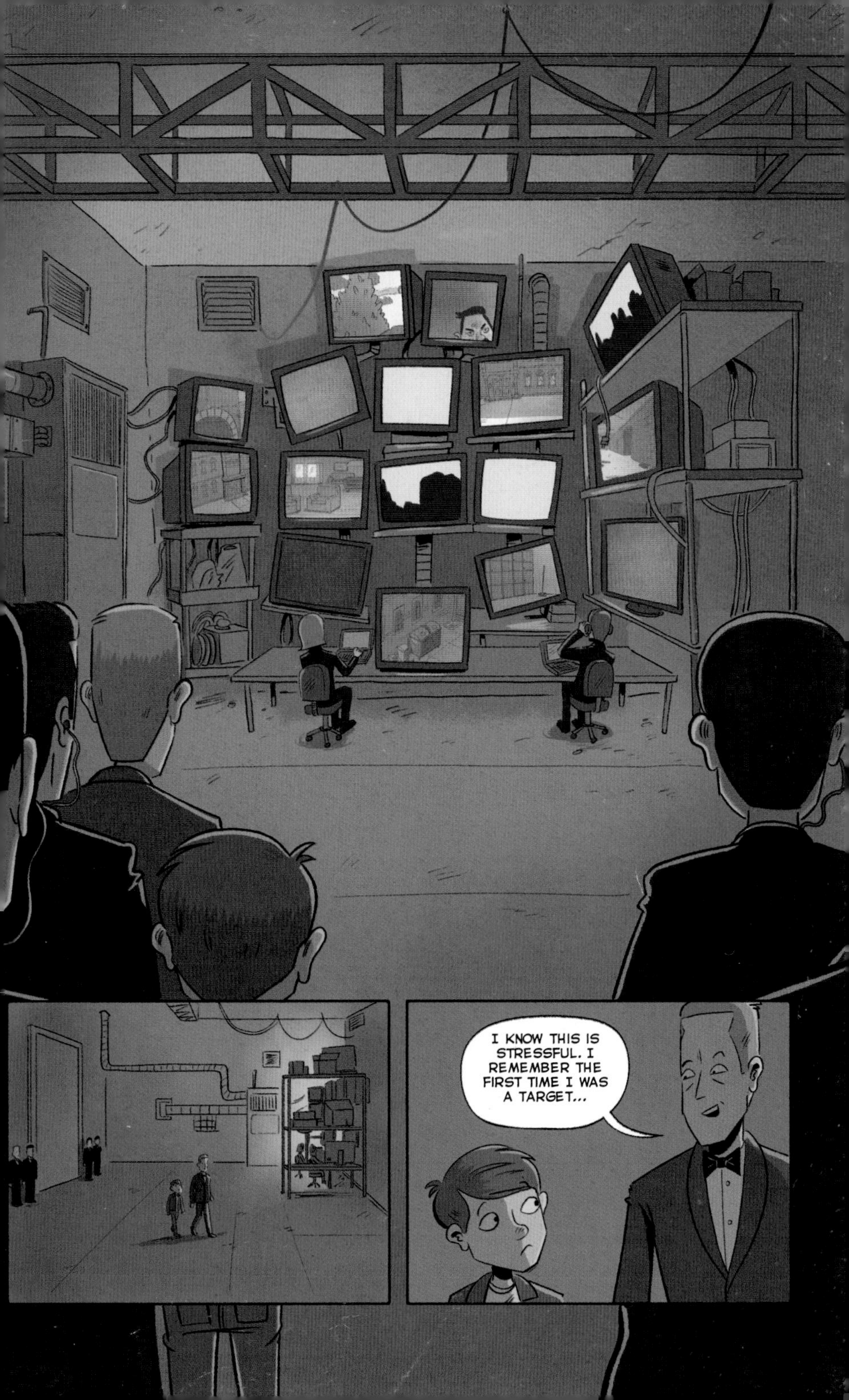
I KNOW THIS IS STRESSFUL. I REMEMBER THE FIRST TIME I WAS A TARGET...

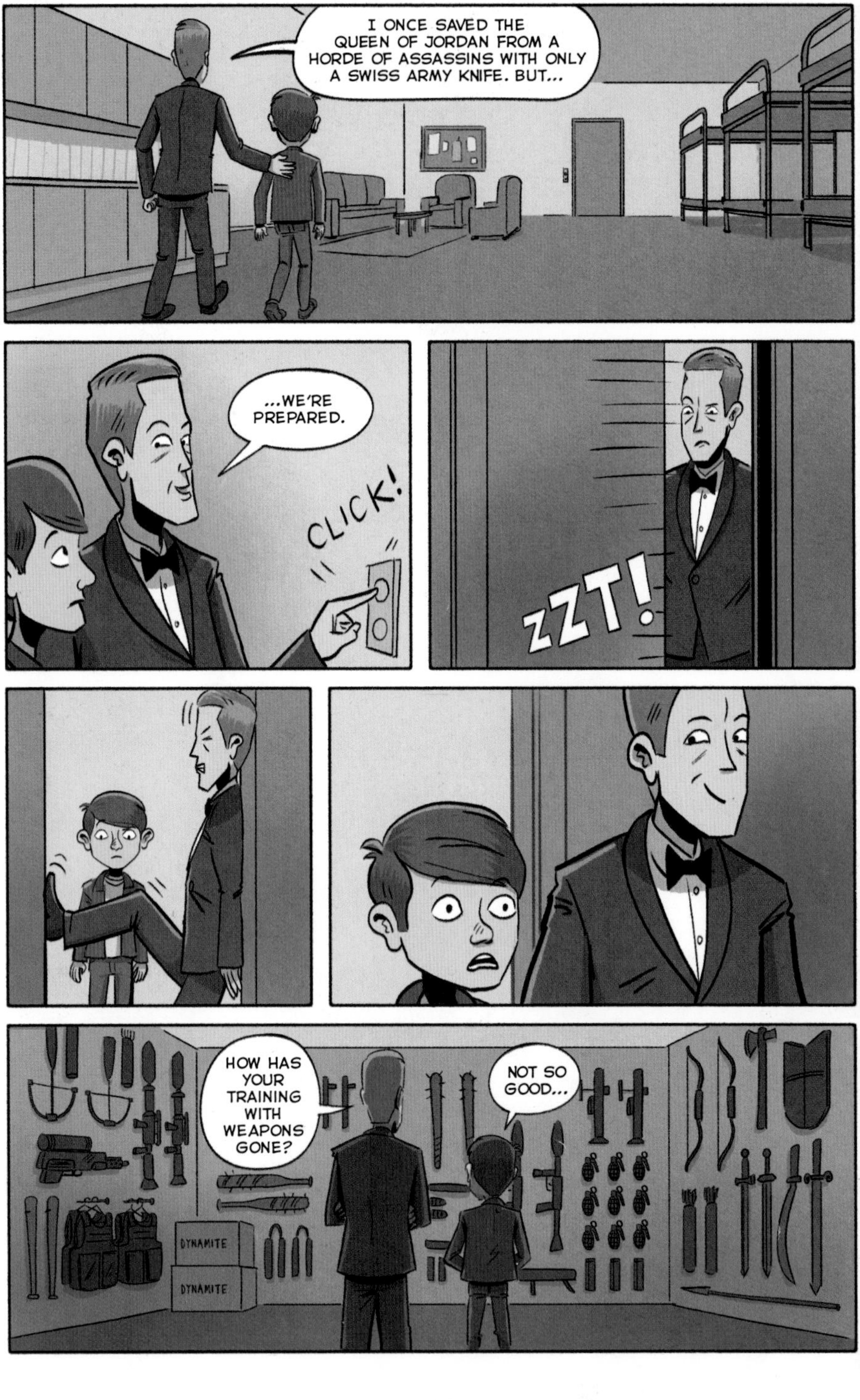
I ONCE SAVED THE QUEEN OF JORDAN FROM A HORDE OF ASSASSINS WITH ONLY A SWISS ARMY KNIFE. BUT...
...WE'RE PREPARED.
CLICK!
zZT!
HOW HAS YOUR TRAINING WITH WEAPONS GONE?
NOT SO GOOD...
DYNAMITE
DYNAMITE

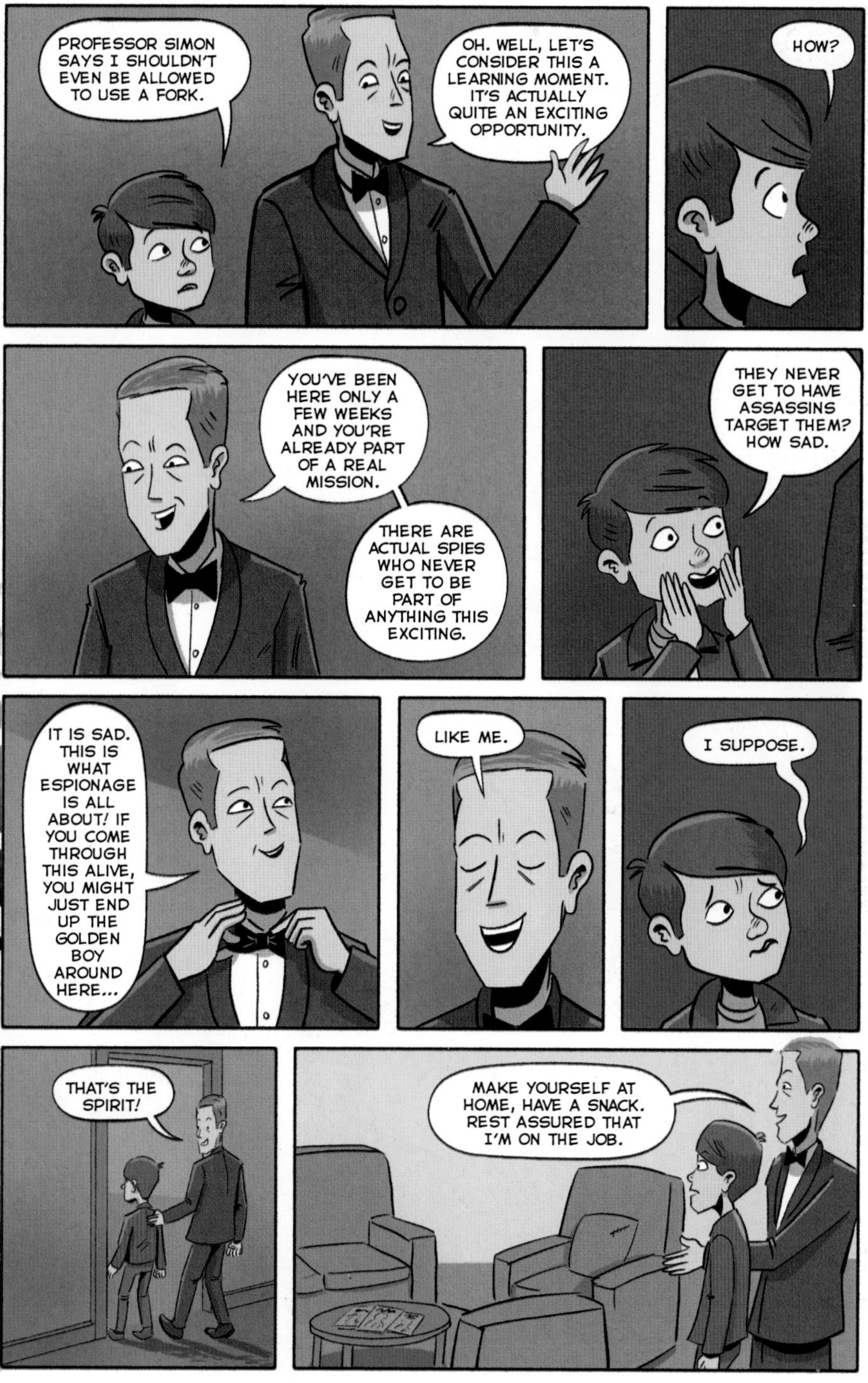
PROFESSOR SIMON SAYS I SHOULDN'T EVEN BE ALLOWED TO USE A FORK.
OH. WELL, LET'S CONSIDER THIS A LEARNING MOMENT. IT'S ACTUALLY QUITE AN EXCITING OPPORTUNITY.
HOW?
YOU'VE BEEN HERE ONLY A FEW WEEKS AND YOU'RE ALREADY PART OF A REAL MISSION.
THERE ARE ACTUAL SPIES WHO NEVER GET TO BE PART OF ANYTHING THIS EXCITING.
THEY NEVER GET TO HAVE ASSASSINS TARGET THEM? HOW SAD.
IT IS SAD. THIS IS WHAT ESPIONAGE IS ALL ABOUT! IF YOU COME THROUGH THIS ALIVE, YOU MIGHT JUST END UP THE GOLDEN BOY AROUND HERE...
LIKE ME.
I SUPPOSE.
THAT'S THE SPIRIT!
MAKE YOURSELF AT HOME, HAVE A SNACK. REST ASSURED THAT I'M ON THE JOB.

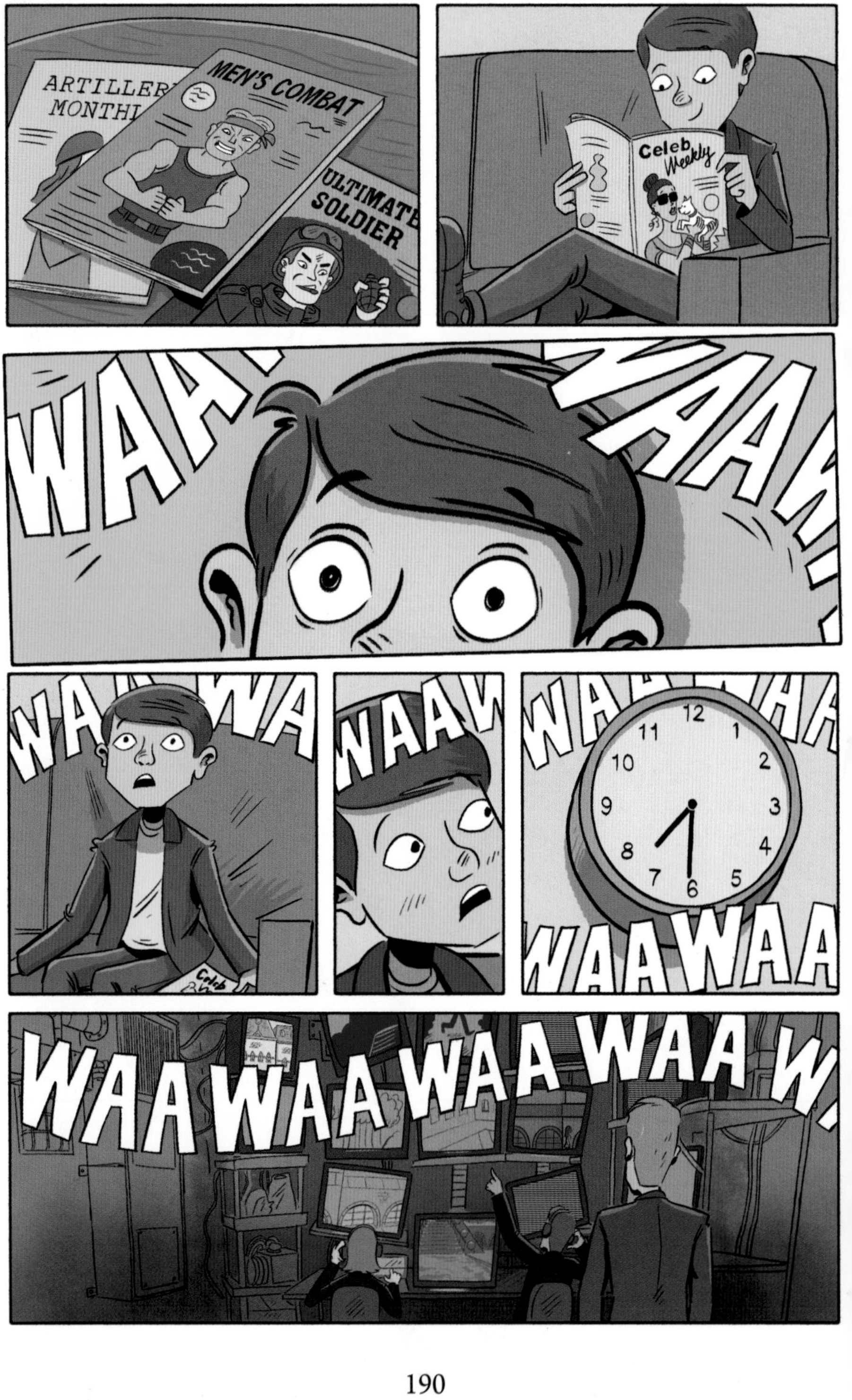
ARTILLER
MONTHL
MEN'S COMBAT
ULTIMATE
SOLDIER
Celeb
Weekly
WAA
WAAW
WAAWA
WAAW
WAAWA
WAAWAA
WAAWAAWAAWAAW

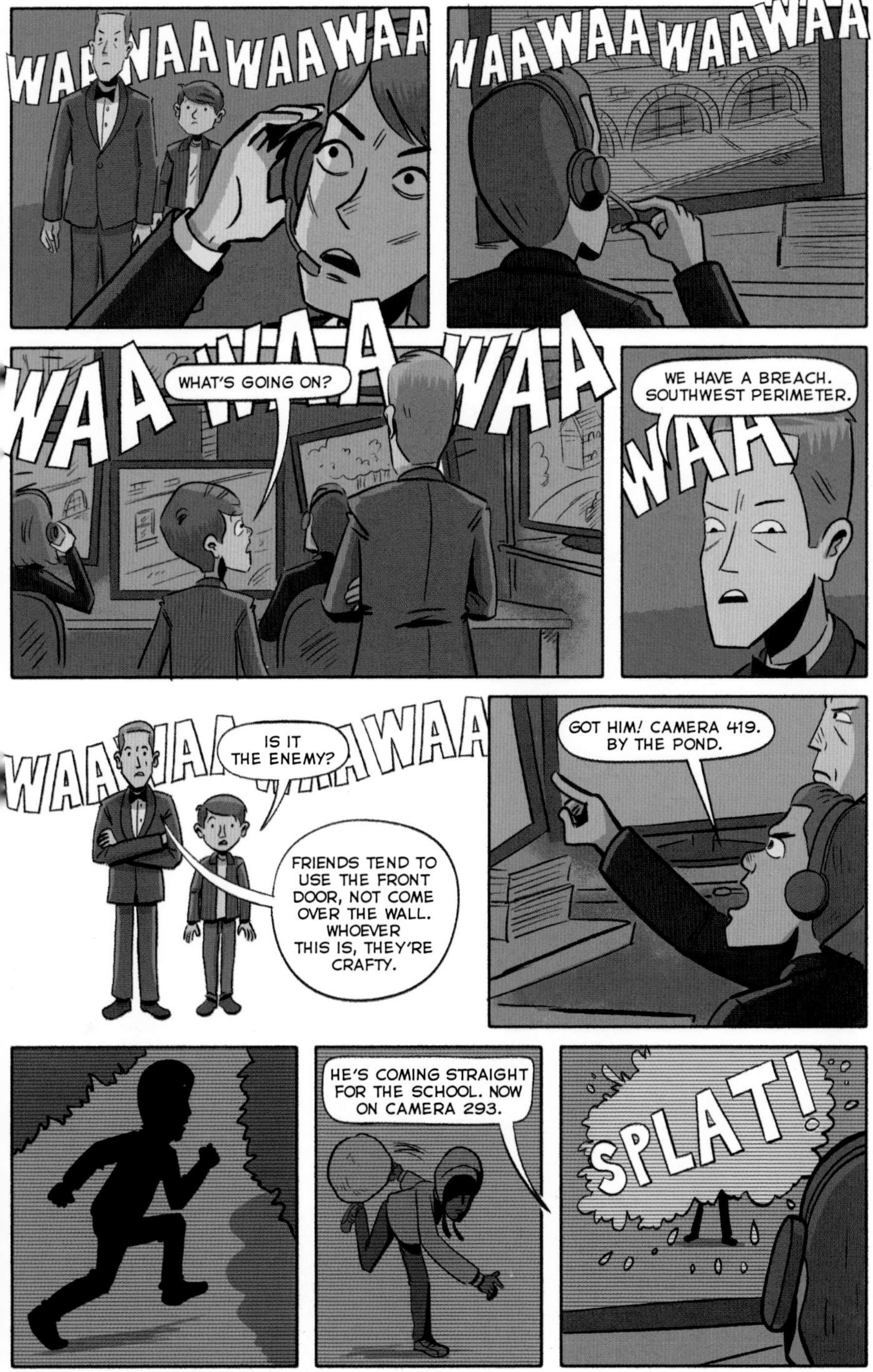
WAAWAAWAAWAA
WAAWAAWAAWAA
WAAWAAWAAWAA
WHAT'S GOING ON?
WE HAVE A BREACH. SOUTHWEST PERIMETER.
WAA
WAAWAAWAAWAA
IS IT THE ENEMY?
FRIENDS TEND TO USE THE FRONT DOOR, NOT COME OVER THE WALL. WHOEVER THIS IS, THEY'RE CRAFTY.
GOT HIM! CAMERA 419. BY THE POND.
HE'S COMING STRAIGHT FOR THE SCHOOL. NOW ON CAMERA 293.
SPLAT!

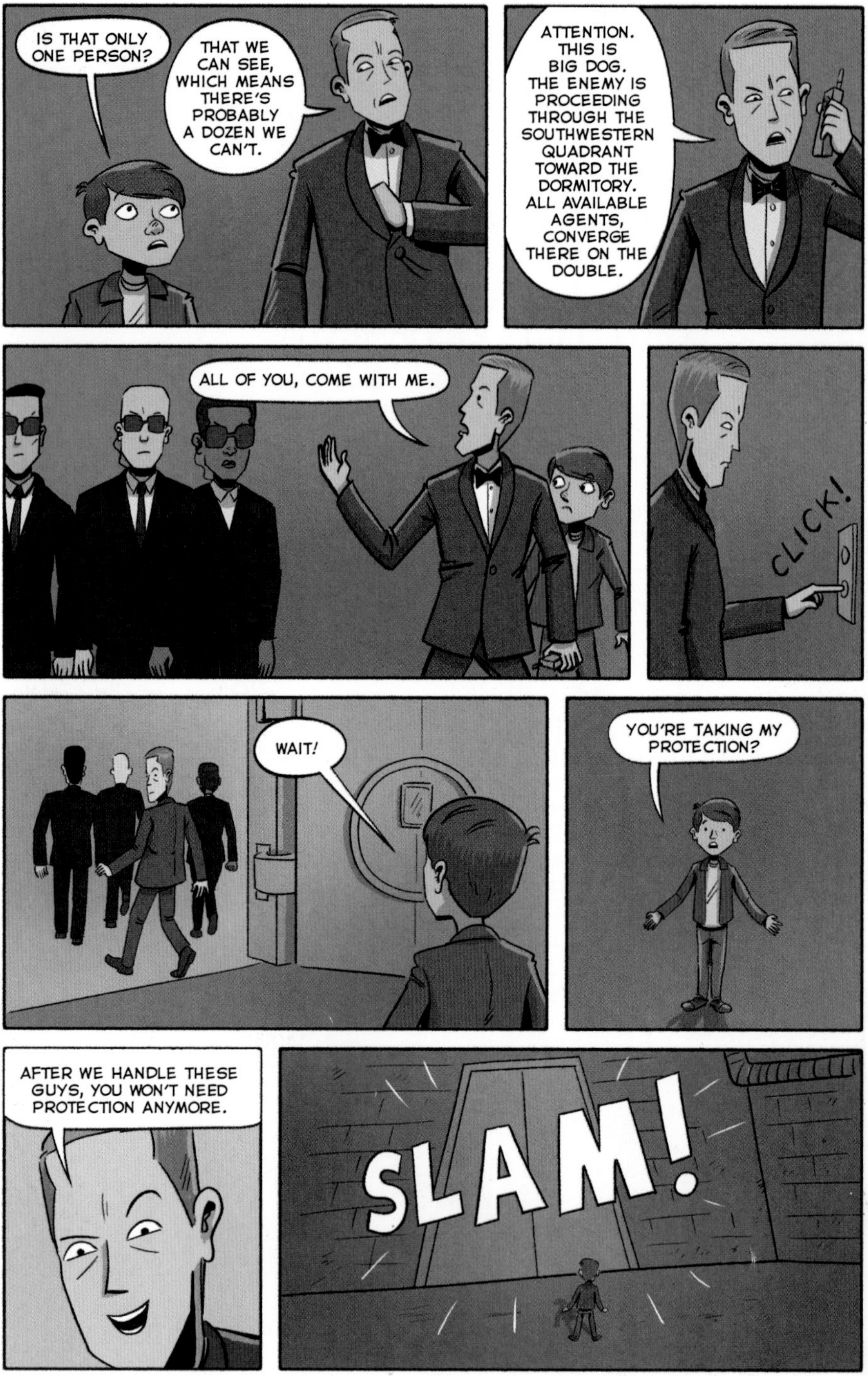
IS THAT ONLY ONE PERSON?
THAT WE CAN SEE, WHICH MEANS THERE'S PROBABLY A DOZEN WE CAN'T.
ATTENTION. THIS IS BIG DOG. THE ENEMY IS PROCEEDING THROUGH THE SOUTHWESTERN QUADRANT TOWARD THE DORMITORY. ALL AVAILABLE AGENTS, CONVERGE THERE ON THE DOUBLE.
ALL OF YOU, COME WITH ME.
CLICK!
WAIT!
YOU'RE TAKING MY PROTECTION?
AFTER WE HANDLE THESE GUYS, YOU WON'T NEED PROTECTION ANYMORE.
SLAM!

IT REALLY LOOKS LIKE THERE'S JUST ONE GUY.

ATTACK!

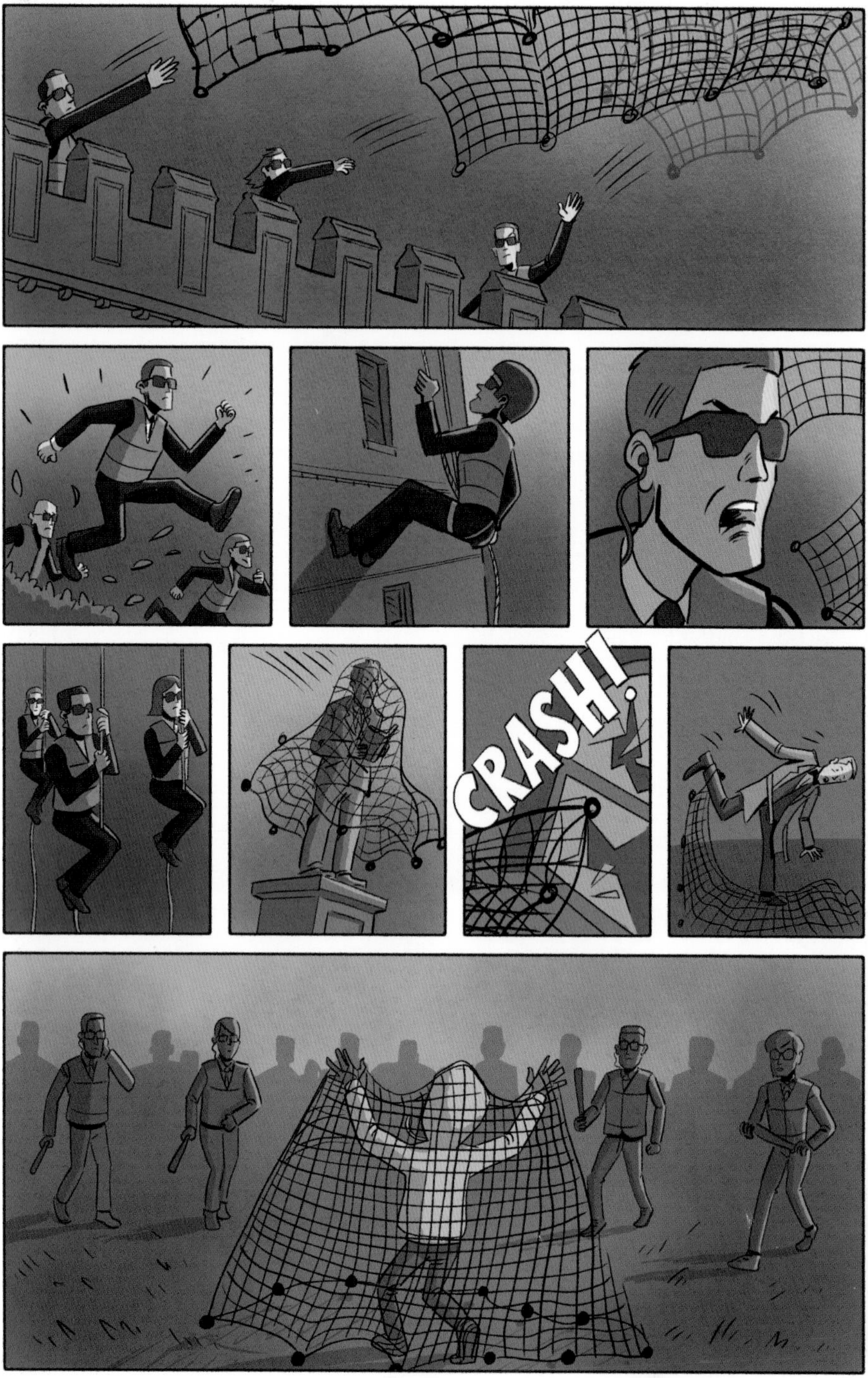
CRASH!

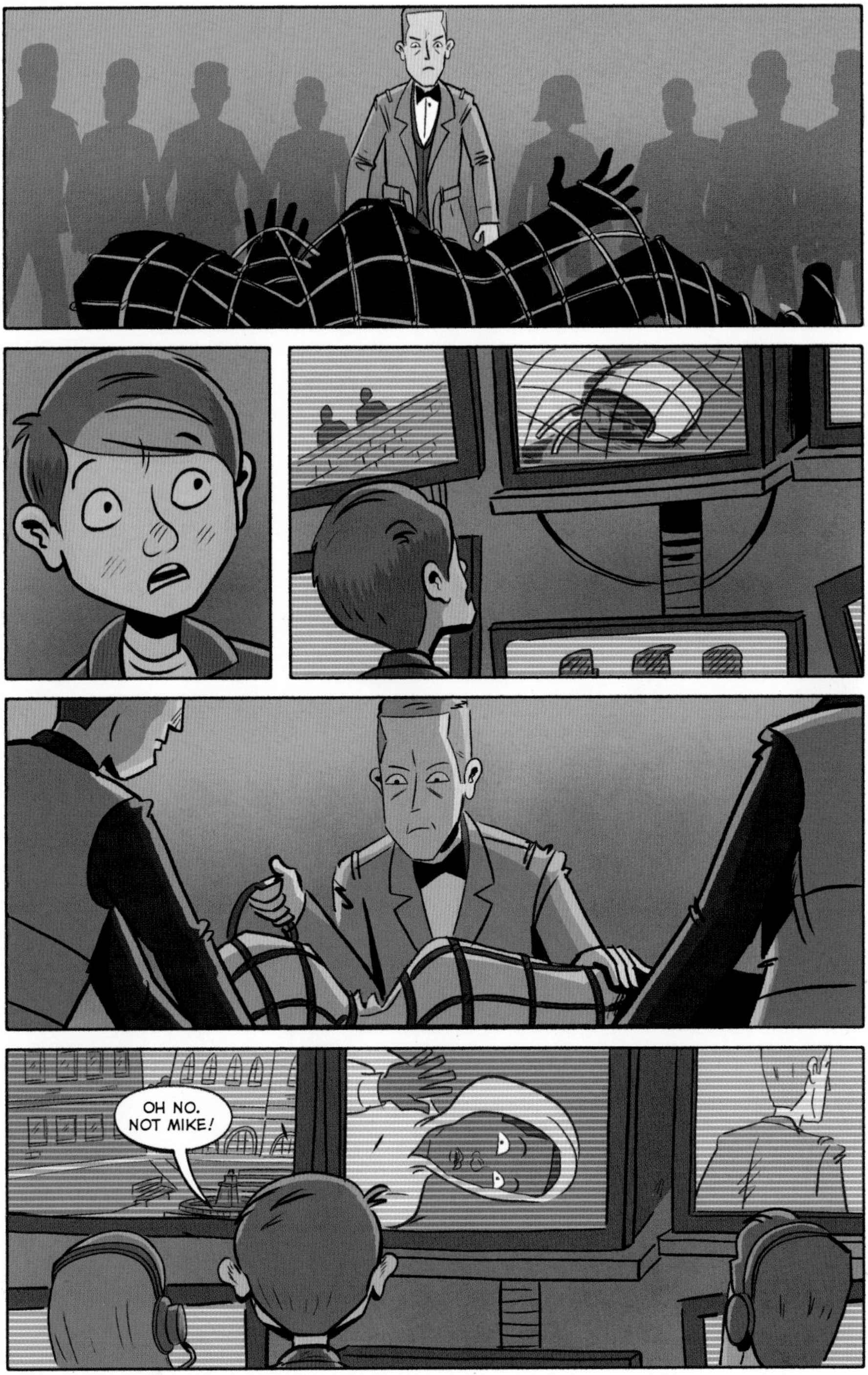
OH NO.
NOT MIKE!

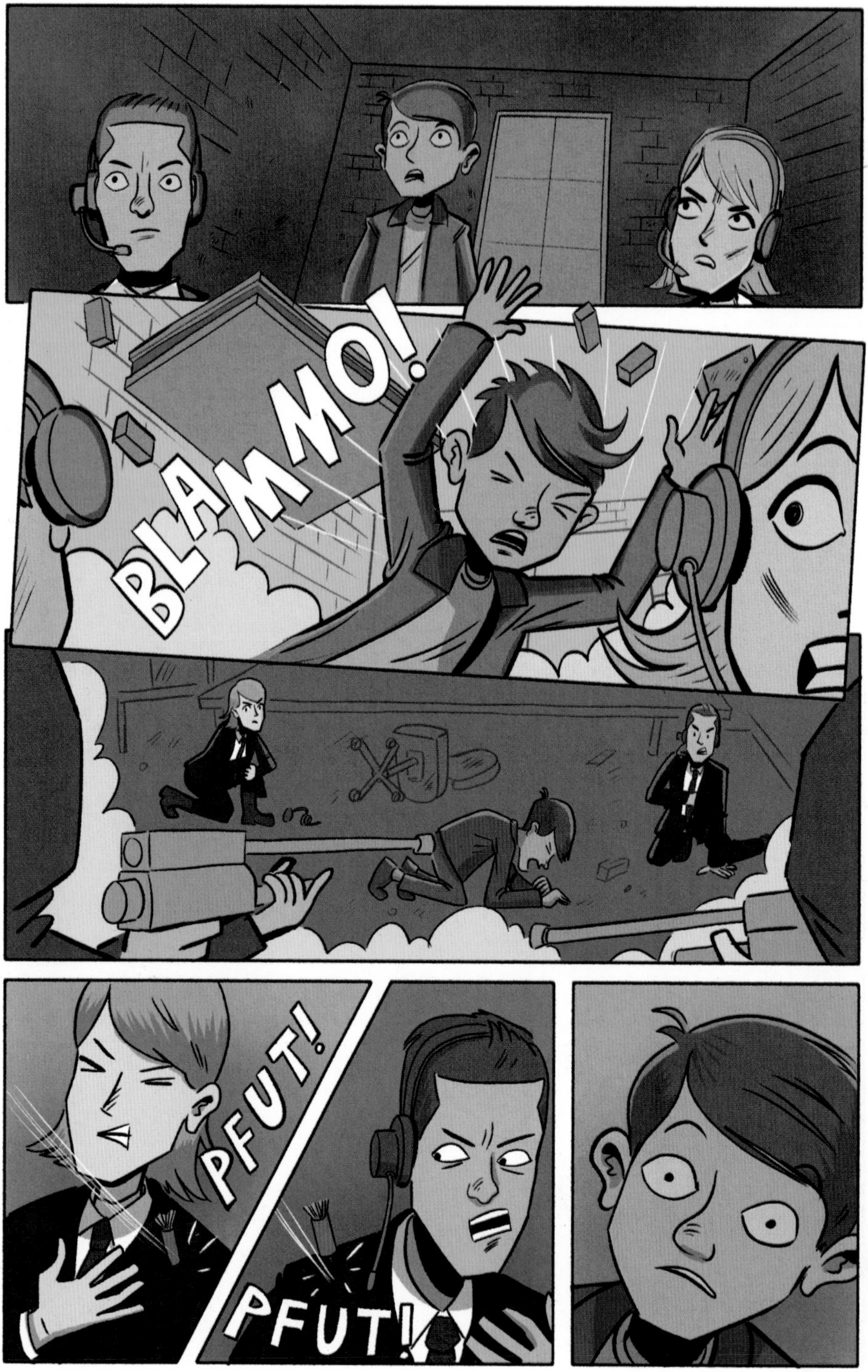
BLAMMO!
PFUT!
PFUT!

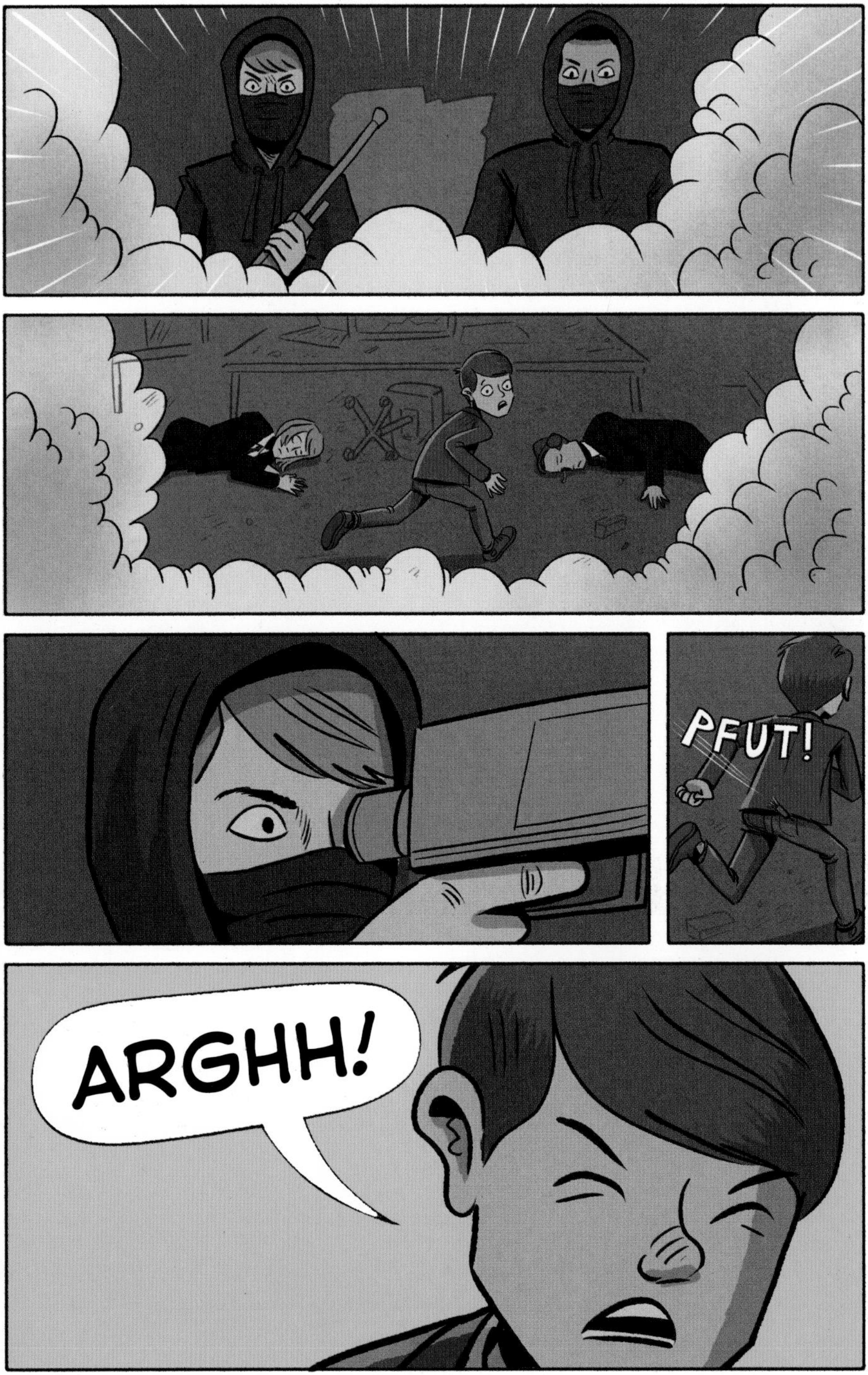
PFUT!
ARGHH!

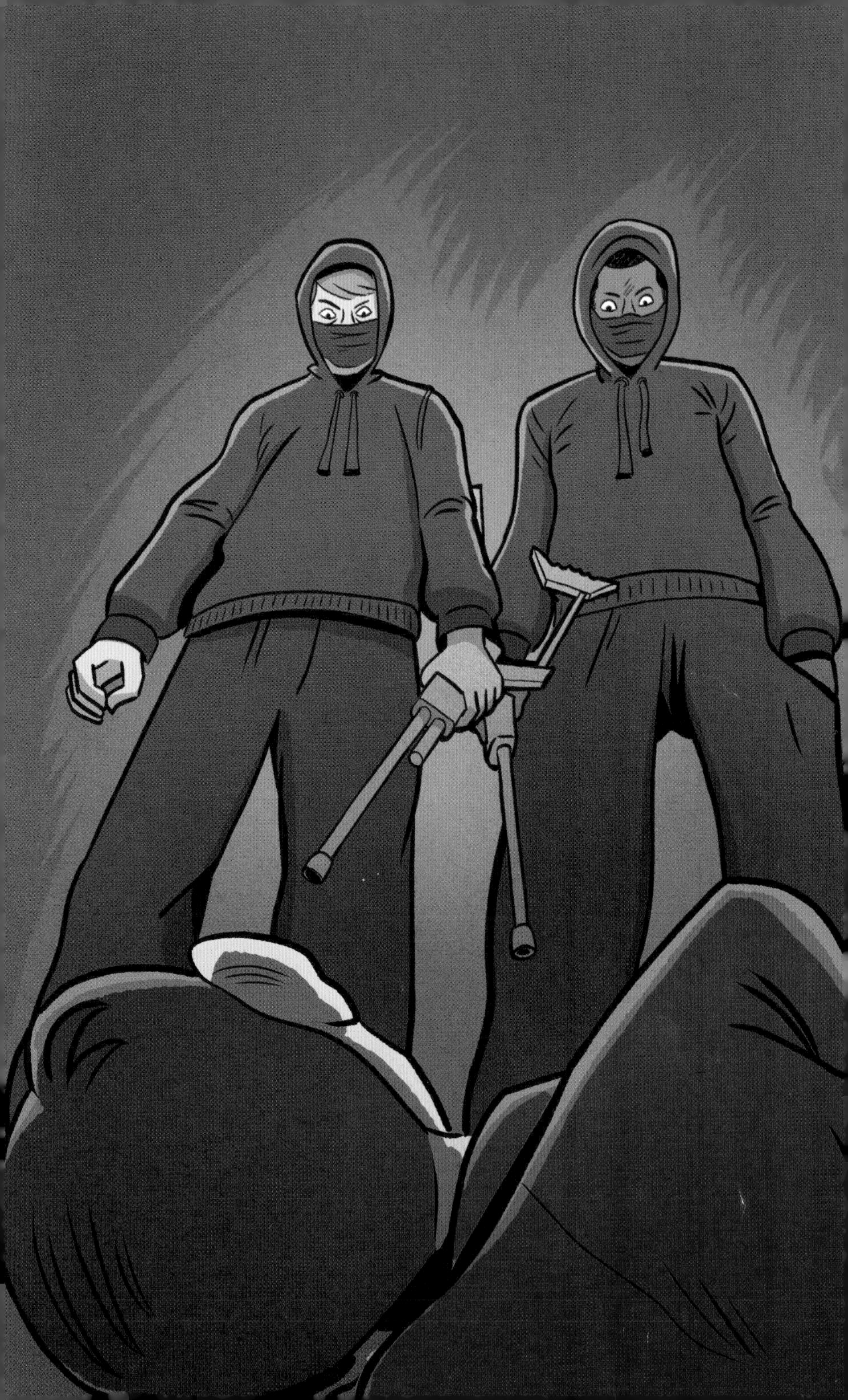

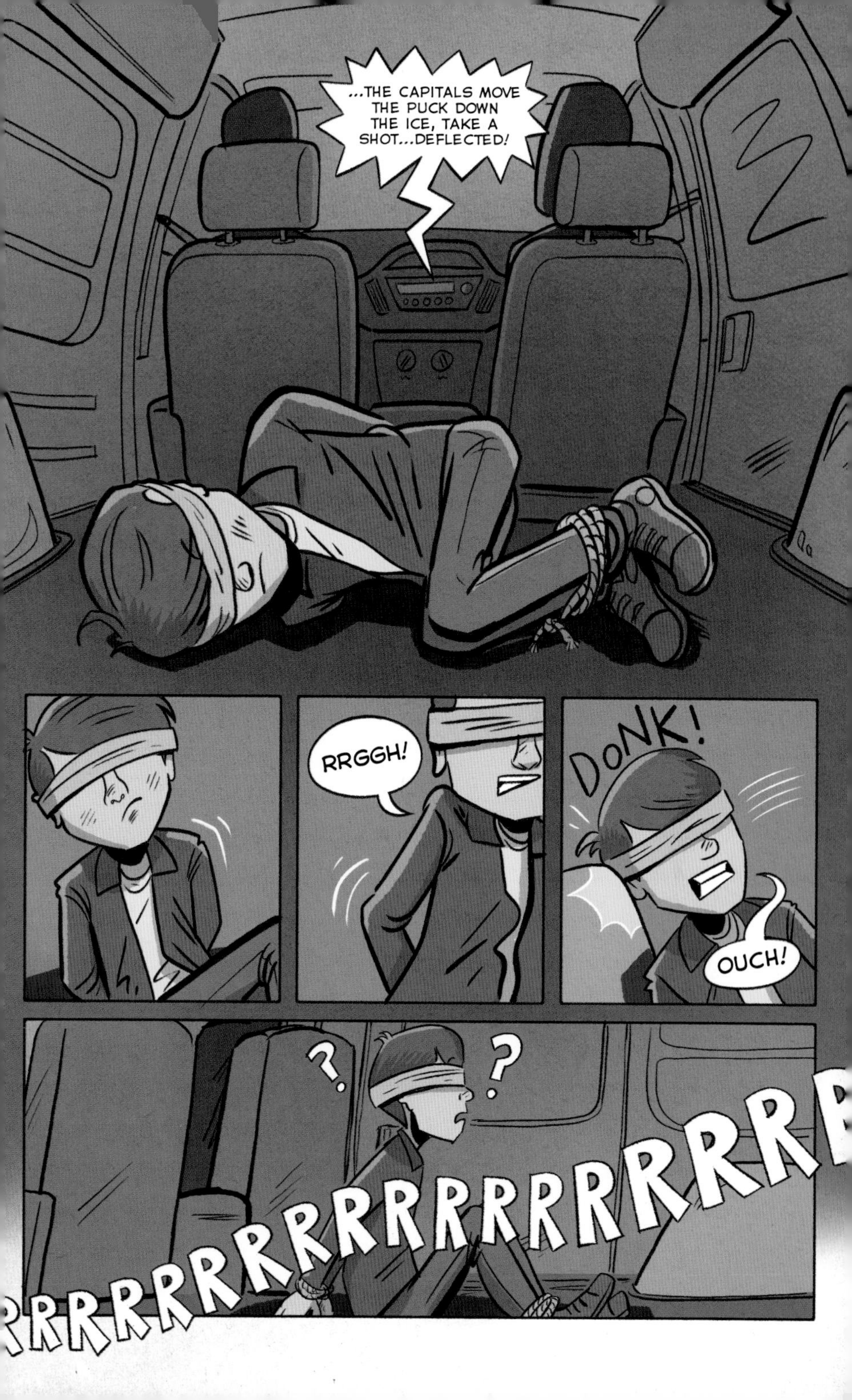
...THE CAPITALS MOVE THE PUCK DOWN THE ICE, TAKE A SHOT...DEFLECTED!
RRGGH!
DONK!
OUCH!
? ?
RRRRRRRRRRRRRRRRRR

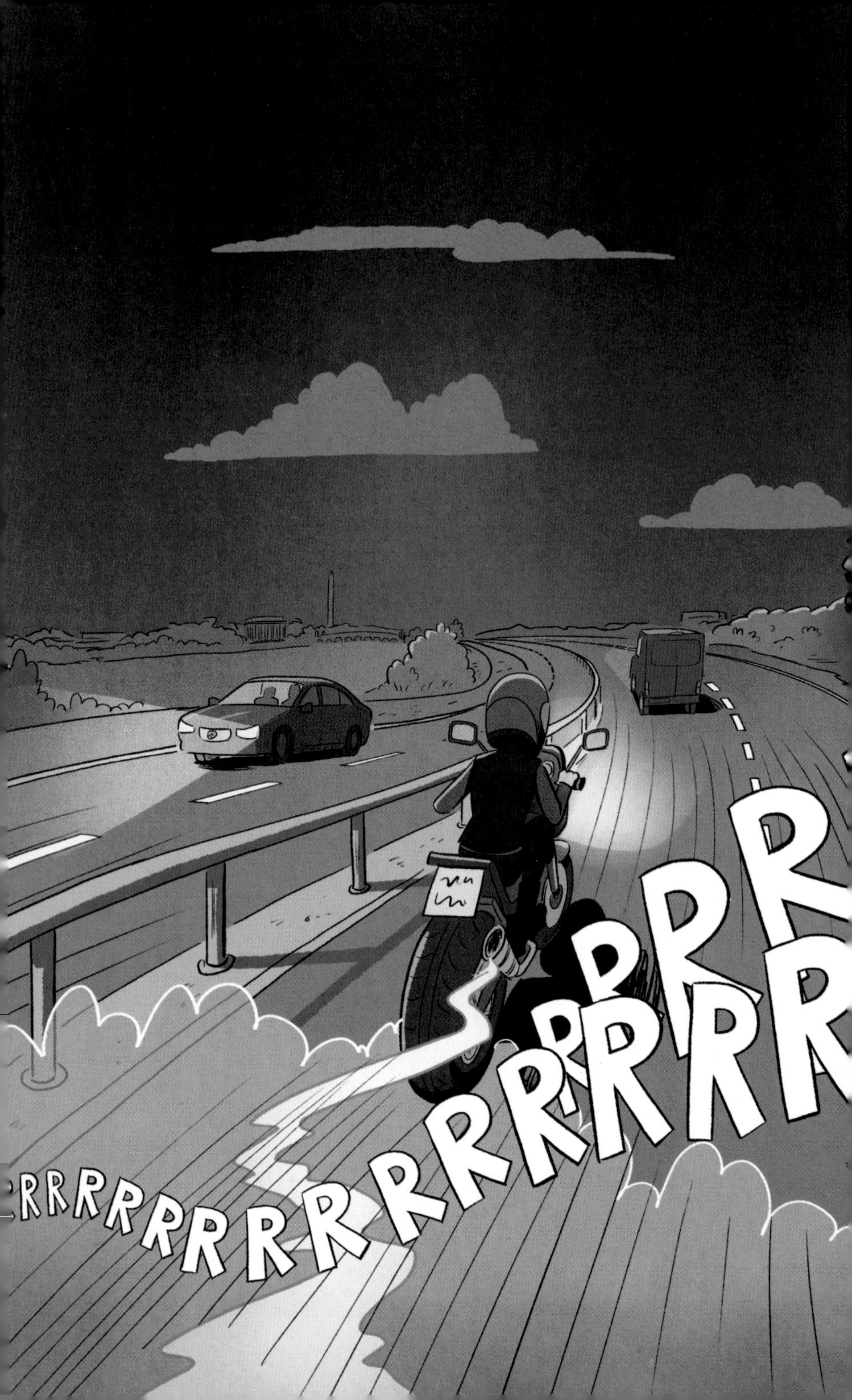
RRRRRRRRRRRRRRRRRR

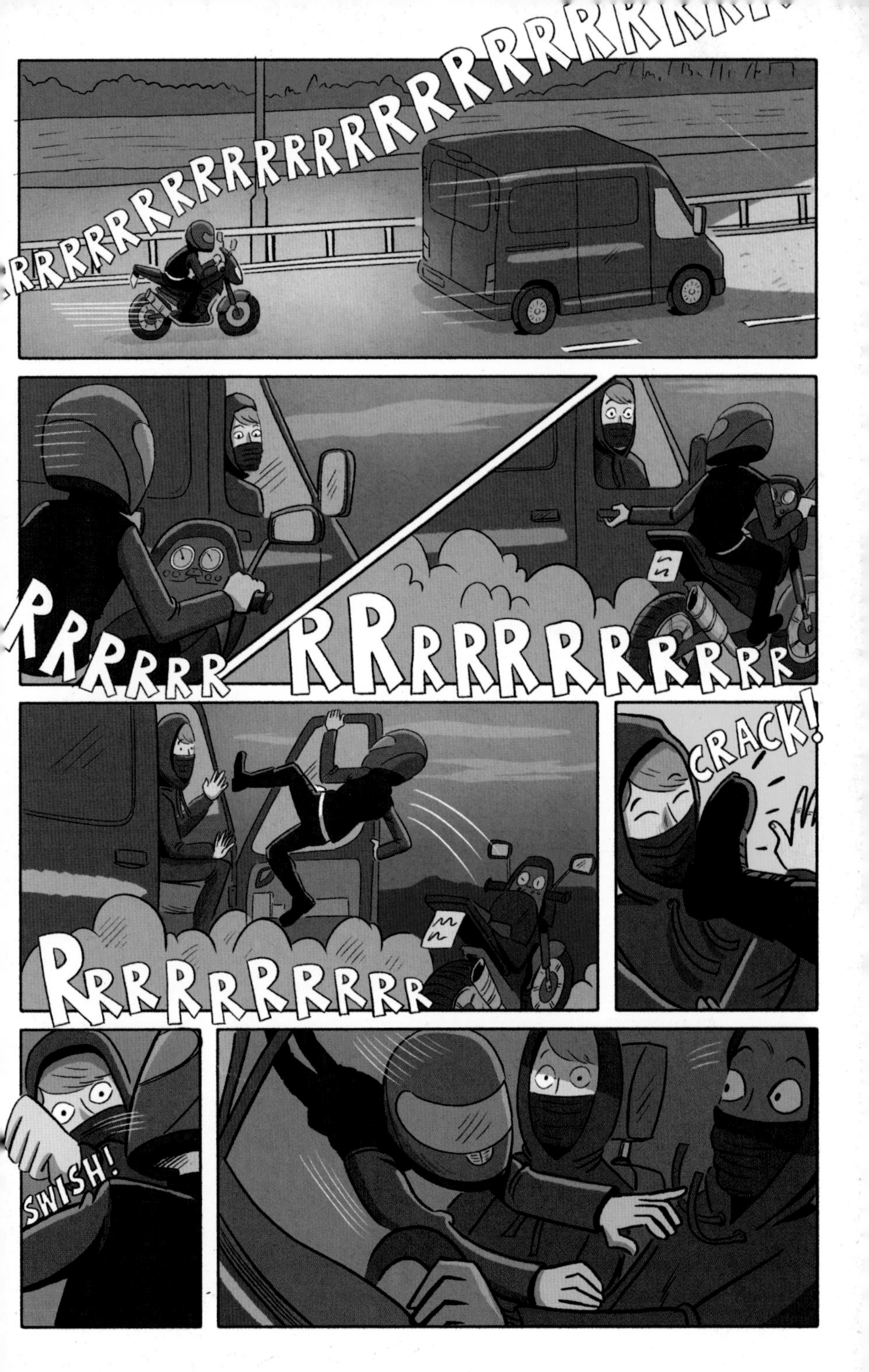
RRRRRRRRRRRRRRRRRRRRRRRR
RRRRRR
RRRRRRRRRRRRR
RRRRRRRRRRRR
CRACK!
SWISH!

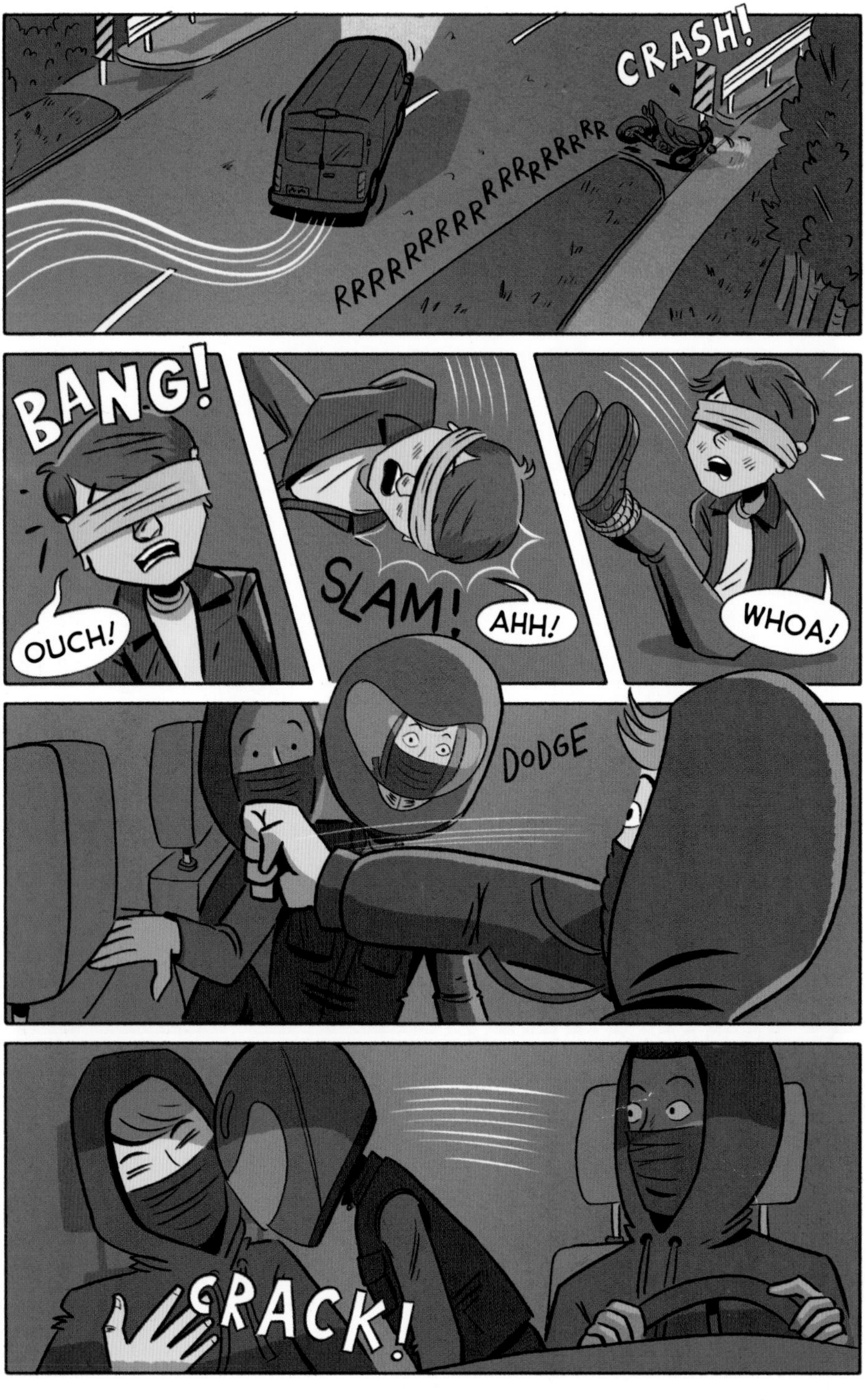
CRASH!
RRRRRRRRRRRRRRRRRRRRR
BANG!
OUCH!
SLAM!
AHH!
WHOA!
DODGE
CRACK!

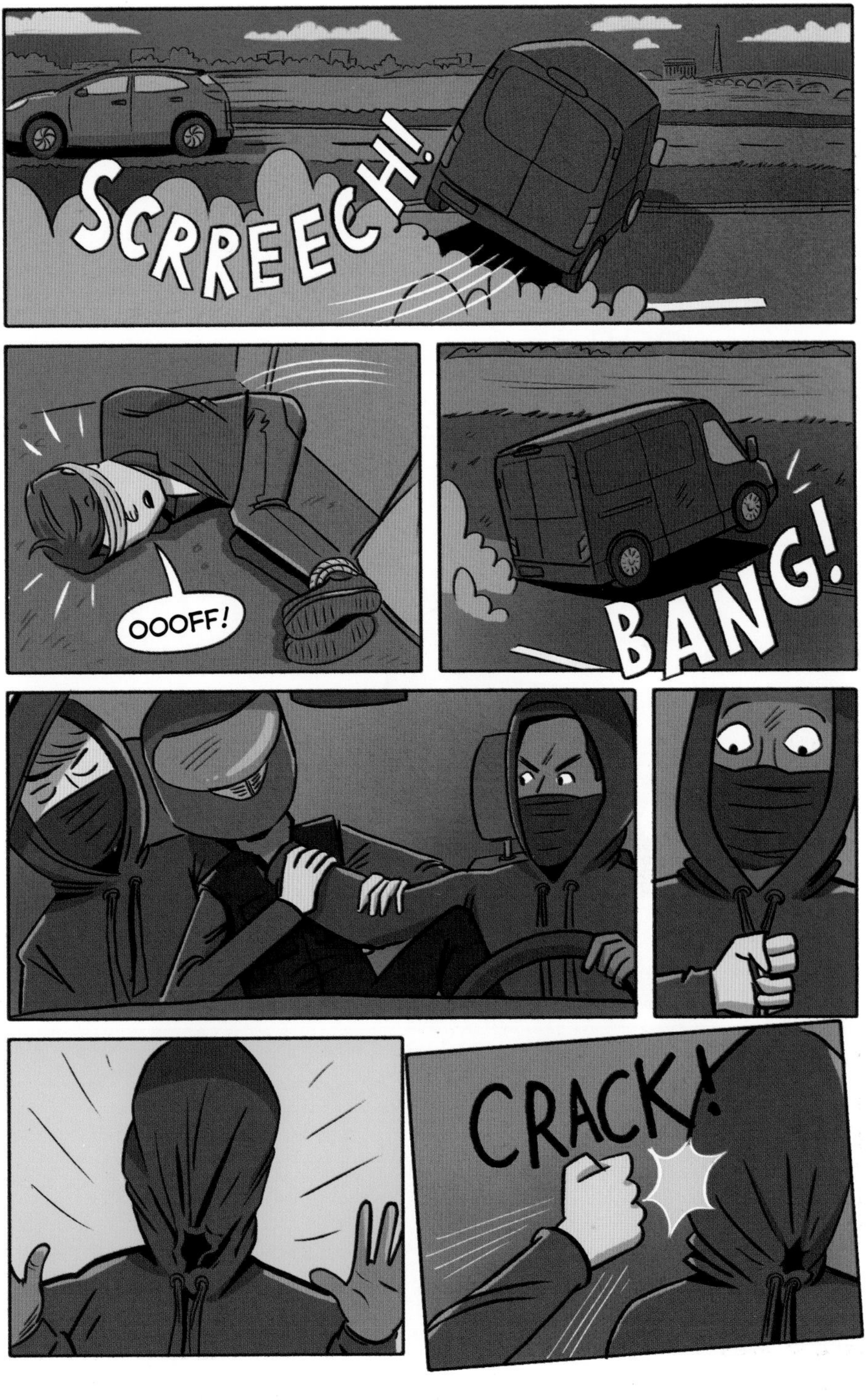
SCRREECH!
OOOFF!
BANG!
CRACK!

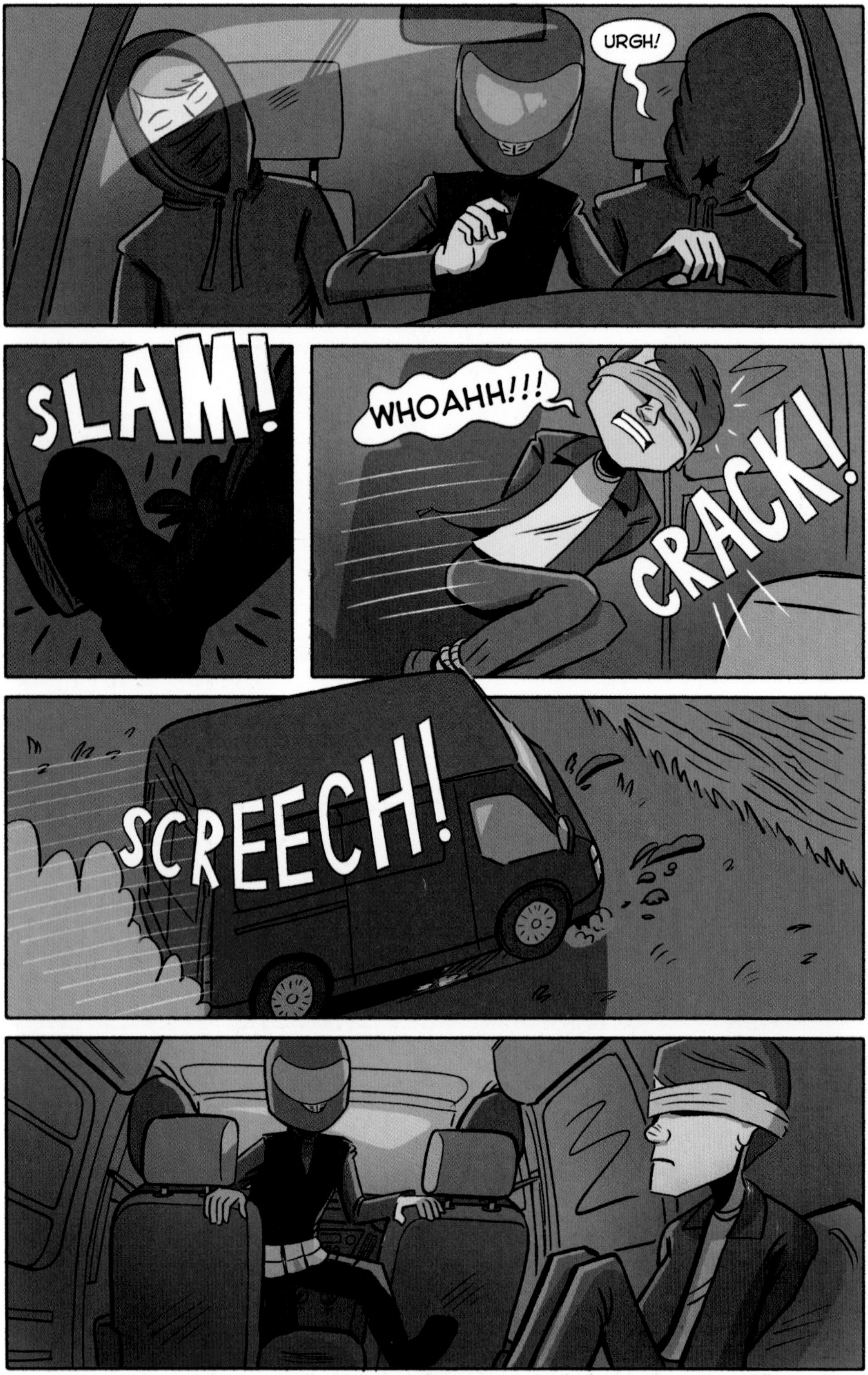
URGH!
SLAM!
WHOAHH!!!
CRACK!
SCREECH!

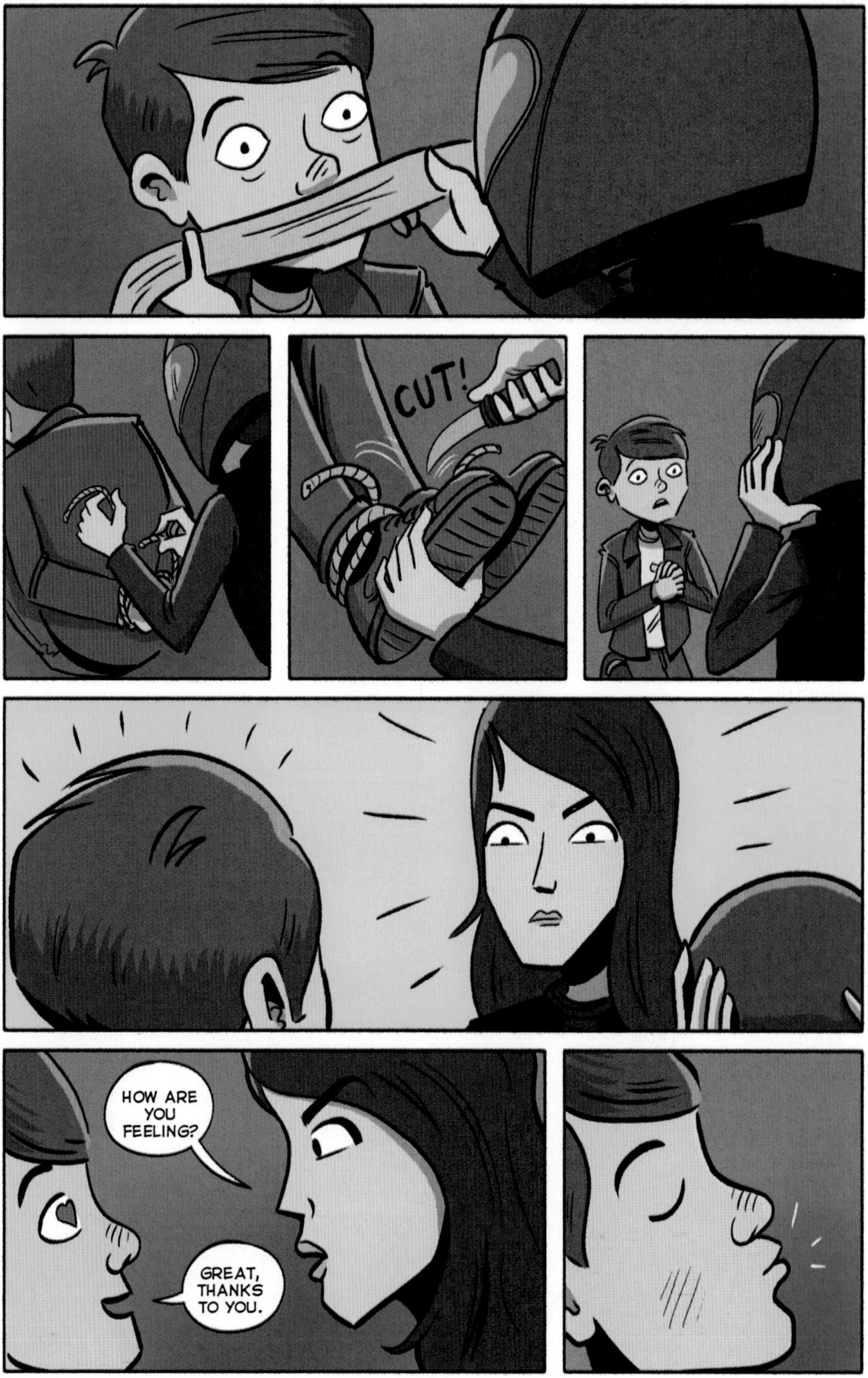
CUT!
HOW ARE YOU FEELING?
GREAT, THANKS TO YOU.

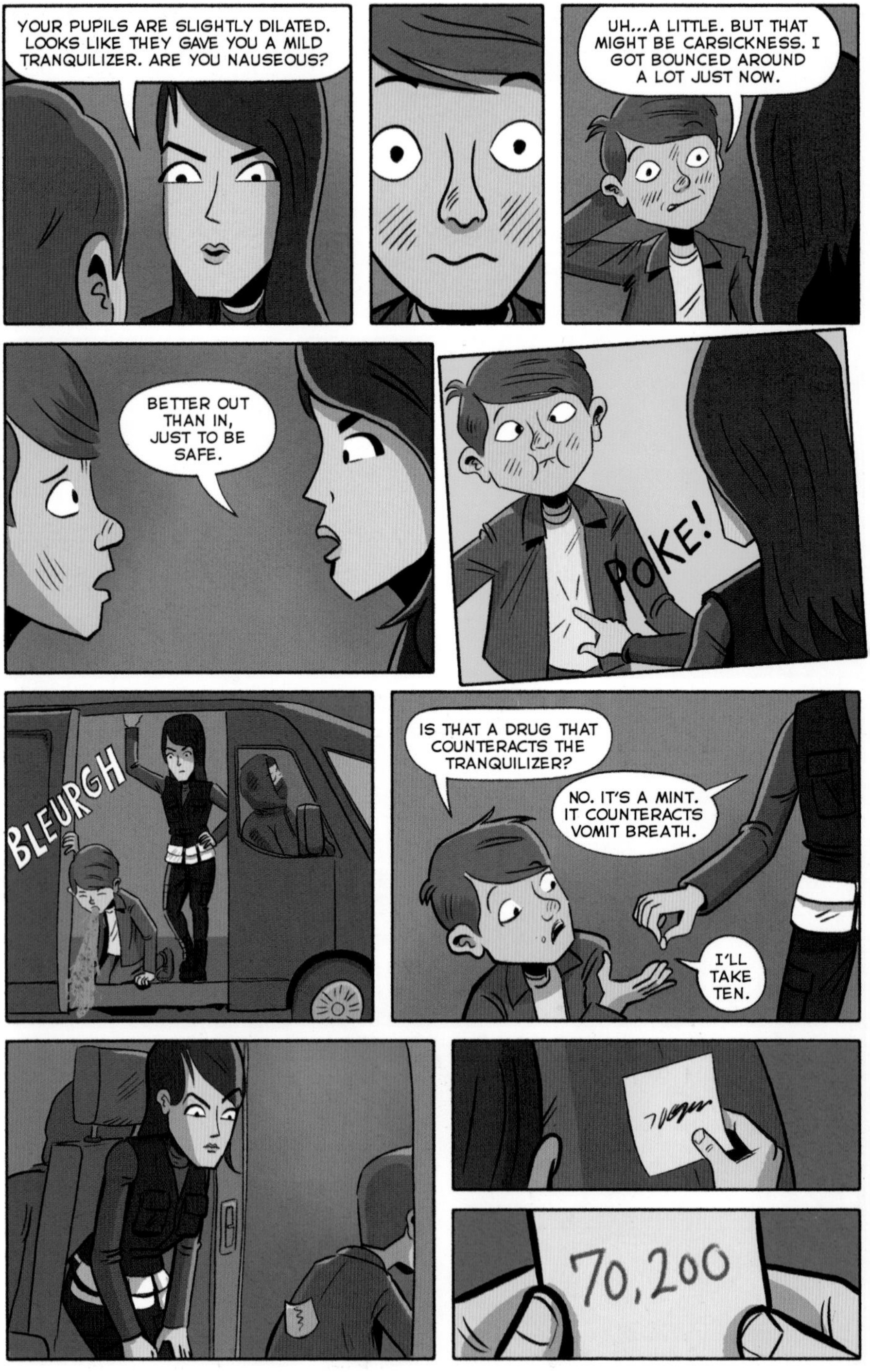
YOUR PUPILS ARE SLIGHTLY DILATED. LOOKS LIKE THEY GAVE YOU A MILD TRANQUILIZER. ARE YOU NAUSEOUS?
UH...A LITTLE. BUT THAT MIGHT BE CARSICKNESS. I GOT BOUNCED AROUND A LOT JUST NOW.
BETTER OUT THAN IN, JUST TO BE SAFE.
POKE!
BLEURGH
IS THAT A DRUG THAT COUNTERACTS THE TRANQUILIZER?
NO. IT'S A MINT. IT COUNTERACTS VOMIT BREATH.
I'LL TAKE TEN.
70,200

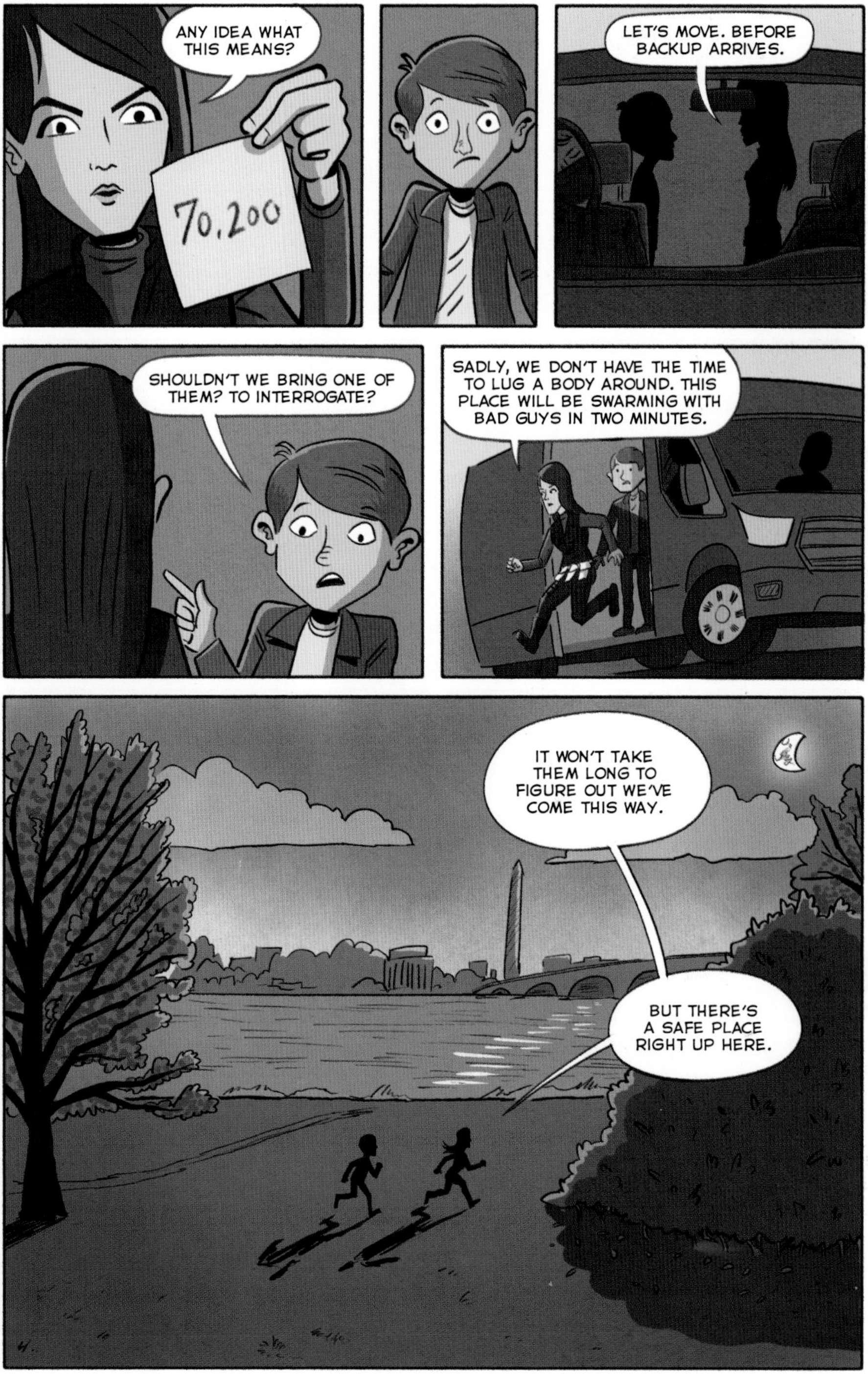
ANY IDEA WHAT THIS MEANS?
70,200
LET'S MOVE. BEFORE BACKUP ARRIVES.
SHOULDN'T WE BRING ONE OF THEM? TO INTERROGATE?
SADLY, WE DON'T HAVE THE TIME TO LUG A BODY AROUND. THIS PLACE WILL BE SWARMING WITH BAD GUYS IN TWO MINUTES.
IT WON'T TAKE THEM LONG TO FIGURE OUT WE'VE COME THIS WAY.
BUT THERE'S A SAFE PLACE RIGHT UP HERE.

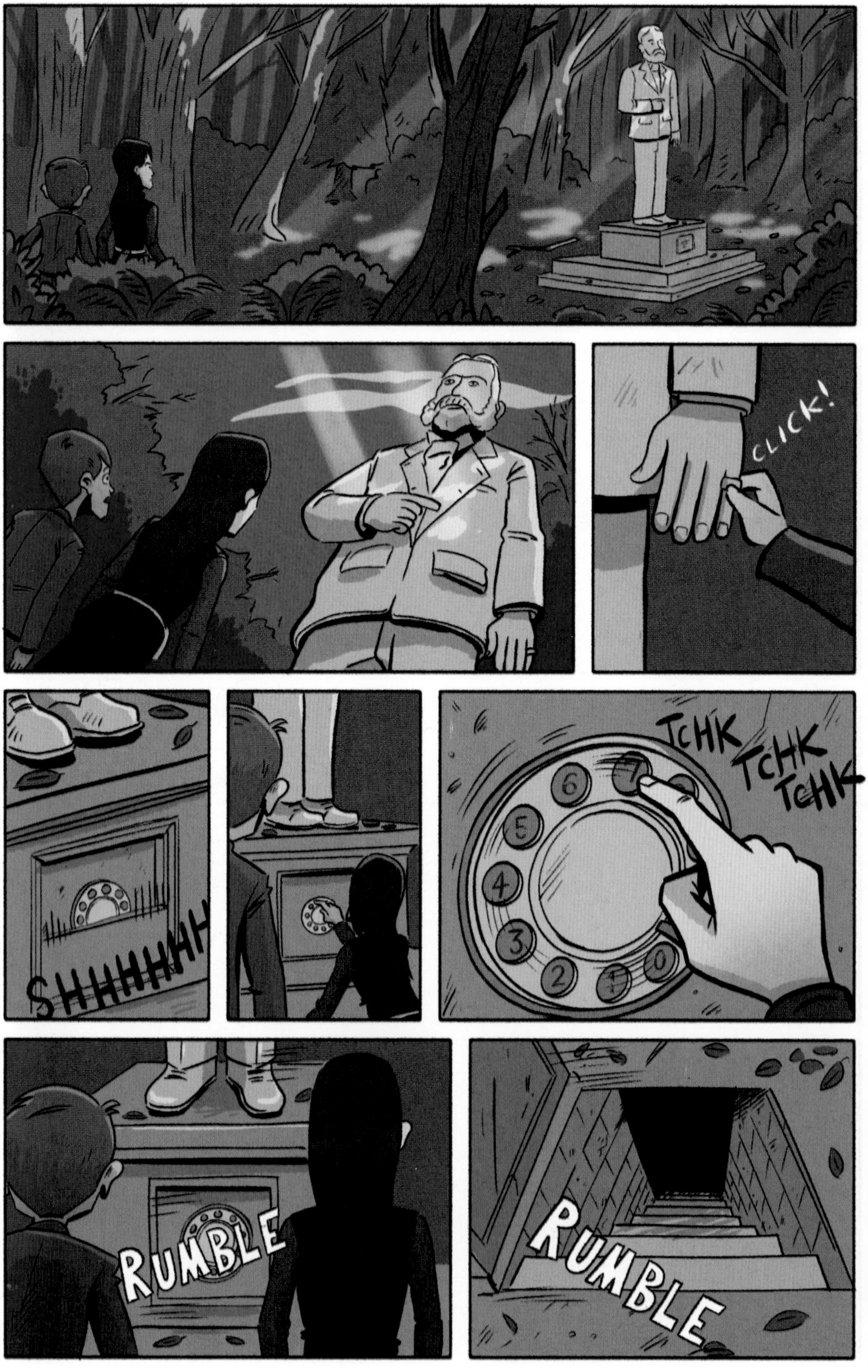
CLICK!
SHHHHHH
TCHK
TCHK
TCHK
RUMBLE
RUMBLE

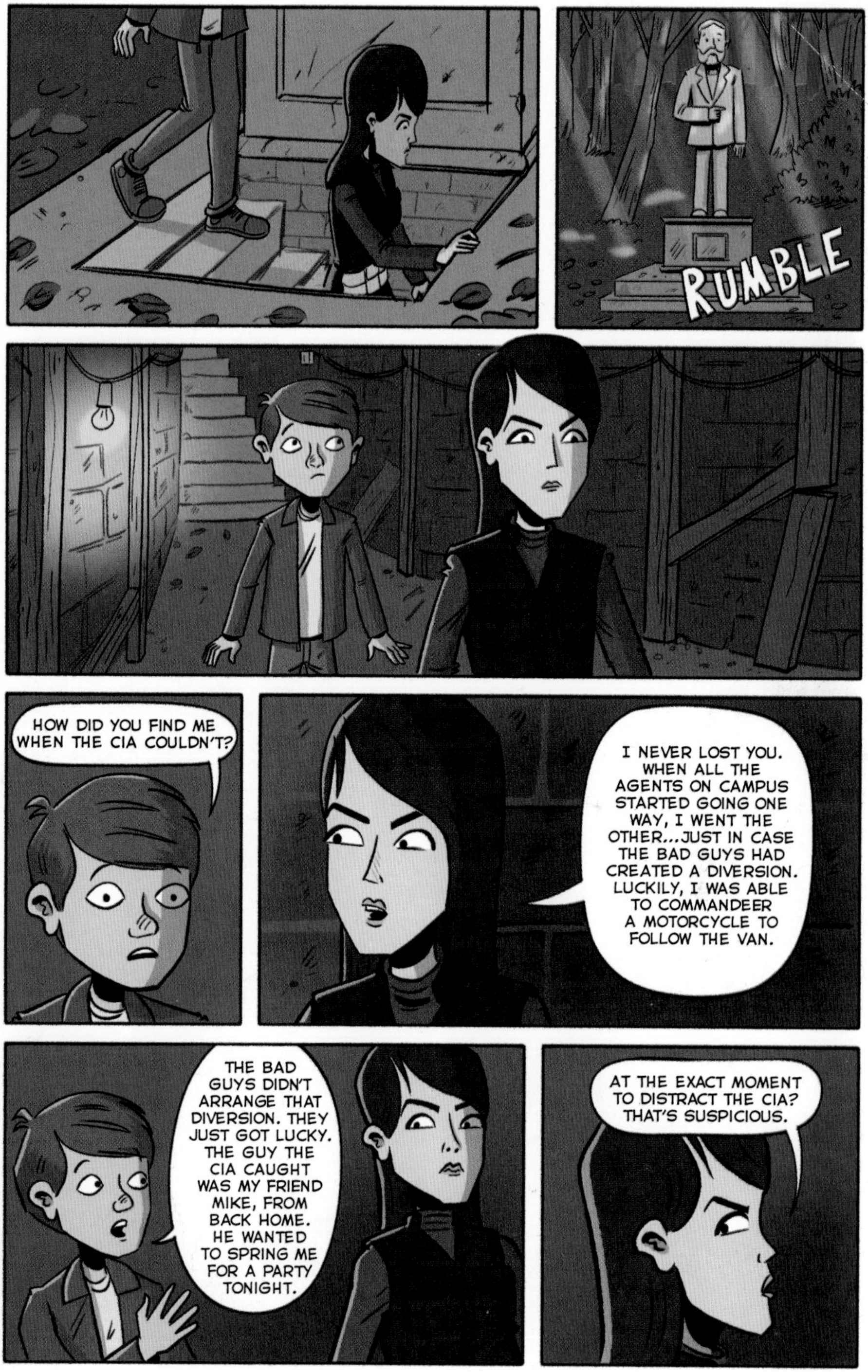
RUMBLE
HOW DID YOU FIND ME WHEN THE CIA COULDN'T?
I NEVER LOST YOU. WHEN ALL THE AGENTS ON CAMPUS STARTED GOING ONE WAY, I WENT THE OTHER...JUST IN CASE THE BAD GUYS HAD CREATED A DIVERSION. LUCKILY, I WAS ABLE TO COMMANDEER A MOTORCYCLE TO FOLLOW THE VAN.
THE BAD GUYS DIDN'T ARRANGE THAT DIVERSION. THEY JUST GOT LUCKY. THE GUY THE CIA CAUGHT WAS MY FRIEND MIKE, FROM BACK HOME. HE WANTED TO SPRING ME FOR A PARTY TONIGHT.
AT THE EXACT MOMENT TO DISTRACT THE CIA? THAT'S SUSPICIOUS.

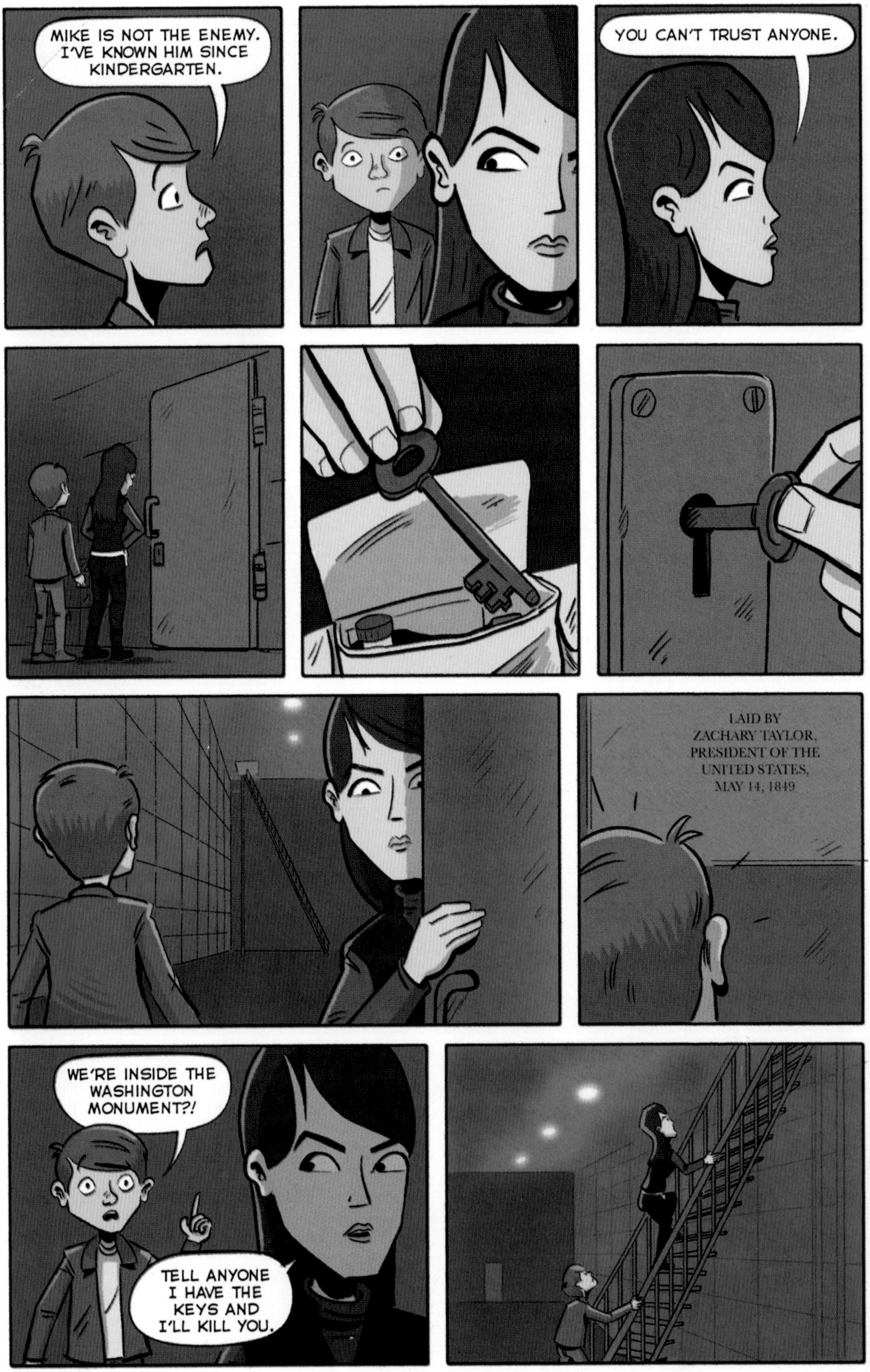
MIKE IS NOT THE ENEMY. I'VE KNOWN HIM SINCE KINDERGARTEN.
YOU CAN'T TRUST ANYONE.
LAID BY ZACHARY TAYLOR, PRESIDENT OF THE UNITED STATES, MAY 14, 1849
WE'RE INSIDE THE WASHINGTON MONUMENT?!
TELL ANYONE I HAVE THE KEYS AND I'LL KILL YOU.

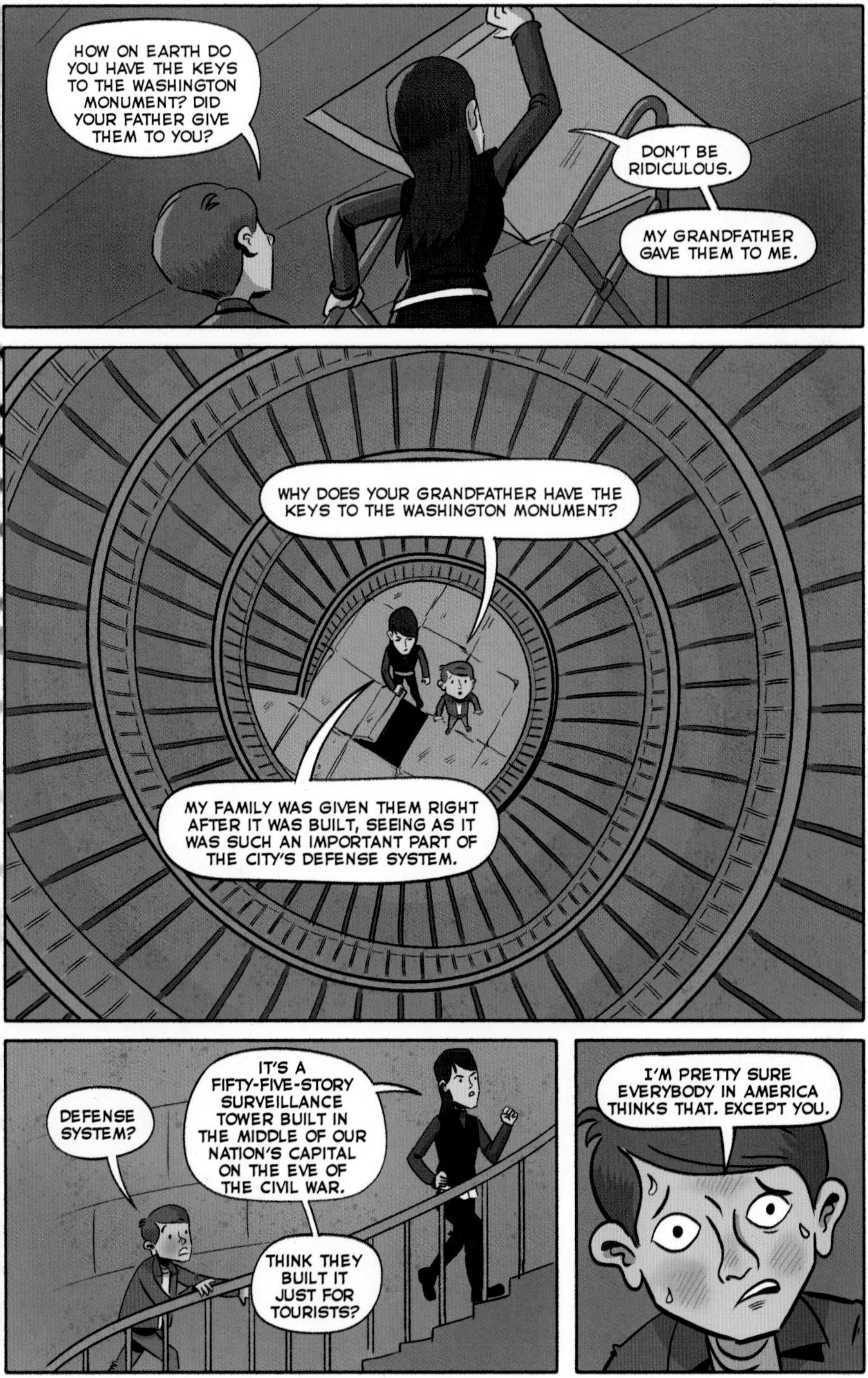
HOW ON EARTH DO YOU HAVE THE KEYS TO THE WASHINGTON MONUMENT? DID YOUR FATHER GIVE THEM TO YOU?
DON'T BE RIDICULOUS.
MY GRANDFATHER GAVE THEM TO ME.
WHY DOES YOUR GRANDFATHER HAVE THE KEYS TO THE WASHINGTON MONUMENT?
MY FAMILY WAS GIVEN THEM RIGHT AFTER IT WAS BUILT, SEEING AS IT WAS SUCH AN IMPORTANT PART OF THE CITY'S DEFENSE SYSTEM.
DEFENSE SYSTEM?
IT'S A FIFTY-FIVE-STORY SURVEILLANCE TOWER BUILT IN THE MIDDLE OF OUR NATION'S CAPITAL ON THE EVE OF THE CIVIL WAR.
THINK THEY BUILT IT JUST FOR TOURISTS?
I'M PRETTY SURE EVERYBODY IN AMERICA THINKS THAT. EXCEPT YOU.

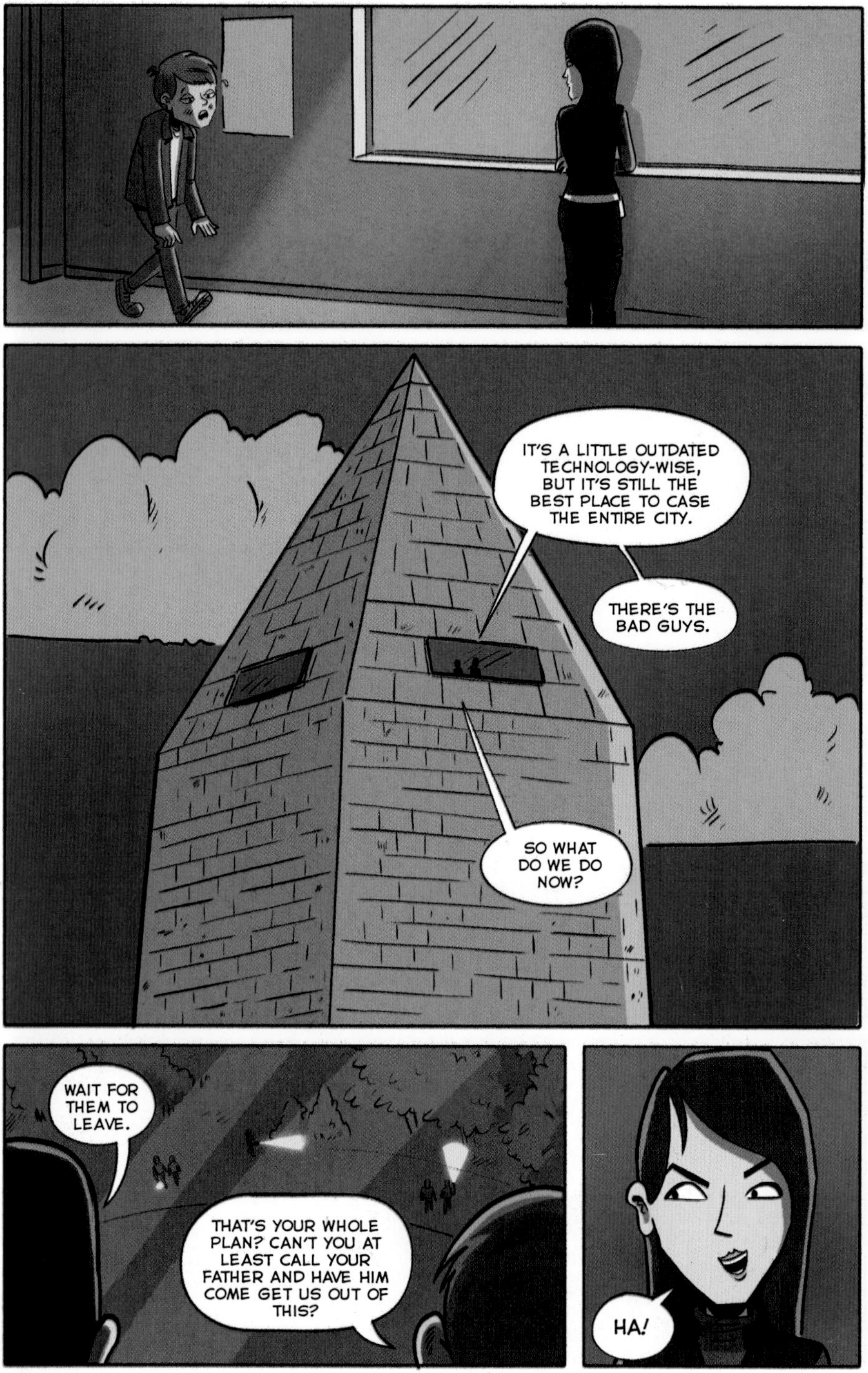
IT'S A LITTLE OUTDATED TECHNOLOGY-WISE, BUT IT'S STILL THE BEST PLACE TO CASE THE ENTIRE CITY.
THERE'S THE BAD GUYS.
SO WHAT DO WE DO NOW?
WAIT FOR THEM TO LEAVE.
THAT'S YOUR WHOLE PLAN? CAN'T YOU AT LEAST CALL YOUR FATHER AND HAVE HIM COME GET US OUT OF THIS?
HA!

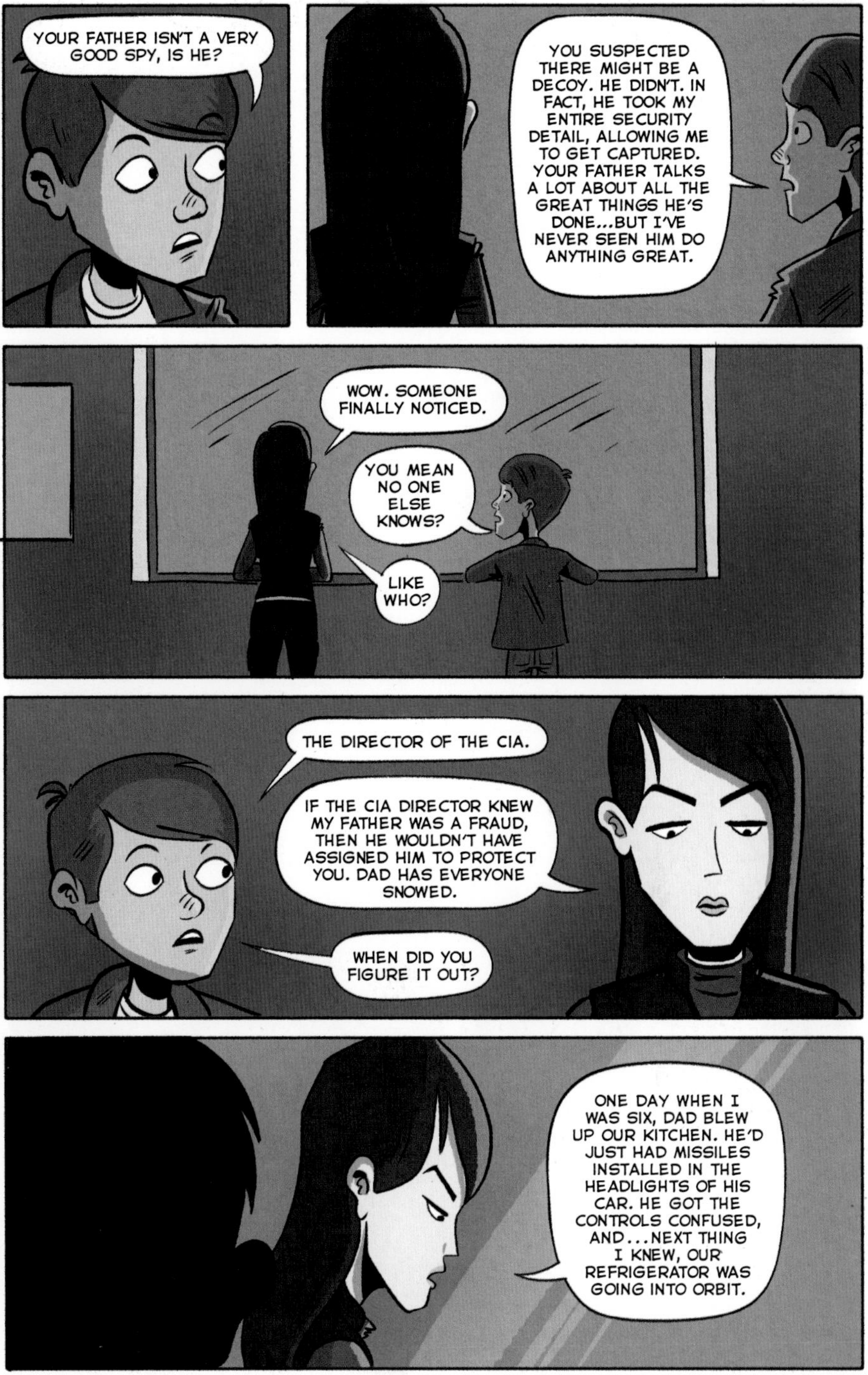
YOUR FATHER ISN'T A VERY GOOD SPY, IS HE?
YOU SUSPECTED THERE MIGHT BE A DECOY. HE DIDN'T. IN FACT, HE TOOK MY ENTIRE SECURITY DETAIL, ALLOWING ME TO GET CAPTURED. YOUR FATHER TALKS A LOT ABOUT ALL THE GREAT THINGS HE'S DONE...BUT I'VE NEVER SEEN HIM DO ANYTHING GREAT.
WOW. SOMEONE FINALLY NOTICED.
YOU MEAN NO ONE ELSE KNOWS?
LIKE WHO?
THE DIRECTOR OF THE CIA.
IF THE CIA DIRECTOR KNEW MY FATHER WAS A FRAUD, THEN HE WOULDN'T HAVE ASSIGNED HIM TO PROTECT YOU. DAD HAS EVERYONE SNOWED.
WHEN DID YOU FIGURE IT OUT?
ONE DAY WHEN I WAS SIX, DAD BLEW UP OUR KITCHEN. HE'D JUST HAD MISSILES INSTALLED IN THE HEADLIGHTS OF HIS CAR. HE GOT THE CONTROLS CONFUSED, AND...NEXT THING I KNEW, OUR REFRIGERATOR WAS GOING INTO ORBIT.

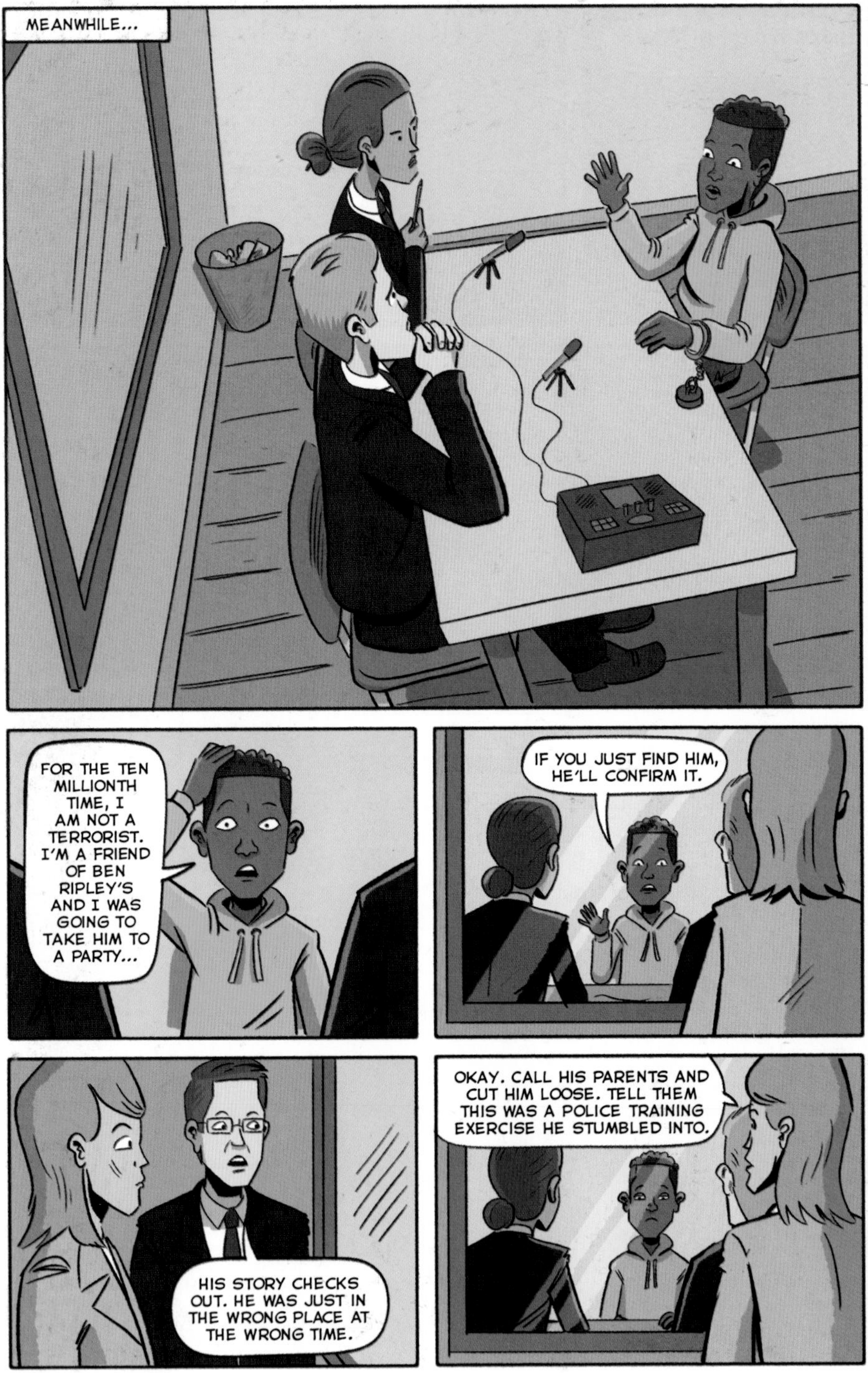
MEANWHILE...
FOR THE TEN MILLIONTH TIME, I AM NOT A TERRORIST. I'M A FRIEND OF BEN RIPLEY'S AND I WAS GOING TO TAKE HIM TO A PARTY...
IF YOU JUST FIND HIM, HE'LL CONFIRM IT.
HIS STORY CHECKS OUT. HE WAS JUST IN THE WRONG PLACE AT THE WRONG TIME.
OKAY. CALL HIS PARENTS AND CUT HIM LOOSE. TELL THEM THIS WAS A POLICE TRAINING EXERCISE HE STUMBLED INTO.

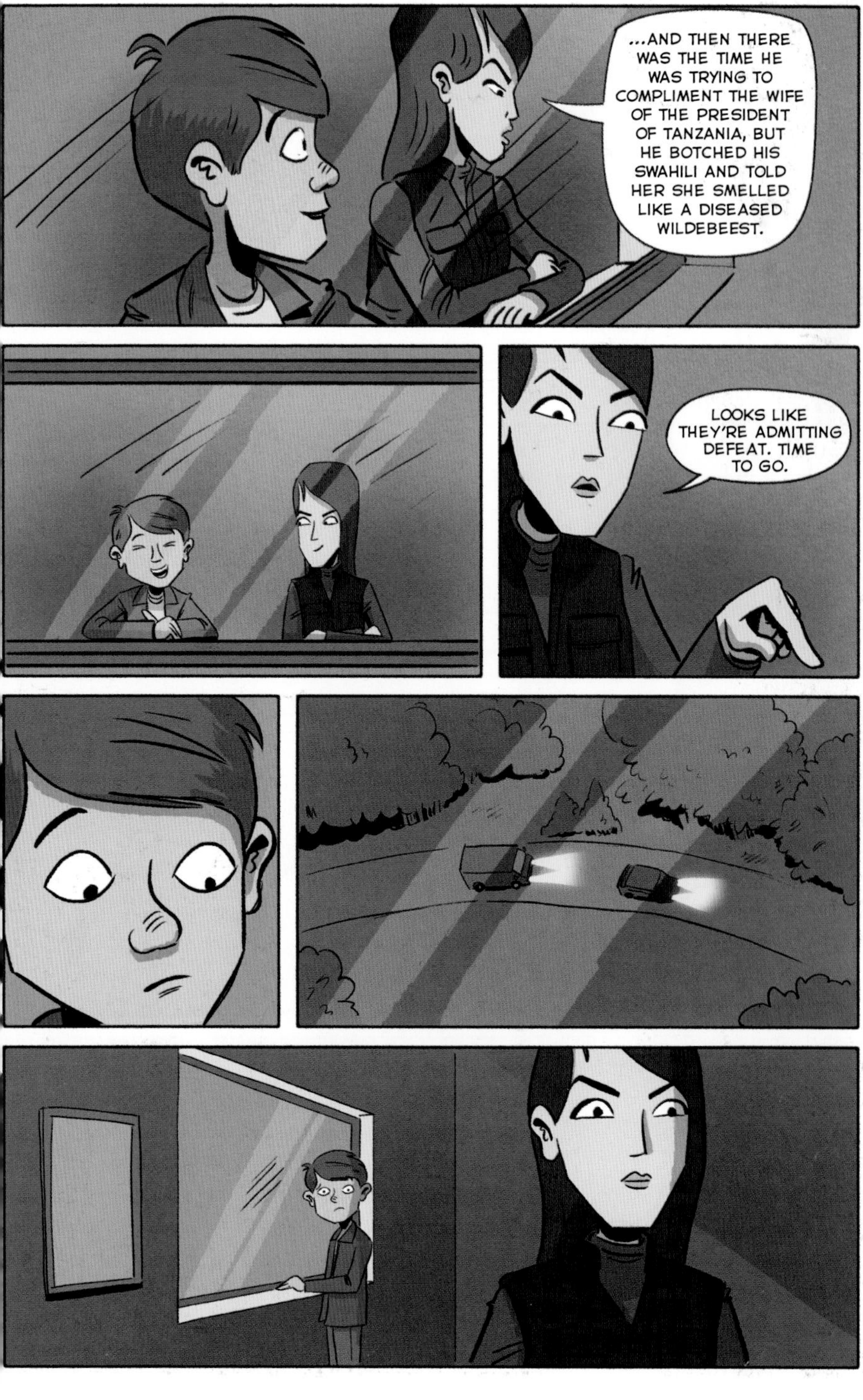
...AND THEN THERE WAS THE TIME HE WAS TRYING TO COMPLIMENT THE WIFE OF THE PRESIDENT OF TANZANIA, BUT HE BOTCHED HIS SWAHILI AND TOLD HER SHE SMELLED LIKE A DISEASED WILDEBEEST.
LOOKS LIKE THEY'RE ADMITTING DEFEAT. TIME TO GO.

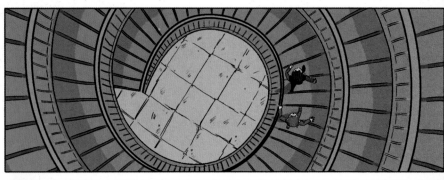

EVERYTHING I TOLD YOU TONIGHT IS CONFIDENTIAL. TELL ANYONE...

...AND YOU'LL KILL ME. I KNOW. WHERE ARE WE GOING?

BACK TO CAMPUS.

I WAS JUST ABDUCTED FROM CAMPUS!

THAT'S WHY WE'RE GOING BACK. IF WE WANT TO FIGURE OUT WHAT'S GOING ON, THAT'S WHERE ALL THE CLUES ARE.

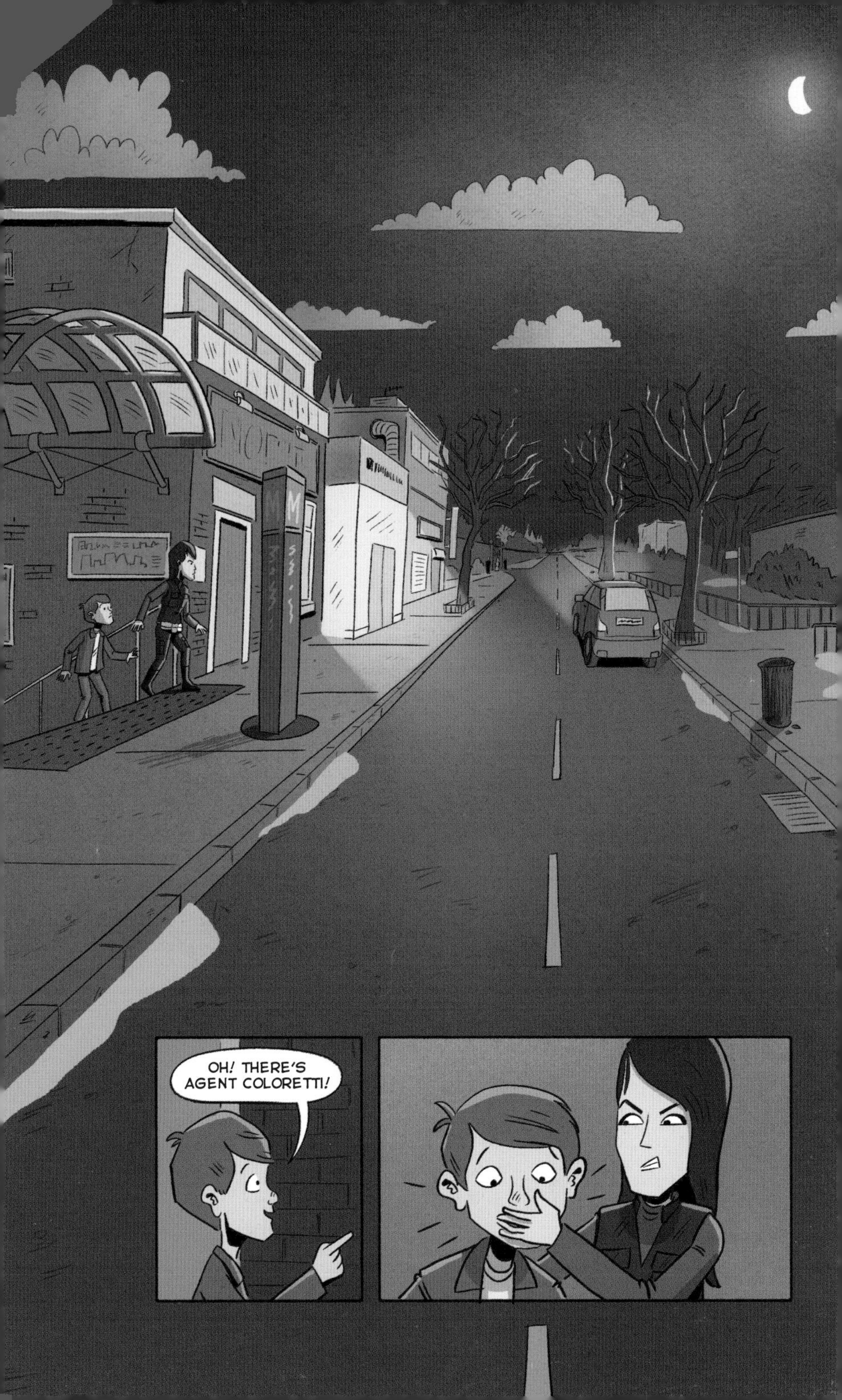
OH! THERE'S AGENT COLORETTI!

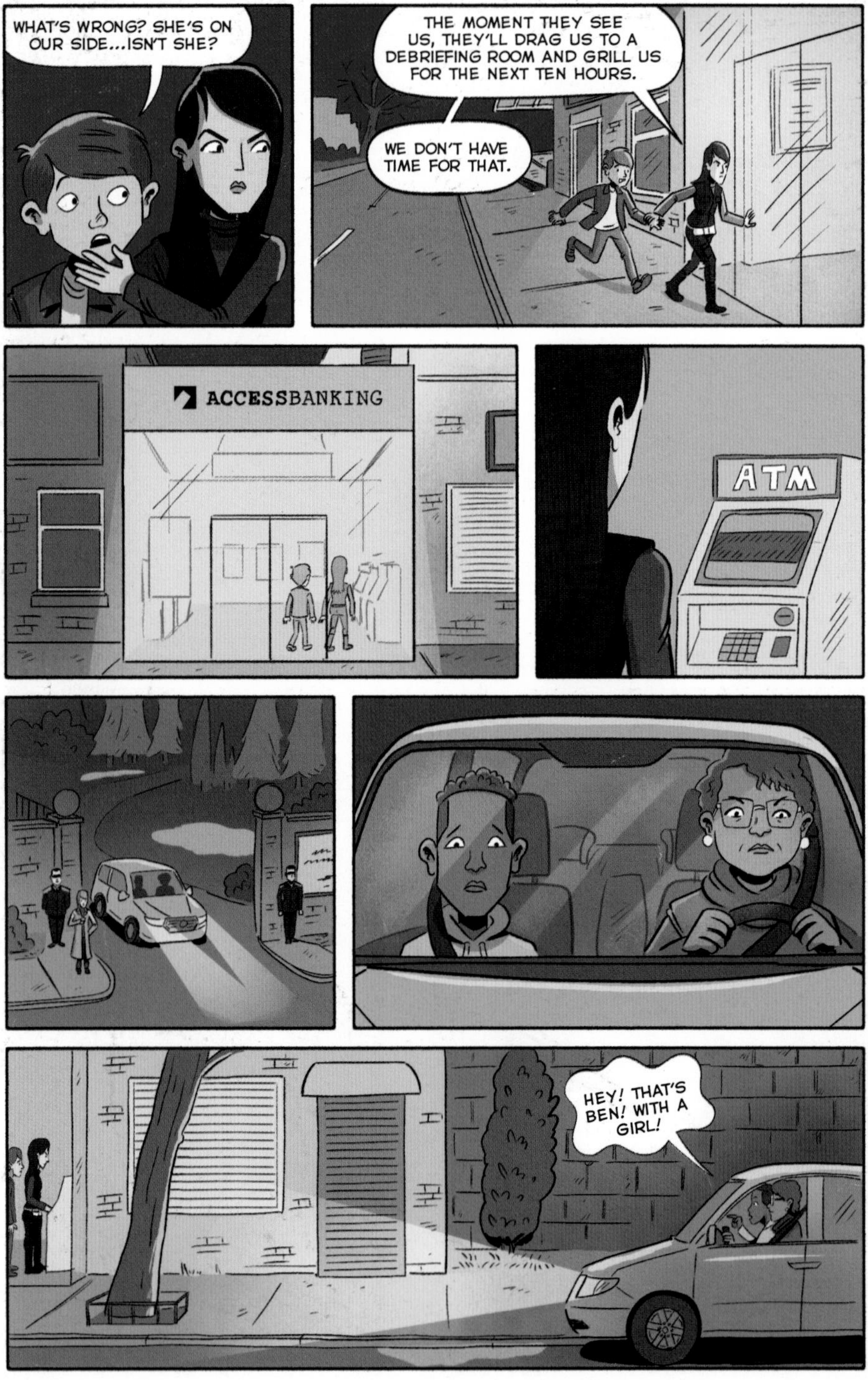
WHAT'S WRONG? SHE'S ON OUR SIDE...ISN'T SHE?
THE MOMENT THEY SEE US, THEY'LL DRAG US TO A DEBRIEFING ROOM AND GRILL US FOR THE NEXT TEN HOURS.
WE DON'T HAVE TIME FOR THAT.
ACCESSBANKING
ATM
HEY! THAT'S BEN! WITH A GIRL!

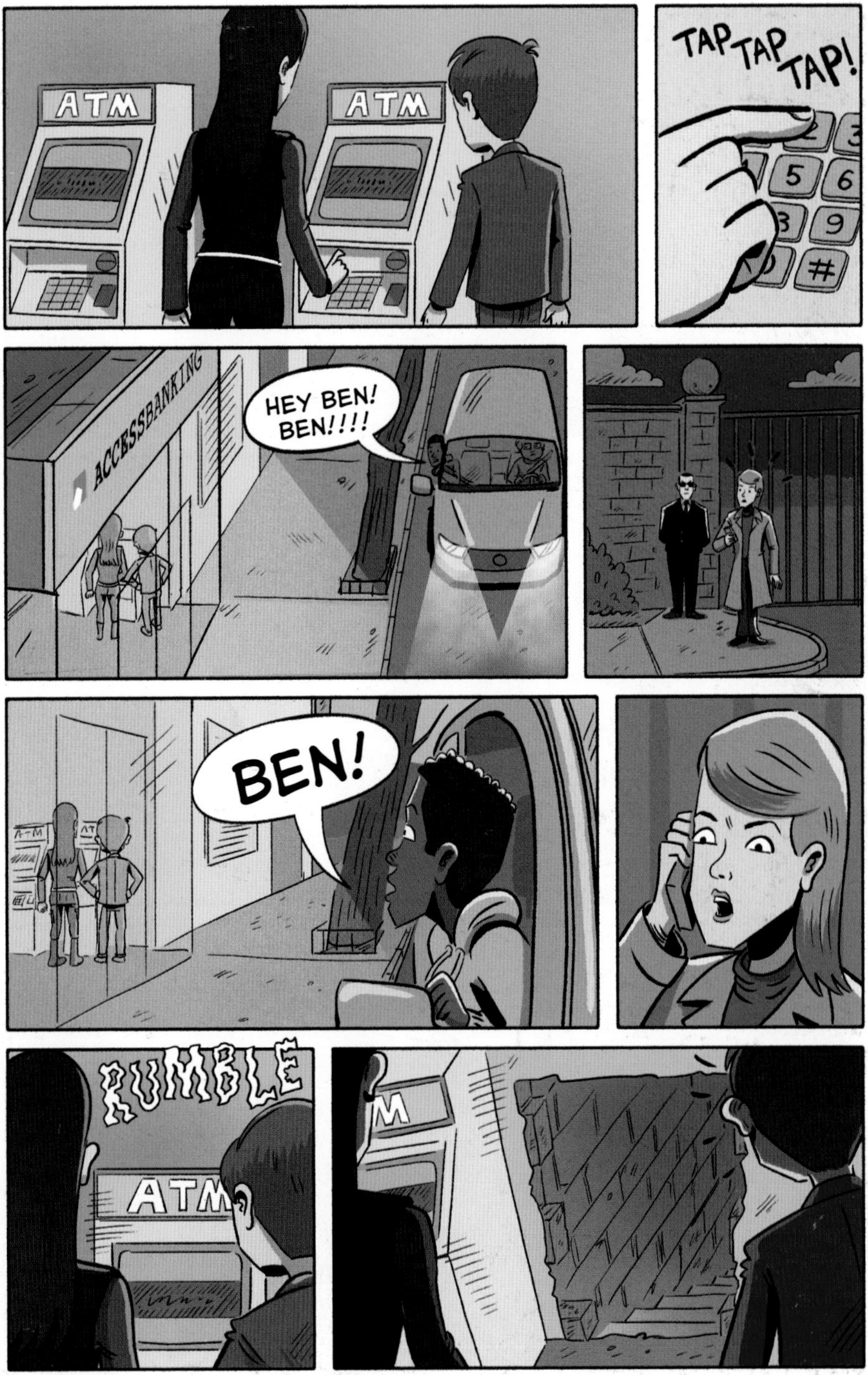

ATM
ATM
TAP TAP TAP!
ACCESSBANKING
HEY BEN! BEN!!!!
BEN!
RUMBLE
ATM

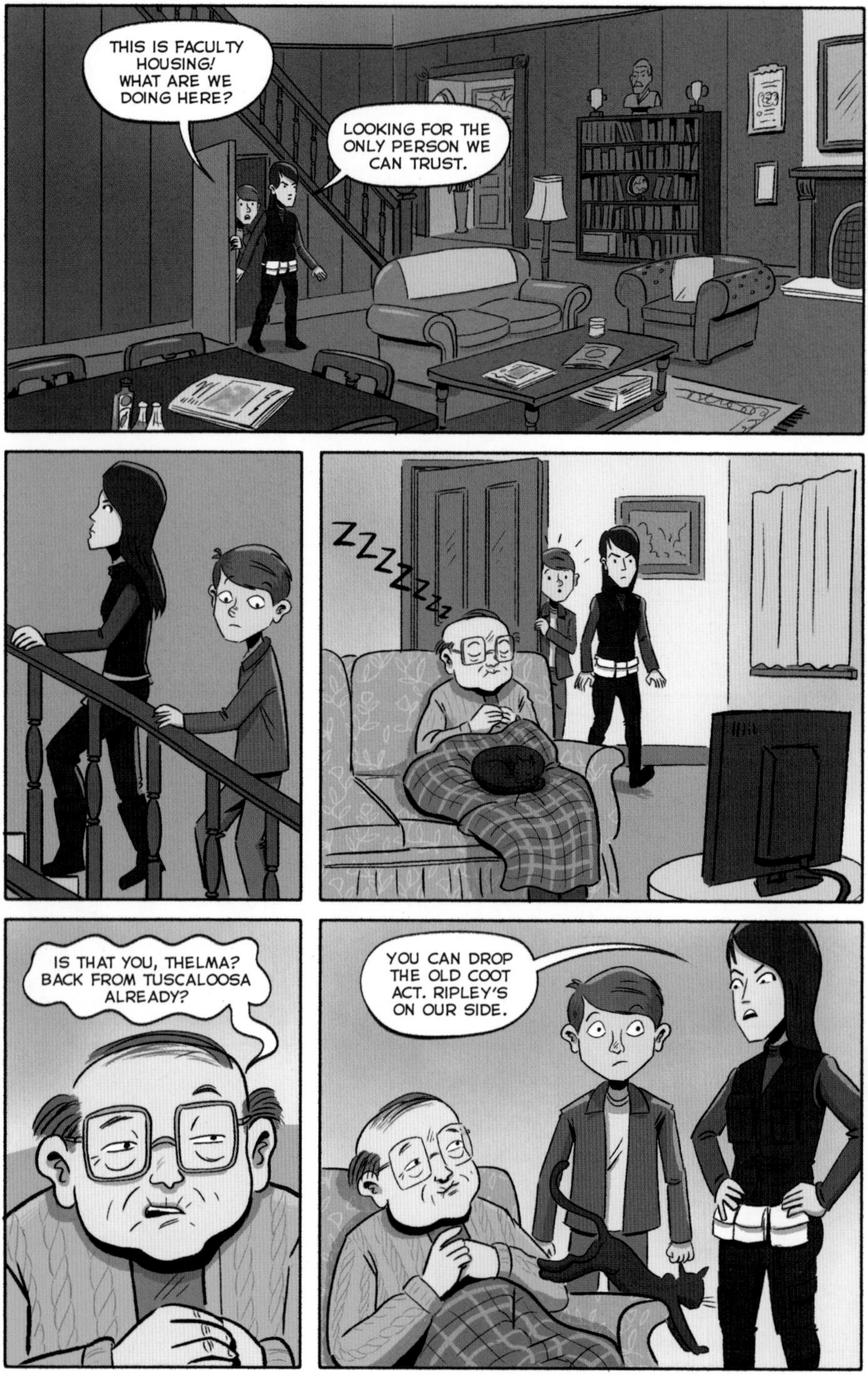
THIS IS FACULTY HOUSING! WHAT ARE WE DOING HERE?
LOOKING FOR THE ONLY PERSON WE CAN TRUST.
ZZZZZZzz
IS THAT YOU, THELMA? BACK FROM TUSCALOOSA ALREADY?
YOU CAN DROP THE OLD COOT ACT. RIPLEY'S ON OUR SIDE.

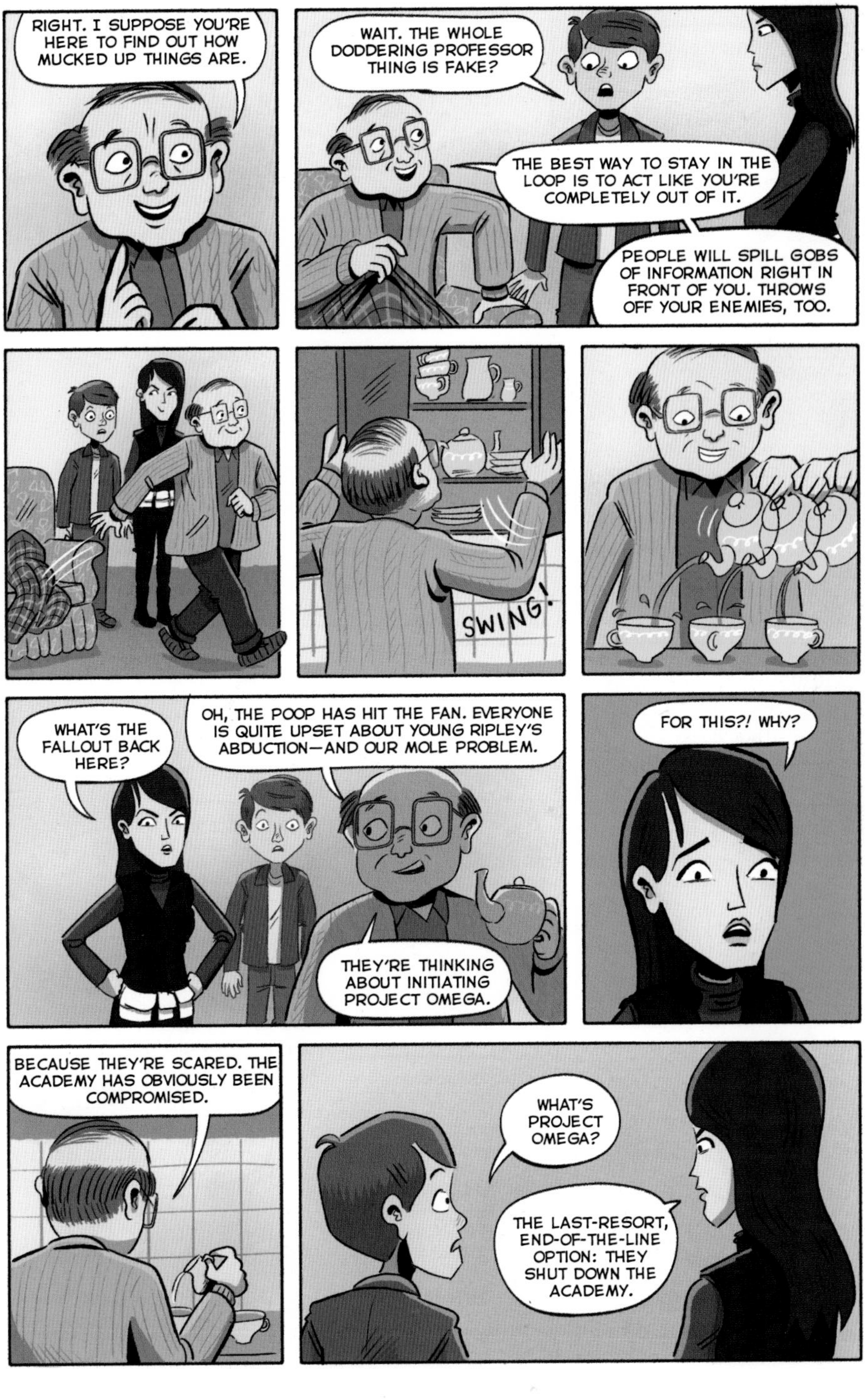
RIGHT. I SUPPOSE YOU'RE HERE TO FIND OUT HOW MUCKED UP THINGS ARE.
WAIT. THE WHOLE DODDERING PROFESSOR THING IS FAKE?
THE BEST WAY TO STAY IN THE LOOP IS TO ACT LIKE YOU'RE COMPLETELY OUT OF IT.
PEOPLE WILL SPILL GOBS OF INFORMATION RIGHT IN FRONT OF YOU. THROWS OFF YOUR ENEMIES, TOO.
SWING!
WHAT'S THE FALLOUT BACK HERE?
OH, THE POOP HAS HIT THE FAN. EVERYONE IS QUITE UPSET ABOUT YOUNG RIPLEY'S ABDUCTION—AND OUR MOLE PROBLEM.
THEY'RE THINKING ABOUT INITIATING PROJECT OMEGA.
FOR THIS?! WHY?
BECAUSE THEY'RE SCARED. THE ACADEMY HAS OBVIOUSLY BEEN COMPROMISED.
WHAT'S PROJECT OMEGA?
THE LAST-RESORT, END-OF-THE-LINE OPTION: THEY SHUT DOWN THE ACADEMY.

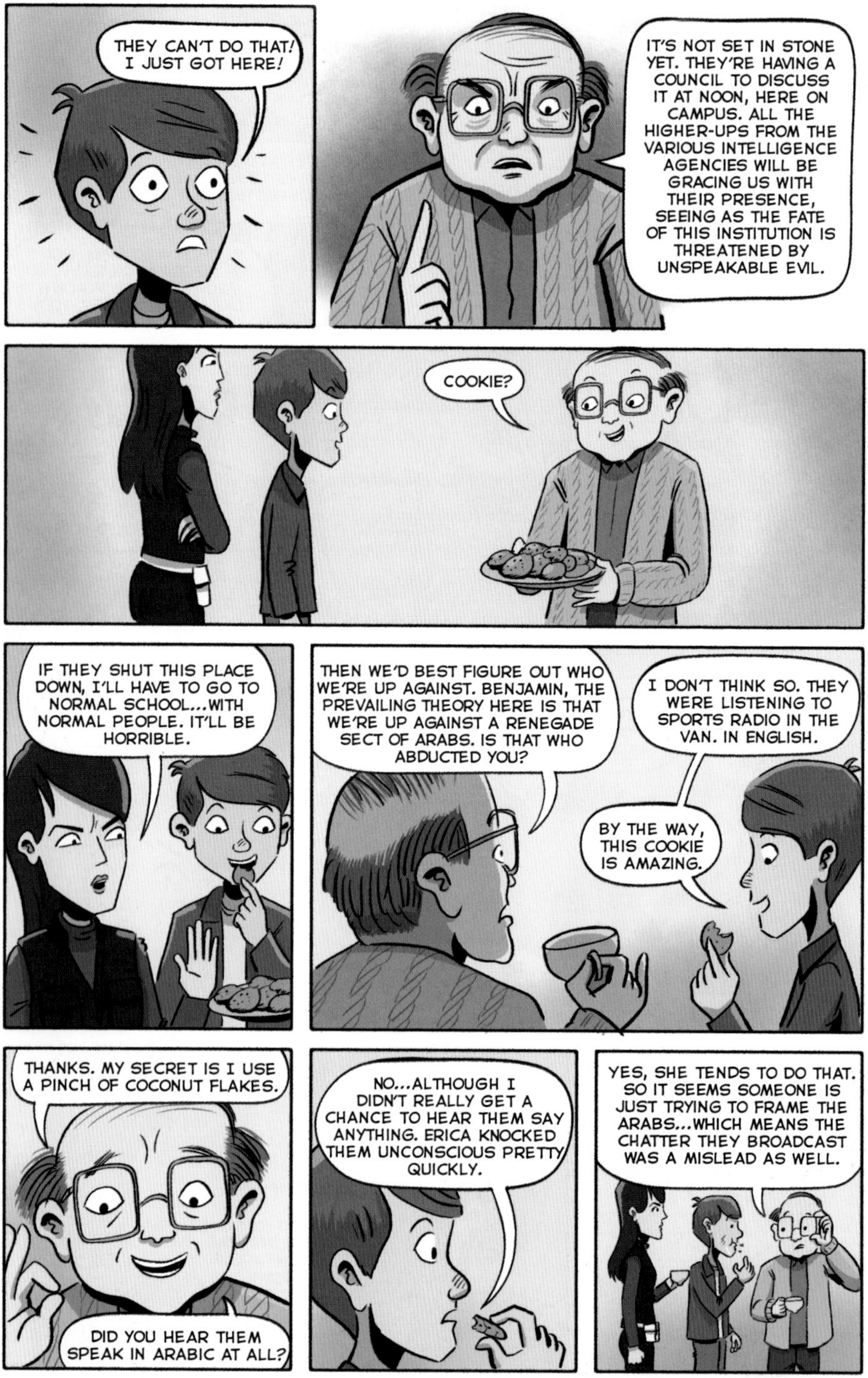

THEY CAN'T DO THAT! I JUST GOT HERE!
IT'S NOT SET IN STONE YET. THEY'RE HAVING A COUNCIL TO DISCUSS IT AT NOON, HERE ON CAMPUS. ALL THE HIGHER-UPS FROM THE VARIOUS INTELLIGENCE AGENCIES WILL BE GRACING US WITH THEIR PRESENCE, SEEING AS THE FATE OF THIS INSTITUTION IS THREATENED BY UNSPEAKABLE EVIL.
COOKIE?
IF THEY SHUT THIS PLACE DOWN, I'LL HAVE TO GO TO NORMAL SCHOOL...WITH NORMAL PEOPLE. IT'LL BE HORRIBLE.
THEN WE'D BEST FIGURE OUT WHO WE'RE UP AGAINST. BENJAMIN, THE PREVAILING THEORY HERE IS THAT WE'RE UP AGAINST A RENEGADE SECT OF ARABS. IS THAT WHO ABDUCTED YOU?
I DON'T THINK SO. THEY WERE LISTENING TO SPORTS RADIO IN THE VAN. IN ENGLISH.
BY THE WAY, THIS COOKIE IS AMAZING.
THANKS. MY SECRET IS I USE A PINCH OF COCONUT FLAKES.
DID YOU HEAR THEM SPEAK IN ARABIC AT ALL?
NO...ALTHOUGH I DIDN'T REALLY GET A CHANCE TO HEAR THEM SAY ANYTHING. ERICA KNOCKED THEM UNCONSCIOUS PRETTY QUICKLY.
YES, SHE TENDS TO DO THAT. SO IT SEEMS SOMEONE IS JUST TRYING TO FRAME THE ARABS...WHICH MEANS THE CHATTER THEY BROADCAST WAS A MISLEAD AS WELL.

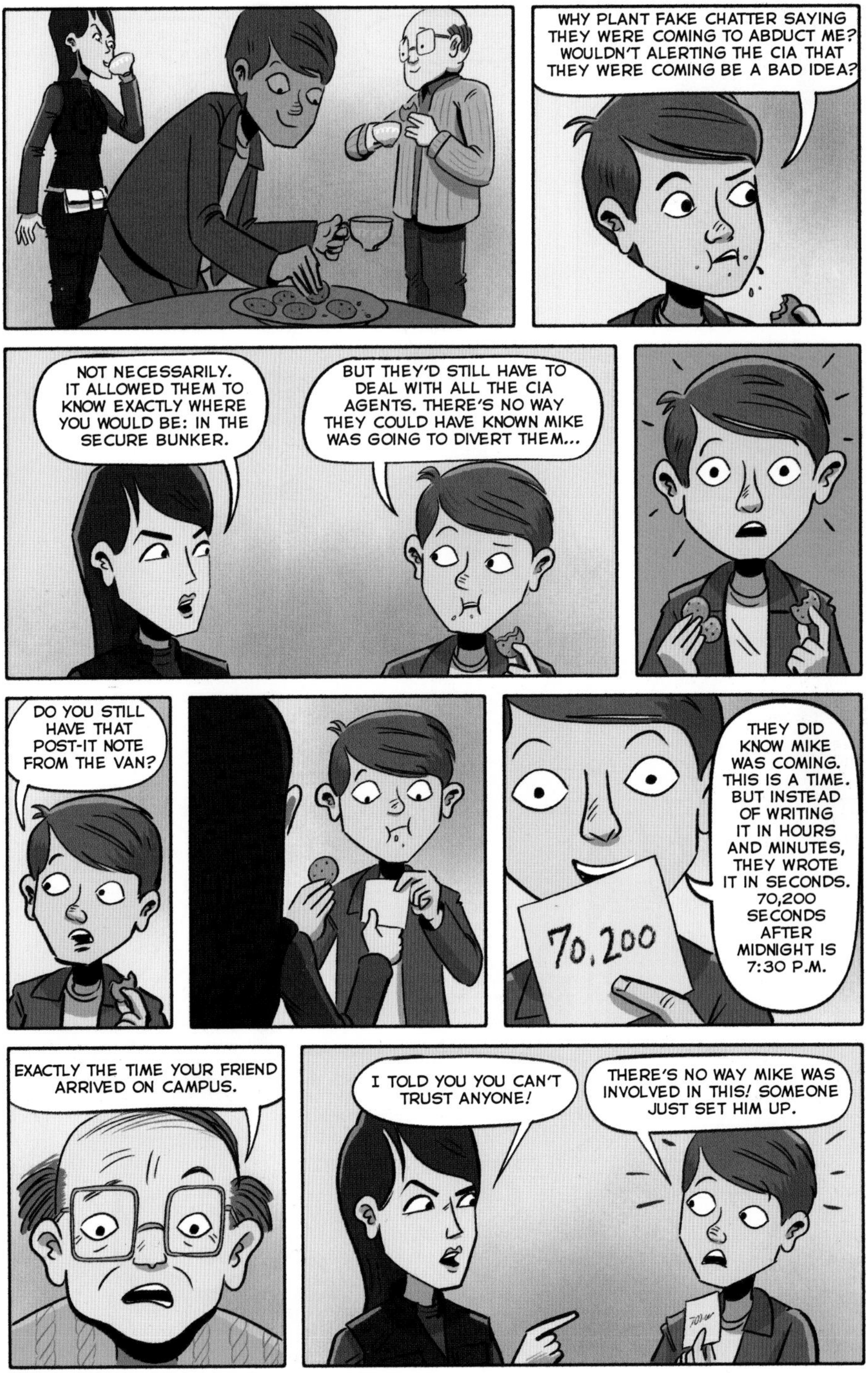
WHY PLANT FAKE CHATTER SAYING THEY WERE COMING TO ABDUCT ME? WOULDN'T ALERTING THE CIA THAT THEY WERE COMING BE A BAD IDEA?
NOT NECESSARILY. IT ALLOWED THEM TO KNOW EXACTLY WHERE YOU WOULD BE: IN THE SECURE BUNKER.
BUT THEY'D STILL HAVE TO DEAL WITH ALL THE CIA AGENTS. THERE'S NO WAY THEY COULD HAVE KNOWN MIKE WAS GOING TO DIVERT THEM...
DO YOU STILL HAVE THAT POST-IT NOTE FROM THE VAN?
70,200
THEY DID KNOW MIKE WAS COMING. THIS IS A TIME. BUT INSTEAD OF WRITING IT IN HOURS AND MINUTES, THEY WROTE IT IN SECONDS. 70,200 SECONDS AFTER MIDNIGHT IS 7:30 P.M.
EXACTLY THE TIME YOUR FRIEND ARRIVED ON CAMPUS.
I TOLD YOU YOU CAN'T TRUST ANYONE!
THERE'S NO WAY MIKE WAS INVOLVED IN THIS! SOMEONE JUST SET HIM UP.

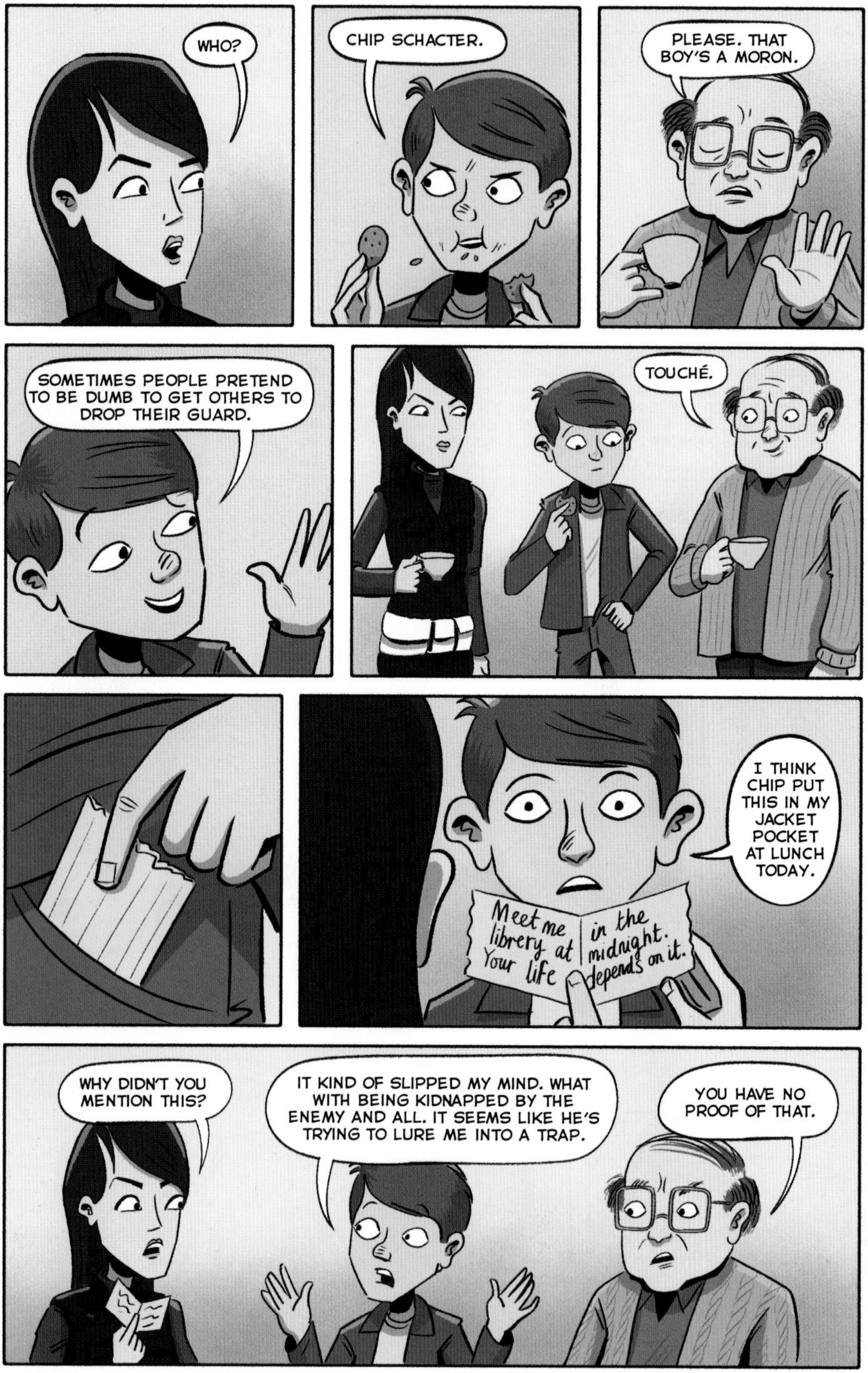
WHO?
CHIP SCHACTER.
PLEASE. THAT BOY'S A MORON.
SOMETIMES PEOPLE PRETEND TO BE DUMB TO GET OTHERS TO DROP THEIR GUARD.
TOUCHÉ.
I THINK CHIP PUT THIS IN MY JACKET POCKET AT LUNCH TODAY.
Meet me librery at Your life
in the midnight. depends on it.
WHY DIDN'T YOU MENTION THIS?
IT KIND OF SLIPPED MY MIND. WHAT WITH BEING KIDNAPPED BY THE ENEMY AND ALL. IT SEEMS LIKE HE'S TRYING TO LURE ME INTO A TRAP.
YOU HAVE NO PROOF OF THAT.

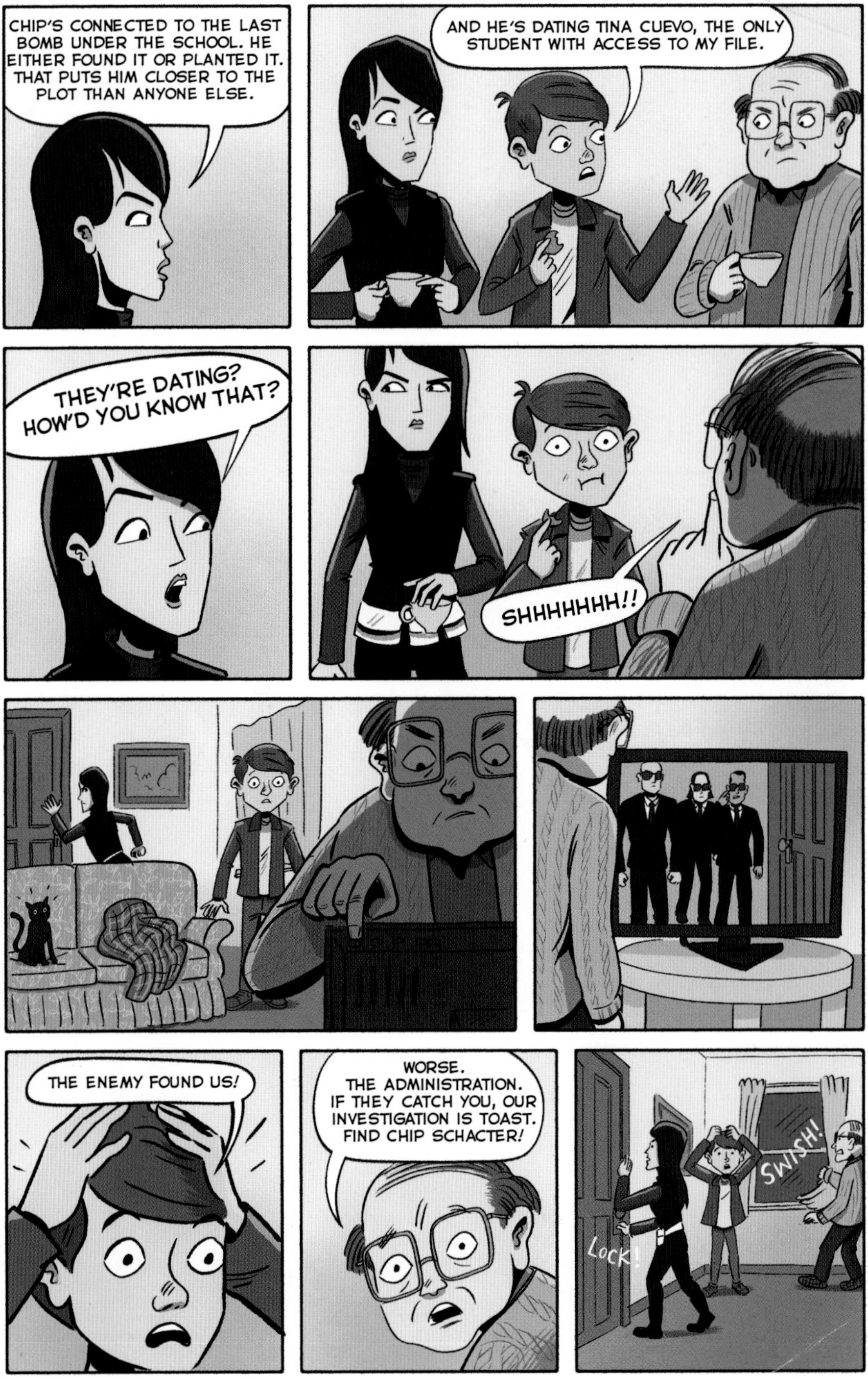
CHIP'S CONNECTED TO THE LAST BOMB UNDER THE SCHOOL. HE EITHER FOUND IT OR PLANTED IT. THAT PUTS HIM CLOSER TO THE PLOT THAN ANYONE ELSE.
AND HE'S DATING TINA CUEVO, THE ONLY STUDENT WITH ACCESS TO MY FILE.
THEY'RE DATING? HOW'D YOU KNOW THAT?
SHHHHHHH!!
THE ENEMY FOUND US!
WORSE. THE ADMINISTRATION. IF THEY CATCH YOU, OUR INVESTIGATION IS TOAST. FIND CHIP SCHACTER!
SWISH!
LOCK!

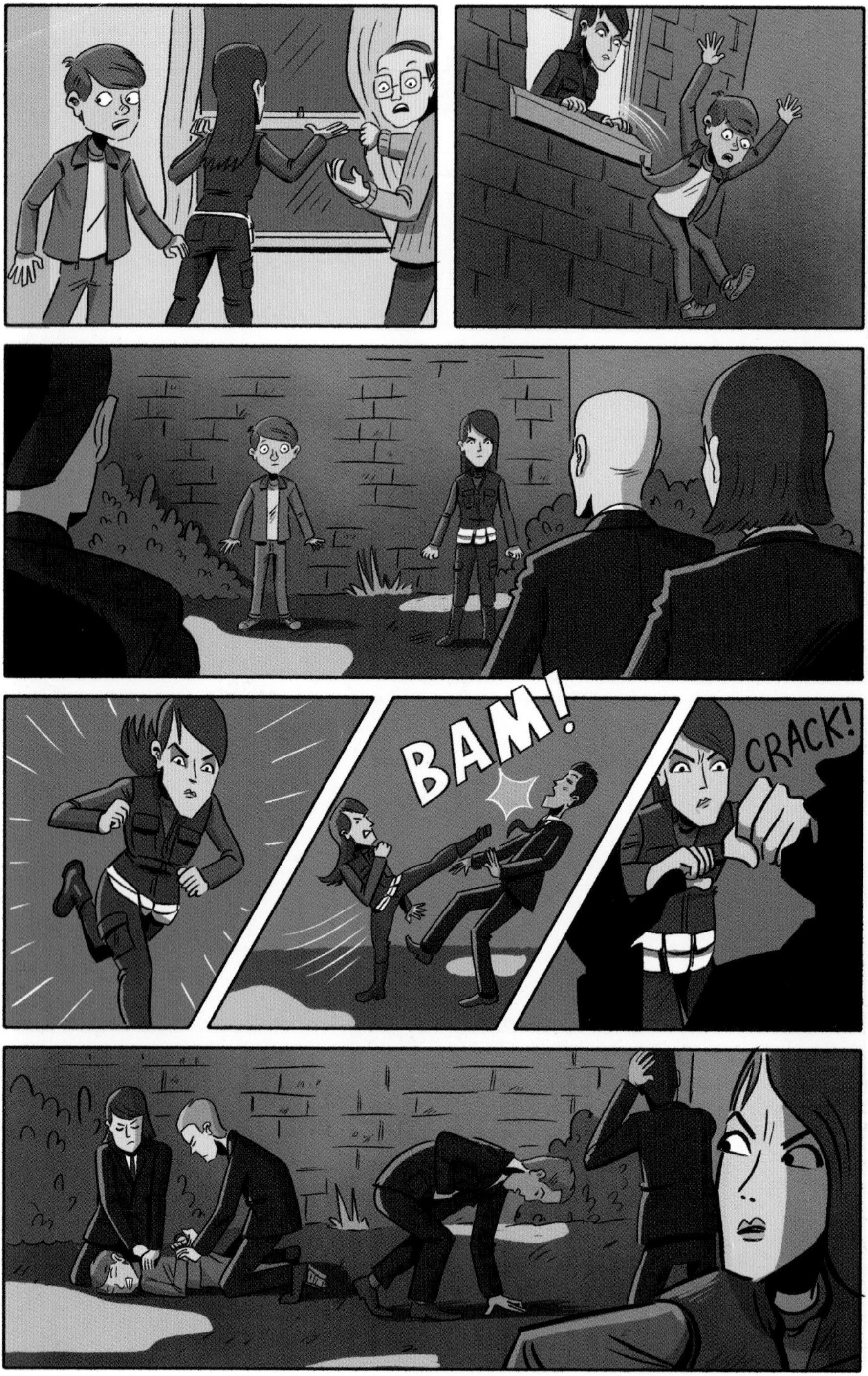
BAM!
CRACK!

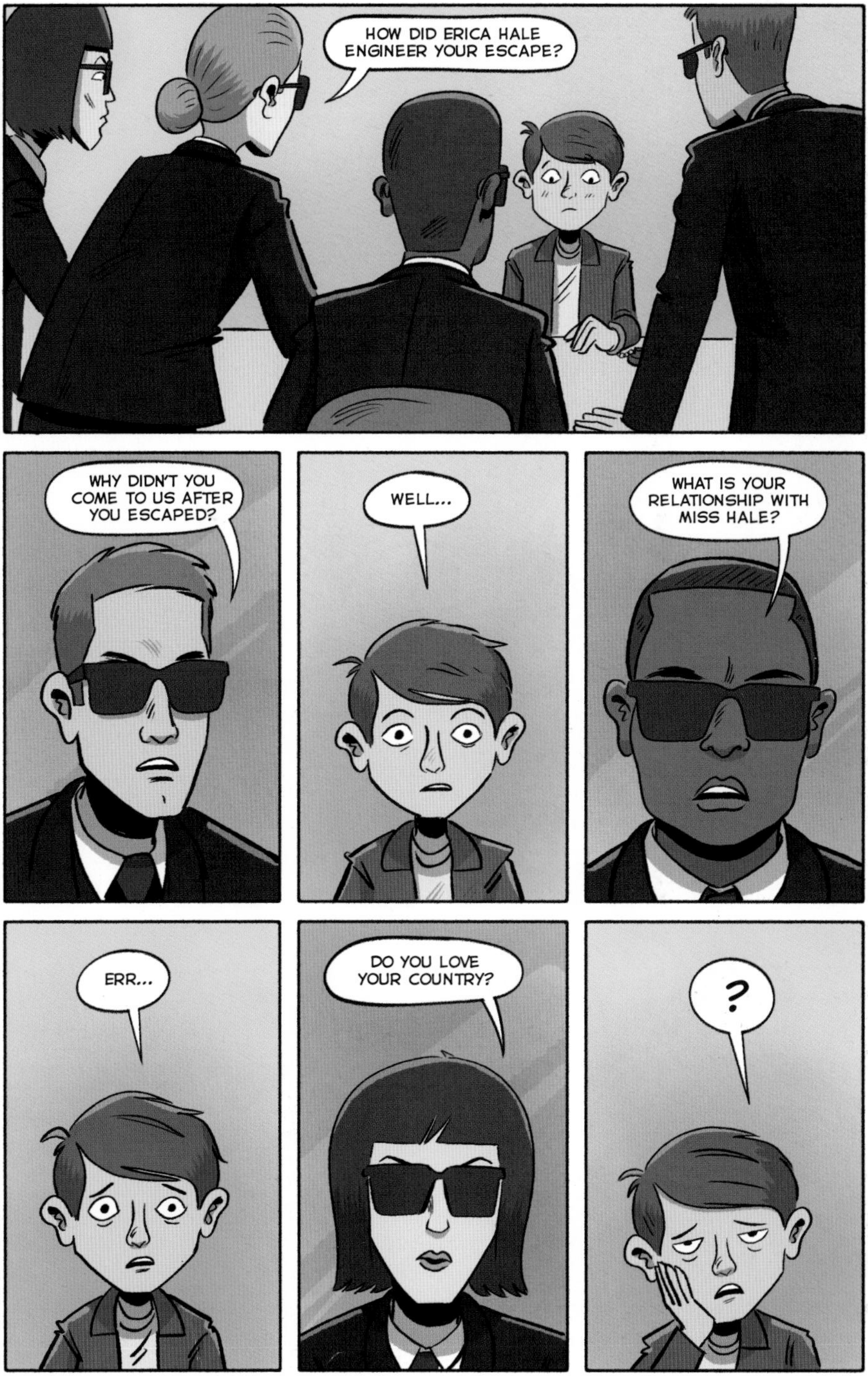
HOW DID ERICA HALE ENGINEER YOUR ESCAPE?
WHY DIDN'T YOU COME TO US AFTER YOU ESCAPED?
WELL...
WHAT IS YOUR RELATIONSHIP WITH MISS HALE?
ERR...
DO YOU LOVE YOUR COUNTRY?
?

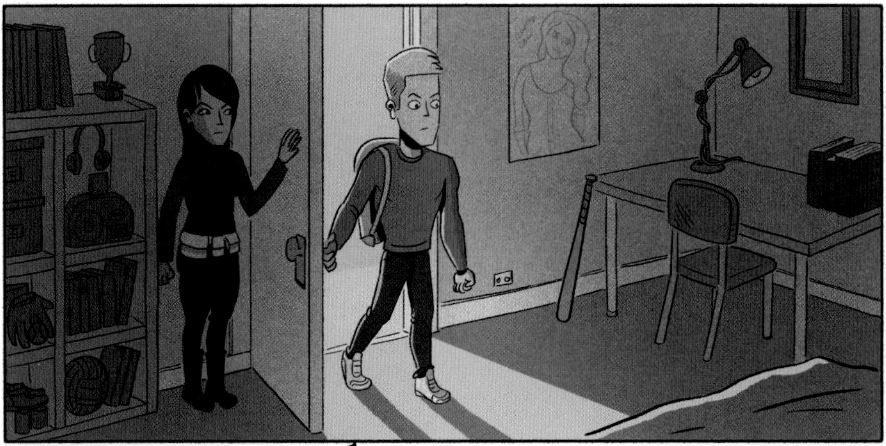

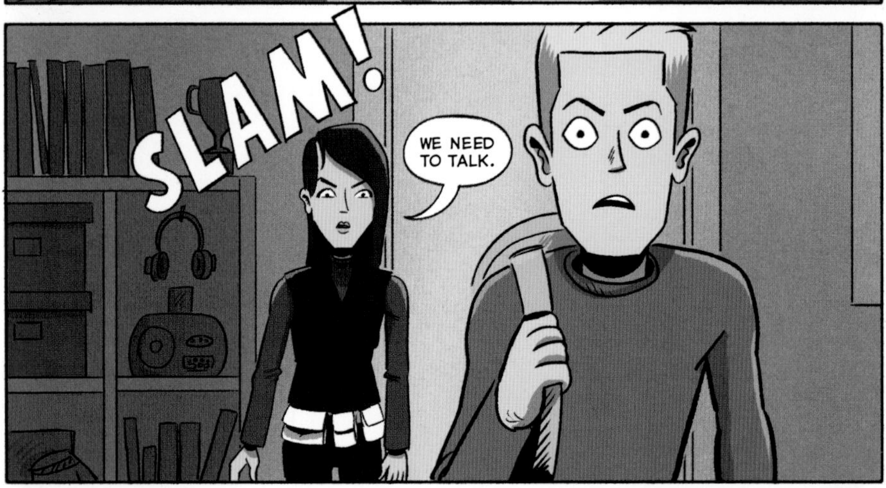
SLAM!
WE NEED TO TALK.

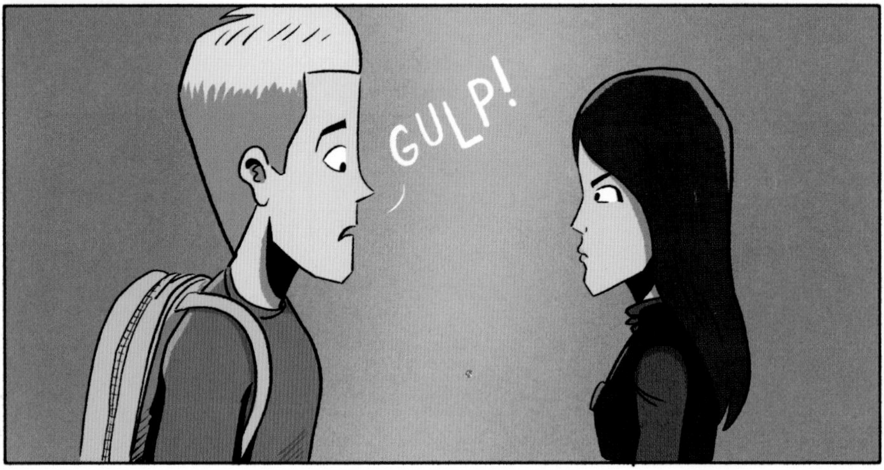
GULP!

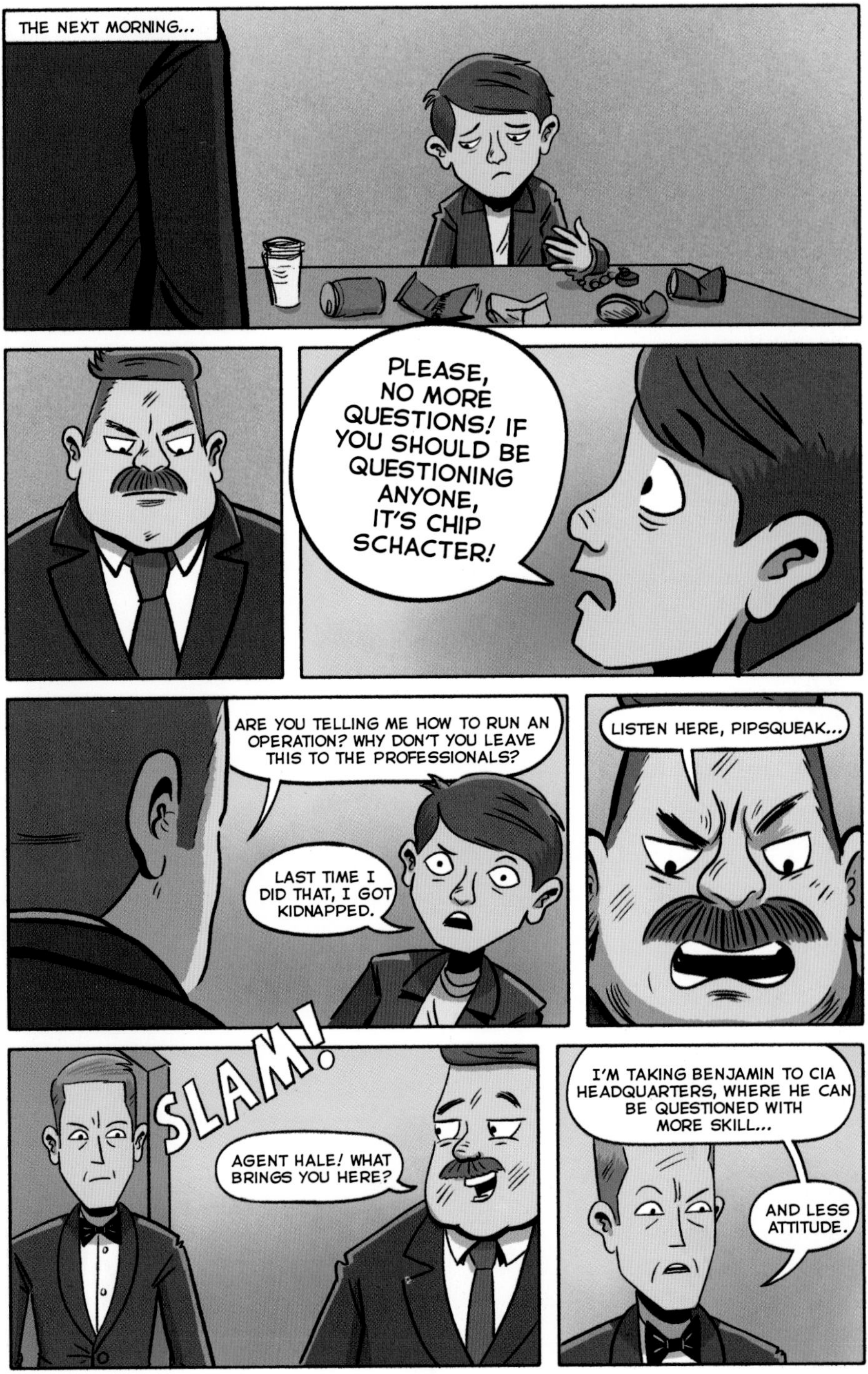
THE NEXT MORNING...
PLEASE, NO MORE QUESTIONS! IF YOU SHOULD BE QUESTIONING ANYONE, IT'S CHIP SCHACTER!
ARE YOU TELLING ME HOW TO RUN AN OPERATION? WHY DON'T YOU LEAVE THIS TO THE PROFESSIONALS?
LAST TIME I DID THAT, I GOT KIDNAPPED.
LISTEN HERE, PIPSQUEAK...
SLAM!
AGENT HALE! WHAT BRINGS YOU HERE?
I'M TAKING BENJAMIN TO CIA HEADQUARTERS, WHERE HE CAN BE QUESTIONED WITH MORE SKILL...
AND LESS ATTITUDE.

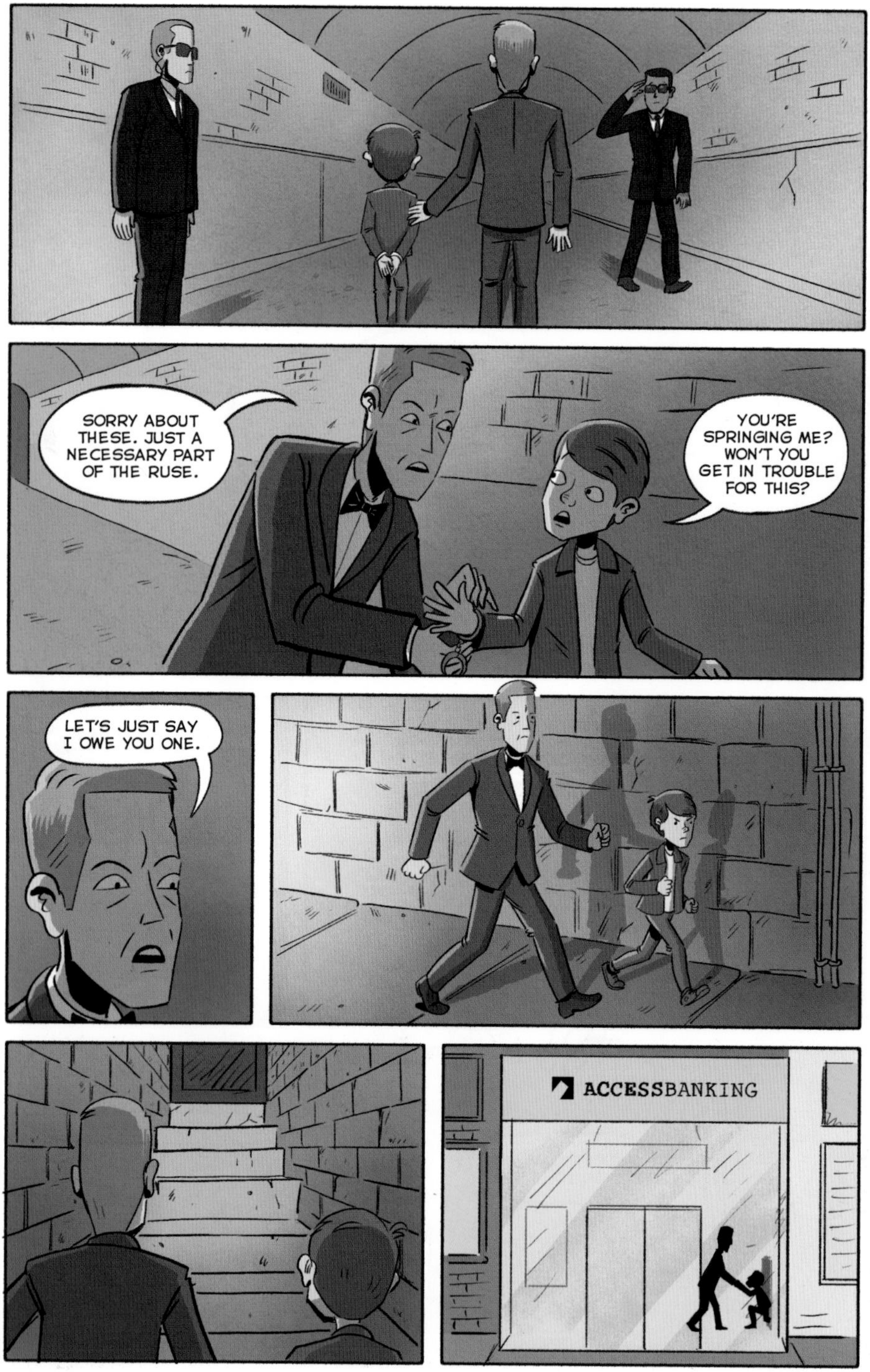
SORRY ABOUT THESE. JUST A NECESSARY PART OF THE RUSE.
YOU'RE SPRINGING ME? WON'T YOU GET IN TROUBLE FOR THIS?
LET'S JUST SAY I OWE YOU ONE.
ACCESSBANKING

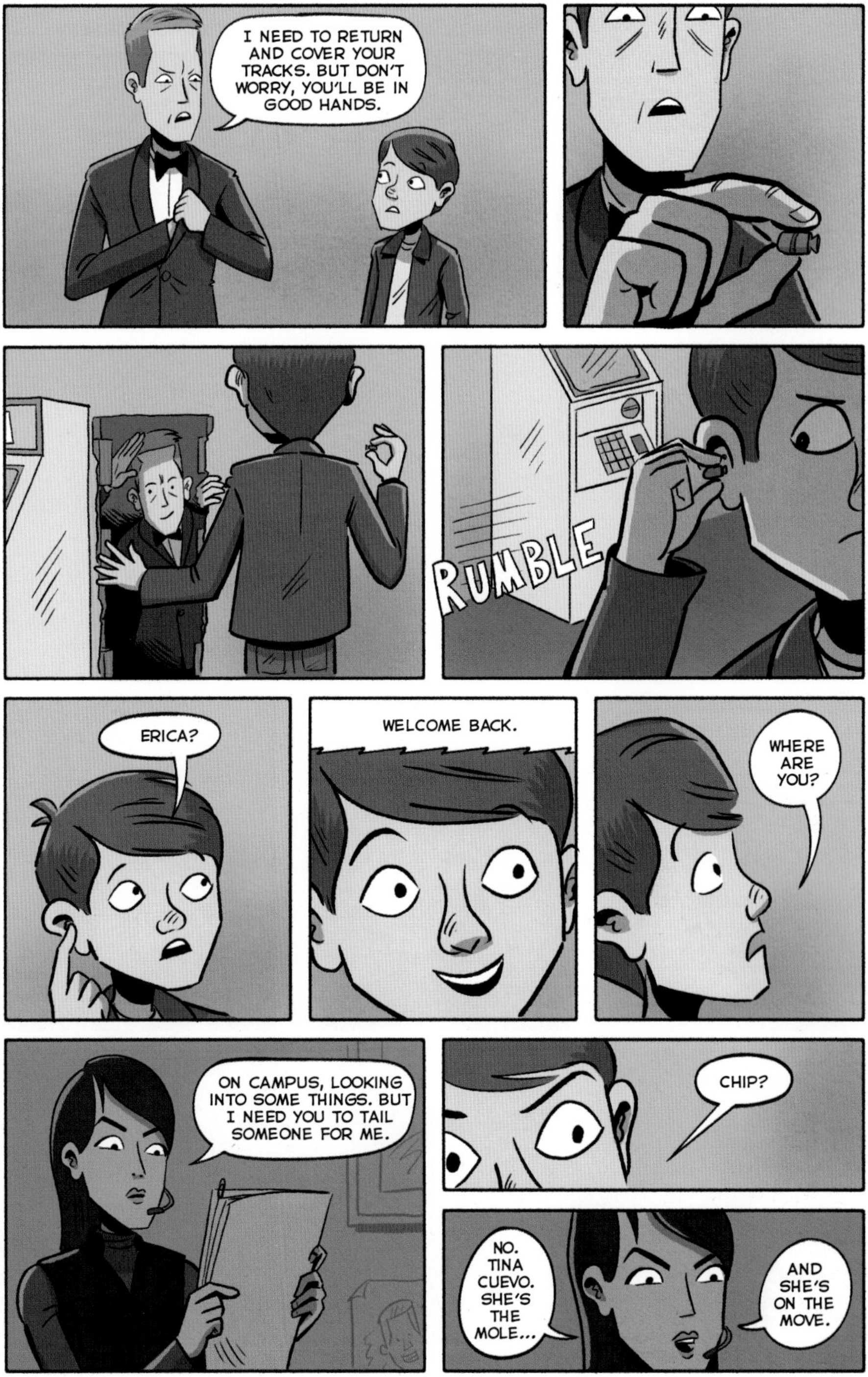
I NEED TO RETURN AND COVER YOUR TRACKS. BUT DON'T WORRY, YOU'LL BE IN GOOD HANDS.
RUMBLE
ERICA?
WELCOME BACK.
WHERE ARE YOU?
ON CAMPUS, LOOKING INTO SOME THINGS. BUT I NEED YOU TO TAIL SOMEONE FOR ME.
CHIP?
NO. TINA CUEVO. SHE'S THE MOLE...
AND SHE'S ON THE MOVE.

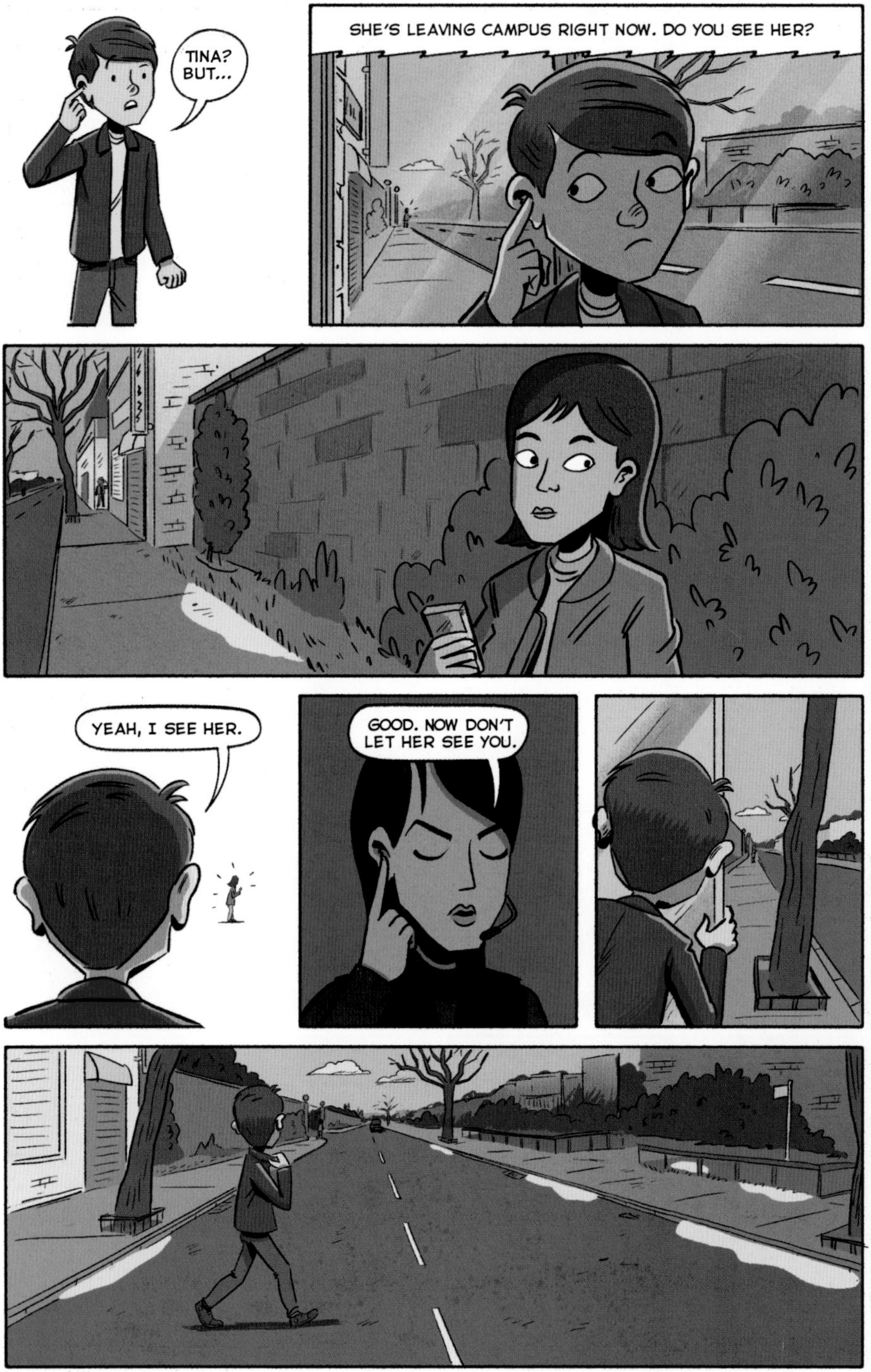
TINA? BUT...
SHE'S LEAVING CAMPUS RIGHT NOW. DO YOU SEE HER?
YEAH, I SEE HER.
GOOD. NOW DON'T LET HER SEE YOU.

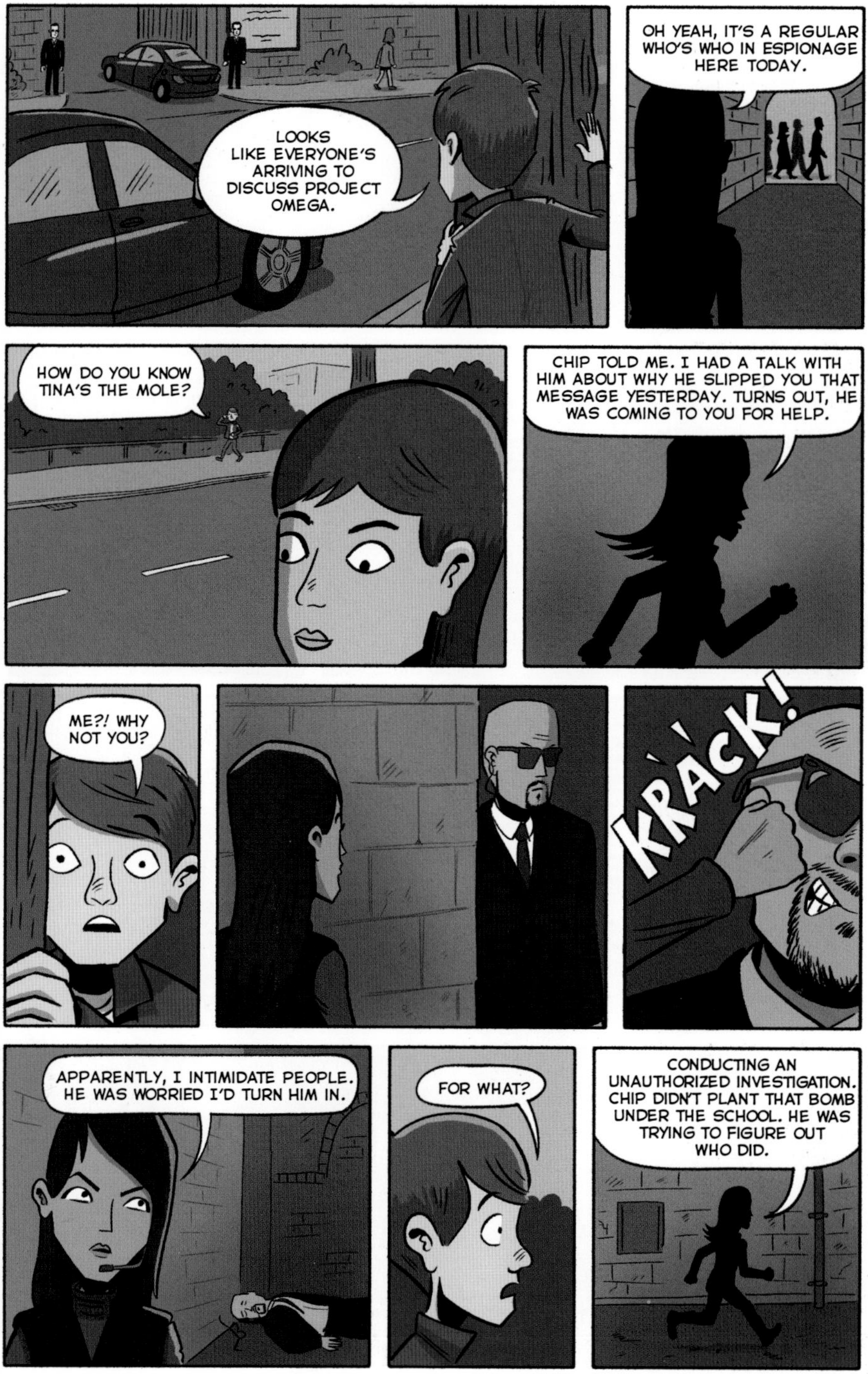
LOOKS LIKE EVERYONE'S ARRIVING TO DISCUSS PROJECT OMEGA.
OH YEAH, IT'S A REGULAR WHO'S WHO IN ESPIONAGE HERE TODAY.
HOW DO YOU KNOW TINA'S THE MOLE?
CHIP TOLD ME. I HAD A TALK WITH HIM ABOUT WHY HE SLIPPED YOU THAT MESSAGE YESTERDAY. TURNS OUT, HE WAS COMING TO YOU FOR HELP.
ME?! WHY NOT YOU?
KRACK!
APPARENTLY, I INTIMIDATE PEOPLE. HE WAS WORRIED I'D TURN HIM IN.
FOR WHAT?
CONDUCTING AN UNAUTHORIZED INVESTIGATION. CHIP DIDN'T PLANT THAT BOMB UNDER THE SCHOOL. HE WAS TRYING TO FIGURE OUT WHO DID.

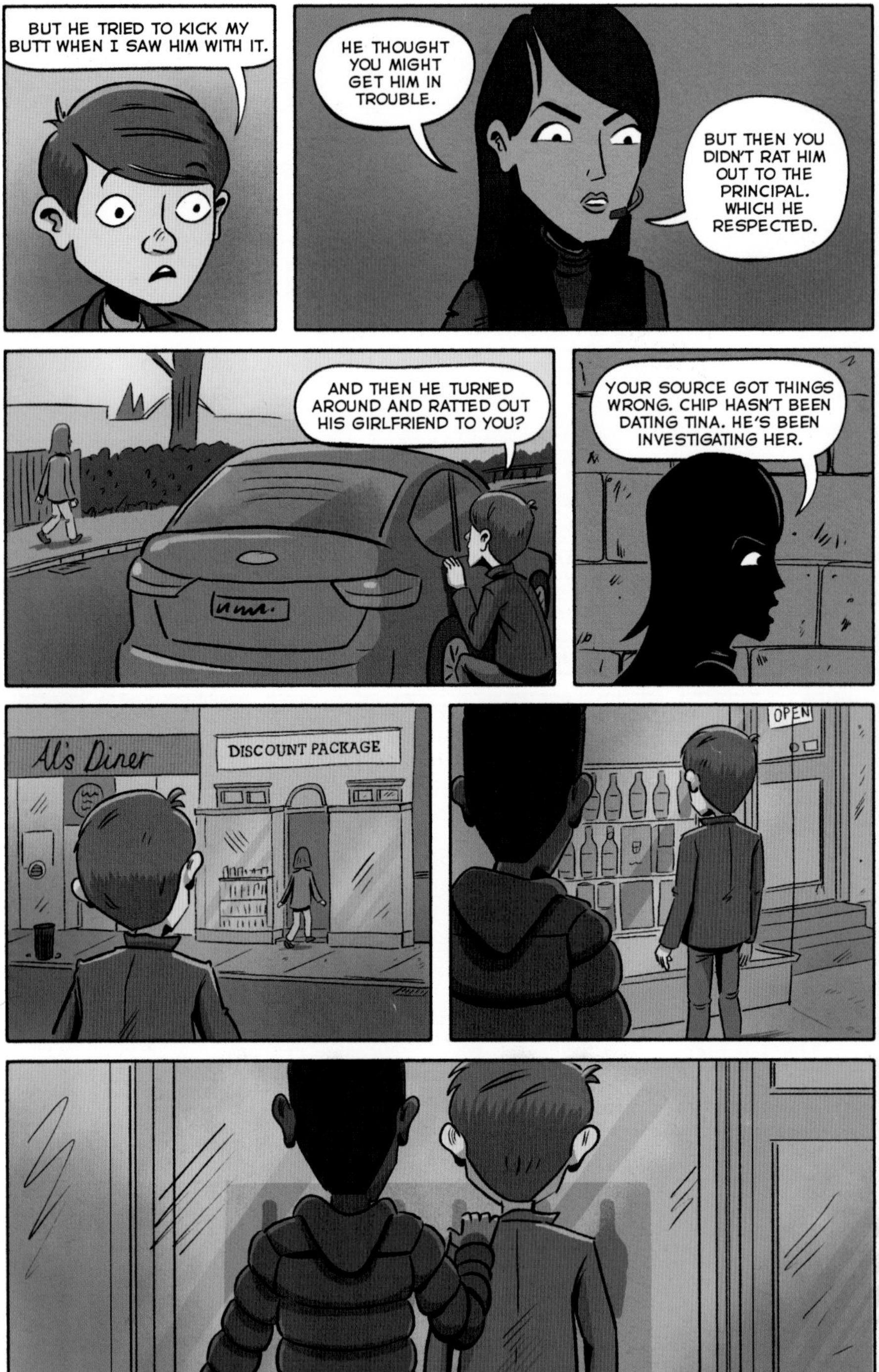
BUT HE TRIED TO KICK MY BUTT WHEN I SAW HIM WITH IT.
HE THOUGHT YOU MIGHT GET HIM IN TROUBLE.
BUT THEN YOU DIDN'T RAT HIM OUT TO THE PRINCIPAL. WHICH HE RESPECTED.
AND THEN HE TURNED AROUND AND RATTED OUT HIS GIRLFRIEND TO YOU?
YOUR SOURCE GOT THINGS WRONG. CHIP HASN'T BEEN DATING TINA. HE'S BEEN INVESTIGATING HER.
Al's Diner
DISCOUNT PACKAGE
OPEN

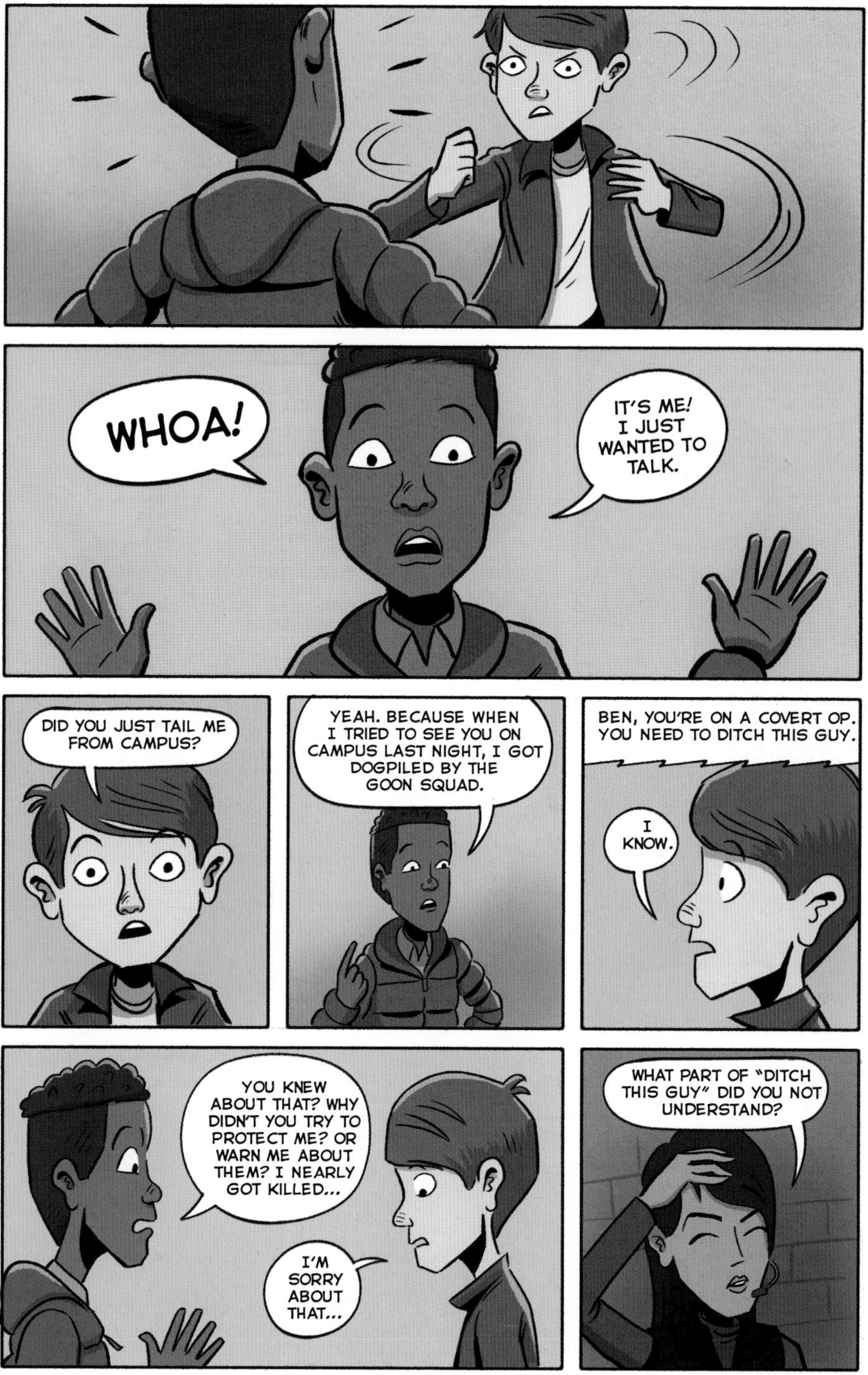
WHOA!
IT'S ME! I JUST WANTED TO TALK.
DID YOU JUST TAIL ME FROM CAMPUS?
YEAH. BECAUSE WHEN I TRIED TO SEE YOU ON CAMPUS LAST NIGHT, I GOT DOGPILED BY THE GOON SQUAD.
BEN, YOU'RE ON A COVERT OP. YOU NEED TO DITCH THIS GUY.
I KNOW.
YOU KNEW ABOUT THAT? WHY DIDN'T YOU TRY TO PROTECT ME? OR WARN ME ABOUT THEM? I NEARLY GOT KILLED...
I'M SORRY ABOUT THAT...
WHAT PART OF "DITCH THIS GUY" DID YOU NOT UNDERSTAND?

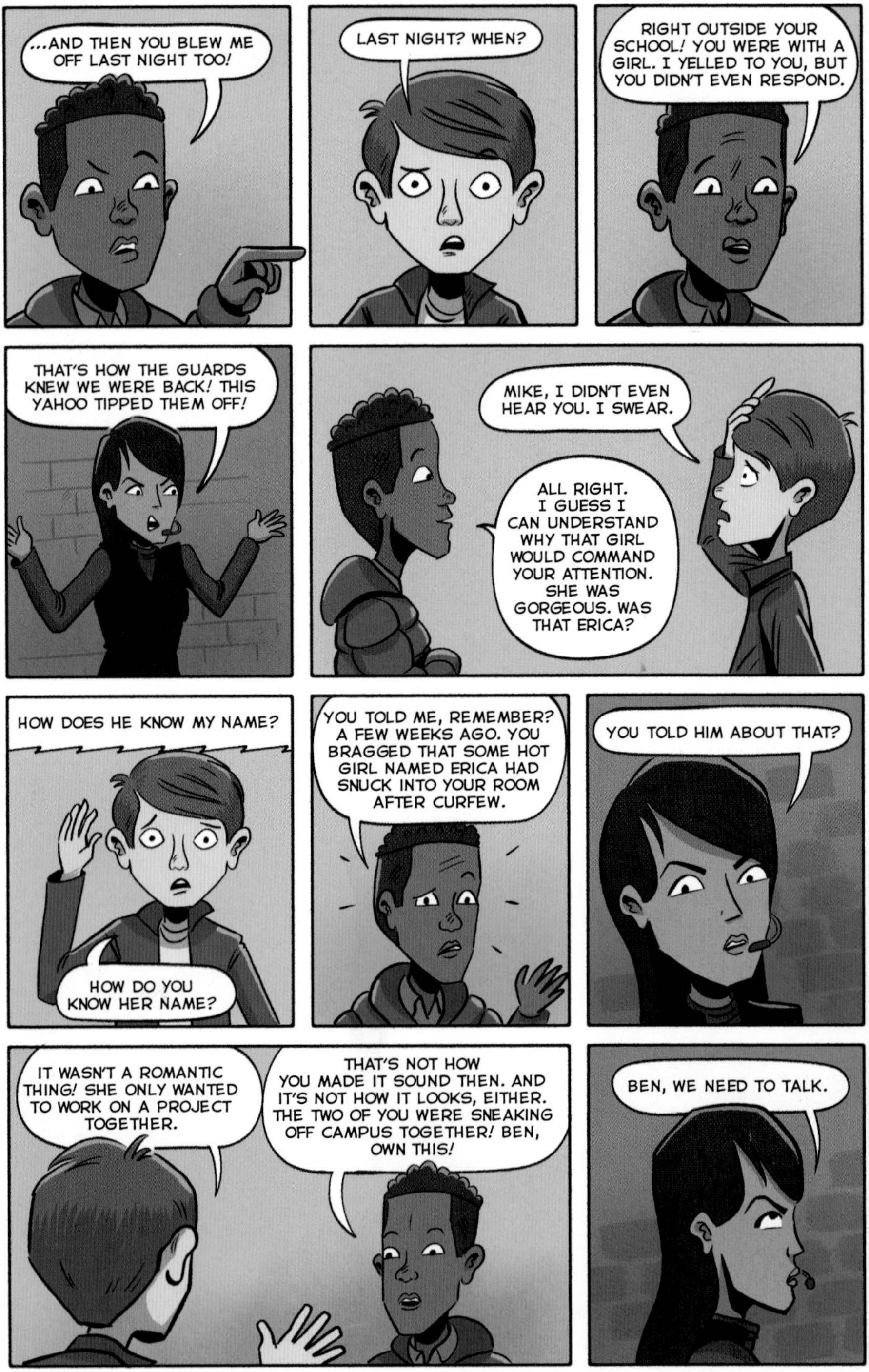
...AND THEN YOU BLEW ME OFF LAST NIGHT TOO!
LAST NIGHT? WHEN?
RIGHT OUTSIDE YOUR SCHOOL! YOU WERE WITH A GIRL. I YELLED TO YOU, BUT YOU DIDN'T EVEN RESPOND.
THAT'S HOW THE GUARDS KNEW WE WERE BACK! THIS YAHOO TIPPED THEM OFF!
MIKE, I DIDN'T EVEN HEAR YOU. I SWEAR.
ALL RIGHT. I GUESS I CAN UNDERSTAND WHY THAT GIRL WOULD COMMAND YOUR ATTENTION. SHE WAS GORGEOUS. WAS THAT ERICA?
HOW DOES HE KNOW MY NAME?
HOW DO YOU KNOW HER NAME?
YOU TOLD ME, REMEMBER? A FEW WEEKS AGO. YOU BRAGGED THAT SOME HOT GIRL NAMED ERICA HAD SNUCK INTO YOUR ROOM AFTER CURFEW.
YOU TOLD HIM ABOUT THAT?
IT WASN'T A ROMANTIC THING! SHE ONLY WANTED TO WORK ON A PROJECT TOGETHER.
THAT'S NOT HOW YOU MADE IT SOUND THEN. AND IT'S NOT HOW IT LOOKS, EITHER. THE TWO OF YOU WERE SNEAKING OFF CAMPUS TOGETHER! BEN, OWN THIS!
BEN, WE NEED TO TALK.

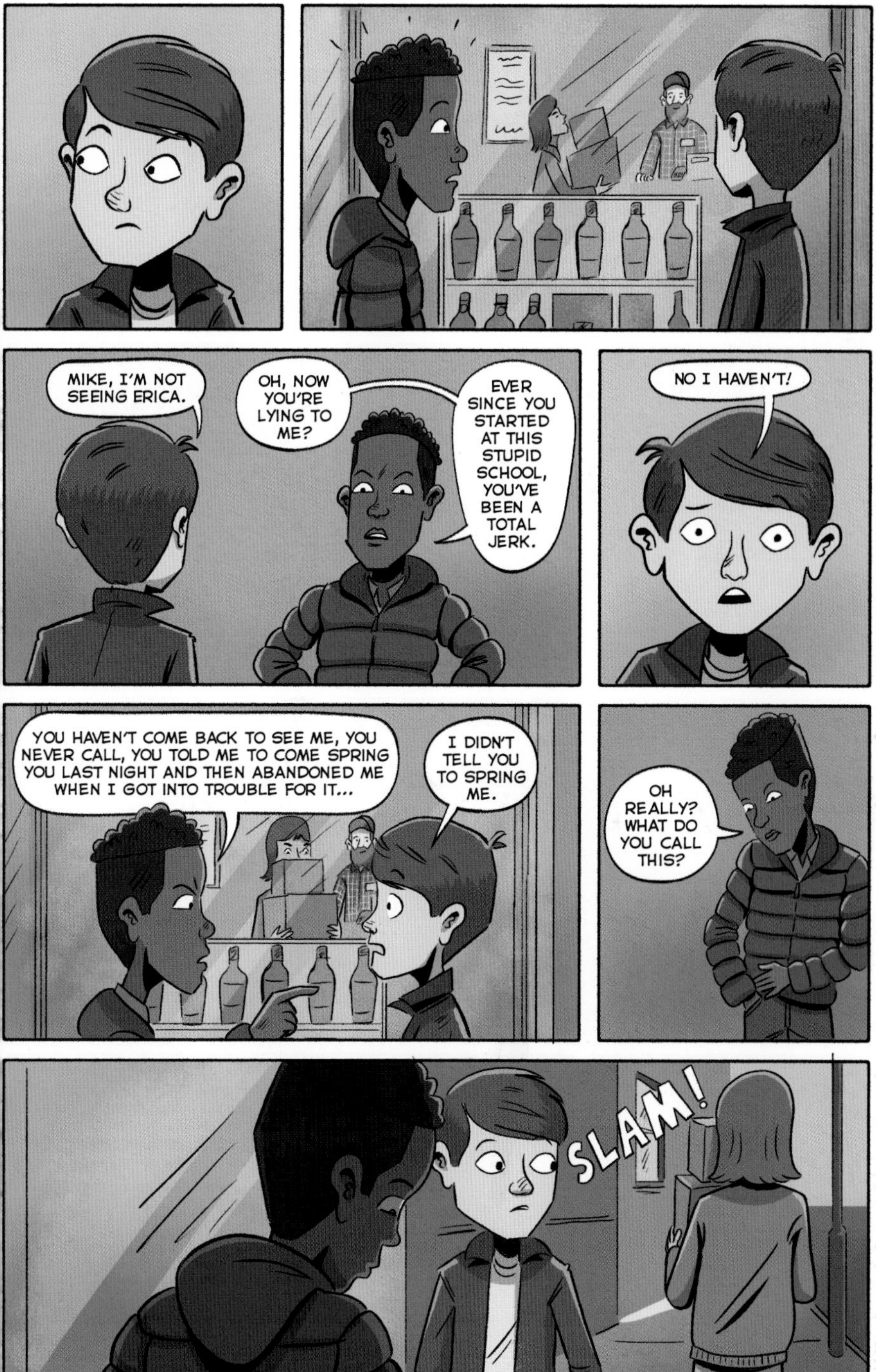
MIKE, I'M NOT SEEING ERICA.
OH, NOW YOU'RE LYING TO ME?
EVER SINCE YOU STARTED AT THIS STUPID SCHOOL, YOU'VE BEEN A TOTAL JERK.
NO I HAVEN'T!
YOU HAVEN'T COME BACK TO SEE ME, YOU NEVER CALL, YOU TOLD ME TO COME SPRING YOU LAST NIGHT AND THEN ABANDONED ME WHEN I GOT INTO TROUBLE FOR IT...
I DIDN'T TELL YOU TO SPRING ME.
OH REALLY? WHAT DO YOU CALL THIS?
SLAM!

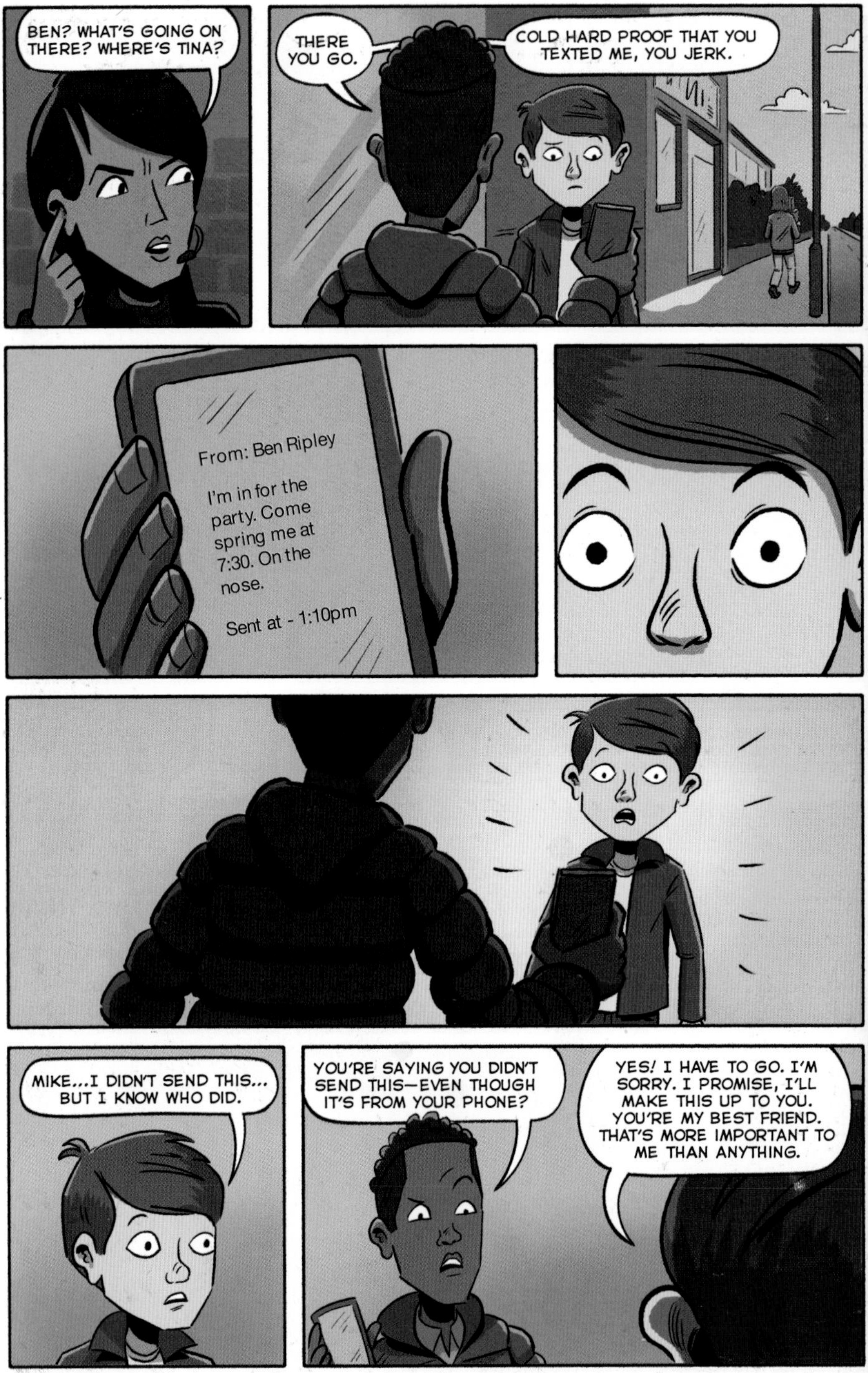
BEN? WHAT'S GOING ON THERE? WHERE'S TINA?
THERE YOU GO.
COLD HARD PROOF THAT YOU TEXTED ME, YOU JERK.
From: Ben Ripley
I'm in for the party. Come spring me at 7:30. On the nose.
Sent at - 1:10pm
MIKE...I DIDN'T SEND THIS... BUT I KNOW WHO DID.
YOU'RE SAYING YOU DIDN'T SEND THIS—EVEN THOUGH IT'S FROM YOUR PHONE?
YES! I HAVE TO GO. I'M SORRY. I PROMISE, I'LL MAKE THIS UP TO YOU. YOU'RE MY BEST FRIEND. THAT'S MORE IMPORTANT TO ME THAN ANYTHING.

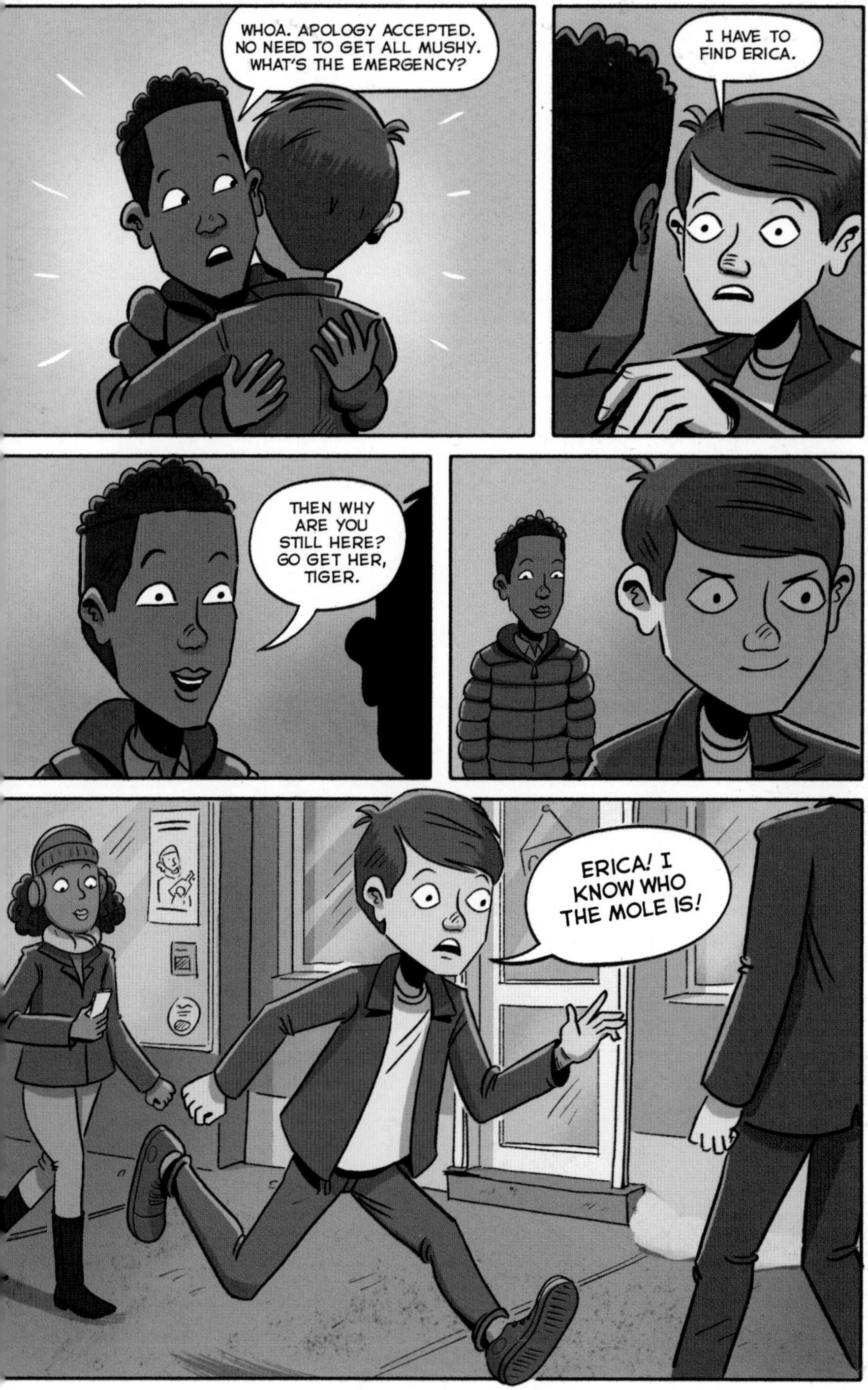

WHOA. APOLOGY ACCEPTED. NO NEED TO GET ALL MUSHY. WHAT'S THE EMERGENCY?
I HAVE TO FIND ERICA.
THEN WHY ARE YOU STILL HERE? GO GET HER, TIGER.
ERICA! I KNOW WHO THE MOLE IS!

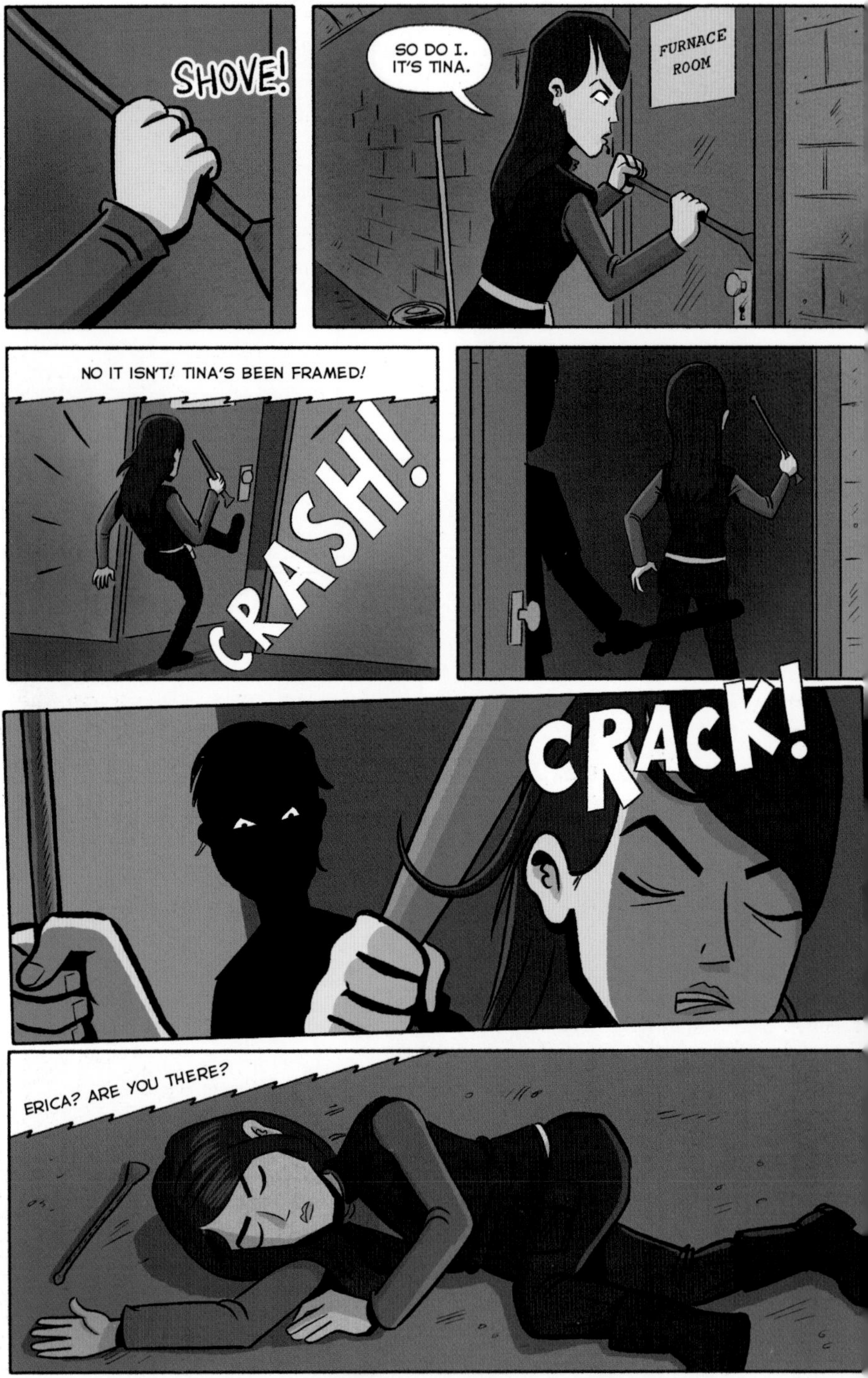
SHOVE!
SO DO I. IT'S TINA.
FURNACE ROOM
NO IT ISN'T! TINA'S BEEN FRAMED!
CRASH!
CRACK!
ERICA? ARE YOU THERE?

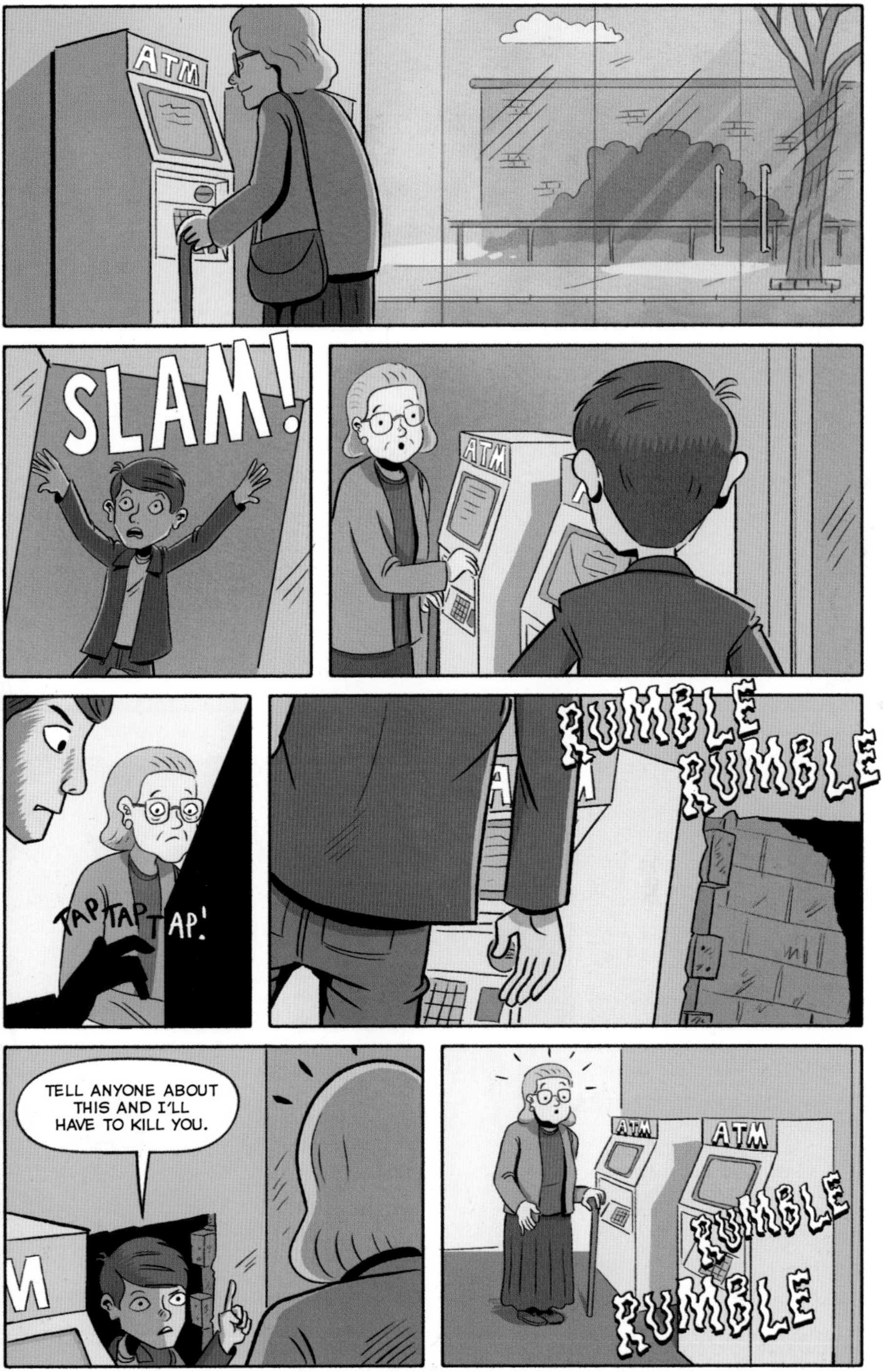
ATM
SLAM!
ATM
TAP TAP TAP!
RUMBLE
RUMBLE
TELL ANYONE ABOUT THIS AND I'LL HAVE TO KILL YOU.
ATM
ATM
RUMBLE
RUMBLE

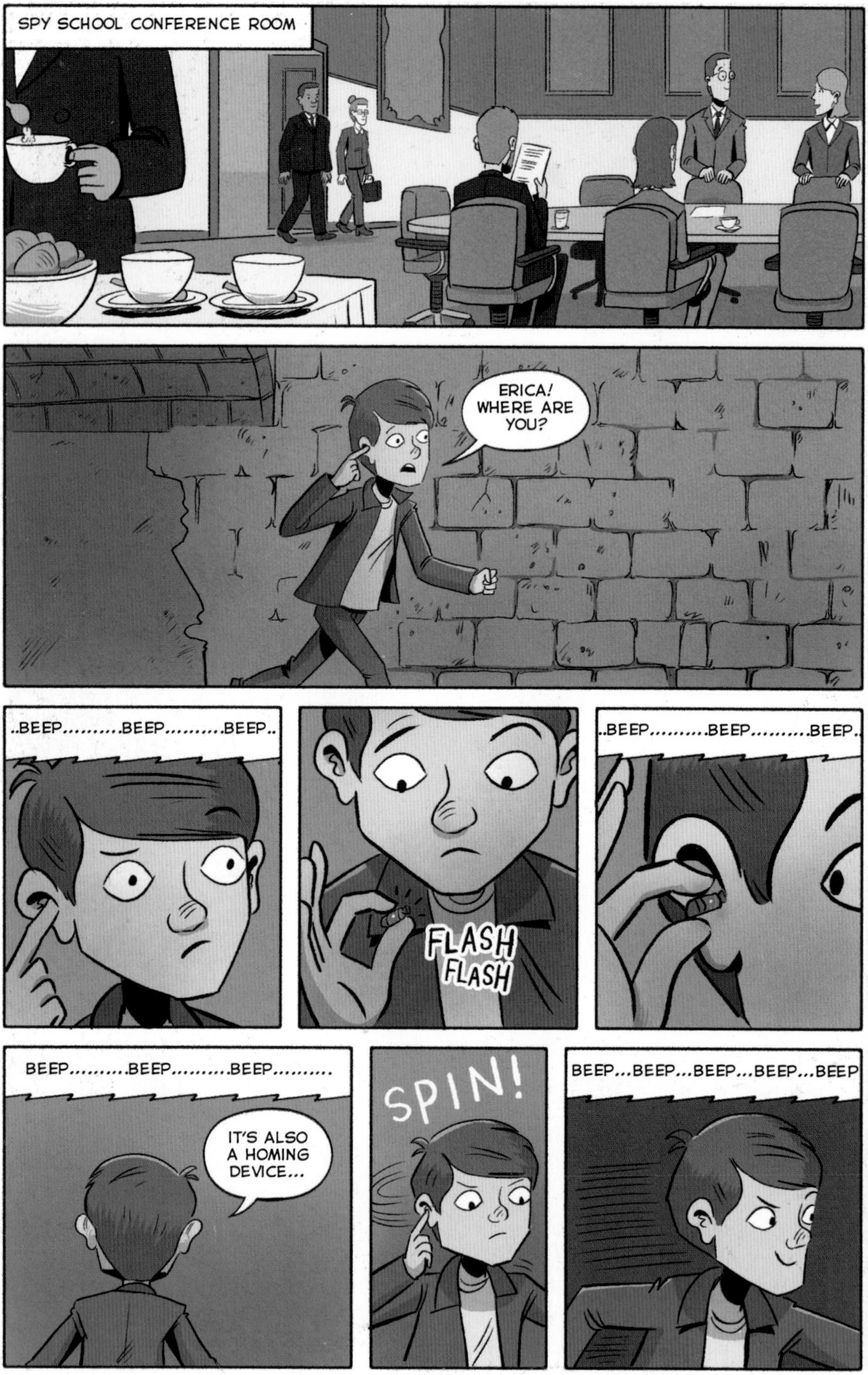
SPY SCHOOL CONFERENCE ROOM
ERICA! WHERE ARE YOU?
..BEEP.........BEEP.........BEEP..
FLASH FLASH
..BEEP.........BEEP.........BEEP..
BEEP.........BEEP.........BEEP.........
IT'S ALSO A HOMING DEVICE...
SPIN!
BEEP...BEEP...BEEP...BEEP...BEEP

BEEP...BEEP...BEEP...BEEP...BEEP...BEEP...BEEP...B...EEP...BEEP...BEEP...BEEP...BEEP...BEEP

BEEP.BEEP.BEEP.BEEP.BEEP.BEEP.BEEP.BEEP.BEEEEEEEEEEEEEEEEEEEEEEEEEEEEEEEEEEEEEEEEEEEEEP.

FURNACE
ROOM

FURNACE
ROOM

CRACK!

243

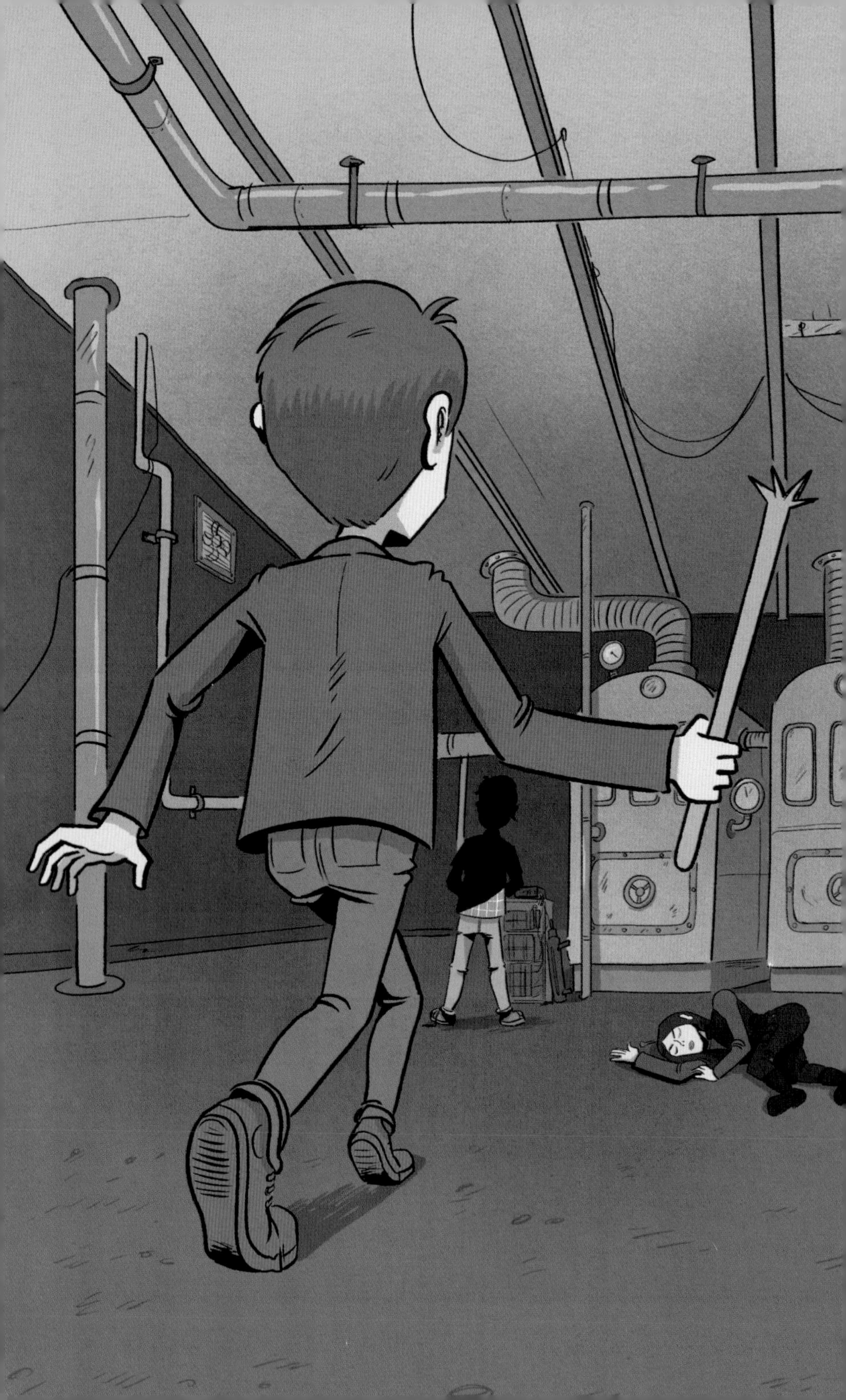

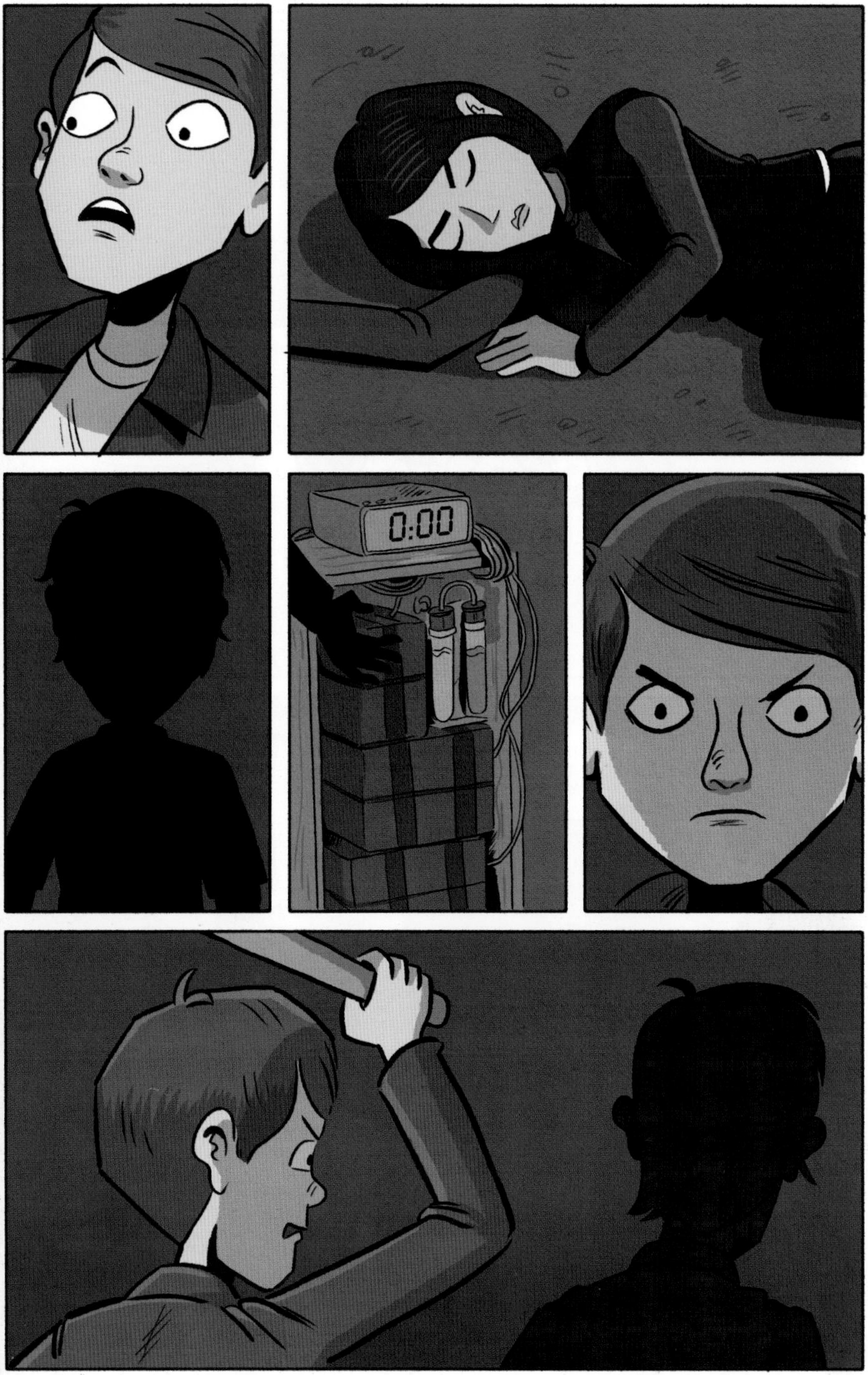
0:00

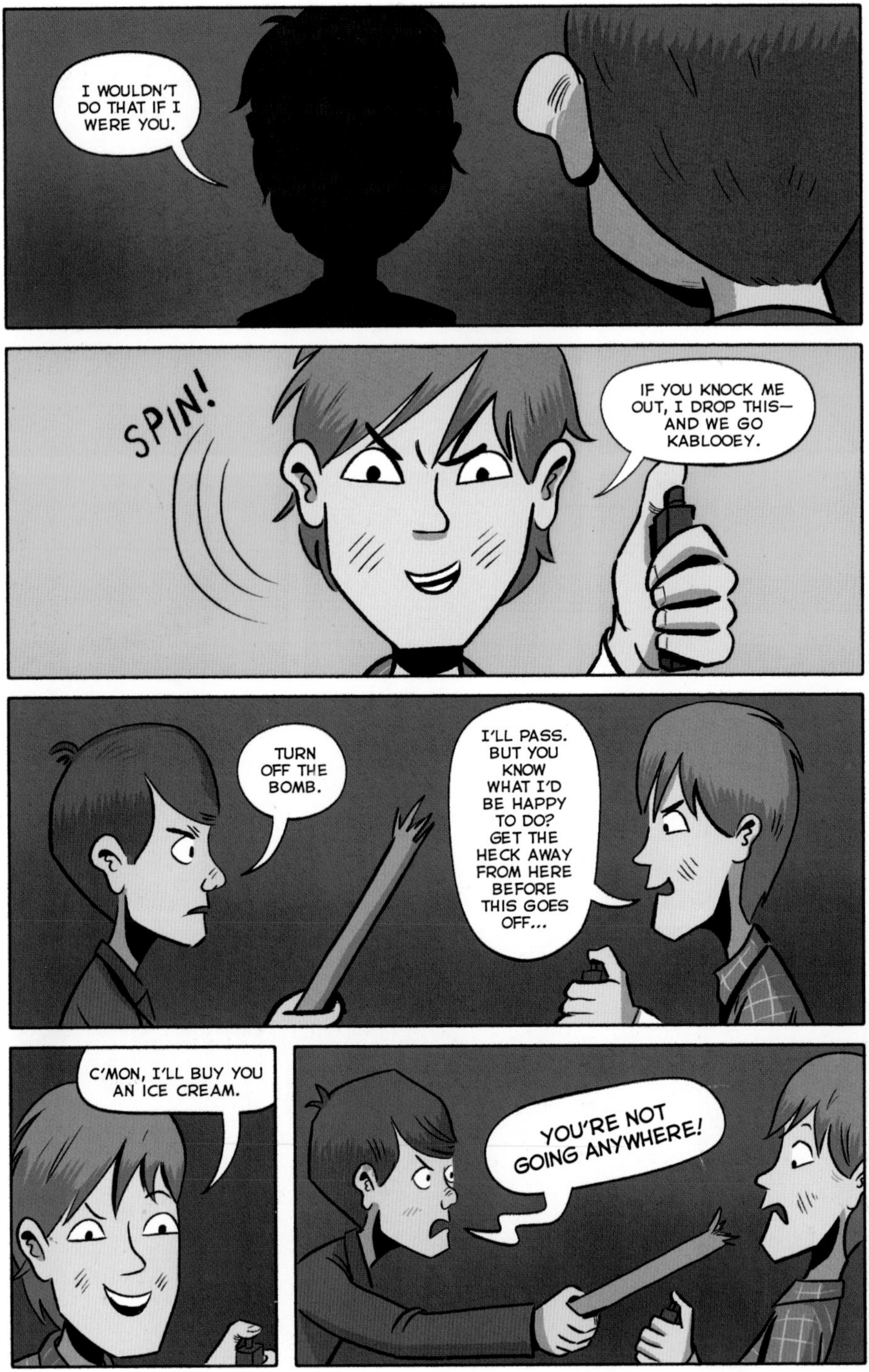
I WOULDN'T DO THAT IF I WERE YOU.
SPIN!
IF YOU KNOCK ME OUT, I DROP THIS— AND WE GO KABLOOEY.
TURN OFF THE BOMB.
I'LL PASS. BUT YOU KNOW WHAT I'D BE HAPPY TO DO? GET THE HECK AWAY FROM HERE BEFORE THIS GOES OFF...
C'MON, I'LL BUY YOU AN ICE CREAM.
YOU'RE NOT GOING ANYWHERE!

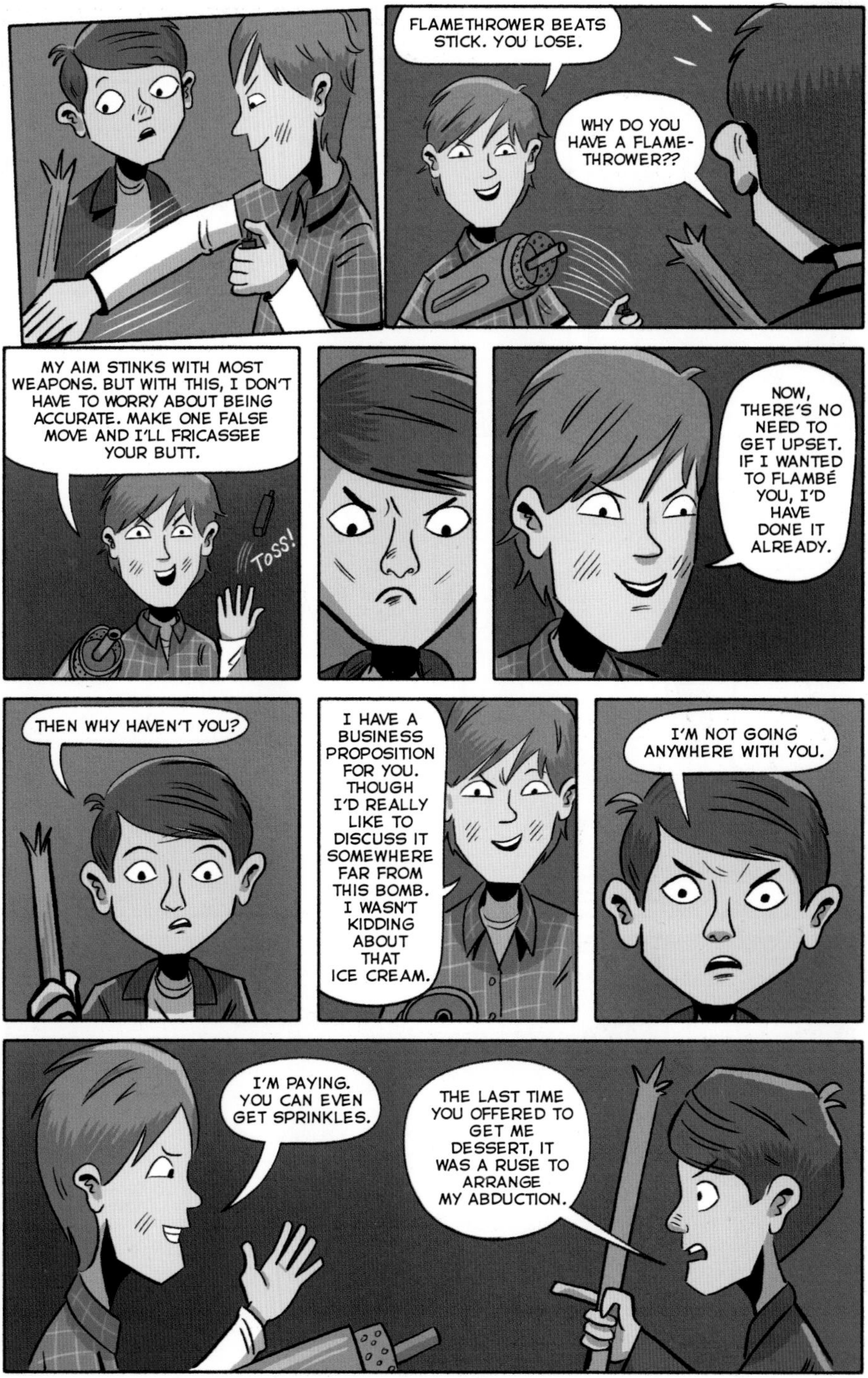
FLAMETHROWER BEATS STICK. YOU LOSE.
WHY DO YOU HAVE A FLAME-THROWER??
MY AIM STINKS WITH MOST WEAPONS. BUT WITH THIS, I DON'T HAVE TO WORRY ABOUT BEING ACCURATE. MAKE ONE FALSE MOVE AND I'LL FRICASSEE YOUR BUTT.
TOSS!
NOW, THERE'S NO NEED TO GET UPSET. IF I WANTED TO FLAMBÉ YOU, I'D HAVE DONE IT ALREADY.
THEN WHY HAVEN'T YOU?
I HAVE A BUSINESS PROPOSITION FOR YOU. THOUGH I'D REALLY LIKE TO DISCUSS IT SOMEWHERE FAR FROM THIS BOMB. I WASN'T KIDDING ABOUT THAT ICE CREAM.
I'M NOT GOING ANYWHERE WITH YOU.
I'M PAYING. YOU CAN EVEN GET SPRINKLES.
THE LAST TIME YOU OFFERED TO GET ME DESSERT, IT WAS A RUSE TO ARRANGE MY ABDUCTION.

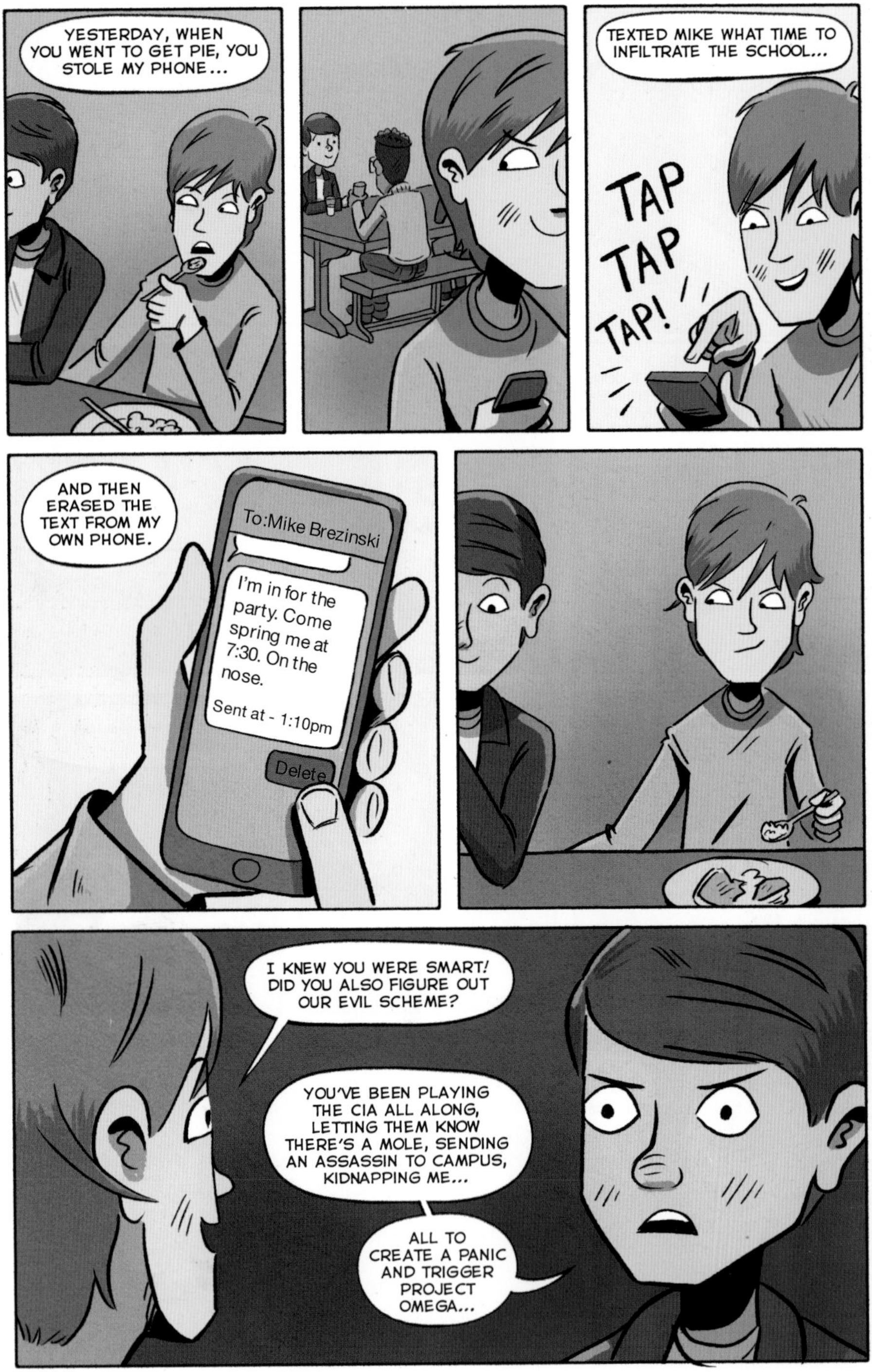
YESTERDAY, WHEN YOU WENT TO GET PIE, YOU STOLE MY PHONE...
TEXTED MIKE WHAT TIME TO INFILTRATE THE SCHOOL...
TAP TAP TAP!
AND THEN ERASED THE TEXT FROM MY OWN PHONE.
To:Mike Brezinski
I'm in for the party. Come spring me at 7:30. On the nose.
Sent at - 1:10pm
Delete
I KNEW YOU WERE SMART! DID YOU ALSO FIGURE OUT OUR EVIL SCHEME?
YOU'VE BEEN PLAYING THE CIA ALL ALONG, LETTING THEM KNOW THERE'S A MOLE, SENDING AN ASSASSIN TO CAMPUS, KIDNAPPING ME...
ALL TO CREATE A PANIC AND TRIGGER PROJECT OMEGA...

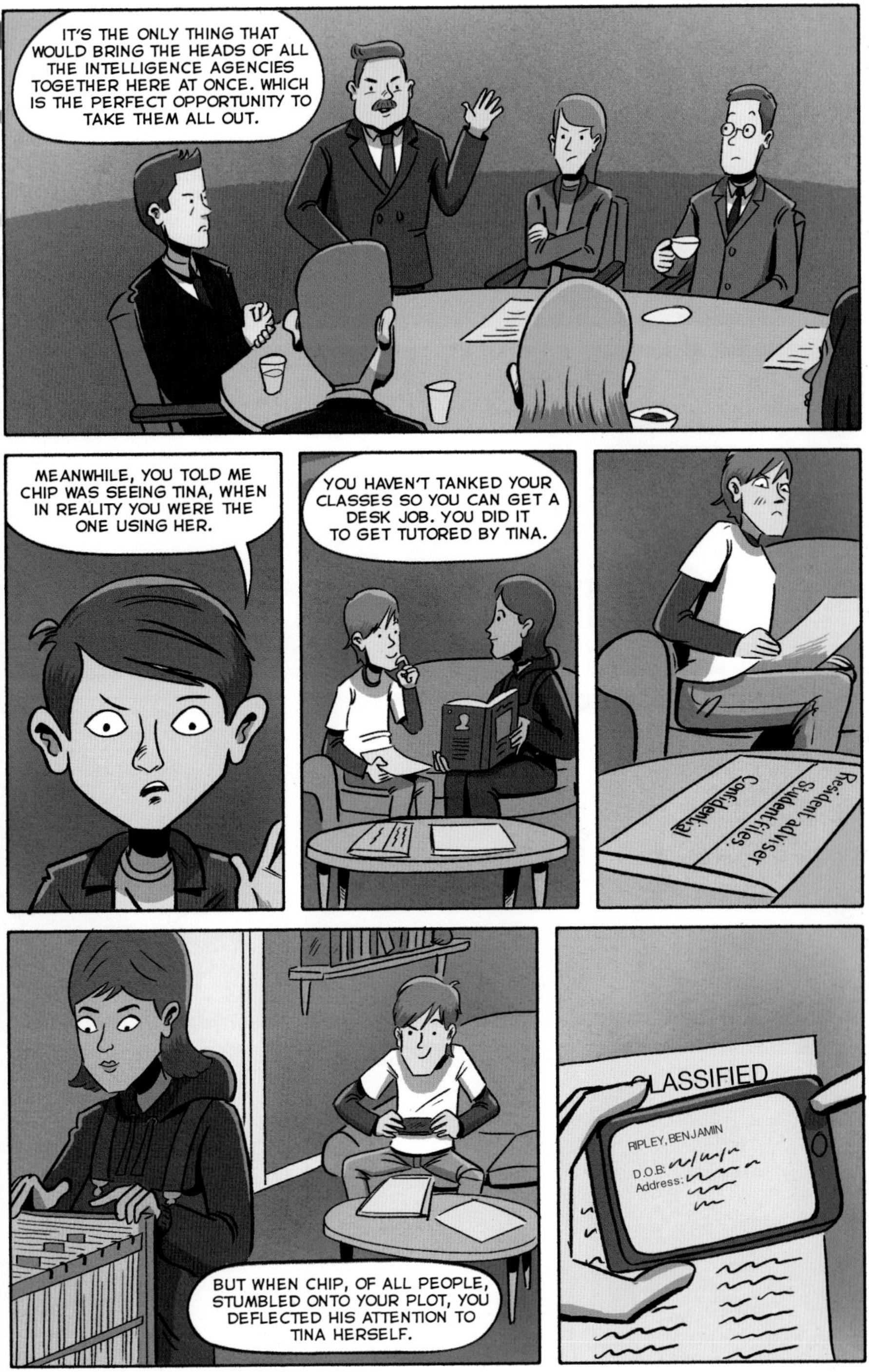
IT'S THE ONLY THING THAT WOULD BRING THE HEADS OF ALL THE INTELLIGENCE AGENCIES TOGETHER HERE AT ONCE. WHICH IS THE PERFECT OPPORTUNITY TO TAKE THEM ALL OUT.
MEANWHILE, YOU TOLD ME CHIP WAS SEEING TINA, WHEN IN REALITY YOU WERE THE ONE USING HER.
YOU HAVEN'T TANKED YOUR CLASSES SO YOU CAN GET A DESK JOB. YOU DID IT TO GET TUTORED BY TINA.
Resident adviser
Student files
Confidential
BUT WHEN CHIP, OF ALL PEOPLE, STUMBLED ONTO YOUR PLOT, YOU DEFLECTED HIS ATTENTION TO TINA HERSELF.
CLASSIFIED
RIPLEY, BENJAMIN
D.O.B:
Address:

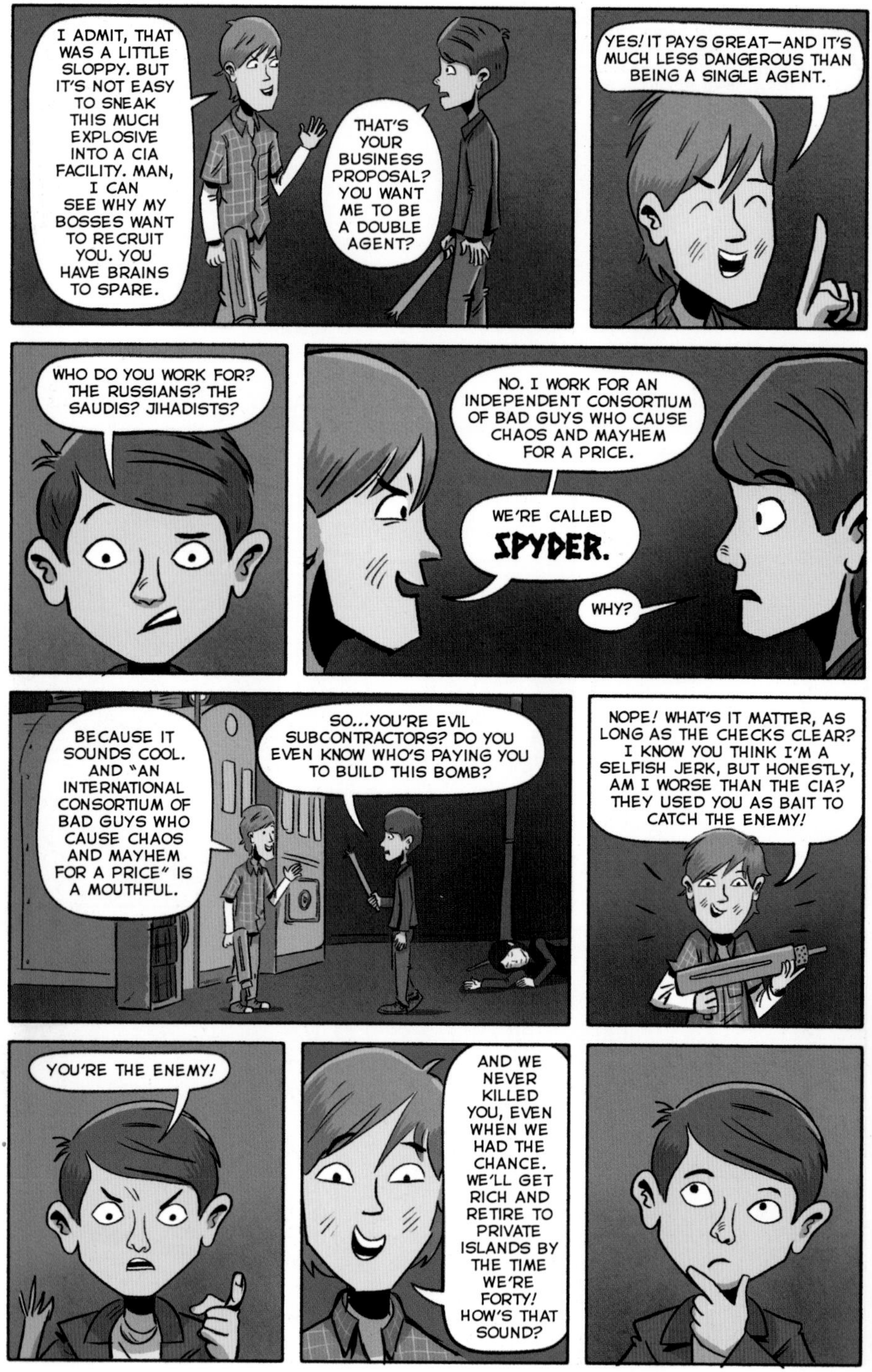
I ADMIT, THAT WAS A LITTLE SLOPPY. BUT IT'S NOT EASY TO SNEAK THIS MUCH EXPLOSIVE INTO A CIA FACILITY. MAN, I CAN SEE WHY MY BOSSES WANT TO RECRUIT YOU. YOU HAVE BRAINS TO SPARE.
THAT'S YOUR BUSINESS PROPOSAL? YOU WANT ME TO BE A DOUBLE AGENT?
YES! IT PAYS GREAT—AND IT'S MUCH LESS DANGEROUS THAN BEING A SINGLE AGENT.
WHO DO YOU WORK FOR? THE RUSSIANS? THE SAUDIS? JIHADISTS?
NO. I WORK FOR AN INDEPENDENT CONSORTIUM OF BAD GUYS WHO CAUSE CHAOS AND MAYHEM FOR A PRICE.
WE'RE CALLED
SPYDER.
WHY?
BECAUSE IT SOUNDS COOL. AND "AN INTERNATIONAL CONSORTIUM OF BAD GUYS WHO CAUSE CHAOS AND MAYHEM FOR A PRICE" IS A MOUTHFUL.
SO...YOU'RE EVIL SUBCONTRACTORS? DO YOU EVEN KNOW WHO'S PAYING YOU TO BUILD THIS BOMB?
NOPE! WHAT'S IT MATTER, AS LONG AS THE CHECKS CLEAR? I KNOW YOU THINK I'M A SELFISH JERK, BUT HONESTLY, AM I WORSE THAN THE CIA? THEY USED YOU AS BAIT TO CATCH THE ENEMY!
YOU'RE THE ENEMY!
AND WE NEVER KILLED YOU, EVEN WHEN WE HAD THE CHANCE. WE'LL GET RICH AND RETIRE TO PRIVATE ISLANDS BY THE TIME WE'RE FORTY! HOW'S THAT SOUND?

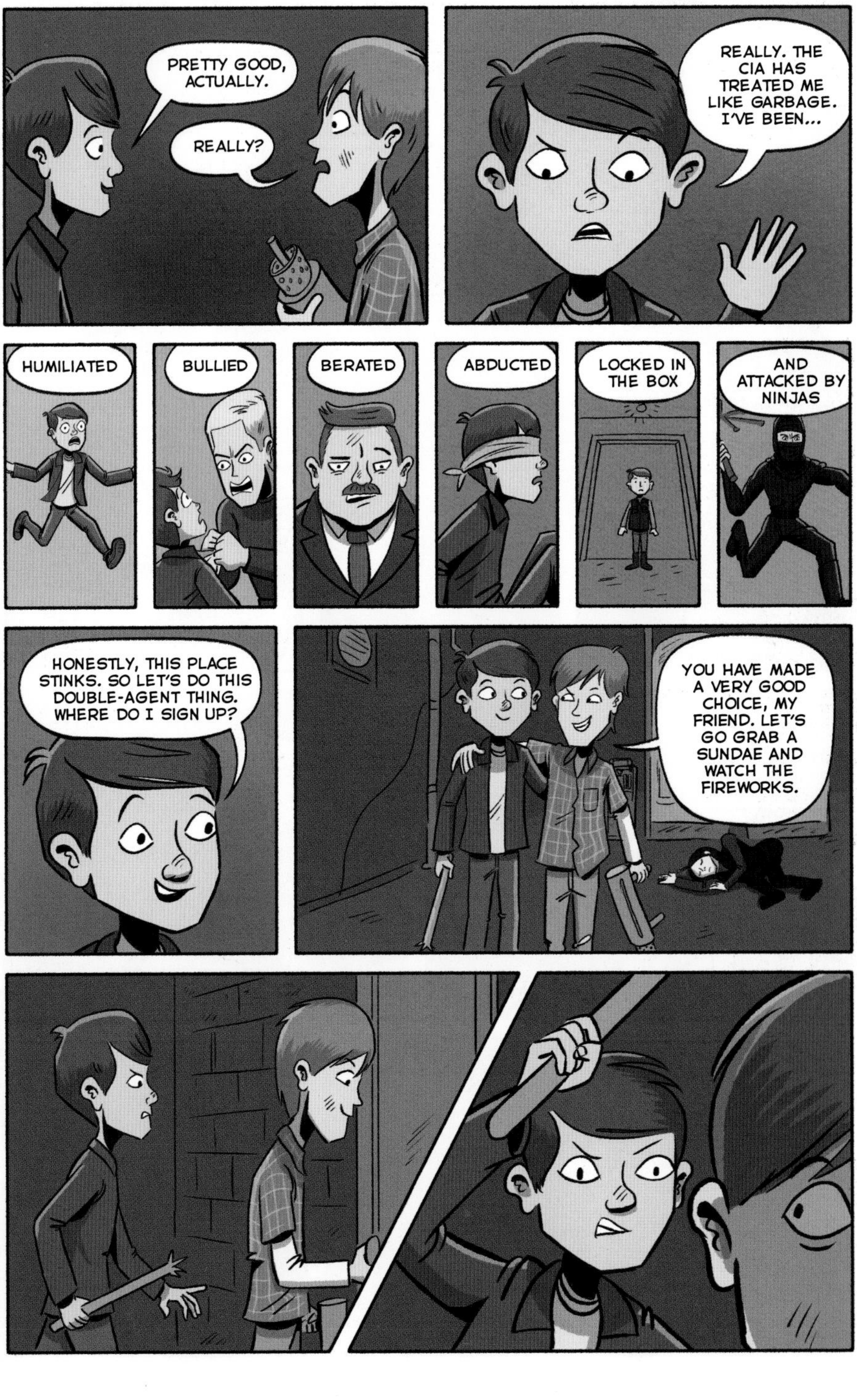
PRETTY GOOD, ACTUALLY.
REALLY?
REALLY. THE CIA HAS TREATED ME LIKE GARBAGE. I'VE BEEN...
HUMILIATED
BULLIED
BERATED
ABDUCTED
LOCKED IN THE BOX
AND ATTACKED BY NINJAS
HONESTLY, THIS PLACE STINKS. SO LET'S DO THIS DOUBLE-AGENT THING. WHERE DO I SIGN UP?
YOU HAVE MADE A VERY GOOD CHOICE, MY FRIEND. LET'S GO GRAB A SUNDAE AND WATCH THE FIREWORKS.

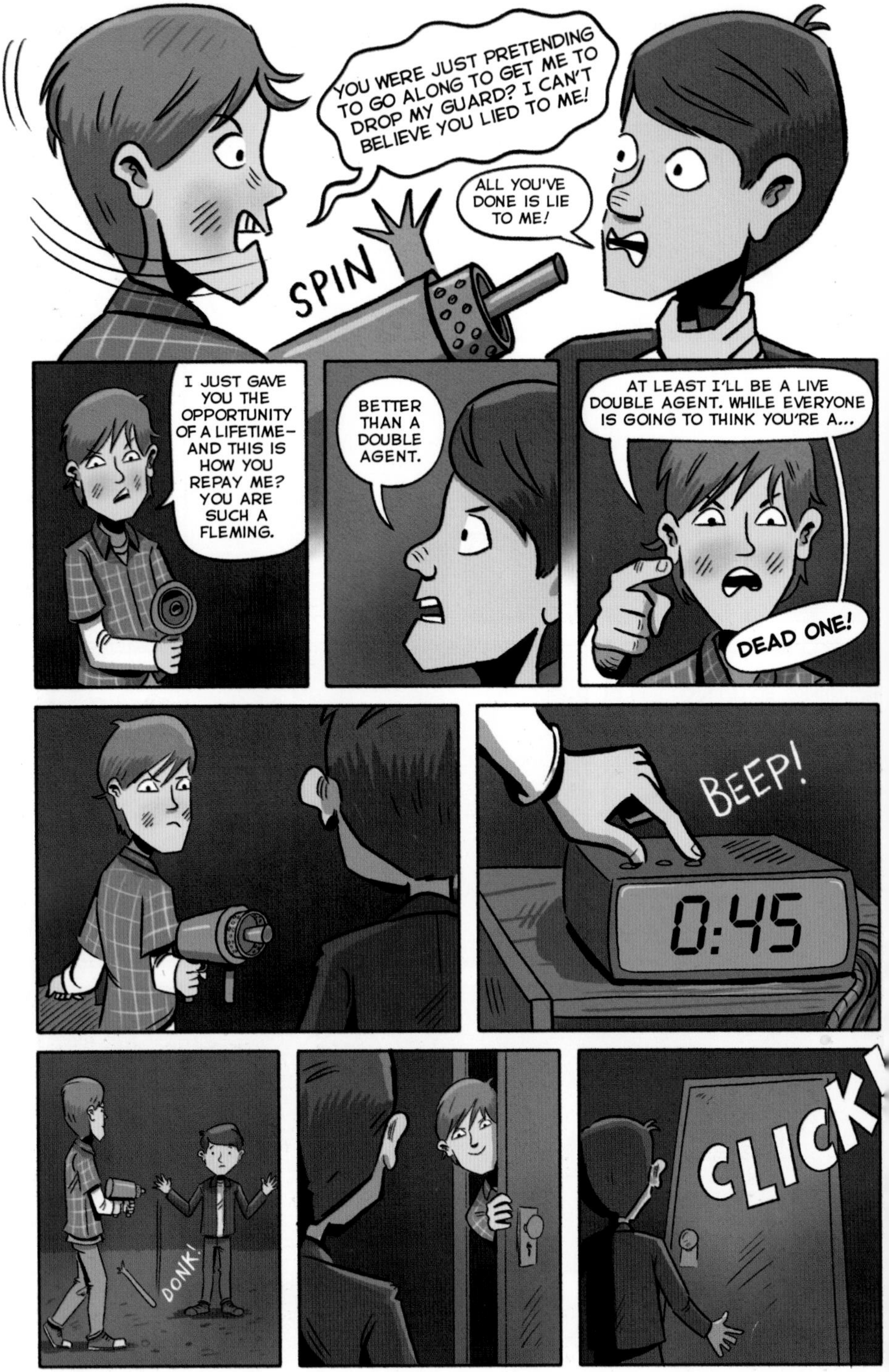
YOU WERE JUST PRETENDING TO GO ALONG TO GET ME TO DROP MY GUARD? I CAN'T BELIEVE YOU LIED TO ME!
ALL YOU'VE DONE IS LIE TO ME!
SPIN
I JUST GAVE YOU THE OPPORTUNITY OF A LIFETIME—AND THIS IS HOW YOU REPAY ME? YOU ARE SUCH A FLEMING.
BETTER THAN A DOUBLE AGENT.
AT LEAST I'LL BE A LIVE DOUBLE AGENT. WHILE EVERYONE IS GOING TO THINK YOU'RE A...
DEAD ONE!
BEEP!
0:45
DONK!
CLICK!

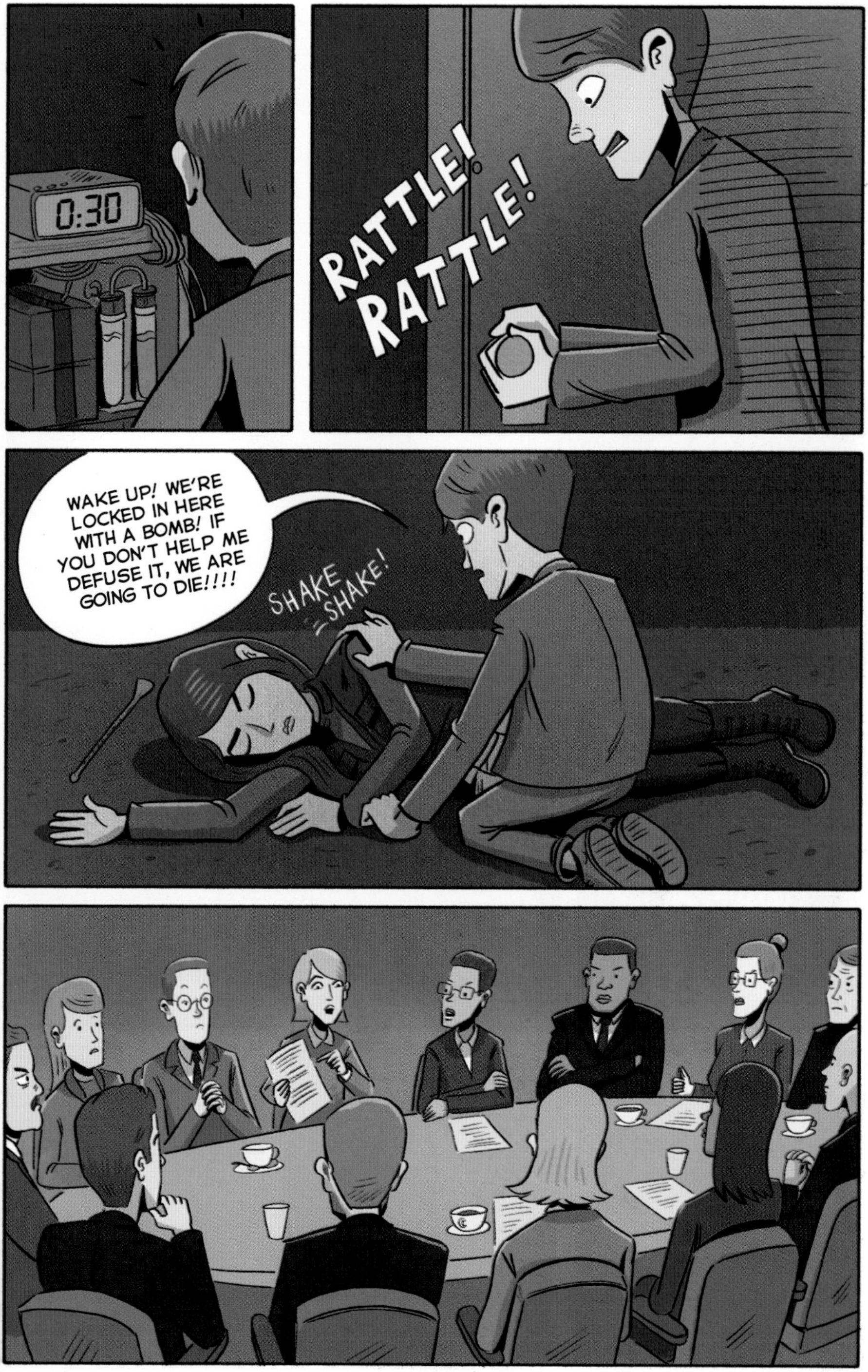
0:30
RATTLE! RATTLE!
WAKE UP! WE'RE LOCKED IN HERE WITH A BOMB! IF YOU DON'T HELP ME DEFUSE IT, WE ARE GOING TO DIE!!!!
SHAKE SHAKE!

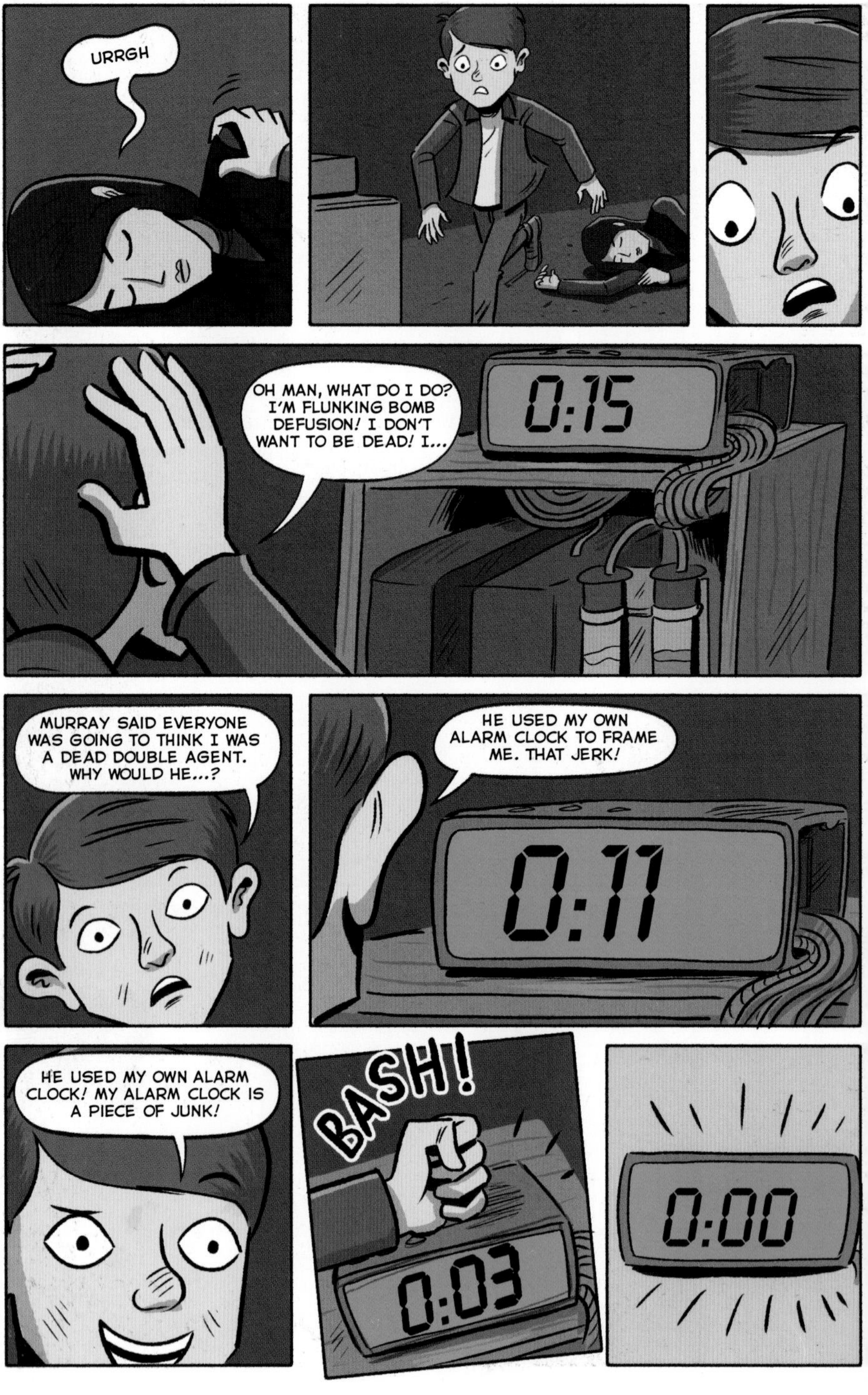
URRGH
OH MAN, WHAT DO I DO? I'M FLUNKING BOMB DEFUSION! I DON'T WANT TO BE DEAD! I...
0:15
MURRAY SAID EVERYONE WAS GOING TO THINK I WAS A DEAD DOUBLE AGENT. WHY WOULD HE...?
HE USED MY OWN ALARM CLOCK TO FRAME ME. THAT JERK!
0:11
HE USED MY OWN ALARM CLOCK! MY ALARM CLOCK IS A PIECE OF JUNK!
BASH!
0:03
0:00

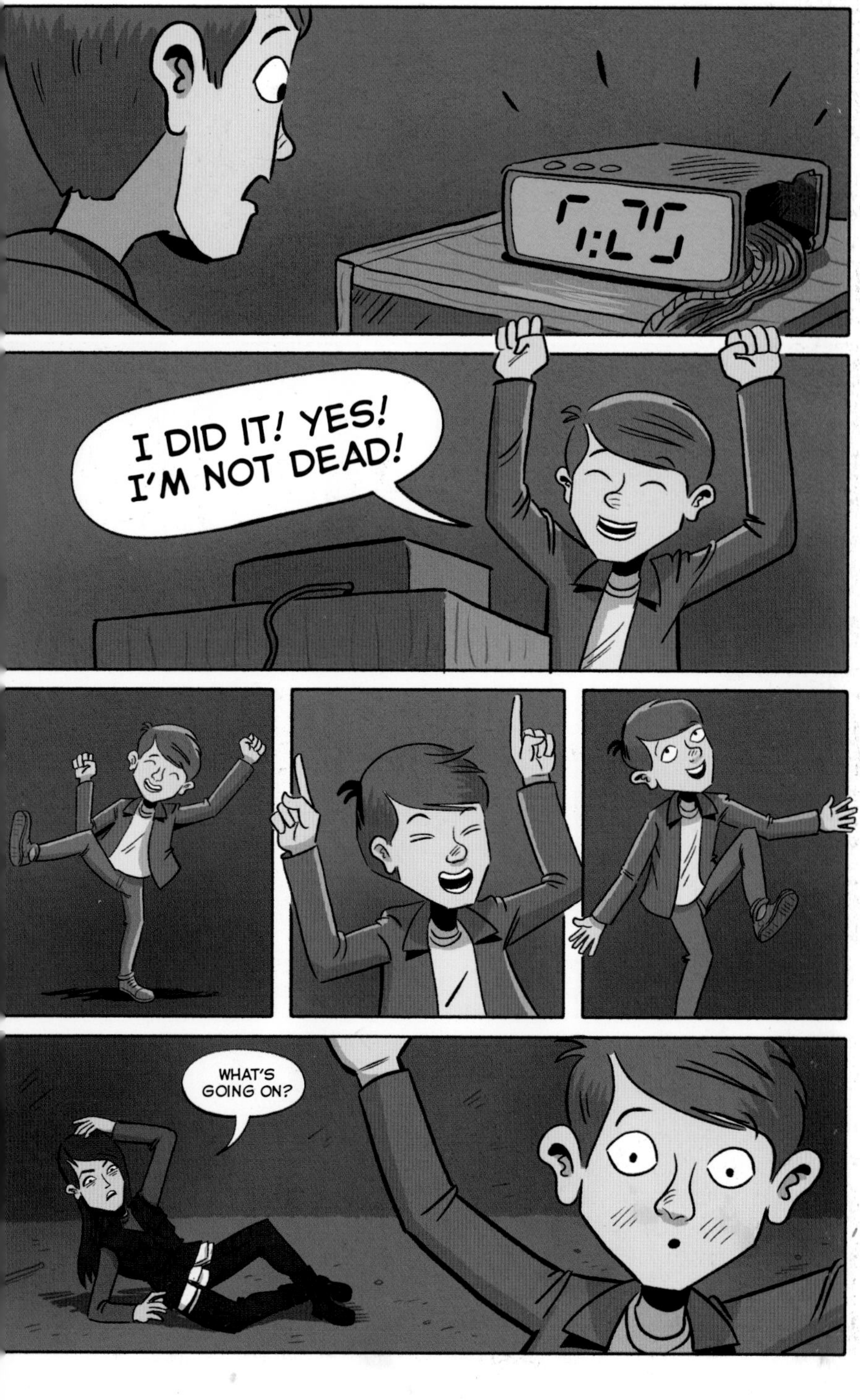
I DID IT! YES! I'M NOT DEAD!
WHAT'S GOING ON?

NOW YOU'RE CONSCIOUS? YOU COULDN'T HAVE COME TO FIVE MINUTES AGO?

YOU STOPPED THE BOMB? NICE WORK.

DID HE TRY TO KILL YOU?

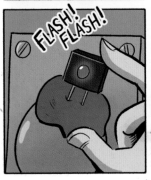

FLASH! FLASH!

NO. HE OFFERED ME A JOB WITH SPYDER.

SPYDER?

THAT'S INTERESTING. WATCH OUT.

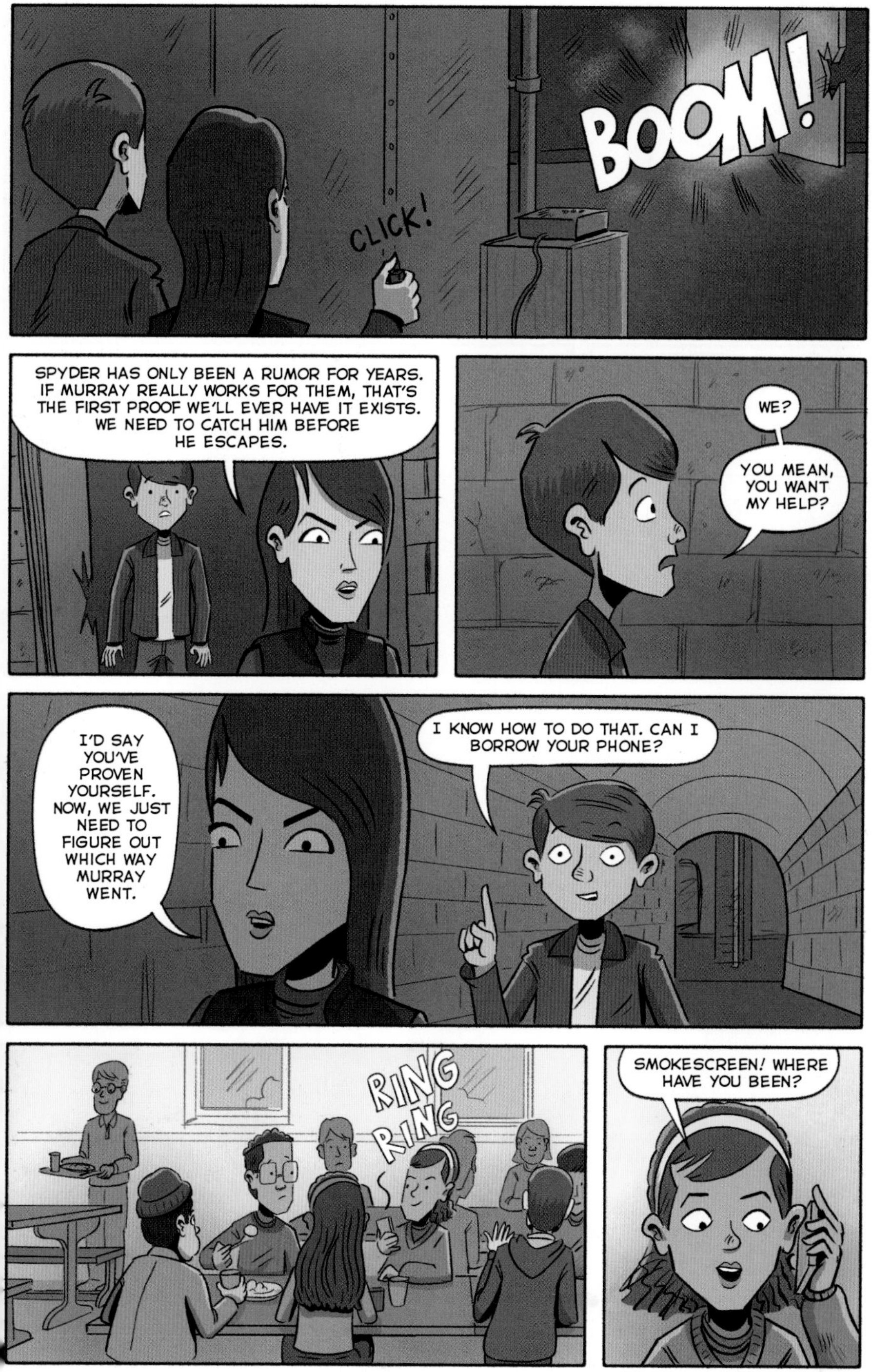
CLICK!
BOOM!
SPYDER HAS ONLY BEEN A RUMOR FOR YEARS. IF MURRAY REALLY WORKS FOR THEM, THAT'S THE FIRST PROOF WE'LL EVER HAVE IT EXISTS. WE NEED TO CATCH HIM BEFORE HE ESCAPES.
WE?
YOU MEAN, YOU WANT MY HELP?
I'D SAY YOU'VE PROVEN YOURSELF. NOW, WE JUST NEED TO FIGURE OUT WHICH WAY MURRAY WENT.
I KNOW HOW TO DO THAT. CAN I BORROW YOUR PHONE?
RING RING
SMOKESCREEN! WHERE HAVE YOU BEEN?

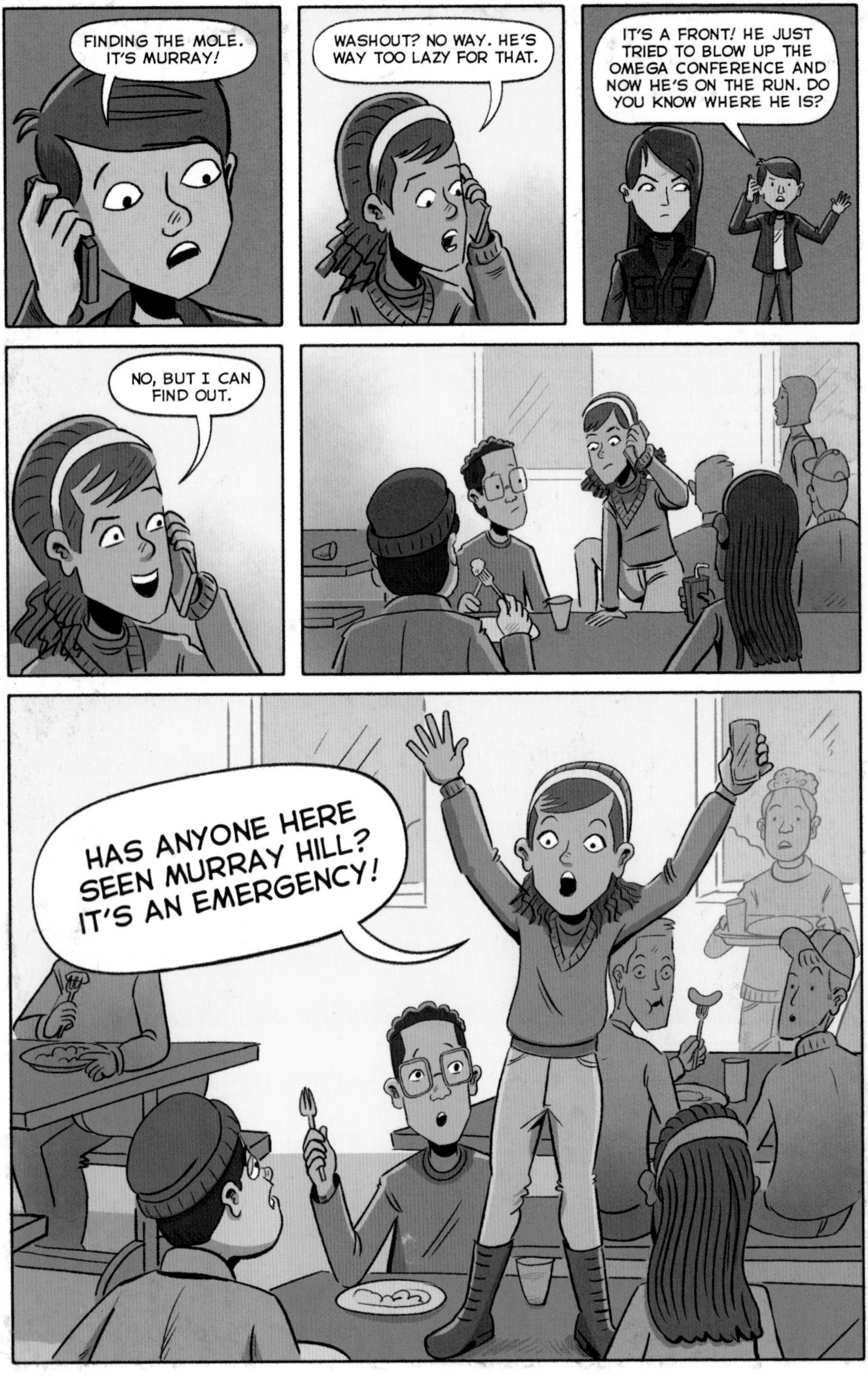
FINDING THE MOLE. IT'S MURRAY!
WASHOUT? NO WAY. HE'S WAY TOO LAZY FOR THAT.
IT'S A FRONT! HE JUST TRIED TO BLOW UP THE OMEGA CONFERENCE AND NOW HE'S ON THE RUN. DO YOU KNOW WHERE HE IS?
NO, BUT I CAN FIND OUT.
HAS ANYONE HERE SEEN MURRAY HILL? IT'S AN EMERGENCY!

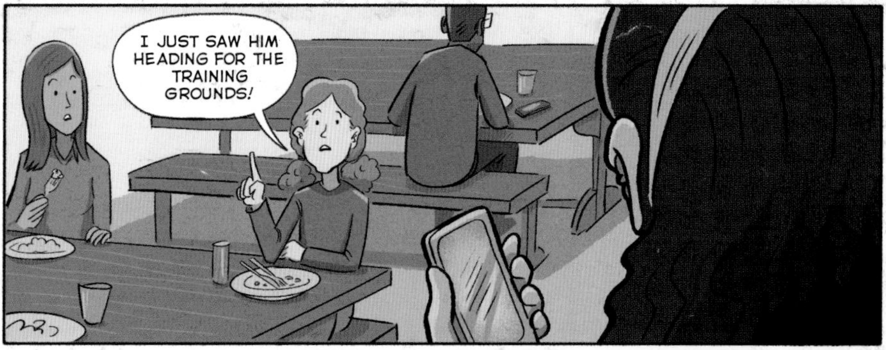
I JUST SAW HIM HEADING FOR THE TRAINING GROUNDS!

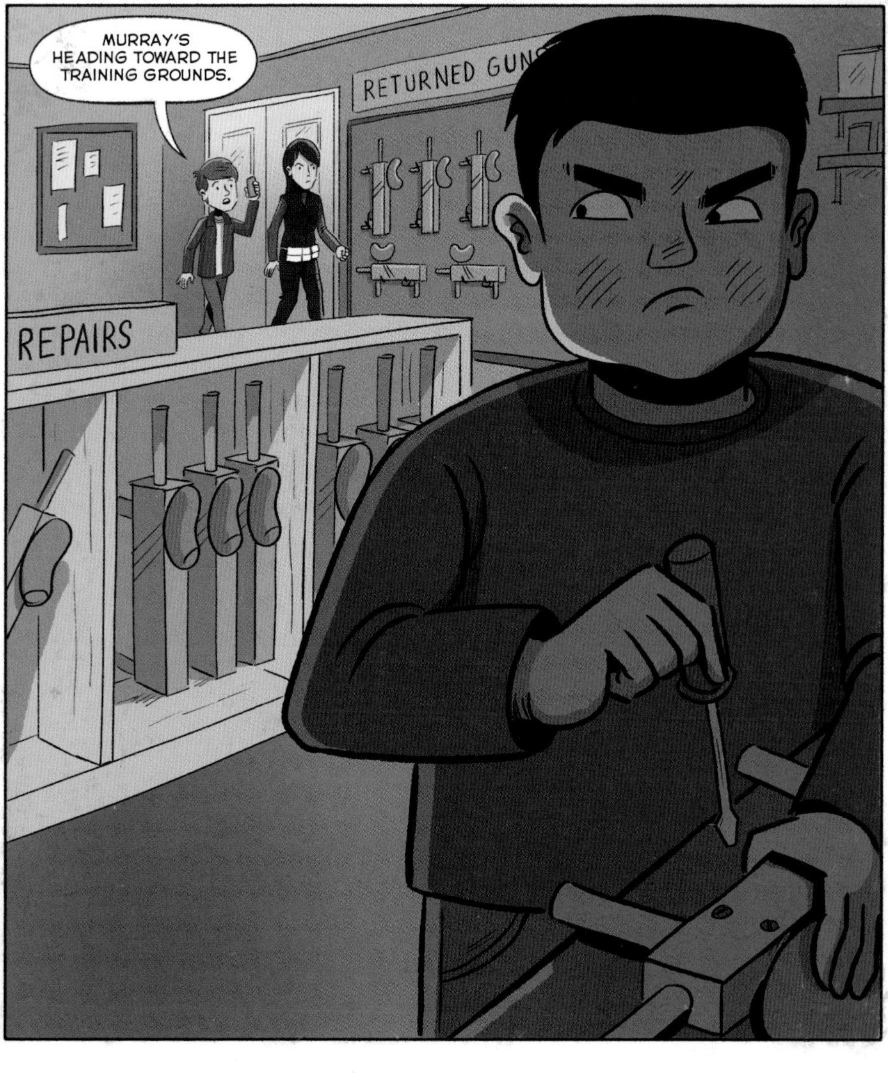
MURRAY'S HEADING TOWARD THE TRAINING GROUNDS.
RETURNED GUN
REPAIRS

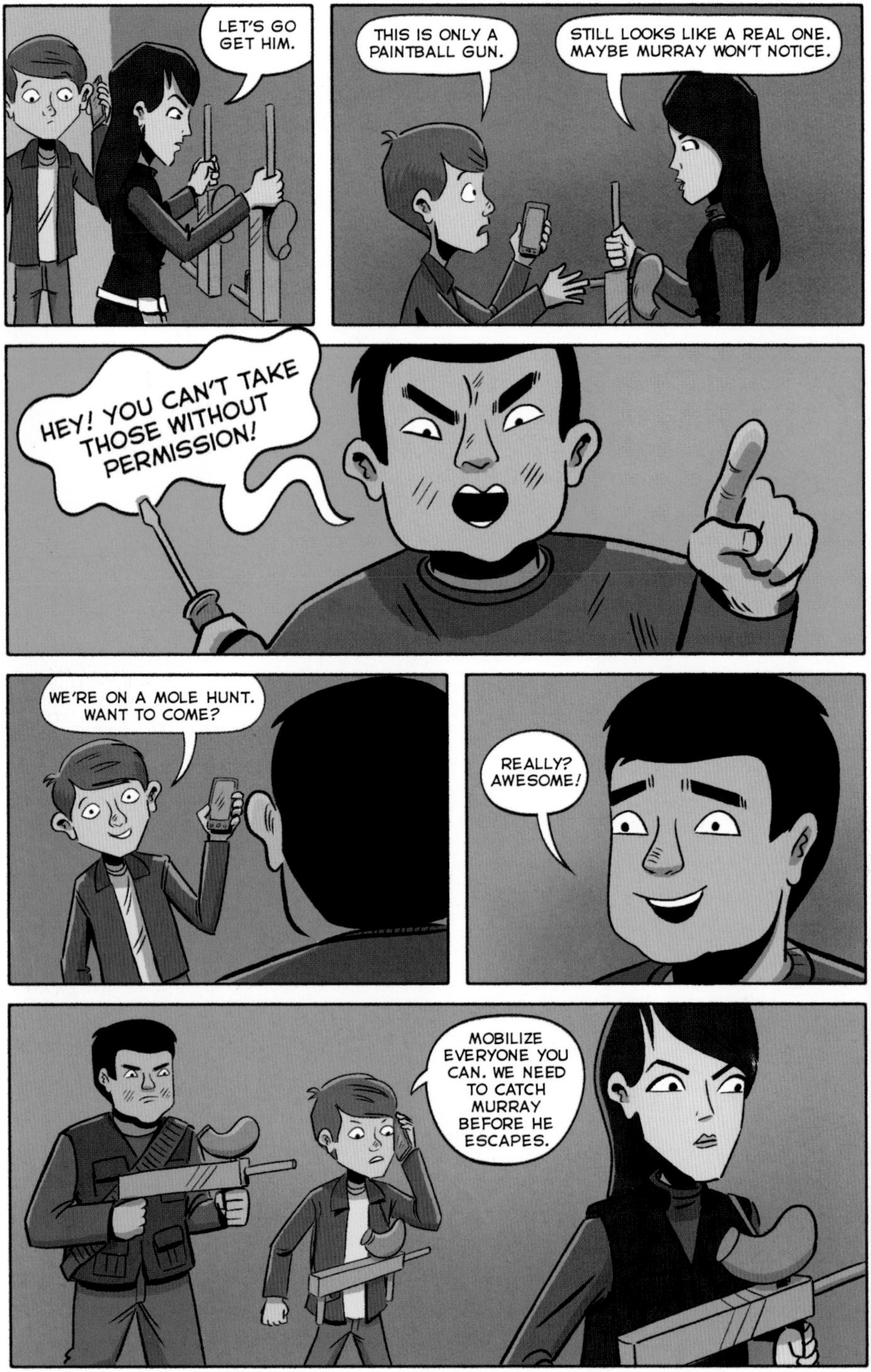
LET'S GO GET HIM.
THIS IS ONLY A PAINTBALL GUN.
STILL LOOKS LIKE A REAL ONE. MAYBE MURRAY WON'T NOTICE.
HEY! YOU CAN'T TAKE THOSE WITHOUT PERMISSION!
WE'RE ON A MOLE HUNT. WANT TO COME?
REALLY? AWESOME!
MOBILIZE EVERYONE YOU CAN. WE NEED TO CATCH MURRAY BEFORE HE ESCAPES.

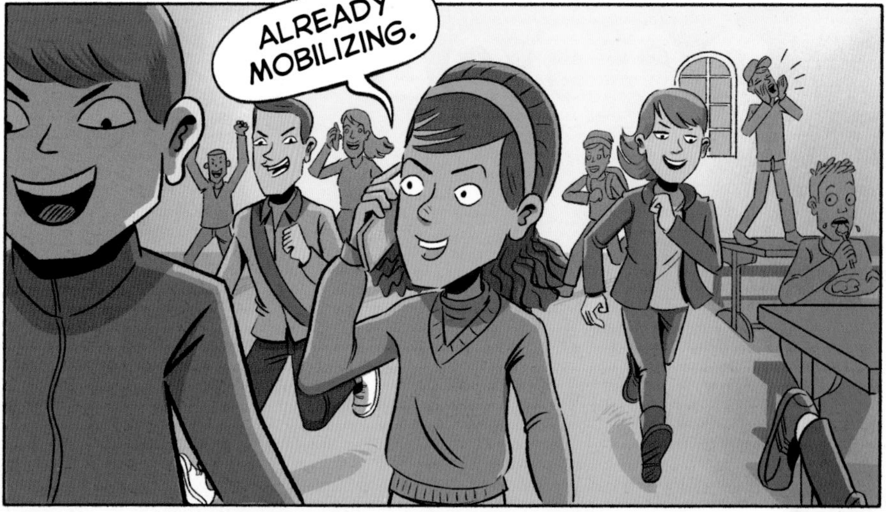
ALREADY MOBILIZING.

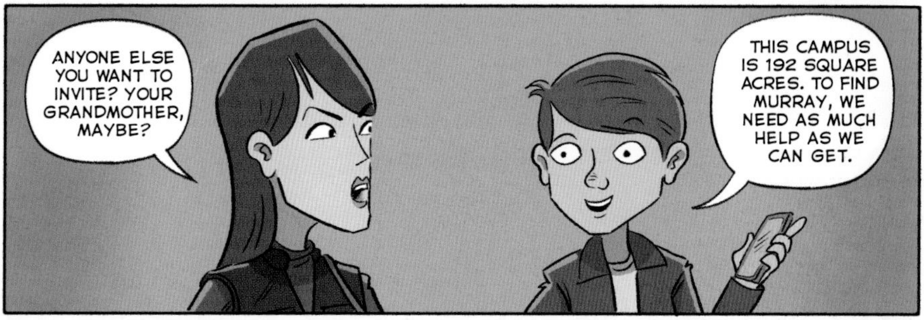
ANYONE ELSE YOU WANT TO INVITE? YOUR GRANDMOTHER, MAYBE?
THIS CAMPUS IS 192 SQUARE ACRES. TO FIND MURRAY, WE NEED AS MUCH HELP AS WE CAN GET.

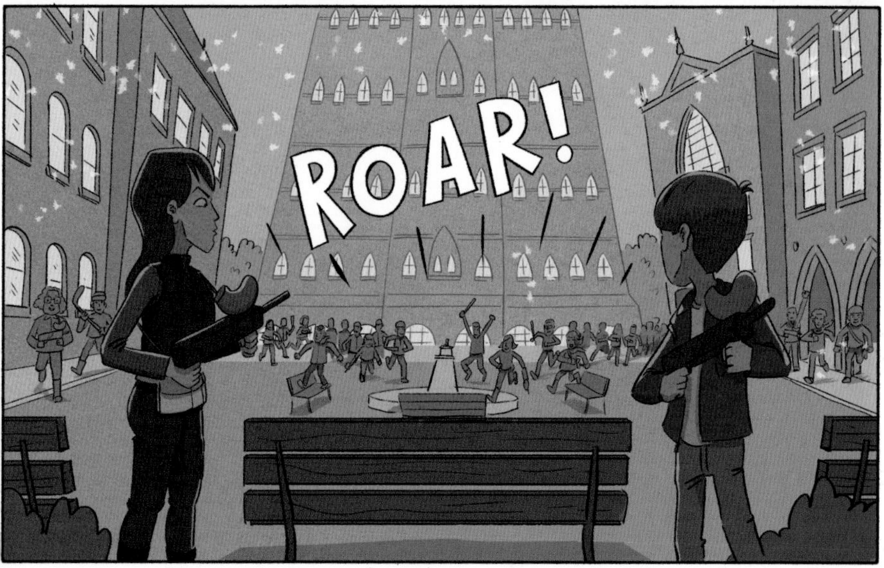
ROAR!

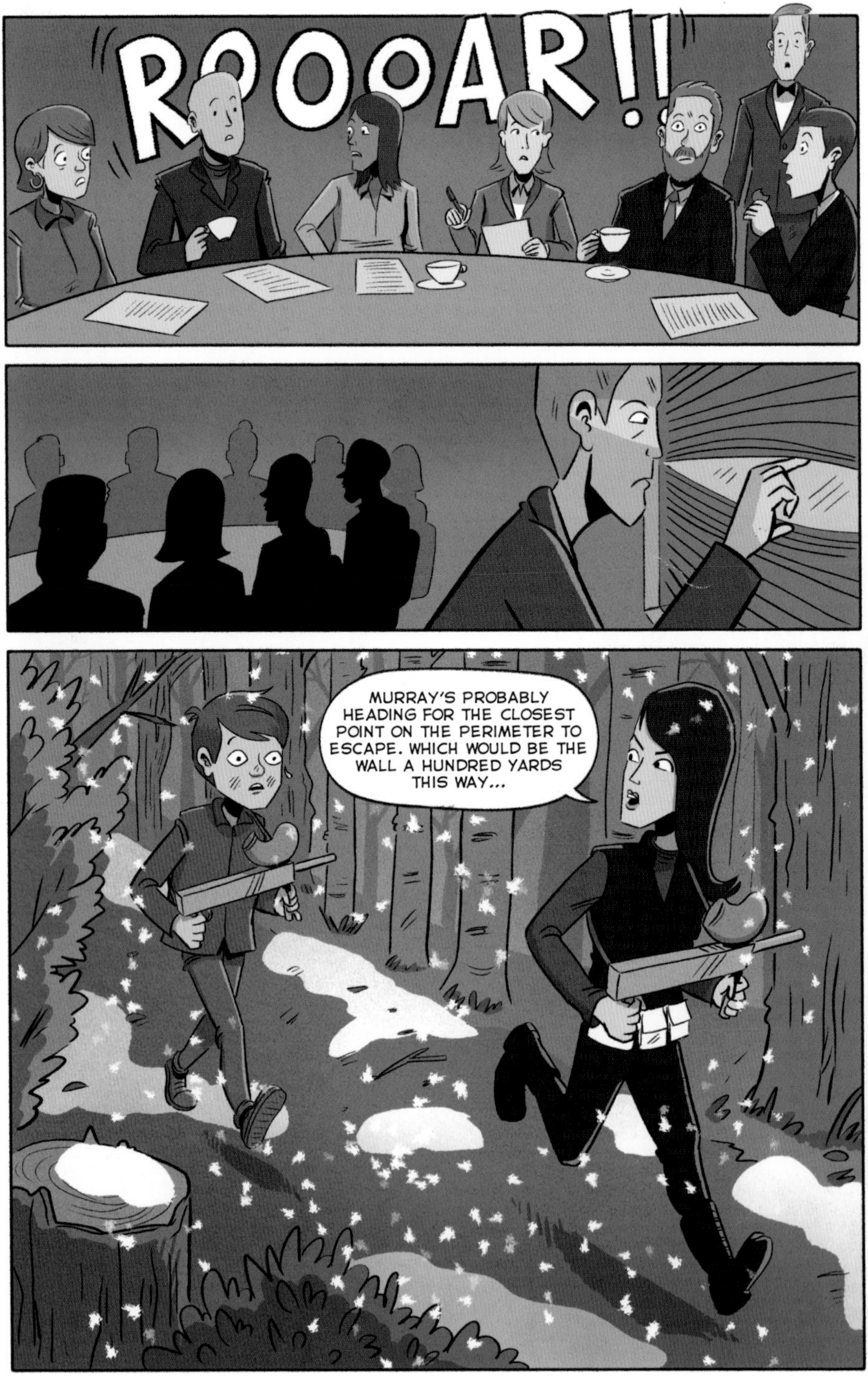
ROOOAR!!
MURRAY'S PROBABLY HEADING FOR THE CLOSEST POINT ON THE PERIMETER TO ESCAPE. WHICH WOULD BE THE WALL A HUNDRED YARDS THIS WAY...

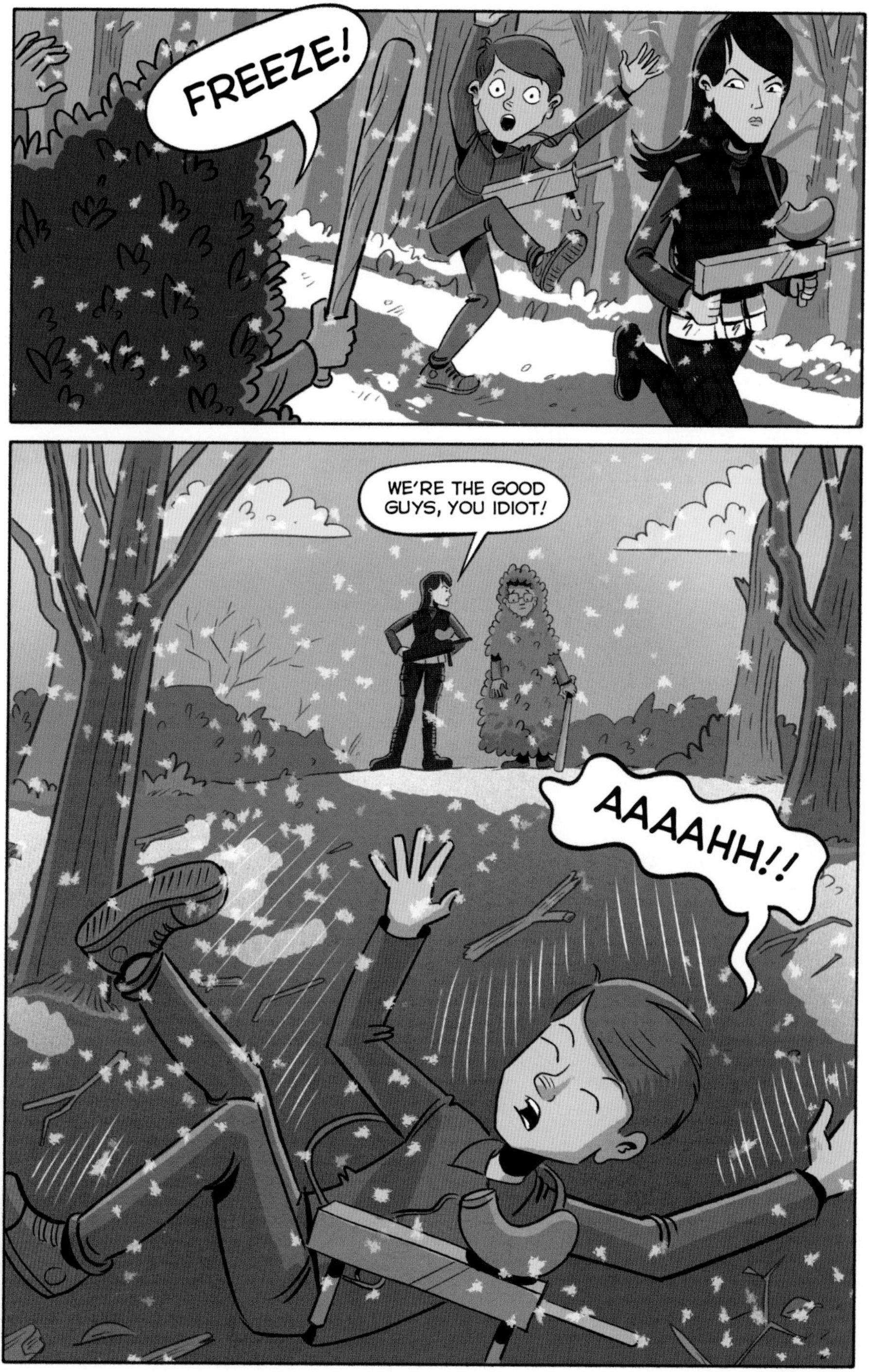
FREEZE!
WE'RE THE GOOD GUYS, YOU IDIOT!
AAAAHH!!

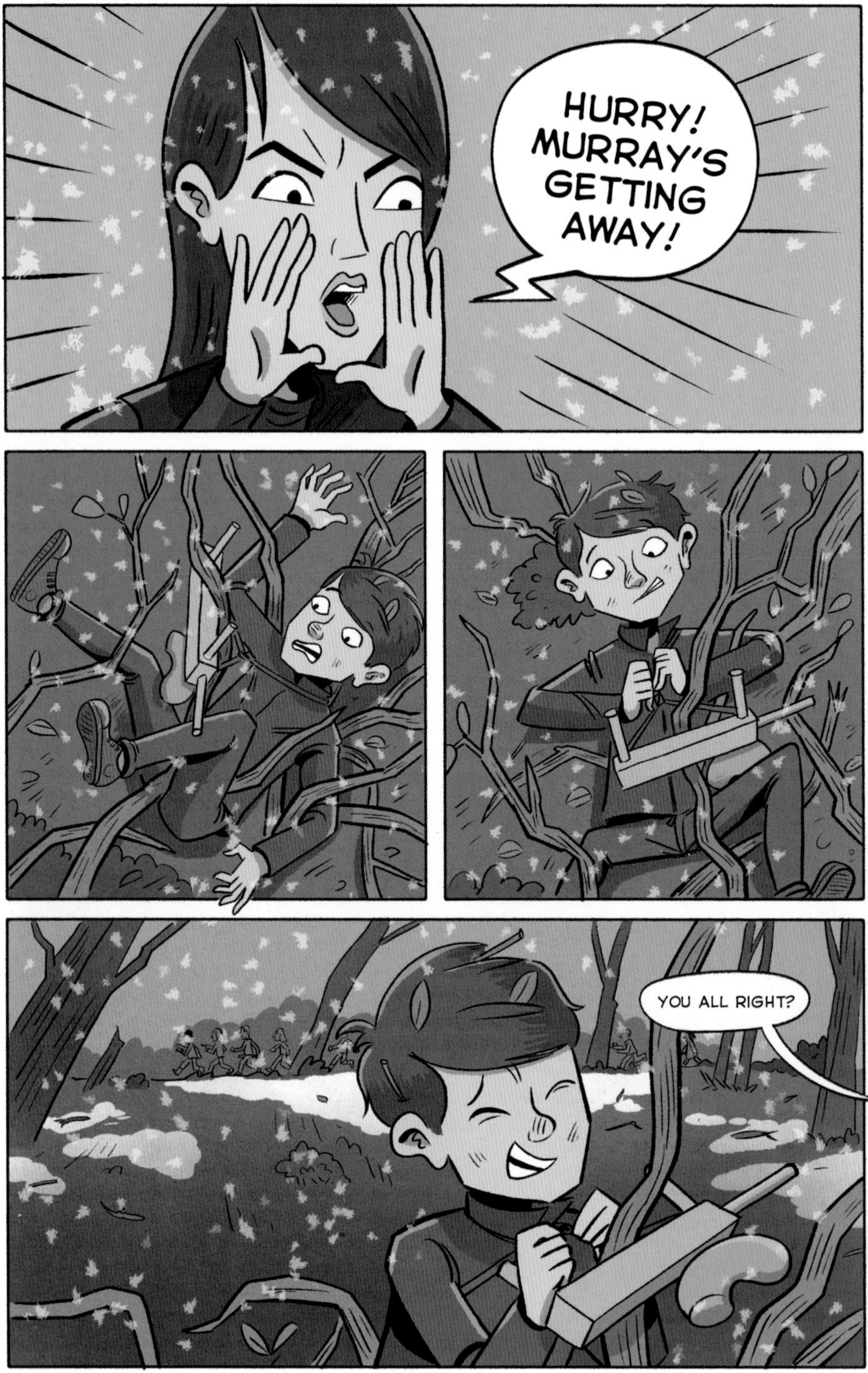
HURRY! MURRAY'S GETTING AWAY!
YOU ALL RIGHT?

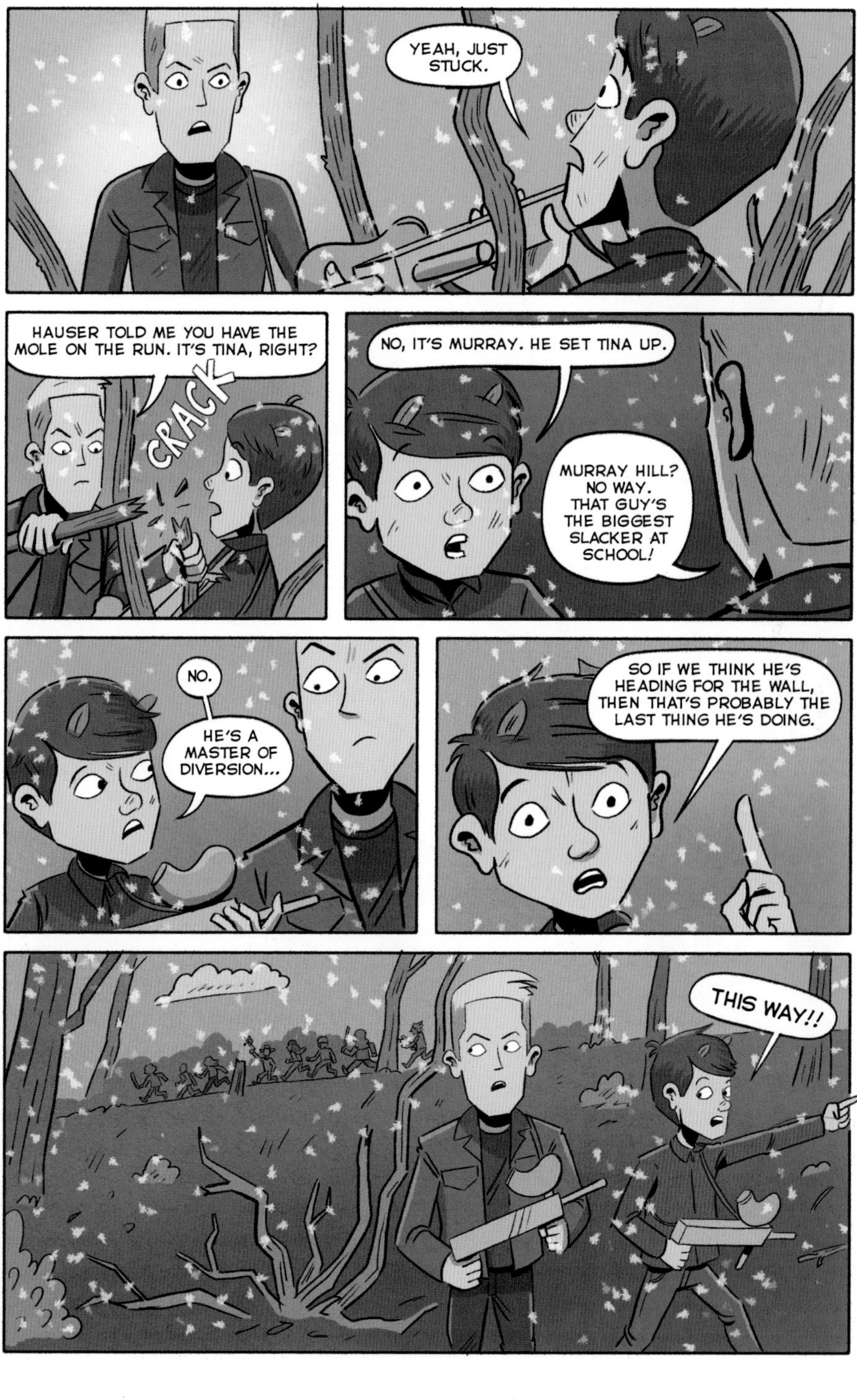
YEAH, JUST STUCK.
HAUSER TOLD ME YOU HAVE THE MOLE ON THE RUN. IT'S TINA, RIGHT?
CRACK
NO, IT'S MURRAY. HE SET TINA UP.
MURRAY HILL? NO WAY. THAT GUY'S THE BIGGEST SLACKER AT SCHOOL!
NO.
HE'S A MASTER OF DIVERSION...
SO IF WE THINK HE'S HEADING FOR THE WALL, THEN THAT'S PROBABLY THE LAST THING HE'S DOING.
THIS WAY!!

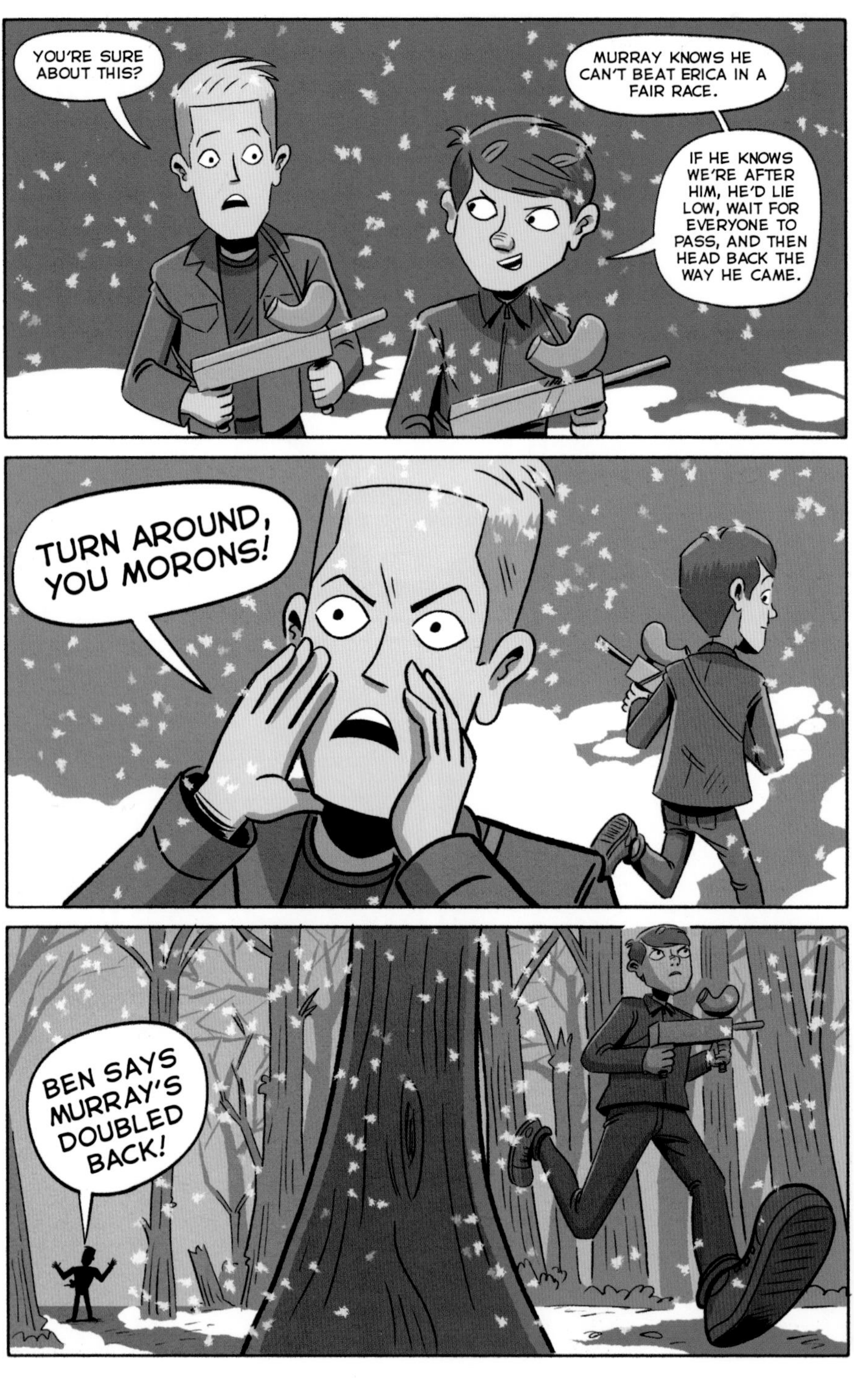
YOU'RE SURE ABOUT THIS?
MURRAY KNOWS HE CAN'T BEAT ERICA IN A FAIR RACE.
IF HE KNOWS WE'RE AFTER HIM, HE'D LIE LOW, WAIT FOR EVERYONE TO PASS, AND THEN HEAD BACK THE WAY HE CAME.
TURN AROUND, YOU MORONS!
BEN SAYS MURRAY'S DOUBLED BACK!

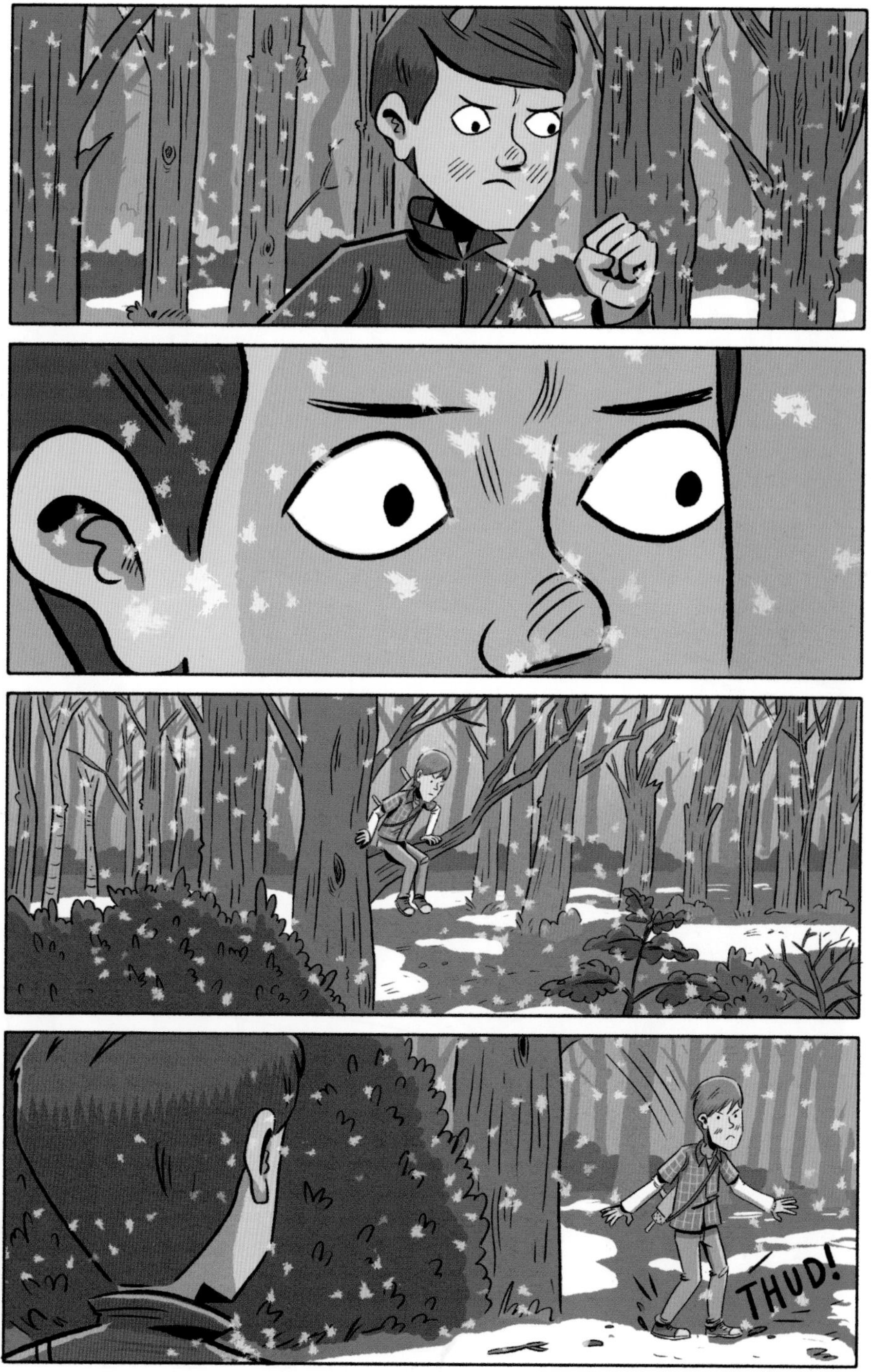
THUD!

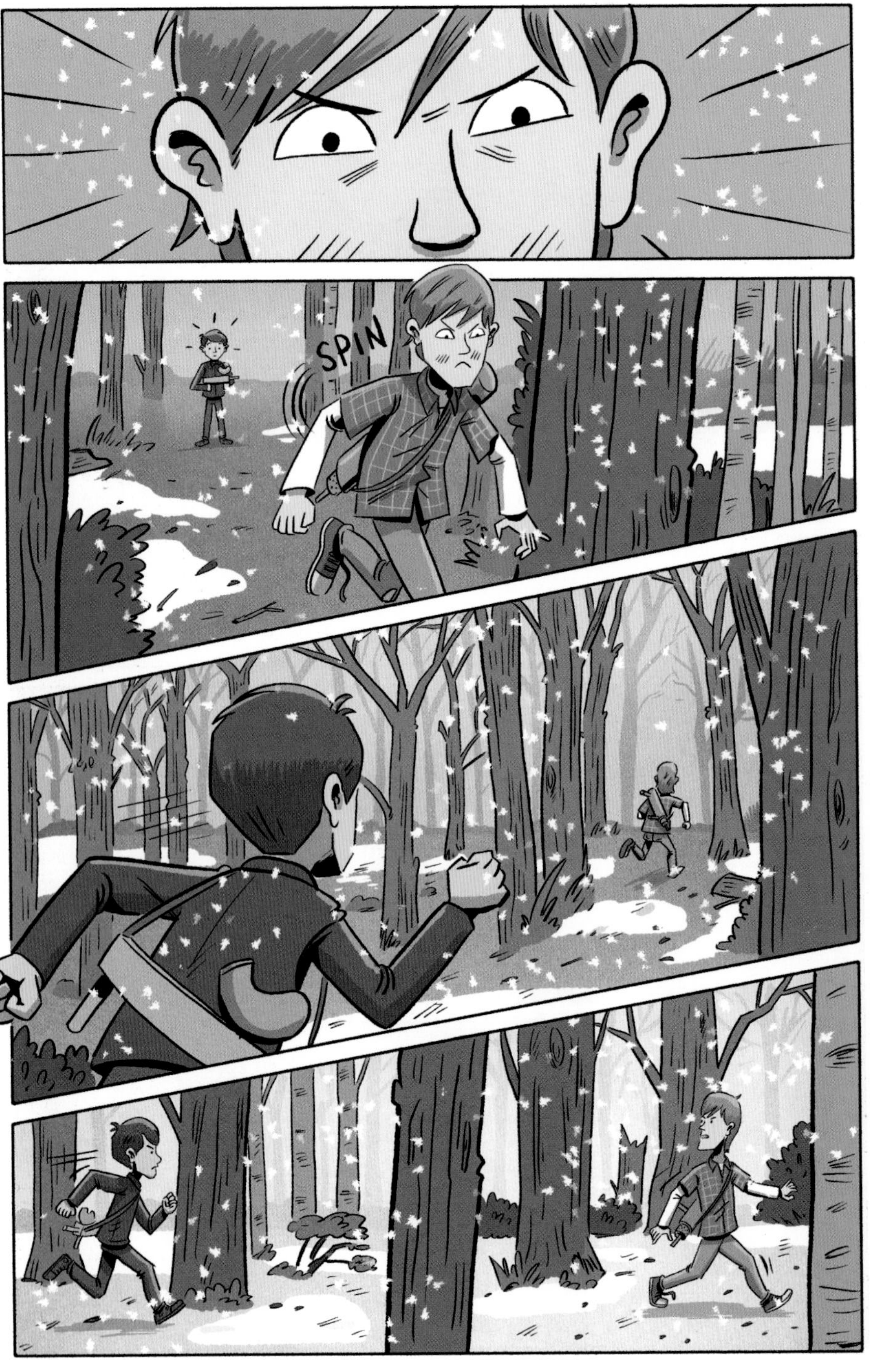
SPIN

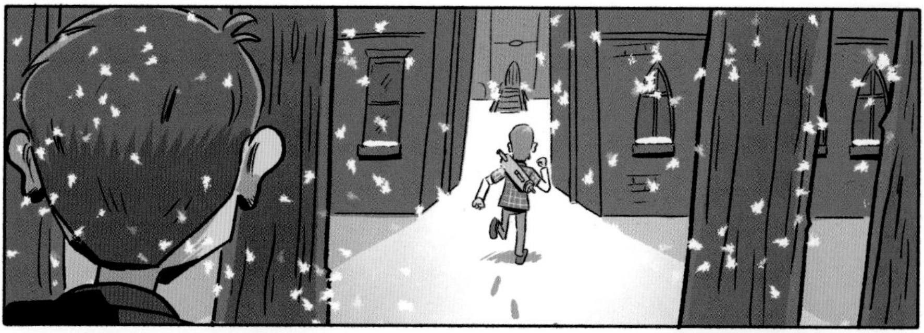

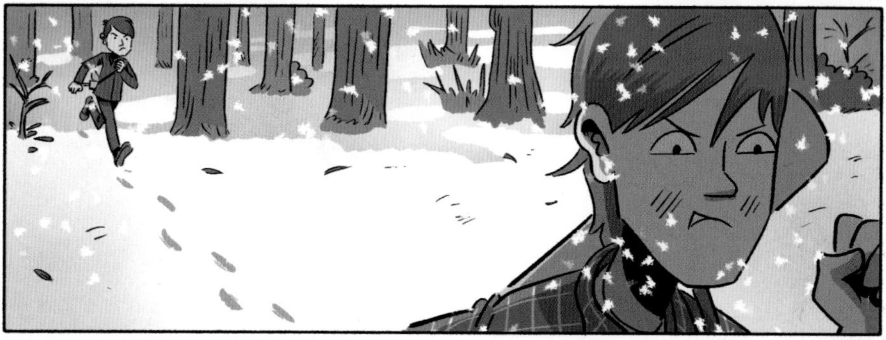

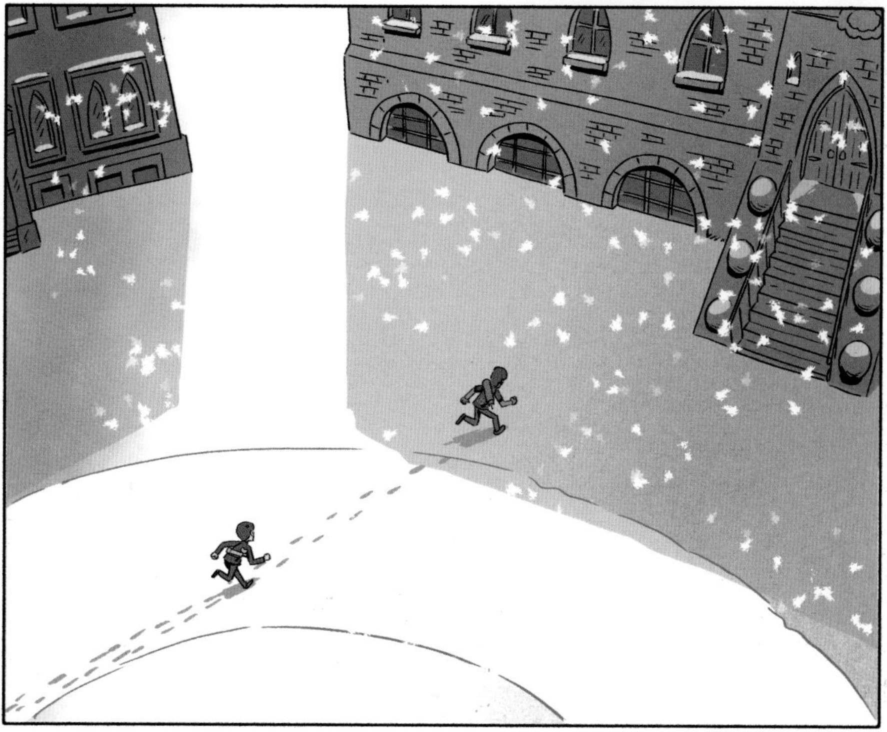

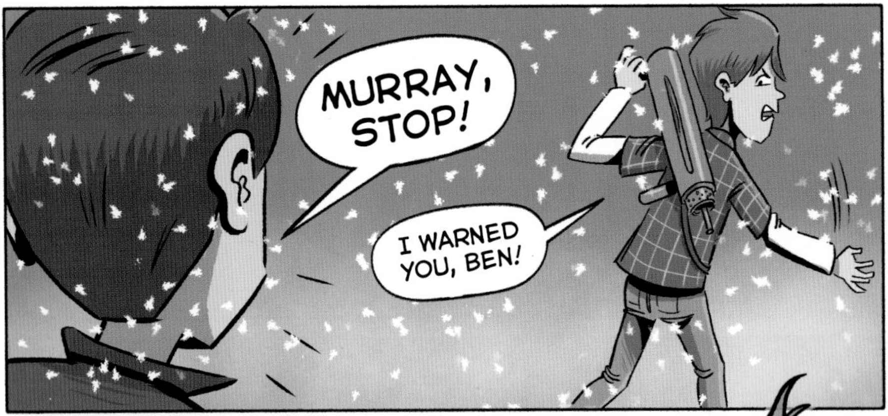
MURRAY, STOP!
I WARNED YOU, BEN!

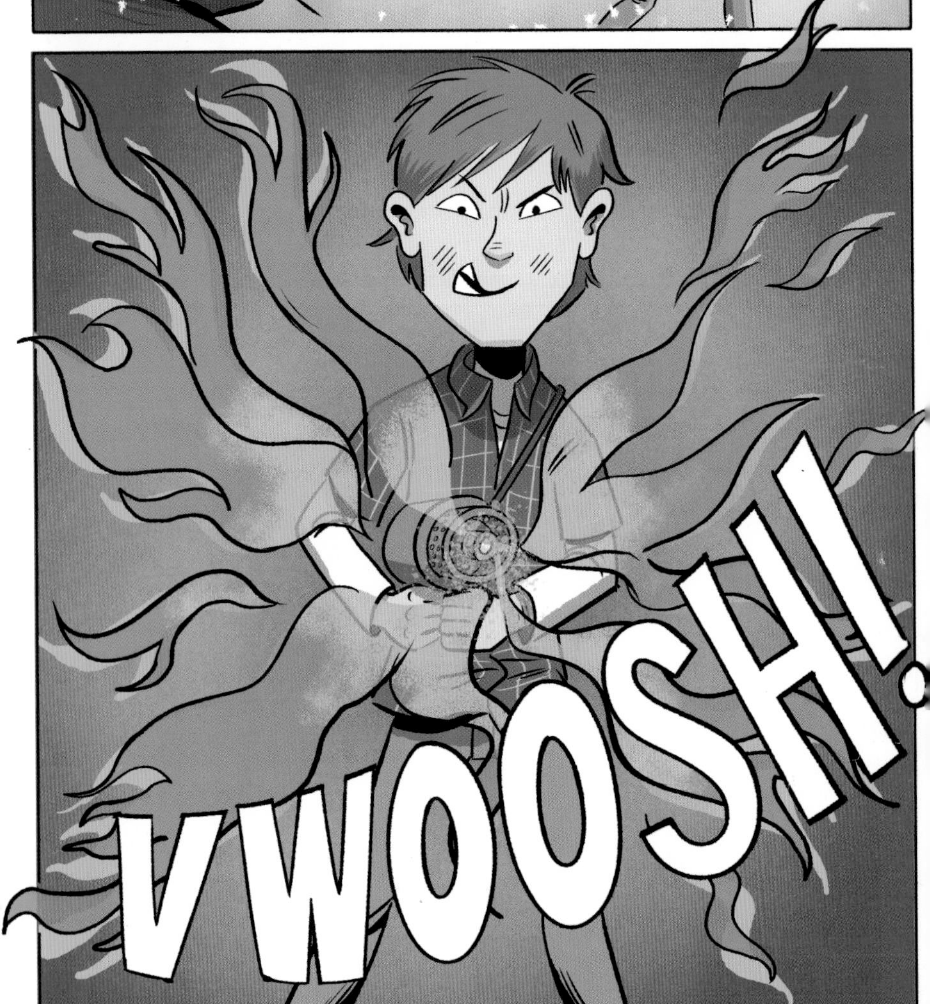
VWOOSH!

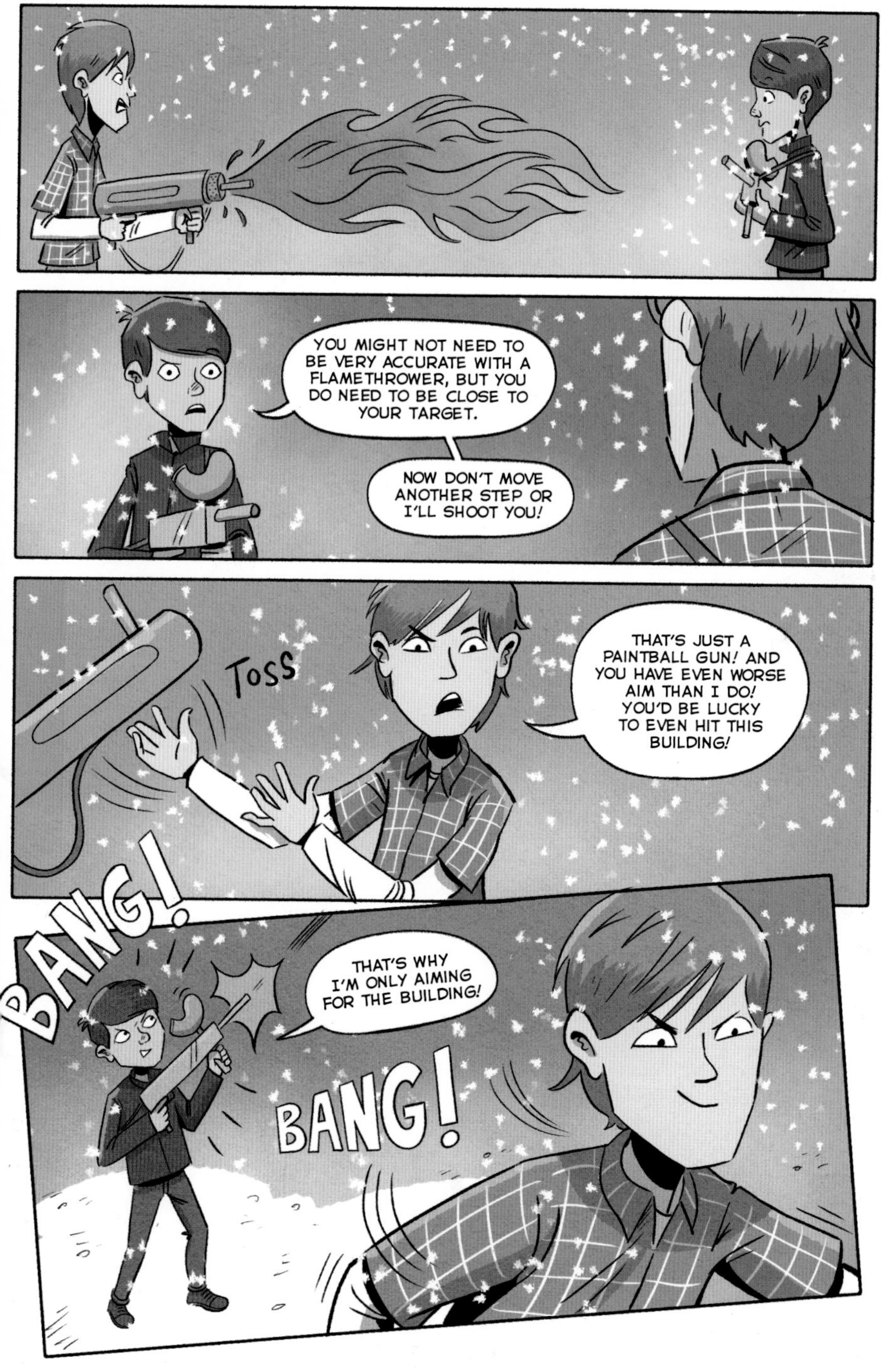
YOU MIGHT NOT NEED TO BE VERY ACCURATE WITH A FLAMETHROWER, BUT YOU DO NEED TO BE CLOSE TO YOUR TARGET.
NOW DON'T MOVE ANOTHER STEP OR I'LL SHOOT YOU!
TOSS
THAT'S JUST A PAINTBALL GUN! AND YOU HAVE EVEN WORSE AIM THAN I DO! YOU'D BE LUCKY TO EVEN HIT THIS BUILDING!
BANG!
THAT'S WHY I'M ONLY AIMING FOR THE BUILDING!
BANG!

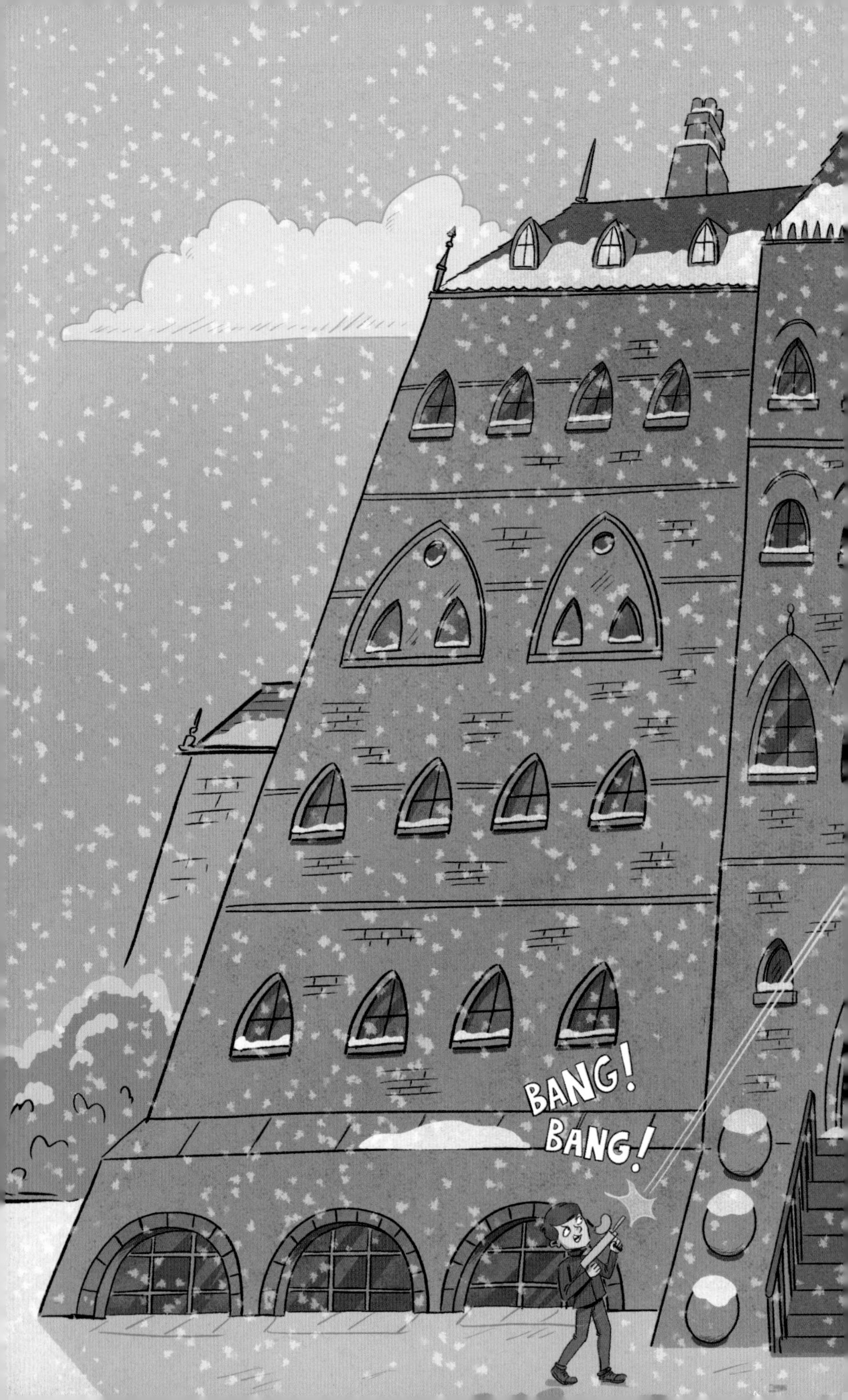
BANG!
BANG!

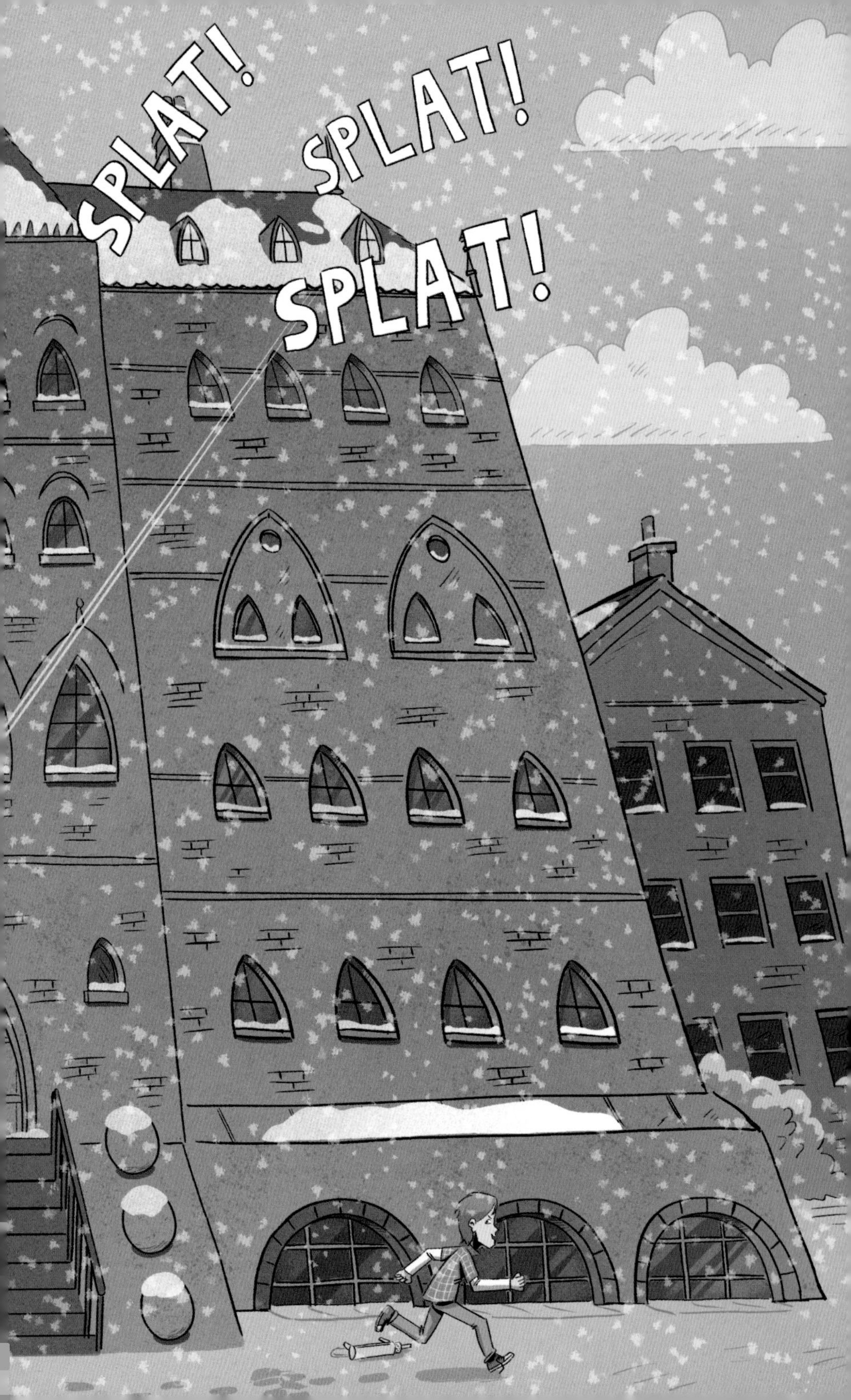
SPLAT!
SPLAT!
SPLAT!

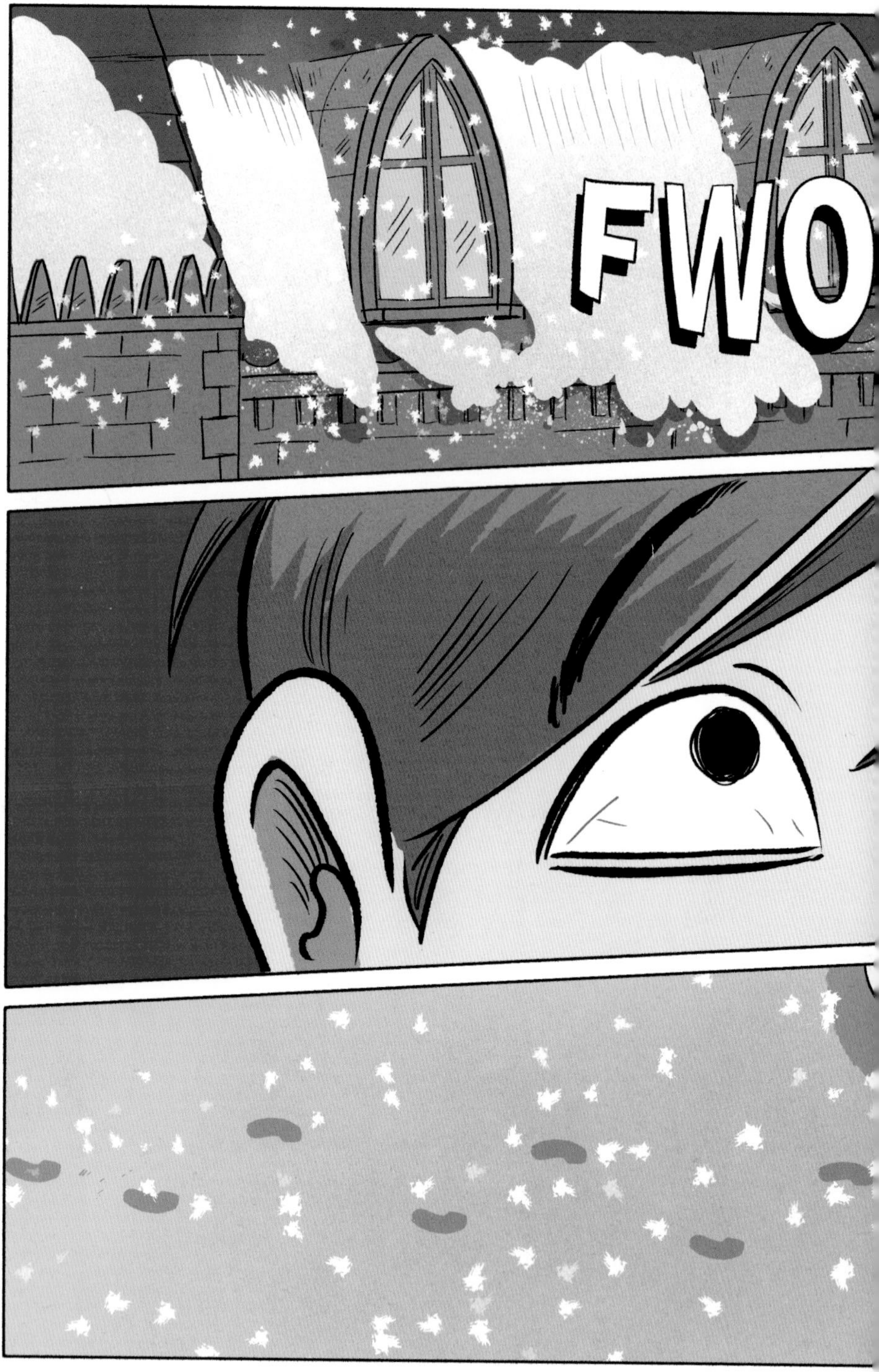
FWO

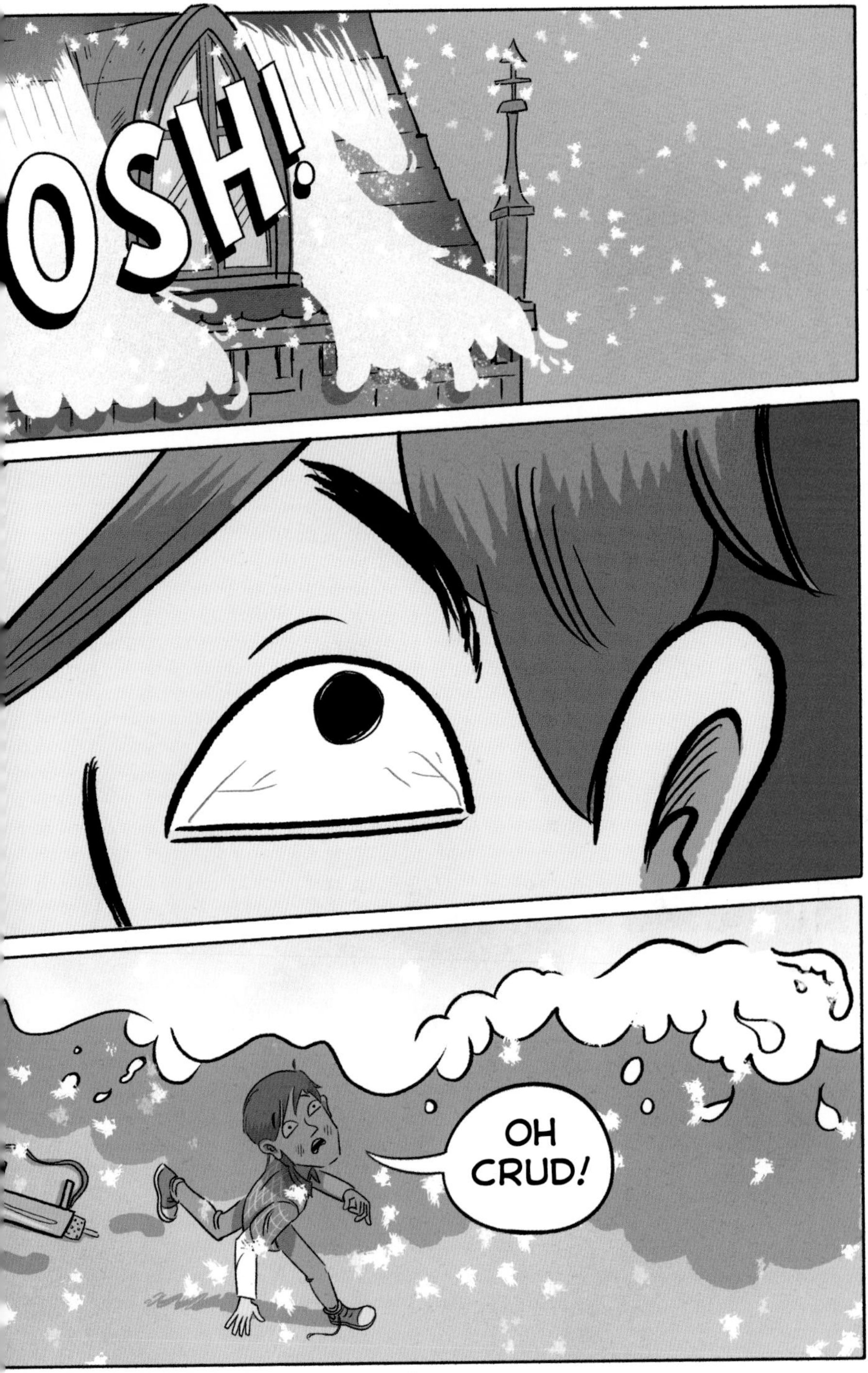
OSH!
OH CRUD!

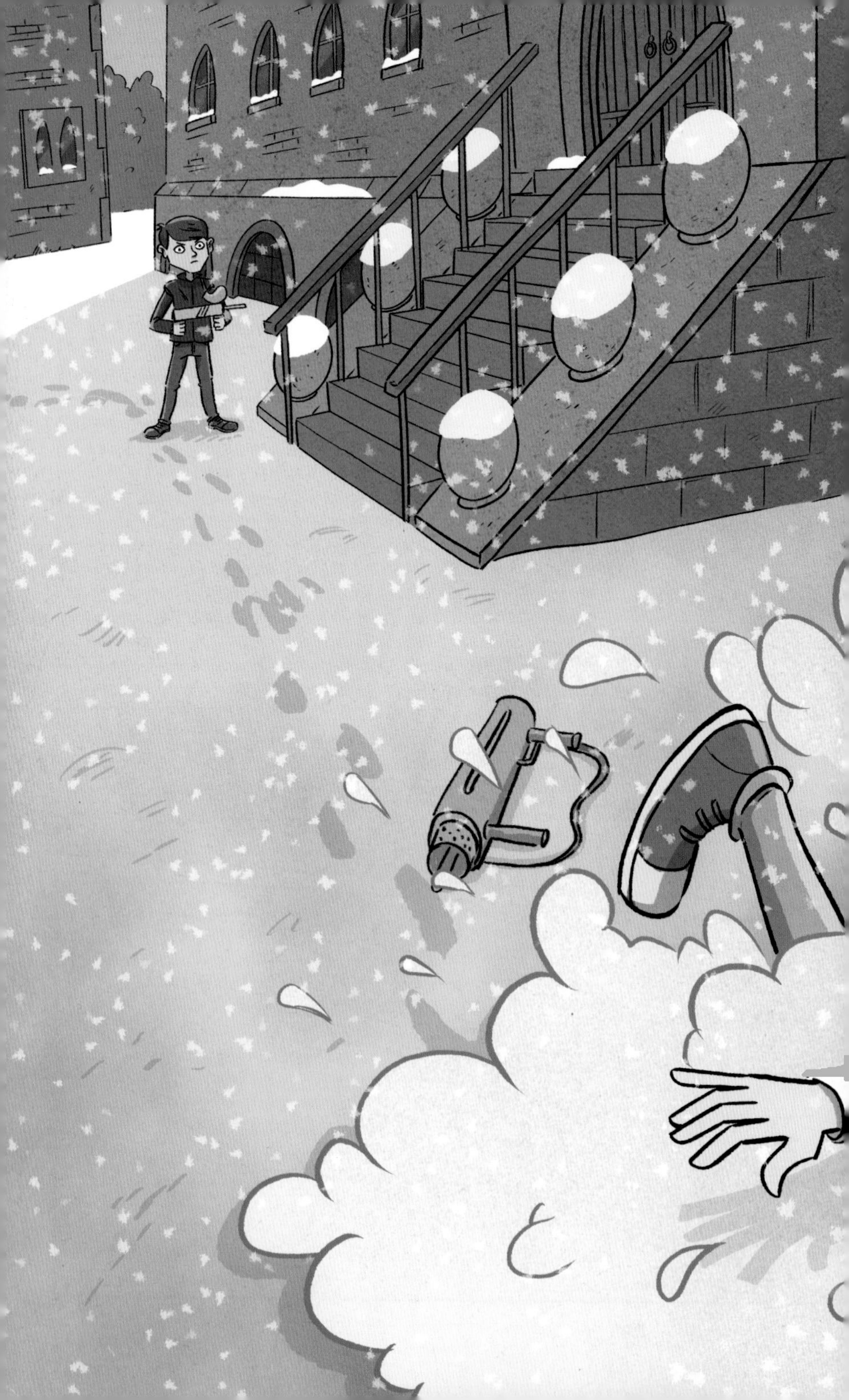

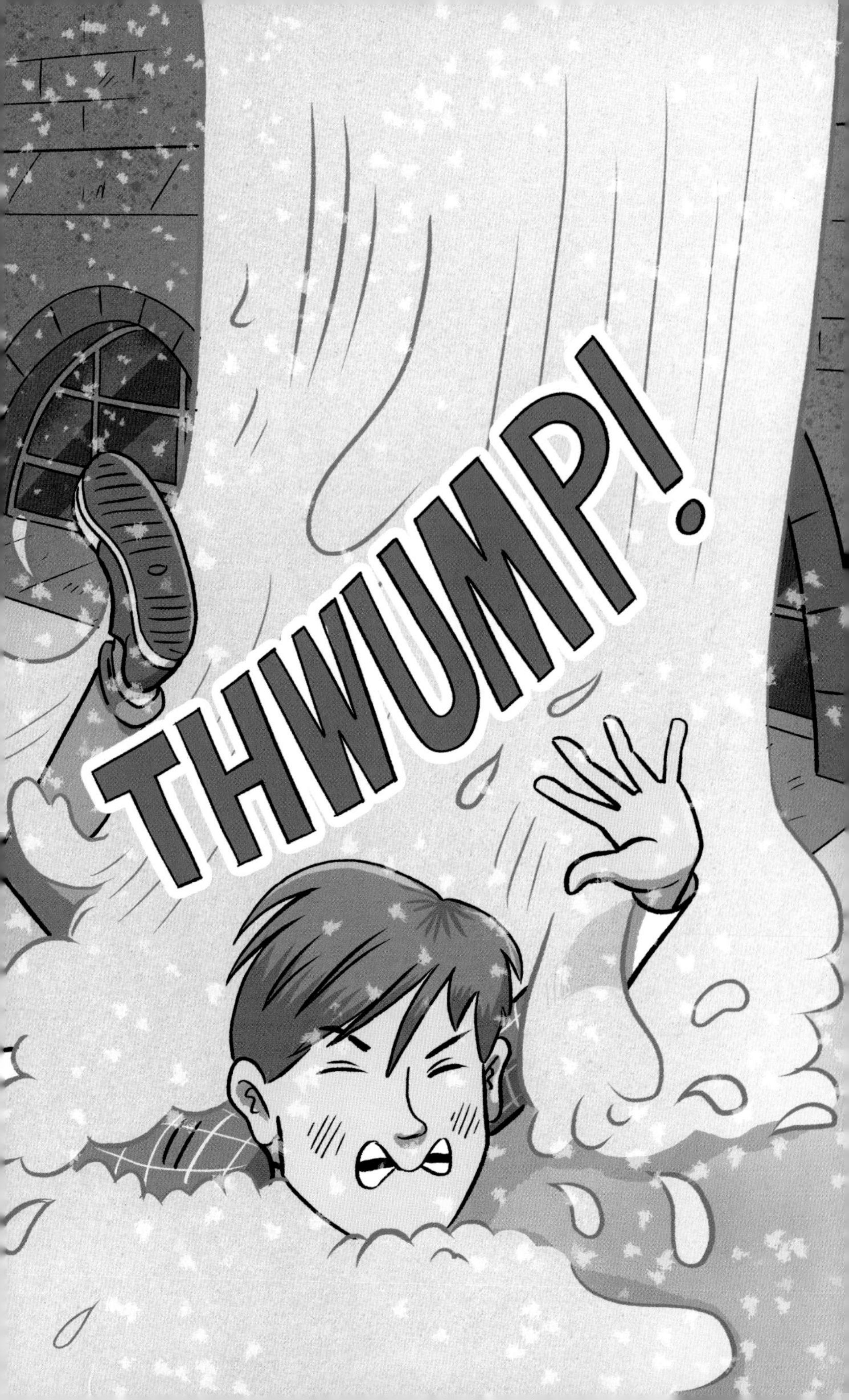
THWUMP!

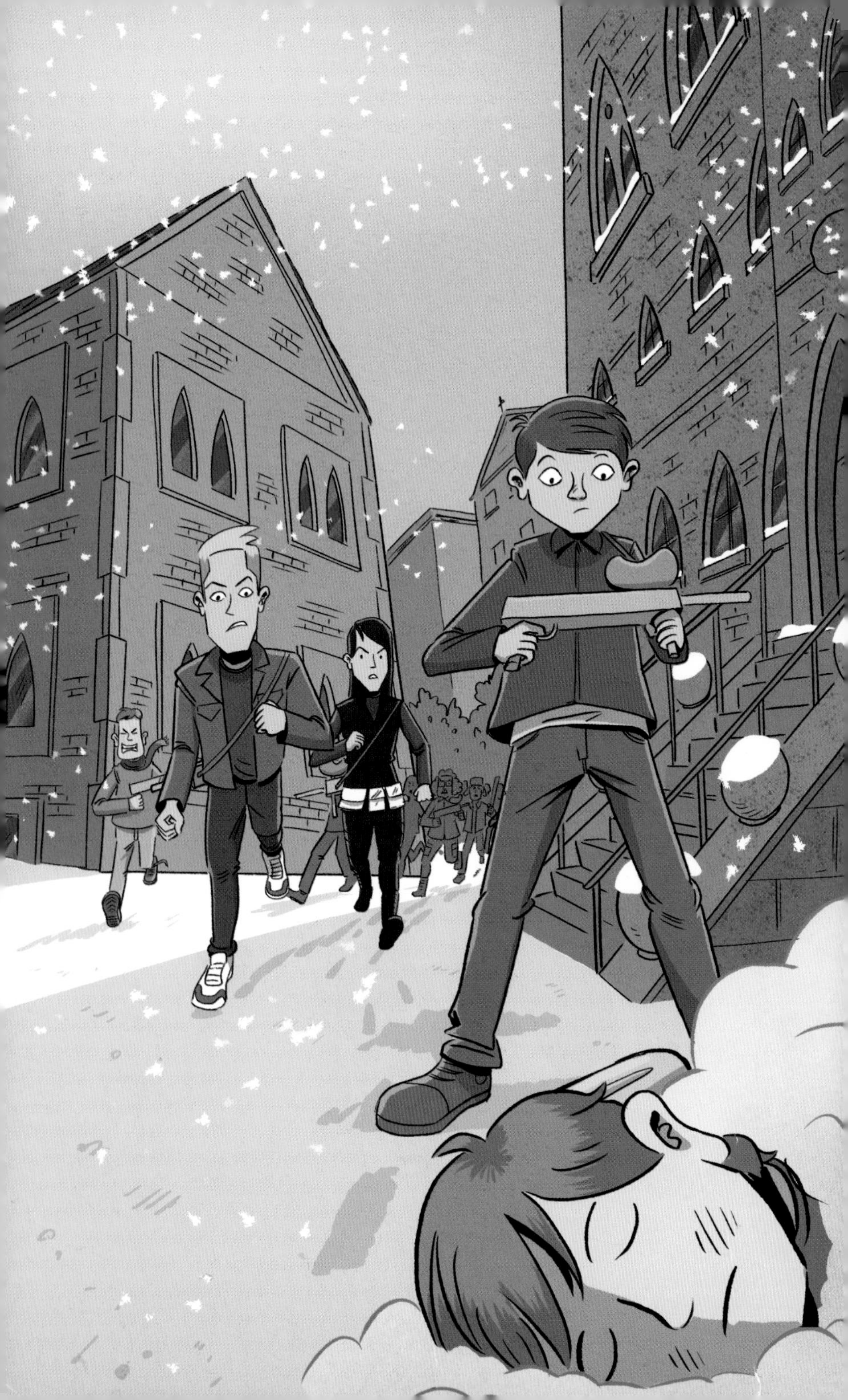

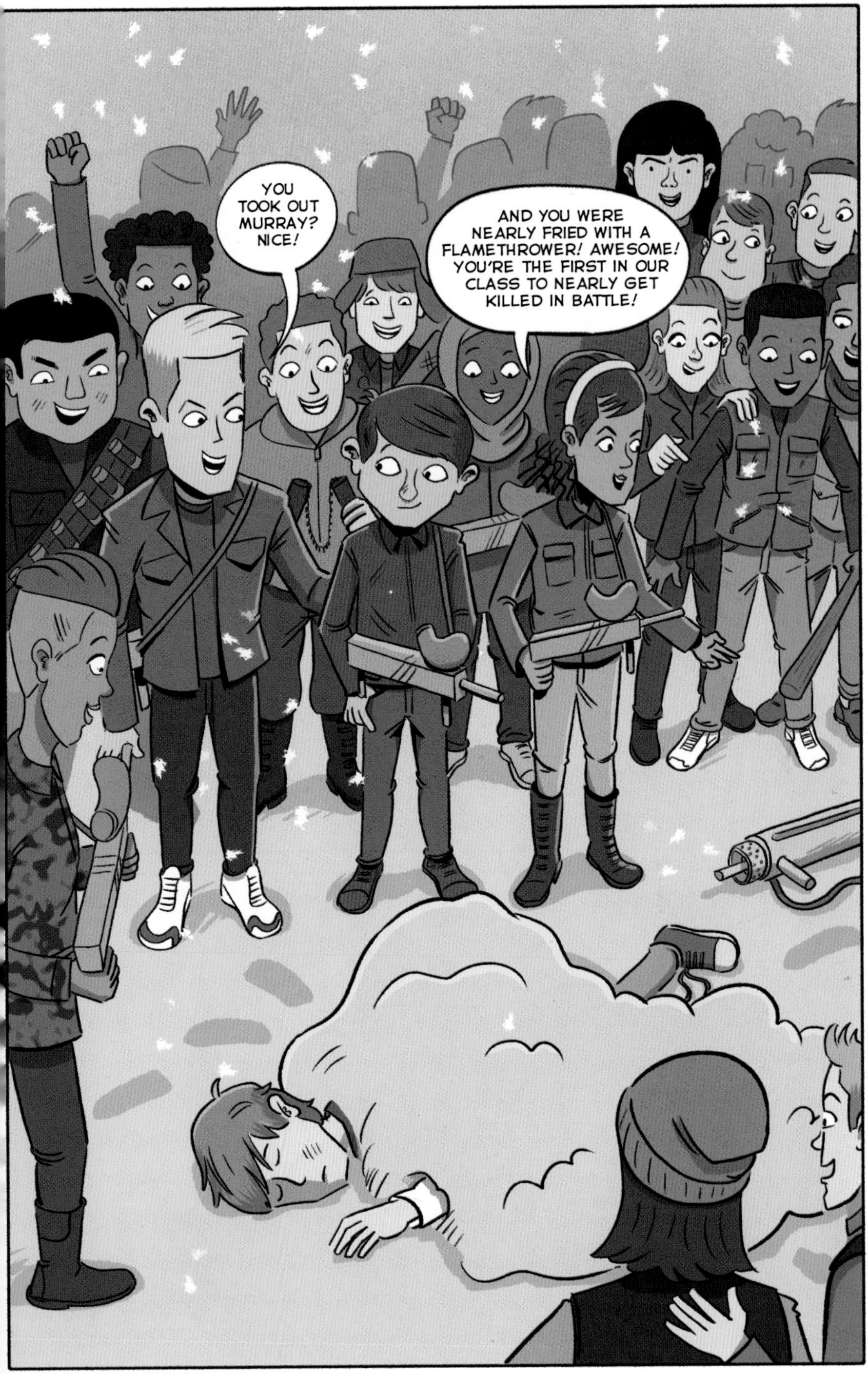
YOU TOOK OUT MURRAY? NICE!
AND YOU WERE NEARLY FRIED WITH A FLAMETHROWER! AWESOME! YOU'RE THE FIRST IN OUR CLASS TO NEARLY GET KILLED IN BATTLE!

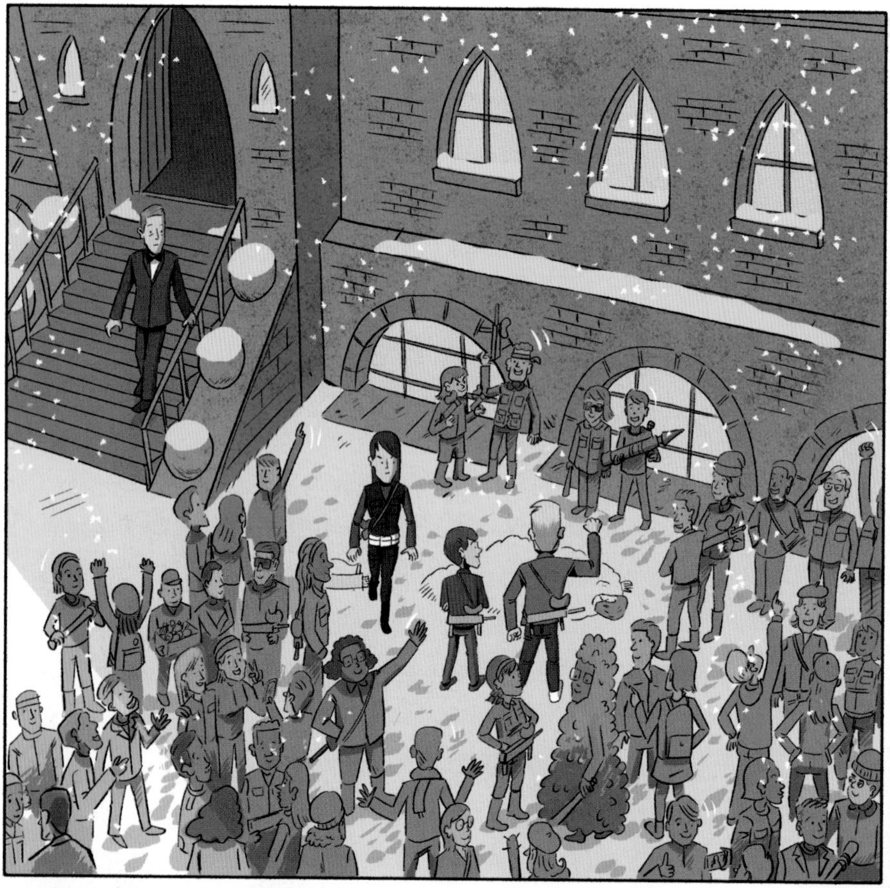

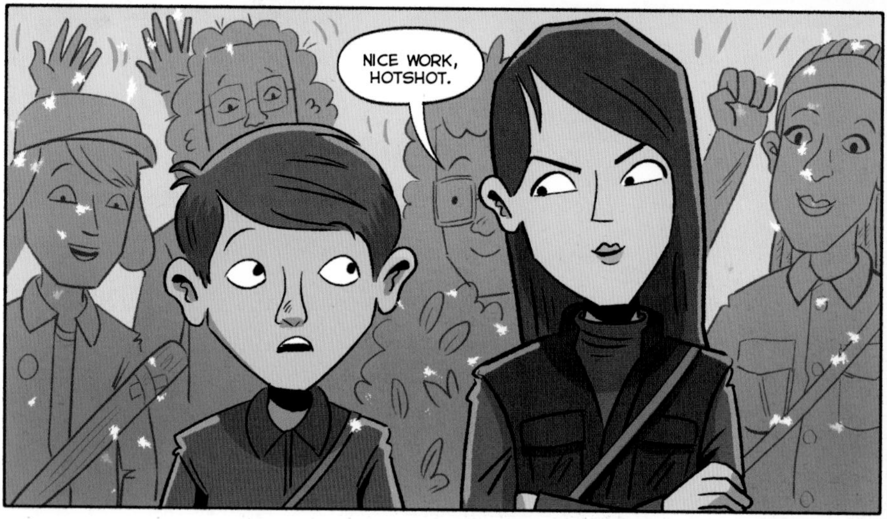
NICE WORK, HOTSHOT.

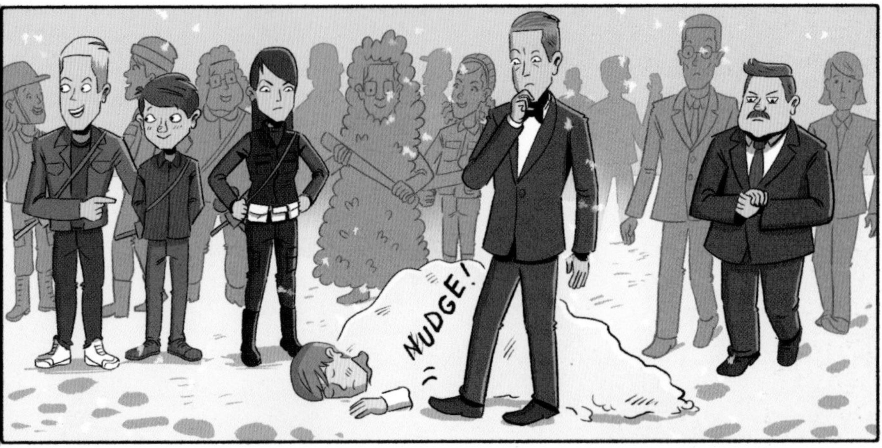
NUDGE!

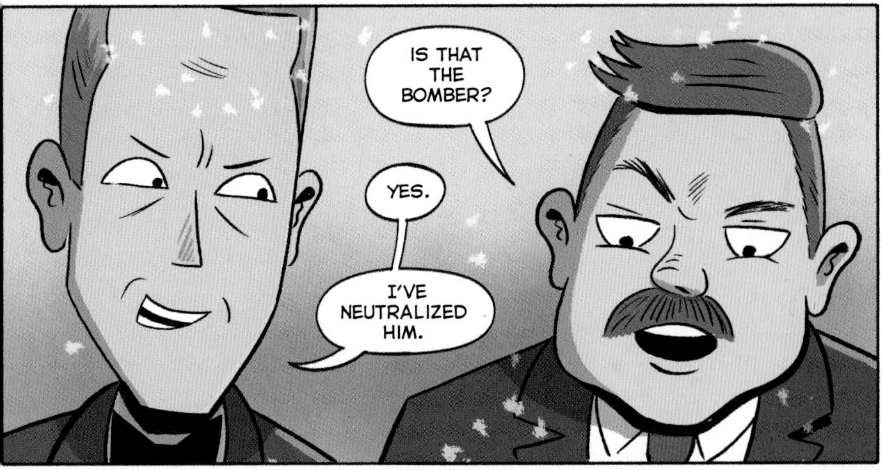
IS THAT THE BOMBER?
YES.
I'VE NEUTRALIZED HIM.

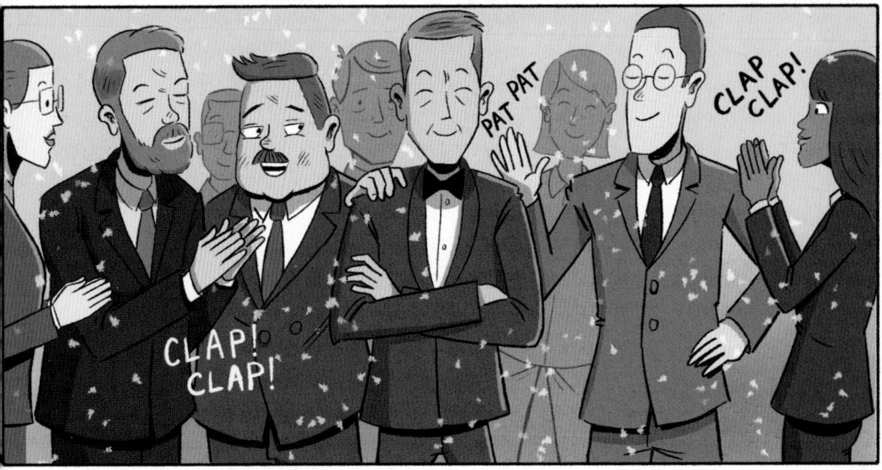
PAT PAT
CLAP CLAP!
CLAP! CLAP!

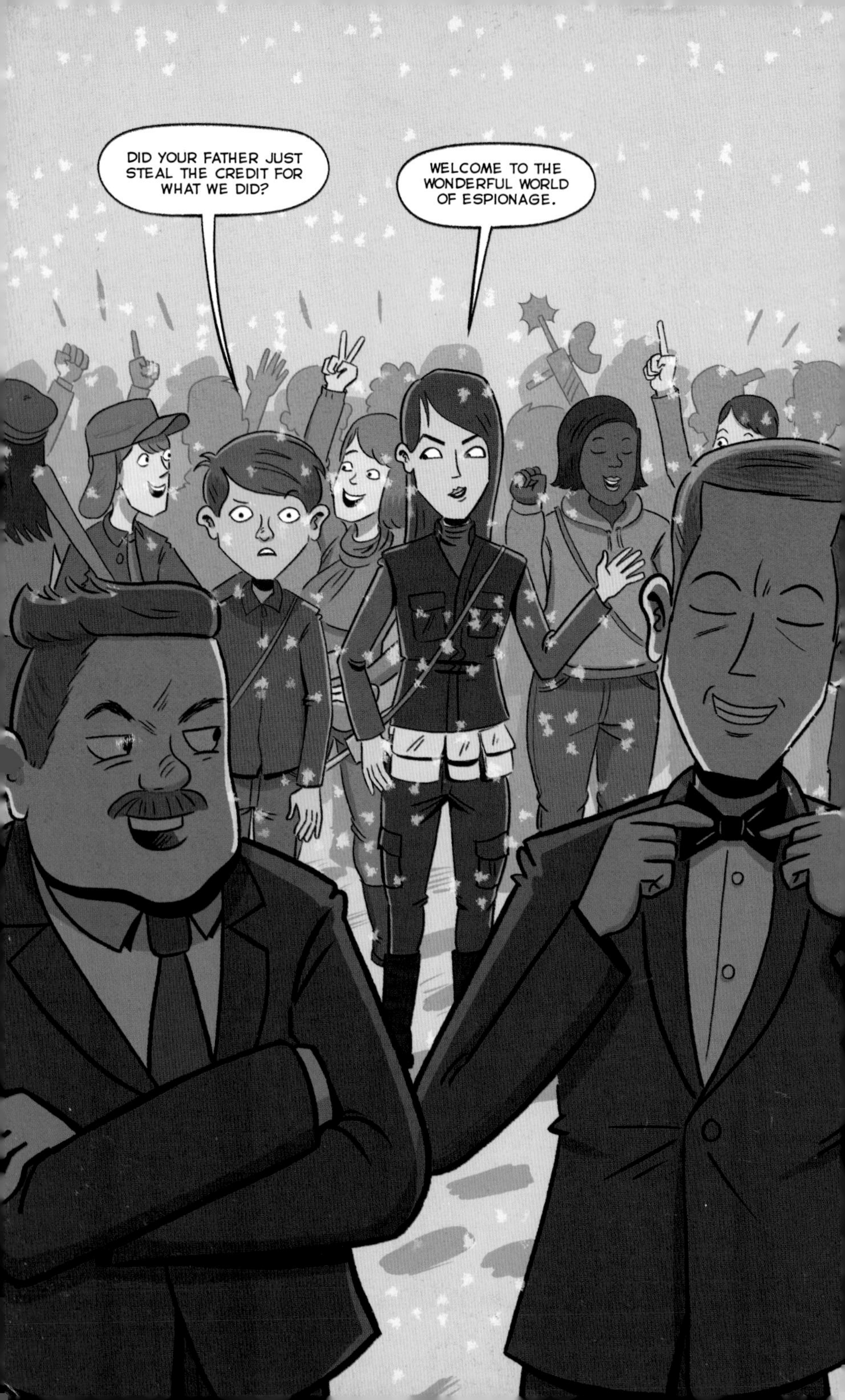
DID YOUR FATHER JUST STEAL THE CREDIT FOR WHAT WE DID?
WELCOME TO THE WONDERFUL WORLD OF ESPIONAGE.

YUMMY BURGER

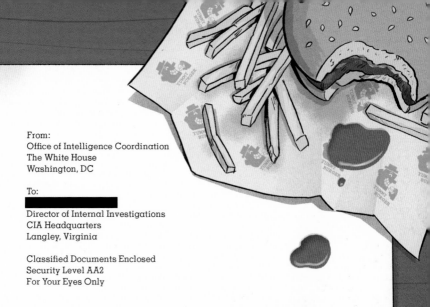

From:
Office of Intelligence Coordination
The White House
Washington, DC

To:
[redacted]
Director of Internal Investigations
CIA Headquarters
Langley, Virginia

Classified Documents Enclosed
Security Level AA2
For Your Eyes Only

After reading the enclosed transcript, it is evident that considerable work lies ahead of us. It appears that reevaluation of [redacted], the governance of the Academy of Espionage and the CIA itself is in order. It is shocking and dismaying that the only person in the entire intelligence community to uncover direct evidence of SPYDER is a first year at the academy. Worse, a first year who didn't even officially qualify for entry. Immediate further investigation into this nefarious organization must proceed at all costs.

To that end, I recommend Benjamin Ripley's acceptance into the school be made official. He has certainly earned it. As he remains a target for SPYDER, he should be given K-24 security status—although at this time, it is probably too early to brief him on Operation Enduring Assault. If he knew that [redacted], he'd probably flip out. Instead, allow him to once again believe he is a normal student at the academy whose life is not in the slightest bit of danger.

In addition, as far as the investigation of SPYDER is concerned, I recommend immediate activation of [redacted], aka Klondike. I am fully aware of the inherent dangers in doing so, but desperate times call for desperate measures. If SPYDER is not neutralized soon, this could portend the end of the intelligence community—and perhaps even the United States of America—as we know it.

My best to Betty and the kids.

[redacted]
Director of Covert Affairs

Acknowledgments

I had never published a graphic novel before, but the idea of doing one became increasingly exciting over the years. The process worked out even better than I had hoped.

The main reason for this is Anjan Sarkar, whose work on this project has exceeded my wildest dreams. His illustrations, his layout, his humor, and his attention to detail have all been amazing. Then, Lucy Ruth Cummins did a wonderful job overseeing the project. Lucy is the artistic genius who has created all of my book covers, so of course she was the perfect person to handle the graphic novel. Also, thanks are due to Justin Chanda, my publisher, who made this whole thing happen, and Krista Vitola, my editor.

Then there's the rest of my awesome team at Simon & Schuster: Erin Toller, Beth Parker, Roberta Stout, Kendra Levin, Catherine Laudone, Anne Zafian, Lisa Moraleda, Jenica Nasworthy, Tom Daly, Chava Wolin, Chrissy Noh, Anna Jarzab, Brian Murray, Devin MacDonald, Christina Pecorale, Victor Iannone, Emily Hutton, Emily Ritter, and Theresa Pang. And massive thanks to my wonderful agent, Jennifer Joel, for making my entire book career possible.

Thanks to the home team: Ronald and Jane Gibbs; Suz, Darragh, and Ciara Howard; Barry and Carole Patmore; Megan Vicente; and Georgia Simon.

And, of course, thanks to my children, Dashiell and Violet, who had been asking me when I was going to do a graphic novel for years. Here it is, kids. I hope you love it as much as I do.